ONE CUNNING PLAN TOO MANY?

(continued from back cover)

Lord Ivan Vorpatril has a problem: unrequited love in general. True, with the men on Barrayar outnumbering the women five to four, his odds aren't good. But Ivan had never thought the odds applied to him. He too has a cunning plan...

If no battle plan survives first contact with the enemy, just imagine what all Miles's closest friends and relatives can do to his romantic strategy!

A CIVIL CAMPAIGN

A COMEDY OF BIOLOGY AND MANNERS

LOIS McMASTER BUJOLD

A Civil Campaign

This is a work of fiction. All the characters and events portrayed in this book are fictional, and any resemblance to real people or incidents is purely coincidental.

Copyright © 1999 by Lois McMaster Bujold

All rights reserved, including the right to reproduce this book or portions thereof in any form.

A Baen Books Original

Baen Publishing Enterprises
P.O. Box 1403
Riverdale, NY 10471
www.baen.com

ISBN: 0-671-57885-5

Cover art by Patrick Turner

First paperback printing, August 2000

Library of Congress Catalog Number 99-16807

Distributed by Simon & Schuster
1230 Avenue of the Americas
New York, NY 10020

Production by Windhaven Press, Auburn, NH
Printed in the United States of America

DEDICATION

For Jane, Charlotte, Georgette, and Dorothy—
long may they rule.

CHAPTER ONE

The big groundcar jerked to a stop centimeters from the vehicle ahead of it, and Armsman Pym, driving, swore under his breath. Miles settled back again in his seat beside him, wincing at a vision of the acrimonious street scene from which Pym's reflexes had delivered them. Miles wondered if he could have persuaded the feckless prole in front of them that being rear-ended by an Imperial Auditor was a privilege to be treasured. Likely not. The Vorbarr Sultana University student darting across the boulevard on foot, who had been the cause of the quick stop, scampered off through the jam without a backward glance. The line of groundcars started up once more.

"Have you heard if the municipal traffic control system will be coming on line soon?" Pym asked, apropos of what Miles counted as their third near-miss this week.

"Nope. Delayed in development again, Lord Vorbohn the Younger reports. Due to the increase in fatal lightflyer incidents, they're concentrating on getting the automated air system up first."

Pym nodded, and returned his attention to the crowded road. The Armsman was a habitually fit man, his graying temples seeming merely an accent to his

1

brown-and-silver uniform. He'd served the Vorkosigans as a liege-sworn guard since Miles had been an Academy cadet, and would doubtless go on doing so till either he died of old age, or they were all killed in traffic.

So much for short cuts. Next time they'd go around the campus. Miles watched through the canopy as the taller new buildings of the University fell behind, and they passed through its spiked iron gates into the pleasant old residential streets favored by the families of senior professors and staff. The distinctive architecture dated from the last un-electrified decade before the end of the Time of Isolation. This area had been reclaimed from decay in the past generation, and now featured shady green Earth trees, and bright flower boxes under the tall narrow windows of the tall narrow houses. Miles rebalanced the flower arrangement between his feet. Would it be seen as redundant by its intended recipient?

Pym glanced aside at his slight movement, following his eye to the foliage on the floor. "The lady you met on Komarr seems to have made a strong impression on you, m'lord . . ." He trailed off invitingly.

"Yes," said Miles, uninvitingly.

"Your lady mother had high hopes of that very attractive Miss Captain Quinn you brought home those times." Was that a wistful note in Pym's voice?

"Miss Admiral Quinn, now," Miles corrected with a sigh. "So had I. But she made the right choice for her." He grimaced out the canopy. "I've sworn off falling in love with galactic women and then trying to persuade them to immigrate to Barrayar. I've concluded my only hope is to find a woman who can already stand Barrayar, and persuade her to like me."

"And does Madame Vorsoisson like Barrayar?"

"About as well as I do." He smiled grimly.

"And, ah . . . the second part?"

"We'll see, Pym." *Or not, as the case may be.* At least the spectacle of a man of thirty-plus, going courting seriously for the first time in his life—the first time in the Barrayaran style, anyway—promised to provide hours of entertainment for his interested staff.

Miles let his breath and his nervous irritation trickle out through his nostrils as Pym found a place to park near Lord Auditor Vorthys's doorstep, and expertly wedged the polished old armored groundcar into the inadequate space. Pym popped the canopy; Miles climbed out, and stared up at the three-story patterned tile front of his colleague's home.

Georg Vorthys had been a professor of engineering failure analysis at the Imperial University for thirty years. He and his wife had lived in this house for most of their married life, raising three children and two academic careers, before Emperor Gregor had appointed Vorthys as one of his hand-picked Imperial Auditors. Neither of the Professors Vorthys had seen any reason to change their comfortable lifestyle merely because the awesome powers of an Emperor's Voice had been conferred upon the retired engineer; Madame Dr. Vorthys still walked every day to her classes. *Dear no, Miles!* the Professora had said to him, when he'd once wondered aloud at their passing up this opportunity for social display. *Can you imagine moving all those books?* Not to mention the laboratory and workshop jamming the entire basement.

Their cheery inertia proved a happy chance, when they invited their recently-widowed niece and her young son to live with them while she completed her own education. Plenty of room, the Professor had boomed jovially, the top floor is so empty since the children left. So close to classes, the Professora had pointed out practically. *Less than six kilometers from Vorkosigan House!* Miles had exulted in his mind, adding a polite murmur of encouragement aloud. And so Ekaterin Nile Vorvayne Vorsoisson had arrived. *She's here, she's here!* Might she be looking down at him from the shadows of some upstairs window even now?

Miles glanced anxiously down the all-too-short length of his body. If his dwarfish stature bothered her, she'd shown no signs of it so far. Well and good. Going on to the aspects of his appearance he could control: no food stains spattered his plain gray tunic, no unfortunate street detritus clung to the soles of his polished half-boots. He checked his distorted reflection in the groundcar's rear

canopy. Its convex mirroring widened his lean, if slightly
hunched, body to something resembling his obese clone-
brother Mark, a comparison he primly ignored. Mark was,
thank God, not here. He essayed a smile, for practice;
in the canopy, it came out twisted and repellent. No dark
hair sticking out in odd directions, anyway.

"You look just fine, my lord," Pym said in a bracing
tone from the front compartment. Miles's face heated,
and he flinched away from his reflection. He recovered
himself enough to take the flower arrangement and
rolled-up flimsy Pym handed out to him with, he hoped,
a tolerably bland expression. He balanced the load in
his arms, turned to face the front steps, and took a deep
breath.

After about a minute, Pym inquired helpfully from
behind him, "Would you like me to carry anything?"

"No. Thank you." Miles trod up the steps and wiggled
a finger free to press the chime-pad. Pym pulled out a
reader, and settled comfortably in the groundcar to await
his lord's pleasure.

Footsteps sounded from within, and the door swung
open on the smiling pink face of the Professora. Her
gray hair was wound up on her head in her usual style.
She wore a dark rose dress with a light rose bolero,
embroidered with green vines in the manner of her
home District. This somewhat formal Vor mode, which
suggested she was just on her way either in or out, was
belied by the soft buskins on her feet. "Hello, Miles.
Goodness, you're prompt."

"Professora." Miles ducked a nod to her, and smiled
in turn. "Is she here? Is she in? Is she well? You said this
would be a good time. I'm not too early, am I? I thought
I'd be late. The traffic was miserable. You're going to be
around, aren't you? I brought these. Do you think she'll
like them?" The sticking-up red flowers tickled his nose
as he displayed his gift while still clutching the rolled-up
flimsy, which had a tendency to try to unroll and escape
whenever his grip loosened.

"Come in, yes, all's well. She's here, she's fine, and
the flowers are very nice—" The Professora rescued the
bouquet and ushered him into her tiled hallway, closing

the door firmly behind them with her foot. The house was dim and cool after the spring sunshine outside, and had a fine aroma of wood wax, old books, and a touch of academic dust.

"She looked pretty pale and fatigued at Tien's funeral. Surrounded by all those relatives. We really didn't get a chance to say more than two words each." *I'm sorry* and *Thank you*, to be precise. Not that he'd wanted to talk much to the late Tien Vorsoisson's family.

"It was an immense strain for her, I think," said the Professora judiciously. "She'd been through so much horror, and except for Georg and myself—and you—there wasn't a soul there to whom she could talk truth about it. Of course, her first concern was getting Nikki through it all. But she held together without a crack from first to last. I was very proud of her."

"Indeed. And she is . . . ?" Miles craned his neck, glancing into the rooms off the entry hall: a cluttered study lined with bookshelves, and a cluttered parlor lined with bookshelves. No young widows.

"Right this way." The Professora conducted him down the hall and out through her kitchen to the little urban back garden. A couple of tall trees and a brick wall made a private nook of it. Beyond a tiny circle of green grass, at a table in the shade, a woman sat with flimsies and a reader spread before her. She was chewing gently on the end of a stylus, and her dark brows were drawn down in her absorption. She wore a calf-length dress in much the same style as the Professora's, but solid black, with the high collar buttoned up to her neck. Her bolero was gray, trimmed with simple black braid running around its edge. Her dark hair was drawn back to a thick braided knot at the nape of her neck. She looked up at the sound of the door opening; her brows flew up and her lips parted in a flashing smile that made Miles blink. *Ekaterin.*

"Mil—my Lord Auditor!" She rose in a flare of skirt; he bowed over her hand.

"Madame Vorsoisson. You look well." She looked wonderful, if still much too pale. Part of that might be the effect of all that severe black, which also made her eyes show a brilliant blue-gray. "Welcome to Vorbarr Sultana. I brought these . . ." He gestured, and the Professora set the flower arrangement down on the table. "Though they hardly seem needed, out here."

"They're lovely," Ekaterin assured him, sniffing them in approval. "I'll take them up to my room later, where they will be very welcome. Since the weather has brightened up, I find I spend as much time as possible out here, under the real sky."

She'd spent nearly a year sealed in a Komarran dome. "I can understand that," Miles said. The conversation hiccuped to a brief stop, while they smiled at each other.

Ekaterin recovered first. "Thank you for coming to Tien's funeral. It meant so much to me."

"It was the least I could do, under the circumstances. I'm only sorry I couldn't do more."

"But you've already done so much for me and Nikki—" She broke off at his gesture of embarrassed denial and instead said, "But won't you sit down? Aunt Vorthys—?" She drew back one of the spindly garden chairs.

The Professora shook her head. "I have a few things to attend to inside. Carry on." She added a little cryptically, "You'll do fine."

She went back into her house, and Miles sat across from Ekaterin, placing his flimsy on the table to await its strategic moment. It half-unrolled, eagerly.

"Is your case all wound up?" she asked.

"That case will have ramifications for years to come, but I'm done with it for now," Miles replied. "I just turned in my last reports yesterday, or I would have been here to welcome you earlier." Well, that and a vestigial sense that he'd ought to let the poor woman at least get her bags unpacked, before descending in force.

"Will you be sent out on another assignment now?"

"I don't think Gregor will let me risk getting tied up elsewhere till after his marriage. For the next couple of months, I'm afraid all my duties will be social ones."

"I'm sure you'll do them with your usual flair."

God, I hope not. "I don't think flair is exactly what my Aunt Vorpatril—she's in charge of all the Emperor's wedding arrangements—would wish from me. More like, shut up and do what you're told, Miles. But speaking of paperwork, how's your own? Is Tien's estate settled? Did you manage to recapture Nikki's guardianship from that cousin of his?"

"Vassily Vorsoisson? Yes, thank heavens, there was no problem with that part."

"So, ah, what's all this, then?" Miles nodded at the cluttered table.

"I'm planning my course work for the next session at university. I was too late to start this summer, so I'll begin in the fall. There's so much to choose from. I feel so ignorant."

"Educated is what you aim to be coming out, not going in."

"I suppose so."

"And what will you choose?"

"Oh, I'll start with basics—biology, chemistry . . ." She brightened. "One real horticulture course." She gestured at her flimsies. "For the rest of the season, I'm trying to find some sort of paying work. I'd like to feel I'm not totally dependent on the charity of my relatives, even if it's only my pocket money."

That seemed almost the opening he was looking for, but Miles's eye caught sight of a red ceramic basin, sitting on the wooden planks forming a seat bordering a raised garden bed. In the middle of the pot a red-brown blob, with a fuzzy fringe like a rooster's crest growing out of it, pushed up through the dirt. If it was what he thought . . . He pointed to the basin. "Is that by chance your old bonsai'd skellytum? Is it going to live?"

She smiled. "Well, at least it's the start of a new skellytum. Most of the fragments of the old one died on the way home from Komarr, but that one took."

"You have a—for native Barrayaran plants, I don't suppose you can call it a green thumb, can you?"

"Not unless they're suffering from some pretty serious plant diseases, no."

"Speaking of gardens." Now, how to do this without jamming his foot in his mouth too deeply. "I don't think, in all the other uproar, I ever had a chance to tell you how impressed I was with your garden designs that I saw on your comconsole."

"Oh." Her smile fled, and she shrugged. "They were no great thing. Just twiddling."

Right. Let them not bring up any more of the recent past than absolutely necessary, till time had a chance to blunt memory's razor edges. "It was your Barrayaran garden, the one with all the native species, which caught my eye. I'd never seen anything like it."

"There are a dozen of them around. Several of the District universities keep them, as living libraries for their biology students. It's not really an original idea."

"Well," he persevered, feeling like a fish swimming upstream against this current of self-deprecation, "*I* thought it was very fine, and deserved better than just being a ghost garden on the holovid. I have this spare lot, you see . . ."

He flattened out his flimsy, which was a ground plot of the block occupied by Vorkosigan House. He tapped his finger on the bare square at the end. "There used to be another great house, next to ours, which was torn down during the Regency. ImpSec wouldn't let us build anything else—they wanted it as a security zone. There's nothing there but some scraggly grass, and a couple of trees that somehow survived ImpSec's enthusiasm for clear lines of fire. And a criss-cross of walks, where people made mud paths by taking short cuts, and they finally gave up and put some gravel down. It's an extremely boring piece of ground." So boring he had completely ignored it, till now.

She tilted her head, to follow his hand as it blocked out the space on the ground plan. Her own long finger made to trace a delicate curve, but then shyly withdrew. He wondered what possibility her mind's eye had just seen, there.

"Now, *I* think," he went on valiantly, "that it would be a splendid thing to install a Barrayaran garden—all native species—open to the public, in this space. A sort of gift from the Vorkosigan family to the city of Vorbarr Sultana. With running water, like in your design, and walks and benches and all those civilized things. And those discreet little name tags on all the plants, so more people could learn about the old ecology and all that." There: art, public service, education—was there any bait he'd left off his hook? Oh yes, money. "It's a happy chance that you're looking for a summer job," *chance, hah, watch and see if I leave anything to chance,* "because I think you'd be the ideal person to take this on. Design and oversee the installation of the thing. I could give you an unlimited, um, generous budget, and a salary, of course. You could hire workmen, bring in whatever you needed."

And she would have to visit Vorkosigan House practically *every day*, and consult *frequently* with its resident lord. And by the time the shock of her husband's death had worn away, and she was ready to put off her forbidding formal mourning garb, and every unattached Vor bachelor in the capital showed up on her doorstep, Miles could have a lock on her affections that would permit him to fend off the most glittering competition. It was too soon, wildly too soon, to suggest courtship to her crippled heart; he had that clear in his head, even if his own heart howled in frustration. But a straightforward business friendship just might get past her guard. . . .

Her eyebrows had flown up; she touched an uncertain finger to those exquisite, pale unpainted lips. "This is exactly the sort of thing I wish to train to do. I don't know how to do it *yet*."

"On-the-job training," Miles responded instantly. "Apprenticeship. Learning by doing. You have to start sometime. You can't start sooner than now."

"But what if I make some dreadful mistake?"

"I do intend this be an *ongoing* project. People who are enthusiasts about this sort of thing always seem to be changing their gardens around. They get bored with the same view all the time, I guess. If you come up with better ideas later, you can always revise the plan. It will provide variety."

"I don't want to waste your money."

If she ever became Lady Vorkosigan, she would have to get over that quirk, Miles decided firmly.

"You don't have to decide here on the spot," he purred, and cleared his throat. *Watch that tone, boy. Business.* "Why don't you come to Vorkosigan House tomorrow, and walk over the site in person, and see what ideas it stirs up in your mind. You really can't tell anything by looking at a flimsy. We can have lunch, afterward, and talk about what you see as the problems and possibilities then. Logical?"

She blinked. "Yes, very." Her hand crept back curiously toward the flimsy.

"What time may I pick you up?"

"Whatever is convenient for you, Lord Vorkosigan. Oh, I take that back. If it's after twelve hundred, my aunt will be back from her morning class, and Nikki can stay with her."

"Excellent!" Yes, much as he liked Ekaterin's son, Miles thought he could do without the assistance of an active nine-year-old in this delicate dance. "Twelve hundred it will be. Consider it a deal." Only a little belatedly, he added, "And how does Nikki like Vorbarr Sultana, so far?"

"He seems to like his room, and this house. I think he's going to get a little bored, if he has to wait until his school starts to locate boys his own age."

It would not do to leave Nikolai Vorsoisson out of his calculations. "I gather then that the retro-genes took, and he's in no more danger of developing the symptoms of Vorzohn's Dystrophy?"

A smile of deep maternal satisfaction softened her face. "That's right. I'm so pleased. The doctors in the clinic here in Vorbarr Sultana report he had a very clean and complete cellular uptake. Developmentally, it should be just as if he'd never inherited the mutation at all." She glanced across at him. "It's as if I'd had a five-hundred-kilo weight lifted from me. I could fly, I think."

So you should.

Nikki himself emerged from the house at this moment, carrying a plate of cookies with an air of consequence, followed by the Professora with a tea tray and cups. Miles and Ekaterin hastened to clear a place on the table.

"Hello, Nikki," said Miles.

"Hi, Lord Vorkosigan. Is that your groundcar out front?"

"Yes."

"It's a barge." This observation was delivered without scorn, as a point of interest.

"I know. It's a relic of my father's time as Regent. It's armored, in fact—has a massive momentum."

"Oh yeah?" Nikki's interest soared. "Did it ever get shot at?"

"I don't believe that particular car ever did, no."

"Huh."

When Miles had last seen Nikki, the boy had been wooden-faced and pale with concentration, carrying the taper to light his father's funeral offering, obviously anxious to get his part of the ceremony right. He looked much better now, his brown eyes quick and his face mobile again. The Professora settled and poured tea, and the conversation became general for a time.

It became clear shortly that Nikki's interest was more in the food than in his mother's visitor; he declined a flatteringly grownup offer of tea, and with his great-aunt's permission snagged several cookies and dodged back indoors to whatever he'd been occupying himself with before. Miles tried to remember what age he'd been when his own parents' friends had stopped seeming part of the furniture. Well, except for the military men in his father's train, of course, who'd always riveted his attention. But then, Miles had been military-mad from the time he could walk. Nikki was jump-ship mad, and would probably light up for a jump pilot. Perhaps Miles could provide one sometime, for Nikki's delectation. A happily married one, he corrected this thought.

He'd laid his bait on the table, Ekaterin had taken it; it was time to quit while he was winning. But he knew for a fact that she'd already turned down one premature offer of remarriage from a completely unexpected quarter. *Had* any of Vorbarr Sultana's excess Vor males found her yet? The capital was crawling with young officers, rising bureaucrats, aggressive entrepreneurs, men of ambition and wealth and rank drawn to the empire's heart. But not, by a ratio of almost five to three, with their sisters. The parents of the preceding generation had taken galactic sex-selection technologies much too far in their foolish passion for male heirs, and the very sons they'd so cherished—Miles's contemporaries—had inherited the resulting mating mess. Go to any formal party in Vorbarr Sultana these days, and you could practically taste the damned testosterone in the air, volatilized by the alcohol no doubt.

"So, ah . . . have you had any other callers yet, Ekaterin?"

"I only arrived a week ago."

That was neither yes nor no. "I'd think you'd have the bachelors out in force in no time." Wait, he hadn't meant to point that out . . .

"Surely," she gestured down her black dress, "this will keep them away. If they have any manners at all."

"Mm, I'm not so sure. The social scene is pretty intense just now."

She shook her head and smiled bleakly. "It makes no difference to me. I had a decade of . . . of marriage. I don't need to repeat the experience. The other women are welcome to the bachelors; they can have my share, in fact." The conviction in her face was backed by an uncharacteristic hint of steel in her voice. "That's one mistake I don't have to make twice. I'll never remarry."

Miles controlled his flinch, and managed a sympathetic, interested smile at this confidence. *We're just friends. I'm not hustling you, no, no. No need to fling up your defenses, milady, not for me.*

He couldn't make this go faster by pushing harder; all he could do was screw it up worse. Forced to be satisfied with his one day's progress, Miles finished his tea, exchanged a few more pleasantries with the two women, and took his leave.

Pym hurried to open the groundcar door as Miles skipped down the last three steps in one jump. He flung himself into the passenger seat, and as Pym slipped back into the driver's side and closed the canopy, waved grandly. "Home, Pym."

Pym eased the groundcar into the street, and inquired mildly, "Go well, did it, m'lord?"

"Just exactly as I had planned. She's coming to Vorkosigan House tomorrow for lunch. As soon as we get home, I want you to call that gardening service—get them to get a crew out tonight and give the grounds an extra going-over. And talk to—no, *I'll* talk to Ma Kosti. Lunch must be . . . exquisite, yes. Ivan always says women like food. But not too heavy. Wine—does she drink wine in the daytime, I wonder? I'll offer it, anyway. Something from the estate. And tea if she doesn't choose the wine, I know she drinks tea. Scratch the wine. And get the house cleaning crew in, get all those covers off the first floor furniture—off all the furniture. I want to give her a tour of the house while she still doesn't realize . . . No, wait. I wonder . . . if the place was a dreadful bachelor mess, perhaps it would stir up her pity. Maybe instead I ought to clutter it up some more, used glasses strategically piled up, the odd fruit peel under the sofa—a silent appeal, *Help us! Move in and straighten this poor fellow out*—or would that be more likely to frighten her off? What do you think, Pym?"

Pym pursed his lips judiciously, as if considering whether it was within his Armsman's duties to spike his lord's taste for street theater. He finally said in a cautious tone, "If I may presume to speak for the household, I *think* we should prefer to put our best foot forward. Under the circumstances."

"Oh. All right."

Miles fell silent for a few moments, staring out the canopy as they threaded through the crowded city streets, out of the University district and across a mazelike corner of the Old Town, angling back toward Vorkosigan House. When he spoke again, the manic humor had drained from his voice, leaving it cooler and bleaker.

"We'll be picking her up tomorrow at twelve hundred. You'll drive. You will always drive, when Madame Vorsoisson or her son are aboard. Figure it in to your duty schedule from now on."

"Yes, m'lord." Pym added a carefully laconic, "My pleasure."

The seizure disorder was the last souvenir that ImpSec Captain Miles Vorkosigan had brought home from his decade of military missions. He'd been lucky to get out of the cryo-chamber alive and with his mind intact; Miles was fully aware that many did not fare nearly so well. Lucky to be merely medically discharged from the Emperor's Service, not buried with honors, the last of his glorious line, or reduced to some animal or vegetative existence. The seizure-stimulator the military doctors had issued him to bleed off his convulsions was very far from being a cure, though it was supposed to keep them from happening at random times. Miles drove, and flew his lightflyer—but only alone. He never took passengers anymore. Pym's batman's duties had been expanded to include medical assistance; he had by now witnessed enough of Miles's disturbing seizures to be grateful for this unusual burst of level-headedness.

One corner of Miles's mouth crooked up. After a moment, he asked, "And how did you ever capture Ma Pym, back in the old days, Pym? Did you put your best foot forward?"

"It's been almost eighteen years ago. The details have gone a bit fuzzy." Pym smiled a little. "I was a senior sergeant at the time. I'd taken the ImpSec advanced course, and was assigned to security duty at Vorhartung Castle. She had a clerk's job in the archives there. I thought, I wasn't some boy anymore, it was time I got serious . . . though I'm not just sure that wasn't an idea she put into my head, because she claims she spotted me first."

"Ah, a handsome fellow in uniform, I see. Does it every time. So why'd you decide to quit the Imperial Service and apply to the Count-my-father?"

"Eh, it seemed the right progression. Our little daughter'd come along by then, I was just finishing my twenty-years hitch, and I was facing whether or not to continue my enlistment. My wife's family was here, and her roots, and she didn't particularly fancy following the flag with children in tow. Captain Illyan, who knew I was District-born, was kind enough to give me a tip, that your father had a place open in his Armsmen's score.

And a recommendation, when I nerved up to apply. I figured a Count's Armsman would be a more settled job, for a family man."

The groundcar arrived at Vorkosigan House; the ImpSec corporal on duty opened the gates for them, and Pym pulled around to the porte cochère and popped the canopy.

"Thank you, Pym," Miles said, and hesitated. "A word in your ear. Two words."

Pym made to look attentive.

"When you chance to socialize with the Armsmen of other Houses ... I'd appreciate it if you wouldn't mention Madame Vorsoisson. I wouldn't want her to be the subject of invasive gossip, and, um ... she's no business of everyone and his younger brother anyway, eh?"

"A loyal Armsman does not gossip, m'lord," said Pym stiffly.

"No, of course not. Sorry, I didn't mean to imply ... um, sorry. Anyway. The other thing. I'm maybe guilty of saying a little too much myself, you see. I'm not actually courting Madame Vorsoisson."

Pym tried to look properly blank, but a confused expression leaked into his face. Miles added hastily, "I mean, not *formally*. Not *yet*. She's ... she's had a difficult time, recently, and she's a touch ... skittish. Any premature declaration on my part is likely to be disastrous, I'm afraid. It's a timing problem. Discreet is the watchword, if you see what I mean?"

Pym attempted a discreet but supportive-looking smile.

"We're just good friends," Miles reiterated. "Anyway, we're going to be."

"Yes, m'lord. I understand."

"Ah. Good. Thank you." Miles climbed out of the groundcar, and added over his shoulder as he headed into the house, "Find me in the kitchen when you've put the car away."

Ekaterin stood in the middle of the blank square of grass with gardens boiling up in her head.

"If you excavated there," she pointed, "and piled it

up on that side, you'd gain enough slope for the water flow. A bit of a wall there, too, to block off the street noise and to heighten the effect. And the walkway curving down—" She wheeled, to encounter Lord Vorkosigan watching her, smiling, his hands stuffed in his gray trouser pockets. "Or would you prefer something more geometrical?"

"Beg pardon?" He blinked.

"It's an aesthetic question."

"I, uh . . . aesthetics are not exactly my area of expertise." He said this in a tone of sad confession, as though it might be something of which she was previously unaware.

Her hands sketched the bones of the projected piece, trying to call structure out of the air. "Do you want an illusion of a natural space, Barrayar before it was touched by man, with the water seeming like rocks and a creek, a slice of backcountry in the city—or something more in the nature of a metaphor, with the Barrayaran plants in the interstices of these strong human lines—probably in concrete. You can do really wonderful things with water and concrete."

"Which is better?"

"It's not a question of better. It's a question of what you are trying to say."

"I hadn't thought of it as a political statement. I'd thought of it as a gift."

"If it's your garden, it will be seen as a political statement whether you intended it or not."

The corner of his lip quirked as he took this in. "I'll have to think about that. But there's no doubt in your mind something could be done with the area?"

"Oh, none." The two Earth trees, seemingly stuck in the flat ground at random, would have to go. That silver maple was punky in the heartwood and would be no loss, but the young oak was sound—perhaps it could be moved. The terraformed topsoil must also be salvaged. Her hands twitched with the desire to start digging into the dirt then and there. "It's an extraordinary space to find preserved in the middle of Vorbarr Sultana." Across the street, a commercial office building rose a dozen stories high. Fortunately, it angled to the north and did not block out much light. The hiss and huff of groundcar fans made continuous counterpoint along the busy thoroughfare crossing the top end of the block, where she'd mentally placed her wall. Across the park on the opposite side, a high gray stone wall topped with iron spikes was already in place; treetops rising beyond it half-screened from view the great house holding down the center of the block.

"I'd invite you to sit while I think about it," said Lord Vorkosigan, "but ImpSec never put in benches—they didn't want to encourage loitering around the Regent's residence. Suppose you run up both contrasting designs on your comconsole, and bring them to me for review. Meanwhile, shall we walk round to the house? I think my cook will have lunch ready soon."

"Oh . . . all right . . ." With only one backward glance at the entrancing possibilities, Ekaterin let him lead her away.

They angled across the park. Around the corner of the gray wall at Vorkosigan House's front entrance, a concrete kiosk sheltered a guard in Imperial Security undress greens. He coded open the iron gate for the little Lord Auditor and his guest, and watched them pass through it, exchanging a short formal nod for Vorkosigan's thank-you half-salute, and smiling pleasantly at Ekaterin.

The somber stone of the mansion rose before them, four stories high in two major wings. What seemed dozens of windows frowned down. The short semicircle of drive curled around a brilliantly healthy patch of green grass and under a portico, which sheltered carved double doors flanked by tall narrow windows.

"Vorkosigan House is about two hundred years old, now. It was built by my great-great-great grandfather, the seventh Count, in a moment of historically unusual family prosperity ended by, among other things, the building of Vorkosigan House," Lord Vorkosigan told her cheerfully. "It replaced some decaying clan fortress down in the old Caravanserai area, and not before time, I gather."

He started to hold his hand to a palm-lock, but the doors eased soundlessly open before he could even touch it. His brows twitched up, and he bowed her inside.

Two guardsmen in Vorkosigan brown-and-silver livery stood at attention, flanking the entrance to the black-and-white stone-paved foyer. A third liveried man, Pym, the tall driver whom she'd met when Vorkosigan had picked her up earlier, was just turning away from the door security control panel; he too braced before his lord. Ekaterin was daunted. She had not received the impression when she'd seen him on Komarr that Vorkosigan maintained the old Vor formalities to quite this extent. Though not totally formal—instead of being sternly expressionless, the large guardsmen all smiled down at them, in a friendly and most welcoming manner.

"Thank you, Pym," said Vorkosigan automatically, and paused. After a moment regarding them back with a quizzical bent to his brows, he added, "I thought you were on night shift, Roic. Shouldn't you be asleep?"

The largest and youngest of the guards stood more stiffly to attention, and murmured, "M'lord."

"*M'lord* is not an answer. *M'lord* is an evasion," Vorkosigan said, in a tone more of observation than censure. The guard ventured a subdued smile. Vorkosigan sighed, and turned from him. "Madame Vorsoisson, permit me to introduce the rest of the Vorkosigan Armsmen presently seconded to me—Armsman Jankowski, Armsman Roic. Madame Vorsoisson."

She ducked her head, and they both nodded back, murmuring, "Madame Vorsoisson," and "My pleasure, Madame."

"Pym, you can let Ma Kosti know we're here. Thank you, gentlemen, that *will* be all," Vorkosigan added, with peculiar emphasis.

With more subdued smiles, they melted away down the back passage. Pym's voice drifted back, "See, what did I tell you—" His further explication to his comrades, whatever it was, was quickly muffled by distance into an unintelligible mutter.

Vorkosigan rubbed his lips, recovered his hostly cordiality, and turned back to her again. "Would you like to take a walk around the house before lunch? Many people find it of historical interest."

Personally, she thought it would be utterly fascinating, but she didn't want to come on like some goggling backcountry tourist. "I don't wish to trouble you, Lord Vorkosigan."

His mouth flickered to dismay and back again to earnest welcome. "No trouble. A pleasure, in fact." His gaze at her grew oddly intent.

Did he want her to say yes? Perhaps he was very proud of his possessions. "Then thank you. I should like that very much."

It was the right answer. His cheer returned in force, and he immediately motioned her to the left. A formal antechamber gave way to a wonderful library running the length of the end of the wing; she had to tuck her hands in her bolero pockets to keep them from diving at the old printed books with leather bindings which lined parts of the room from floor to ceiling. He bowed her out glass doors at the end of the library and across a back garden where several generations of servitors had clearly left very little room for any improvements. She thought she might plunge her arm to the elbow into the soil of the perennial beds. Apparently determined to be thorough, he led on into the cross-wing and down to an enormous wine cellar stocked with produce of various Vorkosigan District country farms. They passed through a subbasement garage. The gleaming armored groundcar was there, and a red enameled lightflyer tucked into a corner.

"Is that yours?" Ekaterin said brightly, nodding to the lightflyer.

His answer was unusually brief. "Yes. But I don't fly it much any more."

Oh. Yes. His seizures. She could have kicked herself. Fearing that some tangled attempt to apologize could only make it worse, she followed his shortcut up through a huge and redolent kitchen complex. There Vorkosigan formally introduced her to his famous cook, a plump middle-aged woman named Ma Kosti, who smiled broadly at Ekaterin and thwarted her lord's attempt to sample his lunch-in-preparation. Ma Kosti made it plain she felt her vast domain was underutilized—but how much could one short man eat, after all? He should be encouraged to bring in more company; hope you will come again soon, and often, Madame Vorsoisson.

Ma Kosti benignly shooed them on their way again, and Vorkosigan conducted Ekaterin through a bewildering succession of formal receiving rooms and back to the paved foyer. "Those are the public areas," he told her. "The second floor is all my own territory." With an infectious enthusiasm, he hustled her up the curving staircase to show off a suite of rooms he assured her had once been occupied by the famous General Count Piotr himself, and which were now his own. He made sure to point out the excellent view of the back gardens from the suite's sitting room.

"There are two more floors, plus the attics. The attics of Vorkosigan House are something to behold. Would you like to see them? Is there anything you'd particularly like to see?"

"I don't know," she said, feeling a little overwhelmed. "Did you grow up here?" She stared around the well-appointed sitting room, trying to picture the child-Miles therein, and decide whether she was grateful he'd stopped short of hauling her through his bedroom, just visible through the end door.

"In fact, for the first five or six years of my life, we lived at the Imperial Residence with Gregor," he replied. "My parents and my grandfather had some little, um, disagreement in the early years of the Regency, but then they were reconciled, and Gregor went off to the preparatory academy. My parents moved back here; they claimed the third floor the way I've marked off the second. Heir's privilege. Several generations in one house works best if it's a very *large* house. My grandfather had these rooms till he died, when I was about seventeen. I had a room on my parents' floor, though not in the same wing. They chose it for me because

Illyan said it had the worst angle of fire from . . . um, it has a good view of the garden too. Would you care to . . . ?" He turned, gestured, smiled over his shoulder, and led her out and up another flight, around a corner, and part way down a long hall.

The room into which they turned did have a good window on the garden, but any traces of the boy Miles had been were erased. It was now done up as a bland guest room, with scant personality beyond what was lent it by the fabulous house itself. "How long were you here?" she asked, staring around.

"Till last winter, actually. I moved downstairs after I was medically discharged." He jerked up his chin in his habitual nervous tic. "During the decade I served in ImpSec, I was home so seldom, I never thought to need more."

"At least you had your own bath. These houses from the Time of Isolation are sometimes—" She broke off, as the door she casually opened proved instead to be a closet. The door next to it must lead into the bath. A soft glow of light came on automatically.

The closet was stuffed with uniforms—Lord Vorkosigan's old military uniforms, she realized from the size of them, and the superior tailoring. He wouldn't have been able to use standard-issue gear, after all. She recognized black fatigues, Imperial dress and undress greens, and the glittering brilliance of the formal parade red-and-blues. An array of boots stood guard along the floor from side to side. They'd all been put away clean, but the close concentrated aroma of him still permeated the warm dry air that puffed against her face like a caress. She inhaled, stunned by the military-masculine patchouli. It seemed to flow from her nose to her body directly, circumventing her brain. He stepped anxiously to her side, watching her face; the well-chosen scent he wore that she'd noticed in the cool air of his groundcar, a flattering spicy-citrus overlying clean male, was suddenly intensified by his proximity.

It was the first moment of spontaneous sensuality she'd felt since Tien's death. *Oh, since years before Tien's death.* It was embarrassing, yet oddly comforting too. *Am*

I alive below the neck after all? She was abruptly aware that this was a bedroom.

"What's this one?" She kept her voice from squeaking upward much, and reached to pull out an unfamiliar gray uniform on its hanger, a heavy short jacket with epaulettes, many closed pockets, and white trim, with matching trousers. The stripes on the sleeves and assorted collar-pins encoding rank were a mystery to her, but there seemed to be a lot of them. The fabric had that odd fire-proof feel one found only in seriously expensive field gear.

His smile softened. "Well, now." He slipped the jacket off the hanger she clutched, and held it up briefly. "You've never met Admiral Naismith, have you. He was my favorite covert ops persona. He—I—ran the Dendarii Free Mercenary Fleet for ImpSec for years."

"You pretended to be a galactic admiral?"

"—Lieutenant Vorkosigan?" he finished wryly. "It started as a pretense. I made it real." One corner of his mouth zigged up, and with a murmur of *Why not?*, he hung the jacket over the doorknob and slipped out of his gray tunic, revealing a fine white shirt. A shoulder holster she'd not guessed he wore held a hand-weapon flat to his left side. *Even here, he goes armed?* It was only a heavy-duty stunner, but he seemed to wear it as unselfconsciously as he wore his shirt. *I suppose if you are a Vorkosigan, that's how you dress every day.*

He traded the tunic for the jacket and pulled it on; his suit trousers were so close a color match, he hardly needed to don the uniform pants to present his effect, or effect his presentation. He stretched, and on the return came to a posture totally unlike anything she'd seen in him before: relaxed, extended, somehow filling the space beyond his undersized body. One arm came out to prop him casually against the doorframe, and his tilted smile turned into something blazing. In a dead-pan-perfect flat Betan accent that seemed never to have heard of the concept of the Vor caste, he said, "Aw, don't let that dull dirt-sucking Barrayaran bring you down. Stick with me, lady, and I'll show you the galaxy." Ekaterin, startled, stepped back a pace.

He jerked up his chin, still grinning dementedly, and began fastening the clasps. His hands reached the jacket waist, straightened the band, and paused. The ends were a couple of centimeters short of meeting at the middle, and the clasp notably failed to seat itself even when he gave it a covert tug. He stared down in such obvious dismay at this treasonous shrinkage, Ekaterin choked on a giggle.

He glanced up at her, and a rueful smile lit his eyes in response to the crinkle of her own. His voice returned to Barrayaran-normal. "I haven't had this on for over a year. Seems we outgrow our past in more ways than one." He hitched back out of the uniform jacket. "Hm. Well, you met my cook. Food's not a job for her, it's a sacred calling."

"Maybe it shrank in the wash," she offered in attempted consolation.

"Bless you. No." He sighed. "The Admiral's deep cover was fraying badly even before he was killed. Naismith's days were numbered anyway."

His voice made light of this loss, but she'd seen the scars on his chest left by the needle-grenade. Her mind circled back to the seizure she'd witnessed, on the living room floor of her and Tien's cramped apartment on Komarr. She remembered the look in his eyes after the epileptic storm had passed: mental confusion, shame, helpless rage. The man had driven his body far past its limits, in the belief, apparently, that unsupported will could conquer anything.

So it can. For a time. Then time ran out—no. Time ran on. There was no end to time. *But you come to the end of yourself, and time runs on, and leaves you.* Her years with Tien had taught her that, if nothing else.

"I suppose I ought to give these to Nikki to play with." He gestured casually at the row of uniforms. But his hands carefully straightened the gray jacket again on its hanger, brushed invisible lint, and hooked it back into its place in the bar. "While he still can, and is young enough to want to. He'll outgrow them in another year or so, I think."

Her breath drew in. *I think that would be obscene.* These

relics had clearly been life and death to him. What possessed him, to make-believe they were no more than a child's playthings? She couldn't think how to discourage him from this horrifying notion without sounding as though she scorned his offer. Instead, after the moment's silence threatened to stretch unbearably, she blurted, "Would you go back? If you could?"

His gaze grew distant. "Well, now . . . now that's the strangest thing. I think I would feel like a snake trying to crawl back into its shed dead skin. I miss it every minute, and I have no wish at all to go back." He looked up, and twinkled at her. "Needle grenades are a learning experience, that way."

This was his idea of a joke, apparently. She wasn't sure if she wanted to kiss him and make it well, or run away screaming. She managed a faint smile.

He shrugged on his plain civilian tunic, and the sinister shoulder holster disappeared from view again. Closing the closet door firmly, he took her on a spin around the rest of the third floor; he pointed out his absent parents' suite, but to Ekaterin's secret relief did not offer to take her inside the succession of rooms. It would have felt very odd to wander through the famous Count and Countess Vorkosigan's intimate space, as though she were some voyeur.

They finally fetched up back on "his" floor, at the end of the main wing in a bright room he called the Yellow Parlor, which he apparently used as a dining room. A small table was elegantly set up for lunch for two. Good, they were not expected to dine downstairs in that elaborately-paneled cavern with the table that extended to seat forty-eight; ninety-six in a squeeze, if a second table, cleverly secreted behind the wainscoting, was brought out in parallel. At some unseen signal, Ma Kosti appeared with luncheon on a cart: soup, tea, an exquisite salad involving cultured shrimp and fruit and nuts. She left her lord and his guest discreetly alone after the initial flourishing serving, though a large silver tray with a domed cover which she left sitting atop the cart at Lord Vorkosigan's elbow promised more delights to come.

"It's a great house," Lord Vorkosigan told Ekaterin between bites, "but it gets really quiet at night. Lonely. It's not meant to be this empty. It needs to be filled up with life again, the way it used to be in my father's heyday." His tone was almost disconsolate.

"The Viceroy and Vicereine will be returning for the Emperor's wedding, won't they? It should be full again at Midsummer," she pointed out helpfully.

"Oh, yes, and their whole entourage. *Everyone* will be back on planet for the wedding." He hesitated. "Including my brother Mark, come to think of it. I suppose I should warn you about Mark."

"My uncle once mentioned you had a clone. Is that him, um . . . it?"

"*It* is the preferred Betan pronoun for a hermaphrodite; definitely him. Yes."

"Uncle Vorthys didn't say why you—or was it your parents?—had a clone made, except that it was complicated, and I should ask you." The explanation that leapt most readily to mind was that Count Vorkosigan had wanted an undeformed replacement for his soltoxin-damaged heir, but that obviously wasn't the case.

"That's the complicated part. *We* didn't. Some Komarran expatriates exiled to Earth did, as part of a much-too-baroque plot against my father. I guess when they couldn't get up a military revolution, they thought they'd try some biological warfare on a budget. They got an agent to filch a tissue sample from me—it couldn't have been that hard, I'd had hundreds of medical treatments and tests and biopsies as a child—and farmed it out to one of the less savory clone lords on Jackson's Whole."

"My word. But Uncle Vorthys said your clone didn't look like you—did he grow up without your, um, pre-natal damage, then?" She gave him a short nod, but kept her eyes politely on his face. She'd already encountered his somewhat erratic sensitivity about his birth defects. *Teratogenic, not genetic*, he'd made sure she understood.

"If it had been that simple . . . He actually started to grow as he should, so they had to body-sculpt him down to my size. And shape. It was pretty gruesome. They'd

intended him to pass close inspection as my replacement, so when I did things like have my busted leg
bones replaced with synthetics, his got surgically
replaced too. I know exactly how much that must have
hurt. And they forced him to study to pass for me. All
the years I thought I was an only child, he was developing the worst case of sibling rivalry you ever saw. I
mean, think about it. Never allowed to be yourself,
constantly—under threat of torture, in fact—compared
with your older brother . . . By the time the plot fell
through, he was on a fair way to being driven crazy."

"I should think so! But . . . how did you rescue him
from the Komarrans?"

He was silent for a little, then said, "He kind of
turned up on his own, at the last. As soon as he came
within my Betan mother's orbit—well, you can imagine.
Betans have very strict and clear convictions about
parental responsibilities to clones. It surprised the hell
out of him, I think. He knew he had a brother, God
knows he'd had his face ground into that fact, but he
wasn't expecting parents. He certainly wasn't expecting
Cordelia Vorkosigan. The family has adopted him, I
suppose is the simplest way of thinking about it. He was
here on Barrayar for a while, then last year my mother
sent him off to Beta Colony, to attend university and
get therapy under the supervision of my Betan grandmother."

"That sounds good," she said, pleased with the bizarre
tale's happy ending. The Vorkosigans stood by their own,
it seemed.

"Mm, maybe. Reports leaking back from my grandmother suggest it's been pretty rocky for him. You see,
he's got this obsession—perfectly understandable—about
differentiating himself from me, so's no one could ever
mistake one of us for the other ever again. Which is
fine by me, don't get me wrong. I think it's a great idea.
But . . . but he could have gotten a facial mod, or body
sculpture, or growth hormones, or changed his eye color
or bleached his hair, or anything but . . . instead what
he decided to do was gain a great deal of weight. At
my height, the effect is damned startling. I think he likes

it that way. Does it on purpose." He stared rather broodingly at his plate. "I thought his Betan therapy might
do something about that, but apparently not."

A scrabble at the edge of the tablecloth made
Ekaterin start; a determined-looking half-grown black-
and-white kitten hauled itself up over the side, tiny claws
like pitons, and made for Vorkosigan's plate. He smiled
absently, picked a couple of remaining shrimp from his
salad, and deposited them before the little beast; it
growled and purred through its enthusiastic chewing.
"The gate guard's cat keeps having these kittens," he
explained. "I admire their approach to life, but they do
turn up . . ." He picked the large cover off the tray, and
deposited it over the creature, trapping it. The
undaunted purr resonated against the silver hemisphere
like some small machine stripping its gears. "Dessert?"

The silver tray was loaded with eight different dessert pastries, so alarmingly beautiful Ekaterin thought
it an aesthetic crime to eat them without making a vid
recording for posterity first. "Oh, my." After a long
pause, she pointed at one with thick cream and glazed
fruit like jewels. Vorkosigan slipped it onto a waiting
plate, and handed it across. He stared at the array
longingly, but did not select one for himself, Ekaterin
noticed. He was not in the least fat, she thought indignantly; when he'd played Admiral Naismith he must have
been practically emaciated. The pastry tasted as wonderful as it looked, and Ekaterin's contribution to the
conversation ceased for a short time. Vorkosigan
watched her, smiling in, apparently, vicarious pleasure.

As she was scraping up the last molecules of cream
from her plate with her fork, footsteps sounded in the
hall, and men's voices. She recognized Pym's rumble,
saying, " . . . no, m'lord's in conference with his new
landscape designer. I really don't think he wishes to be
disturbed."

A drawling baritone replied, "Yeah, yeah, Pym. Nor
did I. It's official business from m'mother."

A look of extreme annoyance flashed over
Vorkosigan's face, and he bit off an expletive too
muffled to quite make out. As his visitor loomed in the

doorway to the Yellow Parlor, his expression went very
bland.

The man Pym was failing to impede was a young officer, a tall and startlingly handsome captain in undress
greens. He had dark hair, laughing brown eyes, and a
lazy smile. He paused to sweep Vorkosigan a mocking
half-bow, saying, "Hail, O Lord Auditor coz. My God,
is that a Ma Kosti lunch I spy? Tell me I'm not too late.
Is there anything left? Can I lick your crumbs?" He
stepped inside, and his eye swept over Ekaterin. "Oh ho!
Introduce me to your *landscape designer*, Miles!"

Lord Vorkosigan said, somewhat through his teeth,
"Madame Vorsoisson, may I make you known to my feck-
less cousin, Captain Ivan Vorpatril. Ivan, Madame
Vorsoisson."

Undaunted by this disapproving editorial, Vorpatril
grinned, bowed deeply over her hand, and kissed it. His
lips lingered an appreciative second too long, but at least
they were dry and warm; she didn't have to overcome
an impolite impulse to wipe her hand on her skirt, when
he at last released it. "And are you taking commissions,
Madame Vorsoisson?"

Ekaterin was not quite sure whether to be amused
or offended at his cheerful leer, but amused seemed
safer. She permitted herself a small smile. "I'm only just
starting."

Lord Vorkosigan put in, "Ivan lives in an apartment.
I believe there is a flowerpot on his balcony, but the
last time I looked, its contents were dead."

"It was *winter*, Miles." A faint mewing from the silver dome at his elbow distracted him. He stared at the
cover, curiously tilted it up on one side, said, "Ah. One
of you," and let it back down. He wandered around the
table, spied the unused dessert plate, smiled beatifically,
and helped himself to two of the pastries and the leftover fork at his cousin's plate. Returning to the empty
place opposite, he settled his spoils, dragged up a chair,
and seated himself between Lord Vorkosigan and
Ekaterin. He regarded the mews of protest rising in
volume from the dome, sighed, retrieved the feline
prisoner, and settled it on his lap atop the fine cloth

napkin, occupying it with a liberal smear of cream on its paws and face. "Don't let me interrupt you," he added around his first bite.

"We were just finishing," said Vorkosigan. "Why are you *here*, Ivan?" He added under his breath, "And why couldn't three bodyguards keep you out? Do I have to give orders to shoot to kill?"

"My strength is great because my cause is just," Vorpatril informed him. "My mother has sent me with a list of chores for you as long as my arm. With foot-notes." He drew a roll of folded flimsies from his tunic, and waved them at his cousin; the kitten rolled on its back and batted at them, and he amused himself briefly, batting back. "Tik-tik-tik!"

"Your determination is relentless because you're more afraid of your mother than you are of my guardsmen."

"So are you. So are your guardsmen," observed Lord Vorpatril, downing another bite of dessert.

Vorkosigan swallowed an involuntary laugh, then recovered his severe look again. "Ah . . . Madame Vorsoisson, I can see I'm going to have to deal with this. Perhaps we'd best break off for today." He smiled apologetically at her, and pushed back his chair.

Lord Vorkosigan doubtless had important security matters to discuss with the young officer. "Of course. Um, it was good to meet you, Lord Vorpatril."

Impeded by the kitten, the captain didn't rise, but he nodded a most cordial farewell. "Madame Vorsoisson, a pleasure. I hope we'll see each other again soon."

Vorkosigan's smile went thin; she rose with him, and he shepherded her out into the hall, raising his wristcom to his lips and murmuring, "Pym, please bring the car around front." He gestured onward, and fell into step beside her down the corridor. "Sorry about Ivan."

She didn't quite see what he felt the need to apologize for, so concealed her bewilderment in a shrug.

"So do we have a deal?" he went on. "Will you take on my project?"

"Maybe you'd better see a few possible designs, first."

"Yes, of course. Tomorrow . . . or you can call me whenever you're ready. You have my number?"

"Yes, you gave me several of them back on Komarr. I still have them."

"Ah. Good." They turned down the great stairway, and his face went thoughtful. At the bottom, he looked up at her and added, "And do you still have that little memento?"

He meant the tiny model Barrayar, pendant on a chain, souvenir of the grim events they couldn't talk about in any public forum. "Oh, yes."

He paused hopefully, and she was stricken that she couldn't pull the jewelry out of her black blouse and demonstrate it on the spot, but she'd thought it too valuable to wear everyday; it was put away, carefully wrapped, in a drawer in her aunt's house. After a moment, the sound of the groundcar came from the porte cochère, and he ushered her back out the double doors.

"Good day, then, Madame Vorsoisson." He shook her hand, firmly and without holding it for too long, and saw her into the groundcar's rear compartment. "I guess I'd better go straighten out Ivan." As the canopy closed and the car pulled away, he turned to stalk back indoors. By the time the car bore her smoothly out the gates, he'd vanished from view.

Ivan set one of the used salad plates down on the floor, and plunked the kitten next to it. He had to admit, a young animal of almost any kind made an excellent prop; he'd noted the way Madame Vorsoisson's cool expression had softened as he'd noodled with the furry little verminoid. Where had Miles found that astonishing widow? He sat back, and watched the kitten's pink tongue flash over the sauce, and reflected glumly on his own last night's outing.

His date had seemed such a *possible* young woman: University student, away from home for the first time, bound to be impressed with an Imperial Vor officer. Bold of gaze and not a bit shy; she'd picked *him* up in *her* lightflyer. Ivan was expert in the uses of a lightflyer for breaking down psychological barriers and creating the proper mood. A few gentle swoops and you could almost always evoke some of those cute little shrieks where the young lady clung closer, her chest rising and falling as her breath came faster through parted and increasingly-kissable lips. *This* girl, however . . . he hadn't come so near to losing his last meal in a lightflyer since being trapped by Miles in one of his manic phases for an updraft demonstration over Hassadar. She'd laughed, fiendishly, while Ivan had smiled helplessly through clenched teeth, his knuckles whitening on the seat straps.

Then, in the restaurant she'd picked, they'd met up oh-so-casually with that surly pup of a graduate student, and the playlet began to fall into place. She'd been *using* him, dammit, to test the pup's devotion to her cause; and the cur had rolled over and snarled right on cue. *How do you do, sir. Oh, isn't this your uncle you said was in the Service? I beg your pardon. . . .* The smooth way he'd managed to turn the overly respectful offer of a chair into a subtle insult had been worthy of, of Ivan's shortest relative, practically. Ivan had escaped early, silently wishing them joy of each other. Let the punishment fit the crime. He didn't know what was happening with young Barrayaran girls these days. They were turning almost . . . almost *galactic*, as if they'd been taking lessons from Miles's formidable friend Quinn. His mother's acerbic recommendation that he stick to women of his own age and class seemed almost to begin to make sense.

Light footsteps echoed from the hall, and his cousin appeared in the doorway. Ivan considered, and dismissed, an impulse to favor Miles with a vivid account of last night's debacle. Whatever emotion was tightening Miles's lips and pulling his head down into that bulldog-with-a-hair-up-its-butt look, it was very far from promising sympathy.

"Rotten timing, Ivan," Miles bit out.

"What, did I spoil your tête-à-tête? *Landscape designer*, eh? *I* could develop a sudden interest in a landscape like that, too. What a profile."

"Exquisite," Miles breathed, temporarily distracted by some inner vision.

"And her face isn't bad, either," Ivan added, watching him.

Miles almost took the bait right then, but he muffled his initial response in a grimace. "Don't get greedy. Weren't you telling me you have that sweetheart deal with Madame Vor-what's-her-name?" He pulled back his chair and slumped into it, crossing his arms and his ankles and watching Ivan through narrowed eyes.

"Ah. Yes. Well. That seems to have fallen through."

"You amaze me. Was the compliant husband not so compliant after all?"

"It was all so unreasonable. I mean, they're cooking up their kid in a uterine replicator. It's not like someone even *can* graft a little bastard onto the family tree these days. In any case, he's nailed down a post in the colonial administration, and is whisking her off to Sergyar. He scarcely even let us make a civil good-bye." It had been an unpleasant scene with oblique death threats, actually. It might have been mitigated by the slightest sign of regret, or even concern for Ivan's health and safety, on her part, but instead she'd spent the moment hanging on her husband's arm and looking impressed by his territorial trumpeting. As for the pubescent prole terrorist with the lightflyer whom he'd next tried to persuade to mend his broken heart . . . he suppressed a shudder.

Ivan shrugged off his retrospective moment of depression, and went on, "But a widow, a real live young widow! Do you know how hard they are to find these days? I know fellows in HQ who'd give their right hands for a friendly widow, except they have to save them for those long, lonely nights. However did you luck onto this honey-pot?"

His cousin didn't deign to answer. After a moment, he gestured to the flimsy, rolled up beside Ivan's empty plate. "So what's all this?"

"Ah." Ivan flattened it out, and handed it across the table. "It's the agenda for your upcoming meeting with the Emperor, the Empress-to-be, and my mother. She's pinning Gregor to the wall on all the final details about the wedding. Since you are to be Gregor's Second, your presence is requested and required."

"Oh." Miles glanced down the contents. A puzzled

line appeared between his brows, and he looked up again at Ivan. "Not that this isn't important, but shouldn't you be on duty at Ops right now?"

"Ha," said Ivan glumly. "Do you know what those bastards have done to me?"

Miles shook his head, brows rising inquisitively.

"I have been formally seconded to my mother—my *mother*—as aide-de-camp till the wedding's over. I joined the Service to get *away* from my mother, blast it. And now she's suddenly my chain of command!"

His cousin's brief grin was entirely without sympathy. "Until Laisa is safely hitched to Gregor, and can take over her duties as his political hostess, your mother may be the most important person in Vorbarr Sultana. Don't underestimate her. I've seen planetary invasion plans less complex than what's being booted about for this Imperial Wedding. It's going to take all Aunt Alys's generalship to bring it off."

Ivan shook his head. "I knew I should have put in for off-planet duty while I still could. Komarr, Sergyar, some dismal embassy, anywhere but Vorbarr Sultana."

Miles's face sobered. "I don't know, Ivan. Short of a surprise attack, this is the most politically important event of—I was about to say, of the year, but I really think, of our lifetimes. The more little heirs Gregor and Laisa can put between you and me and the Imperium, the safer we'll be. Us *and* our families."

"We don't have families yet," Ivan pointed out. *So, is that what's on his mind with the pretty widow? Oh ho!*

"Would we have dared? *I* sure thought about the issue, every time I got close enough to a woman to . . . never mind. But this wedding needs to run on rails, Ivan."

"I'm not arguing with that," said Ivan sincerely. He reached down to dissuade the kitten, who had licked the plate clean, from trying to sharpen its claws on his polished boots. A few moments spent petting it in his lap bought it off from that enthusiasm, and it settled down, purring, to the serious business of digesting and growing more hairs to shed on Imperial uniforms. "So what's your widow's first name, say again?" Miles hadn't actually imparted that bit of information, yet.

"Ekaterin," Miles sighed. His mouth seemed to caress all four syllables before reluctantly parting with them.

Oh, yeah. Ivan thought back over every bit of chaff his cousin had ever inflicted upon him for his numerous love affairs. *Did you think I was a stone, for you to sharpen your wits upon?* Opportunities to even the score seemed to hover on the horizon like rain clouds after a long drought. "Grief-stricken, is she, you say? Seems to me she could use someone with a sense of humor, to cheer her up. Not you, you're clearly in one of your funks. Maybe I ought to volunteer to show her the town."

Miles had poured himself more tea and been just about to put his feet up on a neighboring chair; at this, they came back down with a thump. "Don't even think about it. This one is *mine*."

"Really? You secretly betrothed already? Quick work, coz."

"No," he admitted grudgingly.

"You have some sort of an understanding?"

"Not yet."

"So she is not, in point of fact, anyone's but her own. At present."

Uncharacteristically, Miles took a slow sip of tea before responding. "I mean to change that. When the time is right, which it surely is not yet."

"Hey, all's fair in love and war. Why can't I try?"

Miles snapped back, "If you step in this, it *will* be war."

"Don't let your exalted new status go to your head, coz. Even an Imperial Auditor can't order a woman to sleep with him."

"Marry him," Miles corrected frostily.

Ivan tilted his head, his grin spreading. "My God, you *are* gone completely over the edge. Who'd have guessed it?"

Miles bared his teeth. "Unlike you, *I* have never pretended to not be interested in that fate. *I* have no brave bachelor speeches to eat. Nor a juvenile reputation as a local stud to maintain. Or live down, as the case may be."

"My, we are snarky today."

Miles took a deep breath; before he could speak, Ivan put in, "Y'know, that head-down hostile scrunch makes you look more hunch-backed. You ought to watch that."

After a long, chill silence, Miles said softly, "Are you challenging my ingenuity . . . Ivan?"

"Ah . . ." It didn't take long to grope for the right answer. "No."

"Good," Miles breathed, settling back. "Good . . ." Another long and increasingly disturbing silence followed this, during which his cousin studied Ivan through narrowed eyes. At last, he seemed to come to some internal decision. "Ivan, I'm asking for your word as Vorpatril—just between you and me—that you will leave Ekaterin alone."

Ivan's brows flew up. "That's a little pushy, isn't it? I mean, doesn't she get a vote?"

Miles's nostrils flared. "You have no real interest in her."

"How do you know? How do *I* know? I barely had a chance to say hello before you hustled her out."

"I know you. For you, she's interchangeable with the next ten women you chance to meet. Well, she's not interchangeable for me. I propose a treaty. You can have all the rest of the women in the universe. I just want this one. I think that's fair."

It was one of those Miles-arguments again, which always seemed to result oh-so-logically in Miles getting whatever Miles wanted. Ivan recognized the pattern; it hadn't changed since they were five years old. Only the content had evolved. "The problem is, the rest of the women in the universe are not yours to dispense, either," Ivan pointed out triumphantly. After a couple of decades practice, he *was* getting quicker at this. "You're trying to trade something you don't have for—something you don't have."

Thwarted, Miles settled back in his chair and glowered at him.

"Seriously," said Ivan, "isn't your passion a trifle

sudden, for a man who just parted company with the estimable Quinn at Winterfair? Where have you been hiding this Kat, till now?"

"Ekaterin. I met her on Komarr," Miles replied shortly.

"During your case? This *is* recent, then. Hey, you haven't told me all about your first case, Lord Auditor coz. I must say, all that uproar about their solar mirror sure seems to have petered out into nothing." He waited expectantly, but Miles did not pick up on this invitation. He must not be in one of his voluble moods. *Either you can't turn him on, or you can't turn him off.* Well, if there was a choice, taciturn was probably safer for the innocent bystanders than spring-wound. Ivan added after a moment, "So does she have a sister?"

"No."

"They never do." Ivan heaved a sigh. "Who is she, really? Where does she live?"

"She is Lord Auditor Vorthys's niece, and her husband suffered a ghastly death barely two months ago. I doubt she's in the mood for your humor."

She wasn't the only one so disinclined, it appeared. Damn, but Miles seemed stuck in prick-mode today. "Eh, he got mixed up in one of *your* affairs, did he? That'll teach him." Ivan leaned back, and grinned sourly. "That's one way to solve the widow shortage, I suppose. Make your own."

All the latent amusement which had parried Ivan's sallies till now was abruptly wiped from his cousin's face. His back straightened as much as it could, and he leaned forward, his hands gripping his chair arms. His voice dropped to an arctic pitch. "I will thank you, Lord Vorpatril, to take care not to repeat that slander. Ever."

Ivan's stomach lurched in surprise. He had seen Miles come the Lord Auditor a couple of times now, but never before at *him*. The freezing gray eyes suddenly had all the expression of a pair of gun barrels. Ivan opened his mouth, then closed it, more carefully. What the *hell* was going on here? And how did someone so short manage to project that much menace? Years of practice, Ivan supposed. *And conditioning.* "It was a *joke*, Miles."

"I don't find it very damned amusing." Miles rubbed his wrists, and frowned into the middle distance. A muscle jumped in his jaw; he jerked up his chin. After a moment, he added more bleakly, "I won't be telling you about the Komarran case, Ivan. It's slit-your-throat-before-reading stuff, and no horseshit. I will tell you this, and I expect it to go no further. Etienne Vorsoisson's death was a mess and a murder, and I surely failed to prevent it. But I did not cause it."

"For God's sake Miles, I didn't really think you—"

"However," his cousin raised his voice to override this, "all the evidence which proves this is now as classified as it's possible to be. It follows, that should such an accusation be made against me, I can't publicly access the facts or testimony to *disprove* it. Think about the consequences of that for one minute, *if* you please. Especially if . . . if my suit prospers."

Ivan sucked on his tongue for a moment, quelled. Then he brightened. "But . . . Gregor has access. Who could argue with him? Gregor could pronounce you clear."

"My foster-brother the Emperor, who appointed me Auditor as a favor to my father? Or so everyone says?"

Ivan shifted uncomfortably. So, Miles had heard that one, had he? "The people who count know better. Where *do* you pick this stuff up, Miles?"

A dry shrug, and a little hand-gesture, was the only reply he got. Miles was growing unnervingly political, these days. Ivan had slightly less interest in becoming involved with Imperial politics than in holding a plasma arc to his head and pulling the trigger. It wasn't that he ran away screaming whenever the loaded topics arose; that would draw too much attention. Saunter off slowly, that was the ticket. Miles . . . Miles the maniacal maybe had the nerve for a political career. The dwarf always did have that little suicidal streak. *Better you than me, boy.*

Miles, who had fallen into a study of his half-boots, looked up again. "I know I have no right to demand a damned thing from you, Ivan. I still owe you for . . . for the events of last fall. And the dozen other times you saved my neck, or tried to. All I can do is ask. Please.

I don't get many chances, and this one matters the world to me." A crooked smile.

Damn that smile. Was it Ivan's fault, that he had been born undamaged while his cousin had been born crippled? No, blast it. It was bloody bungled politics that had wrecked him, and you'd think it would be a lesson to him, but no. Demonstrably, even sniper fire couldn't stop the hyperactive little git. In between inspiring you to strangle him with your bare hands, he could make you proud enough to cry. At least, Ivan had taken care no one could see his face, when he'd watched from the Council floor as Miles had taken his Auditor's oath with that terrifying intensity, before all the assembled panoply of Barrayar last Winterfair. So small, so wrecked, so obnoxious. So incandescent. *Give the people a light, and they'll follow it anywhere.* Did Miles know how dangerous he was?

And the little paranoid actually believed Ivan had the magic to entice any woman Miles really wanted away from him. His fears were more flattering to Ivan than he would ever let on. But Miles had so few humilities, it seemed almost a sin to take this one away from him. Bad for his soul, eh.

"All right." Ivan sighed. "But I'm only giving you first shot, mind. If she tells you to take a hike, I think I should have just as much right to be next in line as the other fellow."

Miles half relaxed. "That's all I'm asking." Then tensed again. "Your word as Vorpatril, mind."

"My word as Vorpatril," Ivan allowed grudgingly, after a very long moment.

Miles relaxed altogether, looking much more cheerful. A few minutes of desultory conversation about the agenda for Lady Alys's planning session segued into an enumeration of Madame Vorsoisson's manifold virtues. If there was one thing worse than enduring his cousin's preemptive jealousy, Ivan decided, it was listening to his romantically hopeful *burbling.* Clearly, Vorkosigan House was not going to be a good place to hide out from Lady Alys this afternoon, nor, he suspected, for many afternoons to come. Miles wasn't even interested in a spot of recreational drinking; when he started to explain to Ivan his several new plans for gardens, Ivan pleaded duty, and escaped.

As he found his way down the front stairs, it dawned on Ivan that Miles had done him *again*. He'd obtained exactly what he wanted, and Ivan wasn't even sure how it had happened. Ivan hadn't had any intention of giving up his name's word on this one. The very suggestion had been quite offensive, when you looked at it from a certain angle. He frowned in frustration.

It was all wrong. If this Ekaterin woman was indeed that fine, she deserved a man who'd hustle for her. And if the widow's love for Miles was to be tested, it would certainly be better done sooner than later. Miles had no sense of proportion, of restraint, of . . . of self-preservation. How devastating it would be, if she decided to throw him back. It would be the ice-water bath therapy all over again. *Next time, I should hold his head under longer. I let him up too soon, that was my mistake . . .*

It would be almost a public service, to dangle the alternatives in front of the widow before Miles got her mind all turned inside out like he did everyone else's. But . . . Miles had extracted his word from Ivan, with downright ruthless determination. Forced it, practically, and a forced oath was no oath at all.

The way around this dilemma occurred to Ivan between one step and the next; his lips pursed in a sudden whistle. The scheme was nearly . . . Milesian. Cosmic justice, to serve the dwarf a dish with his own sauce. By the time Pym let him out the front door, Ivan was smiling again.

CHAPTER TWO

Kareen Koudelka slid eagerly into the window seat of the orbital shuttle, and pressed her nose to the port. All she could see so far was the transfer station and its starry background. After endless minutes, the usual clanks and yanks signaled undocking, and the shuttle spun away from the station. The thrilling colored arc of Barrayar's terminator slid past her view as the shuttle began its descent. The western three-quarters of North Continent still glowed in its afternoon. She could see the *seas*. Home again, after nearly a year. Kareen settled back in her seat, and considered her mixed feelings.

She wished Mark were with her, to compare notes. And how did people like Miles, who had been off-world maybe fifty times, handle the cognitive dissonance? He'd had a student year on Beta Colony too, when even younger than she. She realized she had a lot more questions to ask him about it now, if she could work up the nerve.

So Miles Vorkosigan really was an Imperial Auditor now. It was hard to imagine him as one of those stiff old sticks. Mark had expended considerable nervous wit at the news, before sending off a congratulatory message by tight-beam, but then, Mark had a Thing about Miles. *Thing* was not accepted psychoscientific terminology, she'd been informed by his twinkling therapist, but there was scarcely another term with the scope and flexibility to take in the whole complexity of the . . . Thing.

Her hand drifted down in an inventory, tugging her shirt and smoothing her trousers. The eclectic mix of garb—Komarran-style pants, Barrayaran bolero, a synthasilk shirt from Escobar—wasn't going to shock her family. She pulled an ash-blond curl out straight and looked up at it cross-eyed. Her hair was almost grown out again to the length and style she'd had when she'd left. Yes, all the important changes were on the inside, privately; she might reveal them or not, in her own time, as seemed right or safe. *Safe?* she queried herself in bemusement. She was letting Mark's paranoias rub off on her. Still . . .

With a reluctant frown, she drew her Betan earrings from her ears, and tucked them into her bolero pocket. Mama had hung around with Countess Cordelia enough; she might well be able to decode their Betan meaning. This was the style that said: Yes, I'm a consenting and contraceptive-protected adult, but I am presently in an exclusive relationship, so please do not embarrass us both by asking. Which was rather a lot to encrypt in a few twists of metal, and the Betans had a dozen more styles for other nuances; she'd graduated through a couple of them. The contraceptive implant the earrings advertised could now just ride along in secret, no one's business but her own.

Kareen considered briefly the comparison of Betan earrings with related social signals in other cultures: the wedding ring, certain styles of clothing or hats or veils or facial hair or tattoos. All such signals could be subverted, as with unfaithful spouses whose behavior belied their outward statement of monogamy, but really the Betans seemed very good about keeping congruent to theirs. Of course, they had so many choices. Wearing a false signal was highly disapproved, socially. *It screws it up for the rest of us,* a Betan had once explained to her. *The whole idea is to eliminate the weird guessing-games.*

You had to admire their honesty. No wonder they did so well at the sciences. In all, Kareen decided, there was a lot about the sometimes appallingly sensible Betan-born Countess Cordelia Vorkosigan that she thought she might understand much better now. But Tante Cordelia wouldn't be back home to talk with till nearly the Emperor's wedding at Midsummer, sigh.

She set the ambiguities of the flesh abruptly aside as Vorbarr Sultana drew into view below. It was evening, and a glorious sunset painted the clouds as the shuttle made its final descent. City lights in the dusk made the groundscape magical. She could pick out dear, familiar landmarks, the winding river, a *real* river after a year of those measly fountains the Betans put in their underground world, the famous bridges—the folk song in four languages about them rippled through her mind—the main monorail lines . . . then the rush of landing, and the final whine to a true stop at the shuttleport. *Home, home, I'm home!* It was all she could do to keep from stampeding over the bodies of all the slow old people ahead of her. But at last she was through the flex-tube ramp and the last maze of tube and corridor. *Will they be waiting? Will they all be there?*

They did not disappoint her. They were all there, every one, standing in their own little squad, staking out the best space by the pillars closest to the exit doors: Mama clutching a huge bouquet of flowers, and Olivia, holding up a big decorated sign with rainbow ribbons streaming that said WELCOME HOME KAREEN!, and Martya, jumping up and down as she saw her, and Delia looking very cool and grownup, and Da himself, still wearing his Imperial undress greens from the day's work at HQ, leaning on his stick and grinning. The group-hug was all that Kareen's homesick heart had ever imagined, bending the sign and squashing the flowers. Olivia giggled and Martya shrieked and even Da rubbed water from his eyes. Passers-by stared; male passers-by stared longingly, and tended to blunder into walls. Commodore Koudelka's all-blond commando team, the junior officers from HQ joked. Kareen wondered if Martya and Olivia still tormented them on purpose. The poor boys kept trying to surrender, but so far, none of the sisters had taken prisoners except Delia, who'd apparently conquered that Komarran friend of Miles's at Winterfair—an ImpSec commodore, no less. Kareen could hardly wait to get home and hear all the details of the engagement.

All talking at once, except for Da, who'd given up years ago and now just listened benignly, they herded off to collect Kareen's luggage and meet the groundcar. Da and Mama had evidently borrowed the big one from Lord Vorkosigan for the occasion, along with Armsman Pym to drive it, so that they all might fit in the rear compartment. Pym greeted her with a hearty welcome-home from his liege-lord and himself, piled her modest valises in beside him, and they were off.

"I thought you would come home wearing one of those topless Betan sarongs," Martya teased her, as the groundcar pulled away from the shuttleport and headed toward town.

"I thought about it." Kareen buried her grin in her armload of flowers. "It's just not warm enough here."

"You didn't actually wear one *there*, did you?"

Fortunately, before Kareen was forced to either answer or evade this, Olivia piped up, "When I saw Lord Vorkosigan's car I thought Lord Mark might have come home with you after all, but Mama said not. Won't he be coming back to Barrayar for the wedding?"

"Oh, yes. He actually left Beta Colony before I did, but he stopped on the way at Escobar to . . ." she hesitated, "to attend to some business of his." Actually, Mark had gone to cadge weight-loss drugs, more powerful than those his Betan therapist would prescribe for him, from a clinic of refugee Jacksonian doctors in which he had a financial interest. He would doubtless check out the business health of the clinic at the same time, so it wasn't an outright lie.

Kareen and Mark had come close to having their first real argument over this dubious choice of his, but it was, Kareen recognized, indeed his choice. Body-control issues lay near the core of his deepest troubles; she was developing an instinct—if she didn't flatter herself, close to a real understanding—of when she could push for his good. And when she just had to wait, and let Mark wrestle with Mark. It had been a somewhat terrifying privilege to watch and listen, this past year, as his therapist coached him; and an exhilarating experience to participate, under the therapist's supervision, in the partial healing he was achieving. And to learn there were more important aspects to love than a mad rush for connection: confidentiality, for one. Patience for another. And, paradoxically and most urgently in Mark's case, a certain cool and distant autonomy. It had taken her months to figure that one out. She wasn't about to try to explain it to her noisy, teasing, loving family in the back of a groundcar.

"You've become good friends . . ." her mother trailed off invitingly.

"He needed one." *Desperately*.

"Yes, but is he your *boy*friend?" Martya had no patience with subtlety, preferring clarity.

"He seemed sweet on you when he was here last year," Delia observed. "And you've been running around with him all year on Beta Colony. Is he slow off the gun?"

Olivia added, "I suppose he's bright enough to be interesting—I mean, he's Miles's twin, he has to be—but *I* thought he was a bit creepy."

Kareen stiffened. *If you'd been cloned a slave, raised by terrorists to be a murderer, trained by methods tantamount to physical and psychological torture, and had to kill people to escape, you'd likely seem a little creepy too. If you weren't a twitching puddle.* Mark was no puddle, more power to him. Mark was creating himself anew with an all-out effort no less heroic for being largely invisible to the outside observer. She pictured herself trying to explain this to Olivia or Martya, and gave up instantly. Delia . . . no, not even Delia. She needed only to mention Mark's four semiautonomous subpersonalities, each with his own nickname, for the conversation to slide downhill permanently. Describing the fascinating way they all worked together to support the fragile economy of his

personality would not thrill a family of Barrayarans
obviously testing for an acceptable in-law.

"Down, girls," Da put in, smiling in the dimness of
the groundcar compartment, and earning Kareen's
gratitude. But then he added, "Still, if we are about to
receive a go-between from the Vorkosigans, I'd like some
warning to prepare my mind for the shock. I've known
Miles all his life. Mark . . . is another matter."

Could they picture no other role for a man in her
life than potential husband? Kareen was by no means
sure Mark was a potential husband. He was still working his heart out on becoming a potential human being.
On Beta Colony, it had all seemed so clear. She could
almost feel the murky doubt rising around her. She was
glad now she'd ditched her earrings. "I shouldn't think
so," she said honestly.

"Ah." He settled back, clearly relieved.

"Did he really get hugely fat on Beta Colony?" asked
Olivia brightly. "I shouldn't think his Betan therapist
would have let him. I thought they were supposed to
fix that. I mean, he was fat when he left *here*."

Kareen suppressed an urge to tear her hair, or better still, Olivia's. "Where did you hear that?"

"Mama said Lady Cordelia said her mother said,"
Olivia recited the links of the gossip-chain, "when she
was back here at Winterfair for Gregor's betrothal."

Mark's grandmother had been a good Betan god-
mother to both bewildered Barrayaran students this
past year. Kareen had known that she was a pipeline
of information to her concerned daughter about the
progress of her strange clone-son, with the sort of
frankness only two Betans could have; Gran'tante
Naismith often talked about the messages she'd sent
or received, and passed on news and greetings. The
possibility of Tante Cordelia talking to Mama was the
one she hadn't considered, Kareen realized. After all,
Tante Cordelia had been on Sergyar, Mama was
here. . . . She found herself frantically calculating backward, comparing two planetary calendars. Had she and
Mark become lovers yet, by Barrayaran Winterfair when
the Vorkosigans had last been home? No, whew.

Whatever Tante Cordelia knew now, she hadn't known it then.

"I thought the Betans could tweak your brain chemistry around any way they wanted," said Martya. "Couldn't they just normalize him, blip, like that? Why's it take so long?"

"That's just the point," Kareen said. "Mark spent most of his life having his body and mind forcibly jerked around by other people. He needs the time to figure out who he is when people *aren't* pumping him full of stuff from the outside. Time to establish a baseline, his therapist says. He has a Thing about drugs, you see." Though not, evidently, the ones he got himself from refugee Jacksonians. "When he's ready—well, never mind."

"Did his therapy make *any* progress, then?" Mama asked dubiously.

"Oh, yes, lots," said Kareen, glad to be able to say something unequivocally positive about Mark at last.

"What kind?" asked her puzzled mother.

Kareen pictured herself gibbering, *Well, he's gotten completely over his torture-induced impotence, and been trained how to be a gentle and attentive lover. His therapist says she's terribly proud of him, and Grunt is just ecstatic. Gorge would be a reasonable gourmand, if it weren't for his being co-opted by Howl to meet Howl's needs, and it was me who figured out that was what was really going on with the eating binges. Mark's therapist congratulated me for my observation and insight, and loaded me down with catalogs for five different Betan therapist training programs, and told me she'd help me find scholarships if I was interested. She doesn't quite know what to do about Killer yet, but Killer doesn't bother me. I can't deal with Howl. And that's one year's progress. And oh yes, through all this private stress and strain Mark maintained top standing in his high-powered finance school, does anybody care?* "It's pretty complicated to explain," she managed at last.

Time to change the subject. Surely someone else's love interest could be publicly dissected. "Delia! Does your Komarran commodore know Gregor's Komarran fiancée? Have you met her yet?"

Delia perked up. "Yes, Duv knew Laisa back on Komarr. They shared some, um, academic interests."

Martya chimed in, "She's cute, short, and plump. She has the most striking blue-green eyes, and she's going to set a fashion in padded bras. *You'll* be right in. Did you gain weight this year?"

"We've all met Laisa," Mama intervened before this theme could be developed into acrimony. "She seems very nice. Very intelligent."

"Yes," said Delia, shooting Martya a look of scorn. "Duv and I hope Gregor doesn't waste her in public relations, though she'll have to do some, of course. She has Komarran training in economics. She could run Ministerial committees, Duv says, if they'd let her. At least the Old Vor can't shuffle her off to be a brood mare. Gregor and Laisa have already let it be quietly known they plan to use uterine replicators for their babies."

"Are they getting any argument about that from the high traditionalists?" Kareen asked.

"If they do, Gregor's said he'll send 'em to argue with Lady Cordelia." Martya giggled. "If they dare."

"She'll hand them back their heads on a plate if they try," Da said cheerfully. "And they know she can. Besides, we can always help out by pointing to Kareen and Olivia as proof positive that replicators give fine results."

Kareen grinned. Olivia smiled more faintly. Their family's own demographics marked the arrival of that galactic technology on Barrayar; the Koudelkas had been among the first ordinary Barrayarans to chance the new gestation method, for their two younger daughters. Being presented to all and sundry like a prize agricultural exhibit at a District Fair got to be a weary pain after a while, but Kareen supposed it was a public service. There'd been much less of that lately, as the technology became widely accepted, at least in the cities and by those who could afford it. For the first time, she wondered how the Control Sisters, Delia and Martya, had felt about it.

"What do the Komarrans think of the marriage, does your Duv say?" Kareen asked Delia.

"It's a mixed reception, but what else do you expect from a conquered world? The Imperial Household means to put all the positive propaganda spin on it they can, of course. Right down to doing the wedding over again on Komarr in the Komarran style, poor Gregor and Laisa. All ImpSec leaves are canceled from now till after the second ceremony, so that means Duv's and my wedding plans are on hold till then." She heaved a large sigh. "Well, I'd rather have his undivided attention when I do finally get it. He's scrambling to get on top of his new job, and as the first Komarran to head Komarran Affairs he knows every eye in the Imperium is on him. Especially if anything goes wrong." She grimaced. "Speaking of people's heads on plates."

Delia had changed, this past year. Last time she'd spoken of Imperial events, the conversation had revolved around what to wear, not that color-coordinating the Koudelkas wasn't a challenge in its own right. Kareen began to think she might like this Duv Galeni fellow. A brother-in-law, hm. It was a concept to get used to.

And then the groundcar rounded the last corner, and home loomed up. The Koudelkas' residence was the end house in a block-row, a capacious three stories high and with a greedy share of windows overlooking a crescent-shaped park, smack in the middle of the capital and not half a dozen blocks from Vorkosigan House itself. The young couple had purchased it twenty-five years ago, when Da had been personal military aide to the Regent, and Mama had quit her ImpSec post as bodyguard to Gregor and his foster-mother Lady Cordelia in order to have Delia. Kareen couldn't begin to calculate how much its value must have appreciated since then, though she bet Mark could. An academic exercise—who could bear to sell the dear old place, creaky as it was? She bounded out of the car, wild with joy.

It was late in the evening before Kareen had a chance to talk privately with her parents. First there had to be the unpacking, and the distribution of presents, and the reclaiming of her room from the stowage her sisters had ruthlessly dumped there during her absence. Then there was the big family dinner, with all three of her best old girlfriends invited. Everybody talked and talked, except Da of course, who sipped wine and looked smug to be sitting down to dinner with eight women. In all the camouflaging chatter Kareen only gradually became aware that she was wrapping away in private silence the things that mattered most intensely to her. That felt very strange.

Now she perched on the bed in her parents' room as they readied for sleep. Mama was running through her set series of isometric exercises, as she'd done every night for as long as Kareen could remember. Even after two body-births and all those years, she still maintained an athlete's muscle tone. Da limped across the room and set his swordstick up by his side of the bed, sat awkwardly, and watched Mama with a little smile. His hair was all gray now, Kareen noticed; Mama's braided mane still maintained her tawny blond without cosmetic assistance, though it was getting a silvery sheen to it. Da's clumsy hands began the task of removing his half-boots. Kareen's eye was having trouble readjusting. Barrayarans in their mid-fifties looked like Betans in their mid-seventies, or even mid-eighties; and her parents had lived hard in their youth, through war and service. Kareen cleared her throat.

"About next year's," she began with a bright smile, "school."

"You *are* planning on the District University, aren't you?" said Mama, chinning herself gently on the bar hung from the ceiling joists, swinging her legs out horizontally, and holding them there for a silent count of twenty. "We didn't pinch marks to provide you with a galactic education to have you quit halfway. That would be heartbreaking."

"Oh, yes, I want to keep going. I want to go back to Beta Colony." There.

A brief silence. Then Da, plaintively: "But you just got *home*, lovie."

"And I wanted to come home," she assured him. "I wanted to see you all. I just thought . . . it wasn't too soon to begin planning. Knowing it's a big thing."

"Campaigning?" Da raised an eyebrow.

She controlled irritation. It wasn't as though she were a little girl begging for a pony. This was her whole life on the line, here. "Planning. Seriously."

Mama said slowly, perhaps because she was thinking or perhaps because she was folding herself upside-down, "Do you know what you would study this time? The work you selected last year seemed a trifle ... eclectic."

"I did well in all my classes," Kareen defended herself.

"All fourteen completely unrelated courses," murmured Da. "This is true."

"There was so *much* to choose from."

"There is much to choose from at Vorbarr Sultana District," Mama pointed out. "More than you could learn in a couple of lifetimes, even Betan lifetimes. And the commute is much less costly."

But Mark won't be at Vorbarr Sultana. He'll be back on Beta. "Mark's therapist was telling me about some scholarships in her field."

"Is that your latest interest?" asked Da. "Psycho-engineering?"

"I'm not sure," she said honestly. "It *is* interesting, the way they do it on Beta." But was it psychology in general that entranced her, or just Mark's psychology? She couldn't really say. Well ... maybe she could. She just didn't entirely like how the answer sounded.

"No doubt," said Mama, "any practical galactic medical or technical training would be welcome back here. If you could focus on one long enough to ... The problem is money, love. Without Lady Cordelia's scholarship, we couldn't have dreamed of sending you off world. And as far as I know, her next year's grant has already been awarded to another girl."

"I didn't expect to ask her for anything more. She's done so much for me already. But there is the possibility of a Betan scholarship. And I could work this summer. That, plus what you would have spent anyway on the District University ... you wouldn't expect a little thing like money to stop, say, Lord Miles?"

"I wouldn't expect plasma arc fire to stop Miles." Da grinned. "But he is, shall we say, a special case."

Kareen wondered momentarily what fueled Miles's famous drive. Was it frustrated anger, like the kind now heating her determination? How *much* anger? Did Mark, in his exaggerated wariness of his progenitor and twin, realize something about Miles that had eluded her? "Surely we can come up with some solution. If we all try."

Mama and Da exchanged a look. Da said, "I'm afraid things are a bit in the hole to start with. Between schooling for all of you, and your late grandmother Koudelka's illness . . . we mortgaged the house by the sea two years ago."

Mama chimed in, "We'll be renting it out this summer, all but a week. We figure with all the events at Midsummer we'll hardly have time to get out of the capital anyway."

"And your mama is now teaching self-defense and security classes for Ministerial employees," Da added. "So she's doing all she can. I'm afraid there aren't too many sources of cash left that haven't already been pressed into service."

"I enjoy the teaching," Mama said. Reassuring him? She added to Kareen, "And it's better than selling the summer place to clear the debt, which for a time we were afraid we'd have to do."

Lose the house by the sea, focus of her childhood? Kareen was horrified. Lady Alys Vorpatril herself had given the house on the eastern shore to the Koudelkas for a wedding present, all those years ago; something about saving her and baby Lord Ivan's lives in the War of Vordarian's Pretendership. Kareen hadn't known finances were so tight. Until she counted up the number of sisters ahead of her, and multiplied their needs . . . um.

"It could be worse," Da said cheerfully. "Think of what floating this harem would have been like back in the days of dowries!"

Kareen smiled dutifully—he'd been making that joke for at least fifteen years—and fled. She was going to have to come up with another solution. By herself.

❖   ❖   ❖

The decor of the Green Room in the Imperial Residence was superior to that of any other conference chamber in which Miles had ever been trapped. Antique silk wall coverings, heavy drapes and thick carpeting gave it a hushed, serious, and somewhat submarine air, and the elegant tea laid out in elaborate service on the inlaid sideboard beat the extruded-food-in-plastic of the average military meeting all hollow. Spring sunshine streamed through the windows to make warm golden bars across the floor. Miles had been watching them hypnotically shift as the morning stretched.

An inescapable military tone was lent to the proceedings by the presence of three men in uniform: Colonel Lord Vortala the Younger, head of the ImpSec task force assigned to provide security for the Emperor's wedding; Captain Ivan Vorpatril, dutifully keeping notes for Lady Alys Vorpatril, just as he would have done as aide to his commander at any military HQ conference; and Commodore Duv Galeni, chief of Komarran Affairs for ImpSec, preparing for the day when the whole show would be replayed on Komarr. Miles wondered if Galeni, forty and saturnine, was picking up ideas for his own wedding with Delia Koudelka, or whether he had enough sense of self-preservation to hide out and leave it all to the highly competent, not to mention assertive, Koudelka women. All five of them. Miles would offer Vorkosigan House to Duv as a sanctuary, except the girls would certainly track him there.

Gregor and Laisa seemed to be holding up well so far. Emperor Gregor in his mid-thirties was tall and thin, dark and dry. Dr. Laisa Toscane was short, with ash-blond curls and blue-green eyes that narrowed often in amusement, and a figure that made Miles, for one, just want to sort of fall over on top of her and burrow in for the winter. No treason implied; he did not begrudge Gregor his good fortune. In fact, Miles regarded the months of public ceremony which were keeping Gregor from that consummation as a cruelty little short of sadistic. Assuming, of course, that they *were* keeping . . .

The voices droned on; Miles's thoughts drifted further. Dreamily, he wondered where he and Ekaterin

might hold their future wedding. In the ballroom of
Vorkosigan House, in the eye of the Empire? The place
might not hold a big enough mob. He wanted witnesses,
for this. Or did he, as heir to his father's Countship,
have a political obligation to stage it at the Vorkosigan's
District capital of Hassadar? The modern Count's Residence at Hassadar had always seemed more like a hotel
than a home, attached as it was to all those District
bureaucratic offices lining the city's main square. The
most romantic site would be the house at Vorkosigan
Surleau, in the gardens overlooking the Long Lake. An
outdoor wedding, yes, he bet Ekaterin would like that.
In a sense, it would give Sergeant Bothari a chance to
attend, and General Piotr too. *Did you ever believe such
a day would come for me, Grandfather?* The attraction of
that venue would depend on the time of year, of
course—high summer would be glorious, but it wouldn't
seem so romantic in a mid-winter sleet storm. He wasn't
at all sure he could bring Ekaterin up to the matrimo-
nial fence before fall, and delaying the ceremony till next
spring would be as agonizing as what was being done
to Gregor. . . .

Laisa, across the conference table from Miles, flipped
over the next page of her stack of flimsies, read down
it for a few seconds, and said, "You people can't be
serious!" Gregor, seated beside her, looked alarmed, and
leaned to peer over her shoulder.

Oh, we must have got to page twelve already. Quickly,
Miles found his place again on the agenda, and sat up
and tried to look attentive.

Lady Alys gave him a dry glance, before turning her
attention to Laisa. This half-year-long nuptial ordeal,
from the betrothal ceremonies this past Winterfair to
the wedding upcoming at Midsummer, was the cap and
crown of Lady Alys's career as Gregor's official hostess.
She'd made it clear that Things Would Be Done
Properly.

The problem came in defining the term *Properly*. The
most recent wedding of a ruling emperor had been the
scrambling mid-war union of Gregor's grandfather
Emperor Ezar to the sister of the soon-to-be-late Mad

Emperor Yuri, which for a number of sound historical and aesthetic reasons Alys was loath to take as a model. Most other emperors had been safely married for years before they landed on the throne. Prior to Ezar one had to go back almost two hundred years, to the marriage of Vlad Vorbarra le Savante and Lady Vorlightly, in the most gaudily archaic period of the Time of Isolation.

"They didn't really make the poor bride strip to the buff in front of all their wedding guests, did they?" Laisa asked, pointing out the offending passage of historical quotation to Gregor.

"Oh, Vlad had to strip too," Gregor assured her earnestly. "The in-laws would have insisted. It was in the nature of a warranty inspection. Just in case any mutations turned up in future offspring, each side wanted to be able to assert it wasn't *their* kin's fault."

"The custom has largely died out in recent years," Lady Alys remarked, "except in some of the backcountry districts in certain language groups."

"She means the Greekie hicks," Ivan helpfully interpreted this for offworld-born Laisa. His mother frowned at this bluntness.

Miles cleared his throat. "The Emperor's wedding may be counted on to reinvigorate any old customs it takes up and displays. Personally, I'd prefer that this not be one of them."

"Spoilsport," said Ivan. "*I* think it would reintroduce a lot of excitement to wedding parties. It could be a better draw than the competitive toasting."

"Followed later in the evening by the competitive vomiting," Miles murmured. "Not to mention the thrilling, if erratic, Vor crawling races. I think you won one of those once, didn't you, Ivan?"

"I'm surprised you remember. Aren't you usually the first to pass out?"

"Gentlemen," said Lady Alys coldly. "We have a *great* deal of material yet to get through in this meeting. And *neither* of you is leaving till we are finished." She let that hang quellingly in the air for a moment, for emphasis, then went on. "I wouldn't expect to exactly reproduce that old custom, Laisa, but I put it on the list because it does represent something of cultural importance to the more conservative Barrayarans. I was hoping we might come up with an updated version which would serve the same psychological purpose."

Duv Galeni's dark brows lowered in a thoughtful frown. "Publish their gene scans?" he suggested.

Gregor grimaced, but then took his fiancée's hand and gripped it, and smiled at her. "I'm sure Laisa's would be just fine."

"Well, of course it is," she began. "My parents had it checked before I ever went into the uterine replicator—"

Gregor kissed her palm. "Yes, and I'll bet you were a darling blastocyst."

She grinned giddily at him. Alys smiled faintly, in brief indulgence. Ivan looked mildly nauseated. Colonel Vortala, ImpSec trained and with years of experience on the Vorbarr Sultana scene, managed to look pleasantly blank. Galeni, nearly as good, appeared only a little stiff.

Miles took this strategic moment to lean across and ask Galeni in an undertone, "Kareen's home, has Delia told you?"

Galeni brightened. "Yes. I expect I'll see her tonight."

"I want to do something for a welcome-home. I was thinking of inviting the whole Koudelka clan for dinner soon. Interested?"

"Sure—"

Gregor tore his besotted gaze from Laisa's, leaned back, and said mildly, "Thank you, Duv. And what other ideas does anyone have?"

Gregor was clearly not interested in making his gene-scan public knowledge. Miles thought through several regional variants of the old custom. "You could make it a sort of a levee. Each set of parental in-laws, or whoever you think ought to have the right and the voice, plus a physician of their choice gets to visit the opposite member of the couple on the morning of the wedding, for a brief physical. Each delegation publicly announces itself satisfied at some appropriate point of the ceremony. Private inspection, public assurance. Modesty, honor, and paranoia all get served."

"And you could be given your tranquilizers at the same time," Ivan pointed out, with gruesome cheer. "Bet you'll both need 'em by then."

"Thank you, Ivan," murmured Gregor. "So thoughtful." Laisa could only nod in amused agreement.

Lady Alys's eyes narrowed in calculation. "Gregor, Laisa? Is that idea mutually acceptable?"

"It works for me," said Gregor.

"I don't think my parents would mind going along with it," said Laisa. "Um . . . who would stand in for your parents, Gregor?"

"Count and Countess Vorkosigan will be taking their place on the wedding circle, of course," said Gregor. "I'd assume it would be them . . . ah, Miles?"

"Mother wouldn't blink," said Miles, "though I can't guarantee she wouldn't make rude comments about Barrayarans. Father . . ."

A more politically-guarded silence fell around the table. More than one eye drifted to Duv Galeni, whose jaw tightened slightly.

"Duv, Laisa." Lady Alys tapped one perfectly enameled fingernail on the polished tabletop. "Komarran socio-political response on this one. Frankly, please."

"I have no *personal* objection to Count Vorkosigan," said Laisa.

Galeni sighed. "Any . . . ambiguity that we can side-step, I believe we should."

Nicely put, Duv. You'll be a politician yet. "In other words, sending the Butcher of Komarr to ogle their nekkid sacrificial maiden would be about as popular as plague with the Komarrans back home," Miles put in, since no one else could. Well, Ivan maybe. Lady Alys would have had to grope for several more moments to come up with a polite locution for the problem. Galeni shot him a medium-grateful glower. "Perfectly understandable," Miles went on. "If the lack of symmetry isn't too obvious, send Mother and Aunt Alys as the delegation from Gregor's side, with maybe one of the female cousins from his mother Princess Kareen's family. It'll fly for the Barrayaran conservatives because guarding the genome always was women's work."

The Barrayarans around the table grunted agreement. Lady Alys smiled shortly, and ticked off the item.

A complicated, and lengthy, debate ensued over whether the couple should repeat their vows in all four of Barrayar's languages. After that came thirty minutes of discussion on how to handle domestic and galactic newsfeeds, in which Miles adroitly, and with Galeni's strong support, managed to avoid collecting any more tasks requiring his personal handling. Lady Alys flipped to the next page, and frowned. "By the way, Gregor, have you decided what you're going to do about the Vorbretten case yet?"

Gregor shook his head. "I'm trying to avoid making any public utterance on that one for the moment. At least till the Council of Counts gets done trampling about in it. Whichever way they fall out, the loser's appeal will doubtless land in my lap within minutes of their decision."

Miles glanced at his agenda in confusion. The next item read *Meal Schedules*. "Vorbretten case?"

"Surely you've heard the scandal—" began Lady Alys. "Oh, that's right, you were on Komarr when it broke. Didn't Ivan fill you in? Poor René. The whole family's in an uproar."

"Has something happened to René Vorbretten?" Miles asked, alarmed. René had been a couple of years ahead of Miles at the Academy, and looked to be following in his brilliant father's footsteps. Commodore Lord Vorbretten had been a star protégé of Miles's father on the General Staff, until his untimely, if heroic, death by Cetagandan fire in the war of the Hegen Hub a decade past. Less than a year later, old Count Vorbretten had died, some said in grief for the loss of his beloved eldest son; René had been forced to give up his promising military career and take up his duties as Count of his family's District. Three years ago, in a whirlwind romance that had been the delight of Vorbarr Sultana, he'd married the gorgeous eighteen-year-old daughter of the wealthy Lord Vorkeres. *Them what has, gets*, as they said in the backcountry.

"Well . . ." said Gregor, "yes and no. Um . . ."

"Um *what?*"

Lady Alys sighed. "Count and Countess Vorbretten, having decided it was time to start carrying out their family duties, very sensibly decided to use the uterine replicator for their first-born son, and have any detected defects repaired in the zygote. For which, of course, they both had complete gene scans."

"René found he was a mutie?" Miles asked, astonished. Tall, handsome, athletic René? René, who spoke four languages in a modulated baritone that melted female hearts and male resistance, played three musical instruments entrancingly, and had perfect singing pitch to boot? René, who could make *Ivan* grind his teeth in sheer physical jealousy?

"Not exactly," said Lady Alys, "unless you count being one-eighth Cetagandan ghem as a defect."

Miles sat back. "Whoops." He took this in. "When did this happen?"

"Surely you can do the math," murmured Ivan.

"Depends on which line it came through."

"The male," said Lady Alys. "Unfortunately."

Right. René's grandfather, the seventh Count-Vorbretten-to-be, had indeed been born in the middle of the Cetagandan occupation. The Vorbrettens, like many Barrayarans, had done what they needed to survive. . . . "So René's great-grandma was a collaborator. Or . . . was it something nastier?"

"For what it's worth," said Gregor, "what little surviving documentation ImpSec has unearthed suggests it was probably a voluntary and rather extended liaison, with one—or more—of the high-ranking ghem-officers occupying their District. At this range, one can't tell if it was love, self-interest, or an attempt to buy protection for her family in the only coin she had."

"It could have been all three," said Lady Alys. "Life in a war zone isn't simple."

"In any case," said Gregor, "it seems not to have been a matter of rape."

"Good God. So, ah, do they know which ghem-lord was René's ancestor?"

"They could in theory send his gene scan to

Cetaganda and find out, but as far as I know they haven't elected to do so yet. It's rather academic. What is . . . something other than academic is the apparent fact that the seventh Count Vorbretten was not the son of the sixth Count."

"They were calling him René Ghembretten last week at HQ," Ivan volunteered. Gregor grimaced.

"I'm astounded the Vorbrettens let this leak out," said Miles. "Or was it the doctor or the medtechs who betrayed them?"

"Mm, therein hangs yet more of the tale," said Gregor. "They had no intention of doing so. But René told his sisters and his brother, thinking they had a right to know, and the young Countess told her parents. And from there, well, who knows. But the rumor eventually came to the ears of Sigur Vorbretten, who is the direct descendant of the sixth Count's younger brother, and incidentally the son-in-law of Count Boriz Vormoncrief. Sigur has somehow—and there's a counter-suit pending about his methods—obtained a copy of René's gene scan. And Count Vormoncrief has brought suit before the Council of Counts, on his son-in-law's behalf, to claim the Vorbretten descent and District for Sigur. And there it sits."

"Ow. Ow! So . . . is René still Count, or not? He was presented and confirmed in his person by the Council, with all the due forms—hell, I was there, come to think of it. A Count doesn't *have* to be the previous Count's son—there've been nephews, cousins, skips to other lines, complete breaks due to treason or war—has anyone mentioned Lord Midnight, the fifth Count Vortala's horse, yet? If a horse can inherit a Countship, I don't see what's the theoretical objection to a Cetagandan. Part-Cetagandan."

"I doubt Lord Midnight's father was married to his mother, either," Ivan observed brightly.

"Both sides were claiming that case as a precedent, last I heard," Lord Vortala, himself a descendant of the infamous fifth Count, put in. "One because the horse was confirmed as heir, t' other because the confirmation was later revoked."

Galeni, listening in fascination, shook his head in wonder, or something like that. Laisa sat back and gnawed gently on her knuckle, and kept her mouth straight. Her eyes only crinkled slightly.

"How's René taking it all?" asked Miles.

"He seems to have become rather reclusive lately," said Alys, in a worried tone.

"I . . . maybe I'll call on him."

"That would be a good thing," said Gregor gravely. "Sigur is attempting in his suit to attach everything René inherited, but he's let it be known he'd be willing to settle for just the Countship and its entailments. Too, I suppose there are some trifles of property inherited through the female lines which aren't under question."

"In the meanwhile," Alys said, "Sigur has sent a note to my office requesting his rightful place in the wedding procession and the oath-takings as Count Vorbretten. And René has sent a note requesting Sigur be barred from the ceremonies if the case has not yet been settled in his favor. So, Gregor? Which one lays his hands between Laisa's when she's confirmed as Empress, if the Council of Counts hasn't made up what passes for its collective mind by then?"

Gregor rubbed the bridge of his nose, and squeezed his eyes shut briefly. "I don't know. We may have to have both of them. Provisionally."

"Together?" said Lady Alys, her lip curling in dismay. "Tempers are running high, I heard." She glowered at Ivan. "Exacerbated by the humor certain low-minded persons seem to find in what is actually an exquisitely painful situation."

Ivan began to smile, then apparently thought better of it.

"One trusts they will not choose to mar the dignity of the occasion," said Gregor. "Especially if their appeal to me is still hanging fire. I suppose I should find some way to let them know that, gently. I am presently constrained to avoid them . . ." His eye fell on Miles. "Ah, Lord Auditor Vorkosigan. This sounds like a task very much within your purview. Would you be so kind as to remind them both of the delicacy of their positions, if things look to be getting out of hand at any point?"

Since the official job description of an Imperial Auditor was, in effect, Whatever You Say, Gregor, Miles could hardly argue with this. Well, it could have been worse. He shuddered to think of how many chores he might have been assigned by now if he'd been so stupid as to *not* show up for this meeting. "Yes, Sire," he sighed. "I'll do my best."

"The formal invitations begin to go out soon," Lady Alys said. "Let me know if there are any changes." She turned over the last page. "Oh, and have your parents said yet exactly when they'll be arriving, Miles?"

"I've assumed you would know before I did. Gregor?"

"Two Imperial ships are assigned to the Viceroy's pleasure," said Gregor. "If there are no crises on Sergyar to impede him, Count Vorkosigan implied he'd like to be here in better time than last Winterfair."

"Are they coming together? I thought Mother might come early again, to support Aunt Alys," said Miles.

"I love your mother dearly, Miles," Lady Alys sighed, "but after the betrothal, when I suggested she come home to help me with these preparations, she suggested Gregor and Laisa ought to elope."

Gregor and Laisa both looked quite wistful at the thought, and held hands under the table. Lady Alys frowned uneasily at this dangerous breath of mutiny.

Miles grinned. "Well, of course. That's what *she* did. After all, it worked for her."

"I don't think she was serious, but with Cordelia, one can never quite tell. It's just appalling how this whole subject brings out the Betan in her. I can only be grateful she's on Sergyar just now." Lady Alys glowered at her flimsy, and added, "Fireworks."

Miles blinked, then realized this wasn't a prediction of the probable result of the clash in social views between his Betan mother and his Barrayaran aunt, but rather, the last—thank God—item on today's agenda.

"Yes!" said Gregor, smiling eagerly. All the Barrayarans round the table, including Lady Alys, perked up at this. An inherent cultural passion for things that went boom, perhaps.

"On what schedule?" Lady Alys asked. "There will of course be the traditional display on Midsummer Day, the evening after the Imperial Military Review. Do you want displays every night on the three days intervening till the wedding, as well as on the wedding night?"

"Let me see that budget," Gregor said to Ivan. Ivan called it up for him. "Hm. We wouldn't want the people to become jaded. Let other organizations, such as the city of Vorbarr Sultana or the Council of Counts, foot the displays on the intervening nights. And up the budget for the post-wedding display by fifty percent, from my personal purse as Count Vorbarra."

"Ooh," said Ivan appreciatively, and entered the changes. "Nice."

Miles stretched. Done at last.

"Oh, yes, I almost forgot," added Lady Alys. "Here is your meal schedule, Miles."

"My what?" Without thinking, he accepted the flimsy from her hand.

"Gregor and Laisa have dozens of invitations during the week between the Review and the Wedding from assorted organizations which wish to honor them—and themselves—ranging from the Imperial Veterans' Corps to the Honorable Order of City Bakers. And Bankers. And Brewers. And Barristers. Not to mention the rest of the alphabet. Far more than they can possibly accept, of course. They will do as many of the most critical ones as they can fit in, but after that, you will have to take the next tier, as Gregor's Second."

"Did any of these people actually invite me, in my own person?" Miles asked, scanning down the list. There were at least thirteen meals or ceremonies in three days on it. "Or are they getting a horrible surprise? I can't eat all this!"

"Throw yourself on that unexploded dessert, boy!" Ivan grinned. "It's your duty to save the Emperor from indigestion."

"Of course they'll know. You may expect to be called upon to make a number of thank-you speeches appropriate to the various venues. And here," his mother added, "is your schedule, Ivan."

Ivan's grin faded into a look of dismay, as he stared at his own list. "I didn't know there were that many guilds in this damned town . . ."

A wonderful thought occurred to Miles—he might be able to take Ekaterin along to a sedate selection of these. Yes, let her see Lord Auditor Vorkosigan in action. And her serene and sober elegance would add no little validation to *his* consequence. He sat up straighter, suddenly consoled, and folded the flimsy and slipped it into his tunic.

"Can't we send Mark to some of these?" asked Ivan plaintively. "He'll be back in town for this bash. And he's a Vorkosigan too. Outranks a Vorpatril, surely. And if there's one thing the lad can do, it's eat."

Galeni's brows rose in reluctant agreement with this last assessment, though the look on his face was a study in grim bemusement. Miles wondered if Galeni too was reflecting that Mark's other notable talent was assassination. *At least he doesn't eat what he kills.*

Miles began to glower at Ivan, but Aunt Alys beat him to it. "Control your wit, if you please, Ivan. Lord Mark is neither the Emperor's Second, nor an Imperial Auditor, nor of any great experience in delicate social situations. And despite all Aral and Cordelia could do for him last year, most people still regard his position within the family as rather ambiguous. Nor is he, I'm given to understand, stable enough yet to be safely subjected to stress in very public arenas. Despite his therapy."

"It was a *joke*," Ivan muttered defensively. "How do you expect us to all get through this alive if we're not allowed to have a sense of humor?"

"Exert yourself," his mother advised him brutally.

On these daunting words, the meeting broke up.

CHAPTER THREE

A cool spring drizzle misted onto Miles's hair as he stepped into the shelter of the Vorthys's doorway. In the gray air, the gaudy tile front of the house was subdued, becoming a patterned subtlety. Ekaterin had inadvertently delayed this meeting by sending him her proposed garden designs over the comconsole. Fortunately, he hadn't had to *feign* indecision over the choice; both layouts were very fine. He trusted they would still be able to spend hours this afternoon, heads bent together over the vid display, comparing and discussing the fine points.

A fleeting memory of the erotic dream from which he'd awoken this morning warmed his face. It had been a replay of his and Ekaterin's first meeting in the garden here, but in this version her welcome had taken a much more, um, exciting and unexpected turn. Except why had his stupid unconscious spent so much worry about tell-tale grass-stains on the knees of his trousers, when it could have been manufacturing even more fabulous moments of abundance for his dream-self? And then he'd woken up too damned soon. . . .

The Professora opened the door to him, and smiled a welcome. "Come in, Miles." She added, as he entered her hallway, "Have I ever mentioned before how much I appreciate the fact that you call before you visit?"

Her house did not have its usual hushed, librarylike quiet. There seemed to be a party going on. Startled, Miles swiveled his head toward the archway on his left. A clink of plates and glassware and the scent of tea and apricot pastries wafted from the parlor.

Ekaterin, smiling politely but with two little parallel lines of tension between her brows, sat enthroned in her uncle's overstuffed chair in the corner, holding a teacup. Ranged around the room, perched on more decorative chairs, were three men, two in Imperial undress greens and one in a civilian tunic and trousers.

Miles didn't recognize the heavy-set fellow who wore major's tabs, along with Ops pins, on his high collar. The other officer was Lieutenant Alexi Vormoncrief, whom Miles knew slightly. His pins, too, indicated he now worked in Ops. The third man, in the finely-cut civilian togs, was highly adept at avoiding work of any kind, as far as Miles knew. Byerly Vorrutyer had never joined the Service; he'd been a town clown for as long as Miles had been acquainted with him. Byerly had impeccable taste in everything but his vices. Miles would have been loath to introduce Ekaterin to him even *after* she was safely betrothed.

"Where did *they* come from?" Miles asked the Professora in an undertone.

"Major Zamori I had as an undergraduate student, fifteen years ago," the Professora murmured back. "He brought me a book he said he thought I would like. Which is true; I already had a copy. Young Vormoncrief came to compare pedigrees with Ekaterin. He thought they might be related, he said, as his grandmother was a Vorvane. Aunt to the Minister for Heavy Industries, you know."

"I know that branch, yes."

"They have spent the past hour establishing that, while the Vorvanes and the Vorvaynes are indeed of the same root stock, the families split off at least five generations back. I don't know why By Vorrutyer is here. He neglected to supply me with an excuse."

"There is no excuse for By." But Miles thought he could see exactly why the three of them were there, lame stories and all, and she was clutching her teacup in the corner and looking trapped. Couldn't they do better than those palpably transparent tales? "Is my cousin Ivan here?" he added dangerously. Ivan worked in Ops, come to think of it. Once was happenstance, twice was coincidence . . .

"Ivan Vorpatril? No. Oh, dear, is he likely to turn up? I'm out of pastries. I had bought them for the Professor's dessert tonight. . . ."

"I trust not," muttered Miles. He fixed a polite smile on his face, and swung into the Professora's parlor. She followed after him.

Ekaterin's chin came up, and she smiled and put down her cup-shield. "Oh, Lord Vorkosigan! I'm so glad you're here. Um . . . do you know these gentlemen?"

"Two out of three, Madame. Good morning, Vormoncrief. Hello, Byerly."

The three acquaintances exchanged guarded nods. Vormoncrief said politely, "Good morning, my Lord Auditor."

"Major Zamori, this is Lord Auditor Miles Vorkosigan," the Professora supplied.

"Good day, sir," said Zamori. "I've heard of you." His gaze was direct and fearless, despite his being so heavily outnumbered by Vor lords. But then, Vormoncrief was a mere stripling of a lieutenant, and Byerly Vorrutyer didn't rank at all. "Did you come to see Lord Auditor Vorthys? He just stepped out."

Ekaterin nodded. "He went for a walk."

"In the rain?"

The Professora rolled her eyes slightly, by which Miles guessed her husband had skipped off and left her to play duenna to her niece by herself.

"No matter," Miles went on. "In fact, I have some little business with Madame Vorsoisson." And if they took that to mean a Lord Auditor's Imperial business, and not merely Lord Vorkosigan's private business, who was he to correct them?

"Yes," Ekaterin nodded in confirmation of this.

"My apologies for interrupting you all," Miles added, by way of a broad hint. He did not sit down, but leaned against the frame of the archway, and crossed his arms. No one moved.

"We were just discussing family trees," Vormoncrief explained.

"At some length," murmured Ekaterin.

"Speaking of strange pedigrees, Alexi, Lord Vorkosigan and I were almost related much more closely," Byerly remarked. "I feel quite a familial attachment to him."

"Really?" said Vormoncrief, looking puzzled.

"Oh, yes. One of my aunts on the Vorrutyer side was once married to his father. So Aral Vorkosigan is actually some sort of virtual, if not virtuous, uncle to me. But she died young, alas—ruthlessly pruned from the tree— without bearing me a cousin to cut the future Miles out of his inheritance." Byerly cocked a brow at Miles. "Was she fondly remembered, in your family dinner conversations?"

"We never much discussed the Vorrutyers," said Miles.

"How odd. We never much discussed the Vorkosigans, either. Hardly at all, in fact. Such a resounding silence, one feels."

Miles smiled, and let just such a silence stretch between them, curious to see who would flinch first. By's eye began to glint appreciation, but the first whose nerve broke was one of the innocent bystanders.

Major Zamori cleared his throat. "So, Lord Auditor Vorkosigan. What's the final word on the Komarr accident, really? Was it sabotage?"

Miles shrugged, and let By and his habitual needling drop from his attention. "After six weeks of sifting through the data, Lord Auditor Vorthys and I returned a probable cause of pilot error. We debated the possibility of pilot suicide, but finally discarded the idea."

"And which was your opinion?" asked Zamori, sounding interested. "Accident or suicide?"

"Mm. I felt suicide would explain a lot about certain physical aspects of the collision," Miles replied, sending up a silent prayer of apology to the soul of the slandered pilot. "But since the dead pilot neglected to supply us with any supporting evidence, such as notes or messages or therapy records, we couldn't make it an official verdict. Don't quote me," he added, for verisimilitude.

Ekaterin, sheltered in her uncle's chair, nodded understanding to him of this official lie, perhaps adding it to her own repertoire of deflections.

"So what do you think of this Komarran marriage of the Emperor's?" Vormoncrief added. "I suppose you must approve of it—you're in it."

Miles took note of his dubious tone. Ah yes, Vormoncrief's uncle Count Boriz Vormoncrief, being just outside the spatter-zone, had inherited the leadership of the shrinking Conservative Party after the fall of Count Vortrifrani. The Conservative party's response to future-Empress Laisa had been lukewarm at best, though, prudently, no overt hostility had been permitted to leak into their public stances where someone— i.e., ImpSec—would have been compelled to take notice of it. Still, just because Boriz and Alexi were related didn't by any means guarantee they shared the same political views. "I think it's great," said Miles. "Dr. Toscane is brilliant and beautiful, and Gregor, well, it's high time he produced an heir. And you have to figure, if nothing else it leaves one more Barrayaran woman for the rest of us."

"Well, it leaves one more Barrayaran woman for *one* of us," Byerly Vorrutyer corrected this sweetly. "Unless you are proposing something delightfully outré."

Miles's smile thinned as he contemplated By. Ivan's wit, wearing as it could sometimes grow, was saved from being offensive by a certain ingenuousness. Unlike Ivan, Byerly never insulted anyone unintentionally.

"You gentlemen should all pay a visit to Komarr," Miles recommended genially. "Their domes are just chock full of lovely women, all with clean gene scans and galactic educations. And the Toscanes aren't the only clan fielding an heiress. Many of the Komarran ladies are rich—Byerly." He restrained himself from helpfully explaining to all present that Madame

Vorsoisson's feckless late husband had left her destitute, first because Ekaterin was sitting right there, with her eyebrows tilted at him, and secondly because he couldn't imagine that By, for one, didn't already know it.

Byerly smiled faintly. "Money isn't everything, they say."

Check. "Still, I'm sure you could make yourself pleasant, if you ever chose to try."

By's lip quirked. "Your faith in me is touching, Vorkosigan."

Alexi Vormoncrief said sturdily, "A daughter of the Vor is good enough for me, thanks. I've no need or taste for off-world exotica."

While Miles was still trying to work out if this was an intended slur on his Betan mother—with By, he would have been sure, but Vormoncrief had never struck him as over-supplied with subtlety—Ekaterin said brightly, "I'll just step up to my room and get those data disks, shall I?"

"If you please, Madame." Miles trusted By had not made her the object of any of his guerrilla conversational techniques. If so, Miles might have a little private word with his ersatz cousin. Or maybe even send his Armsmen to do so, just like the good old days. . . .

She rose, and made her way to the hall and up the stairs. She did not return. Vormoncrief and Zamori eventually exchanged disappointed looks, and noises about *time to be going*, and made to rise. The military raincoat Vormoncrief shrugged on had had time to dry since his arrival, Miles noted with disapproval. The gentlemen courteously took their leave of their putative hostess, the Professora.

"Tell Madame Vorsoisson I'll bring that disk of jumpship designs around for Nikki as soon as I may," Major Zamori assured the Professora, glancing up the stairway.

Zamori's been here often enough to know Nikki already? Miles regarded his regular profile uneasily. He seemed tall, too, though not as tall as Vormoncrief; it was his bulk that helped make his presence loom like that. Byerly was slim enough that his height was not so apparent.

They lingered a moment in an awkward crowded gaggle in the tiled hall, but Ekaterin did not descend again, and at last they gave up and let themselves be shepherded out the front door. It was raining harder now, Miles saw with some satisfaction. Zamori plunged off into the shower, head-down. The Professora closed the door on them with a grimace of relief.

"You and Ekaterin can use the comconsole in my study," she directed Miles, and turned to start collecting the plates and cups left derelict in her parlor.

Miles trod across the hall into her office-cum-library, and looked around. Yes, this would be a fine and cozy spot for his conference. The front window was propped open to catch a fresh draft. Voices from the porch carried through the damp air with unfortunate clarity.

"By, you don't think *Vorkosigan* is dangling after Madame Vorsoisson, is he?" That was Vormoncrief.

Byerly Vorrutyer replied indifferently, "Why not?"

"You'd think she'd be revolted. No, it must be just some leftover business from his case."

"I wouldn't wager on that. I know women enough who would hold their noses and take the plunge for a Count's heir even if he came covered in green fur."

Miles's fist clenched, then carefully unclenched. *Oh, yeah? So why didn't you ever supply me with that list, By?* Not that Miles cared *now* . . .

"I don't claim to understand women, but Ivan's the catch I could see them going for," Vormoncrief said. "If the assassins had been a little more competent, way back when, *he* might have inherited the Vorkosigans' Countship. Too bad. My uncle says he'd be an ornament to our party, if he didn't have that family alliance with Aral Vorkosigan's damned Progressives."

"Ivan Vorpatril?" Byerly snorted. "Wrong type of party for him, Alexi. He only goes to the kind where the wine flows freely."

Ekaterin appeared in the archway and smiled crookedly at Miles. He considered slamming the window shut, hard. There were technical difficulties with that idea; it had a crank-latch. Ekaterin too had caught the voices—how soon? She drifted in, and cocked her head, and lifted an inquiring and unrepentant brow at him, as if to say, *At it again, are you?* Miles managed a brief embarrassed smile.

"Ah, here's your driver at last," Byerly added. "Lend me your coat, Alexi; I don't wish to damp my lovely new suit. What do you think of it? The color flatters my skin tone, no?"

"Hang your skin tone, By."

"Oh, but my tailor assured me it does. Thank you. Good, he's opening the canopy. Now for the dash through the wet; well, you can dash. I shall saunter with dignity, in this ugly but inarguably waterproof Imperial garment. Off we go now . . ." Two sets of footsteps faded into the drizzle.

"He *is* a character, isn't he?" said Ekaterin, half-laughing.

"Who? Byerly?"

"Yes. He's *very* snarky. I could scarcely believe the things he dared to say. Or keep my face straight."

"I scarcely believe the things By says either," said Miles shortly. He pulled a second chair around in front of the comconsole as close to the first as he dared, and settled her. "Where did they all come from?" Besides the Ops department of Imperial Headquarters, apparently. *Ivan, you rat, you and I are going to have a talk about what sort of gossip you sprinkle around at work. . . .*

"Major Zamori called on the Professora last week," said Ekaterin. "He seems a pleasant enough fellow. He had a long chat with Nikki—I was impressed with his patience."

Miles was impressed with his *brains*. Damn the man, for spotting Nikki as one of the few chinks in Ekaterin's armor.

"Vormoncrief first turned up a few days ago. I'm afraid he's a bit of a bore, poor man. Vorrutyer just came in with him this morning; I'm not sure he was exactly invited."

"He's found a new victim to sponge off, I suppose," said Miles. Vorrutyers seemed to come in two flavors, flamboyant and reclusive; By's father, the youngest son of his generation, was a misanthropic pinchmark of the second category, and never came near the capital if he could help it. "By's notoriously without visible means of support."

"He puts up a good front, if so," said Ekaterin judiciously.

Upper-class poverty was a dilemma with which Ekaterin could identify, Miles realized. He hadn't intended his remark as a ploy to gain sympathy for Byerly Vorrutyer. Blast.

"I think Major Zamori was a bit put out when they arrived on top of his visit," Ekaterin went on. She added fretfully, "I don't know why they're *here*."

Check your mirror, Miles refrained from advising her. He let his brows rise. "Truly?"

She shrugged, and smiled a little bitterly. "They mean well, I guess. Maybe I was naïve to think this," she gestured down her black dress, "would be enough to relieve me of having to deal with the nonsense. Thanks for trying to ship them to Komarr for me, though I'm not sure it took. My hints don't seem to be working. I don't wish to be rude."

"Why not?" said Miles, hoping to encourage this trend of thought. Though rudeness might not work on By; it would be just as likely to excite him into making it a contest. Miles suppressed a morbid urge to inquire if there'd been any *more* unattached gentlemen turn up on her front step this week, or if he'd just viewed the whole inventory. He really didn't want to hear the answer. "But enough of this, as you say, nonsense. Let's talk about my garden."

"Yes, let's," she said gratefully, and set up the two vid models, which they'd dubbed *the backcountry garden* and *the urban garden* respectively, on her aunt's comconsole. Their heads bent together side by side, just as Miles had pictured. He could smell the dusky perfume of her hair.

The backcountry garden was a naturalistic display, with bark pathways curling through thickly planted native species on contoured banks, a winding stream, and scattered wooden benches. The urban garden had strong rectangular terraces of poured plascrete, which were walks and benches and channels for the water all together. In a series of skillful, penetrating questions, Ekaterin managed to elicit from him that his heart really favored the backcountry garden, however much his eye was seduced by the plascrete fountains. As he watched in fascination, she modified the backcountry design to give the ground more slope and the stream more prominence, winding in an S-curve that originated in a rock fall and ended in a small grotto. The central circle where the paths intersected was transformed to traditional patterned brick, with the Vorkosigan crest, the stylized maple leaf backed by the three overlapping triangles representing the mountains, picked out in contrasting paler brick. The whole was dropped further below street level, to give the banks more room to climb, and to muffle the city noise.

"Yes," he said at last, in considerable satisfaction. "That's the plan. Go with it. You can start lining up your contractors and bids."

"Are you sure you really want to go on?" said Ekaterin. "I'm now out of my experience, I'm afraid. All my designs have been virtual ones, till this."

"Ah," said Miles smugly, having anticipated this last-minute waffle. "Now is the moment to put you in direct touch with my man of business, Tsipis. He's had to arrange every sort of maintenance and building work on the Vorkosigan properties in the last thirty years. He knows who all the reputable and reliable people are, and where we can draw labor or materials from the Vorkosigan estates. He'll be delighted to walk you through the whole thing." *In fact, I've let him know I'll have his head if he's not delighted every minute.* Not that Miles had had to lean very hard; Tsipis found all aspects of business management utterly fascinating, and would drone on for hours about them. It made Miles laugh, if painfully, to realize how often in his space mercenary command he'd saved a day by drawing not on his ImpSec training, but on one of old Tsipis's scorned lessons. "If you're willing to be his pupil, he'll be your slave."

Tsipis, carefully primed, answered the comconsole in his office in Hassadar himself, and Miles made the necessary introductions. The new acquaintance went well; Tsipis was elderly, long married, and genuinely interested in the project at hand. He drew Ekaterin almost instantly out of her wary shyness. By the time he'd finished his first lengthy conversation with her, she'd shifted from *I can't possibly* mode to possession of a flow-chart checklist and a coherent plan which would, with luck, result in groundbreaking as early as the following week. Oh yes. This was going to do well. If there was one thing Tsipis appreciated, it was a quick study. Ekaterin was one of those *show once* people whom Miles, in his mercenary days, had found more precious than unexpected oxygen in the emergency reserve. And she didn't even know she was unusual.

"Good heavens," she remarked, organizing her notes after Tsipis had cut the com. "What an education that man is. I think I should be paying you."

"Payment," said Miles, reminded. "Yes." He drew a credit chit from his pocket. "Tsipis has set up the account for you to pay all expenses incurred. This is your own fee for the accepted design."

She checked it in the comconsole. "Lord Vorkosigan, this is too much!"

"No, it's not. I had Tsipis scout the prices for similar design work from three different professional companies." They happened to be the top three in the business, but would he have hired anything less for Vorkosigan House? "This is an average of their bids. He can show them to you."

"But I'm an amateur."

"Not for damn long."

Wonder of wonders, this actually won a smile of increasing self-confidence. "All I did was assemble some pretty standard design elements."

"So, ten percent of that is for the design elements. The other ninety percent is for knowing how to arrange them."

Hah, she didn't argue with *that*. You couldn't be that good and not know it, somewhere in your secret heart, however much you'd been abused into affecting public humility.

This was, he recognized, a good bright note on which to end. He didn't want to linger to the point of boring her, as Vormoncrief had evidently done. Was it too early to . . . no, he'd try. "By the way, I'm putting together a dinner party for some old friends of mine—the Koudelka family. Kareen Koudelka, who is a sort of protégé of my mother's, is just back from a school year on Beta Colony. She's hit the ground running, but as soon as I can determine a date when everyone's free, I'd like to have you come too, and meet them."

"I wouldn't want to intrude—"

"Four daughters," he overrode this smoothly, "Kareen's the youngest. And their mother, Drou. And Commodore Koudelka, of course. I've known them all my life. And Delia's fiancé, Duv Galeni."

"A family with five women in it? All at once?" An envious note sounded plainly in her voice.

"I'd think you'd enjoy them a lot. And vice versa."

"I haven't met many women in Vorbarr Sultana . . . they're all so busy . . ." She glanced down at her black skirt. "I really ought not to go to parties just yet."

"A *family* party," he emphasized, tacking handily into this wind. "Of course I mean to invite the Professor and the Professora." Why not? He had, after all, ninety-six chairs.

"Perhaps . . . that would be unexceptionable."

"Excellent! I'll get back to you on the dates. Oh, and be sure to call Pym to notify the House guards when your workmen are due, so he can add them to his security schedule."

"Certainly."

And on that carefully-balanced note, warm yet not too personal, he made his excuses and decamped.

So, the enemy was now thronging her gates. *Don't panic, boy.* By the time of the dinner party, he might have her up to the pitch of accepting some of his wedding-week engagements. And by the time they'd been seen publicly paired at half a dozen of those, well, who knew.

Not me, unfortunately.

He sighed, and sprinted off through the rain to his waiting car.

Ekaterin wandered back to the kitchen, to see if her aunt needed any more help with the clean up. She was guiltily afraid she was too late, and indeed she found the Professora sitting at the kitchen table with a cup of tea and stack of, judging by the bemused look on her face, undergraduate essays.

Her aunt frowned fiercely, and scribbled with her stylus, then looked up and smiled. "All done, dear?"

"More like, just started. Lord Vorkosigan chose the backcountry garden. He really wants me to go ahead."

"I never doubted it. He's a decisive man."

"I'm sorry for all the interruptions this morning." Ekaterin made a gesture in the direction of the parlor.

"I don't see why *you're* apologizing. You didn't invite them."

"Indeed, I didn't." Ekaterin held up her new credit chit, and smiled. "But Lord Vorkosigan has already paid me for the design! I can give you rent for Nikki and me now."

"Good heavens, you don't owe us rent. It doesn't cost us anything to let you have the use of those empty rooms."

Ekaterin hesitated. "You can't say the food we eat comes free."

"If you wish to buy some groceries, go ahead. But I'd much prefer you saved it toward your schooling in the fall."

"I'll do both." Ekaterin nodded firmly. Carefully managed, the credit chit would spare her having to beg her father for spending money for the next several months. Da was not ungenerous, but she didn't want to hand him the right to give her reams of unwanted advice and suggestions as to how to run her life. He'd made it plain at Tien's funeral that he was unhappy she hadn't chosen to come home, as befit a Vor widow, or gone to live with her late husband's mother, though the senior Madame Vorsoisson hadn't invited them.

And how had he imagined Ekaterin and Nikki could

fit in his modest flat, or find any educational opportunities in the small South Continent town to which he'd retired? Sasha Vorvayne seemed a man oddly defeated by his life, at times. He'd always made the conservative choices. Mama had been the daring one, but only in the little ways she could fit into the interstices of her role as a bureaucrat's wife. Had the defeat become contagious, toward the end? Ekaterin sometimes wondered if her parents' marriage had been, in some subtler way, almost as much of a secret mismatch as her own.

A white-haired head passed the window; a rattle, and the back door opened to reveal her Uncle Vorthys, Nikki in tow. The Professor stuck his head inside, and whispered dramatically, "Are they gone? Is it safe to come back?"

"All clear," reported his wife, and he lumbered into the kitchen.

He was burdened with a large bag, which he dumped on the table. It proved to contain replacements, several times over, for the pastries that had been consumed earlier.

"Do you think we have enough now?" the Professora inquired dryly.

"No artificial shortages," declaimed her husband. "I remember when the girls were going through that phase. Up to our elbows in young men at all hours, and not a crumb left in the house at the end of the day. I never understood your generous strategy." He explained aside to Ekaterin, "I wanted to cut their numbers by offering them spotty vegetables, and chores. The ones who came back after *that*, we would know were serious. Eh, Nikki? But for some reason, the women wouldn't let me."

"Feel free to offer them all the rotten vegetables and chores you can think of," Ekaterin told him. *Alternately, we could lock the doors and pretend no one is home. . . .* She sat down glumly beside her aunt, and helped herself to a pastry. "Did you and Nikki get your share, finally?"

"We had coffee and cookies and milk at the bakery," her uncle assured her.

Nikki licked his lips happily, and nodded confirmation. "Uncle Vorthys says all those fellows want to marry you," he added in apparent disbelief. "Is that really true?"

Thank you, dear Uncle, Ekaterin thought wryly. She'd been wondering how to explain it all to a nine-year-old boy. Though Nikki didn't seem to find the idea nearly as horrifying as she did. "That would be illegal," she murmured. "Outré, even." She smiled faintly at By Vorrutyer's jibe.

Nikki scorned the joke. "You know what I mean! Are you going to pick one of 'em?"

"No, dear," she assured him.

"Good." He added after a moment of silence, "Though if you *did*, a major would be better than a lieutenant."

"Ah . . . why?"

Ekaterin watched with interest as Nikki struggled to evolve *Vormoncrief is a patronizing Vor bore*, but to her relief, the vocabulary escaped him. He finally fell back on, "Majors make more money."

"A very practical point," Uncle Vorthys observed, and, perhaps still mistrusting his wife's generosity, packed up about half of his new stock of pastries to carry off and hide in his basement laboratory. Nikki tagged along.

Ekaterin leaned her elbows on the kitchen table, rested her chin on her hands, and sighed. "Uncle Vorthys's strategy might not be such a bad idea, at that. The threat of chores might get rid of Vormoncrief, and would certainly repel Vorrutyer. I'm not so sure it would work on Major Zamori, though. The spotty vegetables might be good all round."

Aunt Vorthys sat back, and regarded her with a quizzical smile. "So what do you want me to do, Ekaterin? Start telling your potential suitors you're not at home to visitors?"

"Could you? With my work on the garden starting, it would be the truth," said Ekaterin, considering this.

"Poor boys. I almost feel sorry for them."

Ekaterin smiled briefly. She could feel the pull of that

sympathy, like a clutching hand, drawing her back into the dark. It made her skin crawl.

Every night now, lying down alone without Tien, was like a taste of some solitary heaven. She could stretch her arms and legs out all the way to the sides of the bed, reveling in the smooth space, free of compromise, confusion, oppression, negotiation, deference, placation. Free of Tien. Through the long years of their marriage she had become almost numb to the ties that had bound her to him, the promises and the fear, his desperate needs, his secrets and lies. When the straps of her vows had been released at last by his death, it was as if her whole soul had come awake, tingling painfully, like a limb when circulation was restored. *I did not know what a prison I was in, till I was freed.* The thought of voluntarily walking back into such a marital cell again, and locking the door with another oath, made her want to run screaming.

She shook her head. "I don't need another dependent."

Her aunt's brows quirked. "You don't need another Tien, that's certain. But not all men are like Tien."

Ekaterin's fist tightened, thoughtfully. "But I'm still like me. I don't know if I can *be* intimate, and not fall back into the bad old ways. Not give myself away down to the very bottom, and then complain I'm empty. The most horrible thought I have, looking back on it all, is that it wasn't all Tien's fault. I *let* him get worse and worse. If he'd chanced to marry a woman who would have stood up to him, who would have *insisted* . . ."

"Your line of logic makes my head ache," her aunt observed mildly.

Ekaterin shrugged. "It's all moot now."

After a long moment of silence, the Professora asked curiously, "So what do you think of Miles Vorkosigan?"

"He's all right. *He* doesn't make me cringe."

"I thought—back on Komarr—he seemed a bit interested in you himself."

"Oh, that was just a joke," Ekaterin said sturdily. Their joke had gone a little beyond the line, perhaps, but they had both been tired, and punchy at their release from those days and hours of fearsome strain . . . his flashing smile, and the brilliant eyes in his weary face, blazed in her memory. It had to have been a joke. Because if it weren't a joke . . . she would have to run screaming. And she was much too tired to get up. "But it's been nice to find someone genuinely interested in gardens."

"Mmm," said her aunt, and turned over another essay.

The afternoon sun of the Vorbarr Sultana spring warmed the gray stone of Vorkosigan House into something almost mellow, as Mark's hired groundcar turned in to the drive. The ImpSec gate guard at the kiosk was not one of the men Mark had met last year. The guard was respectful but meticulous, going as far as checking Mark's palm print and retina scan before waving them through with a mumbled grunt that might have been an apologetic "M'lord." Mark stared up through the car's canopy as they wound up the drive to the front portico.

Vorkosigan House again. Home? His cozy student apartment back on Beta Colony seemed more like home now than did this vast stone pile. But although he was hungry, horny, tired, tense, and jump-lagged, at least he wasn't throwing up in a paroxysm of anticipated terror this time. It was just Vorkosigan House. He could handle it. And as soon as he got inside, he could call Kareen, yes! He released the canopy the instant the car sighed to the pavement, and turned to help Enrique unload.

Mark's feet had barely hit the concrete when Armsman Pym popped out of the front doors, and gave him a snappy, yet somehow reproachful, salute. "My Lord Mark! You should have called us from the shuttleport, m'lord. We'd have picked you up properly."

"That's all right, Pym. I don't think all our gear would have fit in the armored car anyway. Don't worry, there's still plenty for you to do." The hired freight van which had followed them from the shuttleport cleared the gate guard and chuffed up the drive to wheeze to a halt behind them.

"Holy saints," murmured Enrique out of the corner of his mouth, as Mark hurried to help him hoist the DELICATE crate, which had ridden between them in the ground car, out to the pavement. "You really *are* Lord Vorkosigan. I'm not sure I totally believed you, till now."

"I really am Lord *Mark*," Mark corrected this. "Get it straight. It matters, here. I am not now, nor do I ever aspire to be, the heir to the Countship." Mark nodded toward the new short figure exiting the mansion through the carved double doors, now swung welcoming-wide. "*He's* Lord Vorkosigan."

Miles didn't look half-bad, despite the peculiar rumors about his health which had leaked back to Beta Colony. Someone had taken a hand in improving his civilian wardrobe, judging by the sharp gray suit he wore, and he filled it properly, not so sickly-thin as he'd still been when Mark had last seen him here almost a year ago. He advanced on Mark with a grin, his hand held out. They managed to exchange a firm, brotherly handshake. Mark was desperate for a hug, but not from Miles.

"Mark, dammit, you took us by surprise. You're supposed to call from orbit when you get in. Pym would have been there to pick you up."

"So I've been advised."

Miles stood back and looked him over, and Mark flushed in self-consciousness. The meds Lilly Durona had given him had permitted him to piss away more fat in less time than was humanly natural, and he'd stuck religiously to the strict regimen of diet and liquids to combat the corrosive side effects. She'd said the drug-complex wasn't addictive, and Mark believed her; he couldn't wait to get off the loathsome stuff. He now weighed very little more than when he'd last set foot on Barrayar, just as planned. Killer was released from his fleshly cage, able to defend them again if he absolutely had to. . . . But Mark hadn't anticipated how flabby and gray he was going to look, as though he were melting and slumping like a candle in the sun.

And indeed, the next words out of his brother's mouth were, "Are you feeling all right? You don't look so good."

"Jump lag. It will pass." He grinned tightly. He wasn't sure if it was the drugs, Barrayar, or missing

Kareen that put him more on edge, but he was sure of the cure. "Have you heard from Kareen? Did she get in all right?"

"Yes, she got here fine, last week. What's that peculiar crate with all the layers?"

Mark wanted to see Kareen more than anything in the universe, but first things first. He turned to Enrique, who was goggling in open fascination at him and his progenitor-twin.

"I brought a guest. Miles, I'd like you to meet Dr. Enrique Borgos. Enrique, my brother Miles, Lord Vorkosigan."

"Welcome to Vorkosigan House, Dr. Borgos," Miles said, and shook hands in automatic politeness. "Your name sounds Escobaran, yes?"

"Er, yes, er, Lord Vorkosigan."

Wonders, Enrique managed to get it right this time. Mark had only been coaching him on Barrayaran etiquette for ten straight days. . . .

"And what are you a doctor of?" Miles glanced again, worriedly, at Mark; Mark guessed he was evolving alarmed theories about his clone-brother's health.

"Not medicine," Mark assured Miles. "Dr. Borgos is a biochemist and genetic entomologist."

"Words . . . ? No, that's etymologist. Bugs, that's right." Miles's eye was drawn again to the big steel-wound shock-cushioned crate at their feet. "Mark, why does that crate have air holes?"

"Lord Mark and I are going to be working together," the gangling scientist told Miles earnestly.

"I assume we have some room to spare for him," Mark added.

"God, yes, help yourselves. The House is yours. I moved last winter to the big suite on the second floor of the east wing, so the whole of the north wing is unoccupied now above the ground floor. Except for the room on the fourth floor that Armsman Roic has. He sleeps days, so you might want to give him some margin. Father and Mother will bring their usual army with them when they get here towards Midsummer, but we can rearrange things then if necessary."

"Enrique hopes to set up a little temporary laboratory, if you don't mind," Mark said.

"Nothing explosive, I trust? Or toxic?"

"Oh, no, no, Lord Vorkosigan," Enrique assured him. "It's not like that at all."

"Then I don't see why not." He glanced down, and added in a fainter tone, "Mark . . . why do the air holes have *screens* in them?"

"I'll explain everything," Mark assured him airily, "as soon as we get unloaded and I pay off these hired drivers." Armsman Jankowski had appeared at Pym's elbow while the introductions had been going forth. "The big blue valise is mine, Pym. Everything else goes with Dr. Borgos."

By press-ganging the drivers, the van was unloaded quickly to the staging area of the black-and-white tiled entry hall. A moment of alarm occurred when Armsman Jankowski, tottering along under a load of what Mark knew to be hastily-packed laboratory glassware, stepped on a black-and-white kitten, well-camouflaged by the tiles. The outraged creature emitted an ear-splitting yowl, spat, and shot off between Enrique's feet, nearly tripping the Escobaran, who was just then balancing the very expensive molecular analyzer. It was saved by a grab from Pym.

They'd almost been caught, during their midnight raid on the padlocked lab that had liberated the all-important notes and irreplaceable specimens, when Enrique had insisted on going back for the damned analyzer. Mark would have taken it as some sort of cosmic I-told-you-so if Enrique had dropped it *now*. *I'll buy you a whole new lab when we get to Barrayar*, he'd kept trying to convince the Escobaran. Enrique had seemed to think Barrayar was still stuck in the Time of Isolation, and he wasn't going to be able to obtain anything here more scientifically complex than an alembic, a still, and maybe a trepanning chisel.

Settling in their digs took still more time, as the ideal spot Enrique immediately tried to select for his new lab was the mammoth, modernized, brilliantly-lit, and abundantly-powered kitchen. Upon Pym's inquiry, Miles hastily arrived to defend this turf for his cook, a formidable woman whom he seemed to regard as essential to the smooth running not only of his household but also of his new political career. After a low-voiced explanation from Mark that the phrase *The House is yours* was a mere polite locution, and not meant to be taken literally, Enrique was persuaded to settle for a secondary laundry room in the half-basement of the north wing, not nearly so spacious, but with running water and waste disposal facilities. Mark promised a shopping trip for whatever toys and tools and benches and hoods and lighting Enrique's heart desired just as soon as possible, and left him to start arranging his treasures. The scientist showed no interest whatsoever in the selection of a bedroom. Mark figured he'd probably end up dragging a cot into his new lab, and settling there like a brooding hen defending her nest.

Mark threw his valise into the same room he'd occupied last year, and returned to the laundry to make ready to pitch his proposal to his big brother. It had all seemed to make such splendid sense, back on Escobar, but Mark hadn't known Enrique so well then. The man was a genius, but God Almighty he needed a keeper. Mark thought he understood the whole mess with the bankruptcy proceedings and the fraud suits perfectly, now. "Let me do the talking, understand?" Mark told Enrique firmly. "Miles is an important man here, an Imperial Auditor, *and* he has the ear of the Emperor himself. His support could give us a big boost." More importantly, his active opposition could be fatal to the scheme; he could kill it with a word. "I know how to work him. Just agree with everything I say, and don't try to add any embellishments of your own."

Enrique nodded eagerly, and followed him like an over-sized puppy through the maze of the house till they tracked Miles down in the great library. Pym was just setting out a spread of tea, coffee, Vorkosigan wines, two varieties of District-brewed beer, and a tray of assorted hors d'oeuvres that looked like a stained-glass window done in food. The Armsman gave Mark a cordial welcome-home nod, and withdrew to leave the two brothers to their reunion.

"How handy," Mark said, pulling up a chair next to the low table. "Snacks. It just so happens I have a new product for you to taste-test, Miles. I think it could prove very profitable."

Miles flicked up an interested eyebrow, and leaned forward as Mark unwrapped a square of attractive red foil to reveal a soft white cube. "Some sort of cheese, is it?"

"Not exactly, though it is an animal product, in a sense. This is the unflavored base version. Flavors and colors can be added as desired, and I'll show you some of those later when we've had time to mix them up. It's nutritious as hell, though—a perfectly balanced blend of carbohydrates, proteins, and fats, with all the essential vitamins in their proper proportions. You could live on a diet of this stuff alone, and water, if you had to."

"I lived on it for three months straight!" Enrique put in proudly. Mark shot him a slight frown, and he subsided.

Mark seized one of the silver knives on the tray, cut the cube into four parts, and popped a portion into his mouth. "Try it!" he said around his chewing. He stopped short of a dramatic mumble of *yum, yum!* or other convincing sound effects. Enrique too reached for a piece. More cautiously, so did Miles. He hesitated, with the fragment at his lips, to find both his watchers hanging on his gesture. His brows twitched up; he chewed. A breathless silence fell. He swallowed.

Enrique, scarcely able to contain himself, said, "How d'you like it?"

Miles shrugged. "It's . . . all right. Bland, but you said it was unflavored. Tastes better than a lot of military rations I've eaten."

"Oh, military rations," said Enrique. "Now, there's an application I hadn't thought of—"

"We'll get to that phase later," said Mark.

"So what makes it so potentially profitable?" asked Miles curiously.

"Because, through the miracle of modern bioengineering, it can be made practically for free. Once the customer has purchased, or perhaps licensed, his initial supply of butter bugs, that is."

A slight but noticeable silence. "His what?"

Mark pulled out the little box from his jacket pocket, and carefully lifted the lid. Enrique sat up expectantly. "This," said Mark, and held the box out toward his brother, "is a butter bug."

Miles glanced down into the box, and recoiled. "*Yuk!* That is the most disgusting thing I've seen in my life!"

Inside the box, the thumb-sized worker butter bug scrabbled about on its six stubby legs, waved its antennae frantically, and tried to escape. Mark gently pushed its tiny claws back from the edges. It chittered its dull brown vestigial wing carapaces, and crouched to drag its white, soft, squishy-looking abdomen to the safety of one corner.

Miles leaned forward again, to peer in revolted fascination. "It looks like a cross between a cockroach, a termite, and a . . . and a . . . and a pustule."

"We have to admit, its physical appearance is not its main selling point."

Enrique looked indignant, but refrained from denying this last statement out loud.

"Its great value lies in its efficiency," Mark went on. It was a good thing they hadn't started out by showing Miles a whole colony of butter bugs. Or worse, a queen butter bug. They could work up to the queen butter bugs much later, once they'd dragged their prospective patron over the first few psychological humps. "These things eat almost any kind of low-grade organic feedstocks. Corn stalks, grass clippings, seaweed, you name it. Then, inside their gut, the organic matter is processed by a carefully-orchestrated array of symbiotic bacteria into . . . bug butter curds. Which the butter bugs regur—return through their mouths and pack into special cells, in their hive, all ready for humans to harvest. The raw butter curds—"

Enrique, unnecessarily, pointed to the last fragment still sitting on the foil.

"Are perfectly edible at this point," Mark went on more loudly, "though they can be flavored or processed further. We're considering more sophisticated product development by adding bacteria to provide desirable flavors to the curds right in the bug's guts, so even that processing step won't be necessary."

"Bug vomit," said Miles, working through the implications. "You fed me bug vomit." He touched his hand to his lips, and hastily poured himself some wine. He looked at the butter bug, looked at the remaining fragment of curd, and drank deeply. "You're insane," he said with conviction. He drank once more, carefully swishing the wine around in his mouth for a long time before swallowing.

"It's just like honey," Mark said valiantly, "only different."

Miles's brow wrinkled, as he considered this argument. "Very different. Wait. Is that what was in that crate you brought in, these vomit bugs?"

"*Butter* bugs," Enrique corrected frostily. "They pack most efficiently—"

"*How many* . . . butter bugs?"

"We rescued twenty queen-lines in various stages of development before we left Escobar, each supported by about two hundred worker bugs," Enrique explained. "They did very well on the trip—I was so proud of the girls—they more than doubled their numbers en route. Busy, busy! Ha, ha!"

Miles's lips moved in calculation. "You've carted upwards of *eight thousand* of those revolting things into *my house*?"

"I can see what you're worried about," Mark cut in quickly, "and I assure you, it won't be a problem."

"I don't think you can, but what won't be a problem?"

"Butter bugs are highly controllable, ecologically speaking. The worker bugs are sterile; only the queens can reproduce, and they're parthenogenetic—they don't become fertile till treated with special hormones. Mature queens can't even move, unless their human keeper moves them. Any worker bug that might chance to get out would just wander about till it died, end of story."

Enrique made a face of distress at this sad vision. "Poor thing," he muttered.

"The sooner, the better," said Miles coldly. "Yuk!"

Enrique looked reproachfully at Mark, and began in a low voice, "You promised he'd help us. But he's just like all the others. Short-sighted, emotional, unreasoning—"

Mark held up a restraining hand. "Calm down. We haven't even gotten to the main part yet." He turned to Miles. "Here's the real pitch. We think Enrique can develop a strain of butter bugs to eat *native Barrayaran* vegetation, and convert it into humanly-digestible food."

Miles's mouth opened, then shut again. His gaze sharpened. "Go on . . ."

"Picture it. Every farmer or settler out in the backcountry could keep a hive of these butter bugs, which would crawl around eating all that free alien food that you folks go to so much trouble to eradicate with all the burning and terraforming treatments. And not only would the farmers get free food, they would get free fertilizer as well. Butter bug guano is terrific for plants—they just sop it up, and grow like crazy."

"Oh." Miles sat back, an arrested look in his eyes. "I know someone who is very interested in fertilizers . . ."

Mark went on, "I want to put together a development company, here on Barrayar, to both market the existing butter bugs, and create the new strains. I figure with a science genius like Enrique and a business genius like me," *and let us not get the two mixed up*, "well, there's no limit to what we can get."

Miles frowned thoughtfully. "And what did you get on Escobar, if I may ask? Why bring this genius and his product all the way here?"

Enrique would have got about ten years in jail, if I hadn't come along, but let's not go into that. "He didn't have me to handle the business, then. And the Barrayaran application is just absolutely compelling, don't you think?"

"If it can be made to work."

"The bugs can work to process Earth-descended organic matter right now. We'll market that as soon as we can, and use the proceeds to finance the basic research on the other. I can't set a timetable for that till Enrique has had more time to study Barrayaran biochemistry. Maybe a year or two, to, ah, get all the bugs out." Mark grinned briefly.

"Mark . . ." Miles frowned at the butter bug box, now sitting closed on the table. Tiny scratching noises arose from it. "It sounds logical, but I don't know if logic is going to sell to the proles. Nobody will want to eat food that comes out of something that looks like *that*. Hell, they won't want to eat anything it *touches*."

"People eat honey," argued Mark. "And that comes out of bugs."

"Honeybees are . . . sort of cute. They're furry, and they have those classy striped uniforms. And they're armed with their stings, just like little swords, which makes people respect them."

"Ah, I see—the insect version of the Vor class," Mark murmured sweetly. He and Miles exchanged edged smiles.

Enrique said, in a bewildered tone, "So do you think if I put stings on my butter bugs, Barrayarans would like them better?"

"No!" said Miles and Mark together.

Enrique sat back, looking rather hurt.

"So." Mark cleared his throat. "That's the plan. I'll be setting up Enrique in a proper facility as soon as I have time to find something suitable. I'm not sure whether here in Vorbarr Sultana or out in Hassadar would be better—if this takes off, it could bring in a lot of business, which you might like for the District."

"True . . ." allowed Miles. "Talk to Tsipis."

"I plan to. Do you begin to see why I think of them as money bugs? And do you think you might want to invest? Nothing like getting in on the ground floor, and all that."

"Not . . . at this time. Thanks all the same," said Miles neutrally.

"We, ah, do appreciate the temporary space, you know."

"No problem. Or at least . . ." his eye chilled, "it had better not be."

In the conversational lull that followed, Miles was apparently recalled to his place as a host, and he offered up the food and drinks. Enrique chose beer, and treated them to a dissertation on the history of yeast in human food production, going back to Louis Pasteur, with side comments on parallels between yeast organisms and the butter bugs' symbiotes. Miles drank more wine and didn't say much. Mark nibbled from the grand platter of delectable hors d'oeuvres and calculated the day when he would come to the end of his weight-loss drugs. Or maybe he would just flush the rest tonight.

Eventually Pym, who was apparently playing butler in Miles's reduced bachelor household, came in to collect the plates and glasses. Enrique eyed his brown uniform with interest, and asked about the meaning and history of the silver decorations on the collar and cuffs. This actually drew Miles out briefly, as he supplied Enrique with a few highlights of family history (politely omitting their prominent place in the aborted Barrayaran invasion of Escobar a generation ago), the past of Vorkosigan House, and the story of the Vorkosigan crest. The Escobaran seemed fascinated by the fact that the mountains-and-leaf design had originated as a Count's mark to seal the bags of District tax revenues. Mark was encouraged to believe Enrique was developing a social grace after all. Perhaps he would develop another one soon. One could hope.

When enough time had passed that, Mark calculated, he and Miles could feel they'd accomplished their unaccustomed and still awkward fraternal bonding ritual, he made noises about *finishing unpacking*, and the welcome-home party broke up. Mark guided Enrique back to his new lab, just to be sure he got there all right.

"Well," he said heartily to the scientist. "That went better than I expected."

"Oh, yes," said Enrique vaguely. He had that foggy look in his eyes that betokened visions of long-chain molecules dancing in his head: a good sign. The Escobaran was apparently going to survive his traumatic transplant. "And I've had this wonderful idea how to get your brother to like my butter bugs."

"Great," said Mark, somewhat at random, and left him to it. He headed up the back stairs two at a time to his bedroom and its waiting comconsole, to call Kareen, Kareen, *Kareen*.

CHAPTER FOUR

Ivan had finished his mission of delivering one hundred hand-calligraphed Imperial wedding invitations to Ops HQ for subsequent off-world distribution to select serving officers, when he encountered Alexi Vormoncrief, also passing out through the security scanners in the building's lobby.

"Ivan!" Alexi hailed him. "Just the man! Wait up."

Ivan paused by the automated doors, mentally composing a likely mission order from She Who Must Be Obeyed Till After The Wedding in case he needed to effect an escape. Alexi was not the most stultifying bore in Vorbarr Sultana—several gentlemen of the older generation currently vied for that title—but he certainly qualified as an understudy. On the other hand, Ivan was extremely curious to know if the seeds he'd dropped in Alexi's ear a few weeks back had borne any amusing fruit.

Alexi finished negotiating security and bustled over, a little breathless. "I'm just off duty, are you? Can I treat you to a round, Ivan? I have a bit of news, and you deserve to be the first to know." He rocked on his heels.

If Alexi was buying, why not? "Sure."

Ivan accompanied Alexi across the street to the

convenient tavern that the Ops officers regarded as their collective property. The place was something of an institution, having gone into business some ten or fifteen minutes after Ops had opened its then-new building soon after the Pretender's War. The decor was calculatedly dingy, tacitly preserving it as a male bastion.

They slid into a table toward the back; a man in well-cut civvies lounging at the bar turned his head as they passed. Ivan recognized By Vorrutyer. Most town clowns didn't frequent the officers' bars, but By could turn up anywhere. He had the damnedest connections. By raised a hand in mock-salute to Vormoncrief, who, expansively, beckoned him over to join them. Ivan raised a brow. Byerly was on record as despising the company of his fellows who, as he put it, came unarmed to the battle of wits. Ivan couldn't imagine why he was cultivating Vormoncrief. Opposites attracting?

"Sit, sit," Vormoncrief told By. "I'm buying."

"In that case, certainly," said By, and settled in smoothly. He gave Ivan a cordial nod; Ivan returned it a trifle warily. He didn't have Miles present as a verbal shield-wall. By never baited Ivan while Miles was around. Ivan wasn't quite sure if it was because his cousin ran subtle interference, or because By preferred the more challenging target. Maybe Miles ran interference by *being* the more challenging target. On the other hand, maybe his cousin regarded Ivan as his own personal archery butt, and just didn't want to share. Family solidarity, or mere Milesian possessiveness?

They punched their orders into the server, and Alexi tapped in his credit chit. "Oh, my sincere condolences, by the way, on the death of your cousin Pierre," he said to Byerly. "I kept forgetting to mention that, because you don't wear your House blacks. You really should, you know. You have the right, your blood ties are close enough. Did they finally determine the cause of death?"

"Oh, yes. Heart failure, dropped him like a stone."

"Instant?"

"As far as anyone could tell. Being a ruling Count,

his autopsy was thorough. Well, if the man hadn't been such an antisocial recluse, someone might have come across the body before his brain spoiled."

"So young, hardly fifty. It's a shame he died without issue."

"It's a greater shame that rather more of my Vorrutyer uncles didn't die without issue." By sighed. "I'd have a new job."

"I didn't know you hankered after the Vorrutyers' District, By," said Ivan. "Count Byerly? A political career?"

"God forfend. I have no desire whatsoever to join that hall full of fossils arguing in Vorhartung Castle, and the District bores me to tears. Dreary place. If only my fecund cousin Richars were not such a very complete son-of-a-bitch—no insult intended to my late aunt—I would wish him joy of his prospects. If he can obtain them. Unfortunately, he *does* take joy in them, which quite takes the joy out of it all for me."

"What's wrong with Richars?" asked Alexi blankly. "Seemed a solid enough fellow to me, the few times I've met him. Politically sound."

"Never mind, Alexi."

Alexi shook his head in wonderment. "By, don't you have any proper family feeling?"

By dismissed this with an airy what-would-you? gesture. "I haven't any proper family. My principal feeling is revulsion. With perhaps one or two exceptions."

Ivan's brow wrinkled, as he unraveled By's patter. "*If* he can obtain them? What impediment would Richars have?" Richars was eldest son of the eldest uncle, adult, and as far as Ivan knew, in his right mind. Historically, being a son-of-a-bitch had never been considered a valid excuse for exclusion from the Council of Counts, else it would have been a much thinner body. It was only being a bastard that eliminated one. "No one's discovered he's a secret Cetagandan, like poor René Vorbretten, have they?"

"Unfortunately, no." By glanced across at Ivan, an oddly calculating look starting in his eyes. "But Lady Donna—I believe you know her, Ivan—lodged a formal declaration of impediment with the Council the day after Pierre died, which has temporarily blocked Richars's confirmation."

"I'd heard something. Wasn't paying attention." Ivan hadn't seen Pierre's younger sister Lady Donna in the flesh—and what delicious flesh it had once been—since she'd divested her third spouse and semiretired to the Vorrutyer's District to become her brother's official hostess and unofficial District deputy. It was said she had more clout in the day-to-day running of the District than Pierre. Ivan could believe it. She must be almost forty now; he wondered if she'd started to run to fat yet. On her, it might look good. Ivory skin, wicked black hair to her hips, and smoldering brown eyes like embers. . . .

"Oh, I'd wondered why Richars's confirmation was taking so long," said Alexi.

By shrugged. "We'll see if Lady Donna can make her case stick when she gets back from Beta Colony."

"My mother thought it odd she left before the funeral," said Ivan. "She hadn't heard of any bad blood between Donna and Pierre."

"Actually, they got along rather well, for my family. But the need was urgent."

Ivan's own fling with Donna had been memorable. He'd been a callow new officer, she'd been ten years older and temporarily between spouses. They hadn't talked much about their relatives. He'd never told her, he realized, how her mind-melting lessons had saved his ass a few years later, during that near-disastrous diplomatic mission to Cetaganda. He really ought to call on her, when she got back from Beta Colony. Yes, she might be depressed about those accumulating birthdays, and need cheering up . . .

"So what's the substance of her declaration of impediment?" asked Vormoncrief. "And what's Beta Colony got to do with it?"

"Ah, we shall have to see how that plays out when Donna gets back. It will be a surprise. I wish her every success." A peculiar smile quirked By's lips.

Their drinks arrived. "Oh, very good." Vormoncrief raised his glass high. "Gentlemen, to matrimony. I have sent the Baba!"

Ivan paused with his glass halfway to his lips. "Beg pardon?"

"I've met a woman," said Alexi smugly. "In fact, I might say I have met *the* woman. For which I thank you, Ivan. I would never have known of her existence but for your little hint. By's seen her once—she's suitable in every way to be Madame Vormoncrief, don't you think, By? Great connections—she's Lord Auditor Vorthys's niece—how did you find out about her, Ivan?"

"I . . . met her at my cousin Miles's. She's designing a garden for him." *How did Alexi get so far, so fast?*

"I didn't know Lord Vorkosigan had any interest in gardens. No accounting for taste. In any case, I managed to get her father's name and address through this casual conversation about family trees. South Continent. I had to buy a round-trip ticket for the Baba, but she's one of the most exclusive go-betweens—not that there are many left—in Vorbarr Sultana. Hire the best, I say."

"Madame Vorsoisson has accepted you?" said Ivan, stunned. *I never intended it to go to this. . . .*

"Well, I assume she will. When the offer arrives. Almost no one uses the old formal system anymore. She'll take it as a romantic surprise, I hope. Bowl her right over." His smugness was tinged with anxiety, which he soothed with a large gulp of his beer. By Vorrutyer swallowed a sip of wine and whatever words he'd been about to utter.

"Think she'll accept?" Ivan said cautiously.

"A woman in her situation, why should she refuse? It will give her a household of her own again, which she must be used to, and how else can she get one? She's true Vor, she will surely appreciate the nicety. *And* it steals a march on Major Zamori."

She hadn't accepted yet. There was still hope. This wasn't celebration, this was nervous babbling seeking the sedation of drink. Sound idea—Ivan took a long gulp. Wait . . . "Zamori? I didn't tell Zamori about the widow."

Ivan had selected Vormoncrief with care, as a plausible enough threat to put the wind up Miles without actually posing a real danger to his suit. For status, a mere no-lord Vor surely couldn't compete with a Count's heir and Imperial Auditor. Physically . . . hm. Maybe he hadn't thought enough about that one. Vormoncrief was a well-enough looking man. Once Madame Vorsoisson was outside of Miles's charismatic jamming-field, the comparison might be . . . rather painful. But Vormoncrief was a blockhead—surely she couldn't pick him over . . . *and how many married blockheads do you know? Somebody picked 'em. It can't be that much of an impediment.* But Zamori—Zamori was a serious man, and no fool.

"Something I let slip, I fear." Vormoncrief shrugged. "No matter. He's not Vor. It gives me an edge with her family Zamori can't touch. She married Vor before, after all. And she must know a woman alone has no business raising a son. It'll be a financial stretch, but I think if I take a firm hand I can convince her to fire him off to a real Vor school soon after the knot is tied. Make a man of him, knock that little obnoxious streak right out of him before it becomes a habit."

They finished their beer; Ivan ordered the next round. Vormoncrief went off to find the head.

Ivan chewed on his knuckle, and stared at By.

"Problems, Ivan?" By inquired easily.

"My cousin Miles is courting Madame Vorsoisson. He told me to back off her under pain of his ingenuity."

By's brows twitched up. "Then watching him annihilate Vormoncrief should amuse you. Or would it be the other way around that would charm?"

"He's going to eviscerate me out my ass when he finds out I tipped Vormoncrief onto the widow. And Zamori, oh God."

By smiled briefly with one side of his mouth. "Now, now. I was there. Vormoncrief bored her to tears."

"Yes, but . . . maybe her situation isn't comfortable. Maybe she would take the first ticket out that was offered . . . wait, you? How did you come there?"

"Alexi . . . leaks. It's a habit of his."

"Didn't know you were wife-hunting."

"I'm not. Don't panic. Nor am I about to inflict a Baba—good lord, what an anachronism—on the poor woman. Though I may note that *I* did not bore her. She was even a little intrigued, I fancy. Not bad for a first reconnaissance. I may take Vormoncrief along on my future amorous starts, for flattering contrast." By glanced up, to be sure the object of their analysis was not on the way back, and leaned forward and lowered his voice to a more confidential tone. But he did not go on to carve the block further or more wittily. Instead he murmured, "You know, I think my cousin Lady Donna would be very glad of your support in her upcoming case. You could be of real use to her. You have the ear of a Lord Auditor—short, but surprisingly convincing in his new role, I was impressed—Lady Alys, Gregor himself. Important people."

"They're important. I'm not." Why the hell was By flattering *him*? He must want something—badly.

"Would you be willing to meet with Lady Donna, when she returns?"

"Oh." Ivan blinked. "That, gladly. But . . ." He thought it through. "I'm not quite sure what she expects to accomplish. Even if she blocks Richars, the Countship can only go to one of his sons or younger brothers. Unless you're planning mass murder at the next family reunion, which is more exertion than I'd expect of you, I don't see how it delivers any benefit to you."

By smiled briefly. "I said I don't want the Countship. Meet with Donna. She will explain it all to you."

"Well . . . all right. Good luck to her, anyway."

By sat back. "Good."

Vormoncrief returned, to dither about his Vor mating ploys into his second beer. Ivan tried without success to change the subject. Byerly drifted off just before it was his turn to buy the next round. Ivan made excuses involving obscure Imperial duties, and escaped at last.

How to avoid Miles? He couldn't put in for transfer to some distant embassy till this damned wedding was over. That would be too late. Desertion was a possibility, he thought morosely—maybe he could go off and join the Kshatryan Foreign Legion. No, with all Miles's galactic connections, there wasn't a cranny of the wormhole nexus, no matter how obscure, sure to be safe from his wrath. And ingenuity. Ivan would have to trust to luck, Vormoncrief's stultifying personality, and for Zamori—kidnapping? Assassination? Maybe introduce him to more women? Ah, yes! Not to Lady Donna, though. That one, Ivan proposed to keep for himself.

Lady Donna. *She* was no pubescent prole. Any husband who dared to trumpet in her presence risked being sliced off at the knees. Elegant, sophisticated, assured . . . a woman who knew what she wanted, and how to ask for it. A woman of his own class, who understood the game. A little older, yes, but with lifespans extending so much these days, what of that? Look at the Betans; Miles's Betan grandmother, who must be ninety if she was a day, was reported to have a gentleman-friend of eighty. Why hadn't he thought of Donna earlier?

Donna. Donna, Donna, Donna. Mmm. This was one meeting he wouldn't miss for worlds.

"I set her to wait in the antechamber to the library, m'lord," Pym's familiar rumble came to Kareen's ears. "Would you like me to bring you anything, or ah, anything?"

"No. Thank you," came Lord Mark's lighter voice in reply from the front hall. "Nothing, that will be all, thank you."

Mark's footsteps echoed off the stone paving: three rapid strides, two skips, a slight hesitation, and a more measured footfall to the archway into the antechamber. *Skips? Mark?* Kareen bounced to her feet as he rounded the corner. Oh, my, *surely* it could not have been good for him to lose that much weight that quickly—instead of the familiar excessively round solidity, he looked all *saggy*, except for his grin, and his blazing eyes—

"Ah! Stand right there!" he ordered her, seized a footstool, placed it before her knees, climbed up, and flung his arms around her. She wrapped her arms around him in turn, and the conversation was buried for a moment in frantic kisses given and received and returned redoubled.

He came up for air long enough to inquire, "How

did you get here?" then didn't let her answer for another minute.

"Walked," she said breathlessly.

"Walked! It must be a kilometer and a half!"

She put her hands on his shoulders, and backed off far enough to focus her eyes on his face. He was too pale, she thought disapprovingly, almost pasty. Worse, his buried resemblance to Miles was edging toward the surface with his bones, an observation she knew would horrify him. She kept it to herself. "So? My father used to walk to work here every day in good weather, stick and all, when he was the Lord Regent's aide."

"If you'd called, I would have sent Pym with the car—hell, better, I'd have come myself. Miles says I can use his lightflyer whenever I want."

"A lightflyer, for six blocks?" she cried indignantly, between a couple more kisses. "On a beautiful spring morning like this?"

"Well, they don't have slidewalks here . . . mmm. . . . Oh, that's good . . ." He nuzzled her ear, inhaled her tickling curls, and planted a spiral line of kisses from her earlobe to her collarbone. She hugged him tight. The kisses seemed to burn across her skin like little fiery footprints. "Missed you, missed you, missed you . . ."

"Missed you missed you missed you too." Though they *could* have traveled home together, if he hadn't insisted on his Escobaran detour.

"At least the walk made you all warm . . . you could come up to my room, and take off all those hot clothes . . . can Grunt come out to play, hmm . . . ?"

"*Here*? In *Vorkosigan House*? With all the Armsmen around?"

"It's where I live, presently." This time, he broke off and leaned back to eye-focusing distance. "And there's only three Armsmen, and one sleeps in the daytime." A worried frown started between his eyes. "Your house . . . ?" he ventured.

"Worse. It's full of parents. And sisters. *Gossipy* sisters."

"Rent a room?" he offered after a puzzled moment.

She shook her head, groping for an explanation of muddled feelings she hardly understood herself.

"We could borrow Miles's lightflyer . . ."

This brought an involuntary giggle to her lips. "There's *really* not enough room. Even if we both took your nasty meds."

"Yes, he can't have been thinking, when he purchased that thing. Better a huge aircar, with vast comfortable upholstered seats. That you can fold down. Like that armored groundcar he has, left over from the Regency— hey! We could crawl in the back, mirror the canopy . . ."

Kareen shook her head, helplessly.

"*Anywhere* on Barrayar?"

"That's the trouble," she said. "Barrayar."

"In orbit . . . ?" He pointed skyward in hope.

She laughed, painfully. "I don't *know*, I don't know . . ."

"Kareen, what's wrong?" He was looking very alarmed, now. "Is it something I've done? Something I said? What have I—are you still mad about the drugs? I'm sorry. I'm sorry. I'll stop them. I'll, I'll gain the weight back. Whatever you want."

"It's not *that*." She stepped back half a pace further, though neither let go of the other's hands. She cocked her head. "Though I *don't* understand why being a body narrower should make you suddenly look half a head shorter. What a bizarre optical illusion. Why should mass translate to height, psychologically? But no. It's not you. It's me."

He clutched her hands and stared in earnest dismay. "I don't understand."

"I've been thinking about it the whole ten days, waiting for you to get home here. About you, about us, about me. All week, I've been feeling stranger and stranger. On Beta Colony, it seemed so right, so logical. Open, official, approved. Here . . . I haven't been able to tell my parents about us. I tried to work up to it. I haven't even been able to tell my sisters. Maybe, if we'd come home together, I wouldn't have lost my nerve, but . . . but I did."

"Were . . . are you thinking about that Barrayaran

folktale where the girl's lover ended up with his head in a pot of basil, when her relatives caught up with him?"

"Pot of basil? No!"

"*I* thought about it . . . I think your sisters could, y'know, if they teamed up. Hand me my head, I mean. And I know your mother could; she trained you all."

"How I wish Tante Cordelia were here!" Wait, that was perhaps an unfortunate remark, in the context. Pots of basil, good God. Mark was so paranoid . . . *quite.* Never mind. "I wasn't thinking of you, at all."

"Oh." His voice went rather flat.

"That's not what I mean! I was thinking of you day and night. Of us. But I've been so uncomfortable, since I got back. It's like I can just feel myself, folding back up into my old place in this Barrayaran culture-box. I can feel it, but I can't stop it. It's horrible."

"Protective coloration?" His tone suggested he could understand a desire for camouflage. His fingers noodled back along her collarbone, crept around her neck. One of his wonderful neck rubs would feel so good, just now . . . He'd worked so hard, to learn to touch and be touched, to overcome the panic and the flinching and the hyperventilation. He was breathing faster now.

"Something like that. But I hate secrets and lies."

"Can't you just . . . tell your family?"

"I tried. I just couldn't. Could you?"

He looked nonplused. "You want me to? It would be the basil for sure."

"No, no, I mean hypothetically."

"I could tell *my* mother."

"*I* could tell *your* mother. She's Betan. She's another world, the other world, the one where we were so right. It's *my* mother I can't talk to. And I always could, before." She found she was trembling, a little. Mark could feel it through her hands; she could tell by the stricken look in his eyes as he raised his face to hers.

"I don't understand how it can feel so right there, and so wrong here," Kareen said. "It should be not wrong here. Or not right there. Or something."

"That makes no sense. Here or there, what's the difference?"

"If there's no difference, why did you go to so much trouble to lose all that weight before you would set foot on Barrayar again?"

His mouth opened, and closed. He finally got out, "Well, so. It's only for a couple of months. I can take a couple of months."

"It gets worse. Oh, Mark! I can't go back to Beta Colony."

"What? Why not? We'd planned—you'd planned—is it that your parents suspect, about us? Have they forbidden you—"

"It's not that. At least, I don't think it is. It's just money. Or just no money. I couldn't have gone, last year, without the Countess's scholarship. Mama and Da say they're strapped, and I don't know how I can earn so much in just the few months." She bit her lip in renewed determination. "But I mean to think of something."

"But if you can't—but I'm not done yet, on Beta Colony," he said plaintively. "I have another year of school, and another year of therapy."

Or more. "But you do mean to come back to Barrayar, after, don't you?"

"Yes, I think. But a whole year apart—" He gripped her tighter, as though looming parents were bearing down upon them to rip her from his grasp on the spot. "It would be . . . excessively stressful, without you," he mumbled in muffled understatement into her flesh.

After a moment, he took a deep breath, and peeled himself away from her. He kissed her hands. "There's no need to panic," he addressed her knuckles earnestly. "There's months to figure something out. Anything could happen." He looked up, and feigned a normal smile. "I'm glad you're here anyway. You have to come see my butter bugs." He hopped down from the footstool.

"Your what?"

"Why does everyone seem to have so much trouble with that name? I thought it was simple enough. Butter bugs. And if I hadn't gone by Escobar, I would never have run across 'em, so that much good has come of it all. Lilly Durona tipped me on to them, or rather, onto Enrique, who was in a spot of trouble. Great biochemist, no financial sense. I bailed him out of jail, and helped him rescue his experimental stocks from the idiot creditors who'd confiscated 'em. You'd have laughed, to watch us blundering around in that raid on his lab. Come on, come see."

As he towed her by the hand through the great house, Kareen asked dubiously, "Raid? On Escobar?"

"Maybe raid is the wrong word. It was entirely peaceful, miraculously enough. *Burglary*, perhaps. I actually got to dust off some of my old training, believe it or not."

"It doesn't sound very . . . legal."

"No, but it was moral. They were Enrique's bugs—he'd made 'em, after all. And he loves them like pets. He cried when one of his favorite queens died. It was very affecting, in a bizarre sort of way. If I hadn't been wanting to strangle him at just that moment, I'd have been very moved."

Kareen was just starting to wonder if those cursed weight-loss meds had any psychological side-effects Mark hadn't seen fit to confide to her, when they arrived at what she recognized as one of Vorkosigan House's basement laundry rooms. She hadn't been back in this part of the house since she'd played hide-and-seek here with her sisters as children. The windows high in the stone walls let in a few strips of sunlight. A lanky fellow with crisp dark hair, who looked no older than his early twenties at the outside, was puttering distractedly about among piles of half-unpacked boxes.

"Mark," he greeted them. "I must have more shelving. And benches. And lighting. And more heat. The girls are sluggish. You promised."

"Check the attics first, before you go running out to buy stuff new," Kareen suggested practically.

"Oh, good idea. Kareen, this is Dr. Enrique Borgos, from Escobar. Enrique, this is my . . . my *friend*, Kareen

Koudelka. My best friend." Mark held tightly and possessively to her hand as he announced this. But Enrique merely nodded vaguely at her.

Mark turned to a broad covered metal tray, balanced precariously on a crate. "Don't look yet," he said over his shoulder to her.

A memory of life with her older sisters whispered through Kareen's mind—*Open your mouth and close your eyes, and you will get a big surprise*... Prudently, she ignored his directive and advanced to see what he was doing.

He lifted the tray's cover to reveal a writhing mass of brown-and-white shapes, chittering faintly and crawling over one another. Her startled eye sorted out the details—insectoid, big, lots of legs and waving feelers—

Mark plunged his hand in amongst the heaving masses, and she blurted, "Eck!"

"It's all right. They don't bite or sting," he assured her with a grin. "Here, see? Kareen, meet butter bug. Bug, Kareen."

He held out a single bug, the size of her thumb, in his palm.

Does he really want me to touch that thing? Well, she'd got through Betan sex education, after all. What the hell. Torn between curiosity and revulsion, she held out her hand, and Mark tipped the bug into it.

Its little clawed feet tickled her skin, and she laughed nervously. It was quite the most incredibly ugly live thing she'd ever seen in her life. Though she had perhaps dissected nastier items in her Betan xenozoology course last year; nothing looked its best after pickling. The bugs didn't smell too bad, just sort of green, like mown hay. It was the scientist who needed to wash his shirt.

Mark embarked on an explanation of how the bugs reprocessed organic matter in their really disgusting-looking abdomens, complicated by pedantic technical corrections about the biochemical details from his new friend Enrique. It all made sense biologically, as far as Kareen could tell.

Enrique pulled a single petal from a pink rose which lay piled with half a dozen others in a box. The box, also balanced on a stack of crates, bore the mark of one of Vorbarr Sultana's premier florists. He set the petal in her palm next to the bug; the bug clutched it in its front claws, and began nibbling off the tender edge. He smiled fondly at the creature. "Oh, and Mark," he added, "the girls need more food as soon as possible. I got these this morning, but they won't last the day." He waved at the florist's box.

Mark, who had been anxiously watching Kareen contemplate the bug in her hand, seemed to notice the roses for the first time. "Where did you get the flowers? Wait, you bought *roses* for *bug fodder?*"

"I asked your brother how to get some Earth-descended botanical matter that the girls would like. He said, call there and order it. Who is Ivan? But it was terribly expensive. We're going to have to rethink the budget, I'm afraid."

Mark smiled thinly, and seemed to count to five before answering. "I see. A *slight* miscommunication, I fear. Ivan is our cousin. You will doubtless not be able to avoid meeting him sooner or later. There is Earth-descended botanical matter available much more cheaply. I believe you can collect some outside—no, maybe I'd better not send you out alone. . . ." He stared at Enrique with an expression of deeply mixed emotion, rather the way Kareen stared at the butter bug in her palm. It was about halfway through munching down the rose petal now.

"Oh, and I *must* have a lab assistant as soon as possible," Enrique added, "if I am to plunge unimpeded into my new studies. And access to whatever the natives here may know about their local biochemistry. Mustn't waste precious time reinventing the wheel, you know."

"I believe my brother has some contacts at Vorbarr Sultana University. And at the Imperial Science Institute. I'm sure he could get you access to anything that isn't security-related." Mark chewed gently on his lip, his brows drawn down in a momentarily downright Milesian expression of furious thought. "Kareen . . . didn't you say you were looking for a job?"

"Yes . . ."

"Would *you* like a job as an assistant? You had those couple of Betan biology courses last year—"

"Betan training?" Enrique perked up. "Someone with Betan training, in this benighted place?"

"Only a couple of undergraduate courses," Kareen explained hastily. "And there are *lots* of folks on Barrayar with galactic training of all sorts." *What does he think this is, the Time of Isolation?*

"It's a start," said Enrique, in a tone of judicious approval. "But I was going to ask, Mark, do we have enough money to hire anyone yet?"

"Mm," said Mark.

"You, out of money?" said Kareen to Mark, startled. "What did you *do* on Escobar?"

"I'm not *out*. It's just tied up in a lot of nonliquid ways right now, and I spent quite a bit more than I'd budgeted—it's only a temporary cash-flow problem. I'll get it sorted out at the end of the next period. But I have to confess, I was really glad I could put Enrique and his project up here free for a little while."

"We could sell shares again," Enrique suggested. "That's what I did before," he added in an aside to Kareen.

Mark winced. "I think not. I know I explained to you about *closely-held*."

"People do raise venture capital that way," Kareen observed.

Mark informed her under his breath, "But they don't normally sell shares to five hundred and eighty percent of their company."

"Oh."

"I was going to pay them all back," Enrique protested indignantly. "I was so close to breakthrough, I couldn't stop then!"

"Um . . . excuse us a moment, Enrique." Mark took Kareen by her free hand, led her into the corridor outside the laundry room, and shut the door firmly. He turned to her. "He doesn't need an assistant. He needs a *mother*. Oh, God, Kareen, you have no idea what a boon it would be if you could help me ride herd on the man. I could give *you* the credit chits with a quiet mind, and you could keep the records and dole out his pocket-money, and keep him out of dark alleys and not let him pick the Emperor's flowers or talk back to ImpSec guards or whatever suicidal thing he comes up with next. The thing is, um . . ." He hesitated. "*Would* you be willing to take shares as collateral against your salary, at least till the end of the period? Doesn't give you much spending money, I know, but you said you meant to save . . ."

She stared dubiously at the butter bug, still tickling her palm as it finished off the last of its rose petal. "Can you really give me shares? Shares of what? But . . . if this doesn't work out as you hope, I wouldn't have anything else to fall back on."

"It will work," he promised urgently. "I'll make it work. I own fifty-one percent of the enterprise. I'm having Tsipis help me officially register us as a research and development company, out of Hassadar."

She would be betting their future together on Mark's odd foray into bioentrepreneurship, and she wasn't even sure he was in his right mind. "What, ah, does your Black Gang think of all this?"

"It's not their department in any way."

Well, that was reassuring. This was apparently the work of his dominant personality, Lord Mark, serving the whole man, and not a ploy of one of his sub-personas for its own narrow ends. "Do you really think Enrique is that much of a genius? Mark, I thought that smell back in the lab was the bugs at first, but it was him. When was his last bath?"

"He probably forgot to take one. Feel free to remind him. He won't be offended. In fact, think of it as part of your job. Make him wash and eat, take charge of his credit chit, organize the lab, make him look both ways before crossing the street. *And* it would give you an excuse to hang out here at Vorkosigan House."

Put like that . . . besides, Mark was giving her that pleading-puppy-eyes look. In his own strange way Mark was almost as good as Miles at drawing one into doing things one suspected one would later regret deeply. Infectious obsession, a Vorkosigan family trait.

"Well . . ." A little chittering *burp* made her look down. "Oh, no, Mark! Your bug is sick." Several milliliters of thick white liquid dripped from the bug's mandibles onto her palm.

"What?" Mark surged forward in alarm. "How can you tell?"

"It's throwing up. Ick! Could it be jump-lag? That makes some people nauseous for days." She looked around frantically for a place to deposit the creature before it exploded or something. Would bug diarrhea be next?

"Oh. No, that's all right. They're supposed to do that. It's just producing its bug butter. *Good* girl," he crooned to the bug. At least, Kareen trusted he was addressing the bug.

Firmly, Kareen took his hand, turned it palm-up, and dumped the now-slimy bug into it. She wiped her hand on his shirt. "Your bug. You hold it."

"Our bugs . . . ?" he suggested, though he accepted it without demur. "Please . . . ?"

The goop didn't smell bad, actually. In fact, it had a scent rather like roses, roses and ice cream. She nevertheless found the impulse to lick the stickiness off her hand to be quite resistible. Mark . . . was less so. "Oh, very well." *I don't know how he talks me into things like this.* "It's a deal."

CHAPTER FIVE

Armsman Pym admitted Ekaterin to the grand front hall of Vorkosigan House. Belatedly, she wondered if she ought to be using the utility entrance, but in his tour of a couple of weeks ago Vorkosigan hadn't shown her where it was. Pym was smiling at her in his usual very friendly way, so perhaps it was all right for the moment.

"Madame Vorsoisson. Welcome, welcome. How may I serve you?"

"I had a question for Lord Vorkosigan. It's rather trivial, but I thought, if he was right here, and not busy . . ." She trailed off.

"I believe he's still upstairs, madame. If you would be pleased to wait in the library, I'll fetch him at once."

"I can find my way, thank you," she fended off his proffered escort. "Oh, wait—if he's still asleep, please don't—" But Pym was already ascending the stairs.

She shook her head, and wandered through the antechamber to the left toward the library. Vorkosigan's Armsmen seemed impressively enthusiastic, energetic, and attached to their lord, she had to concede. And astonishingly cordial to visitors.

She wondered if the library harbored any of those

wonderful old hand-painted herbals from the Time of Isolation, and whether she might borrow—she came to a halt. The chamber had an occupant: a short, fat, dark-haired young man who crouched at a comconsole that sat so incongruously among the fabulous antiques. It was displaying a collection of colored graphs of some kind. He glanced up at the sound of her step on the parquet.

Ekaterin's eyes widened. *At my height,* Lord Vorkosigan had complained, *the effect is damned startling.* But it wasn't the soft obesity that startled nearly so much as the resemblance to, what did they call it for a clone, to his progenitor, which was half-buried beneath the . . . why did she instantly think of it as a barrier of flesh? His eyes were the same intense gray as Miles's—as Lord Vorkosigan's, but their expression was closed and wary. He wore black trousers and a black shirt; his belly burgeoned from an open backcountry-style vest which conceded the spring weather outside only by being a green so dark as to be almost black.

"Oh. You must be Lord Mark. I'm sorry," she spoke to that wariness.

He sat back, his finger touching his lips in a gesture very like one of Lord Vorkosigan's, but then going on to trace his doubled chin, pinching it between thumb and finger in an emphatic variation clearly all his own. "I, on the other hand, am tolerably pleased."

Ekaterin flushed in confusion. "I didn't mean—I didn't mean to intrude."

His eyebrows flicked up. "You have the advantage of me, milady." The timbre of his voice was very like his brother's, perhaps a trifle deeper; his accent was an odd amalgam, neither wholly Barrayaran nor wholly galactic.

"Not milady, merely Madame. Ekaterin Vorsoisson. Excuse me. I'm, um, your brother's landscape consultant. I just came in to check what he wants done with the maple tree we're taking down. Compost, firewood—" She gestured at the cold carved white marble fireplace. "Or if he just wants me to sell the chippings to the arbor service."

"Maple tree, ah. That would be Earth-descended botanical matter, wouldn't it?"

"Why, yes."

"I'll take any chopped-up bits he doesn't want."

"Where . . . would you want it put?"

"In the garage, I suppose. That would be handy."

She pictured the heap dumped in the middle of Pym's immaculate garage. "It's a rather large tree."

"Good."

"Do you garden . . . Lord Mark?"

"Not at all."

The decidedly disjointed conversation was interrupted by a booted tread, and Armsman Pym leaning around the doorframe to announce, "M'lord will be down in a few minutes, Madame Vorsoisson. He says, please don't go away." He added in a more confiding tone, "He had one of his seizures last night, so he's a little slow this morning."

"Oh, dear. And they give him such a headache. I shouldn't trouble him till he's had his painkillers and black coffee." She turned for the door.

"No, no! Sit down, madame, sit, please. M'lord would be right upset with me if I botched his orders." Pym, smiling anxiously, motioned her urgently toward a chair; reluctantly, she sat. "There now. Good. Don't move." He watched her a moment as if to make sure she wasn't going to bolt, then hurried off again. Lord Mark stared after him.

She hadn't thought Lord Vorkosigan was the sort of Old Vor who threw his boots at his servants' heads when he was displeased, but Pym did seem edgy, so who knew? She looked around again to find Lord Mark leaning back in his chair, steepling his fingers and watching her curiously.

"Seizures . . . ?" he said invitingly.

She stared back at him, not at all sure what he was asking. "They leave him with the most dreadful hangover the next day, you see."

"I'd understood they were practically cured. Is this not, in fact, the case?"

"Cured? Not if the one I witnessed was a sample. Controlled, he says."

His eyes narrowed. "So, ah . . . where did you see this show?"

"The seizure? It was on my living room floor, actually. In my old apartment on Komarr," she felt compelled to explain at his look. "I met him during his recent Auditorial case there."

"Oh." His gaze flicked up and down, taking in her widow's garb. Construing . . . what?

"He has this little headset device his doctors made for him, which is supposed to trigger them when he chooses, instead of randomly." She wondered if the one he'd had last night was medically induced, or if he'd left it for too long again and suffered the more severe, spontaneous version. He'd claimed to have learned his lesson, but—

"He neglected to supply me with all those complicating details, for some reason," Lord Mark murmured. An oddly unhumorous grin flashed over his face and was gone. "Did he explain to you how he came by them in the first place?"

His attention upon her had grown intent. She groped for the right balance between truth and discretion. "Cryo-revival damage, he told me. I once saw the scars on his chest from the needle grenade. He's lucky he's alive."

"Huh. Did he also mention that at the time he encountered the grenade, he was trying to save my sorry ass?"

"No . . ." She hesitated, taking in his defiantly lifted chin. "I don't think he's supposed to talk much about his, his former career."

He smiled thinly, and drummed his fingers on the comconsole. "My brother has this bad little habit of editing his version of reality to fit his audience, y'see."

She could understand why Lord Vorkosigan was loath to display any weakness. But was Lord Mark angry about something? Why? She sought to find some more neutral topic. "Do you call him your brother, then, and not your progenitor?"

"Depends on my mood."

The subject of their discussion arrived then, curtailing

the conversation. Lord Vorkosigan wore one of his fine gray suits and polished half-boots, his hair was neatly combed but still damp, and the faint scent of his cologne carried from his shower-warmed skin. This dapper impression of greet-the-morning energy was unfortunately belied by his gray-toned face and puffy eyes; the general effect was of a corpse reanimated and dressed for a party. He managed a macabre smile in Ekaterin's direction, and a suspicious squint at his clone-brother, and lowered himself stiffly into an armchair between them. "Uh," he observed.

He looked appallingly just like that morning-after on Komarr, minus the bloodstains and scabs. "Lord Vorkosigan, you should not have gotten up!"

He gave her a little wave of his fingers which might have been either agreement or denial, then Pym arrived in his wake bearing a tray with coffeepot, cups, and a basket covered with a bright cloth from which wafted an enticing aroma of warm spiced bread. Ekaterin watched with fascination as Pym poured out the first cup and folded his lord's hand around it; Lord Vorkosigan sipped, inhaled—it looked like his first breath of the day—sipped again, and looked up and blinked. "Good morning, Madame Vorsoisson." His voice only sounded a little underwater.

"Good morning—oh—" Pym poured her a cup too before she could forestall him. Lord Mark shut off his comconsole graphs and added sugar and cream to his, and studied his progenitor-brother with obvious interest. "Thank you," Ekaterin said to Pym. She hoped Vorkosigan had ingested his painkillers upstairs, first thing; by his rapidly-improving color and easing movement, she was fairly sure he had.

"You're up early," Vorkosigan said to her.

She almost pointed out the time, in denial of this, then decided that might be impolitic. "I was excited to be starting my first professional garden. The sod crew are out rolling up the grass in the park this morning, and collecting the terraformed topsoil. The tree crew will be along shortly to transplant the oak. It occurred to me to ask if you wanted the maple for firewood, or compost."

"Firewood. Sure. We burn wood now and then, when we're being deliberately archaic for show—it impresses the hell out of my mother's Betan visitors—and there're always the Winterfair bonfires. There's a pile out back behind some bushes. Pym can show you."

Pym nodded genial confirmation.

"I've laid claim to the leaves and chippings," Lord Mark put in, "for Enrique."

Lord Vorkosigan shrugged, and held a hand palm-out in a warding gesture. "That's between you and your eight thousand little friends."

Lord Mark appeared to find no mystery in this obscure remark; he nodded thanks. Having, apparently, accidentally routed her employer out of bed, Ekaterin wondered if it would be too rude to dash out again immediately. She ought probably to stay long enough to drink at least one cup of Pym's coffee. "If all goes well, the excavation can start tomorrow," she added.

"Ah, good. Did Tsipis put you in the way of collecting all your water and power connection permits?"

"Yes, that's all under control. And I've learned more than I expected about Vorbarr Sultana's infrastructure."

"It's a lot older and stranger than you'd think. You should hear Drou Koudelka's war stories some time, about how they escaped through the sewers after collecting the Pretender's head. I'll see if I can get her going at the dinner party."

Lord Mark leaned his elbow on the comconsole, nibbled gently on his knuckle, and idly rubbed his throat.

"A week from tomorrow night seems to be the date I can round up everyone," Lord Vorkosigan added. "Will that work for you?"

"Yes, I think so."

"Good." He shifted around, and Pym hastened to pour him more coffee. "I'm sorry I missed the garden groundbreaking. I really meant to come out and watch that with you. Gregor sent me out-country a couple of days ago on what turned out to be a fairly bizarre errand, and I didn't get back till late last night."

"Yes, what was that all about?" Lord Mark put in. "Or is it an Imperial secret?"

"No, unfortunately. In fact, it's already gossip all over town. Maybe it will divert attention from the Vorbretten case. Though I'm not sure if you can call it a *sex* scandal, exactly." A tilted grimace. "Gregor told me, 'You're half-Betan, Miles, you're *just* the Auditor to handle this one.' I said, 'Thanks, Sire.'"

He paused for his first bite of sweet spiced bread, washed down with another swallow of coffee, and warmed to his theme. "Count Vormuir came up with this wonderful idea how to solve his District's underpopulation problem. Or so he imagined. Are you up on the latest hot demographic squabbles among the Districts, Mark?"

Lord Mark waved a negating hand, and reached for the bread basket. "I haven't been following Barrayaran politics for the past year."

"This one goes back further than that. Among our father's early reforms, when he was Regent, was that he managed to impose uniform simplified rules for ordinary subjects who wanted to change Districts, and switch their oaths to their new District Count. Since every one of the sixty Counts was trying to attract population to his District at the expense of his brother Counts, Da somehow greased this through the Council, even though everyone was also trying to prevent their own liege people from leaving them. Now, each Count has a lot of discretion about how he runs his District, how he structures his District government, how he imposes his taxes, supports his economy, what services he provides his people, whether Progressive or Conservative or a party of his own invention like that loon Vorfolse down on the south coast, and on and on. Mother describes the Districts as sixty sociopolitical culture dishes. I'd add, economic, too."

"That part, I've been studying," Lord Mark allowed. "It matters to where I place my investments."

Vorkosigan nodded. "Effectively, the new law gave every Imperial subject the right to vote local government with their feet. Our parents drank champagne with dinner the night the vote slipped through, and Mother grinned for days. I must have been about six, because we were living here by then, I remember. The long-term effect, as you can imagine, has been a downright biological competition. Count Vorenlightened makes it good for his people, his District grows, his revenues increase. His neighbor Count Vorstodgy makes it too tough, and he leaks people like a sieve, and his revenues drop. *And* he gets no sympathy from his brother Counts, because his loss is their gain."

"Ah, ha," said Mark. "And is the Vorkosigan's District winning or losing?"

"We're just treading water, I think. We've been losing people to the Vorbarr Sultana economy since forever. And a hell of a lot of loyalists followed the Viceroy to Sergyar last year. On the other hand, the District University and new colleges and medical complexes in Hassadar have been a big draw. Anyway, Count Vormuir has been a long-time loser in this demographic game. So, he implemented what he fondly imagined to be a wildly Progressive personal—I might say, very personal—solution."

Ekaterin's cup was empty, but she'd lost all desire to leave. She could listen to Lord Vorkosigan by the hour, she thought, when he was on like this. He was entirely awake and alive now, engrossed in his story.

"Vormuir," Vorkosigan went on, "bought himself thirty uterine replicators and imported some techs to run them, and started, ah, manufacturing his own liege people. His own personal crèche, as it were, but with only one sperm donor. Guess who."

"Vormuir?" Mark hazarded.

"None other. It's the same principle as a harem, I guess. Only different. Oh, and he's only making little girls, at present. The first batch of them are almost two years old. I saw them. Appallingly cute, en masse."

Ekaterin's eyes widened at this vision of a whole thundering cadre of little girls. The impact must be something like a child-garden—or, depending on the decibel level, a girl-grenade. *I always wanted daughters.* Not just one, lots—sisters, the like of which she had never had.

Too late now. None for her, dozens for Vormuir—the pig, it wasn't fair! She was bemusedly aware that she ought to be feeling outrage, but what she really felt was outraged envy. What had Vormuir's wife—wait. Her brows lowered. "Where is he getting the eggs? His Countess?"

"That's the next little legal wrinkle in this mess," Vorkosigan went on enthusiastically. "His Countess, who has four half-grown children of her—and his—own, wants nothing to do with this. In fact, she isn't talking to him, and has moved out. One of his Armsmen told Pym, very privately, that the last time he attempted to impose a, um, conjugal visit upon her, and threatened to batter down her door, she dumped a bucket of water out the window on him—this was mid-winter—and then threatened to personally warm him with her plasma arc. And then threw down the bucket and screamed at him that if he was that much in love with plastic tubes, he could use that one. Do I have that right, Pym?"

"Not the precise quote I was given, but close enough, m'lord."

"Did she hit him?" Mark asked, sounding quite interested.

"Yes," said Pym, "both times. I understand her aim is superior."

"I suppose that made the plasma arc threat convincing."

"Speaking professionally, when one is standing next to the target, an assailant with *bad* aim is actually more alarming. Nevertheless, the Count's Armsmen persuaded him to come away."

"But we digress." Vorkosigan grinned. "Ah, thank you, Pym." The attentive Armsman, blandly, poured his lord more coffee, and refilled Mark and Ekaterin's cups.

Vorkosigan went on, "There is a commercial replicator crèche in Vormuir's District capital, which has been growing babies for the well-to-do for several years now. When a couple present themselves for this service, the techs routinely harvest more than one egg from the wife, that being the more complex and expensive part of the proceedings. The backup eggs are kept frozen for a certain length of time, and if not claimed by then, are discarded. Or they are supposed to be. Count Vormuir hit upon a clever economy. He had his techs collect all the viable discards. He was very proud of this angle, when he was explaining it all to me."

Now *that* was appalling. Nikki had been, to her cost, a body-birth, but it might well have been different. If Tien had had sense, or if she'd stood up for simple prudence instead of letting herself be seduced by the romantic drama of it all, they might have chosen a replicator-gestation. Imagine learning that her longed-for daughter was now the property of an eccentric like Vormuir . . . "Do any of the women know?" asked Ekaterin. "The ones whose egg cells were . . . can you call it stolen?"

"Ah, not at first. Rumors, however, had begun to leak out, hence the Emperor was moved to dispatch his newest Imperial Auditor to investigate." He bowed at her, sitting. "As for whether it can be called theft— Vormuir claims to have violated no Barrayaran law whatsoever. He claims it quite smugly. I shall be consulting with several of Gregor's Imperial lawyers over the next few days, and trying to figure out if that is in fact true. On Beta Colony, they could hang him out to dry for this, and his techs with him, but of course on Beta Colony, he'd never have got this far."

Lord Mark shifted in his station chair. "So how many little girls does Vormuir have by now?"

"Eighty-eight live births, plus thirty more coming along in the replicators. Plus his first four. A hundred and twenty-two children for that idiot, not one for— anyway, I gave him an order in the Emperor's Voice to start no more until Gregor had ruled on his ingenious scheme. He was inclined to protest, but I pointed out that since all his replicators were full anyway, and would be for the next seven or so months, he wasn't really much discommoded by this. He shut up, and went off to consult with *his* lawyers. And I flew back to Vorbarr Sultana and gave Gregor my verbal report, and went home to bed."

He'd left out confession of his seizure in this description, Ekaterin noted. What was Pym about, to have so pointedly mentioned it?

"There ought to be a law," Lord Mark said.

"There ought to be," his brother replied, "but there isn't. This is Barrayar. Lifting the Betan legal model wholesale strikes me as a recipe for revolution, and besides, a lot of their particular conditions don't apply here. There are a dozen galactic codes which address these issues in addition to the Betan. I left Gregor last night muttering about appointing a select committee to study them all and recommend a Joint Council ruling. And me on it, for my sins. I hate committees. I much prefer a nice clean chain of command."

"Only if you're at the top of it," Lord Mark observed dryly.

Lord Vorkosigan conceded this with a sardonic wave. "Well, yes."

Ekaterin asked, "But will you be able to corner Vormuir with a new law? Surely his situation would have to be, um . . . grandfathered."

Lord Vorkosigan grinned briefly. "Exactly the problem. We've got to nail Vormuir under some existing rule, bent to fit, to discourage imitators, while shoving the new law, in whatever form it finally takes, through the Counts and Ministers. We can't use a rape charge; I looked up all the technical definitions, and they just don't stretch that way."

Lord Mark asked, in a worried voice, "Did the little girls seem abused or neglected?"

Lord Vorkosigan glanced up at him rather sharply. "I'm not the expert on crèche care you are, but they seemed all right to me. Healthy . . . noisy . . . they screeched and giggled a lot. Vormuir told me he had two full-time nurturers for every six children, in shifts. He also went on about his frugal plans for having the older ones care for the younger ones, later on, which gave an unsettling hint of just how far he's thinking of expanding this genetic enterprise. Oh, and we can't get him for slavery, either, because they all really are actually his daughters. And the theft-of-the-eggs angle is extremely ambiguous under current rules." In a peculiarly exasperated tone he added, "Barrayarans!" His clone-brother gave him an odd look.

Ekaterin said slowly, "In Barrayaran customary law, when Vor-caste families split because of death or other reasons, the girls are supposed to go to their mothers or mother's kin, and the boys to their fathers. Don't these girls belong to their mothers?"

"I looked at that one, too. Leaving aside the fact that Vormuir isn't married to any of them, I suspect very few of the mothers would actually want the girls, and all of them would be pretty upset."

Ekaterin wasn't altogether sure about the first part of this, but he certainly had the second dead-to-rights.

"And if we forced them into their mothers' families, what punishment would there be in it to Vormuir? His District would still be richer by a hundred and eighteen girls, and he wouldn't even have to feed them." He set aside his half-eaten piece of spice bread, and frowned. Lord Mark selected a second, no, third slice, and nibbled on it. A glum silence fell.

Ekaterin's brows drew down in thought. "By your account, Vormuir is much taken with economies, of scale and otherwise." Only long after Nikki's birth had she wondered if Tien had pushed for the old-fashioned way because it had seemed much cheaper. *We won't have to wait until we can afford it* had been a potent argument, in her eager ears. Vormuir's motivation seemed as much economic as genetic: ultimately, wealth for his District and therefore for him. This techno-harem was intended to become future taxpayers, along with the husbands he no doubt assumed they would draw in, to support him in his old age. "In effect, the girls are the Count's acknowledged bastards. I'm sure I read somewhere . . . in the Time of Isolation, weren't Imperial and count-palatine female bastards entitled to a dowry, from their high-born father? And it required some sort of Imperial permission . . . the dowry almost was the sign of legal acknowledgment. I'll bet the Professora would know all the historical details, including the cases where the dowries had to be dragged out by force. Isn't an Imperial permission effectively an Imperial order? Couldn't Emperor Gregor set Count Vormuir's dowries for the girls . . . high?"

"Oh." Lord Vorkosigan sat back, his eyes widening with delight. "Ah." An evil grin leaked between his lips. "Arbitrarily high, in fact. Oh . . . *my*." He looked across at her. "Madame Vorsoisson, I believe you have hit on a possible solution. I will certainly pass the idea along as soon as I may."

Her heart lifted in response to his obvious pleasure—well, all right, actually it was a sort of razor-edged glee; anyway, he smiled at her smile at his smile. She could only hope she'd done some little bit to ease his morning-after headache. A chiming clock began sounding in the antechamber. Ekaterin glanced at her chrono. Wait, how could it possibly be this late? "Oh, my word, the time. My tree crew will be here any moment. Lord Vorkosigan, I must excuse myself."

She jumped to her feet, and made polite farewells to Lord Mark. Both Pym and Lord Vorkosigan escorted her personally to the front door. Vorkosigan was still very stiff; she wondered how much pain his forced motion denied, or defied. He encouraged her to stop in again, any time she had the least question, or needed anything at all, and dispatched Pym to show her where to have the crew stack the maple wood, and stood in the doorway and watched them both till they turned the corner of the great house.

Ekaterin glanced back over her shoulder. "He didn't look very well this morning, Pym. You really shouldn't have let him get out of bed."

"Oh, I know it, ma'am," Pym agreed morosely. "But what's a mere Armsman to do? I haven't the authority to countermand his orders. What he really needs, is looking after by someone who won't stand his nonsense. A proper Lady Vorkosigan would do the trick. Not one of those shy, simpering ingenues all the young lords seem to be looking to these days, he'd just ride right over her. He needs a woman of experience, to stand up to him." He smiled apologetically down at her.

"I suppose so," sighed Ekaterin. She hadn't really thought about the Vor mating scene from the Armsmen's point of view. Was Pym hinting that his lord had such an ingenue in his eye, and his staff was worried it was some sort of mismatch?

Pym showed her the wood cache, and made a sensible suggestion for placing Lord Mark's compost heap near it rather than in the underground garage, assuring her it would be just fine there. Ekaterin thanked him and headed back toward the front gates.

Ingenues. Well, if a Vor wanted to marry within his caste, he almost had to look to the younger cohort, these days. Vorkosigan did not strike her as a man who would be happy with a woman who was not up to his intellectual weight, but how much choice did he have? Presumably any woman with brains enough to be interesting to him in the first place would not be so foolish as to reject him for his physical . . . it was no business of hers, she told herself firmly. And it was absurd to allow the vision of this imaginary ingenue, offering him an imaginary devastating insult about his disabilities, to raise one's real blood pressure. Completely absurd. She marched off to oversee the dismantling of the bad tree.

Mark was just reaching to reactivate the comconsole when Miles wandered back into the library, smiling absently. Mark turned to watch his progenitor-brother start to fling himself back into his armchair, only to hesitate, and lower himself more carefully. Miles stretched his shoulders as if to loosen knotted muscles, leaned back, and stuck his feet out. He picked up his half-eaten piece of bread, remarked cheerfully, "That went well, don't you think?" and bit into it.

Mark eyed him doubtfully. "What went well?"

"The co'versation." Miles chased his bite with the last of his cold coffee. "So, you've met Ekaterin. Good. What did you two find to talk about, before I got downstairs?"

"You. Actually."

"Ah?" Miles's face lit, and he sat up a little straighter. "What did she say about me?"

"We mainly discussed your seizures," Mark said grimly. "She seemed to know a great deal more about them than you had seen fit to confide to me."

Miles subsided, frowning. "Hm. That's not the aspect

of me I'm really anxious to have her dwell on. Still, it's good she knows. I wouldn't want to be tempted to conceal a problem of that magnitude again. I've learned my lesson."

"Oh, really." Mark glowered at him.

"I sent you the basic facts," his brother protested in response to this look. "You didn't need to dwell on all the gory medical details. You were on Beta Colony; there was nothing you could do about it anyway."

"They're my fault."

"Rubbish." Miles really did do a very good offended snort; Mark decided it was a touch of his—their—Aunt Vorpatril in it that gave it that nice upper-class edge. Miles waved a dismissive hand. "It was the sniper's doing, followed by more medical random factors than I can calculate. Done's done; I'm alive again, and I mean to stay that way this time."

Mark sighed, realizing reluctantly that if he wanted to wallow in guilt, he'd get no cooperation from his big brother. Who, it appeared, had other things on his mind.

"So what did you think of her?" Miles asked anxiously.

"Who?"

"*Ekaterin*, who else?"

"As a landscape designer? I'd have to see her work."

"No, no, no! Not as a landscape designer, though she's good at that *too*. As the next Lady Vorkosigan."

Mark blinked. "What?"

"What do you mean, *what*? She's beautiful, she's smart—dowries, ye gods, how perfect, Vormuir will split—she's incredibly level-headed in emergencies. Calm, y'know? A lovely calm. I adore her calm. I could swim in it. Guts *and* wit, in one package."

"I wasn't questioning her fitness. That was a merely a random noise of surprise."

"She's Lord Auditor Vorthys's niece. She has a son, Nikki, almost ten. Cute kid. Wants to be a jump-pilot, and I think he has the determination to make it. Ekaterin wants to be a garden designer, but I think she could go on to be a terraformer. She's a little too quiet, sometimes—she needs to build up her self-confidence."

"Perhaps she was just waiting to get a word in edge-wise," Mark suggested.

Miles paused, stricken—briefly—by doubt. "Do you think I talked too much, just now?"

Mark waved his fingers in a little perish-the-thought gesture, and poked through the bread basket for any lurking spice bread crumbs. Miles stared at the ceiling, stretched his legs, and counter-rotated his feet.

Mark thought back over the woman he had just seen here. Pretty enough, in that elegant brainy-brunette style Miles liked. Calm? Perhaps. Guarded, certainly. Not very expressive. Round blondes were much sexier. Kareen was wonderfully expressive; she'd even managed to rub some of those human skills off on him, he thought in his more optimistic moments. Miles was plenty expressive too, in his own unreliable way. Half of it was horseshit, but you were never sure which half.

Kareen, Kareen, Kareen. He must *not* take her attack of nerves as a rejection of him. *She's met someone she likes better, and is dumping us,* whispered someone from the Black Gang in the back of his head, and it wasn't the lustful Grunt. *I know a few ways to get rid of excess fellows like that. They'd never even find the body.* Mark ignored the vile suggestion. *You have no place in this, Killer.*

Even if she had met someone else, say, on the way home, all lonely by herself because he'd insisted on taking that other route, she had the compulsive honesty to tell him so if it were so. Her honesty was at the root of their present contretemps. She was constitutionally incapable of walking around pretending to be a chaste Barrayaran maiden unless she was. It was her unconscious solution to the cognitive dissonance of having one foot planted on Barrayar, the other on Beta Colony.

All Mark knew was that if it came down to a choice between Kareen and oxygen, he'd prefer to give up oxygen, thanks. Mark considered, briefly, laying his sexual frustrations open to his brother for advice. Now would be the perfect opportunity, trading on Miles's newly-revealed infatuation. Trouble was, Mark was by no means sure which side Miles would be *on*. Commodore Koudelka had been Miles's mentor and friend, back when Miles had been a fragile youth hopelessly wild for a military career. Would Miles be sympathetic, or would he lead, Barrayaran-style, the posse seeking Mark's head? Miles was being terrifically Vorish these days.

Yes, and so after all his exotic galactic romances, Miles had finally settled on the Vor next door. If settled was the term—the man mouthed certainties that the twitching of his body belied. Mark's brow wrinkled in puzzlement. "Does Madame Vorsoisson know this?" he asked at last.

"Know what?"

"That you're, um . . . hustling her for the next Lady Vorkosigan." And what an *odd* way to say, *I love her, and I want to marry her.* It was very Miles, though.

"Ah." Miles touched his lips. "That's the tricky part. She's very recently widowed. Tien Vorsoisson was killed rather horribly less than two months ago, on Komarr."

"And you had what, to do with this?"

Miles grimaced. "Can't give you the details, they're classified. The public explanation is a breath-mask accident. But in effect, I was standing next to him. You know how that one feels."

Mark flipped up a hand, in sign of surrender; Miles nodded, and went on. "But she's still pretty shaken up. By no means ready to be courted. Unfortunately, that doesn't stop the competition around here. No money, but she's beautiful, and her bloodlines are impeccable."

"Are you choosing a wife, or buying a horse?"

"I am describing how my Vor rivals think, thank you. Some of them, anyway." His frown deepened. "Major Zamori, I don't trust. He may be smarter."

"You have rivals already?" *Down, Killer. He didn't ask for your help.*

"God, yes. And I have a theory about where they came from . . . never mind. The important thing is for me to make friends with her, get close to her, without setting off her alarms, without offending her. Then, when the time is right—well, then."

"And, ah, when are you planning to spring this stunning surprise on her?" Mark asked, fascinated.

Miles stared at his boots. "I don't know. I'll recognize

the tactical moment when I see it, I suppose. If my sense of timing hasn't totally deserted me. Penetrate the perimeter, set the trip lines, plant the suggestion—strike. Total victory! Maybe." He counter-rotated his feet the other way.

"You have your campaign all plotted out, I see," said Mark neutrally, rising. Enrique would be glad to hear the good news about the free bug fodder. And Kareen would be here for work soon—her organizational skills had already had notable effect on the zone of chaos surrounding the Escobaran.

"Yes, exactly. So take care not to foul it up by tipping my hand, if you please. Just play along."

"Mm, I wouldn't dream of interfering." Mark made for the door. "Though I'm not at all sure *I'd* choose to structure *my* most intimate relationship as a war. Is she the enemy, then?"

His timing was perfect; Miles's feet had come down and he was still sputtering just as Mark passed the door. Mark stuck his head back through the frame to add, "I hope her aim is as good as Countess Vormuir's."

Last word: I win. Grinning, he exited.

CHAPTER SIX

"Hello?" came a soft alto voice from the door of the laundry room-cum-laboratory. "Is Lord Mark here?"

Kareen looked up from assembling a new stainless steel rack on wheels to see a dark-haired woman leaning diffidently through the doorway. She wore very conservative widow's garb, a long-sleeved black shirt and skirt set off only by a somber gray bolero, but her pale face was unexpectedly young.

Kareen put down her tools and scrambled to her feet. "He'll be back soon. I'm Kareen Koudelka. Can I help you?"

A smile illuminated the woman's eyes, all too briefly. "Oh, you must be the student friend who is just back from Beta Colony. I'm glad to meet you. I'm Ekaterin Vorsoisson, the garden designer. My crew took out that row of amelanchier bushes on the north side this morning, and I wondered if Lord Mark wanted any more compost."

So that's what those scrubby things had been called. "I'll ask. Enrique, can we use any um, amel-whatsit bush chippings?"

Enrique leaned around his comconsole display and

peered at the newcomer. "Is it Earth-descended organic matter?"

"Yes," replied the woman.

"Free?"

"I suppose. They were Lord Vorkosigan's bushes."

"We'll try some." He disappeared once more behind the churning colored displays of what Kareen had been assured were enzymatic reactions.

The woman stared curiously around the new lab. Kareen followed her gaze proudly. It was all beginning to look quite orderly and scientific and attractive to future customers. They'd painted the walls cream white; Enrique had picked the color because it was the exact shade of bug butter. Enrique and his comconsole occupied a niche in one end of the room. The wet-bench was fully plumbed, set up with drainage into what had once been the washtub. The dry-bench, with its neat array of instruments and brilliant lighting, ran along the wall all the way to the other end. The far end was occupied by racks each holding a quartet of meter-square custom-designed new bughouses. As soon as Kareen had the last set assembled, they could release the remaining queen-lines from their cramped travel box into their spacious and sanitary new homes. Tall shelves on both sides of the door held their proliferating array of supplies. A big plastic waste bin brimmed with a handy supply of bug fodder; a second provided temporary storage for bug guano. The bugshit had not proved nearly as smelly or abundant as Kareen had expected, which was nice, as the task of cleaning the bughouses daily had fallen to her. Not half bad for a first week's work.

"I must ask," said the woman, her eye falling on the heaped-up maple bits in the first bin. "What does he want all those chippings *for*?"

"Oh, come in, and I'll show you," said Kareen enthusiastically. The dark-haired woman responded to Kareen's friendly smile, drawn in despite her apparent reserve.

"I'm the Head Bug Wrangler of this outfit," Kareen went on. "They were going to call me the lab assistant, but I figured as a shareholder I ought to at least be able to pick my own job title. I admit, I don't have any other wranglers to be the head of, yet, but it never hurts to be optimistic."

"Indeed." The woman's faint smile was not in the least Vor-supercilious; drat it, she hadn't said if it was Lady or Madame Vorsoisson. Some Vor could get quite huffy about their correct title, especially if it was their chief accomplishment in life so far. No, if this Ekaterin were that sort, she would have made a point of the *Lady* at the first possible instant.

Kareen unlatched the steel-screen top of one of the bug hutches, reached in, and retrieved a single worker-bug. She was getting quite good at handling the little beasties without wanting to puke by now, as long as she didn't look too closely at their pale pulsing abdomens. Kareen held out the bug to the gardener, and began a tolerably close copy of Mark's Better Butter Bugs for a Brighter Barrayar sales talk.

Though Madame Vorsoisson's eyebrows went up, she didn't shriek, faint, or run away at her first sight of a butter bug. She followed Kareen's explanation with interest, and was even willing to hold the bug and feed it a maple leaf. There was something very *bonding* about feeding live things, Kareen had to admit; she would have to keep that ploy in mind for future pre-sentations. Enrique, his interest piqued by the voices drifting past his comconsole discussing his favorite subject, wandered over and did his best to queer her pitch by adding long, tedious technical footnotes to Kareen's streamlined explanations. The garden designer's interest soared visibly when Kareen got to the part about future R&D to create a Barrayaran-vegetation-consuming bug.

"If you could teach them to eat strangle-vines, South Continent farmers would buy and keep colonies for that alone," Madame Vorsoisson told Enrique, "whether they produced edible food as well or not."

"Really?" said Enrique. "I didn't know that. Are you familiar with the local planetary botany?"

"I'm not a fully-trained botanist—yet—but I have some practical experience, yes."

"Practical," echoed Kareen. A week of Enrique had given her a new appreciation for the quality.

"So let's see this bug manure," the gardener said.

Kareen led her to the bin and unsealed the lid. The woman peered in at the heap of dark, crumbly matter, leaned over, sniffed, ran her hand through it, and let some sift out through her fingers. "Good heavens."

"What?" asked Enrique anxiously.

"This looks, feels, and smells like the finest compost I've ever seen. What kind of chemical analysis are you getting off it?"

"Well, it depends on what the girls have been eating, but—" Enrique burst into a kind of riff on the periodic table of the elements. Kareen followed the significance of about half of it.

Madame Vorsoisson, however, looked impressed. "Could I have some to try on my plants at home?" she asked.

"Oh, yes," said Kareen gratefully. "Carry away all you want. There's getting to be rather a lot of it, and I'm really beginning to wonder where would be a safe place to dispose of it."

"Dispose of it? If this is half as good as it looks, put it up in ten-liter bags and sell it! Everyone who's trying to grow Earth plants here will be willing to try it."

"Do you think so?" said Enrique, anxious and pleased. "I couldn't get anyone interested, back on Escobar."

"This is Barrayar. For a long time, burning and composting was the only way to terraform the soil, and it's still the cheapest. There was never enough Earth-life based compost to both keep old ground fertile and break in new lands. Back in the Time of Isolation they even had a war over horse manure."

"Oh, yeah, I remember that one from my history class." Kareen grinned. "A *little* war, but still, very . . . symbolic."

"Who fought who?" asked Enrique. "And why?"

"I suppose the war was really over money and traditional Vor privilege," Madame Vorsoisson explained to him. "It had been the custom, in the Districts where the Imperial cavalry troops were quartered, to distribute the products of the stables free to any prole who showed up to cart it away, first-come first-served. One of the more financially pressed Emperors decided to keep it all for Imperial lands or sell it. This issue somehow got attached to a District inheritance squabble, and the fight was on."

"What finally happened?"

"In *that* generation, the rights fell to the District Counts. In the following generation, the Emperor took them back. And in the generation after that—well, we didn't have much horse cavalry anymore." She went to the sink to wash, adding over her shoulder, "There is still a customary distribution every week from the Imperial Stables here in Vorbarr Sultana, where the ceremonial cavalry squad is kept. People come in their groundcars, and carry off a bag or two for their flower beds, just for old time's sake."

"Madame Vorsoisson, I've lived for four years in butter bug guts," Enrique told her earnestly as she dried her hands.

"Mm," she said, and won Kareen's heart on the spot by receiving this declaration with no more risibility than a slight helpless widening of her eyes.

"We really need someone on the macro-level as a native guide to the native vegetation," Enrique went on. "Do you think *you* could help us out?"

"I suppose I could give you some sort of quick overview, and some ideas about where to go to next. But you'd really need a District agronomy officer—Lord Mark can surely access the one in the Vorkosigan's District for you."

"There, you see already," cried Enrique. "I didn't even know there was such a thing as a District agronomy officer."

"I'm not sure Mark does, either," Kareen added doubtfully.

"I'll bet the Vorkosigans' manager, Tsipis, could guide you," Madame Vorsoisson said.

"Oh, do you know Tsipis? Isn't he a lovely man?" said Kareen.

Madame Vorsoisson nodded instant agreement. "I've

not met him in person yet, but he's given me ever so much help over the comconsole with Lord Vorkosigan's garden project. I mean to ask him if I could come down to the District to collect stones and boulders from the Dendarii Mountains to line the stream bed—the water in the garden is going to take the form of a mountain stream, you see, and I fancied Lord Vorkosigan would appreciate the home touch."

"Miles? Yes, he loves those mountains. He used to ride up into them all the time when he was younger."

"Really? He hasn't talked much to me about that part of his life—"

Mark appeared at the door at that moment, tottering along under a large box of laboratory supplies. Enrique relieved him of it with a glad cry, and carried it off to the dry bench, and began unpacking the awaited reagents.

"Ah, Madame Vorsoisson," Mark greeted her, catching his breath. "Thank you for the maple chippings. They seem to be a hit. Have you met everyone?"

"Just now," Kareen assured him.

"She likes our bugs," said Enrique happily.

"Have you tried the bug butter yet?" Mark asked.

"Not yet," Madame Vorsoisson said.

"Would you be willing to? I mean, you did see the bugs, yes?" Mark smiled uncertainly at this new potential customer/test subject.

"Oh . . . all right." The gardener's return smile was a trifle crooked. "A small bite. Why not."

"Give her a taste test, Kareen."

Kareen pulled one of the liter tubs of bug butter from the stack on the shelf, and pried it open. Sterilized and sealed, the stuff would keep indefinitely at room temperature. She'd harvested this batch just this morning; the bugs had responded most enthusiastically to their new fodder. "Mark, we're going to need more of these containers. Bigger ones. A liter of bug butter per bughouse per day is going to add up to a lot of bug butter after a while." Pretty soon, actually. Especially when they hadn't been able to persuade anyone in the household to eat more than a mouthful apiece. The Armsmen had taken to avoiding this corridor.

"Oh, the girls will make more than that, now they're fully fed," Enrique informed them cheerfully over his shoulder from the bench.

Kareen stared thoughtfully at the twenty tubs she'd put up this morning, atop the small mountain from the last week. Fortunately, there was a lot of storage space in Vorkosigan House. She scrounged up one of the disposable spoons kept ready for sampling, and offered it to Madame Vorsoisson. Madame Vorsoisson accepted it, blinked uncertainly, scooped a sample from the tub, and took a brave bite. Kareen and Mark anxiously watched her swallow.

"Interesting," she said politely after a moment.

Mark slumped.

Her brows knotted in sympathy; she glanced at the stack of tubs. After a moment she offered, "How does it respond to freezing? Have you tried running it through an ice cream freezer, with some sugar and flavoring?"

"Actually, not yet," said Mark. His head tilted in consideration. "Hm. D'you think that would work, Enrique?"

"Don't see why not," responded the scientist. "The colloidal viscosity doesn't break down when exposed to subzero temperatures. It's thermal acceleration which alters the protein microstructure and hence texture."

"Gets kind of rubbery when you cook it," Mark translated this. "We're working on it, though."

"Try freezing," Madame Vorsoisson suggested. "With, um, perhaps a more dessert-sounding name?"

"Ah, marketing," Mark sighed. "That's the next step now, isn't it?"

"Madame Vorsoisson said she would test out the bug shit on her plants for us," Kareen consoled him.

"Oh, great!" Mark smiled again at the gardener. "Hey, Kareen, you want to fly down to the District with me day after tomorrow, and help me scout sites for the future facility?"

Enrique paused in his unpacking to unfocus his gaze into the air, and sigh, *"Borgos Research Park."*

"Actually, I was thinking of calling it *Mark Vorkosigan Enterprises*," Mark said. "D'you suppose I ought to spell it out in full? MVK Enterprises might have some potential for confusion with Miles."

"*Kareen's Butter Bug Ranch*," Kareen put in sturdily.

"We'll obviously have to have a shareholder's vote." Mark smirked.

"But you'd win automatically," Enrique said blankly.

"Not necessarily," Kareen told him, and shot Mark a mock-glower. "Anyway, Mark, we were just talking about the District. Madame Vorsoisson has to go down there and collect rocks. And she told Enrique she could help him with figuring out Barrayaran native botany. What if we all go together? Madame Vorsoisson says she's never met Tsipis except over the comconsole. We could introduce her and make a sort of picnic out of it all."

And she wouldn't end up alone with Mark, and exposed to all sorts of . . . temptation, and confusion, and resolve-melting neck rubs, and back rubs, and ear-nibbling, and . . . she didn't want to think about it. They'd got on very *professionally* all week here at Vorkosigan House, very comfortably. Very busily. Busy was good. Company was good. Alone together was . . . um.

Mark muttered under his breath to her, "But then we'd have to take Enrique, and . . ." By the look on his face, *alone together* had been just what he'd had in mind.

"Oh, c'mon, it'll be fun." Kareen took the project firmly in hand. A very few minutes of persuasion and schedule-checking and she had the quartet committed, with an early start set and everything. She made a mental note to arrive at Vorkosigan House in plenty of time to make sure Enrique was bathed, dressed, and ready for public display.

Quick, light footsteps sounded from the corridor, and Miles rounded the doorjamb like a trooper swinging himself through a shuttle hatch. "Ah! Madame Vorsoisson," he panted. "Armsman Jankowski only just told me you were here." His gaze swept the room, taking in the demonstration in progress. "You didn't let them feed you that bug vom—bug stuff, did you? Mark—!"

"It's not half bad, actually," Madame Vorsoisson assured him, earning a relieved look from Mark, followed by a see-what-did-I-tell you jerk of his chin at his brother. "It may possibly need a little product development before it's ready to market."

Miles rolled his eyes. "Just a tad, yes."

Madame Vorsoisson glanced at her chrono. "My excavation crew will be back from lunch any minute. It was nice to meet you, Miss Koudelka, Dr. Borgos. Until day after tomorrow, then?" She picked up the bag of tubs packed with bug manure Kareen had put up for her, smiled, and excused herself. Miles followed her out.

He was back in a couple of minutes, having evidently seen her to the door at the end of the corridor. "Good God, Mark! I can't believe you fed her that bug vomit. How could you!"

"Madame Vorsoisson," said Mark with dignity, "is a very sensible woman. When presented with compelling facts, *she* doesn't let a thoughtless emotional response overcome her clear reason."

Miles ran his hands through his hair. "Yeah, I know."

Enrique said, "Impressive, actually. She seemed to understand what I wanted to say even before I spoke."

"And after you spoke, too," said Kareen mischievously. "That's even more impressive."

Enrique grinned sheepishly. "Was I too technical, do you think?"

"Evidently not in this case."

Miles's brows drew down. "What's going on the day after tomorrow?"

Kareen answered sunnily, "We're all going down to the District together to visit Tsipis and look around for various things we need. Madame Vorsoisson's promised to introduce Enrique to Barrayaran native botany on site, so he can start to design what modifications he'll need to make to the new bugs later."

"*I* was going to take her on her first tour of the District. I have it all planned out. Hassadar, Vorkosigan Surleau, the Dendarii Gorge—I have to make exactly the right first impression."

"Too bad," said Mark unsympathetically. "Relax. We're

only going to have lunch in Hassadar and scout around a bit. It's a big District, Miles, there'll be plenty left for you to show off later."

"Wait, I know! I'll go with you. Expedite things, yeah."

"There are only four seats in the lightflyer," Mark pointed out. "I'm flying, Enrique needs Madame Vorsoisson, and I'm damned if I'm going to leave Kareen behind in order to pack *you*." He somehow smiled fondly at her and glowered at his brother simultaneously.

"Yeah, Miles, you're not even a stockholder," Kareen supported this.

With a driven glare, Miles decamped, going off up the corridor muttering, " . . . can't *believe* he fed her *bug* vomit. If only I'd gotten here before—Jankowski, dammit, you and I are going to have a little—"

Mark and Kareen followed him out the door. They stood in the corridor watching this retreat. "What in the world's bit him?" Kareen asked in wonder.

Mark grinned evilly. "He's in love."

"With his gardener?" Kareen's brows rose.

"Causality's the other way around, I gather. He met her on Komarr during his recent case. He hired her as his gardener to create a little propinquity. He's courting her in secret."

"In secret? Why? She seems perfectly eligible to me—she's Vor, even—or is her rank only by marriage? But I shouldn't think that would matter to Miles. Or—are *her* relatives against it, because of his—?" A vague gesture down her body implied Miles's putative mutations. She frowned in outrage at the scent of this romantically doleful scenario. How dare they look down on Miles for—

"Ah, secret *from* her, as I understand it."

Kareen wrinkled her nose. "Wait, what?"

"You'll have to get him to explain it. It made no sense to me. Not even by Miles's standards of sense." Mark frowned thoughtfully. "Unless he's having a major outbreak of sexual shyness."

"Sexually shy, Miles?" Kareen scoffed. "You met that Captain Quinn he had in tow, didn't you?"

"Oh, yes. I've met several of his girlfriends, in fact. The most appalling bunch of bloodthirsty amazons you ever saw. God, they were frightening." Mark shuddered in memory. "Of course, they were all pissed as hell at me at the time for getting him killed, which I suppose accounts for some of it. But I was just thinking . . . you know, I really wonder if he picked them—or if they picked him? Maybe, instead of being such a great seducer, he's just a man who can't say no. It would certainly explain why they were *all* tall aggressive women who were used to getting what they wanted. But now—maybe for the first time—he's up against trying to pick for himself. And he doesn't know *how.* He hasn't had any practice." A slow grin spread across Mark's broad face at this vision. "Ooh. I wanna watch."

Kareen punched his shoulder. "Mark, that's not nice. Miles *deserves* to meet the right woman. I mean, he's not getting any younger, is he?"

"Some of us get what they deserve. Others of us get luckier than that." He captured her hand, and nuzzled the inside of her wrist, making the hairs stand up on her arm.

"Miles always says you make your own luck. Stop that." She repossessed her hand. "If sweat-equity is going to pay my way back to Beta Colony, I need to get back to work." She retreated into the lab; Mark followed.

"Was Lord Vorkosigan very upset?" Enrique asked anxiously as they reappeared. "But Madame Vorsoisson *said* she didn't mind trying our bug butter—"

"Don't worry about it, Enrique," Mark told him jovially. "My brother is just being a prick because he has something on his mind. If we're lucky, he'll go take it out on his Armsmen."

"Oh," said Enrique. "That's all right, then. I have a plan to bring him around."

"Yeah?" said Mark skeptically. "What plan?"

"It's a surprise," said the scientist, with a sly grin, or at any rate, as sly as he could bring off, which really wasn't very. "If it works, that is. I'll know in a few more days."

Mark shrugged, and glanced at Kareen. "You know what he's got up his sleeve?"

She shook her head, and settled herself on the floor once more with her rack-assembly project. "You might try pulling an ice cream freezer out of yours, though. Ask Ma Kosti first. Miles seems to have showered her with every piece of food service equipment imaginable. I think he was trying to bribe her into resisting the employment offers from all his friends." Kareen blinked, seized by inspiration.

Product development, too right. Never mind the appliances, the resource they had right here in Vorkosigan House was human genius. *Frustrated* human genius; Ma Kosti pressed the hard-working entrepreneurs to come to a special lunch in her kitchen every day, and sent trays of snacks to the lab betimes. And the cook was already soft on Mark, even after just a week; he so obviously appreciated her art. They were well on their way to bonding.

She jumped up and handed Mark the screwdriver. "Here. Finish this."

Grabbing six tubs of bug butter, she headed for the kitchen.

Miles climbed from the old armored groundcar, and paused a moment on the flower-bordered curving walkway to stare enviously at René Vorbretten's entirely modern townhouse. Vorbretten House perched on the bluff overlooking the river, nearly opposite to Vorhartung Castle. Civil war as urban renewal: the creaky old fortified mansion which had formerly occupied the space had been so damaged in the Pretender's War that the previous Count and his son, when they'd returned to the city with Aral Vorkosigan's victorious forces, had decided to knock it flat and start over. In place of dank, forbidding, and defensively useless old stone walls, truly effective protection was now supplied by optional force-fields. The new mansion was light and open and airy, and took full advantage of the excellent views of the Vorbarr Sultana cityscape up and down stream. It doubtless had enough bathrooms for all the Vorbretten Armsmen. And Miles bet René didn't have troubles with *his* drains.

And if Sigur Vorbretten wins his case, René will lose it all. Miles shook his head, and advanced to the arched doorway, where an alert Vorbretten Armsman stood ready to lead Miles to his liege-lord's presence, and Pym, no doubt, to a good gossip downstairs.

The Armsman brought Miles to the splendid sitting room with the window-wall looking across the Star Bridge toward the castle. This morning, however, the wall was polarized to near-darkness, and the Armsman had to wave on lights as they entered. René was sitting in a big chair with his back to the view. He sprang to his feet as the Armsman announced, "Lord Auditor Vorkosigan, m'lord."

René swallowed, and nodded dismissal to his Armsman, who withdrew silently. At least René appeared sober, well-dressed, and depilated, but his handsome face was dead pale as he nodded formally to his visitor. "My Lord Auditor. How may I serve you?"

"Relax, René, this isn't an official visit. I just dropped by to say hello."

"Oh." René exhaled visible relief, the sudden stiffness in his face reverting to mere tiredness. "I thought you were . . . I thought Gregor might have dispatched you with the bad news."

"No, no, no. After all, the Council can't very well vote without telling you." Miles nodded vaguely toward the river, and the Council's seat beyond it; René, recalled to his hostly duties, depolarized the window and pulled chairs around for himself and Miles to take in the view while they talked. Miles settled himself across from the young Count. René had thought quickly enough to drag up a rather low chair for his august visitor, so Miles's feet didn't dangle in air.

"But you might have been—well, I don't know what you might have been," said René ruefully, sitting down and rubbing his neck. "I wasn't expecting you. Or anyone. Our social life has evaporated with amazing speed. Count and Countess Ghembretten are apparently not good people to know."

"Ouch. You've heard that one, have you?"

"My Armsmen heard it first. The joke's all over town, isn't it?"

"Eh, yeah, sort of." Miles cleared his throat. "Sorry I wasn't by earlier. I was on Komarr when your case broke, and I only heard about it when I got back, and then Gregor sent me up-country, and, well, screw the excuses. I'm sorry as hell this thing has happened to you. I can flat guarantee the Progressives don't want to lose you."

"Can you? I thought I had become a deep embarrassment to them."

"A vote's a vote. With turnover among the Counts literally a once-in-a-lifetime event—"

"Usually," René put in dryly.

Miles shrugged this off. "Embarrassment is a passing emotion. If the Progressives lose you to Sigur, they lose that vote for the next generation. They'll back you." Miles hesitated. "They are backing you, aren't they?"

"More or less. Mostly. Some." René waved an ironic hand. "Some are thinking that if they vote against Sigur and lose, they'll have made a permanent enemy in the Council. And a vote, as you say, is a vote."

"What do the numbers look like, can you tell yet?"

René shrugged. "A dozen certain for me, a dozen certain for Sigur. My fate will be decided by the men in the middle. Most of whom aren't speaking with the Ghembrettens this month. I don't think it looks good, Miles." He glanced across at his visitor, his expression an odd mix of sharpness and hesitancy. In a neutral tone he added, "And do you know how Vorkosigan's District is going to vote yet?"

Miles had realized he would have to answer that question if he saw René. So, no doubt, did every other Count or Count's Deputy, which also explained the sudden dip in René's social life lately; those who weren't avoiding him were avoiding the issue. With a couple of weeks to think it through behind him, Miles had his answer ready. "We're for you. Could you doubt it?"

René managed a rueful smile. "I had been almost

certain, but then there is that large radioactive hole the Cetagandans once put in the middle of your District."

"History, man. Do I help your vote-count?"

"No," sighed René. "I'd already factored you in."

"Sometimes, one vote makes all the difference."

"It makes me crazy to think it might be that close," René confessed. "I hate this. I wish it were over."

"Patience, René," Miles counseled. "Don't throw away any advantage just because of an attack of nerves." He frowned thoughtfully. "Seems to me what we have here are two coequal legal precedents, jostling each other for primacy. A Count chooses his own successor, with the consent of the Council by their vote of approval, which is how Lord Midnight got in."

René's smile twisted. "If a horse's ass can be a Count, why not the whole horse?"

"I think that *was* one of the fifth Count Vortala's arguments, actually. I wonder if any transcripts of those sessions still exist in the archives? I must read them someday, if they do. Anyway, Midnight clearly established that direct blood relationship, though customary, was not required, and even if Midnight's case is rejected, there are dozens of other less memorable precedents on that score anyway. Count's choice before Count's blood, unless the Count has neglected to make a choice. Only then does male primogeniture come into play. Your grandfather was confirmed as heir in his . . . his mother's husband's lifetime, wasn't he?" Miles had been confirmed as his own father's heir during the Regency, while his father had been at the height of his power to ram it through the Council.

"Yes, but fraudulently, according to Sigur's suit. And a fraudulent result is no result."

"I don't suppose the old man might have known? And is there any way to prove it, if he did? Because if he knew your grandfather was not his son, his confirmation was legal, and Sigur's case evaporates."

"If the sixth Count knew, we haven't been able to find a scrap of evidence. And we've been turning the family archives inside out for weeks. I shouldn't think he could have known, or he would surely have killed the boy. And the boy's mother."

"I'm not so sure. The Occupation was a strange time. I'm thinking about how the bastard war played out in the Dendarii region." Miles blew out his breath. "Ordinary known Cetagandan by-blows were usually aborted or killed as soon as possible. Occasionally, the guerrillas used to make a sort of gruesome game of planting the little corpses for the occupying soldiers to find. Used to unnerve the hell out of the Cetagandan rank and file. First was their normal human reaction, and second, even the ones who were so brutalized by then as not to care realized anywhere we slipped in a dead baby, we could just as well have slipped in a bomb."

René grimaced distaste, and Miles realized belatedly that the lurid historical example might have acquired a new personal edge for him. He hurried on, "The Cetagandans weren't the only people to object to that game. Some Barrayarans hated it too, and took it as a blot on our honor—Prince Xav, for example. I know he argued vehemently with my grandfather against it. Your great—the sixth Count could well have been in agreement with Xav, and what he did for your grandfather a sort of silent answer."

René tilted his head, looking struck. "I never thought of that. He *was* a friend of old Xav's, I believe. But there's still no proof. Who knows what a dead man knew, but never spoke of?"

"If you have no proof, neither does Sigur."

René brightened slightly. "That's true."

Miles gazed again at the magnificent view along the urbanized river valley. A few small boats chugged up and down the narrowing stream. In former eras, Vorbarr Sultana had been as far inland as navigation from the sea could get, as the rapids and falls here blocked further commercial transport. Since the end of the Time of Isolation, the dam and locks just upstream from the Star Bridge had been destroyed and rebuilt three times.

Across from where they sat in Vorbretten House, Vorhartung Castle's crenellations loomed up through the spring-green treetops, gray and archaic. The traditional meeting-place of the Council of Counts had overlooked—in both senses of the word, Miles thought dryly—all these transformations. When there wasn't a war on, waiting for old Counts to die in order to effect change could be a slow process. One or two popped off a year, on average these days, but the pace of generational turn-over was slowing still further as life spans extended. Having two seats open at once, and both up for grabs by either a Progressive or a Conservative heir, was fairly unusual. Or rather, René's seat was up for grabs between the two main parties. The other was more mysterious.

Miles asked René, "Do you have any idea what was the substance of Lady Donna Vorrutyer's motion of impediment against her cousin Richars taking the Vorrutyer Countship? Have you heard any talk?"

René waved a hand. "Not much, but then, who's talking to me, these days? Present company excepted." He shot Miles a covertly grateful look. "Adversity does teach who your real friends are."

Miles was embarrassed, thinking of how long it had taken him to get over here. "Don't take me for more virtuous than I am, René. I would have to be the last person on Barrayar to argue that carrying a bit of off-planet blood in one's veins should disqualify one for a Countship."

"Oh. Yes. You're half-Betan, that's right. But in your case, at least it's the correct half."

"Five-eighths Betan, technically. Less than half a Barrayaran." Miles realized he'd just left himself open for a pot shot about his height, but René didn't take aim. Byerly Vorrutyer would never have let a straight-line like that pass unexploited, and Ivan would have at least dared to grin. "I usually try to avoid bringing people's attention to the math."

"Actually, I did have a few thoughts on Lady Donna," René said. "Her case just might end up impinging on you Vorkosigans after all."

"Oh?"

René, drawn out of his bleak contemplation of his own dilemma, grew more animated. "She placed her motion of impediment and took off immediately for Beta Colony. What does that suggest to you?"

"I've been to Beta Colony. There are so many possibilities I can scarcely begin to sort them out. The first and simplest thought is that she's gone to collect some sort of obscure evidence about her cousin Richars's ancestry, genes, or crimes."

"Have you ever met Lady Donna? *Simple* isn't how I'd describe her."

"Mm, there's that. I should ask Ivan for a guess, I suppose. I believe he slept with her for a time."

"I don't think I was around town then. I was out on active duty during that period." A faint regret for his abandoned military career crept into René's voice, or maybe Miles was projecting. "But I'm not surprised. She had a reputation for collecting men."

Miles cocked an interested eyebrow at his host. "Did she ever collect you?"

René grinned. "I somehow missed that honor." He returned the ironic glance. "And did she ever collect you?"

"What, with *Ivan* available? I doubt she ever looked down far enough to notice me."

René opened his hand, as if to deflect Miles's little flash of self-deprecation, and Miles bit his tongue. He was an Imperial Auditor now; public whining about his physical lot in life sat oddly on the ear. He *had* survived. No man could challenge him now. But would even an Auditorship be enough to induce the average Barrayaran woman to overlook the rest of the package? *So it's a good thing you're not in love with an average woman, eh, boy?*

René went on, "I was thinking about your clone Lord Mark, and your family's push to get him recognized as your brother."

"He *is* my brother, René. My legal heir and everything."

"Yes, yes, so your family has argued. But what if Lady Donna has been following that controversy, and how you made it come out? I'll bet she's gone off to Beta Colony to have a clone made of poor old Pierre, and is going to bring it back to offer as his heir in place of Richars. Somebody had to try that, sooner or later."

"It's . . . certainly possible. I'm not sure how it would fly with the fossils. They damn near choked on Mark, year before last." Miles frowned in thought. Could this damage Mark's position? "I heard she was practically running the District for Pierre these last five years. If she could get herself appointed the clone's legal guardian, she could continue to run it for the next twenty. It's unusual to have a female relative be a Count's guardian, but there are some historical precedents."

"Including that Countess who was legally declared a male in order to inherit," René put in. "And then had that bizarre suit later about her marriage."

"Oh, yeah, I remember reading about that one. But there was a civil war on, at the time, which broke down the barriers for her. Nothing like being on the side of the right battalions. No civil war here except for whatever lies between Donna and Richars, and I've never heard an inside story on that feud. I wonder . . . if you're right—would she use a uterine replicator for the clone, or would she have the embryo implanted as a body-birth?"

"Body-birth seems weirdly incestuous," René said, with a grimace of distaste. "You do wonder about the Vorrutyers, sometimes. I hope she uses a replicator."

"Mm, but she never had a child of her own. She's what, forty or so . . . and if the clone were growing inside her own body, she'd at least be sure to have it—excuse me, him—as thoroughly personally guarded as possible. Much harder to take away from her, that way, or to argue that someone else should be his guardian. Richars, for example. Now that would be a sharp turn of events."

"With Richars as guardian, how long do you think the child would live?"

"Not past his majority, I suspect." Miles frowned at this scenario. "Not that his death wouldn't be impeccable."

"Well, we'll find out Lady Donna's plan soon," said René. "Or else her case will collapse by default. Her three months to bring her evidence are almost up. It seems a generous allotment of time, but I suppose in the old days they had to allow everyone a chance to get around on horseback."

"Yes, it's not good for a District to leave its Countship empty for so long." One corner of Miles's mouth turned up. "After all, you wouldn't want the proles to figure out they could live without us."

René's brows twitched acknowledgment of the jibe. "Your Betan blood is showing, Miles."

"No, only my Betan upbringing."

"Biology isn't destiny?"

"Not anymore, it's not."

The light music of women's voices echoed up the curving staircase into the sitting room. A low alto burble Miles thought he recognized was answered by a silvery peal of laughter.

René sat up, and turned around; his lips parted in a half smile. "They're back. And she's laughing. I haven't heard Tatya laugh in weeks. Bless Martya."

Had that been Martya Koudelka's voice? The thump of a surprising number of feminine feet rippled up the stairs, and three women burst into Miles's appreciative view. *Yes.* The two blond Koudelka sisters, Martya and Olivia, set off the dark good looks of the shorter third woman. The young Countess Tatya Vorbretten had bright hazel eyes, wide-set in a heart-shaped face with a foxy chin. And dimples. The whole delightful composition was framed by ringlets of ebony hair that bounced as she now did.

"Hooray, René!" said Martya, the owner of the alto voice. "You're *not* still sitting alone here in the dark and gloom. Hi, Miles! Did you finally come to cheer René up? Good for you!"

"More or less," said Miles. "I didn't realize you all knew each other so well."

Martya tossed her head. "Olivia and Tatya were in school together. I just came along for the ride, and to boot them into motion. Can you believe, on this beautiful morning, they wanted to stay *in?*"

Olivia smiled shyly, and she and Countess Tatya clung together for a brief supportive moment. Ah, yes. Tatya

Vorkeres had not been a countess back in those private-school days, though she had certainly already been a beauty, and an heiress.

"Where all did you go?" asked René, smiling at his wife.

"Just shopping in the Caravanserai. We stopped for tea and pastries at a café in the Great Square, and caught the changing of the guard at the Ministry." The Countess turned to Miles. "My cousin Stannis is a directing officer in the fife and drum corps of the City Guard now. We waved at him, but of course he couldn't wave back. He was on duty."

"I was sorry we hadn't made you come out with us," said Olivia to René, "but now I'm glad. You would have missed Miles."

"It's all right, ladies," said Martya stoutly. "Instead I vote we make René escort us all to the Vorbarr Sultana Hall tomorrow night. I *happen* to know where I can get four tickets."

This was seconded and voted in without reference to the Count, but Miles couldn't see him offering much resistance to a proposal that he escort three beautiful women to hear music that he adored. And indeed, with a somewhat sheepish glance at Miles, he allowed himself to be persuaded. Miles wondered how Martya had cornered the tickets, which were generally sold out a year or two in advance, on such short notice. Was she drawing on her sister Delia's ImpSec connections, perhaps? This whole thing smelled of Team Koudelka in action.

The Countess smiled and held up a hand-calligraphed envelope. "Look, René! Armsman Kelso handed this to me as we came in. It's from Countess Vorgarin."

"Looks like an invitation to me," said Martya in a tone of vast satisfaction. "See, things aren't so bad as you feared."

"Open it," urged Olivia.

Tatya did so; her eyes raced down the handwriting. Her face fell. "Oh," she said in a flattened tone. The delicate paper half-crumpled in her tight fist.

"What?" said Olivia anxiously.

Martya retrieved the paper, and read down it in turn. "The cat! It's an *un*-invitation! To her baby daughter's naming party. ' . . . afraid you would not be comfortable,' my eye! The coward. The cat!"

Countess Tatya blinked rapidly. "That's all right," she said in a muffled voice. "I hadn't been planning to go anyway."

"But you said you were going to wear—" René began, then closed his mouth abruptly. A muscle jumped in his jaw.

"All the women—and their mothers—who missed catching René these last ten years are being just . . . just . . ." Martya sputtered to Miles, "*feline.*"

"That's an insult to cats," said Olivia. "*Zap* has better character."

René glanced across at Miles. "I couldn't help noticing . . ." he said in an extremely neutral voice, "we haven't received a wedding invitation from Gregor and Dr. Toscane as yet."

Miles held up a reassuring hand. "Local invitations haven't been sent out yet. I know that for a fact." This was not the moment to mention that inconclusive little political discussion on the subject he'd sat in on a few weeks ago at the Imperial Residence, Miles decided.

He stared around the tableau, Martya fuming, Olivia stricken, the Countess chilled, René flushed and stiff. Inspiration struck. *Ninety-six chairs.* "I'm giving a little private dinner party in two nights time. It's in honor of Kareen Koudelka and my brother Mark getting home from Beta Colony. Olivia will be there, and all the Koudelkas, and Lady Alys Vorpatril and Simon Illyan, and my cousin Ivan and several other valued friends. I'd be honored if you both would join us."

René managed a pained smile at this palpable charity. "Thank you, Miles. But I don't think—"

"Oh, Tatya, yes, you've got to come," Olivia broke in, squeezing her old friend's arm. "Miles is finally unveiling his lady-love for us all to meet. Only Kareen's seen her so far. We're all just dying of curiosity."

René's brows went up. "You, Miles? I thought you

were as confirmed a bachelor as your cousin Ivan. Married to your career."

Miles grimaced furiously at Olivia, and twitched at René's last words. "I had this little medical divorce from my career. Olivia, where did you ever get the idea that Madame Vorsoisson—she's my landscape designer, you see, René, but she's Lord Auditor Vorthys's niece, I met her on Komarr, she's just recently widowed and *certainly* not—not ready to be anybody's lady-love. Lord Auditor Vorthys and the Professora will be there too, you see, a family party, nothing inappropriate for her."

"For who?" asked Martya.

"Ekaterin," escaped his mouth before he could stop it. All four lovely syllables.

Martya grinned unrepentantly at him. René and his wife looked at each other—Tatya's dimple flashed, and René pursed his lips thoughtfully.

"Kareen said Lord Mark said you said," Olivia said innocently. "Who was lying, then?"

"Nobody, dammit, but—but—" He swallowed, and prepared to run down the drill one more time. "Madame Vorsoisson is . . . is . . ." Why was this getting harder to explain with practice, instead of easier? "Is in formal mourning for her late husband. I have every intention of declaring myself to her when the time is right. The time is not right. So I have to wait." He gritted his teeth. René was now leaning his chin on his hand, his finger across his lips, and his eyes alight. "And I *hate waiting*," Miles burst out.

"Oh," said René. "I see."

"Is she in love with you too?" asked Tatya, with a furtive fond glance at her husband.

God, the Vorbrettens were as gooey as Gregor and Laisa, and after three years, too. This marital enthusiasm was a damned contagious disease. "I don't know," Miles confessed in a smaller voice.

"He told Mark he's courting her in secret," Martya put in to the Vorbrettens. "It's a secret *from* her. We're all still trying to figure that one out."

"Is the entire city party to my private conversations?" Miles snarled. "I'm going to strangle Mark."

Martya blinked at him with manufactured innocence. "Kareen had it from Mark. *I* had it from Ivan. Mama had it from Gregor. And Da had it from Pym. If you're trying to keep a secret, Miles, why are you going around telling everyone?"

Miles took a deep breath.

Countess Vorbretten said demurely, "Thank you, Lord Vorkosigan. My husband and I would be pleased to come to your dinner party." She dimpled at him.

His breath blew out in a, "You're welcome."

"Will the Viceroy and Vicereine be back from Sergyar?" René asked Miles. His voice was tinged with political curiosity.

"No. In fact. Though they're due quite soon. This is *my* party. My last chance to have Vorkosigan House to myself before it fills up with the traveling circus." Not that he didn't look forward to his parents' return, but his head-of-the-House role had been rather . . . pleasant, these past few months. Besides, introducing Ekaterin to Count and Countess Vorkosigan, her prospective future parents-in-law, was something he wished to choreograph with the utmost care.

He'd surely done his social duty by now. Miles rose with some dignity, and bid everyone farewell, and politely offered Martya and Olivia a ride, if they wished it. Olivia was staying on with her friend the Countess, but Martya took him up on it.

Miles gave Pym a fishy look as the Armsman opened the groundcar canopy for them to enter the rear compartment. Miles had always put down Pym's extraordinary ability to collect gossip, a most valuable skill to Miles in his new post, to Pym's old ImpSec training. He hadn't quite realized Pym might be *trading*. Pym, catching the look but not its cause, went a bit blander than usual, but seemed otherwise unaffected by his liege-lord's displeasure.

In the rear compartment with Martya as they pulled away from Vorbretten House and swung down toward the Star Bridge, Miles seriously considered dressing her down for roasting him about Ekaterin in front of the Vorbrettens. He was an Imperial Auditor now, by God—

or at least by Gregor. But then he'd get no further information out of her. He controlled his temper.

"How do the Vorbrettens seem to be holding up, from your view?" he asked her.

She shrugged. "They're putting up a good front, but I think they're pretty shaken. René thinks he's going to lose the case, and his District, and everything."

"So I gathered. And he might, if he doesn't make more push to keep it." Miles frowned.

"He's hated the Cetagandans ever since they killed his da in the war for the Hegen Hub. Tatya says it just spooks him, to think the Cetagandans are *in* him." She added after a moment, "I think it spooks her a little, too. I mean . . . now we know why that branch of the Vorbrettens suddenly acquired that extraordinary musical talent, after the Occupation."

"I'd made that connection too. But she seems to be standing by him." Unpleasant, to think this mischance might cost René his marriage as well as his career.

"It's been hard on her too. She likes being a Countess. Olivia says, back in their school days, envy sometimes made the other girls mean to Tatya. Being picked out by René was kind of a boost for her, not that the rest of them couldn't see it coming, with her glorious soprano. She does adore him."

"So you think their marriage will weather this?" he asked hopefully.

"Mm . . ."

"Mm . . . ?"

"This whole thing began when they were going to start their baby. And they haven't gone ahead. Tatya . . . doesn't talk about that part of things. She'll talk about everything else, but not that."

"Oh." Miles tried to figure out what that might mean. It didn't sound very encouraging.

"Olivia is almost the only one of Tatya's old friends who've shown up, after all this blew up. Even René's sisters have kind of gone to ground, though for the opposite reason I suppose. It's like nobody wants to look her in the eye."

"If you go back far enough, we're all descended from

off-worlders, dammit," Miles growled in frustration. "What's one-eighth? A tinge. Why should it disqualify one of the best people we have? Competence should count for something."

Martya's grin twisted. "If you want sympathy, you've come to the wrong store, Miles. If my da were a Count, it wouldn't matter how competent I was, I still wouldn't inherit. All the brilliance in the world wouldn't matter a bit. If you're just now finding out that this world is unjust, well, you're behind the times."

Miles grimaced. "It's not news to me, Martya." The car pulled up outside Commodore Koudelka's townhouse. "But justice wasn't my job, before." *And power isn't nearly as all-powerful as it looks from the outside.* He added, "But that's probably the one issue I can't help you on. I have the strongest personal reasons for not wanting to reintroduce inheritance through the female line into Barrayaran law. Like, my survival. I like my job very well. I don't want Gregor's."

He popped the canopy, and she climbed out, and gave him a sort of acknowledging salaam for both this last point and the ride. "See you at your dinner party."

"Give my best to the Commodore and Drou," he called after her.

She shot him a bright Team Koudelka smile over her shoulder, and bounced away.

CHAPTER SEVEN

Mark gently banked the lightflyer, to give the rear-seat passengers, Kareen and Madame Vorsoisson, a better view of the Vorkosigan's District capital of Hassadar glittering on the horizon. The weather was cooperating, a beautiful sunny day that breathed promise of imminent summer. Miles's lightflyer was a delight: sleek, fast, and maneuverable, knifing through the soft warm air, and best of all with the controls precisely aligned to be ergonomically perfect for a man just Mark's height. So what if the seat was a little on the narrow side. You couldn't have everything. *For example, Miles can't have this anymore.* Mark grimaced at the thought, and shunted it aside.

"It's lovely land," Madame Vorsoisson remarked, pressing her face to the canopy to take it all in.

"Miles would be flattered to hear you say so," Mark carefully encouraged this trend of thought. "He's pretty stuck on this place."

They were certainly viewing it in the best possible light, literally, this morning. A patchwork of spring verdure in the farms and woods—the woods no less a product of back-breaking human cultivation than the fields—rippled across the landscape. The green was

155

broken up and set off by irregular slashes of Barrayaran native red-brown, in the ravines and creek bottoms and along uncultivable slopes.

Enrique, his nose also pressed to the canopy, said, "It's not at all what I was expecting, from Barrayar."

"What were you expecting?" asked Madame Vorsoisson curiously.

"Kilometers of flat gray concrete, I suppose. Military barracks and people in uniform marching around in lockstep."

"Economically unlikely for an entire planetary surface. Though uniforms, we do have," Mark admitted.

"But once it gets up to several hundred different kinds, the effect isn't so uniform anymore. And some of the colors are a little . . . unexpected."

"Yes, I feel sorry for those Counts who ended up having to pick their House colors last," Mark agreed. "I think the Vorkosigans must have fallen somewhere in the middle. I mean, brown and silver isn't *bad*, but I can't help feeling that the fellows with the blue and gold—or the black and silver—do have a sartorial edge." He could fancy himself in black and silver, with Kareen all blond and tall on his arm.

"It could be worse," Kareen put in cheerfully. "How do you think you'd look in a House cadet's uniform of chartreuse and scarlet, like poor Vorharopulos, Mark?"

"Like a traffic signal in boots." Mark made a wry face. "The lockstep is lacking too, I've gradually come to realize. More like, milling around in a confused herd. It was . . . almost disappointing, at first. I mean, even disregarding enemy propaganda, it's not the image Barrayar itself tries to project, now is it? Though I've learned to kind of like it this way."

They banked again. "Where is the infamous radioactive area?" Madame Vorsoisson asked, scanning the changing scene.

The Cetagandan destruction of the old capital of Vorkosigan Vashnoi had torn the heart out of the Vorkosigan's District, three generations ago. "Southeast of Hassadar. Downwind and downstream," Mark replied. "We won't pass it today. You'll have to get Miles to show it to you sometime." He suppressed a slightly snarky grin. Betan dollars to sand the blighted lands hadn't been on Miles's projected itinerary.

"Barrayar doesn't all look like this," Madame Vorsoisson told Enrique. "The part of South Continent where I grew up was flat as a griddlecake, even though the highest mountain range on the planet—the Black Escarpment—was just over the horizon."

"Was it dull, being so flat?" asked Enrique.

"No, because the horizon was boundless. Stepping outdoors was like stepping into the sky. The clouds, the light, the storms—we had the best sunrises and sunsets ever."

They passed the invisible barrier of Hassadar's air traffic control system, and Mark gave over navigation to the city computers. After a few more minutes and some brief coded transmissions, they were brought gently down on a very private and highly restricted landing pad atop the Count's Residence. The Residence was a large modern building faced with polished Dendarii mountain stone. With its connections to the municipal and District offices, it occupied most of one side of the city's central square.

Tsipis stood waiting by the landing ring, neat and gray and spare as ever, to receive them. He shook hands with Madame Vorsoisson as though they were old friends, and greeted off-worlder Enrique with the grace and ease of a natural diplomat. Kareen gave, and got, a familial hug.

They switched vehicles to a waiting aircar, and Tsipis shepherded them off for a quick tour of three possible sites for their future facility, whatever it was to be named, including an underutilized city warehouse, and two nearby farms. Both farm sites were untenanted because their former inhabitants had followed the Count to his new post on Sergyar, and no one else had wanted to take on the challenge of wrestling profit from their decidedly marginal land, one being swampy and the other rocky and dry. Mark checked the radioactivity plats carefully. They were all Vorkosigan properties already, so there was nothing to negotiate with respect to their use.

"You might even persuade your brother to forgo the rent, if you ask," Tsipis pointed out with enthusiastic frugality about the two rural sites. "He can; your father assigned him full legal powers in the District when he left for Sergyar. After all, the family's not getting any income from the properties now. It would conserve more of your capital for your other startup costs."

Tsipis knew precisely what budget Mark had to work with; they'd gone over his plans via comconsole earlier in the week. The thought of asking Miles for a favor made Mark twitch a little, but . . . was he not a Vorkosigan too? He stared around the dilapidated farm, trying to feel entitled.

He put his head together with Kareen, and they ran over the choices. Enrique was permitted to wander about with Madame Vorsoisson, being introduced to various native Barrayaran weeds. The condition of the buildings, plumbing, and power-grid connections won over condition of the land, and they settled at last on the site with the newer—relatively—and more spacious outbuildings. After one more thoughtful tour around the premises, Tsipis whisked them back to Hassadar.

For lunch, Tsipis led them to Hassadar's most exclusive locale—the official dining room of the Count's Residence, overlooking the Square. The remarkable spread which the staff laid on hinted that Miles had sent down a few urgent behind-the-scenes instructions for the care and feeding of his . . . gardener. Mark confirmed this after dessert when Kareen led Enrique and the widow off to see the garden and fountain in the Residence's inner courtyard, and he and Tsipis lingered over the exquisite vintage of Vorkosigan estate-bottled wine usually reserved for visits from Emperor Gregor.

"So, Lord Mark," said Tsipis, after a reverent sip. "What do you think of this Madame Vorsoisson of your brother's?"

"I think . . . she is not my brother's yet."

"Mm, yes, I'd understood *that* part. Or should I say, it has been explained to me."

"What all has he been telling you about her?"

"It is not so much what he says, as how he says it. And how often he repeats himself."

"Well, that too. If it were anyone but Miles, it would be hilarious. Actually, it's still hilarious. But it's also . . . hm."

Tsipis blinked and smiled in perfect understanding. "Heart-stopping . . . I think . . . is the word I should choose." And Tsipis's vocabulary was always as precise as his haircut. He stared out over the square through the room's tall windows. "I used to see him as a youngster rather often, when I was in company with your parents. He was constantly overmatching his physical powers. But he never cried much when he broke a bone. He was almost frighteningly self-controlled, for a child that age. But once, at the Hassadar District Fair it was, I chanced to see him rather brutally rejected by a group of other children whom he'd attempted to join." Tsipis took another sip of wine.

"Did he cry then?" asked Mark.

"No. Though his face looked very odd when he turned away. Bothari was watching with me—there was nothing the Sergeant could do either, there wasn't any physical threat about it all. But the next day Miles had a riding accident, one of his worst ever. Jumping, which he had been forbidden to do, on a green horse he'd been told not to ride . . . Count Piotr was so infuriated— and frightened—I thought he was going to have a stroke on the spot. I came later to wonder how much of an accident that accident was." Tsipis hesitated. "I always imagined Miles would choose a galactic wife, like his father before him. Not a Barrayaran woman. I'm not at all sure what Miles thinks he's doing with this young lady. Is he setting himself up to go smash again?"

"He claims he has a Strategy."

Tsipis's thin lips curved, and he murmured, "And doesn't he always . . ."

Mark shrugged helplessly. "To tell the truth, I've barely met the woman myself. You've been working with her—what do you think?"

Tsipis tilted his head shrewdly. "She's a quick study, and meticulously honest."

That sounded like faint praise, unless one happened to know those were Tsipis's two highest encomiums.

"Quite well-looking, in person," he added as an afterthought. "Not, ah, nearly as over-tall as I was expecting."

Mark grinned.

"I think she could do the *job* of a future Countess."

"Miles thinks so too," Mark noted. "And picking personnel was supposed to have been one of his major military talents." And the better he got to know Tsipis, the more Mark thought that might be a talent Miles had inherited from his—*their*—father.

"It's not before time, that's certain," Tsipis sighed. "One does wish for Count Aral to have grandchildren while he's still alive to see them."

Was that remark addressed to me?

"You will keep an eye on things, won't you?" Tsipis added.

"I don't know what you think I could do. It's not like I could *make* her fall in love with him. If I had that kind of power over women, I'd use it for myself!"

Tsipis smiled vaguely at the place Kareen had vacated, and back, speculatively, to Mark. "What, and here I was under the impression you had."

Mark twitched. His new-won Betan rationality had been losing ground on the subject of Kareen, this past week, his subpersonas growing restive with his rising tension. But Tsipis was his financial advisor, not his therapist. Nor even—this was Barrayar, after all—his Baba.

"So have you seen any sign at all that Madame Vorsoisson returns your brother's regard?" Tsipis went on rather plaintively.

"No," Mark confessed. "But she's very reserved." And was this lack of feeling, or just frightening self-control? Who could tell from this angle? "Wait, ha, I know! I'll set Kareen onto it. Women gossip to each other about that sort of thing. That's why they go off so long to the ladies' room together, to dissect their dates. Or so Kareen once told me, when I'd complained about being left bereft too long . . ."

"I do like that girl's sense of humor. I've always liked

all the Koudelkas." Tsipis's eye grew glinty for a moment. "You *will* treat her properly, I trust?"

Basil alert, basil alert! "Oh, yes," Mark said fervently. Grunt, in fact, was aching to treat her properly to the limit of his Betan-trained skills and powers right now, if only she'd let him. Gorge, who made a hobby of feeding her gourmet meals, had had a good day today. Killer lurked ready to assassinate any enemy she cared to name, except that Kareen didn't make enemies, she just made friends. Even Howl was strangely satisfied, this week, everyone else's pain being his gain. On this subject, the Black Gang voted as one man.

That lovely, warm, open woman . . . In her presence he felt like some sluggish cold-blooded creature crawling from under a rock where it had crept to die, meeting the unexpected miracle of the sun. He might trail around after her all day, meeping piteously, hoping she would light him again for just one more glorious moment. His therapist had had a few stern words to him on the subject of this addiction—*It's not fair to Kareen to lay such a burden on her, now is it? You must learn to give, from sufficiency, not only take, from neediness.* Quite right, quite right. But dammit, even his *therapist* liked Kareen, and was trying to recruit her for the profession. Everyone liked Kareen, because Kareen liked everyone. They wanted to be around her; she made them feel good inside. They would do anything for her. She had in abundance everything Mark most lacked, and most longed for: good cheer, infectious enthusiasm, empathy, sanity. The woman had the most tremendous future in sales—what a team the two of them might make, Mark for analysis, Kareen for the interface with the rest of humanity . . . The mere thought of losing her, for any reason, made Mark frantic.

His incipient panic attack vanished and his breathing steadied as she reappeared safely, with Enrique and Madame Vorsoisson still in tow. Despite the loss of ambition on everyone's part due to lunch, Kareen got them all up and moving again for the second of the day's tasks, collecting the rocks for Miles's garden. Tsipis had rustled them up a holo-map, directions, and two large, amiable young men with hand tractors and a lift van; the lift van followed the lightflyer as Mark headed them south toward the looming gray spine of the Dendarii Mountains.

Mark brought them down in a mountain vale bordered by a rocky ravine. The area was still more Vorkosigan family property, entirely undeveloped. Mark could see why. The virgin patch of native Barrayaran— well, you couldn't call it forest, quite, though *scrub* summed it up fairly well—extended for kilometers along the forbidding slopes.

Madame Vorsoisson exited the lightflyer, and turned to take in the view to the north, out over the peopled lowlands of the Vorkosigan's District. The warm air softened the farthest horizon into a magical blue haze, but the eye could still see for a hundred kilometers. Cumulous clouds puffed white and, in three widely separated arcs, towered up over silver-gray bases like rival castles.

"Oh," she said, her mouth melting in a smile. "Now *that's* a proper sky. That's the way it should be. I can see why you said Lord Vorkosigan likes it up here, Kareen." Her arms stretched out, half-unconsciously, to their fullest extent, her fingers reaching into free space. "Usually hills feel like walls around me, but this—this is very fine."

The oxlike beings with the lift van landed beside the lightflyer. Madame Vorsoisson led them and their equipment scrambling down into the ravine, there to pick out her supply of aesthetically-pleasing genuine Dendarii rocks and stones for the minions to haul away to Vorbarr Sultana. Enrique followed after like a lanky and particularly clumsy puppy. Since what went down would have to puff and wheeze back up, Mark limited himself to a peek over the edge, and then a stroll around the less daunting grade of the vale, holding hands with Kareen.

When he slipped his arm around her waist and cuddled in close, she melted around him, but when he tried to slip in a subliminal sexual suggestion by nuzzling her breast, she stiffened unhappily and pulled away. Damn.

"Kareen . . ." he protested plaintively.

She shook her head. "I'm sorry. I'm sorry."

"Don't . . . apologize to me. It makes me feel very weird. I want you to want me too, or it's no damn good. I thought you did."

"I did. I do. I'm—" She bit off her words, and tried again. "I thought I was a real adult, a real person, back on Beta Colony. Then I came back here . . . I realize I'm dependent for every bite of food I put in my mouth, for every stitch of clothing, for everything, on my family, and this place. And I always was, even when I was on Beta. Maybe it was all . . . fake."

He clutched her hand; that at least he might not let go of. "You want to be good. All right, I can understand that. But you have to be careful who you let define your *good*. My terrorist creators taught me that one, for damn sure."

She clutched him back, at that feared memory, and managed a sympathetic grimace. She hesitated, and went on, "It's the mutually exclusive definitions that are driving me crazy. I can't be good for both places at the same time. I learned how to be a good girl on Beta Colony, and in its own way, it was just as hard as being a good girl here. And a lot scarier, sometimes. But . . . I felt like I was getting *bigger* inside, if you can see what I mean."

"I think so." He hoped he hadn't provided any of that scary, but suspected he had. All right, he knew he had. There had been some dark times, last year. Yet she had stuck with him. "But you have to choose Kareen's good, not Barrayar's . . ." he took a deep breath, for honesty, "Not even Beta's." *Not even mine?*

"Since I got back, it's like I can't even find myself to ask."

For her, this was a metaphor, he reminded himself. Though maybe he was a metaphor too, inside his head with the Black Gang. A metaphor gone metastatic. Metaphors could do that, under enough pressure.

"I want to go back to Beta Colony," she said in a low, passionate voice, staring out unseeing into the breathtaking space below. "I want to stay there till I'm a *real* grownup, and can be myself wherever I am. Like Countess Vorkosigan."

Mark's brows rose at this idea of a role model for gentle Kareen. But you had to say this for his mother, she didn't take any shit from any one for any reason. It would be preferable, though, if one could catch a bit of that quality without having to walk through war and fire barefoot to get it.

Kareen in distress was like the sun going dark. Apprehensively, he hugged her around the waist again. Fortunately, she read it as support, as intended, and not importunity again, and leaned into him in return.

The Black Gang had their place as emergency shock troops, but they made piss-poor commanders. Grunt would just have to wait some more. He could damn well set up a date with Mark's right hand or something. This one was too important to screw up, oh yeah.

But what if she finally became herself in a way that left no room for him . . . ?

There was nothing to eat, here. Change the subject, quick. "Tsipis seems to like Madame Vorsoisson."

Her face lightened with instant gratitude at this release. *Therefore, I must have been pressuring her.* Howl whimpered, from deep inside; Mark stifled him.

"Ekaterin? I do too."

So she was *Ekaterin* now: first names, good. He would have to send them off to the ladies' room some more. "Can you tell if she likes Miles?"

Kareen shrugged. "She seems to. She's working really hard on his garden and all."

"I mean, is she in love at all? I've never even heard her call him by his first name. How can you be in love with someone you're not on a first-name basis with?"

"Oh, that's a Vor thing."

"Huh." Mark took in this reassurance dubiously. "It's true Miles is being very Vor. I think this Imperial Auditor thing has gone to his head. But do you suppose you could kind of hang around her, and try to pick up some clues?"

"Spy on her?" Kareen frowned disapproval. "Did Miles set you on me for this?"

"Actually, no. It was Tsipis. He's a bit worried for Miles. And—I am too."

"I would like to be friends with her . . ."

Naturally.

"She doesn't seem to have very many. She's had to move a lot. And I think whatever happened to her husband on Komarr was more ghastly than she lets on. The woman is so full of silences, they spill over."

"But will she do for Miles? Will she be good for him?"

Kareen cocked an eyebrow down at him. "Is anyone bothering to ask if Miles will be good for *her?*"

"Um . . . um . . . why not? Count's heir. Well-to-do. An Imperial Auditor, for God's sake. What more could a Vor desire?"

"I don't know, Mark. It likely depends on the Vor. I do know I'd take you and every one of the Black Gang at their most obstreperous for a hundred years before I'd let myself get locked up for a week with Miles. He . . . *takes you over.*"

"Only if you let him." But he warmed inside with the thought that she could really, truly prefer him to the glorious Miles, and suddenly felt less hungry.

"Do you have any idea what it takes to stop him? I still remember being kids, me and my sisters, visiting Lady Cordelia with Mama, and Miles told off to keep us occupied. Which was a really cruel thing to do to a fourteen-year-old boy, but what did I know? He decided the four of us should be an all-girl precision drill team, and made us march around in the back garden of Vorkosigan House, or in the ballroom when it was raining. I think I was four." She frowned into the past. "What Miles needs is a woman who will tell him to go soak his head, or it'll be a disaster. For her, not him." After a moment, she added sapiently, "Though if for her, for him too, sooner or later."

"Ow."

The amiable young men came panting back up out of the ravine then, and took the lift van back down into it. With clanks and thumps, they finished loading, and their van lumbered into the air and headed north. Some time later, Enrique and Madame Vorsoisson appeared, breathless. Enrique, who clutched a huge bundle of native Barrayaran plants, looked quite cheerful. In fact, he actually looked as if he had blood circulation. The scientist probably hadn't been outdoors for years; it was doubtless good for him, despite the fact that he was dripping wet from having fallen in the creek.

They managed to get the plants stuffed in the back, and Enrique half-dried, and everyone loaded up again as the sun slanted west. Mark took pleasure in trying the lightflyer's speed, as they circled the vale one last time and banked northward, back toward the capital. The machine hummed like an arrow, sweet beneath his feet and fingertips, and they reached the outskirts of Vorbarr Sultana again before dusk.

They dropped off Madame Vorsoisson first, at her aunt and uncle's home near the University, with many promises that she would stop in at Vorkosigan House on the morrow and help Enrique look up the scientific names of all his new botanical samples. Kareen hopped out at the corner in front of her family's townhouse, and gave Mark a little farewell kiss on the cheek. *Down, Grunt. That wasn't to your address.*

Mark slipped the lightflyer back into its corner in the subbasement garage of Vorkosigan House, and followed Enrique into the lab to help him give the butter bugs their evening feed and checkup. Enrique did stop short of singing lullabies to the little creepy-crawlies, though he was in the habit of talking, half to them and half to himself, under his breath as he puttered around the lab. The man had worked all alone for too damned long, in Mark's view. Tonight, though, Enrique hummed as he separated his new supply of plants according to a hierarchy known only to himself and Madame Vorsoisson, some into beakers of water and some spread to dry on paper on the lab bench.

Mark turned from weighing, recording, and scattering a few generous scoops of tree bits into the butter bug hutches to find Enrique settling at his comconsole and firing it up. Ah, good. Perhaps the Escobaran was about to commit some more futurely-profitable science. Mark wandered over, preparing to kibitz approvingly.

Enrique was busying himself not with a vertigo-inducing molecular display, but with an array of closely-written text.

"What's that?" Mark asked.

"I promised to send Ekaterin a copy of my doctoral thesis. She *asked*," Enrique explained proudly, and in a tone of some wonder. "*Toward Bacterial and Fungal Suite-Synthesis of Extra-cellular Energy Storage Compounds*. It was the basis of all my later work with the butter bugs, when I finally hit upon them as the perfect vehicle for the microbial suite."

"Ah." Mark hesitated. *It's Ekaterin for you too, now?* Well, if Kareen had got on a first-name basis with the widow, Enrique, also present, couldn't very well have been excluded, could he? "Will she be able to read it?" Enrique wrote just the same way he talked, as far as Mark had seen.

"Oh, I don't expect her to follow the molecular energy-flow mathematics—my faculty advisors had a struggle with those—but she'll get the gist of it, I'm sure, from the animations. Still . . . perhaps I could do something about this abstract, to make it more attractive at first glance. I have to admit, it's a trifle dry." He bit his lip, and bent over his comconsole. After a minute he asked, "Can you think of a word to rhyme with *glyoxylate*?"

"Not . . . off-hand. Try *orange*. Or *silver*."

"Those don't rhyme with anything. If you can't be helpful, Mark, go away."

"What are you *doing*?"

"*Isocitrate*, of course, but that doesn't quite scan . . . I'm trying to see if I can produce a more striking effect by casting the abstract in sonnet form."

"That sounds downright . . . stunning."

"Do you think?" Enrique brightened, and started humming again. "Threonine, serine, polar, molar . . ."

"Dolor," Mark supplied at random. "Bowler." Enrique waved him off irritably. Dammit, Enrique wasn't supposed to be wasting his valuable brain-time writing poetry; he was supposed to be designing long-chain molecule interactions with favorable energy-flows or something. Mark stared at the Escobaran, bent like a pretzel in his comconsole station chair in his concentration, and his brows drew down in sudden worry.

Even Enrique couldn't imagine he might attract a woman with his dissertation, could he? Or was that, *only* Enrique could imagine . . . ? It was, after all, his sole signal success in his short life. Mark had to grant, any woman he *could* attract that way was the right sort for him, but . . . but not this one. Not the one Miles had fallen in love with. Madame Vorsoisson was excessively polite, though. She would doubtless say something kind no matter how appalled she was by the offering. And Enrique, who was as starved for kindness as . . . as someone else Mark knew all too well, would build upon it . . .

Expediting the removal of the Bugworks to its new permanent site in the District seemed suddenly a much more urgent task. Lips pursed, Mark tiptoed quietly out of the lab.

Padding up the hall, he could still hear Enrique's happy murmur, "Mucopolysaccharide, hm, there's a good one, like the rhythm, *mu*-co-*pol*-ee-*sacc*-a-*ride* . . ."

The Vorbarr Sultana shuttleport was enjoying a mid-evening lull in traffic. Ivan stared impatiently around the concourse, and shifted his welcome-home bouquet of musky-scented orchids from his right hand to his left. He trusted Lady Donna would not arrive too jump-lagged and exhausted for a little socialization later. The flowers should strike just the right opening note in this renewal of their acquaintance; not so grand and gaudy as to suggest desperation on his part, but sufficiently elegant and expensive to indicate serious interest to anyone as cognizant of the nuances as Donna was.

Beside Ivan, Byerly Vorrutyer leaned comfortably against a pillar and crossed his arms. He glanced at the bouquet and smiled a little By smile, which Ivan noted but ignored. Byerly might be a source of witty, or half-witty, editorial comment, but he certainly wasn't competition for his cousin's amorous attentions.

A few elusive wisps of the erotic dream he'd had

about Donna last night tantalized Ivan's memory. He would offer to carry her luggage, he decided, or rather, some of it, whatever she had in her hand for which he might trade the flowers. Lady Donna did not travel light, as he recalled.

Unless she came back lugging a uterine replicator with Pierre's clone in it. That, By could handle all by himself; Ivan wasn't touching it with a stick. By had remained maddeningly closed-mouthed about what Lady Donna had gone to obtain on Beta Colony that she thought would thwart her cousin Richars's inheritance, but really, somebody had to try the clone-ploy sooner or later. The political complications might land in his Vorkosigan cousins' laps, but as a Vorpatril of a mere junior line, he could steer clear. *He* didn't have a vote in the Council of Counts, thank God.

"Ah." By pushed off from the pillar and gazed up the concourse, and raised a hand in brief greeting. "Here we go."

Ivan followed his glance. Three men were approaching them. The white-haired, grim-looking fellow on the right, returning By's wave, he recognized even out of uniform as the late Count Pierre's tough senior Armsman—what was his name?—Szabo. Good, Lady Donna had taken help and protection on her long journey. The tall fellow on the left, also in civvies, was one of Pierre's other guardsmen. His junior status was discernible both by his age and by the fact that he was the one towing the float pallet with the three valises aboard. He had an expression on his face with which Ivan could identify, a sort of covert crogglement common to Barrayarans just back from their first visit to Beta Colony, as if he wasn't sure whether to fall to the ground and kiss the concrete or turn around and run back to the shuttle.

The man in the center Ivan had never seen before. He was an athletic-looking fellow of middle height, more lithe than muscular, though his shoulders filled his civilian tunic quite well. He was soberly dressed in black, with the barest pale gray piping making salute to the Barrayaran style of pseudo-military ornamentation in

men's wear. The subtle clothes set off his lean good
looks: pale skin, thick dark brows, close-cropped black
hair, and trim, glossy black beard and mustache. His step
was energetic. His eyes were an electric brown, and
seemed to dart all around as if seeing the place for the
first time, and liking what they saw.

Oh, hell, had Donna picked up a Betan paramour?
This could be annoying. The fellow wasn't a mere boy,
either, Ivan saw as they came up to him and By; he was
at least in his mid-thirties. There was something oddly
familiar about him. Damned if he didn't look a true
Vorrutyer—that hair, those eyes, that smirking swagger.
An unknown son of Pierre's? The secret reason, revealed
at last, why the Count had never married? Pierre
would've had to have been about fifteen when he'd sired
the fellow, but it was possible.

By exchanged a cordial nod with the smiling stranger,
and turned to Ivan. "You two, I think, need no introduction."

"I think we do," Ivan protested.

The fellow's white grin broadened, and he stuck out
a hand, which Ivan automatically took. His grip was firm
and dry. "Lord Dono Vorrutyer, at your service, Lord
Vorpatril." His voice was a pleasant tenor, his accent not
Betan at all, but educated Barrayaran Vor-class.

It was the smiling eyes that did it at last, bright like
embers.

"Aw, *shit*," hissed Ivan, recoiling, and snatching back
his hand. "Donna, you *didn't*." Betan medicine, oh, yeah.
And Betan surgery. They could, and would, do anything
on Beta Colony, if you had the money and could convince them you were a freely consenting adult.

"If I have my way with the Council of Counts, soon
to be Count Dono Vorrutyer," Donna—Dono—whoever—
went on smoothly.

"Or killed on sight." Ivan stared at . . . him, in drain-
ing disbelief. "You don't seriously think you can make
this fly, do you?"

He—she—twitched a brow at Armsman Szabo, who
raised his chin a centimeter. Donna/Dono said, "Oh,
believe me, we went over the risks in detail before

starting out." She/he, whatever, spotted the orchids clutched forgotten in Ivan's left hand. "Why, Ivan, are those for *me*? How sweet of you!" she cooed, wrested them from him, and raised them to her nose. Beard occluded, she blinked demure black eyelashes at him over the bouquet, suddenly and horribly Lady Donna again.

"Don't *do* that in public," said Armsman Szabo through his teeth.

"Sorry Szabo." The voice's pitch plunged again to its initial masculine depth. "Couldn't resist. I mean, it's *Ivan*."

Szabo's shrug conceded the point, but not the issue.

"I'll control myself from now on, I promise." Lord Dono reversed the flowers in his grip and swept them down to his side as though holding a spear, and came to a shoulders-back, feet-apart posture of quasimilitary attention.

"Better," said Szabo judiciously.

Ivan stared in horrified fascination. "Did the Betan doctors make you taller, too?" He glanced down; Lord Dono's half-boot heels were not especially thick.

"I'm the same height I always was, Ivan. Other things have changed, but not my height."

"No, you *are* taller, dammit. At least ten centimeters."

"Only in your mind. One of the many fascinating psychological side effects of testosterone I am discovering, along with the amazing mood-swings. When we get home we can measure me, and I'll prove it to you."

"Yes," said By, glancing around, "I do suggest we continue this conversation in a more private place. Your groundcar is waiting as you instructed, Lord Dono, with your driver." He offered his cousin a little ironic bow.

"You . . . don't need me, to intrude on this family reunion," Ivan excused himself. He began to sidle away.

"Oh, yes we do," said By. With matching evil grins, the two Vorrutyers each took Ivan by an arm, and began to march him toward the exit. Dono's grip was convincingly muscular. The Armsmen followed.

They found the late Count Pierre's official groundcar where By had left it. The alert Armsman-driver in the

Vorrutyers' famous blue-and-gray livery hurried to raise the rear canopy for Lord Dono and his party. The driver looked sidelong at the new lord, but appeared entirely unsurprised by the transformation. The younger Armsman finished stowing the limited luggage and slid into the front compartment with the driver, saying, "Damn, I'm glad to be home. Joris, you would not *believe* what I saw on Beta—"

The canopy lowered on Dono, By, Szabo, and Ivan in the rear compartment, cutting off his words. The car pulled smoothly away from the shuttleport. Ivan twisted his neck, and asked plaintively, "Was that all your luggage?" Lady Donna used to require a second car to carry it all. "Where is the rest of it?"

Lord Dono leaned back in his seat, raised his chin, and stretched his legs out before him. "I dumped it all back on Beta Colony. One case is all my Armsmen are expected to travel with, Ivan. Live and learn."

Ivan noted the possessive, *my* Armsmen. "Are they—" he nodded at Szabo, listening, "are you all in on this?"

"Of course," said Dono easily. "Had to be. We all met together the night after Pierre died, Szabo and I presented the plan, and they swore themselves to me then."

"Very, um . . . loyal of them."

Szabo said, "We've all had a number of years to watch Lady Donna help run the District. Even my men who were less than, mm, personally taken with the plan are District men bred and true. No one wanted to see it fall to Richars."

"I suppose you all have had opportunities to watch him, too, over time," allowed Ivan. He added after a moment, "How'd he manage to piss you *all* off?"

"He didn't do it overnight," said By. "Richars isn't that heroic. It's taken him years of persistent effort."

"I doubt," said Dono in a suddenly clinical tone, "that anyone would care, at this late date, that he tried to rape me when I was twelve, and when I fought him off, drowned my new puppy in retaliation. After all, no one cared at the time."

"Er," said Ivan.

"Give your family credit," By put in, "Richars convinced them all the puppy's death had been your fault. He's always been very good at that sort of thing."

"*You* believed my version," said Dono to By. "Almost the only person to do so."

"Ah, but I'd had my own experiences with Richars by then," said By. He did not volunteer further details.

"I was not yet in your father's service," Szabo pointed out, possibly in self-exculpation.

"Count yourself lucky," sighed Dono. "To describe that household as *lax* would be overly kind. And no one else could impose order till the old man finally stroked out."

"Richars Vorrutyer," Armsman Szabo continued to Ivan, "observing Count Pierre's, er, nervous problems, has counted the Vorrutyer Countship and District as his property anytime these last twenty years. It was never in his interest to see poor Pierre get better, or form a family of his own. I know for a fact that he bribed the relatives of the first young lady to whom Pierre was engaged to break it off, and sell her elsewhere. Pierre's second effort at courtship, Richars thwarted by smuggling the girl's family certain of Pierre's private medical records. The third fiancée's death in that flyer wreck was never proved to be anything but an accident. But Pierre didn't believe it was an accident."

"Pierre . . . believed a lot of strange things," Ivan noted nervously.

"I didn't think it was an accident either," said Szabo dryly. "One of my best men was driving. He was killed too."

"Oh. Um. But Pierre's own death is not suspected . . . ?"

Szabo shrugged. "I believe the family tendency to those circulatory diseases would not have killed Pierre if he hadn't been too depressed to take proper care of himself."

"I *tried*, Szabo," said Dono—Donna—bleakly. "After that episode with the medical records, he was so incredibly paranoid about his doctors."

"Yes, I know." Szabo began to pat her hand, caught

himself, and gave him a soft consoling punch in the shoulder instead. Dono's smile twisted in appreciation.

"In any case," Szabo went on, "it was abundantly plain that no Armsman who was loyal to Pierre—and we all were, God help the poor man—would last five minutes in Richars's service. His first step—and we'd all heard him say so—would be to make a clean sweep of everything and everyone loyal to Pierre, and install his own creatures. Pierre's sister being the first to go, of course."

"If Richars had a gram of self-preservation," murmured Dono fiercely.

"Could he do that?" asked Ivan doubtfully. "Evict you from your home? Have you no rights under Pierre's will?"

"Home, District, and all." Dono smiled grimly. "Pierre made no will, Ivan. He didn't want to name Richars as his successor, wasn't all that fond of Richars's brothers or sons either, and was still, I think, even to the last, hoping to cut him out with an heir of his own body. Hell, Pierre might have expected to live forty more years, with modern medicine. All I would have had as Lady Donna was the pittance from my own dowries. The estate's in the most incredible mess."

"I'm not surprised," said Ivan. "But do you really think you can make this work? I mean, Richars *is* heir-presumptive. And whatever you are now, you weren't Pierre's younger brother at the moment Pierre died."

"That's the most important legal point in the plan. A Count's heir only inherits at the moment of his predecessor's death if he's already been sworn in before the Council. Otherwise, the District isn't inherited till the moment the Counts confirm it. And at that moment—some time in the next couple of weeks—I will be, demonstrably, Pierre's brother."

Ivan's mouth screwed up, as he tried to work this through. Judging by the smooth fit of the black tunic, the lovely great breasts in which he'd once . . . never mind—anyway, they were clearly all gone now. "You've really had surgery for . . . what did you do with . . . you didn't do that hermaphrodite thing, did you? Or where is . . . everything?"

"If you mean my former female organs, I jettisoned 'em with the rest of my luggage back on Beta. You can scarcely find the scars, the surgeon was so clever. They'd put in their time, God knows—can't say as I miss 'em."

Ivan missed them already. Desperately. "I wondered if you might have had them frozen. In case things don't work out, or you change your mind." Ivan tried to keep the hopeful tone out of his voice. "I know there are Betans who switch sexes back and forth three or four times in their lives."

"Yes, I met some of them at the clinic. They were most helpful and friendly, I must say."

Szabo rolled his eyes only slightly. Was Szabo acting as Lord Dono's personal valet now? It was customary for a Count's senior Armsman to do so. Szabo must have witnessed it all, in detail. *Two witnesses. She took two witnesses, I see.*

"No," Dono went on, "if I ever change back—which I have no plans to do, forty years were enough—I'd start all over with fresh cloned organs, just as I've done for this. I could be a virgin again. What a dreadful thought."

Ivan hesitated. He finally asked, "Didn't you need to add a Y chromosome from somewhere? Where'd you get it? Did the Betans supply it?" He glanced helplessly at Dono's crotch, and quickly away. "Can Richars argue that the—the inheriting bit is part-Betan?"

"I thought of that. So I got it from Pierre."

"You didn't have, um, your new male organs cloned from him?" Ivan boggled at this grotesque idea. It made his mind hurt. Was it some kind of techno-incest, or what?

"No, no! I admit, I did borrow a tiny tissue sample from my brother—he didn't need it, by then—and the Betan doctors did use part of a chromosome from it, just for my new cloned parts. My new testicles are a little less than two percent Pierre, I suppose, depending on how you calculate it. If I ever decide to give my prick a nickname, the way some fellows do, I suppose I ought to call it after him. I don't feel much inclined to do so, though. It feels very all-me."

"But are the chromosomes of your body still double-X?"

"Well, yes." Dono frowned uneasily, and scratched his beard. "I expect Richars to try to make a point with that, if he thinks of it. I did look into the retrogenetic treatment for complete somatic transformation. I didn't have time for it, the complications can be strange, and for a gene splice this large the result is usually no better than a partial cellular mosaic, a chimera, hit-or-miss. Sufficient for treating some genetic diseases, but not the legal disease of being some-little-cell-female. But the portion of my tissues responsible for fathering the next little Vorrutyer heir is certifiably XY, and incidentally, made free of genetic disease, damage, and mutation while we were about it. The next Count Vorrutyer won't have a bad heart. Among other things. The prick's always been the most important qualification for a Countship anyway. History says so."

By chuckled. "Maybe they'll just let the prick vote." He made an X gesture down by his crotch, and intoned sonorously, "*Dono, his mark.*"

Lord Dono grinned. "While it wouldn't be the first time a real prick has held a seat in the Council of Counts, I'm hoping for a more complete victory. That's where you come in, Ivan."

"Me? I don't have anything to do with this! I don't *want* anything to do with this." Ivan's startled protests were cut short by the car slowing in front of the Vorrutyers' townhouse and turning in.

Vorrutyer House was a generation older than Vorkosigan House and correspondingly notably more fortresslike. Its severe stone walls threw projections out to the sidewalk in a blunted star pattern, giving crossfire onto what had been a mud street decorated with horse dung in the great house's heyday. It had no windows on the ground floor at all, just a few gun-slits. Thick iron-bound planks, scorning carving or any other decorative effect, formed the double doors into its inner courtyard; they now swung aside at an automated signal, and the groundcar squeezed through the passage. The walls were marked with smears of vehicle enamel from less careful drivers. Ivan wondered if the murder-holes in the dark arched roof, above, were still functional. Probably.

The place had been restored with an eye to defense by the great general Count Pierre "Le Sanguinaire" Vorrutyer himself, who was principally famous as Emperor Dorca's trusted right arm/head thug in the civil war that had broken the power of the independent Counts just before the end of the Time of Isolation. Pierre had made serious enemies, all of whom he had survived into a foul-tongued old age. It had taken the invading Cetagandans and all their techno-weaponry to finally put an end to him, with great difficulty, after an infamous and costly siege—not of this place, of course. Old Pierre's eldest daughter had married an earlier Count Vorkosigan, which was where the Pierre of Mark's middle name had come down from. Ivan wondered what old Pierre would think of his offshoots now. Maybe he would like Richars best. Maybe his ghost still walked here. Ivan shuddered, stepping out onto the dark cobblestones.

The driver took the car off to its garage, and Lord Dono led the way, two steps at a time, up the green-black granite staircase out of the courtyard and into the house. He paused to sweep a glance back over the stony expanse. "First thing is, I'm going to get some more light out here," he remarked to Szabo.

"First thing is, get the title deed in your name," Szabo returned blandly.

"My new name." Dono gave him a short nod, and pushed onward.

The interior of the house was so ill-lit, one couldn't make out the mess, but apparently all had been left exactly as it had been dropped when Count Pierre had last gone down to his District some months ago. The echoing chambers had a derelict, musty odor. They fetched up finally, after laboring up two more gloomy staircases, in the late Count's abandoned bedroom.

"Guess I'll sleep here tonight," said Lord Dono, staring around dubiously. "I want clean sheets on the bed first, though."

"Yes, m'lord," said Szabo.

Byerly cleared a pile of plastic flimsies, dirty clothes, dried fruit rinds, and other detritus from an armchair, and settled himself comfortably, legs crossed. Dono prowled the room, staring rather sadly at his dead brother's few and forlorn personal effects, picking up and putting down a set of hairbrushes—Pierre had been balding—dried-up cologne bottles, small coins. "Starting tomorrow, I want this place cleaned up. I'm not waiting for the title deed for that, if I have to live here."

"I know a good commercial service," Ivan couldn't help volunteering. "They clean Vorkosigan House for Miles when the Count and Countess aren't in residence, I know."

"Ah? Good." Lord Dono made a gesture at Szabo. The Armsman nodded, and promptly collected the particulars from Ivan, noting them down on his pocket audiofiler.

"Richars made two attempts to take possession of the old pile while you were gone," Byerly reported. "The first time, your Armsmen stood firm and wouldn't let him in."

"Good men," muttered Szabo.

"Second time, he came round with a squad of municipal guardsmen and an order he'd conned out of Lord Vorbohn. Your officer of the watch called me, and I was able to get a counter-order from the Lord Guardian of the Speaker's Circle with which to conjure them away. It was quite exciting, for a little while. Pushing and shoving in the doorways . . . no one drew weapons, or was seriously injured, though, more's the pity. We might have been able to sue Richars."

"We've lawsuits enough." Dono sighed, sat on the edge of the bed, and crossed his legs. "But thanks for what you did, By."

By waved this away.

"Below the knees, if you must," said Szabo. "Knees apart is better."

Dono immediately rearranged his pose, crossing his ankles instead, but noted, "By sits that way."

"By is not a good male model to copy."

By made a moue at Szabo, and flipped one wrist out limply. "Really, Szabo, how can you be so cruel? And after I saved your old homestead, too."

Everyone ignored him. "How about Ivan?" Dono asked Szabo, eyeing Ivan speculatively. Ivan was suddenly unsure of where to put his feet, or his hands.

"Mm, fair. The very best model, if you can remember exactly how he moved, would be Aral Vorkosigan. Now, *that* was power in motion. His son doesn't do too badly, either, projecting beyond his real space. Young Lord Vorkosigan is just a bit studied, though. Count Vorkosigan just is."

Lord Dono's thick black brows snapped up, and he rose to stalk across the room, flip a desk chair around, and straddle it, arms crossed along its back. He rested his chin on his arms and glowered.

"Huh! I recognize that one," said Szabo. "Not bad, keep working on it. Try to take up more space with your elbows."

Dono grinned, and leaned one hand on his thigh, elbow cocked out. After a moment, he jumped up again, and went to Pierre's closet, flung the doors wide, and began rooting within. A Vorrutyer House uniform tunic sailed out to land on the bed, followed by trousers and a shirt; then one tall boot after another thumped to the bed's end. Dono reemerged, dusty and bright-eyed.

"Pierre wasn't that much taller than me, and I always could wear his shoes, if I had thick socks. Get a seamstress in here tomorrow—"

"Tailor," Szabo corrected.

"Tailor, and we'll see how much of this I can use in a hurry."

"Very good, m'lord."

Dono began unfastening his black tunic.

"I think it's time for me to go now," said Ivan.

"Please sit down, Lord Vorpatril," said Armsman Szabo.

"Yes, come sit by me, Ivan." Byerly patted his upholstered chair arm invitingly.

"Sit down, Ivan," Lord Dono growled. His burning

eyes suddenly crinkled, and he murmured, "For old time's sake, if nothing else. You used to run *into* my bedroom to watch me undress, not out of it. Must I lock the door and make you play hunt the key again?"

Ivan opened his mouth, raised a furious admonishing finger in protest, thought better of it, and sank to a seat on the edge of the bed. *You wouldn't dare* seemed suddenly a really unwise thing to say to the former Lady Donna Vorrutyer. He crossed his ankles, then hastily uncrossed them again and set his feet apart, then crossed them again, and twined his hands together in vast discomfort. "I don't see what you need me for," he said plaintively.

"So you can witness," said Szabo.

"So you can testify," said Dono. The tunic hit the bed beside Ivan, making him jump, followed by a black T-shirt.

Well, Dono had spoken truly about the Betan surgeon; there weren't any visible scars. His chest sprouted a faint nest of black hairs; his musculature tended to the wiry. The shoulders of the tunic hadn't been padded.

"So you can *gossip*, of course," said By, lips parted in either some bizarre prurient interest, or keen enjoyment of Ivan's embarrassment, or more likely both at once.

"If you think I'm going to say one word about being here tonight to *anyone*—"

With a smooth motion, Dono kicked his black trousers onto the bed atop the tunic. His briefs followed.

"Well?" Dono stood before Ivan with an utterly cheerful leer on his face. "What do you think? Do they do good work on Beta, or what?"

Ivan glanced sidelong at him, and away. "You look . . . normal," he admitted reluctantly.

"Well, show *me* while you're at it," By said.

Dono turned before him.

"Not bad," said By judiciously, "but aren't you a trifle, ah, juvenile?"

Dono sighed. "It was a rush job. Quality, but rush.

I went from the hospital straight to the jumpship for home. The organs are going to have to finish growing *in situ*, the doctors tell me. A few months yet to fully adult morphology. The incisions don't hurt anymore, though."

"Ooh," said By, "puberty. What fun for you."

"On fast-forward, at that. But the Betans have smoothed that out a lot for me. You have to give them credit, they're a people in control of their hormones."

Ivan conceded reluctantly, "My cousin Miles, when he had his heart and lungs and guts replaced, said it took almost a full year for his breathing and energy to be completely back to normal. They had to finish growing back to adult size after they were installed too. I'm sure . . . it will be all right." He added after a helpless moment, "So does it work?"

"I can piss standing up, yeah." Dono reached over and retrieved his briefs, and slid them back on. "As for the other, well, real soon now, I understand. I can hardly wait for my first wet dream."

"But will any woman want to . . . it's not like you're going to be keeping it a secret, who and what you were before . . . how will you, um . . . That's one place Armsman Pygmalion over there," Ivan waved at Szabo, "won't be able to coach you."

Szabo smiled faintly, the most expression Ivan had seen on his face tonight.

"Ivan, Ivan, Ivan." Dono shook his head, and scooped up the House uniform trousers. "I taught *you* how, didn't I? Of all the problems I expect to have . . . puzzling how to lose my male virginity isn't one of them. Really."

"It . . . doesn't seem fair," said Ivan in a smaller voice. "I mean, *we* had to figure all this stuff out when we were thirteen."

"As opposed to, say, twelve?" Dono inquired tightly. "Um."

Dono buckled the trousers—they were not too snug across the hips after all—hitched into the tunic, and frowned at his reflection in the mirror. He bunched handfuls of extra fabric at the sides. "Yeah, that'll do.

The tailor should have it ready by tomorrow night. I want to wear this when I go present my evidence of impediment at Vorhartung Castle."

The blue-and-gray Vorrutyer House uniform was going to look exceptionally good on Lord Dono, Ivan had to concede. Maybe that would be a good day to call in his Vor rights and get a ticket, and take a discreet back seat in the visitor's gallery at the Council of Counts. Just to see what happened, to use one of Gregor's favorite phrases.

Gregor . . .

"Does Gregor know about this?" Ivan asked suddenly. "Did you tell him your plan, before you left for Beta?"

"No, of course not," said Dono. He sat on the bed's edge, and began pulling on the boots.

Ivan could feel his teeth clench. "Are you out of your minds?"

"As somebody or another is fond of quoting—I think it was your cousin Miles—it is always easier to get forgiveness than permission." Dono rose, and went to the mirror to check the effect of the boots.

Ivan clutched his hair. "All right. You two—you three—dragged me up here because you claimed you wanted my help. I'm going to hand you a hint. Free." He took a deep breath. "You can blindside me, and laugh your heads off if you want to. It won't be the first time I've been the butt. You can blindside Richars with my good will. You can blindside the whole Council of Counts. Blindside my cousin Miles—please. I want to watch. But do not, if you value your chances, if you mean this to be anything other than a big, short joke, do *not* blindside Gregor."

Byerly grimaced uncertainly; Dono, turning before the mirror, shot Ivan a penetrating look. "Go to him, you mean?"

"Yes. I can't make you," Ivan went on sternly, "but if you don't, I categorically refuse to have anything more to do with you."

"Gregor can kill it all with a word," said Dono warily. "Before it even launches."

"He can," said Ivan, "but he won't, without strong

motivation. Don't give him that motivation. Gregor does not like political surprises."

"I thought Gregor was fairly easy-going," said By, "for an emperor."

"No," said Ivan firmly. "He is not. He is merely rather quiet. It's not the same thing at all. You don't want to see what he's like pissed."

"What does he look like, pissed?" asked By curiously.

"Identical to what he looks like the rest of the time. That's the scary part."

Dono held up a hand, as By opened his mouth again. "By, aside from the chance to amuse yourself, you pulled Ivan in on this tonight because of his connections, or so you claimed. In my experience, it's a bad idea to ignore your expert consultants."

By shrugged. "It's not like we're paying him anything."

"*I* am calling in some old favors. This costs me. And it's not from a fund I can replace." Dono's glance swept to Ivan. "So what exactly do you suggest we do?"

"Ask Gregor for a brief interview. *Before* you talk to or see anyone else at all, even over the comconsole. Chin up, look him in the eye—" An ungodly thought occurred to Ivan then. "Wait, you didn't ever sleep with *him*, did you?"

Dono's lips, and mustache, twitched up with amusement. "No, unfortunately. A missed opportunity I now regret deeply, I assure you."

"Ah." Ivan breathed relief. "All right. Then just tell him what you plan to do. Claim your rights. He'll either decide to let you run, or he'll impound you. If he cuts you off, well, the worst will be over, and quickly. If he decides to let you run . . . you'll have a silent backer even Richars at his most vicious can't top."

Dono leaned against Pierre's bureau, and drummed his fingers in the dust atop it. The orchids now lay there in a forlorn heap. Wilted, like Ivan's dreams. Dono's lips pursed. "Can you get us in?" he asked at last.

"I, uh . . . I, uh . . ."

His gaze became more urgent, piercing. "Tomorrow?"

"Ah . . ."

"Morning?"

"Not *morning*," By protested faintly.

"Early," insisted Dono.

"I'll . . . seewhatIcando," Ivan managed at last.

Dono's face lit. "*Thank* you!"

The extraction of this reluctant promise had one beneficial side-effect: the Vorrutyers proved willing to let their captive audience go, the better for Ivan to hurry home and call Emperor Gregor. Lord Dono insisted on detailing his car and a driver to take Ivan the short distance to his apartment, thwarting Ivan's faint hope of being mugged and murdered in a Vorbarr Sultana alleyway on the way home and thus avoiding the consequences of this evening's revelations.

Blessedly alone in the back of the groundcar, Ivan entertained a brief prayer that Gregor's schedule would be too packed to admit the proposed interview. But it was more likely he'd be so shocked at Ivan breaking his rule of a low profile, he'd make room at once. In Ivan's experience, the only thing more dangerous to such innocent bystanders as himself than arousing Gregor's wrath was arousing his curiosity.

Once back safely in his little apartment, Ivan locked the door against all Vorrutyers past and present. He'd beguiled his time yesterday imagining entertaining the voluptuous Lady Donna here . . . what a waste. Not that Lord Dono didn't make a passable man, but Barrayar didn't *need* more men. Though Ivan supposed they might reverse Donna's ploy, and send the excess male population to Beta Colony to be altered into the more pleasing form . . . he shuddered at the vision.

With a reluctant sigh, he dug out the security card he'd managed to avoid using for the past several years, and ran it through his comconsole's read-slot.

Gregor's gatekeeper, a man in bland civilian dress who did not identify himself—if you had this access, you were supposed to know—answered at once. "Yes? Ah. Ivan."

"I would like to speak to Gregor, please."

"Excuse me, Lord Vorpatril, but did you mean to use this channel?"

"Yes."

The gatekeeper's brows rose in surprise, but his hand moved to one side, and his image blinked out. The comconsole chimed. Several times.

Gregor's image came up at last. He was still dressed for the day, relieving Ivan's alarmed visions of dragging him out of bed or the shower. The background showed one of the Imperial Residence's cozier sitting rooms. Ivan could just make out a fuzzy view of Dr. Toscane, in the background. She seemed to be adjusting her blouse. Ulp. *Keep it brief. Gregor clearly has better things to do tonight.*

I wish I did.

Gregor's blank expression changed to one of annoyance as he recognized Ivan. "Oh. It's you." The irritated look faded slightly. "You never call me on this channel, Ivan. Thought it had to be Miles. What's up?"

Ivan took a deep breath. "I just came from meeting . . . Donna Vorrutyer at the shuttleport. Back from Beta. You two need to see each other."

Gregor's brows rose. "Why?"

"I'm sure she'd much rather explain it all herself. I have nothing to do with this."

"You do now. Lady Donna's calling in old favors, is she?" Gregor frowned, and added a bit dangerously, "I am not a coin to be bartered in your love affairs, Ivan."

"No, Sire," Ivan agreed fervently. "But you want to see her. Really and truly. As soon as possible. Sooner. Tomorrow. Morning. Early."

Gregor cocked his head. Curiously. "Just how important is this?"

"That's entirely for you to judge. Sire."

"If *you* want nothing to do with it . . ." Gregor trailed off, and stared unnervingly at Ivan. His hand at last tapped on his comconsole control, and he glanced aside at some display Ivan could not see. "I could move . . . hm. How about eleven sharp, in my office."

"Thank you, Sire." *You won't regret this* seemed a much too optimistic statement to add. In fact, adding anything

at all had all the appeal of stepping over a cliff without a grav-suit. Ivan smiled instead, and ducked his head
in a little half-bow.

Gregor's frown grew more thoughtful still, but after
a moment of further contemplation, he returned Ivan's
nod, and cut the com.

CHAPTER EIGHT

Ekaterin sat before the comconsole in her aunt's study, and ran again through the seasonal succession of Barrayaran plants bordering the branching pathways of Lord Vorkosigan's garden. The one sensory effect the design program could not help her model was odor. For that most subtle and emotionally profound effect, she had to rely on her own experience and memory.

On a soft summer evening, a border of scrubwire would emit a spicy redolence that would fill the air for meters around, but its color was muted and its shape low and round. Intermittent stands of chuffgrass would break up the lines, and reach full growth at the right time, but its sickly citrus scent would clash with the scrubwire, and besides, it was on the proscribed list of plants to which Lord Vorkosigan was allergic. Ah— zipweed! Its blond and maroon stripes would provide excellent vertical visual interest, and its faint sweet fragrance would combine well, appetizingly even, with the scrubwire. Put a clump there by the little bridge, and there and there. She altered the program, and ran the succession again. *Much better*. She took a sip of her cooling tea, and glanced at the time.

She could hear her Aunt Vorthys moving about in

the kitchen. Late-sleeper Uncle Vorthys would be down soon, and shortly afterwards Nikki, and aesthetic concentration would be a lost cause. She had only a few days for any last design refinements before she began working with real plants in quantity. And less than two hours before she needed to be showered and dressed and onsite to watch the crew hook up and test the creek's water circulation.

If all went well, she could start laying her supply of Dendarii rocks today, and tuning the gentle burble of the water flow around and over and among them. The sound of the creek was another subtlety the design program could not help her with, though it had addressed environmental noise abatement. The walls and curving terraces were up onsite, and satisfactory; the city-noise-baffling effects were all she'd hoped for. Even in winter the garden would be hushed and restful. Blanketed with snow broken only by the bare up-reaching lines of the woodier scrub, the shape of the space would still please the eye and soothe the mind and heart.

By tonight, the bones of the thing would be complete. Tomorrow, the flesh, in the form of trucked-in, unterraformed native soils from remote corners of the Vorkosigan's District, would arrive. And tomorrow evening before Lord Vorkosigan's dinner party, just for promise, she would put the first plant into the soil: a certain spare rootling from an ancient South Continent skellytum tree. It would be fifteen years or more before it would grow to fill the space allotted for it, but what of that? Vorkosigans had held this ground for two hundred years. Chances were good Vorkosigans would still be there to see it in its maturity. Continuity. With continuity like that, you could grow a *real* garden. Or a real family . . .

The front door chimed, and Ekaterin jumped, abruptly aware she was still dressed in an old set of her uncle's ship knits for pajamas, with her hair escaping the tie at the nape of her neck. Her aunt's step sounded from the kitchen into the tiled hall, and Ekaterin tensed to duck out of the line of sight should it prove some formal visitor. Oh, dear, what if it was Lord Vorkosigan?

She'd waked at dawn with garden revisions rioting through her head, sneaked quietly downstairs to work, and hadn't even brushed her teeth yet—but the voice greeting her aunt was a woman's, and a familiar one at that. *Rosalie, here? Why?*

A dark-haired, fortyish woman leaned around the edge of the archway and smiled. Ekaterin waved back in surprise, and rose to go to the hallway and greet her. It was indeed Rosalie Vorvayne, the wife of Ekaterin's eldest brother. Ekaterin hadn't seen her since Tien's funeral. She wore conservative day-wear, skirt and jacket in a bronze green that flattered her olive skin, though the cut was a little dowdy and provincial. She had her daughter Edie in tow, to whom she said, "Run along upstairs and find your cousin Nikki. I have to talk to your Aunt Kat for a while." Edie had not quite reached the adolescent slouch stage, and thumped off willingly enough.

"What brings you to the capital at this hour?" Aunt Vorthys asked Rosalie.

"Is Hugo and everyone all right?" Ekaterin added.

"Oh, yes, we're all fine," Rosalie assured them. "Hugo couldn't get away from work, so I was dispatched. I plan to take Edie shopping later, but getting her up to catch the morning monorail was a real chore, believe me."

Hugo Vorvayne held a post in the Imperial Bureau of Mines northern regional headquarters in Vordarian's District, two hours away from Vorbarr Sultana by the express. Rosalie must have risen before light for this outing. Her two older sons, grown almost past the surly stage, presumably had been left to their own devices for the day.

"Have you had breakfast, Rosalie?" Aunt Vorthys asked. "Do you want any tea or coffee?"

"We ate on the monorail, but tea would be lovely, thank you, Aunt Vorthys."

Rosalie and Ekaterin both followed their aunt into her kitchen to offer assistance, and as a result all ended up seated around the kitchen table with their steaming cups. Rosalie brought them up to date upon the health of her husband, the events of her household, and the accomplishments of her sons since Tien's funeral. Her eyes narrowed with good humor, and she leaned forward confidingly. "But to answer your question, what brings me here is you, Kat."

"Me?" said Ekaterin blankly.

"Can't you imagine why?"

Ekaterin wondered if it would be rude to say, *No, how should I?* She compromised with an inquiring gesture, and raised eyebrows.

"Your father had a visitor a couple of days ago."

Rosalie's arch tone invited a guessing-game, but Ekaterin could only think of how soon she might finish the social niceties and get away to her work-site. She continued to smile dimly.

Rosalie shook her head in amused exasperation, leaned forward, and tapped her finger on the table beside her cup. "You, my dear, have a very eligible offer."

"Offer of what?" Rosalie wasn't likely to be bringing her a new garden design contract. But surely she couldn't mean—

"Marriage, what else? And from a proper Vor gentleman, too, I'm pleased to report. So old-fashioned of the man, he sent a Baba all the way from Vorbarr Sultana to your da in South Continent—it quite bowled the old man over. Your da called Hugo to pass on the particulars. We decided that after all that baba-ing rather than do it over the comconsole someone ought to tell you the good news in person. We're all so pleased, to think you might be settled again so soon."

Aunt Vorthys sat up, looking considerably startled. She put a finger to her lips.

A Vor gentleman from the capital, old-fashioned and highly conscious of etiquette, Da bowled over, who else could it be but—Ekaterin's heart seemed to stop, then explode. *Lord Vorkosigan? Miles, you rat, how could you do this without asking me first!* Her lips parted in a dizzying mixture of fury and elation.

The arrogant little—! But . . . he to pick *her*, to be his Lady Vorkosigan, chatelaine of that magnificent house and of his ancestral District—there was so much to be done in that beautiful District, so daunting and exciting—and Miles himself, oh, my. That fascinating scarred short body, that burning intensity, to come to *her* bed? His hands had touched her perhaps twice; they might as well have left scorch marks on her skin, so clearly did her body remember those brief pressures. She had not, had not dared, let herself think about him in that way, but now her carnal consciousness of him wrenched loose from its careful suppression and soared. Those humorous gray eyes, that alert, mobile, kissable mouth with its extraordinary range of expression . . . could be hers, all hers. But how *dare* he ambush her like this, in front of all her relatives?

"You're pleased?" Rosalie, watching her face closely, sat back and smiled. "Or should I say, thrilled? Good! And not completely surprised, I daresay."

"Not . . . completely." *I just didn't believe it. I chose not to believe it, because . . . because it would have ruined everything . . .*

"We were afraid you might find it early days, after Tien and all. But the Baba said he meant to steal a march on all his rivals, your da told Hugo."

"He doesn't have any rivals." Ekaterin swallowed, feeling decidedly faint, thinking of the remembered scent of him. But how could he imagine that she—

"He has good hopes for his postmilitary career," Rosalie went on.

"Indeed, he's said so." *It's all kinds of hubris*, Miles had told her once, describing his ambitions for fame to exceed his father's. She'd gathered he didn't expect that fact to slow him down in the least.

"Good family connections."

Ekaterin couldn't help smiling. "A *slight* understatement, Rosalie."

"Not as rich as others of his rank, but well-enough to do, and I never thought you were one to hold out for the money. Though I always did think you needed to look a bit more to your own needs, Kat."

Well, yes, Ekaterin had been dimly aware that the Vorkosigans were not as wealthy as many other families of Count's rank, but Miles had riches enough to drown in by her old straitened standards. She would never have to pinch and scrape again. All her energy, all her thought, could be freed for higher goals—Nikki would have every opportunity—"Plenty enough for me, good heavens!"

But how bizarre of him, to send a Baba all the way to South Continent to talk to her da . . . was he that shy? Ekaterin's heart was almost touched, but for the reflection that it might simply be that Miles gave no thought to how much his wants inconvenienced others. Shy, or arrogant? Or both at once? He could be a most ambiguous man sometimes—charming as . . . as no one she'd ever met before, but elusive as water.

Not just elusive; slippery. Borderline trickster, even. A chill stole over her. Had his garden proposal been nothing more than a trick, a ploy to keep her close under his eye? The full implications began to sink in at last. Maybe he didn't admire her work. Maybe he didn't care about his garden at all. Maybe he was merely manipulating her. She knew herself to be hideously vulnerable to the faintest flattery. Her starvation for the slightest scrap of interest or affection was part of what had kept her self-prisoned in her marriage for so long. A kind of Tien-shaped box seemed to loom darkly before her, like a pitfall trap baited with poisoned love.

Had she betrayed herself again? She'd so much wanted it to be true, wanted to take her first steps into independence, to have the chance to display her prowess. She'd imagined not just Miles, but all the people of the city, amazed and delighted by her garden, and new orders pouring in, the launch of a career. . . .

You can't cheat an honest man, the saying went. Or woman. If Lord Vorkosigan had manipulated her, he'd done so with her full cooperation. Her hot rage was douched with cold shame.

Rosalie was burbling on, " . . . want to tell Lieutenant Vormoncrief the good news yourself, or should we go round through his Baba again?"

Ekaterin blinked her back into focus. "What? Wait, *who* did you say?"

Rosalie stared back. "Lieutenant Vormoncrief. Alexi."

"*That* block?" cried Ekaterin in dawning horror. "Rosalie, never tell me you've been talking about Alexi Vormoncrief this whole time!"

"Why, yes," said Rosalie in dismay. "Who did you think, Kat?"

The Professora blew out her breath and sat back.

Ekaterin was so upset the words escaped her mouth without thought. "I thought you were talking about Miles Vorkosigan!"

The Professora's brows shot up; it was Rosalie's turn to stare. "Who? Oh, good heavens, you don't mean the Imperial Auditor fellow, do you? That grotesque little man who came to Tien's funeral and hardly said a word to anyone? No wonder you looked so odd. No, no, no." She paused to peer more closely at her sister-in-law. "You don't mean to tell me he's been courting you too? How embarrassing!"

Ekaterin took a breath, for balance. "Apparently not."

"Well, that's a relief."

"Um . . . yes."

"I mean, he's a mutie, isn't he? High Vor or no, the family would never urge you to match with a mutie just for money, Kat. Put that right out of your mind." She paused thoughtfully. "Still . . . they're not handing out too many chances to be a Countess. I suppose, with the uterine replicators these days, you wouldn't actually have to have any physical contact. To have children, I mean. And they could be gene-cleaned. These galactic technologies give the idea of a marriage of convenience a whole new twist. But it's not as though you were that desperate."

"No," Ekaterin agreed hollowly. *Just desperately distracted.* She was furious with the man; why should the notion of never ever having to have any physical contact with him make her suddenly want to burst into tears? Wait, no—if Vorkosigan *wasn't* the man who'd sent the Baba, her whole case against him, which had bloomed so violently in her mind just now, collapsed like a house of cards. He was innocent. She was crazy, or headed that way fast.

"I mean," Rosalie went on in a tone of renewed encouragement, "here's Vormoncrief, for instance."

"Here is *not* Vormoncrief," Ekaterin said firmly, grasping for the one certain anchor in this whirlwind of confusion. "Absolutely not. You've never met the man, Rosalie, but take it from me, he's a twittering idiot. Aunt Vorthys, am I right or not?"

The Professora smiled fondly at her. "I would not put it so bluntly, dear, but really, Rosalie, shall we say, I think Ekaterin can do better. There's plenty of time yet."

"Do you think so?" Rosalie took in this assurance doubtfully, but accepted her elder aunt's authority. "It's true Vormoncrief's only a lieutenant, and the descendant of a younger son at that. Oh, dear. What are we to tell the poor man?"

"Diplomacy's the Baba's job," Ekaterin pointed out. "All we have to supply is a straight *no*. She'll have to take it from there."

"That's true," Rosalie allowed, looking relieved. "One of the advantages of the old system, I suppose. Well . . . if Vormoncrief is not the one, he's not the one. You're old enough to know your own mind. Still, Kat, I don't think you ought to be too choosy, or wait too long past your mourning time. Nikki needs a da. And you're not getting any younger. You don't want to end up as one of those odd old women who eke out their lives in their relatives' attics."

Your attic is safe from me under any circumstances, Rosalie. Ekaterin smiled a bit grimly, but did not speak this thought aloud. "No, only the third floor."

The Professora's eyes flicked at her, reprovingly, and Ekaterin flushed. She was not ungrateful, she wasn't. It was just . . . oh, hell. She pushed back her chair.

"Excuse me. I have to go get my shower and get dressed. I'm due at work soon."

"Work?" said Rosalie. "Must you go? I'd hoped to take you out to lunch, and shopping. To celebrate, and look for bride clothes, in the original plan, but I suppose we could convert it to a consolation day instead. What do you say, Kat? I think you could use a little fun. You haven't had much, lately."

"No shopping," said Ekaterin. She remembered the last time she'd been shopping, on Komarr with Lord

Vorkosigan in one of his more lunatic moods, before Tien's death had turned her life inside-out. She didn't think a day with Rosalie could match it. At Rosalie's look of distressed disappointment, she relented. The woman had got up before dawn for this fool's errand, after all. "But I suppose you and Edie could pick me up for lunch, and then bring me back."

"All right . . . where? Whatever are you doing these days, anyway? Weren't you talking about going back to school? You haven't exactly communicated with the rest of the family much lately, you know."

"I've been busy. I have a commission to design and implement a display garden for a Count's townhouse." She hesitated. "Lord Auditor Vorkosigan's, actually. I'll give you directions how to get there before you and Edie go out."

"Vorkosigan is employing you, too?" Rosalie looked surprised, then suddenly militantly suspicious. "He hasn't been . . . you know . . . pushing himself on you at all, has he? I don't care whose son he is, he has no right to impose on you. Remember, you have a brother to stand up for you if you need it." She paused, perhaps to reflect upon a vision of Hugo's probable appalled recoil at being volunteered for this duty. "Or I'd be willing to give him a piece of my mind myself, if you need help." She nodded, now on firmer ground.

"Thank you," choked Ekaterin, beginning to evolve plans for keeping Rosalie and Lord Vorkosigan as far apart as possible. "I'll keep you in mind, if it ever becomes necessary." She escaped upstairs.

In the shower, she tried to recover from the seething chaos Rosalie's misunderstood mission had generated in her brain. Her physical attraction for Miles—Lord Vorkosigan—*Miles*, was no news, really. She'd felt and ignored the pull of it before. It was by no means in despite of his odd body; his size, his scars, his energy, his *differences* fascinated her in their own right. She wondered if people would think her perverse, if they knew the strange way her tastes seemed to be drifting these days. Firmly, she turned the water temperature down to pure cold.

But flatline suppression of all erotic speculation was a legacy of her years with Tien. She owned herself now, owned her own sexuality at last. Free and clear. She could dare to dream. To look. To feel, even. Action was another matter altogether, but drat it, she could *want*, in the solitude of her own skull, and possess that wanting whole.

And he liked her, he did. It was no crime to like her, even if it was inexplicable. And she liked him back, yes. A little too much, even, but that was no one's business but her own. They could go on like this. The garden project wouldn't last forever. By midsummer, fall at the latest, she could turn it and a schedule of instructions over to Vorkosigan House's usual groundskeepers. She might drop by to check on it from time to time. They might even meet. From time to time.

She was starting to shiver. She turned the water temperature back up to as hot as she could stand, so the steam billowed in clouds.

Would it do any harm, to make of him a dream-lover? It seemed invasive. How would she like it, after all, if she discovered she was starring in someone else's pornographic daydreams? Horrified, yes? Disgusted, to be pawed over in some untrusted stranger's thoughts. She imagined herself so portrayed in Miles's thoughts, and checked her horror quotient. It was a little . . . weak.

The obvious solution was to bring dreams and reality into honest congruence. If deleting the dreams wasn't possible, what about making them real? She tried to imagine having a lover. How did people go *about* such things, anyway? She could barely nerve herself to ask for directions on a street corner. How in the world did you ask someone to . . . But reality—reality was too great a risk, ever again. To lose herself and all her free dreams in another long nightmare like her life with Tien, a slow, sucking, suffocating bog closing over her head forever . . .

She jerked the temperature down again, and adjusted the spray so the droplets struck her skin like spicules of ice. Miles was not Tien. He wasn't trying to own her, for heaven's sake, or destroy her; he'd only hired her to make him a garden. Entirely benign. She must be going insane. She trusted it was a temporary insanity. Maybe her hormones had spiked this month. She would just ride it out, and all these . . . unusual thoughts, would just go away on their own. She would look back on herself and laugh.

She laughed, experimentally. The hollow echoes were due to being in the shower, no doubt. She shut off the freezing water, and stepped out.

There was no reason she would have to see him today. He sometimes came out and sat on the wall a while and watched the crew's progress, but he never interrupted. She wouldn't have to talk with him, not till his dinner tomorrow night, and there would be lots of *other* people to talk with then. She had plenty of time to settle her mind again. In the meanwhile, she had a creek to tune.

Lady Alys Vorpatril's office at the Imperial Residence, which handled all matters of social protocol for the Emperor, had expanded of late from three rooms to half of a third-floor wing. There Ivan found himself at the disposal of the fleet of secretaries and assistants Lady Alys had laid on to help handle the wedding. It had sounded a treat, to be working in an office with dozens of women, till he'd discovered they were mostly steely-eyed middle-aged Vor ladies who brooked even less nonsense from him than his mother did. Fortunately, he'd only dated two of their daughters, and both those ventures had ended without acrimony. It could have been much worse.

To Ivan's concealed dismay, Lord Dono and By Vorrutyer were in such good time for their Imperial appointment they stopped up to see him on the way in. Lady Alys's secretary summoned him curtly into the department's outer office, where he found the pair refraining from sitting down and making themselves comfortable. By was dressed in his usual taste, in a maroon suit conservative only by town clown standards. Lord Dono wore his neat Vor-style black tunic and trousers with gray piping and decoration, clearly mourning garb, which not coincidentally set off his newly masculinized good looks. The middle-aged secretary was giving him approving glances from under her eyelashes. Armsman Szabo, in full Vorrutyer House uniform, had taken up that I-am-furniture guard stance by the door, as if covertly declaring there were some kinds of lines of fire it wasn't his job to be in.

No one not on staff wandered the halls of the Imperial Residence by themselves; Dono and By had an escort, in the person of Gregor's senior major-domo. This gentleman turned from some conversation with the secretary as Ivan entered, and eyed him with new appraisal.

"Good morning, Ivan," said Lord Dono cordially.

"Morning, Dono, By." Ivan managed a brief, reasonably impersonal nod. "You, ah, made it, I see."

"Yes, thank you." Dono glanced around. "Is Lady Alys here this morning?"

"Gone off to inspect florists with Colonel Vortala," said Ivan, happy to be able to both tell the truth and avoid being drawn further into whatever schemes Lord Dono might have.

"I must chat with her sometime soon," mused Dono.

"Mm," said Ivan. Lady Donna had not been one of Alys Vorpatril's intimates, being half a generation younger and involved with a different social set than the politically active crowd over which Lady Alys presided. Lady Donna had discarded, along with her first husband, a chance to be a future Countess; though having met that lordling, Ivan thought he could understand the sacrifice. In any case, Ivan had not had any trouble controlling his urge to gossip about this new twist of events with either his mother or any of the sedate Vor matrons she employed. And fascinating as it would be to witness the first meeting of Lady Alys with Lord Dono and all the protocol puzzles he trailed, on the whole Ivan thought he would rather be safely out of range.

"Ready, gentlemen?" said the major-domo.

"Good luck, Dono," said Ivan, and prepared to retreat.

"Yes," said By, "good luck. I'll just stay here and chat with Ivan till you're done, shall I?"

"My list," said the major-domo, "has all of you on it. Vorrutyer, Lord Vorrutyer, Lord Vorpatril, Armsman Szabo."

"Oh, that's an error," said Ivan helpfully. "Only Lord Dono actually needs to see Gregor." By nodded confirmation.

"The list," said the major-domo, "is in the Emperor's own hand. This way, please."

The normally saturnine By swallowed a little, but they all dutifully followed the major-domo down two floors and around the corner to the north wing and Gregor's private office. The major-domo had not demanded Ivan vouch for Dono's identity, Ivan noted, by which he deduced the Residence had caught up with events overnight. Ivan was almost disappointed. He'd so wanted to see somebody else be as boggled as he'd been.

The major-domo touched the palm pad by the door, announced his party, and was bid to enter. Gregor shut down his comconsole desk and looked up as they all trod within. He rose and walked around to lean against it, cross his arms, and eye the group. "Good morning, gentlemen. Lord Dono. Armsman."

They returned a mumble averaging out to *Good morning, Sire*, except for Dono, who stepped forward with his chin up and said in a clear voice, "Thank you for seeing me on such short notice, Sire."

"Ah," said Gregor. "Short notice. Yes." He cast an odd look at By, who blinked demurely. "Please be seated," Gregor went on. He gestured to the leather sofas at the end of the room, and the major-domo hurried to pull around a couple of extra armchairs. Gregor took his usual seat on one of the sofas, turned a little sideways, that he might have full view of his guests' faces in the bright diffuse light from the north-facing windows overlooking his garden.

"I should be pleased to stand, Sire," Armsman Szabo murmured suggestively, but he was not to be permitted to hug the doorway and potential escape; Gregor merely smiled briefly, and pointed at a chair, and Szabo perforce sat, though on the edge. By took a second chair and managed a good simulation of his usual cross-legged ease. Dono sat straight, alert, knees and elbows apart, claiming a space no one disputed; he had the second couch entirely to himself, until Gregor opened an ironic palm, and Ivan was forced to take the place next to him. As far toward the end as possible.

Gregor's face wasn't giving much away, except the obvious fact that the chance of Donna/Dono taking him by surprise had passed sometime in the intervening hours since Ivan's call. Gregor broke the ensuing silence just before Ivan could panic and blurt something.

"So, whose idea was this?"

"Mine, Sire," Lord Dono answered steadily. "My late brother expressed himself forcibly many times—as Szabo and others of the household can witness—that he abhorred the idea of Richars stepping into his place as Count Vorrutyer. If Pierre had not died so suddenly and unexpectedly, he would surely have found a substitute heir. I feel I am carrying out his verbal will."

"So you, ah, claim his posthumous approval."

"Yes. If he had thought of it. Granted, he had no reason to entertain such an extreme solution while he lived."

"I see. Go on." This was Gregor in his classic give-them-enough-rope-to-hang-themselves mode, Ivan recognized. "What support did you assure yourself of, before you left?" He glanced rather pointedly at Armsman Szabo.

"I secured the approval of my Arms—of my late brother's Armsmen, of course," said Dono. "Since it was their duty to guard the disputed property until my return."

"You took their oaths?" Gregor's voice was suddenly very mild.

Ivan cringed. To receive an Armsman's oath before one was confirmed as a Count or Count's heir was a serious crime, a violation of one of the subclauses of Vorlopulous's Law which, among other things, had restricted a Count's Armsmen to a mere squad of twenty. Lord Dono gave Szabo the barest nod.

"We gave our personal words," Szabo put in smoothly.

"Any man may freely give his personal word for his personal acts, Sire."

"Hm," said Gregor.

"Beyond the Vorrutyer Armsmen, the only two people I informed were my attorney, and my cousin By," Lord Dono continued. "I needed my attorney to put certain legal arrangements into motion, check all the details, and prepare the necessary documents. She and all her records are entirely at your disposal, of course, Sire. I'm sure you understand the tactical necessity for surprise. I told no one else before I left, lest Richars take warning and also prepare."

"Except for Byerly," Gregor prompted.

"Except for By," Dono agreed. "I needed someone I could trust in the capital to keep an eye on Richars's moves while I was out of range and incapacitated."

"Your loyalty to your cousin is most . . . notable, Byerly," murmured Gregor.

By eyed him warily. "Thank you, Sire."

"And your remarkable discretion. I do take note of it."

"It seemed a personal matter, Sire."

"I see. Do go on, Lord Dono."

Dono hesitated fractionally. "Has ImpSec passed you my Betan medical files yet?"

"Just this morning. They were apparently a little delayed."

"You mustn't blame that nice ImpSec boy who was following me. I'm afraid he found Beta Colony a trifle overwhelming. And I'm sure the Betans didn't offer them up voluntarily, especially since I told them not to." Dono smiled blandly. "I'm glad to see he rose to the challenge. One would hate to think ImpSec was losing its old edge, after Illyan's retirement."

Gregor, listening with his chin in his hand, gave a little wave of his fingers in acknowledgement of this, on all its levels.

"If you've had a chance to glance over the records," Dono went on, "you will know I am now fully functional as a male, capable of carrying out my social and biological duty of siring the next Vorrutyer heir. Now that the requirement of male primogeniture has been met, I claim the nearest right by blood to the Countship of the Vorrutyer's District, and in light of my late brother's expressed views, I claim Count's choice as well. Peripherally, I also assert that I will make a better Count than my cousin Richars, and that I will serve my District, the Imperium, and you more competently than he ever could. For evidence, I submit my work in the District on Pierre's behalf over the last five years."

"Are you proposing other charges against Richars?" asked Gregor.

"Not at present. The one charge of sufficient seriousness lacked sufficient proof to bring to trial at the time—" Dono and Szabo exchanged a glance.

"Pierre requested an ImpSec investigation of his fiancée's flyer accident. I remember reading the synopsis of the report. You are correct. There was no proof."

Dono managed to shrug acknowledgement without agreement. "As for Richars's lesser offenses, well, no one cared before, and I doubt they'll start caring now. I will not be charging that he is unfit—though I think he is unfit—but rather, maintaining that I am more fit and have the better right. And so I will lay it before the Counts."

"And do you expect to obtain any votes?"

"I would expect a certain small number of votes against Richars from his personal enemies even if I were a horse. For the rest, I propose to offer myself to the Progressive party as a future voting member."

"Ah?" Gregor glanced up at this. "The Vorrutyers were traditionally mainstays of the Conservatives. Richars was expected to maintain that tradition."

"Yes. My heart goes out to the old guard; they were my father's party, and his father's before him. But I doubt many of their hearts will go out to me. Besides, they are a present minority. One must be practical."

Right. And while Gregor was careful to maintain a façade of Imperial even-handedness, no one had any doubt the Progressives were the party he privately favored. Ivan chewed on his lip.

"Your case is going to create an uproar in the Council

at an awkward time, Lord Dono," said Gregor. "My credit with the Counts is fully extended right now in pushing through the appropriations for the Komarran solar mirror repairs."

Dono answered earnestly, "I ask nothing of you, Sire, but your neutrality. Don't quash my motion of impediment. And don't permit the Counts to dismiss me unheard, or hear me only in secret. I want a public debate and a public vote."

Gregor's lips twisted, contemplating this vision. "Your case could set a most peculiar precedent, Lord Dono. With which I would then have to live."

"Perhaps. I would point out that I am playing exactly by the old rules."

"Well . . . perhaps not *exactly*," murmured Gregor.

By put in, "May I suggest, Sire, that if in fact dozens of Counts' sisters were itching to stampede out to galactic medical facilities and return to Barrayar to attempt to step into their brothers' boots, it would have likely happened before now? As a precedent, I doubt it would be all that popular, once the novelty wore off."

Dono shrugged. "Prior to our conquest of Komarr, access to that sort of medicine was scarcely available. Someone had to be the first. It wouldn't even have been me if things had gone differently for poor Pierre." He glanced across at Gregor, eye to eye. "Though I will certainly not be the last. Quashing my case, or brushing it aside, won't settle anything. If nothing else, taking it through the full legal process will force the Counts to explicitly examine their assumptions, and rationalize a set of laws which have managed to ignore the changing times for far too long. You cannot expect to run a galactic empire with rules that haven't been revised or even reviewed since the Time of Isolation." That awful cheerful leer ignited Lord Dono's face suddenly. "In other words, it will be good for them."

A very slight smile escaped Gregor in return, not entirely voluntarily, Ivan thought. Lord Dono was playing Gregor just right—frank, fearless, and up front. But then, Lady Donna had always been observant.

Gregor looked Lord Dono over, and pressed his hand

to the bridge of his nose, briefly. After a moment he said ironically, "And will you be wanting a wedding invitation too?"

Dono's brows flicked up. "If I am Count Vorrutyer by then, my attendance will be both my right and my duty. If I'm not—well, then." After a slight silence, he added wistfully, "Though I always did like a good wedding. I had three. Two were disasters. It's so much nicer to watch, saying over and over to yourself, *It's not me! It's not me!* One can be happy all day afterward on that alone."

Gregor said dryly, "Perhaps your next one will be different."

Dono's chin lifted. "Almost certainly, Sire."

Gregor sat back, and stared thoughtfully at the crew arrayed before him. He tapped his fingers on the sofa arm. Dono waited gallantly, By nervously, Szabo stolidly. Ivan spent the time wishing he were invisible, or that he'd never run across By in that damned bar, or that he'd never met Donna, or that he'd never been born. He waited for the ax, whatever it was going to be, to fall, and wondered which way he ought to dodge.

Instead what Gregor said at last was, "So . . . what's it like?"

Dono's white grin flashed in his beard. "From the inside? My energy's up. My libido's up. I would say it makes me feel ten years younger, except I didn't feel like this when I was thirty, either. My temper's shorter. Otherwise, only the world has changed."

"Ah?"

"On Beta Colony, I scarcely noticed a thing. By the time I got to Komarr, well, the personal space people gave me had approximately doubled, and their response time to me had been cut in half. By the time I hit the Vorbarr Sultana Shuttleport, the change was phenomenal. Somehow, I don't think I got all that result just from my exercise program."

"Huh. So . . . if your motion of impediment fails, will you change back?"

"Not any time soon. I must say, the view from the top of the food chain promises to be downright panoramic. I propose to have my blood and money's worth of it."

Another silence fell. Ivan wasn't sure if everyone was digesting this declaration, or if their minds had all simply shorted out.

"All right . . ." said Gregor slowly at last.

The look of growing curiosity in his eyes made Ivan's skin crawl. *He's going to say it, I just know he is . . .*

"Let's see what happens." Gregor sat back, and gave another little wave of his fingers, as if to speed them on their way. "Carry on, Lord Dono."

"Thank you, Sire," said Dono sincerely.

No one waited around for Gregor to reiterate this dismissal. They all beat a prudent retreat to the corridor before the Emperor could change his mind. Ivan thought he could feel Gregor's eyes boring wonderingly into his back all the way out the door.

"Well," By exhaled brightly, as the major-domo led them down the corridor once more. "That went better than I'd expected."

Dono gave him a sidelong look. "What, was your faith failing, By? I think things went quite as well as I'd hoped for."

By shrugged. "Let's say, I was feeling a bit out of my usual depth."

"That's why we asked Ivan for help. For which I thank you once more, Ivan."

"It was nothing," Ivan denied. "I didn't do anything." *It's not my fault.* He didn't know why Gregor had put him on his short list for this meeting; the Emperor hadn't even asked him anything. Though Gregor was as bad as Miles for plucking clues out of, as far as Ivan could tell, thin air. He couldn't imagine what Gregor had construed from all this. He didn't *want* to imagine what Gregor had construed from all this.

The syncopated clomp of all their boots echoed as they rounded the corner into the East Wing. A calculating look entered Lord Dono's eyes, which put Ivan briefly in mind of Lady Donna, in the least reassuring way. "So what's your mama doing in the next few days, Ivan?"

"She's busy. Very busy. All this wedding stuff, you know. Long hours. I scarcely see her except at work, anymore. Where we are all very busy."

"I have no wish to interrupt her work. I need something more . . . casual. When were you going to see her again not at work?"

"Tomorrow night, at my cousin Miles's dinner party for Kareen and Mark. He told me to bring a date. I said I'd be bringing you as my guest. He was delighted." Ivan brooded on this lost scenario.

"Why, thank you, Ivan!" said Dono promptly. "How thoughtful of you. I accept."

"Wait, no, but that was before—before you—before I knew you—" Ivan sputtered, and gestured at Lord Dono in his new morphology. "I don't think he'll be so delighted now. It will mess up his seating arrangements."

"What, with *all* the Koudelka girls coming? I don't see how. Though I suppose some of them have taken young men in tow by now."

"I don't know about that, except for Delia and Duv Galeni. And if Kareen and Mark aren't—never mind. But I think Miles is trying to slant the sex ratio, to be on the safe side. It's really a party to introduce everyone to his gardener."

"I beg your pardon?" said Dono. They fetched up in the vestibule by the Residence's east doors. The major-domo waited patiently to see the visitors out, in that invisible and unpressing way he could project so well. Ivan was sure he was taking in every word to report to Gregor later.

"His gardener. Madame Vorsoisson. She's this Vor widow he's gone and lost his mind over. He hired her to put a garden in that lot next to Vorkosigan House. She's Lord Auditor Vorthys's niece, if you must know."

"Ah. Quite eligible, then. But how unexpected. Miles Vorkosigan, in love at last? I'd always thought Miles would fancy a galactic. He always gave one the feeling most of the women around here bored him to death. One was never quite certain it wasn't sour grapes, though. Unless it was self-fulfilling prophecy." Lord Dono's smile was briefly feline.

"It was getting a galactic to fancy Barrayar that was the hang-up, I gather," said Ivan stiffly. "Anyway, Lord Auditor Vorthys and his wife will be there, and Illyan with my mother, and the Vorbrettens, as well as all the Koudelkas and Galeni and Mark."

"René Vorbretten?" Dono's eyes narrowed with interest, and he exchanged a glance with Szabo, who gave a tiny nod in return. "I'd like to talk to *him*. He's a pipeline into the Progressives."

"Not this week, he's not." By smirked. "Didn't you hear what Vorbretten found dangling in his family tree?"

"Yes." Lord Dono waved this away. "We all have our little genetic handicaps. I think it would be fascinating to compare notes with him just now. Oh, yes, Ivan, you must bring me. It will be perfect."

For whom? With all that Betan education, Miles was about as personally liberal as it was possible for a Barrayaran Vor male to be, but Ivan still couldn't imagine that he would be thrilled to find Lord Dono Vorrutyer at his dining table.

On the other hand . . . so what? If Miles had something *else* to be irritated about, perhaps it would distract him from that little problem with Vormoncrief and Major Zamori. What better way to confuse the enemy than to multiply the targets? It wasn't as though Ivan would have any obligation to protect Lord Dono from Miles.

Or Miles from Lord Dono, for that matter. If Dono and By considered Ivan, a mere HQ captain, a valuable consultant on the social and political terrain of the capital, how much better a one was a real Imperial Auditor? If Ivan could, as it were, transfer Dono's affections to this new target, he might be able to crawl away entirely unobserved. *Yes.*

"Yes, yes, all right. But this is the last favor I'm going to do for you, Dono, is it understood?" Ivan tried to look stern.

"*Thank* you," said Lord Dono.

CHAPTER NINE

Miles stared at his reflection in the long antique mirror on his grandfather's former bedroom wall, now his own room, and frowned. His best Vorkosigan House uniform of brown and silver was much too formal for this dinner party. He would surely have an opportunity to squire Ekaterin to some venue for which it was actually appropriate, such as the Imperial Residence or the Council of Counts, and she could see and, he hoped, admire him in it then. Regretfully, he shucked the polished brown boots back off and prepared to return to the clothing he'd started with forty-five minutes before, one of his plain gray Auditor's suits, very clean and pressed. Well, slightly less pressed, now, with another House uniform and two Imperial uniforms from his late service tossed atop it on the bed.

He necessarily cycled back through naked, and frowned uneasily at himself again. Someday, if things went well, he must stand before her in his skin, in this very room and place, with no disguise at all.

A moment of panicked longing for Admiral Naismith's gray-and-whites, put away in the closet one floor above, passed over him. No. Ivan would be certain to hoot at him. Worse, Illyan might say something . . .

dry. And it wasn't as though he wanted to explain the little Admiral to his other guests. He sighed, and redonned the gray suit.

Pym stuck his head back through the bedroom door, and smiled in approval, or perhaps relief. "Ah, are you ready now, m'lord? I'll just get these out of your way again, shall I?" The speed with which Pym whipped away the other garments assured Miles he'd made the right choice, or at least, the best choice available to him.

Miles adjusted the thin strip of white shirt collar above the jacket's neck with military precision. He leaned forward to peer suspiciously for gray in his scalp, relocated the couple of strands he'd noted recently, suppressed an impulse to pluck them out, and then combed his hair again. *Enough of this madness.*

He hurried downstairs to recheck the table arrangements in the grand dining room. The table glittered with Vorkosigan cutlery, china, and a forest of wineglasses. The linen was graced with no less than three strategically low, elegant flower arrangements, over which he could see, and which he hoped Ekaterin would enjoy. He'd spent an hour debating with Ma Kosti and Pym over how to properly seat ten women and nine men. Ekaterin would be seated at Miles's right hand, off the head of the table, and Kareen at Mark's, off the foot; that hadn't been negotiable. Ivan would be seated next to his lady guest, in the middle as far from Ekaterin and Kareen as possible, the better to block any possible move of his on anyone else's partner—though Miles trusted Ivan would be fully occupied.

Miles had been an envious bystander to Ivan's brief, meteoric affair with Lady Donna Vorrutyer. In retrospect, he thought perhaps Lady Donna had been more charitable and Ivan less suave than it had seemed to his then-twenty-year-old perspective, but Ivan had certainly made the most of his good luck. Lady Alys, still full of plans for her son's marriage to some more eligible Vor bud, had been a bit rigid about it all; but with all those years of frustrated matchmaking behind her Lady Alys might find Lady Donna looking much better now. After all, with the advent of the uterine replicator and associated galactic biotech, being forty-something was no bar to a woman's reproductive plans at all. Nor being sixty-something, or eighty-something . . . Miles wondered if Ivan had mustered the nerve to ask Lady Alys and Illyan if they had any plans for providing him with a half-sib, or if the possibility hadn't crossed his mind yet. Miles decided he would have to point it out to his cousin at some appropriate moment, preferably when Ivan's mouth was full.

But not tonight. Tonight, everything had to be perfect.

Mark wandered in to the dining room, also frowning. He too was showered and slicked, and dressed in a suit tailored and layered, black on black with black. It lent his short bulk a surprisingly authoritative air. He strolled up the table's side, reading place cards, and reached for a pair.

"Don't even touch them," Miles told him firmly.

"But if I just switch Duv and Delia with Count and Countess Vorbretten, Duv will be as far away from me as we can get him," Mark pleaded. "I can't believe he wouldn't prefer that himself. I mean, as long as he's still next to Delia . . ."

"No. I have to put René next to Lady Alys. It's a favor. He's politicking. Or he damn well should be." Miles cocked his head. "If you're serious about Kareen, you and Duv are going to have to deal, you know. He's going to be one of the family."

"I can't help thinking his feelings about me must be . . . mixed."

"Come now, you saved his life." *Among other things.* "Have you seen him, since you got back from Beta?"

"Once, for about thirty seconds, when I was dropping off Kareen at her home, and he was coming out with Delia."

"So what did he say?"

"He said, *Hello, Mark.*"

"That sounds pretty unexceptionable."

"It was his tone of voice. That dead-level thing he does, y'know?"

"Well, yes, but you can't deduce anything from that."

"Exactly my point."

Miles grinned briefly. And just how serious was Mark about Kareen? He was attentive to her to the point of obsession, and the sense of sexual frustration rising from them both was like heat off a pavement in high summer. Who knew what had passed between them on Beta Colony? *My mother does, probably.* Countess Vorkosigan had better spies than ImpSec did. But if they were sleeping together, it wasn't in Vorkosigan House, according to Pym's informal security reports.

Pym himself entered at this point, to announce, "Lady Alys and Captain Illyan have arrived, m'lord."

This formality was scarcely necessary, as Aunt Alys was right at Pym's elbow, though she nodded brief approval at the Armsman as she passed into the dining room. Illyan strolled in after her, and favored the room with a benign smile. The retired ImpSec chief looked downright dapper, in a dark tunic and trousers that set off the gray at his temples; since their late-life romance had bloomed, Lady Alys had taken a firm hand in improving his somewhat dire civilian wardrobe. The sharp clothes did a lot to camouflage the disturbing vague look that clouded his eyes now and then, damn the enemy who'd so disabled him.

Aunt Alys swept down the table, inspecting the arrangements with a cool air that would have daunted a drill sergeant. "Very good, Miles," she said at last. The *Better than I would have expected of you* was unspoken, but understood. "Though your numbers are uneven."

"Yes, I know."

"Hm. Well, it can't be helped now. I want a word with Ma Kosti. Thank you, Pym, I'll find my way." She bustled out the server's door. Miles let her go, trusting that she would find all in order below, and that she would refrain from prosecuting her ongoing campaign to hire away his cook in the middle of the most important dinner party of his life.

"Good evening, Simon," Miles greeted his former boss. Illyan shook his hand cordially, and Mark's without hesitation. "I'm glad you could make it tonight. Did

Aunt Alys explain to you about Eka—about Madame
Vorsoisson?"

"Yes, and Ivan had a few comments as well. Something on the theme of fellows who fall into the muck-
hole and return with the gold ring."

"I haven't got to the gold ring part yet," said Miles
ruefully. "But that's certainly my plan. I'm looking forward to you all meeting her."

"She's the one, is she?"

"I hope so."

Illyan's smile sharpened at Miles's fervent tone. "Good
luck, son."

"Thanks. Oh, one word of warning. She's still in her
mourning year, you see. Did Alys or Ivan explain—"

He was interrupted by the return of Pym, who
announced that the Koudelka party had arrived, and he
had conveyed them to the library, as planned. It was
time to go play host in earnest.

Mark, who trod on Miles's heels all the way across
the house, paused in the antechamber to the great
library to give himself a desperate look in the mirror
there, and smooth his jacket down over his paunch. In
the library, Kou and Drou waited, all smiles; the
Koudelka girls were raiding the shelves. Duv and Delia
were seated together bent over an old book already.

Greetings were exchanged all around, and Armsman
Roic, on cue, began bringing out the hors d'oeuvres and
drinks. Over the years Miles had watched Count and
Countess Vorkosigan host what seemed a thousand parties and receptions here in Vorkosigan House, scarcely
one without some hidden or overt political agenda.
Surely he could manage this little one in style. Mark,
across the room, made himself properly attentive to
Kareen's parents. Lady Alys arrived from her inspection
tour, gave her nephew a short nod, and went to hang
on Illyan's arm. Miles listened for the door.

His heart beat faster at the sound of Pym's voice and
steps, but the next guests the Armsman ushered in were
only René and Tatya Vorbretten. The Koudelka girls
instantly made Tatya welcome. Things were certainly
starting well. At the sound of action at the distant front

door again, Miles abandoned René to make what he could of his opportunity with Lady Alys, and slipped out to check for the new arrivals. *This* time it was Lord Auditor Vorthys and his wife, and Ekaterin at last, yes!

The Professor and the Professora were gray blurs in his eyes, but Ekaterin glowed like a flame. She wore a sedate evening dress in some silky charcoal-gray fabric, but she was happily handing off a pair of dirty garden gloves to Pym. Her eyes were bright, and her cheeks bore a faint, exquisite flush. Miles concealed in a welcoming smile his thrill to see the pendant model Barrayar he'd given her lying skin-warmed against her creamy breast.

"Good evening, Lord Vorkosigan," she greeted him. "I'm pleased to report the first native Barrayaran plant is now growing in your garden."

"Clearly, I'll have to inspect it." He grinned at her. What a great excuse to nip out for a quiet moment together. Perhaps it might finally give him occasion to declare . . . no. No. Still much too premature. "Just as soon as I get everyone introduced, here." He offered her his arm, and she took it. Her warm scent made him a little dizzy.

Ekaterin hesitated at the party noise already pouring from the library as they approached, her hand tightening on his arm, but she took a breath, and plunged in with him. Since she already knew Mark and the Koudelka girls, whom Miles trusted would soon make her comfortable again, he made her known first to Tatya, who eyed her with interest and exchanged shy pleasantries. He then took her over to the long doors, took a slight breath himself, and introduced her to René, Illyan, and Lady Alys.

Miles was watching so anxiously for the signs of approval in Illyan's expression that he almost missed the blink of terror in Ekaterin's, as she found herself shaking the hand of the legend who'd run the dreaded Imperial Security for thirty iron years. But she rose to the occasion with scarcely a tremor. Illyan, who seemed blithely unconscious of his sinister effect, smiled upon her with all the admiration Miles could have hoped for.

There. Now people could mill about and drink and talk till it was time to herd them all in to be seated for dinner. Were they all in? No, he was still missing Ivan. And one other—should he send Mark to check—?

Ah, not necessary. Here came Dr. Borgos, all on his own. He poked his head around the door and entered diffidently. To Miles's surprise, he was all washed and combed and dressed in a perfectly respectable suit, if in the Escobaran style, that was entirely free of lab stains. Enrique smiled, and came up to Miles and Ekaterin. He reeked not of chemicals, but of cologne.

"Ekaterin, good evening!" he said happily. "Did you get my dissertation?"

"Yes, thank you."

His smile grew shyer still, and he stared down at his shoe. "Did you like it?"

"It was very impressive. Though it was a bit over my head, I'm afraid."

"I don't believe that. I'm sure you got the gist of it . . ."

"You flatter me, Enrique." She shook her head, but her smile said, *And you may flatter me some more.*

Miles went slightly stiff. *Enrique? Ekaterin? She doesn't even call me by my first name yet!* And she would never have accepted a comment on her physical beauty without flinching; had Enrique stumbled on an unguarded route to her heart that Miles had missed?

She added, "I think I followed the introductory sonnet, almost. Is that the usual style, for Escobaran academic papers? It seems very challenging."

"No, I made it up especially." He glanced up at her again, then down at his other shoe.

"It, um, scanned quite perfectly. Some of the rhymes seemed quite unusual."

Enrique brightened visibly.

Good God, Enrique was writing *poetry* to her? Yes, and why hadn't *he* thought of poetry? Besides the obvious reason of his absence of talent in that direction. He wondered if she'd like to read a really clever combat-drop mission plan, instead. Sonnets, damn. All he'd ever come up with in that line were limericks.

He stared at Enrique, who was now responding to her smile by twisting himself into something resembling a tall knotted bread-stick, with dawning horror. *Another* rival? And insinuated into his own household . . . ! *He's a guest. Your brother's guest, anyway. You can't have him assassinated.* Besides, the Escobaran was only twenty-four standard years old; she must see him as a mere puppy. *But maybe she likes puppies . . .*

"Lord Ivan Vorpatril," Pym's voice announced from the doorway. "Lord Dono Vorrutyer." The odd timbre in Pym's voice jerked Miles's head around even before his brain caught up with the unauthorized name accompanying Ivan. *Who?*

Ivan stood well clear of his new companion, but it was obvious by some remark the other was making that they'd come in together. Lord Dono was an intense-looking fellow of middle height with a close-trimmed black spade-beard, wearing Vor-style mourning garb, a black suit edged with gray which set off his athletic body. Had Ivan made a substitution in Miles's guest list without telling him? He should know better than to violate House Vorkosigan's security procedures like that . . . !

Miles strolled up to his cousin, Ekaterin still beside him—well, he hadn't exactly let go of her hand on his arm, but she hadn't tried to draw it from under his hand, either. Miles thought he knew on sight all his Vorrutyer relatives who could claim a lord's rank. Was this a more distant descendant of Pierre Le Sanguinaire, or some by-blow? The man was not young. Damn, where had he seen those electric brown eyes before . . . ?

"Lord Dono. How do you do." Miles proffered his hand, and the lithe man took it in a cheerful grip. Between one breath and the next the clue dropped, bricklike, and Miles added suavely, "You *have* been to Beta Colony, I perceive."

"Indeed, Lord Vorkosigan." Lord Dono's—Lady Donna who was, yes—white grin broadened in his black beard.

Ivan looked on with betrayed disappointment at this lack of a double-take.

"Or should I say, Lord Auditor Vorkosigan," Lord Dono went on. "I don't believe I've had the chance to congratulate you upon your new appointment.'

"Thank you," said Miles. "Permit me to introduce my friend, Madame Ekaterin Vorsoisson . . ."

Lord Dono kissed Ekaterin's hand with slightly too enthusiastic panache, bordering on a mockery of the gesture; Ekaterin returned an uncertain smile. They gavotted through the social niceties, while Miles's wits went on overdrive. Right. Clearly, the former Lady Donna did not have a clone of brother Pierre tucked away in a uterine replicator after all. It was breathtakingly plain what his legal tactic against Pierre's putative heir Richars was going to be instead. *Well, somebody had to try it, sooner or later.* And it would be a privilege to watch. "May I wish you the best of luck in your upcoming suit, Lord Dono?"

"Thank you." Lord Dono met his gaze directly. "Luck, of course, has nothing to do with it. May I discuss it in more detail with you, later on?"

Caution tempered his delight; Miles sidestepped. "I am, of course, but my father's proxy in the Council. As an Auditor, I am obliged to avoid party politics on my own behalf."

"I quite understand."

"But, ah . . . perhaps Ivan could reintroduce you to Count Vorbretten over there. He's dealing with a suit in the Council as well; you could compare valuable notes. And Lady Alys and Captain Illyan, of course. Professora Vorthys would also be extremely interested, I think; don't overlook any comments she might have. She's a noted expert on Barrayaran political history. Carry on, Ivan." Miles nodded demurely disinterested dismissal.

"*Thank* you, Lord Vorkosigan." Lord Dono's eyes were alight with appreciation of all the nuances, as he passed cordially on.

Miles wondered if he could sneak out to the next room and have a laughing fit. Or if he'd better make a vid call . . . He grabbed Ivan in passing, and stood on tiptoe to whisper, "Does Gregor know about this yet?"

"Yes," Ivan returned out of the corner of his mouth. "I made sure of that, first thing."

"Good man. What did he say?"

"Guess."

"*Let's see what happens?*"

"Got it in one."

"Heh." Relieved, Miles let Lord Dono tow Ivan off.

"Why are you laughing?" Ekaterin asked him.

"I am not laughing."

"Your eyes are laughing. I can tell."

He glanced around. Lord Dono had buttonholed René, and Lady Alys and Illyan were circling in curiously. The Professor and Commodore Koudelka were off in a corner discussing, from the snatches of words Miles could overhear, quality control problems in military procurement. He motioned Roic to bring wine, led Ekaterin into the remaining free corner, and brought her up to speed on Lady Donna/Lord Dono and the impending motion of impediment in as few words as he could manage.

"Goodness." Ekaterin's eyes widened, and her left hand stole to touch the back of her right, as if the pressure of Lord Dono's kiss still lingered there. But she managed to keep her other reactions to no more than a quick glance down the room, where Lord Dono was now attracting a crowd including all the Koudelka girls and their mother. "Did you know about this?"

"Not at all. That is, everyone knew she'd spiked Richars and gone to Beta Colony, but not why. It makes perfect sense now, in an absurd kind of way."

"Absurd?" said Ekaterin doubtfully. "I should think it would have taken a great deal of courage." She took a sip of her drink, then added in a thoughtful tone, "And anger."

Miles back-pedaled quickly. "Lady Donna never suffered fools gladly."

"Really?" Ekaterin, an odd look in her eyes, drifted away down the room toward this new show.

Before he could follow her, Ivan appeared at his elbow, a glass of wine already half-empty in his hand. Miles didn't want to talk with Ivan. He wanted to talk with *Ekaterin*. He murmured nonetheless, "That's quite a date you brought. I would never have suspected you of such Betan breadth of taste, Ivan."

Ivan glowered at him. "I might have known I'd get no sympathy from you."

"Bit of a shock, was it?"

"I damn near passed out right there in the shuttleport. Byerly Vorrutyer set me up for it, the little sneak."

"By knew?"

"Sure did. In on it from the beginning, I gather."

Duv Galeni too drifted up, in time to hear this; seeing Duv detached from Delia at last, his future father-in-law Commodore Koudelka and the Professor joined them. Miles let Ivan explain the new arrival, in his own words. Miles's guess was confirmed that Ivan hadn't had any hint of this at the time he'd asked his host's permission to bring Donna to the dinner, smugly plotting his welcome-home campaign upon her, well, not virtue; oh, oh, oh, to have been the invisible eye at the moment Ivan discovered the change . . . !

"Did this catch ImpSec by surprise too?" Commodore Koudelka inquired blandly of Commodore Galeni.

"Wouldn't know. Not my department." Galeni took a firm sip of his wine. "Domestic Affairs' problem."

Both officers glanced around at a peal of laughter from the group at the far end of the room; it was Madame Koudelka's laugh. An echoing cascade of giggles hushed conspiratorially, and Olivia Koudelka glanced over her shoulder at the men.

"What *are* they laughing at?" said Galeni doubtfully.

"Us, probably," growled Ivan, and slouched off to find more wine for his empty glass.

Koudelka stared down the room, and shook his head. "Donna Vorrutyer, good God."

Every woman in the party including Lady Alys was now clustered in evident fascination around Lord Dono, who was gesturing and holding forth to them in lowered tones. Enrique was grazing the hors d'oeuvres, and staring at Ekaterin in bovine rapture. Illyan, abandoned by Alys, was leafing absently through a book, one of the illustrated herbals Miles had laid out earlier.

It was time to serve dinner, Miles decided firmly. Where Ivan *and* Lord Dono would be barricaded behind a wall of older, married ladies and their spouses. He broke away for a quiet word with Pym, who departed to pass the word belowstairs, and returned shortly to formally announce the meal.

The couples resorted themselves and shuffled out of the great library, across the anteroom and the paved hall, and through the intervening series of chambers. Miles, in the lead with Ekaterin recaptured on his arm, encountered Mark and Ivan conspiratorially exiting the formal dining room. They turned around and rejoined the throng. Miles's sudden suspicion was horribly confirmed, out of the corner of his eye, as he passed up the table; his hour of strategic planning with the place cards had just been disarranged.

All his carefully rehearsed conversational gambits were for people now on the other end of the table. Seating was utterly randomized—no, not randomized, he realized. Reprioritized. Ivan's goal had clearly been to get Lord Dono as far away from himself as possible; Ivan now was taking his chair at the far end of the table by Mark, while Lord Dono seated himself in the place Miles had intended for René Vorbretten. Duv, Drou, and Kou had somehow all migrated Miles-ward, farther from Mark. Mark still kept Kareen at *his* right hand, but Ekaterin had been bumped down the other side of the table, beyond Illyan, who was still on Miles's immediate left. It seemed no one had quite dared touch Illyan's card. Miles would now have to speak across Illyan to converse with her, no *sotto voce* remarks possible.

Aunt Alys, looking a little confused, seated herself at Miles's honored right, directly across from Illyan. She'd clearly noticed the switches, but failed Miles's last hope of help by saying nothing, merely letting her eyebrows flick up. Duv Galeni found his future mother-in-law Drou between himself and Delia. Illyan glanced at the cards and seated Ekaterin between himself and Duv, and the *accompli* was *fait*.

Miles kept smiling; Mark, ten places distant, was too far away to catch the *I-will-get-you-for-this-later* edge to it. Maybe it was just as well.

Conversations, though not the ones Miles had anticipated, began anew around the table as Pym, Roic, and Jankowski, playing butler and footmen, bustled about and began to serve. Miles watched Ekaterin with some concern for signs of stress, trapped as she was between her formidable ImpSec seatmates, but her expression remained calm and pleasant as the Armsmen plied her with excellent food and wine.

It wasn't until the second course appeared that Miles realized what was bothering him about the food. He had confidently left the details to Ma Kosti, but this wasn't quite the menu they'd discussed. Certain items were ... different. The hot consommé was now an exquisite cold creamy fruit soup, decorated with edible flowers. In honor of Ekaterin, maybe? The vinegar-and-herb salad dressing had been replaced by something with a pale, creamy base. The aromatic herb spread, passed around with the bread, bore no relation to butter ...

Bug vomit. They've slipped in that damned bug vomit.

Ekaterin twigged to it, too, about the time Pym brought round the bread; Miles spotted it by her slight hesitation, glance through her lashes at Enrique and Mark, and completely dead-pan continuation in spreading her piece and taking a firm bite. By not the smallest other sign did she reveal that she knew what she was swallowing.

Miles tried to indicate to her that she didn't have to eat it by pointing surreptitiously at the little herbed bug-butter crock and desperately raising his eyebrows; she merely smiled and shrugged.

"Hm?" Illyan, between them, murmured with his mouth full.

"Nothing, sir," Miles said hastily. "Nothing at all." Leaping up and screaming, *Stop, stop, you're all eating hideous bug stuff!* to his high-powered guests, would be ... startling. Bug vomit wasn't, after all, poisonous. If nobody told them, they'd never know. He bit into dry bread, and chased it with a large gulp of wine.

The salad plates were removed. Three-quarters of the way down the table, Enrique dinged on his wineglass with his knife, cleared his throat, and stood up.

"Thank you for your attention . . ." He cleared his throat again. "I've enjoyed the hospitality of Vorkosigan House, as I'm sure we all have tonight—" agreeing murmurs rose around the table; Enrique brightened and burbled on. "I have a gift of thanks I would like to present to Lord—to Miles, Lord Vorkosigan," he smiled at his successful precision, "and I thought that now would be a good time."

Miles was seized with certainty that whatever it was, now would be a *terrible* time. He stared down-table at Mark with an inquiring glower, *Do you know what the hell this is all about?* Mark returned an unreassuring *No clue, sorry,* shrug, and eyed Enrique with growing concern.

Enrique removed a box from his jacket and trod up the room to lay it between Miles and Lady Alys. Illyan and Galeni, across the table, tensed in ImpSec-trained paranoia; Galeni's chair slid back slightly. Miles wanted to reassure them that it wasn't likely to be explosive, but with Enrique, how could one be sure? It was bigger than the last box the butter-bug crew had presented to him. Miles prayed for maybe one of those tacky sets of gold-plated dress spurs that had been a brief rage a year ago, mostly among young men who'd never crossed a horse in their lives, anything but . . .

Enrique proudly lifted the lid. It wasn't a bigger butter bug; it was three butter bugs. Three butter bugs whose carapaces flashed brown and silver as they scrabbled over one another, feelers waving . . . Lady Alys recoiled and strangled a squeak; Illyan jerked upright in alarm for her. Lord Dono leaned forward around her in curiosity, and his black brows shot up.

Miles, mouth slightly open, bent to stare in paralyzed fascination. Yes, it was indeed the Vorkosigan crest stenciled in bright silver on each tiny, repulsive brown back; a lace-edge of silver outlined the vestigial wings in exact imitation of the decorations on the sleeves of his Armsmen's uniforms. The replication of his House colors was precise. You could identify the famous crest at a glance. You could probably identify it at a glance from two meters away. Dinner service ground to a halt as Pym, Jankowski, and Roic gathered to look over his shoulder into the box.

Lord Dono glanced from the butter bugs to Miles's face, and back. "Are they . . . are they perhaps a weapon?" he ventured cautiously.

Enrique laughed, and launched into an enthusiastic explanation of his new model butter bugs, complete with the totally unnecessary information that they were the source of the very fine improved bug butter base underlying the soup, salad dressing, and bread spread recipes. Miles's mental picture of Enrique bent over a magnifying glass with a teeny, tiny paintbrush shredded into vapor as Enrique explained that the patterns weren't, oh no, of course not, *applied*, but rather, genetically created, and would breed true with each succeeding generation.

Pym looked at the bugs, glanced at the sleeve of his proud uniform, stared again at the deadly parody of his insignia the creatures now bore, and shot Miles a look of heartbreaking despair, a silent cry which Miles had no trouble interpreting as, *Please, m'lord, please, can we take him out and kill him* now?

From the far end of the table he heard Kareen's worried voice whisper, "What's going on? Why isn't he saying anything? Mark, go look . . ."

Miles leaned back, and grated through his teeth to Pym at the lowest possible volume, "He didn't intend it as an insult." *It just came out that way. My father's, my grandfather's, my House's sigil on those pullulating cockroaches . . . !*

Pym returned him a fixed smile over eyes blazing with fury. Aunt Alys remained rather frozen in place. Duv Galeni had his head cocked to one side, his eyes crinkling and his lips parted in who-knew-what inner reflections, and Miles wasn't about to ask, either. Lord Dono was even worse; he now had his napkin half stuffed into his mouth, and his face was flushed as he snorted through his nose. Illyan watched with his finger to his lips, and almost no expression at all, except for a faint delight in his eyes that made Miles writhe inside. Mark arrived, and bent to look. His face paled, and he glanced sideways at Miles in alarm. Ekaterin had her hand over her mouth; her eyes upon him were dark and wide.

Of all his riveted audience, only one's opinion mattered.

This was the woman whose late unlamented husband had been given over to . . . what displays of temper? What public or private rages? Miles swallowed his gibbering opinion of Enrique, Escobarans, bioengineering, his brother Mark's insane notions of entrepreneurship, and Liveried Vorkosigan Vomit Bugs, blinked, took a deep breath, and smiled.

"Thank you, Enrique. Your talent leaves me speechless. But perhaps you ought to put the girls away now. You wouldn't want them to get . . . tired." Gently, he replaced the lid of the box, and handed it back to the Escobaran. Across from him, Ekaterin softly exhaled. Lady Alys's brows rose in impressed surprise. Enrique marched back happily to his place. Where he proceeded to explain and demonstrate his Vorkosigan butter bugs to everyone who had been seated too far away to see the show, including Count and Countess Vorbretten opposite him. It was a real conversation-stopper, except for an unfortunate crack of laughter from Ivan, quickly choked down at a sharp reproof from Martya.

Miles realized that food had ceased to appear in the previous smooth stream. He motioned the still-transfixed Pym over, and murmured, "Will you bring the next course now, please?" He added in a grim undertone, "*Check* it first."

Pym, jerked back to attention to his duties, muttered, "Yes, m'lord. I understand."

The next course proved to be poached chilled Vorkosigan District lake salmon, without bug butter sauce, just some hastily-cut lemon slices. Good. Miles breathed temporary relief.

Ekaterin at last worked up the nerve to attempt a conversational gambit upon one of her seatmates. One couldn't very well ask an ImpSec officer, *So, how was work today?* so she fell back on what she clearly thought was a more generalized opener. "It's unusual to meet a Komarran in the Imperial Service," she said to Galeni. "Does your family support your career choice?"

Galeni's eyes widened just slightly, and narrowed again at Miles, who realized belatedly that his predinner briefing to Ekaterin, designed to accentuate the positive, hadn't included the fact that most of Galeni's family had died in various Komarran revolts and their aftermaths. And the peculiar relation between Duv and Mark was something he hadn't even begun to figure out how to broach to her. He was frantically trying to guess how to telepathically convey this to Duv, when Galeni replied merely, "My new one does." Delia, who had stiffened in alarm, melted in a smile.

"Oh." It was instantly apparent from Ekaterin's face that she knew she'd misstepped, but not how. She glanced at Lady Alys, who, perhaps still stunned by the butter bugs, was bemusedly studying her plate and missed the silent plea.

Never one to let a damsel flounder in distress, Commodore Koudelka cut in heartily, "So, Miles, speaking of Komarr, do you think their solar mirror repair appropriations are going to fly in Council?"

Oh, perfect segue. Miles flashed his old mentor a brief smile of gratitude. "Yes, I think so. Gregor's thrown his weight behind it, as I'd hoped he would."

"Good," said Galeni judiciously. "That will help on all sides." He gave Ekaterin a short, forgiving nod.

The difficult moment passed; in the relieved pause while people marshaled their contributory bits of political gossip to follow up this welcome lead, Enrique Borgos's cheerful voice floated up the table, disastrously clear:

"—will make so much profit, Kareen, you and Mark can buy yourselves another one of those amazing trips to the Orb when you get back to Beta. As many as you want, in fact." He sighed enviously. "I wish *I* had somebody to go there with."

The Orb of Unearthly Delights was one of Beta Colony's most famous, or notorious, pleasure domes; it had a galactic reputation. If your tastes weren't quite vile enough to direct you on to Jackson's Whole, the range of licensed, medically supervised pleasures which could be purchased at the Orb was enough to boggle most minds. Miles entertained a brief, soaring hope that Kareen's parents had never heard of it. Mark could pretend it was a Betan science museum, anything but—

Commodore Koudelka had just taken a mouthful of wine to chase his last bite of salmon. The atomized spray arced nearly to Delia, seated across from her father. A lungful of wine in a man that age was an alarming event in any case; Olivia patted his back in hesitant worry, as he buried his reddening face in his napkin and gasped. Drou half-pushed her chair back, as she hesitated between going up around the table to assist her husband or, possibly, down the table to strangle Mark. Mark was no help at all; guilty terror drained his fat cheeks of blood, producing a suety, unflattering effect.

Kou got just enough breath back to gasp at Mark, "*You* took *my* daughter to the *Orb?*"

Kareen, utterly panicked, blurted, "It was part of his therapy!"

Mark, panicked worse, added in desperate exculpation, "We got a Clinic discount . . ."

Miles had often thought that he wanted to be there to see the look on Duv Galeni's face when he learned that Mark was his potential brother-in-law. Miles now took the wish back, but it was too late. He'd seen Galeni look frozen before, but never so . . . *stuffed*. Kou was breathing again, which would be reassuring if it weren't for the slight tinge of hyperventilation. Olivia stifled a nervous giggle. Lord Dono's eyes were bright with appreciation; he surely knew all about the Orb, possibly in both his current and former sexual incarnations. The Professora, next to Enrique, leaned forward to take a curious look up and down the table.

Ekaterin looked terribly worried, but not, Miles noted, surprised. Had Mark confided history to her that he hadn't seen fit to trust to his own brother? Or had she and Kareen already become close enough friends to share such secrets, one of those women-things? And if so, what had Ekaterin seen fit to confide to Kareen in return about *him*, and was there any way he could find out . . . ?

Drou, after a notable hesitation, sank back down. An ominous, blighted we-will-discuss-this-later silence fell.

Lady Alys was alive to every nuance; her social self-control was such that only Miles and Illyan were close enough to her to detect her wince. Well able to set a tone no one dared ignore, she weighed in at last with, "The presentation of the mirror repair as a wedding gift has proven most popular with—Miles, *what* has that animal got in its mouth?"

Miles's confused query of *What animal*? was answered before he even voiced it by the thump of multiple little feet across the dining room's polished floor. The half-grown black-and-white kitten was being chased by its all-black litter mate; for a catlet with its mouth stuffed full, it managed to emit an astonishingly loud *mrowr* of possession. It scrabbled across the wide oak boards, then gained traction on the priceless antique hand-woven carpet, till it caught a claw and flipped itself over. Its rival promptly pounced upon it, but failed to force it to give up its prize. A couple of insectoid legs waved feebly among the quivering white whiskers, and a brown-and-silver wing carapace gave a dying shudder.

"My butter bug!" cried Enrique in horror, shoved back his chair, and pounced, rather more effectively, on the feline culprit. "Give it up, you murderess!" He retrieved the mangled bug, much the worse for wear, from the jaws of death. The black kitten stretched itself up his leg, and waved a frantic paw, *Me, me, give me one too!*

Excellent! thought Miles, smiling fondly at the kittens. *The vomit bugs have a natural predator after all!* He was just evolving a rapid-deployment plan for Vorkosigan House's guardcats when his brain caught up with itself. The kitten had already had the butter bug in its mouth when it had scampered into the dining room. Therefore—

"Dr. Borgos, where did that cat find that bug?" Miles asked. "I thought you had them all locked down. In fact," he glanced down the table at Mark, "you promised me they would be."

"Ah . . ." Enrique said. Miles didn't know what chain of thought the Escobaran was thumbing down, but he could see the jerk when he got to the end. "Oh. Excuse me. There's something I have to check in the lab." Enrique smiled unreassuringly, dropped the kitten on his vacated chair, spun on his heel, and hurried out of the dining room toward the back stairs.

Mark said hastily, "I think I'd better go with him," and followed.

Filled with foreboding, Miles set his napkin down, and murmured quietly, "Aunt Alys, Simon, take over for me, would you?" He joined the parade, pausing only long enough to direct Pym to serve more wine. Lots more. Immediately.

Miles caught up with Enrique and Mark at the door of the laundry-cum-laboratory one floor below just in time to hear the Escobaran's cry of *Oh, no!* Grimly, he shouldered past Mark to find Enrique kneeling by a large tray, one of the butter bug houses, which now lay at an angle between the box upon which it had been perched, and the floor. Its screen top was knocked askew. Inside, a single Vorkosigan-liveried butter bug, which was missing two legs on one side, scrambled about in forlorn circles but failed to escape over the side-wall.

"What happened?" Miles hissed to Enrique.

"They're *gone*," Enrique replied, and began to crawl around the floor, looking under things. "Those cursed cats must have knocked the tray over. I'd pulled it out to select your presentation bugs. I wanted the biggest and best. It was all right when I left it . . ."

"*How many* bugs were in this tray?"

"All of them, the entire genetic grouping. About two hundred individuals."

Miles stared around the lab. No Vorkosigan-liveried bugs were visible anywhere. He thought about what a large, old, creaky structure Vorkosigan House really was. Cracks in the floors, cracks in the walls, tiny fissures of access everywhere; spaces under the floorboards, behind the wainscoting, up in the attics, inside the old plastered walls . . .

The worker bugs, Mark had said, *would just wander about*

till they died, end of story . . . "You still have the queen, presumably? You can, ah, recover your genetic resource, eh?" Miles began to walk slowly along the walls, staring down intently. No brown-and-silver flashes caught his straining eye.

"Um," said Enrique.

Miles chose his words carefully. "You assured me the queens couldn't move."

"*Mature* queens can't move, that's true," Enrique explained, climbing to his feet again, and shaking his head. "*Immature* queens, however, can scuttle like lightning."

Miles thought it through; it took only a split-second. Vorkosigan-liveried vomit bugs. Vorkosigan-liveried vomit bugs *all over Vorbarr Sultana.*

There was an ImpSec trick, which involved grabbing a man by the collar and giving it a little half-twist, and doing a thing with the knuckles; applied correctly, it cut off both blood circulation and breath. Miles was absently pleased to see that he hadn't lost his touch, despite his new civilian vocation. He drew Enrique's darkening face down toward his own. Kareen, breathless, arrived at the lab door.

"Borgos. You will have every one of those goddamned vomit bugs, and *especially* their queen, retrieved and accounted for at least six hours before Count and Countess Vorkosigan are due to walk in the door tomorrow afternoon. Because five hours and fifty-nine minutes before my parents arrive here, I am calling in a professional exterminator to take care of the infestation, that means any and all vomit bugs left outstanding, do you understand? No exceptions, no mercy."

"*No, no!*" Enrique managed to wail, despite his lack of oxygen. "You *mustn't . . .*"

"Lord Vorkosigan!" Ekaterin's shocked voice came from the door. It had some of the surprise effect of being hit from ambush by a stunner beam. Miles's hand sprang guiltily open, and Enrique staggered upright again, drawing breath in a huge strangled wheeze.

"Don't stop on my account, Miles," said Kareen coldly. She stalked into the lab, Ekaterin behind her.

"Enrique, you idiot, how *could* you mention the Orb in front of my parents! Have you no sense?"

"You've known him for this long, and you have to ask?" said Mark direfully.

"And how did you—" her angry gaze swung to Mark, "how did he find out about it anyway—Mark?"

Mark shrank slightly.

"Mark never said it was a secret—I thought it sounded romantic. Lord Vorkosigan, please! Don't call an exterminator! I'll get the girls all back, I promise! Somehow—" Tears welled in Enrique's eyes.

"Calm down, Enrique!" Ekaterin said soothingly. "I'm sure," she cast Miles a doubtful look, "Lord Vorkosigan won't order your poor bugs killed. You'll find them again."

"I have a *time* limit here . . ." Miles muttered through his teeth. He could just picture the scene, tomorrow afternoon or evening, of himself explaining to the returning Viceroy and Vicereine just what those tiny retching noises coming from their walls were. Maybe he could shove the task of apprising them onto Mark—

"If you like, Enrique, I'll stay and help you hunt," Ekaterin volunteered sturdily. She frowned at Miles.

The sensation was like an arrow through his heart, *Urk*. Now *there* was a scenario: Ekaterin and Enrique with their heads heroically, and closely, bent together to save the Poor Bugs from the evil threats of the villainous Lord Vorkosigan . . . Grudgingly, he back-pedaled. "After dinner," he suggested. "We'll all come back after dinner and help." Yes, if anyone was going to crawl around on the floor hunting bugs alongside Ekaterin, it would be him, dammit. "The Armsmen too." He pictured Pym's joy at the news of this task, and cringed inside. "For now, perhaps we had better return and make polite conversation and all that," Miles went on. "Except Dr. Borgos, who will be busy."

"I'll stay and help him," Mark offered brightly.

"What?" cried Kareen. "And send me back up there with my parents all alone? *And* my sisters—I'll never hear the end of this from them . . ."

Miles shook his head in exasperation. "Why in God's

name did you take Kareen to the Orb in the first place, Mark?"

Mark stared at him in disbelief. "Why d'you *think*?"

"Well . . . yes . . . but surely you knew it wasn't, um, wasn't, um . . . proper for a young Barrayaran la—"

"Miles, you howling hypocrite!" said Kareen indignantly. "When Gran' Tante Naismith told us you'd been there yourself—*several* times . . . !"

"That was duty," Miles said primly. "It's astounding how much interstellar military and industrial espionage gets filtered through the Orb. You'd better believe Betan security tracks it, too."

"Oh, yeah?" said Mark. "And are we also supposed to believe you never once sampled the services while you were waiting for your contacts—?"

Miles could recognize the moment for a strategic retreat when he saw it. "I think we should all go eat dinner now. Or it will burn up or dry out or something, and Ma Kosti will be very angry with us for spoiling her presentation. And she'll go work for Aunt Alys instead, and we'll all have to go back to eating Reddi-Meals."

This hideous threat reached both Mark and Kareen. Yes, and who *had* inspired his cook to come up with all those tasty bug butter recipes? Ma Kosti surely hadn't volunteered on her own. It reeked of conspiracy.

He exhaled, and offered his arm to Ekaterin. After a moment of hesitation, and a worried glance back at Enrique, she took it, and Miles managed to get them all marshaled out of the lab and back upstairs to the dining room again without anyone bolting off.

"Was all well, belowstairs, m'lord?" Pym inquired in a concerned undervoice.

"We'll talk about it later," Miles returned, equally *sotto voce*. "Start the next course. And offer more wine."

"Should we wait for Dr. Borgos?"

"No. He'll be occupied."

Pym gave a disquieted twitch, but moved off about his duties. Aunt Alys, bless her etiquette, didn't ask for enlargement, but led the conversation immediately onto neutral topics; her mention of the Emperor's wedding diverted most people's thoughts at once. Possibly excepted were the thoughts of Mark and Commodore Koudelka, who eyed each other in wary silence. Miles wondered if he ought to privately warn Kou what a bad idea it would be to pull his swordstick on Mark, or whether that might do more harm than good. Pym topped up Miles's own wineglass before Miles could explain that his whispered instructions hadn't been meant to apply to himself. What the hell. A certain . . . numbness, was beginning to seem like an attractive state.

He was not at all sure if Ekaterin was having a good time; she'd gone all quiet again, and glanced occasionally toward Dr. Borgos's empty place. Though Lord Dono's remarks made her laugh, twice. The former Lady Donna made a startlingly good-looking man, Miles realized on closer study. Witty, exotic, and just possibly heir to a Countship . . . and, come to think of it, with the most appalling unfair advantage in love-making expertise.

The Armsmen cleared away the plates for the main course, which had been grilled vat beef fillet with a very quick pepper garnish, accompanied by a powerful deep red wine. Dessert appeared: sculpted mounds of frozen creamy ivory substance bejeweled with a gorgeous arrangement of glazed fresh fruit. Miles caught Pym, who had been avoiding his eye, by the sleeve in passing, and leaned over for a word behind his hand.

"Pym, is that what I think it is?"

"Couldn't be helped, m'lord," Pym muttered back in wary self-exculpation. "Ma Kosti said it was that or nothing. She's still right furious about the sauces, and says she wants a word with you after this."

"Oh. I see. Well. Carry on."

He picked up his spoon, and took a valiant bite. His guests followed suit doubtfully, except for Ekaterin, who regarded her portion with every evidence of surprised delight, and leaned forward to exchange a smile with Kareen, downtable; Kareen returned her a mysterious but triumphant high-sign. To make it even worse, the stuff was meltingly delicious, seeming to lock into every primitive pleasure-receptor in Miles's mouth at once. The sweet and potent golden dessert wine followed it with an

aromatic shellburst on his palate that complemented the
frozen bug stuff perfectly. He could have cried. He smiled
tightly, and drank, instead. His dinner party limped on
somehow.

Talk of Gregor and Laisa's wedding allowed Miles to
supply a nice, light, amusing anecdote about his duties
in obtaining, and transporting, a wedding gift from the
people of his District, a life-sized sculpture of a guerilla
soldier on horseback done in maple sugar. This won a
brief smile from Ekaterin at last, this time toward the
right fellow. He mentally marshaled a leading question
about gardens to draw her out; she could sparkle, he
was sure, if only she had the right straight line. He
briefly regretted not priming Aunt Alys for this ploy,
which would have been more subtle, but in his original plan, she hadn't been going to be seated right
there—

Miles's pause had lasted just a little too long. Genially
taking his turn to fill it, Illyan turned to Ekaterin.

"Speaking of weddings, Madame Vorsoisson, how long
has Miles been courting you? Have you awarded him
a date yet? Personally, I think you ought to string him
along and make him work for it."

A chill flush plunged to the pit of Miles's stomach.
Alys bit her lip. Even *Galeni* winced.

Olivia looked up in confusion. "I thought we weren't
supposed to mention that yet."

Kou, next to her, muttered, "Hush, lovie."

Lord Dono, with malicious Vorrutyer innocence,
turned to her and inquired, "What weren't we supposed
to mention?"

"Oh, but if Captain Illyan said it, it must be all right,"
Olivia concluded.

Captain Illyan had his brains blown out last year, thought
Miles. *He is not all right. All right is precisely what he is
not . . .*

Her gaze crossed Miles's. "Or maybe . . ."

Not, Miles finished silently for her.

Ekaterin's face, animate and amused moments ago,
was turning to sculpted marble. It was not an instan-
taneous process, but it was relentless, implacable,

geologic. The weight of it, pressing on Miles's heart, was crushing. *Pygmalion in reverse; I turn breathing women to white stone....* He knew that bleak and desert look; he'd seen it one bad day on Komarr, and had hoped never to see it in her lovely face again.

Miles's sinking heart collided with his drunken panic. *I can't afford to lose this one, I can't, I can't.* Forward momentum, forward momentum and bluff, those had won battles for him before.

"Yes, ah, heh, quite, well, so, that reminds me, Madame Vorsoisson, I'd been meaning to ask you—will you marry me?"

Dead silence reigned all along the table.

Ekaterin made no response at all, at first. For a moment, it seemed as though she had not even heard his words, and Miles almost yielded to a suicidal impulse to repeat himself more loudly. Aunt Alys buried her face in her hands. Miles could feel his breathless grin grow sickly, and slide down his face. *No, no. What I should have said—what I meant to say was ... please pass the bug butter? Too late ...*

She visibly unlocked her throat, and spoke. Her words fell from her lips like ice chips, singly and shattering. "How strange. And here I thought you were interested in gardens. Or so you told me."

You lied to me hung in the air between them, unspoken, thunderously loud.

So yell. Scream. Throw something. Stomp on me all up and down, it'll be all right, it'll hurt good—I can deal with that—

Ekaterin took a breath, and Miles's soul rocketed in hope, but it was only to push back her chair, set her napkin down by her half-eaten dessert, turn, and walk away up the table. She paused by the Professora only long enough to bend down and murmur, "Aunt Vorthys, I'll see you at home."

"But dear, will you be all right ...?" The Professora found herself addressing empty air, as Ekaterin strode on. Her steps quickened as she neared the door, till she was almost running. The Professora glanced back and made a helpless, how-could-you-do-this, or maybe that was, how-could-you-do-this-you-idiot, gesture at Miles.

The rest of your life is walking out the door. Do something. Miles's chair fell backwards with a bang as he scrambled out of it. "Ekaterin, wait, we have to talk—"

He didn't run till he passed the doorway, pausing only long enough to slam it, and a couple of intervening ones, shut between the dinner party and themselves. He caught up with her in the entry hall, as she tried the door and fell back; it was, of course, security-locked.

"Ekaterin, wait, listen to me, I can explain," he panted.

She turned to give him a disbelieving stare, as though he were a Vorkosigan-liveried butter bug she'd just found floating in her soup.

"I have to talk to you. You have to talk to me," he demanded desperately.

"Indeed," she said after a moment, white about the lips. "There is something I need to say. Lord Vorkosigan, I resign my commission as your landscape designer. As of this moment, you no longer employ me. I will send the designs and planting schedules on to you tomorrow, to pass on to my successor."

"What good will those do me?!"

"If a garden was what you really wanted from me, then they are all you'll need. Right?"

He tested the possible answers on his tongue. *Yes* was right out. So was *no*. Wait a minute—

"Couldn't I have wanted both?" he suggested hopefully. He continued more strongly, "I wasn't lying to you. I just wasn't saying everything that was on my mind, because, dammit, you weren't ready to hear it, because you aren't half-healed yet from being worked over for ten years by that ass Tien, and I could see it, and you could see it, and even your Aunt Vorthys could see it, and *that's* the truth."

By the jerk of her head, that one had hit home, but she only said, in a dead-level voice, "Please open your door now, Lord Vorkosigan."

"Wait, listen—"

"You have manipulated me enough," she said. "You've played on my . . . my *vanity*—"

"Not vanity," he protested. "Skill, pride, drive—anyone could see you just needed scope, opportunity—"

"You *are* used to getting your own way, aren't you, Lord Vorkosigan. Any way you can." Now her voice was horribly dispassionate. "Trapping me in front of everyone like that."

"That was an accident. Illyan didn't get the word, see, and—"

"Unlike everyone else? You're *worse* than Vormoncrief! I might just as well have accepted *his* offer!"

"Huh? What did Alexi—I mean, no, but, but—whatever you want, I want to give it to you, Ekaterin. Whatever you need. Whatever it is."

"You can't give me my own soul." She stared, not at him, but inward, on what vista he could not imagine. "The garden could have been *my* gift. You took that away too."

Her last words arrested his gibbering. What? Wait, now they were getting down to something, elusive, but utterly vital—

A large groundcar was pulling up outside, under the porte cochère. No more visitors were due; how had they got past the ImpSec gate guard without notification of Pym? Dammit, no interruptions, not *now*, when she was just beginning to open up, or at least open fire—

On the heels of this thought, Pym hurtled through the side doors into the foyer. "Sorry, m'lord—sorry to intrude, but—"

"*Pym.*" Ekaterin's voice was nearly a shout, cracking, defying the tears lacing it. "*Open the damned door and let me out.*"

"*Yes* milady!" Pym snapped to attention, and his hand spasmed to the security pad.

The doors swung wide. Ekaterin stormed blindly through, head-down, into the chest of a startled, stocky, white-haired man wearing a colorful shirt and a pair of disreputable, worn black trousers. Ekaterin bounced off him, and had her hands caught up by the, to her, inexplicable stranger. A tall, tired-looking woman in rumpled travel-skirts, with long roan-red hair tied back at the nape of her neck, stepped up beside them, saying, "What in the world . . . ?"

"Excuse me, miss, are you all right?" the white-haired man rumbled in a raspy baritone. He stared piercingly at Miles, lurching out of the light of the foyer in Ekaterin's wake.

"No," she choked. "I need—I want an auto-cab, please."

"Ekaterin, no, wait," Miles gasped.

"I want an auto-cab *right now*."

"The gate guard will be happy to call one for you," the red-haired woman said soothingly. Countess Cordelia Vorkosigan, Vicereine of Sergyar—*Mother*—stared even more ominously at her wheezing son. "And see you safely into it. Miles, why are you harrying this young lady?" And more doubtfully, "Are we interrupting business, or pleasure?"

From thirty years of familiarity, Miles had no trouble unraveling this cryptic shorthand to be a serious query of, *Have we walked in on, perhaps, an official Auditorial interrogation gone wrong, or is this one of your personal screwups again?* God knew what Ekaterin made of it. One bright note: if Ekaterin never spoke to him again, he'd never be put to explain the Countess's peculiar Betan sense of humor to her.

"My dinner party," Miles grated. "It's just breaking up." *And sinking. All souls feared lost.* It was redundant to ask, *What are you doing here?* His parents' jumpship had obviously made orbit early, and they had left the bulk of their entourage to follow on tomorrow, while they came straight downside to sleep in their own bed. How had he rehearsed this vitally-important, utterly-critical meeting, again? "Mother, Father, let me introduce—*she's getting away!*"

As a new distraction rose from the hallway at Miles's back, Ekaterin slipped through the shadows all the way to the gate. The Koudelkas, having perhaps intelligently concluded that this party was over, were decamping en masse, but the wait-till-we-get-home conversation had undergone a jump-start. Kareen's voice was protesting;

the Commodore's overrode it, saying, "You *will* come home now. You're not staying another minute in this house."

"I *have* to come back. I *work* here."

"Not any more, you don't—"

Mark's harried voice dogged along, "Please, sir, Commodore, Madame Koudelka, you mustn't blame Kareen—"

"You can't stop me!" Kareen declaimed.

Commodore Koudelka's eye fell on the returnees as the rolling altercation piled up in the hallway. "Ha—Aral!" he snarled. "Do you realize what your son has been up to?"

The Count blinked. "Which one?" he asked mildly.

The chance of the light caught Mark's face, as he heard this off-hand affirmation of his identity. Even in the chaos of his hopes pinwheeling to destruction, Miles was glad to have seen the brief awed look that passed over those fat-distorted features. *Oh, Brother. Yeah. This is why men follow this man—*

Olivia tugged her mother's sleeve. "Mama," she whispered urgently, "can I go home with Tatya?"

"Yes, dear, I think that might be a good idea," said Drou distractedly, clearly looking ahead; Miles wasn't sure if she was cutting down Kareen's potential allies in the brewing battle, or just the anticipated noise level.

René and Tatya looked as though they would have been glad to sneak out quietly under the covering fire, but Lord Dono, who had somehow attached himself to their party, paused just long enough to say cheerily, "*Thank* you, Lord Vorkosigan, for a most memorable evening." He nodded cordially to Count and Countess Vorkosigan, as he followed the Vorbrettens to their groundcar. Well, the operation hadn't changed Donna/Dono's vile grip on irony, unfortunately . . .

"Who was that?" asked Count Vorkosigan. "Looks familiar, somehow . . ."

A distracted-looking Enrique, his wiry hair half on-end, prowled into the great hall from the back entry. He had a jar in one hand, and what Miles could only dub Stink-on-a-Stick in the other: a wand with a wad of sickly-sweet scent-soaked fiber attached to its end, which he waved along the baseboards. "Here, buggy, buggy," he cooed plaintively. "Come to Papa, that's the good girls . . ." He paused, and peered worriedly under a side-table. "Buggy-buggy . . . ?"

"Now . . . *that* cries out for an explanation," murmured the Count, watching him in arrested fascination.

Out by the front gate, an auto-cab's door slammed; its fans whirred as it pulled away into the night forever. Miles stood still, listening amid the uproar, till the last whisper of it was gone.

"Pym!" The Countess spotted a new victim, and her voice went a little dangerous. "I seconded you to look after Miles. Would you care to explain this scene?"

There was a thoughtful pause. In a voice of simple honesty, Pym replied, "No, Milady."

"Ask Mark," Miles said callously. "He'll explain everything." Head down, he started for the stairs.

"You rat-coward—!" Mark hissed at him in passing.

The rest of his guests were shuffling uncertainly into the hallway.

The Count asked cautiously, "Miles, are you drunk?"

Miles paused on the third step. "Not yet, sir," he replied. He didn't look back. "Not nearly enough yet. Pym, see me."

He took the steps two at a time to his chambers, and oblivion.

CHAPTER TEN

"**G**ood afternoon, Mark." Countess Vorkosigan's bracing voice spiked Mark's last futile attempts to maintain unconsciousness. He groaned, pulled his pillow from his face, and opened one bleary eye.

He tested responses on his furry tongue. *Countess. Vicereine. Mother.* Strangely enough, *Mother* seemed to work best. "G'fertn'n, M'thur."

She studied him for a moment further, then nodded, and waved at the maid who'd followed in her wake. The girl set down a tea tray on the bedside table and stared curiously at Mark, who had an urge to pull his covers up over himself even though he was still wearing most of last night's clothing. The maid trundled obediently out of Mark's room again at the Countess's firm, "Thank you, that will be all."

Countess Vorkosigan opened the curtains, letting in blinding light, and pulled up a chair. "Tea?" she inquired, pouring without waiting for an answer.

"Yeah, I guess." Mark struggled upright, and rearranged his pillows enough to accept the mug without spilling it. The tea was strong and dark, with cream, the way he liked it, and it scalded the glue out of his mouth.

The Countess poked doubtfully at the empty butter

bug tubs piled on the table. Counting them up, perhaps, because she winced. "I didn't think you'd want breakfast yet."

"No. Thank you." Though his excruciating stomachache was calming down. The tea actually soothed it.

"Neither does your brother. Miles, possibly driven by his new-found need to uphold Vor tradition, sought *his* anesthetic in wine. Achieved it, too, according to Pym. At present, we're letting him enjoy his spectacular hangover without commentary."

"Ah." *Fortunate son.*

"Well, he'll have to come out of his rooms eventually. Though Aral advises not to look for him before tonight." Countess Vorkosigan poured herself a mug of tea too, and stirred in cream. "Lady Alys was very peeved at Miles for abandoning the field before his guests had all departed. She considered it a shameful lapse of manners on his part."

"It was a shambles." One that, it appeared, they were all going to live through. Unfortunately. Mark took another sluicing swallow. "What happened after . . . after the Koudelkas left?" Miles had bailed out early; Mark's own courage had broken when the Commodore had lost his grip to the point of referring to the Countess's mother as a *damned Betan pimp*, and Kareen had flung out the door proclaiming that she would sooner walk home, or possibly to the other side of the continent, before riding one meter in a car with a pair of such hopelessly uncultured, ignorant, benighted Barrayaran *savages*. Mark had fled to his bedroom with a stack of bug butter tubs and a spoon, and locked the door; Gorge and Howl had done their best to salve his shaken nerves.

Reversion under stress, his therapist would no doubt have dubbed it. He'd half hated, half exulted in the sense of not being in charge in his own body, but letting Gorge run to his limit had blocked the far more dangerous *Other*. It was a bad sign when Killer became nameless. He had managed to pass out before he ruptured, but only just. He felt spent now, his head foggy and quiet like a landscape after a storm.

The Countess continued, "Aral and I had an extremely enlightening talk with Professor and Professora Vorthys—now, *there's* a woman who has her head screwed on straight. I wish I'd made her acquaintance before this. They then left to see after their niece, and we had a longer talk with Alys and Simon." She took a slow sip. "Do I understand correctly that the dark-haired young lady who bolted past us last night was my potential daughter-in-law?"

"Not anymore, I don't think," said Mark morosely.

"Damn." The Countess frowned into her cup. "Miles told us practically nothing about her in his, I think I'm justified in calling them *briefs*, to us on Sergyar. If I'd known then half the things the Professora told me later, I'd have intercepted her myself."

"It wasn't my fault she ran off," Mark hastened to point out. "Miles opened his mouth and jammed his boot in there all by himself." He conceded reluctantly after a moment, "Well, I suppose Illyan helped."

"Yes. Simon was pretty distraught, once Alys explained it all to him. He was afraid he'd been told Miles's big secret and then forgot. *I'm* quite peeved at Miles for setting him up like that." A dangerous spark glinted in her eye.

Mark was considerably less interested in Miles's problems than in his own. He said cautiously, "Has, ah . . . Enrique found his missing queen, yet?"

"Not so far." The Countess hitched around in her chair and looked bemusedly at him. "I had a nice long talk with Dr. Borgos, too, once Alys and Illyan left. He showed me your lab. Kareen's work, I understand. I promised him a stay of Miles's execution order upon his girls, after which he calmed down considerably. I will say, his science seems sound."

"Oh, he's brilliant about the things that get his attention. His interests are a little, um, narrow, is all."

The Countess shrugged. "I've been living with obsessed men for the better part of my life. I think your Enrique will fit right in here."

"So . . . you've met our butter bugs?"

"Yes."

She seemed unfazed; *Betan, you know*. He could wish Miles had inherited more of her traits. "And, um . . . has the Count seen them yet?"

"Yes, in fact. We found one wandering about on our bedside table when we woke up this morning."

Mark flinched. "What did you do?"

"We turned a glass over her and left her to be collected by her papa. Sadly, Aral did not spot the bug exploring his shoe before he put it on. That one we disposed of quietly. What was left of her."

After a daunted silence, Mark asked hopefully, "It wasn't the queen, was it?"

"We couldn't tell, I'm afraid. It appeared to have been about the same size as the first one."

"Mm, then not. The queen would have been noticeably bigger."

Silence fell again, for a time.

"I will grant Kou one point," said the Countess finally. "I do have some responsibility toward Kareen. And toward you. I was perfectly aware of the array of choices that would be available to you both on Beta Colony. Including, happily, each other." She hesitated. "Having Kareen Koudelka as a daughter-in-law would give Aral and me great pleasure, in case you had any doubt."

"I never imagined otherwise. Are you asking me if my intentions are honorable?"

"I trust your honor, whether it fits in the narrowest Barrayaran definition or encompasses something broader," the Countess said equably.

Mark sighed. "Somehow, I don't think the Commodore and Madame Koudelka are ready to greet me with reciprocal joy."

"You *are* a Vorkosigan."

"A clone. An imitation. A cheap Jacksonian knock-off." *And crazy to boot.*

"A bloody expensive Jacksonian knock-off."

"Ha," Mark agreed darkly.

She shook her head, her smile growing more rueful. "Mark, I'm more than willing to help you and Kareen reach for your goals, whatever the obstacles. But you have to give me some clue of what your goals *are*."

Be careful how you aim this woman. The Countess was to obstacles as a laser cannon was to flies. Mark studied his stubby, plump hands in covert dismay. Hope, and its attendant, fear, began to stir again in his heart. "I want . . . whatever Kareen wants. On Beta, I thought I knew. Since we got back here, it's been all confused."

"Culture clash?"

"It's not just the culture clash, though that's part of it." Mark groped for words, trying to articulate his sense of the wholeness of Kareen. "I think . . . I think she wants *time.* Time to be herself, to be where she is, who she is. Without being hurried or stampeded to take up one role or another, to the exclusion of all the rest of her possibilities. *Wife* is a pretty damned exclusive role, the way they do it here. She says Barrayar wants to put her in a box."

The Countess tilted her head, taking this in. "She may be wiser than she knows."

He brooded. "On the other hand, maybe I was her secret vice, back on Beta. And here I'm a horrible embarrassment to her. Maybe she'd like me to just shove off and leave her alone."

The Countess raised a brow. "Didn't sound like it last night. Kou and Drou practically had to pry her nails out of our door jamb."

Mark brightened slightly. "There is that."

"And how have your goals changed, in your year on Beta? In addition to adding Kareen's heart's desire to your own, that is."

"Not changed, exactly," he responded slowly. "Honed, maybe. Focused. Modified . . . I achieved some things in my therapy I'd despaired of, of ever making come right in my life. It made me think maybe the rest isn't so impossible after all."

She nodded encouragement.

"School . . . economics school was good. I'm getting quite a tool-kit of skills and knowledge, you know. I'm really starting to know what I'm doing, not just faking it all the time." He glanced sideways at her. "I haven't forgotten Jackson's Whole. I've been thinking about indirect ways to shut down the damned butcher cloning lords there. Lilly Durona has some ideas for life-extension therapies that might be able to compete with their clone-brain transplants. Safer, nearly as effective, *and* cheaper. Draw off their customers, disrupt them economically even if I can't touch them physically. Every scrap of spare cash I've been able to amass, I've been dumping into the Durona Group, to support their R and D. I'm going to own a controlling share of them, if this goes on." He smiled wryly. "And I still want enough money left that no one has power over me. I'm beginning to see how I can get it, not overnight, but steadily, bit by bit. I, um . . . wouldn't mind starting a new agribusiness here on Barrayar."

"And Sergyar, too. Aral was very interested in possible applications for your bugs among our colonists and homesteaders."

"*Was* he?" Mark's lips parted in astonishment. "Even with the Vorkosigan crest on them?"

"Mm, it would perhaps be wise to lose the House livery before pitching them seriously to Aral," the Countess said, suppressing a smile.

"I didn't know Enrique was going to do that," Mark offered by way of apology. "Though you should have seen the look on Miles's face, when Enrique presented them to him. It almost made it worth it. . . ." He sighed at the memory, but then shook his head in renewed despair. "But what good is it all, if Kareen and I can't get back to Beta Colony? *She's* stuck for money, if her parents won't support her. I could offer to pay her way, but . . . but I don't know if that's a good idea."

"Ah," said the Countess. "Interesting. Are you afraid Kareen would feel you had purchased her loyalty?"

"I'm . . . not sure. She's very conscientious about obligations. I want a lover. Not a debtor. I think it would be a bad mistake to accidentally . . . put her in another kind of box. I want to give her *everything*. But I don't know how!"

An odd smile turned the Countess's lip. "When you give each other everything, it becomes an even trade. Each wins all."

Mark shook his head, baffled. "An odd sort of Deal."

"The best." The Countess finished her tea and put down her cup, "Well. I don't wish to invade your privacy. But do remember, you're *allowed* to ask for help. It's part of what families are all about."

"I owe you too much already, milady."

Her smile tilted. "Mark, you don't pay back your parents. You can't. The debt you owe them gets collected by your children, who hand it down in turn. It's a sort of entailment. Or if you don't have children of the body, it's left as a debt to your common humanity. Or to your God, if you possess or are possessed by one."

"I'm not sure that seems fair."

"The family economy evades calculation in the gross planetary product. It's the only deal I know where, when you give more than you get, you aren't bankrupted—but rather, vastly enriched."

Mark took this in. And what kind of parent to him was his progenitor-brother? More than a sibling, but most certainly not his mother. . . . "Can you help Miles?"

"That's more of a puzzle." The Countess smoothed her skirts, and rose. "I haven't known this Madame Vorsoisson all her life the way I've known Kareen. It's not at all clear what I *can* do for Miles—I would say *poor boy*, but from everything I've heard he dug his very own pit and jumped in. I'm afraid he's going to have to dig himself back out. Likely it will be good for him." She gave a firm nod, as though a supplicant Miles were already being sent on his way to achieve salvation alone: *Write when you find good works*. The Countess's idea of maternal concern was damned unnerving, sometimes, Mark reflected as she made her way out.

He was conscious that he was sticky, and itchy, and needed to pee and wash. And he had a pressing obligation to go help Enrique hunt for his missing queen, before she and her offspring built a nest in the walls and started making *more* Vorkosigan butter bugs. Instead, he lurched to his comconsole, sat gingerly, and tried the code for the Koudelkas' residence.

He desperately aligned an array of fast talk in four flavors, depending on whether the Commodore, Madame Koudelka, Kareen, or one of her sisters answered the vid. Kareen hadn't called him this morning: was she sleeping, sulking, locked in? Had her parents bricked her up in the walls? Or worse, thrown her out on the street? Wait, no, that would be all right—she could come live *here*—

His subvocalized rehearsals were wasted. *Call Not Accepted* blinked at him in malignant red letters, like a scrawl of blood hovering over the vid plate. The voice-recognition program had been set to screen him out.

Ekaterin had a splitting headache.

It was all that wine last night, she decided. An appalling amount had been served, including the sparkling wine in the library and the different wines with each of the four courses of dinner. She had no idea how much she'd actually drunk. Pym had assiduously topped up her glass whenever the level had dropped below two-thirds. More than five glasses, anyway. Seven? Ten? Her usual limit was two.

It was a wonder she'd been able to stalk out of that overheated grand dining room without falling over; but then, if she'd been stone sober, could she ever have found the nerve—or was that, the ill-manners—to do so? *Pot-valiant, were you?*

She ran her hands through her hair, rubbed her neck, opened her eyes, and lifted her forehead again from the cool surface of her aunt's comconsole. All the plans and notes for Lord Vorkosigan's Barrayaran garden were now neatly and logically organized, and indexed. Anyone—well, any gardener who knew what they were doing in the first place—could follow them and complete the job in good order. The final tally of all expenses was appended. The working credit account had been balanced, closed, and signed off. She had only to hit the Send pad on the comconsole for it all to be gone from her life forever.

She groped for the exquisite little model Barrayar on its gold chain heaped by the vid plate, held it up, and let it spin before her eyes. Leaning back in the comconsole chair, she contemplated it, and all the memories attached to it like invisible chains. Gold and lead, hope and fear, triumph and pain . . . She squinted it to a blur.

She remembered the day he'd bought it, on their absurd and ultimately very wet shopping trip in the Komarran dome, his face alive with the humor of it all. She remembered the day he'd given it to her, in her hospital room on the transfer station, after the defeat of the conspirators. *The Lord Auditor Vorkosigan Award for Making His Job Easier*, he'd dubbed it, his gray eyes glinting. He'd apologized that it was not the real medal any soldier might have earned for doing rather less than what she'd done that awful night-cycle. It wasn't a gift. Or if it was, she'd been very wrong to accept it from his hand, because it was much too expensive a bauble to be proper. Though *he* had grinned like a fool, Aunt Vorthys, watching, hadn't batted an eye. It was, therefore, a prize. She'd won it herself, paid for it with bruises and terror and panicked action.

This is mine. I will not give it up. With a frown, she drew the chain back over her head and tucked the pendant planet inside her black blouse, trying not to feel like a guilty child hiding a stolen cookie.

Her flaming desire to return to Vorkosigan House and rip her skellytum rootling, so carefully and proudly planted mere hours ago, back out of the ground, had burned out sometime after midnight. For one thing, she would certainly have run afoul of Vorkosigan House's security, if she'd gone blundering about in its garden in the dark. Pym, or Roic, might have stunned her, and been very upset, poor fellows. And then carried her back inside, where . . . Her fury, her wine, and her overwrought imagination had all worn off near dawn, running out at last in secret, muffled tears in her pillow, when the household was long quiet and she could hope for a scrap of privacy.

Why should she even bother? Miles didn't care about the skellytum—he hadn't even gone out to *look* at it last evening. She'd been lugging the awkward thing around in her life for fifteen years, in one form or another, since inheriting the seventy-year-old bonsai from her great-aunt. It had survived death, marriage, a dozen moves, interstellar travel, being flung off a balcony and shattered, more death, another five wormhole jumps, and two subsequent transplantations. It had to be as exhausted as she was. Let it sit there and rot, or dry up and blow away, or whatever its neglected fate was to be. At least she had dragged it back to Barrayar to finish dying. Enough. She was done with it. Forever.

She called her garden instructions back up on the comconsole, and added an appendix about the skellytum's rather tricky post-transplant watering and feeding requirements.

"Mama!" Nikki's sharp, excited voice made her flinch.

"Don't . . . don't *thump* so, dear." She turned in her station chair and smiled bleakly at her son. She was inwardly grateful she hadn't dragged him along to last night's debacle, though she could've pictured him enthusiastically joining poor Enrique on the butter bug hunt. But if Nikki had been present, she could not have left, and abandoned him. Nor yanked him along with her, halfway through his dessert and doubtless protesting in bewilderment. She'd have been mother-bound to her chair, there to endure whatever ghastly, awkward social torment might have subsequently played out.

He stood by her elbow, and bounced. "Last night, did you work out with Lord Vorkosigan when he's gonna take me down to Vorkosigan Surleau and learn to ride his horse? You said you would."

She'd brought Nikki along to the garden work-site several times, when neither her aunt nor uncle could be home with him. Lord Vorkosigan had generously offered to let him have the run of Vorkosigan House on such days, and they'd even hustled up Pym's youngest boy Arthur from his nearby home for a playmate. Ma Kosti had captured Nikki's stomach, heart, and slavish loyalty in very short order, Armsman Roic had played games with him, and Kareen Koudelka had let him help in the lab. Ekaterin had almost forgotten this off-hand invitation, issued by Lord Vorkosigan when he'd turned Nikki back over to her at the end of one workday. She'd made polite-doubtful noises at the time. Miles had assured her the horse in question was very old and gentle, which hadn't exactly been the doubt that had concerned her.

"I . . ." Ekaterin rubbed her temple, which seemed to anchor a lacework of shooting pain inside her head. *Generously . . . ?* Or just more of Miles's campaign of subtle manipulation, now revealed? "I really don't think we ought to impose on him like that. It's such a long way down to his District. If you're really interested in horses, I'm sure we can get you riding lessons somewhere much nearer Vorbarr Sultana."

Nikki frowned in obvious disappointment. "I dunno about horses. But he said he might let me try his lightflyer, on the way down."

"Nikki, you're much too young to fly a lightflyer."

"Lord Vorkosigan said *his* father let *him* fly when he was younger than me. He said his da said he needed to know how to take over the controls in an emergency just as soon as he was physically able. He said he sat him on his lap, and let him take off and land all by himself and everything."

"You're much too big to sit on Lord Vorkosigan's lap!" So was she, she supposed. But if he and she were to—*stop that.*

"Well," Nikki considered this, and allowed, "anyway, he's too little. It'd look goofy. But his lightflyer seat's just right! Pym let me sit in it, when I was helping him polish the cars." Nikki bounced some more. "Can you ask Lord Vorkosigan when you go to work?"

"No. I don't think so."

"Why not?" He looked at her, his brow wrinkling slightly. "Why didn't you go today?"

"I'm . . . not feeling very well."

"Oh. Tomorrow, then? Come on, Mama, *please?*" He hung on her arm, and twisted himself up, and made big eyes at her, grinning.

She rested her throbbing forehead in her hand. "No, Nikki. I don't think so."

"Aw, why *not?* You *said.* Come on, it'll be so great. You don't have to come if you don't want, I s'pose. Why not, why not, why not? Tomorrow, tomorrow, tomorrow?"

"I'm not going to work tomorrow, either."

"Are you that sick? You don't look that sick." He stared at her in startled worry.

"No." She hastened to address that worry, before he started making up dire medical theories in his head. He'd lost one parent this year. "It's just . . . I'm not going to be going back to Lord Vorkosigan's house. I quit."

"Huh?" Now his stare grew entirely bewildered. "*Why*? I thought you *liked* making that garden thing."

"I did."

"Then why'd you quit?"

"Lord Vorkosigan and I . . . had a falling-out. Over, over an ethical issue."

"What? What issue?" His voice was laced with confusion and disbelief. He twisted himself around the other way.

"I found he'd . . . lied to me about something." *He promised he'd never lie to me.* He'd feigned that he was very interested in gardens. He'd arranged her life by subterfuge—and then told everyone else in Vorbarr Sultana. He'd pretended he didn't love her. He'd as much as promised he'd never ask her to marry him. He'd *lied*. Try explaining *that* to a nine-year-old boy. Or to any other rational human being of any age or gender, her honesty added bitterly. *Am I insane yet?* Anyway, Miles hadn't actually *said* he wasn't in love with her, he'd just . . . implied it. Avoided saying much on the subject at all, in fact. Prevarication by misdirection.

"Oh," said Nikki, eyes wide, daunted at last.

The Professora's blessed voice interrupted from the archway. "Now, Nikki, don't be pestering your mother. She has a very bad hangover."

"A *hang*over?" Nikki clearly had trouble fitting the words *mother* and *hangover* into the same conceptual space. "She said she was sick."

"Wait till you're older, dear. You'll doubtless discover the distinction, or lack of it, for yourself. Run along now." His smiling great-aunt guided him firmly away. "Out, out. Go see what your Uncle Vorthys is up to downstairs. I heard some very odd noises a bit ago."

Nikki let himself be chivvied out, with a disturbed backward glance over his shoulder.

Ekaterin put her head back down on the comconsole, and shut her eyes.

A clink by her head made her open them again; her aunt was setting down a large glass of cool water and holding out two painkiller tablets.

"I had some of those this morning," said Ekaterin dully.

"They appear to have worn off. Drink all the water, now. You clearly need to rehydrate."

Dutifully, Ekaterin did so. She set the glass down, and squeezed her eyes open and shut a few times. "That really was *the* Count and Countess Vorkosigan last night, wasn't it." It wasn't really a question, more a plea for denial. After nearly stampeding over them in her desperate flight out the door, she'd been halfway home in the auto-cab before her belated realization of their identity had dawned so horribly. The great and famous Viceroy and Vicereine of Sergyar. What business had they, to look so like ordinary people at a moment like that? *Ow, ow, ow.*

"Yes. I'd never met them to speak to at any length before."

"Did you . . . speak to them at length last night?" Her aunt and uncle had been almost an hour behind her, arriving home.

"Yes, we had quite a nice chat. I was impressed. Miles's mother is a very sensible woman."

"Then why is her son such a . . . never mind." *Ow.* "They must think I'm some sort of hysteric. How did I get the nerve to just stand up and walk out of a formal dinner in front of all those . . . and Lady *Alys Vorpatril* . . . and at *Vorkosigan House.* I can't believe I did that." After a brooding moment, she added, "I can't believe *he* did that."

Aunt Vorthys did not ask, *What?*, or *Which he?* She did purse her lips, and look quizzically at her niece. "Well, I don't suppose you had much choice."

"No."

"After all, if you hadn't left, you'd have had to answer Lord Vorkosigan's question."

"I . . . didn't . . . ?" Ekaterin blinked. Hadn't her actions been answer enough? "Under *those* circumstances? Are you mad?"

"He knew it was a mistake the moment the words were out of his mouth, I daresay, at least judging from that ghastly expression on his face. You could see everything just drain right out of it. Extraordinary. But I can't help wondering, dear—if you'd wanted to say *no*, why didn't you? It was the perfect opportunity to do so."

"I . . . I . . ." Ekaterin tried to collect her wits, which seemed to be scattering like sheep. "It wouldn't have been . . . *polite*."

After a thoughtful pause, her aunt murmured, "You might have said, 'No, thank you.' "

Ekaterin rubbed her numb face. "Aunt Vorthys," she sighed, "I love you dearly. But please go away now."

Her aunt smiled, and kissed her on the top of her head, and drifted out.

Ekaterin returned to her twice-interrupted brooding. Her aunt was right, she realized. Ekaterin *hadn't* answered Miles's question. And she hadn't even noticed she hadn't answered.

She recognized this headache, and the knotted stomach that went with it, and it had nothing to do with too much wine. Her arguments with her late husband Tien had never involved physical violence directed against her, though the walls had suffered from his clenched fists a few times. The rows had always petered out into days of frozen, silent rage, filled with unbearable tension and a sort of grief, of two people trapped together in the same always-too-small space walking wide around each other. She had almost always broken first, backed down, apologized, placated, anything to make the pain stop. *Heartsick*, perhaps, was the name of the emotion.

I don't want to go back there again. Please don't ever make me go back there again.

Where am I, when I am at home in myself? Not here, for all the increasing burden of her aunt and uncle's charity. Not, certainly, with Tien. Not with her own father. With . . . Miles? She had felt flashes of profound ease in his company, it was true, brief perhaps, but calm like deep water. There had also been moments when she'd wanted to whack him with a brick. Which was the real Miles? Which was the real Ekaterin, for that matter?

The answer hovered, and it scared her breathless. But she'd picked wrong before. She had no judgment in these man-and-woman matters, she'd proved that.

She turned back to the comconsole. A note. She should write some sort of cover note to go with the returned garden plans.

I think they will be self-explanatory, don't you?

She pressed the Send pad on the comconsole, and stumbled back upstairs to pull the curtains and lie down fully dressed on her bed until dinner.

Miles slouched into the library of Vorkosigan House, a mug of weak tea clutched in his faintly trembling hand. The light in here was still too bright this evening. Perhaps he ought to seek refuge in a corner of the garage instead. Or the cellar. Not the wine cellar—he shuddered at the thought. But he'd grown entirely bored with his bed, covers pulled over his head or not. A day of that was enough.

He stopped abruptly, and lukewarm tea sloshed onto his hand. His father was at the secured comconsole, and his mother was at the broad inlaid table with three or four books and a mess of flimsies spread out before her. They both looked up at him, and smiled in tentative greeting. It would probably seem surly of him to back out and flee.

"G'evening," he managed, and shambled past them to find his favorite chair, and lower himself carefully into it.

"Good evening, Miles," his mother returned. His father put his console on hold, and regarded him with bland interest.

"How was your trip home from Sergyar?" Miles went on, after about a minute of silence.

"Entirely without incident, happily enough," his mother said. "Till the very end."

"Ah," said Miles. "That." He brooded into his tea mug.

His parents humanely ignored him for several minutes, but whatever they'd been separately working on seemed to not hold their attention anymore. Still, nobody left.

"We missed you at breakfast," the Countess said finally. "And lunch. And dinner."

"I was still throwing up at breakfast," said Miles. "I wouldn't have been much fun."

"So Pym reported," said the Count.

The Countess added astringently, "Are you done with that now?"

"Yeh. It didn't help." Miles slumped a little further, and stretched his legs out before him. "A life in ruins with vomiting is still a life in ruins."

"Mm," said the Count in a judicious tone, "though it does make it easy to be a recluse. If you're repulsive enough, people spontaneously avoid you."

His wife twinkled at him. "Speaking from experience, love?"

"Naturally." His eyes grinned back at her.

More silence fell. His parents did not decamp. Obviously, Miles concluded, he wasn't repulsive enough. Perhaps he should emit a menacing belch.

He finally started, "Mother—you're a woman—"

She sat up, and gave him a bright, encouraging Betan smile. "Yes . . . ?"

"Never mind," he sighed. He slumped again.

The Count rubbed his lips and regarded him thoughtfully. "Do you have anything to *do*? Any miscreants to go Imperially Audit, or anything?"

"Not at present," Miles replied. After a contemplative moment he added, "Fortunately for them."

"Hm." The Count tamped down a smile. "Perhaps you are wise." He hesitated. "Your Aunt Alys gave us a blow-by-blow account of your dinner party. With editorials. She was particularly insistent that I tell you she *trusts*," Miles could hear his aunt's cadences mimicked in his father's voice, "you would not have fled the scene of any other losing battle the way you deserted last night."

Ah. Yes. His parents had been left with the mopping up, hadn't they. "But there was no hope of being shot dead in the dining room if I stayed with the rear guard."

His father flicked up an eyebrow. "And so avoid the subsequent court martial?"

"Thus conscience doth make cowards of us all," Miles intoned.

"I am sufficiently your partisan," said the Countess, "that the sight of a pretty woman running screaming, or at least swearing, into the night from your marriage proposal rather disturbs me. Though your Aunt Alys says you scarcely left the young lady any other choice. It's hard to say what else she could have done *but* walk out. Except squash you like a bug, I suppose."

Miles cringed at the word *bug*.

"Just how bad—" the Countess began.

"Did I offend her? Badly enough, it seems."

"Actually, I was about to ask, just how bad *was* Madame Vorsoisson's prior marriage?"

Miles shrugged. "I only saw a little of it. I gather from the pattern of her flinches that the late unlamented Tien Vorsoisson was one of those subtle feral parasites who leave their mates scratching their heads and asking, *Am I crazy? Am I crazy?*" She wouldn't have those doubts if she married *him*, ha.

"Aah," said his mother, in a tone of much enlightenment. "One of *those*. Yes. I know the type of old. They come in all gender-flavors, by the way. It can take years to fight your way out of the mental mess they leave in their wake."

"I don't *have* years," Miles protested. "I've *never* had years." And then pressed his lips shut at the little flicker of pain in his father's eyes. Well, who knew what Miles's second life expectancy was, anyway. Maybe he'd started his clock all over, after the cryorevival. Miles slumped lower. "The hell of it is, I knew better. I'd had way too much to drink, I panicked when Simon . . . I never meant to ambush Ekaterin like that. It was *friendly* fire . . ."

He went on after a little, "I had this great plan, see. I thought it could solve everything in one brilliant swoop. She has this real passion for gardens, and her husband had left her effectively destitute. So I figured, I could help her jump-start the career of her dreams, slip her some financial support, and get an excuse to see her nearly every day, *and* get in ahead of the competition. I had to practically wade through the fellows panting after her in the Vorthys's parlor, the times I went over there—"

"For the purpose of panting after her in her parlor, I take it?" his mother inquired sweetly.

"No!" said Miles, stung. "To consult about the garden I'd hired her to make in the lot next door."

"Is *that* what that crater is," said his father. "In the dark, from the groundcar, it looked as though someone tried to shell Vorkosigan House and missed, and I'd wondered why no one had reported it to us."

"It is not a *crater*. It's a sunken garden. There's just . . . just no plants in it yet."

"It has a very nice shape, Miles," his mother said soothingly. "I went out and walked through it this afternoon. The little stream is very pretty indeed. It reminds me of the mountains."

"That was the idea," said Miles, primly ignoring his father's mutter of . . . *after a Cetagandan bombing raid on a guerilla position* . . .

Then Miles sat bolt upright in sudden horror. *Not quite no plants.* "Oh, God! I never went out to look at her skellytum! Lord Dono came in with Ivan—did Aunt Alys explain to you about Lord Dono?—and I was distracted, and then it was time for dinner, and I never had the chance afterwards. Has anyone watered—? Oh, shit, no wonder she was angry. I'm dead meat twice over—!" He melted back into his puddle of despair.

"So, let me get this straight," said the Countess slowly, studying him dispassionately. "You took this destitute widow, struggling to get on her own feet for the first time in her life, and dangled a golden career opportunity before her as bait, just to tie her to you and cut her off from other romantic possibilities."

That seemed an uncharitably bald way of putting it. "Not . . . not *just*," Miles choked. "I was trying to do her a good turn. I never imagined she'd quit—the garden was everything to her."

The Countess sat back, and regarded him with a horribly thoughtful expression, the one she acquired when you'd made the mistake of getting her full, undivided attention. "Miles . . . do you remember that unfortunate incident with Armsman Esterhazy and the game of cross-ball, when you were about twelve years old?"

He hadn't thought of it in years, but at her words, the memory came flooding back, still tinged with shame and fury. The Armsmen used to play cross-ball with him, and sometimes Elena and Ivan, in the back garden of Vorkosigan House: a low-impact game, of minimum threat to his then-fragile bones, but requiring quick reflexes and good timing. He'd been elated the first time he'd won a match against an actual adult, in this case Armsman Esterhazy. He'd been shaken with rage, when a not-meant-to-be-overheard remark had revealed to him that the game had been a setup. Forgotten. But not forgiven.

"Poor Esterhazy had thought it would cheer you up, because you were depressed at the time about some, I forget which, slight you'd suffered at school," the Countess said. "I still remember how furious you were when you figured out he'd *let* you win. Did you ever carry on about that one. We thought you'd do yourself a harm."

"He stole my victory from me," grated Miles, "as surely as if he'd cheated to win. *And* he poisoned every subsequent real victory with doubt. I had a *right* to be mad."

His mother sat quietly, expectantly.

The light dawned. Even with his eyes squeezed shut, the intensity of the glare hurt his head.

"Oh. Noooo," groaned Miles, muffled into the cushion he jammed over his face. "*I* did *that* to *her?*"

His remorseless parent let him stew in it, a silence sharper-edged than words.

"*I* did *that* to *her . . .*" he moaned, pitifully.

Pity did not seem to be forthcoming. He clutched the cushion to his chest. "Oh. God. That's exactly what I did. She said it herself. She said the garden could have been *her* gift. And I'd taken it away from her. Too. Which made no sense, since it was she who'd just quit . . . I thought she was starting to argue with me. I was so pleased, because I thought, if only she would argue with me . . ."

"You could win?" the Count supplied dryly.

"Uh . . . yeah."

"Oh, son." The Count shook his head. "Oh, poor son." Miles did not mistake this for an expression of sympathy. "The only way you win *that* war is to start with unconditional surrender."

"That *you* is plural, note," the Countess put in.

"I *tried* to surrender!" Miles protested frantically. "The woman was taking no prisoners! I tried to get her to stomp me, but she wouldn't. She's too dignified, too, oversocialized, too, too . . ."

"Too smart to lower herself to your level?" the Countess suggested. "Dear me. I think I'm beginning to like this Ekaterin. And I haven't even finished being properly introduced to her yet. *I'd like you to meet—she's getting away!* seemed a little . . . truncated."

Miles glared at her. But he couldn't keep it up. In a smaller voice, he said, "She sent all the garden plans back to me this afternoon, on the comconsole. Just like she'd said she would. I'd set it to code-buzz me if any call originating from her came in. I damn near killed myself, getting over to the machine. But it was just a data packet. Not even a personal note. *Die, you rat* would have been better than this . . . this *nothing*." After a fraught pause, he burst out, "What do I do *now*?"

"Is that a rhetorical question, for dramatic effect, or are you actually asking my advice?" his mother inquired tartly. "Because I'm not going to waste my breath on you unless you're finally paying attention."

He opened his mouth for an angry reply, then closed it. He glanced for support to his father. His father opened his hand blandly in the direction of his mother. Miles wondered what it would be like, to be in such practiced teamwork with someone that it was as though you coordinated your one-two punches telepathically. *I'll never get the chance to find out. Unless.*

"I'm paying attention," he said humbly.

"The . . . the kindest word I can come up with for it is *blunder*—was yours. You owe the apology. Make it."

"*How*? She's made it abundantly clear she doesn't want to speak to me!"

"*Not* in person, good God, Miles. For one thing, I can't imagine you could resist the urge to babble, and blow yourself up. Again."

What is it about all my relatives, that they have so little faith in—

"Even a live comconsole call is too invasive," she continued. "Going over to the Vorthys's in person would be much too invasive."

"The way *he's* been going about it, certainly," murmured the Count. "General Romeo Vorkosigan, the one-man strike force."

The Countess gave him a faintly quelling flick of her eyelash. "Something rather more controlled, I think," she continued to Miles. "About all you can do is write her a note, I suppose. A short, succinct note. I realize you don't do *abject* very well, but I suggest you exert yourself."

"D'you think it would work?" Faint hope glimmered at the bottom of a deep, deep well.

"*Working* is not what this is about. You can't still be plotting to make love and war on the poor woman. You'll send an apology because you owe it, to her and to your own honor. Period. Or else don't bother."

"Oh," said Miles, in a very small voice.

"Cross-ball," said his father. Reminiscently. "Huh."

"The knife is in the target," sighed Miles. "To the hilt. You don't have to twist." He glanced across at his mother. "Should the note be handwritten? Or should I just send it on the comconsole?"

"I think your *just* just answered your own question. If your execrable handwriting has improved, it would perhaps be a nice touch."

"Proves it wasn't dictated to your secretary, for one thing," put in the Count. "Or worse, composed by him at your order."

"Haven't got a secretary yet." Miles sighed. "Gregor hasn't given me enough work to justify one."

"Since work for an Auditor hinges on awkward crises arising in the Empire, I can't very well wish more for you," the Count said. "But no doubt things will pick up after the wedding. Which will have one less crisis because of the good work you just did on Komarr, I might say."

He glanced up, and his father gave him an understanding nod; yes, the Viceroy and Vicereine of Sergyar were most definitely in the need-to-know pool about the late events on Komarr. Gregor had undoubtedly sent on a copy of Miles's eyes-only Auditor's report for the Viceroy's perusal. "Well . . . yes. At the very least, if the conspirators had maintained their original schedule, there'd have been several thousand innocent people killed that day. It would have marred the festivities, I think."

"Then you've earned some time off."

The Countess looked momentarily introspective. "And what did Madame Vorsoisson earn? We had her aunt give us her eyewitness description of their involvement. It sounded like a frightening experience."

"The public gratitude of the Empire is what she *should* have earned," said Miles, in reminded aggravation. "Instead, it's all been buried deep-deep under the ImpSec security cap. No one will ever know. All her courage, all her cool and clever moves, all her bloody *heroism*, dammit, was just . . . made to disappear. It's not fair."

"One does what one has to, in a crisis," said the Countess.

"No." Miles glanced up at her. "Some people do. Others just fold. I've seen them. I know the difference. Ekaterin—she'll never fold. She can go the distance, she can find the speed. She'll . . . she'll *do*."

"Leaving aside whether we are discussing a woman or a horse," said the Countess—dammit, Mark had said practically the same thing, what was *with* all Miles's nearest and dearest?—"everyone has their folding-point, Miles. Their mortal vulnerability. Some just keep it in a nonstandard location."

The Count and Countess gave each other one of

those Telepathic Looks again. It was extremely annoying. Miles squirmed with envy.

He drew the tattered shreds of his dignity around him, and rose. "Excuse me. I have to go . . . water a plant."

It took him thirty minutes of wandering around the bare, crusted garden in the dark, with his hand-light wavering and the water from his mug dribbling over his fingers, to even *find* the blasted thing. In its pot, the skellytum rootling had looked sturdy enough, but out here, it looked lost and lonely: a scrap of life the size of his thumb in an acre of sterility. It also looked disturbingly limp. Was it wilting? He emptied the cup over it; the water made a dark spot in the reddish soil that began to evaporate and fade all too quickly.

He tried to imagine the plant full grown, five meters high, its central barrel the size, and shape, of a sumo wrestler, its tendril-like branches gracing the space with distinctive corkscrew curves. Then he tried to imagine himself forty-five or fifty years old, which was the age to which he'd have to survive to see that sight. Would he be a reclusive, gnarled bachelor, eccentric, shrunken, invalidish, tended only by his bored Armsmen? Or a proud, if stressed, paterfamilias with a serene, elegant, dark-haired woman on his arm and half a dozen hyperactive progeny in tow? Maybe . . . maybe the hyperactivity could be toned down in the gene-cleaning, though he was sure his parents would accuse him of cheating. . . .

Abject.

He went back inside Vorkosigan House to his study, where he sat himself down to attempt, through a dozen drafts, the best damned *abject* anybody'd ever seen.

CHAPTER ELEVEN

Kareen leaned over the porch rail of Lord Auditor Vorthys's house and stared worriedly at the close-curtained windows in the bright tile front. "Maybe there's no one home."

"I said we should have called before we came here," said Martya, unhelpfully. But then came a rapid thump of steps from within—surely not the Professora's—and the door burst open.

"Oh, hi, Kareen," said Nikki. "Hi, Martya."

"Hello, Nikki," said Martya. "Is your mama home?"

"Yeah, she's out back. You want to see her?"

"Yes, please. If she's not too busy."

"Naw, she's only messing with the garden. Go on through." He gestured them hospitably in the general direction of the back of the house, and thumped back up the stairs.

Trying not to feel like a trespasser, Kareen led her sister through the hall and kitchen and out the back door. Ekaterin was on her knees on a pad by a raised flower bed, grubbing out weeds. The discarded plants were laid out beside her on the walk, roots and all, in rows like executed prisoners. They shriveled in the westering sun. Her bare hand slapped another green corpse down at the end of the row. It looked therapeutic. Kareen wished *she* had something to kill right now. Besides Martya.

Ekaterin glanced up at the sound of their footsteps, and a ghost of a smile lightened her pale face. She jammed her trowel into the dirt, and rose to her feet. "Oh, hello."

"Hi, Ekaterin." Not wishing to plunge too baldly into the purpose of her visit, Kareen added, with a wave of her arm, "This is pretty." Trees, and walls draped with vines, made the little garden into a private bower in the midst of the city.

Ekaterin followed her glance. "It was a hobby-project of mine, when I lived here as a student, years ago. Aunt Vorthys has kept it up, more or less. There are a few things I'd do differently now . . . Anyway," she gestured at the graceful wrought-iron table and chairs, "won't you sit down?"

Martya took prompt advantage of the invitation, seating herself and resting her chin on her hands with a put-upon sigh.

"Would you like anything to drink? Tea?"

"Thanks," said Kareen, also sitting. "Nothing to drink, thanks." This household lacked servants to dispatch on such errands; Ekaterin would have to go off and rummage in the kitchen with her own hands to supply her guests. And the sisters would be put to it to guess whether to follow prole rules, and all troop out to help, or impoverished-high-Vor rules, and sit and wait and pretend they didn't notice there weren't any servants. Besides, they'd just eaten, and her dinner still sat like a lump in Kareen's stomach even though she'd barely picked at it.

Kareen waited until Ekaterin was seated to venture cautiously, "I just stopped by to find out—that is, I'd wondered if, if you'd heard anything from . . . from Vorkosigan House?"

Ekaterin stiffened. "No. Should I have?"

"Oh." What, Miles the monomaniacal hadn't made it all up to her by now? Kareen had pictured him at Ekaterin's door the following morning, spinning damage-control propaganda like mad. It wasn't that Miles was so irresistible—she, for one, had always found him quite resistible, at least in the romantic sense, not that he'd ever exactly turned his attention on her—but he was certainly the most *relentless* human being she'd ever met. What was the man doing all this time? Her anxiety grew. "I'd thought—I was hoping—I'm awfully worried about Mark, you see. It's been almost two days. I was hoping you might have . . . heard something."

Ekaterin's face softened. "Oh, Mark. Of course. No. I'm sorry."

Nobody cared enough about Mark. The fragilities and fault lines of his hard-won personality were invisible to them all. They'd load him down with impossible pressures and demands as though he were, well, Miles, and assume he'd never break. . . . "My parents have forbidden me to call anyone at Vorkosigan House, or go over there or anything," Kareen explained, tight-voiced. "They insisted I give them my word before they'd even let me out of the house. And *then* they stuck me with a snitch." She tossed her head in the direction of Martya, now slumping with almost equal surliness.

"It wasn't *my* idea to be your bodyguard," protested Martya. "Did I get a vote? No."

"Da and Mama—especially Da—have gone all Time-of-Isolation over this. It's just crazy. They're all the time telling you to grow up, and then when you do, they try to make you stop. And shrink. It's like they want to cryofreeze me at twelve forever. Or stick me back in the replicator and lock down the lid." Kareen bit her lip. "And I don't fit in there anymore, *thank* you."

"Well," said Ekaterin, a shade of sympathetic amusement in her voice, "at least you'd be safe there. I can understand the parental temptation of that."

"You're making it worse for yourself, you know," said Martya to Kareen, with an air of sisterly critique. "If you hadn't carried on like a madwoman being locked in an attic, I bet they wouldn't have gone nearly so rigid."

Kareen bared her teeth at Martya.

"There's something to that in both directions," said Ekaterin mildly. "Nothing is more guaranteed to make one start acting like a child than to be treated like one. It's so infuriating. It took me the longest time to figure out how to stop falling into that trap."

"Yes, exactly," said Kareen eagerly. "You understand! So—how did *you* make them stop?"

"You can't make them—whoever your particular *them* is—do anything, really," said Ekaterin slowly. "Adulthood isn't an award they'll give you for being a good child. You can waste . . . years, trying to get someone to give that respect to you, as though it were a sort of promotion or raise in pay. If only you do enough, if only you are *good enough*. No. You have to just . . . take it. Give it to yourself, I suppose. Say, *I'm sorry you feel like that*, and walk away. But that's hard." Ekaterin looked up from her lap where her hands had been absently rubbing at the yard dirt smeared on them, and remembered to smile. Kareen felt an odd chill. It wasn't just her reserve that made Ekaterin daunting, sometimes. The woman went down and down, like a well to the middle of the world. Kareen bet even Miles couldn't shift her around at his will and whim.

How hard is it to walk away? "It's like they're *that* close," she held up her thumb and finger a few millimeters apart, "to telling me I have to choose between my family and my lover. And it makes me scared, and it makes me furious. Why shouldn't I have both? Would it be considered too much of a good thing, or what? Leaving aside that it'd be a horrid guilt to lay on poor Mark—he knows how much my family means to me. A family is something he didn't have, growing up, and he romanticizes it, but still."

Her flattened hands beat a frustrated tattoo on the garden tabletop. "It all comes back to the damned money. If I were a *real* adult, I'd have my own income. And I could walk away, and they'd know I could, and they'd have to back off. They think they have me trapped."

"Ah," said Ekaterin faintly. "That one. Yes. That one is very real."

"Mama accused *me* of only doing short-term thinking, but I'm not! The butter bug project—it's like school all over again, short-term deprivation for a really major pay-off down the line. I've studied the analyses Mark did with Tsipis. It's not a get-rich-quick scheme. It's a get-rich-*big* scheme. Da and Mama don't have a clue how big. They imagine I've spent my time with Mark playing around, but I've been working my tail off, and I know *exactly* why. Meanwhile I have over a month's salary tied up in shares in the basement of Vorkosigan House, and *I don't know what's happening over there!*" Her fingers were white where they gripped the table edge, and she had to stop for breath.

"I take it you haven't heard from Dr. Borgos, either?" said Martya cautiously to Ekaterin.

"Why . . . no."

"I felt almost sorry for him. He was trying so hard to please. I hope Miles hasn't really had all his bugs killed."

"Miles never threatened *all* his bugs," Kareen pointed out. "Just the escapees. As for me, I wish Miles *had* strangled him. I'm sorry you made him stop, Ekaterin."

"Me!" Ekaterin's lips twisted with bemusement.

"What, Kareen," scoffed Martya, "just because the man revealed to everybody that you were a practicing heterosexual? You know, you really didn't play that one right, considering all the Betan possibilities. If only you'd spent the last few weeks dropping the right kind of hints, you could have had Mama and Da falling to their knees in thanks that you were only messing around with Mark. Though I do wonder about your taste in men."

What Martya doesn't know about my sampling of Betan possibilities, Kareen decided firmly, *won't hurt me.* "Or else they really would have locked me in the attic."

Martya waved this away. "Dr. Borgos was terrorized enough. It's really unfair to drop a normal person down in Vorkosigan House with the Chance Brothers and expect him to just cope."

"Chance Brothers?" Ekaterin inquired.

Kareen, who had heard the jibe before, gave it the bare grimace it deserved.

"Um," Martya had the good grace to look embarrassed. "It was a joke that was going around. Ivan passed it on to me." When Ekaterin continued to look blankly at her, she added reluctantly. "You know—Slim and Fat."

"Oh." Ekaterin didn't laugh, though she smiled briefly; she looked as though she was digesting this tidbit, and wasn't sure if she liked the aftertaste.

"You think Enrique is normal?" said Kareen to her sister, wrinkling her nose.

"Well . . . at least he's a change from the sort of Lieutenant Lord Vor-I'm-God's-Gift-to-Women we usually meet in Vorbarr Sultana. He doesn't back you into a corner and gab on endlessly about military history and ordnance. He backs you into a corner and gabs on endlessly about biology, instead. Who knows? He might be good husband material."

"Yeah, if his wife didn't mind dressing up as a butter bug to lure him to bed," said Kareen tartly. She made antennae of her fingers, and wriggled them at Martya.

Martya snickered, but said, "I think he's the sort who needs a managing wife, so he can work fourteen hours a day in his lab."

Kareen snorted. "She'd better seize control immediately. Yeah, Enrique has biotech ideas the way Zap the Cat has kittens, but it's a near-certainty that whatever profit he gets from them, he'll lose."

"Too trusting, do you think? Would people take advantage of him?"

"No, just too absorbed. It would come to the same thing in the end, though."

Ekaterin sighed, a distant look in her eyes. "I wish I could work *four* hours at a stretch without chaos erupting."

"Oh," said Martya, "but you're another. One of those people who pulls amazing things out of their ears, that is." She glanced around the tiny, serene garden. "You're wasted in domestic management. You're definitely R and D."

Ekaterin smiled crookedly. "Are you saying I don't need a husband, I need a wife? Well, at least that's a *slight* change from my sister-in-law's urgings."

"Try Beta Colony," Kareen advised, with a melancholy sigh.

The conversation grounded for a stretch upon this beguiling thought. The muted city street noises echoed over the walls and around the houses, and the slanting sunlight crept off the grass, putting the table into cool pre-evening shade.

"They really are utterly revolting bugs," Martya said after a time. "No one in their right mind will ever buy them."

Kareen hunched at this discouraging non-news. The bugs *did too* work. Bug butter was science's almost-perfect food. There *ought* to be a market for it. People were so prejudiced. . . .

A slight smile turned Martya's lip, and she added, "Though the brown and silver was just perfect. I thought Pym was going to pop."

"If only I'd known what Enrique was up to," mourned Kareen, "I could have stopped him. He'd been babbling on about his surprise, but I didn't pay enough attention—I didn't know he *could* do that to the bugs."

Ekaterin said, "I could have realized it, if I'd given it any thought. I scanned his thesis. The real secret is in the suite of microbes." At Martya's raised eyebrows, she explained, "It's the array of bioengineered microorganisms in the bugs' guts that do the real work of breaking down what the bugs eat and converting it into, well, whatever the designer chooses. Enrique has dozens of ideas for future products beyond food, including a wild application for environmental radiation cleanup that might excite . . . well. Anyway, keeping the microbe ecology balanced—tuned, Enrique calls it—is the most delicate part. The bugs are just self-assembling and self-propelled packaging around the microbe suite. Their shape is semi-arbitrary. Enrique just grabbed the most efficient functional elements from a dozen insect species, with no attention at all to the aesthetics."

"Most likely." Slowly, Kareen sat up. "Ekaterin . . . *you* do aesthetics."

Ekaterin made a throwaway gesture. "In a sense, I guess."

"Yes, you do. Your hair is always right. Your clothes always look better than anyone else's, and I don't think it's that you're spending more money on them."

Ekaterin shook her head in rueful agreement.

"You have what Lady Alys calls *unerring taste*, I think," Kareen continued, with rising energy. "I mean, look at this garden. Mark, Mark does money, and deals. Miles does strategy and tactics, and inveigling people into doing what he wants." Well, maybe not always; Ekaterin's lips tightened at the mention of his name. Kareen hurried on. "I still haven't figured out what I do. You—you do beauty. I really envy that."

Ekaterin looked touched. "Thank you, Kareen. But it really isn't anything that—"

Kareen waved away the self-deprecation. "No, listen, this is important. Do you think you could make a *pretty* butter bug? Or rather, make butter bugs pretty?"

"I'm no geneticist—"

"I don't mean that part. I mean, could you *design* alterations to the bugs so's they don't make people want to lose their lunch when they see one. For Enrique to apply."

Ekaterin sat back. Her brows sank down again, and an absorbed look grew in her eyes. "Well . . . it's obviously possible to change the bugs' colors and add surface designs. That has to be fairly trivial, judging from the speed with which Enrique produced the . . . um . . . Vorkosigan bugs. You'd have to stay away from fundamental structural modifications in the gut and mandibles and so on, but the wings and wing carapaces are already nonfunctional. Presumably they could be altered at will."

"Yes? Go on."

"Colors—you'd want to look for colors found in nature, for biological appeal. Birds, beasts, flowers . . . fire . . ."

"*Can* you think of something?"

"I can think of a dozen ideas, offhand." Her mouth curved up. "It seems too easy. Almost any change would be an improvement."

"Not just any change. Something *glorious*."

"A glorious butter bug." Her lips parted in faint

delight, and her eyes glinted with genuine cheer for the first time this visit. "Now, *that's* a challenge."

"Oh, would you, could you? *Will* you? Please? I'm a shareholder, I have as much authority to hire you as Mark or Enrique. Qualitatively, anyway."

"Heavens, Kareen, you don't have to pay me—"

"*Never*," said Kareen with passion, "ever suggest they don't have to pay you. What they pay for, they'll value. What they get for free, they'll take for granted, and then demand as a right. Hold them up for all the market will bear." She hesitated, then added anxiously, "You will take shares, though, won't you? Ma Kosti did, for the product development consultation she did for us."

"I must say, Ma Kosti made the bug butter ice cream work," Martya admitted. "And that bread spread wasn't bad either. It was all the garlic, I think. As long as you didn't think about where the stuff came from."

"So what, have you ever thought about where regular butter and ice cream come from? And meat, and liver sausage, and—"

"I can about guarantee you the beef filet the other night came from a nice, clean vat. Tante Cordelia wouldn't have it any other way at Vorkosigan House."

Kareen gestured this aside, irritably. "How long do you think it would take you, Ekaterin?" she asked.

"I don't know—a day or two, I suppose, for preliminary designs. But surely we'd have to meet with Enrique and Mark."

"I can't go to Vorkosigan House." Kareen slumped. She straightened again. "Could we meet *here*?"

Ekaterin glanced at Martya, and back to Kareen. "I can't be a party to undercutting your parents, or going behind their backs. But this is certainly legitimate business. We could all meet here if you'll get their permission."

"Maybe," said Kareen. "Maybe. If they have another day or so to calm down . . . As a last resort, you could meet with Mark and Enrique alone. But I want to be here, if I can. I know I can sell the idea to them, if only I have a chance." She stuck out her hand to Ekaterin. "Deal?"

Ekaterin, looking amused, rubbed the soil from her

hand against the side of her skirt, leaned across the table, and shook on the compact. "Very well."

Martya objected, "You know Da and Mama will stick me with having to tag along, if they think Mark will be here."

"So, *you* can persuade them you're not needed. You're kind of an insult anyway, you know."

Martya stuck out a sisterly tongue at this, but shrugged a certain grudging agreement.

The sound of voices and footsteps wafted from the open kitchen window; Kareen looked up, wondering if Ekaterin's aunt and uncle had returned. And if maybe one of *them* had heard anything from Miles or Tante Cordelia or . . . But to her surprise, ducking out the door after Nikki came Armsman Pym, in full Vorkosigan House uniform, as neat and glittery as though ready for the Count's inspection. Pym was saying, "—I don't know about that, Nikki. But you know you're welcome to come play with my son Arthur at our flat, any time. He was asking after you just last night, in fact."

"Mama, Mama!" Nikki bounced to the garden table. "Look, Pym's here!"

Ekaterin's expression closed as though shutters had fallen across her face. She regarded Pym with extreme wariness. "Hello, Armsman," she said, in a tone of utter neutrality. She glanced across at her son. "Thank you, Nikki. Please go in now."

Nikki departed, with reluctant backward glances. Ekaterin waited.

Pym cleared his throat, smiled diffidently at her, and gave her a sort of half-salute. "Good evening, Madame Vorsoisson. I trust I find you well." His gaze went on to take in the Koudelka sisters; he favored them with a courteous, if curious, nod. "Hello, Miss Martya, Miss Kareen. I . . . this is unexpected." He looked as though he was riffling through revisions to some rehearsed speech.

Kareen wondered frantically if she could pretend that her prohibition from speaking with anyone from the Vorkosigan household was meant to apply only to the immediate family, and not the Armsmen as well.

She smiled back with longing at Pym. Maybe *he* could talk to *her*. Her parents hadn't—couldn't—enforce their paranoid rule on anyone else, anyhow. But after his pause Pym only shook his head, and turned his attention back to Ekaterin.

Pym drew a heavy envelope from his tunic. Its thick cream paper was sealed with a stamp bearing the Vorkosigan arms—just like on the back of a butter bug—and addressed in ink in clear, square writing with only the words: *Madame Vorsoisson.* "Ma'am. Lord Vorkosigan directs me to deliver this into your hand. He says to say, he's sorry it took so long. It's on account of the drains, you see. Well, *m'lord* didn't say that, but the accident did delay things all round." He studied her face anxiously for her response to this.

Ekaterin accepted the envelope and stared at it as if it might contain explosives.

Pym stepped back, and gave her a very formal nod. When, after a moment, no one said anything, he gave her another half-salute, and said, "Didn't mean to intrude, ma'am. My apologies. I'll just be on my way now. Thank you." He turned on his heel.

"Pym!" His name, breaking from Kareen's lips, was almost a shriek; Pym jerked, and swung back. "Don't you dare just go off like that! What's *happening* over there?"

"Isn't that breaking your word?" asked Martya, with clinical detachment.

"Fine! Fine! *You* ask him, then!"

"Oh, very well." With a beleaguered sigh, Martya turned to Pym. "So tell me, Pym, what did happen to the drains?"

"I don't care about the drains!" Kareen cried. "I care about Mark! And my shares."

"So? Mama and Da say *you* aren't allowed to talk to anyone from Vorkosigan House, so you're out of luck. *I* want to know about the drains."

Pym's brows rose as he took this in, and his eyes glinted briefly. A sort of pious innocence informed his voice. "I'm most sorry to hear that, Miss Kareen. I trust the Commodore will see his way clear to lift our quarantine very soon. Now, *m'lord* told *me* I was not to hang about and distress Madame Vorsoisson with any ham-handed attempts at making things up to her, nor pester her by offering to wait for a reply, nor annoy her by watching her read his note. Very nearly his exact words, those. He never ordered me not to talk with you young ladies, however, not anticipating that you would be here."

"Ah," said Martya, in a voice dripping with, in Kareen's view, unsavory delight. "So you can talk to me and Kareen, but not to Ekaterin. And Kareen can talk to Ekaterin and me—"

"Not that I'd want to talk to you," Kareen muttered.

"—but not to you. That makes me the only person here who can talk to everybody. How . . . nice. *Do* tell me about the drains, dear Pym. Don't tell me they backed up again."

Ekaterin slipped the envelope into the inside pocket of her bolero, leaned her elbow on her chair arm and her chin on her hand, and sat listening with her dark eyebrows crinkling.

Pym nodded. "I'm afraid so, Miss Martya. Late last night, Dr. Borgos—" Pym's lips compressed at the name "—being in a great hurry to return to the search for his missing queen, took two days' harvest of bug butter—about forty or fifty kilos, we estimated later—which was starting to overflow the hutches on account of Miss Kareen not being there to take care of things properly, and flushed it all down the laboratory drain. Where it encountered some chemical conditions which caused it to . . . set. Like soft plaster. Entirely blocking the main drain, which, in a household with over fifty people in it—all the Viceroy and Vicereine's staff having arrived yesterday, and my fellow Armsmen and their families—caused a pretty immediate and pressing crisis."

Martya had the bad taste to giggle. Pym merely looked prim.

"Lord Auditor Vorkosigan," Pym went on, with a bare glance under his eyelashes at Ekaterin, "being of previous rich military experience with drains, he informed us, responded at once and without hesitation to his mother's piteous plea, and drafted and led a picked strike-force to the subbasement to deal with the dilemma. Which was me and Armsman Roic, in the event."

"Your courage and, um, utility, astound me," Martya intoned, staring at him with increasing fascination.

Pym shrugged humbly. "The necessity of wading knee-deep in bug butter, tree root bits, and, er, all the other things that go into drains, could not be honorably refused when following a leader who had to wade, um, knee-deeper. Being as how m'lord knew exactly what he was doing, it didn't actually take us very long, and there was much rejoicing in the household. But I was made later than intended for bringing Madame Vorsoisson her letter on account of everyone getting a slow start, this morning."

"What happened to Dr. Borgos?" asked Martya, as Kareen gritted her teeth, clenched her hands, and bounced in her chair.

"My suggestion that he be tied upside-down to the subbasement wall while the, um, *liquid* level rose being most unfairly rejected, I believe the Countess had a little talk with him, afterwards, about what kinds of materials could and could not be safely committed to Vorkosigan House's drains." Pym heaved a sigh. "Milady is quite too gentle and kindly."

The story having apparently finally wound to its conclusion, Kareen punched Martya on the shoulder and hissed, "Ask him how is *Mark*."

A little silence stretched, while Pym waited benignly for his translator, and Kareen reflected that it probably *would* take someone with a sense of humor as arcane as Pym's to get along so well with Miles as an employer. At last, Martya broke down and said ungraciously, "So, how's the fat one?"

"*Lord Mark*," Pym replied with faint emphasis, "having narrowly escaped injury in an attempt to consume—" his mouth paused, open, while he changed course in mid-sentence, "though quite visibly depressed by the unfortunate turn of events night before last, has been kept busy in assisting Dr. Borgos in his bug recovery."

Kareen decoded "visibly depressed" without difficulty. *Gorge has got out. Probably Howl, as well.* Oh, hell, and Mark had been doing so well in keeping the Black Gang subordinated. . . .

Pym went on smoothly, "I think I may speak for the entire Vorkosigan household when I say that we all wish Miss Kareen may return as soon as possible and restore order. Lacking information on the events in the Commodore's family, Lord Mark has been uncertain how to proceed, but that should be remedied now." His eyelid shivered in a ghost of a wink at Kareen. Ah yes, Pym was former ImpSec and proud of it; thinking sideways in two directions simultaneously was no mystery to him. Throwing her arms around his boots and screaming, *Help, help! Tell Tante Cordelia I'm being held prisoner by insane parents!* would be entirely redundant, she realized with satisfaction. Intelligence was about to flow.

"Also," Pym added in the same bland tone, "the piles of bug butter tubs lining the basement hall are beginning to be a problem. They toppled on a maid yesterday. The young lady was very upset."

Even the silently listening Ekaterin's eyes widened at this image. Martya snickered outright. Kareen suppressed a growl.

Martya glanced sideways at Ekaterin, and added somewhat daringly, "And so how's the skinny one?"

Pym hesitated, followed her glance, and finally replied, "I'm afraid the drain crisis brightened his life only temporarily."

He sketched a bow at all three ladies, leaving them to construe the stygian blackness of a soul that could find fifty kilos of bug butter in the main drain an *improvement* in his gloomy world. "Miss Martya, Miss Kareen, I hope we may see all the Koudelkas at Vorkosigan House again soon. Madame Vorsoisson, allow me to excuse myself, and apologize for any discomfort I may have inadvertently caused you. Speaking only for my own house, and Arthur, may I ask if Nikki may still be permitted to visit us?"

"Yes, of course," said Ekaterin faintly.

"Good evening, then." He touched his forehead amiably, and trod off to let himself out the garden gate in the narrow space between the houses.

Martya shook her head in amazement. "Where *do* the Vorkosigans find their *people*?"

Kareen shrugged. "I suppose they get the cream of the Empire."

"So do a lot of high Vor, but they don't get a *Pym*. Or a Ma Kosti. Or a—"

"I heard Pym came personally recommended by Simon Illyan, when he was head of ImpSec," said Kareen.

"Oh, I see. They *cheat*. That accounts for it."

Ekaterin's hand strayed to touch her bolero, beneath which that fascinating cream envelope lay hidden, but to Kareen's intense disappointment, she didn't take it out and break it open. She doubtless wouldn't read it in front of her uninvited guests. It was, therefore, time to shove off.

Kareen got to her feet. "Ekaterin, thank you so much. You've been more help to me than anybody—" *in my own family*, she managed to bite back. There was no point in deliberately ticking off Martya, when she'd allowed this grudging and partial allegiance against the parental opposition. "And I'm deadly serious about the bug redesign. Call me as soon as you have something ready."

"I'll have something tomorrow, I promise." Ekaterin walked the sisters to the gate, and closed it behind them.

At the end of the block, they were more or less ambushed by Pym, who waited leaning against the parked armored groundcar.

"Did she read it?" he asked anxiously.

Kareen nudged Martya.

"Not in front of *us*, Pym," said Martya, rolling her eyes.

"Huh. Damn." Pym stared up the block at the tile front of Lord Auditor Vorthys's house, half concealed in the trees. "I was hoping—damn."

"How *is* Miles, really?" asked Martya, following his glance and then cocking her head.

Pym absently scratched the back of his neck. "Well, he's over the vomiting and moaning part. Now he's taken to wandering around the house muttering to himself, when there's nothing to distract him. Starved for action, *I'd* say. The way he took to the drain problem was right frightening. From my point of view, you understand."

Kareen did. After all, wherever Miles bolted off to, Pym would be compelled to follow. No wonder all Miles's household watched his courtship with bated breath. She pictured the conversations belowstairs: *For God's sake, can't somebody please get the little git laid, before he drives us all as crazy as he is?* Well, no, most of Miles's people were sufficiently under his spell, they probably wouldn't put it in quite such harsh terms. But she bet it came to about that.

Pym abandoned his futile surveillance of Madame Vorsoisson's house and offered the sisters a ride; Martya, possibly looking ahead to parental cross-examination later, politely declined for them both. Pym drove off. Trailed by her personal snitch, Kareen departed in the opposite direction.

Ekaterin returned slowly to the garden table, and sat again. She pulled the envelope from her left inner pocket, and turned it over, staring at it. The cream-colored paper had impressive weight and density. The back flap was indented in the pattern of the Vorkosigans' seal, pressed deeply and a little off-center into the thick paper. Not machine embossed; some hand had put it there. *His* hand. A thumb-smear of reddish pigment filled the grooves and brought out the pattern, in the highest of high Vor styles, more formal than a wax seal. She raised the envelope to her nose, but if there was any scent of him lingering from his touch, it was too faint to be certain of.

She sighed in anticipated exhaustion, and carefully opened it. Like the address, the sheet inside was hand-written.

Dear Madame Vorsoisson, it began. *I am sorry.*
This is the eleventh draft of this letter. They've all started

*with those three words, even the horrible version in rhyme,
so I guess they stay.*

Her mind hiccuped to a stop. For a moment, all she
could wonder was who emptied his wastebasket, and if
they could be bribed. Pym, probably, and likely not. She
shook the vision from her head, and read on.

*You once asked me never to lie to you. All right, so. I'll
tell you the truth now even if it isn't the best or cleverest thing,
and not abject enough either.*

*I tried to be the thief of you, to ambush and take prisoner
what I thought I could never earn or be given. You were not
a ship to be hijacked, but I couldn't think of any other plan
but subterfuge and surprise. Though not as much of a surprise as what happened at dinner. The revolution started
prematurely because the idiot conspirator blew up his secret
ammo dump and lit the sky with his intentions. Sometimes
those accidents end in new nations, but more often they end
badly, in hangings and beheadings. And people running into
the night. I can't be sorry I asked you to marry me, because
that was the one true part in all the smoke and rubble, but
I'm sick as hell I asked you so badly.*

*Even though I'd kept my counsel from you, I should at
least have done you the courtesy to keep it from others as well,
till you'd had the year of grace and rest you'd asked for. But
I became terrified you'd choose another first.*

What *other* did he imagine her choosing, for God's
sake? She'd wanted no one. Vormoncrief was impossible.
Byerly Vorrutyer didn't even pretend to be serious.
Enrique Borgos? *Eep.* Major Zamori, well, Zamori
seemed kindly enough. But dull.

She wondered when *not dull* had become her prime
criterion for mate selection. About ten minutes after
she'd first met Miles Vorkosigan, perhaps? Damn the
man, for ruining her taste. And judgment. And . . .
and . . .

She read on.

*So I used the garden as a ploy to get near to you. I delib-
erately and consciously shaped your heart's desire into a trap.
For this I am more than sorry. I am ashamed.*

*You'd earned every chance to grow. I'd like to pretend
I didn't see it would be a conflict of interest for me to be*

*the one to give you some of those chances, but that would
be another lie. But it made me crazy to watch you constrained to tiny steps, when you could be outrunning time.
There is only a brief moment of apogee to do that, in most
lives.*

*I love you. But I lust after and covet so much more than
your body. I wanted to possess the power of your eyes, the way
they see form and beauty that isn't even there yet and draw
it up out of nothing into the solid world. I wanted to own
the honor of your heart, unbowed in the vilest horrors of those
bleak hours on Komarr. I wanted your courage and your will,
your caution and serenity. I wanted, I suppose, your soul,
and that was too much to want.*

She put the letter down, shaken. After a few deep
breaths, she took it up again.

*I wanted to give you a victory. But by their essential nature
triumphs can't be given. They must be taken, and the worse
the odds and the fiercer the resistance, the greater the honor.
Victories can't be gifts.*

*But gifts can be victories, can't they. It's what you said.
The garden could have been your gift, a dowry of talent, skill,
and vision.*

*I know it's too late now, but I just wanted to say, it would
have been a victory most worthy of our House.*

Yours to command,

Miles Vorkosigan.

Ekaterin rested her forehead in her hand, and closed
her eyes. She regained control of her breathing again
in a few gulps.

She sat up again, and reread the letter in the fading light. Twice. It neither demanded nor requested nor
seemed to anticipate reply. Good, because she doubted
she could string two coherent clauses together just now.
What did he expect her to make of this? Every sentence
that didn't start with *I* seemed to begin with *But*. It
wasn't just honest, it was *naked*.

With the back of her dirty hand, she swiped the
water from her eyes across her hot cheeks to cool and
evaporate. She turned over the envelope and stared
again at the seal. In the Time of Isolation, such incised
seals had been smeared with blood, to signify a lord's

most personal protestation of loyalty. Subsequently, soft pigment sticks had been invented for rubbing over the indentations, in a palette of colors of various fashionable meanings. Wine red and purple had been popular for love letters, pink and blue for announcements of births, black for notifications of deaths. This seal-rubbing was the very most conservative and traditional color, red-brown.

The reason for that, Ekaterin realized with a blurred blink, was that it *was* blood. Conscious melodrama on Miles's part, or unthinking routine? She had not the slightest doubt that he was perfectly capable of melodrama. In fact, she was beginning to suspect he reveled in it, when he got the chance. But the horrible conviction grew on her, staring at the smear and imagining him pricking his thumb and applying it, that for him it had been as natural and original as breathing. She bet he even owned one of those daggers with the seal concealed in the hilt for the purpose, which the high lords had used to wear. One could buy imitation reproductions of them in antique and souvenir shops, with soft and blunted metal blades because nobody ever actually nicked themselves anymore to testify in blood. Genuine seal daggers with provenance from the Time of Isolation, on the rare occasions when they appeared on the market, were bid up to tens and hundreds of thousands of marks.

Miles probably used his for a letter opener, or to clean under his fingernails.

And when and how had he ever hijacked a ship? She was unreasonably certain he hadn't plucked that comparison out of the air.

A helpless puff of a laugh escaped her lips. If she ever saw him again, she would say, *People who've been in Covert Ops shouldn't write letters while high on fast-penta*.

Though if he really was suffering a virulent outbreak of truthfulness, what about that part that started, *I love you*? She turned the letter over, and read that bit again. Four times. The tense, square, distinctive letters seemed to waver before her eyes.

Something was missing, though, she realized as she

read the letter through one more time. Confession was there in plenty, but nowhere was any plea for forgiveness, absolution, penance, or any begging to call or see her again. No entreaty that she respond in any way. It was very strange, that stopping-short. What did it mean? If this was some sort of odd ImpSec code, well, she didn't own the cipher.

Maybe he didn't ask for forgiveness because he didn't expect it was possible to receive it. That seemed a cold, dry place to be left standing. . . . Or was he just too bleakly arrogant to beg? Pride, or despair? Which? Though she supposed it could be both—*On sale now*, her mind supplied, *this week only, two sins for the price of one!* That . . . that sounded very *Miles*, somehow.

She thought back over her old, bitter domestic arguments with Tien. How she had hated that awful dance between break and rejoining, how many times she had short-circuited it. If you were going to forgive each other eventually, why not do it now and save days of stomach-churning tension? Straight from sin to forgiveness, without going through any of the middle steps of repentance and restitution. . . . Just go on, just do it. But they hadn't gone on, much. They'd always seemed to circle back to the start-point again. Maybe that was why the chaos had always seemed to replay in an endless loop. Maybe they hadn't learned enough, when they'd left out the hard middle parts.

When you'd made a real mistake, how did you continue? How to go on rightly from the bad place where you found yourself, on and not back again? Because there was never really any going back. Time erased the path behind your heels.

Anyway, she didn't want to go back. Didn't want to know less, didn't want to be smaller. She didn't wish these words unsaid—her hand clutched the letter spasmodically to her chest, then carefully flattened out the creases against the tabletop. She just wanted the pain to stop.

The next time she saw him, did she have to answer his disastrous question? Or at least, know what the answer was? Was there another way to say *I forgive you* short of *Yes, forever*, some third place to stand? She desperately wanted a third place to stand right now.

I can't answer this right away. I just can't.

Butter bugs. She could do butter bugs, anyway—

The sound of her aunt's voice, calling her name, shattered the spinning circle of Ekaterin's thoughts. Her uncle and aunt must be back from their dinner out. Hastily, she stuffed the letter back in its envelope and hid it again in her bolero, and scrubbed her hands over her eyes. She tried to fit an expression, any expression, onto her face. They all felt like masks.

"Coming, Aunt Vorthys," she called, and rose to collect her trowel, carry the weeds to the compost, and go into the house.

CHAPTER TWELVE

The door-chime to his apartment rang as Ivan was alternating between slurping his first cup of coffee of the morning and fastening his uniform shirtsleeves. Company, at this hour? His brows rose in puzzlement and some curiosity, and he trod to the entryway to answer its summons.

He was yawning behind his hand as the door slid back to reveal Byerly Vorrutyer, and so he was too slow to hit the Close pad again before By got his leg through. The safety sensor, alas, brought the door to a halt rather than crushing By's foot. Ivan was briefly sorry the door was edged with rounded rubber instead of, say, a honed razor-steel flange.

"Good morning, Ivan," drawled By through the shoe-wide gap.

"What the hell are you doing up so early?" Ivan asked suspiciously.

"So late," said By, with a small smile.

Well, that made a little more sense. Upon closer examination, By was looking a bit seedy, with a beard shadow and red-rimmed eyes. Ivan said firmly, "I don't want to hear any more about your cousin Dono. Go away."

"Actually, this is about your cousin Miles."

Ivan eyed his ceremonial dress sword, sitting nearby in an umbrella canister made from an old-fashioned artillery shell. He wondered if driving it down on By's shod foot hard enough to make him recoil would allow getting the door shut and locked again. But the canister was just out of reach from the doorway. "I don't want to hear anything about my cousin Miles, either."

"It's something I judge he needs to know."

"Fine. You go tell him, then."

"I . . . would really rather not, all things considered."

Ivan's finely tuned shit-detectors began to blink red, in some corner of his brain usually not active at this hour. "Oh? What things?"

"Oh, you know . . . delicacy . . . consideration . . . family feeling . . ."

Ivan made a rude noise through his lips.

" . . . the fact that he controls a valuable vote in the Council of Counts . . ." By went on serenely.

"It's my Uncle Aral's vote Dono is after," Ivan pointed out. "Technically. He arrived back in Vorbarr Sultana four nights ago. Go hustle him." *If you dare.*

By bared his teeth in a pained smile. "Yes, Dono told me all about the Viceroy's grand entrance, and the assorted grand exits. I don't know how you managed to escape the wreckage unscathed."

"Had Armsman Roic let me out the back door," said Ivan shortly.

"Ah, I see. Very prudent, no doubt. But in any case, Count Vorkosigan has made it quite well known that he leaves his proxy to his son's discretion in nine votes out of ten."

"That's his business. Not mine."

"*Do* you have any more of that coffee?" By eyed the cup in his hand longingly.

"No," Ivan lied.

"Then perhaps you would be so kind as to make me some more. Come, Ivan, I appeal to your common humanity. It's been a very long and tedious night."

"I'm sure you can find someplace open in Vorbarr Sultana to sell you coffee. On your way home." Maybe he wouldn't leave the sword in its scabbard . . .

By sighed, and leaned against the doorframe, crossing his arms as if for a lengthy chat. His foot stayed planted. "What *have* you heard from your cousin the Lord Auditor in the last few days?"

"Nothing."

"And what do you think about that?"

"When Miles decides what I should think, I'm sure he'll tell me. He always does."

By's lip curled up, but he tamped it straight again. "Have you tried to talk to him?"

"Do I look that stupid? You heard about the party. The man crashed and burned. He'll be impossible for days. My Aunt Cordelia can hold his head under water this time, thanks."

By raised his brows, perhaps taking this last remark for an amusing metaphor. "Now, now. Miles's little *faux pas* wasn't irredeemable, according to Dono, whom I take to be a shrewder judge of women than we are." By's face sobered, and his eyes grew oddly hooded. "But it's about to become so, if nothing is done."

Ivan hesitated. "What do you mean?"

"Coffee, Ivan. And what I have to pass on to you is not, most definitely not, for the public hallway."

I'm going to regret this. Grudgingly, Ivan hit the Door-open pad and stood aside.

Ivan handed By coffee and let him sit on his sofa. Probably a strategic error. If By sipped slowly enough, he could spin out this visit indefinitely. "I'm on my way to work, mind," Ivan said, lowering himself into the one comfortable chair, across from the sofa.

By took a grateful sip. "I'll make it fast. Only my sense of Vorish duty keeps me from my bed even now."

In the interests of speed and efficiency, Ivan let this one pass. He gestured for By to proceed, preferably succinctly.

"I went to a little private dinner with Alexi Vormoncrief last night," By began.

"How exciting for you," growled Ivan.

By waved his fingers. "It proved to have moments of interest. It was at Vormoncrief House, hosted by Alexi's uncle Count Boriz. One of those little behind-the-scenes love-fests that give *party* politics its name, you know. It seems my complacent cousin Richars heard about Lord Dono's return at last, and hurried up to town to investigate the truth of the rumors. What he found alarmed him sufficiently to, ah, begin to exert himself on behalf of his vote-bag in the upcoming decision in the Council of Counts. As Count Boriz influences a significant block of Conservative Party votes in the Council, Richars, nothing if not efficient, started his campaign with him."

"Get to the point, By," sighed Ivan. "What has all this to do with my cousin Miles? It's got nothing to do with *me*; serving officers are officially discouraged from playing politics, you know."

"Oh, yes, I'm quite aware. Also present, incidentally, were Boriz's son-in-law Sigur Vorbretten, and Count Tomas Vormuir, who apparently had a little run-in with your cousin in his Auditorial capacity recently."

"The lunatic with the baby factory that Miles shut down? Yeah, I heard about that."

"I knew Vormuir slightly, before this. Lady Donna used to go target-shooting with his Countess, in happier times. Quite the gossips, those girls. At any rate, as expected, Richars opened his campaign with the soup, and by the time the salad was served had settled upon a trade with Count Boriz: a vote for Richars in exchange for allegiance to the Conservatives. This left the rest of the dinner, from entrée to dessert through the wine, free to drift onto other topics. Count Vormuir expanded much upon his dissatisfaction with his Imperial Audit, which rather brought your cousin, as it were, onto the table."

Ivan blinked. "Wait a minute. What were you doing hanging out with Richars? I thought you were on the other side in this little war."

"Richars thinks I'm spying on Dono for him."

"And are you?" If Byerly was playing both ends against the middle in this, Ivan cordially hoped he'd get both hands burned.

A sphinxlike smile lifted By's lips. "Mm, shall we say, I tell him what he needs to know. Richars is quite proud of his cunning, for planting me in Dono's camp."

"Doesn't he know about you getting the Lord Guardian of the Speaker's Circle to block him from taking possession of Vorrutyer House?"

"In a word, no. I managed to stay behind the curtain on that one."

Ivan rubbed his temples, wondering which of his cousins By was actually lying to. It wasn't his imagination; talking with the man *was* giving him a headache. He hoped By had a hangover. "Go on. Speed it up."

"Some standard Conservative bitching was exchanged about the costs of the proposed Komarran solar mirror repairs. Let the Komarrans pay for it, they broke it, didn't they, and so on as usual."

"They will be paying for it. Don't they know how much of our tax revenues are based in Komarran trade?"

"You surprise me, Ivan. I didn't know you paid attention to things like that."

"I don't," Ivan denied hastily. "It's common knowledge."

"Discussion of the Komarran incident brought up, again, our favorite little Lord Auditor, and dear Alexi was moved to unburden himself of his personal grievance. It seems the beautiful Widow Vorsoisson bounced his suit. After much trouble and expense on his part, too. All those fees to the Baba, you know."

"Oh." Ivan brightened. "Good for her." She was refusing everybody. Miles's domestic disaster was provably *not Ivan's fault*, yes!

"Sigur Vorbretten, of all people, next offered up a garbled version of Miles's recent dinner party, complete with a vivid description of Madame Vorsoisson storming out in the middle of it after Miles's calamitous public proposal of marriage." By tilted his head. "Even taking Dono's version of the dialogue over Sigur's, whatever did possess the man, anyway? I always thought Miles more reliably suave."

"Panic," said Ivan. "I believe. I was at the other end of the table." He brooded briefly. "It can happen to the best of us." He frowned. "How the hell did Sigur get hold of the story? *I* sure haven't been passing it out. Has Lord Dono been blabbing?"

"Only to me, I trust. But Ivan, there were nineteen people at that party. Plus the Armsmen and servants. It's all over town, and growing more dramatic and delicious with each reiteration, I'm sure."

Ivan could just picture it. Ivan could just picture it coming to Miles's ears, and the smoke pouring back out of them. He winced deeply. "Miles . . . Miles will be homicidal."

"Funny you should say that." By took another sip of coffee, and regarded Ivan very blandly. "Putting together Miles's investigation on Komarr, Administrator Vorsoisson's death in the middle of it, Miles's subsequent proposition of his widow, and her theatrical—in Sigur's version, though Dono claims she was quite dignified, under the circumstances—public rejection of it, plus five Conservative Vor politicians with long-time grudges against Aral Vorkosigan and all his works, *and* several bottles of fine Vormoncrief District wine, a Theory was born. And evolved rapidly, in a sort of punctuated equilibrium, to a full-grown Slander even as I watched. It was just fascinating."

"Oh, shit," whispered Ivan.

By gave him a sharp look. "You anticipate me? Goodness, Ivan. What unexpected depths. You can imagine the conversation; I had to sit through it. Alexi piping about the damned mutant daring to court the Vor lady. Vormuir opining it was bloody convenient, say what, the husband killed in some supposed-accident in the middle of Vorkosigan's case. Sigur saying, But there weren't any charges, Count Boriz eyeing him like the pitiful waif he is and rumbling, There wouldn't be— the Vorkosigans have had ImpSec under their thumb for thirty years, the only question is whether was it collusion between the wife and Vorkosigan? Alexi leaping to the defense of his lady-love—the man just *does not* take a hint—and declaring her innocent, unsuspecting till Vorkosigan's crude proposal finally tipped his hand. Her storming out was Proof! Proof!—actually, he said it three times, but he was pretty drunk by then— that she, at least, now realized Miles had cleverly made away with her beloved spouse to clear his way to her, and she ought to know, she was there. And he bet she would be willing to reconsider his own proposal now! Since Alexi is a known twit, his seniors were not altogether convinced by his arguments, but willing to give the widow the benefit of the doubt for the sake of family solidarity. And so on."

"Good God, By. Couldn't you stop them?"

"I attempted to inject sanity to the limit available to me without, as you military types say, blowing my cover. They were far too entranced with their creation to pay me much heed."

"If they bring that murder charge against Miles, he'll wipe the floor with them all. I guarantee he will *not* suffer those fools gladly."

By shrugged. "Not that Boriz Vormoncrief wouldn't be delighted to see an indictment laid against Aral Vorkosigan's son, but as I pointed out to them, they haven't enough proof for that, and for—whatever—reason, aren't likely to get any, either. No. A *charge* can be disproved. A charge can be defended against. A charge proved false can draw legal retaliation. There won't be a charge."

Ivan was less sure. The mere hint of the idea had surely put the wind up Miles.

"But a wink," By went on, "a whisper, a snicker, a joke, a deliciously horrific anecdote . . . who can get a grip on such vapor? It would be like trying to fight fog."

"You think the Conservatives will embark on a smear campaign using this?" said Ivan slowly, chilled.

"I think . . . that if Lord Auditor Vorkosigan wishes to exert any kind of damage control, he needs to mobilize his resources. Five swaggering tongues are sleeping it off this morning. By tonight, they'll be flapping again. I would not presume to suggest strategies to My Lord Auditor. He's a big boy now. But as a, shall we say, courtesy, I present him the advantage of early intelligence. What he does with it is up to him."

"Isn't this more a matter for ImpSec?"

"Oh, ImpSec." By waved a dismissive hand. "I'm sure they'll be on top of it. But—*is* it a matter for ImpSec, y'see? Vapor, Ivan. Vapor."

This is slit your throat before reading stuff, and no horseshit, Miles had said, in a voice of terrifying conviction. Ivan shrugged, carefully. "How would I know?"

By's little smile didn't shift, but his eyes mocked. "How, indeed."

Ivan glanced at the time. Ye gods. "I have to report to work now, or my mother will bitch," he said hastily.

"Yes, Lady Alys is doubtless at the Residence waiting for you already." Taking the hint for a change, Byerly rose. "I don't suppose you can use your influence upon her to get *me* issued a wedding invitation?"

"I have no influence," said Ivan, edging By towards the door. "If Lord Dono is Count Dono by then, maybe you can get him to take you along."

By acknowledged this with a wave, and strolled off down the corridor, yawning. Ivan stood for a moment after the door hissed shut, rubbing his forehead. He pictured himself presenting By's news to Miles, assuming his distraught cousin had sobered up by now. He pictured himself ducking for cover. Better yet, he pictured himself deserting it all, possibly for the life of a licensed male prostitute at Beta's Orb. Betan male prostitutes did have female customers, yes? Miles had been there, and told him not-quite-all about it. Fat Mark and Kareen had even been there. But *he'd* never even once made it to the Orb, dammit. Life was unfair, that was what.

He slouched to his comconsole, and punched in Miles's private code. But all he stirred up was the answering program, a new one, all very official announcing that the supplicant had reached *Lord Auditor Vorkosigan*, whoop-te-do. Except he hadn't. Ivan left a message for his cousin to call him on urgent private business, and cut the com.

Miles probably wasn't even awake yet. Ivan dutifully promised his conscience he'd try again later today, and if that still didn't draw a response, drag himself over to Vorkosigan House to see Miles tonight. Maybe. He sighed, and shoved off to don the tunic of his undress greens, and head out for the Imperial Residence and the day's tasks.

❖   ❖   ❖

Mark rang the chime on the Vorthys's door, shifted from foot to foot, and gritted his teeth in anxiety. Enrique, let out of Vorkosigan House for the occasion, stared around in fascination. Tall, thin, and twitchy, the ectomorphic Escobaran made Mark feel more like a squat toad than ever. He should have given more thought to the ludicrous picture they presented when together . . . ah. Ekaterin opened the door to them, and smiled welcome.

"Lord Mark, Enrique. Do come in." She gestured them out of the afternoon glare into a cool tiled entry hall.

"Thank you," said Mark fervently. "Thank you so much for this, Madame Vorsoisson—Ekaterin—for setting this up. Thank you. Thank you. You don't know how much this means to me."

"Goodness, don't thank me. It was Kareen's idea."

"Is she here?" Mark swiveled his head in search of her.

"Yes, she and Martya were just a few minutes ahead of you both. This way . . ." Ekaterin led them to the right, into a book-crammed study.

Kareen and her sister sat in spindly chairs ranged around a comconsole. Kareen was beautiful and tight-lipped, her fists clenched in her lap. She looked up as he entered, and her smile twisted bleakly upward. Mark surged forward, stopped, stammered her name inaudibly, and seized her rising hands. They exchanged a hard grip.

"I'm allowed to talk to you now," Kareen told him, with an irritated toss of her head, "but only about business. I don't know what they're so paranoid about. If I wanted to elope, all I'd have to do is step out the door and walk six blocks."

"I, I . . . I'd better not say anything, then." Reluctantly, Mark released her hands, and backed off a step. His eyes drank her in like water. She looked tired and tense, but otherwise all right.

"Are *you* all right?" Her gaze searched him in turn.

"Yeah, sure. For now." He returned her a wan smile, and looked vaguely at Martya. "Hi, Martya. What are you doing here?"

"I'm the duenna," she told him, with a grimace quite as annoyed as her sister's. "It's the same principle as putting a guard on the picket line after the horses are stolen. Now, if they'd sent me along to Beta Colony, *that* might have been of some use. To me, at least."

Enrique folded himself into the chair next to Martya, and said in an aggrieved tone, "Did *you* know Lord Mark's mother was a *Betan Survey captain?*"

"Tante Cordelia?" Martya shrugged. "Sure."

"A *Betan Astronomical Survey captain*. And nobody even thought to mention it! A *Survey captain*. And nobody even *told* me."

Martya stared at him. "Is it important?"

"Is it important. Is it important! Holy saints, you people!"

"It was thirty years ago, Enrique," Mark put in wearily. He'd been listening to variations on this rant for two days. The Countess had acquired another worshipper in Enrique. His conversion had doubtless helped save his life from all his coreligionists in the household, after the incident with the drains in the nighttime.

Enrique clasped his hands together between his knees, and gazed up soulfully into the air. "I gave her my dissertation to read."

Kareen, her eyes widening, asked, "Did she understand it?"

"Of *course* she did. She was a *Betan Survey commander*, for God's sake! Do you have any idea how those people are chosen, what they do? If I'd completed my postgraduate work with honors, instead of all that stupid misunderstanding with the arrest, I could have hoped, only hoped, to put in an application, and even then I wouldn't have had a prayer of beating out all the Betan candidates, if it weren't for their off-worlder quotas holding open some places specifically for non-Betans." Enrique was breathless with the passion of this speech. "She said she would recommend my work to the attention of the Viceroy. And she said my sonnet was very ingenious. I composed a sestina in her honor in my head while I was catching bugs, but I haven't had time to get it down yet. Survey captain!"

"It's . . . not what Tante Cordelia is most famous for, on Barrayar," Martya offered after a moment.

"The woman is wasted here. *All* the women are wasted here." Enrique subsided grumpily. Martya turned half-around, and gave him an odd raised-brows look.

"How's the bug roundup going?" Kareen asked him anxiously.

"One hundred twelve accounted for. The queen is still missing." Enrique rubbed the side of his nose in reminded worry.

Ekaterin put in, "Thank you, Enrique, for sending me the butter bug vid model so promptly yesterday. It speeded up my design experiments vastly."

Enrique smiled at her. "My pleasure."

"Well. Perhaps I ought to move along to my presentations," said Ekaterin. "It won't take long, and then we can discuss them."

Mark lowered his short bulk into the last spindly chair, and stared mournfully across the gap at Kareen. Ekaterin sat in the comconsole chair, and keyed up the first vid. It was a full-color three-dimensional representation of a butter bug, blown up to a quarter of a meter long. Everyone but Enrique and Ekaterin recoiled.

"Here, of course, is our basic utility butter bug," Ekaterin began. "Now, I've only run up four modifications so far, because Lord Mark indicated time was of the essence, but I can certainly make more. Here's the first and easiest."

The shit-brown-and-pus-white bug vanished, to be replaced with a much classier model. This bug's legs and body were patent-leather black, as shiny as a palace guardsman's boots. A thin white racing stripe ran along the edges of the now-elongated black wing carapaces, which hid the pale pulsing abdomen from view. "Ooh," said Mark, surprised and impressed. How could such small changes have made such a large difference? "Yeah!"

"Now here's something a little brighter."

The second bug also had patent-black legs and body parts, but now the carapaces were more rounded, like fans. A rainbow progression of colors succeeded each other in curved stripes, from purple in the center through blue-and-green-and-yellow-and-orange to red on the edge.

Martya sat up. "Oh, now *that's* better. That's actually *pretty*."

"I don't think this next one will quite be practical," Ekaterin went on, "but I wanted to play with the range of possibilities."

At first glance, Mark took it for a rose bud bursting into bloom. Now the bug's body parts were a matte leaf-green faintly edged with a subtle red. The carapaces looked like flower petals, in a delicate pale yellow blushing with pink in multiple layers; the abdomen too was a matching yellow, blending with the flower atop and receding from the eye's notice. The spurs and angles of the bug's legs were exaggerated into little blunt thorns.

"Oh, oh," said Kareen, her eyes widening. "I want that one! I vote for that one!"

Enrique looked quite stunned, his mouth slightly open. "Goodness. Yes, that could be done . . ."

"This design might possibly work for—I suppose you'd call them—the farmed or captive bugs," said Ekaterin. "I think the carapace petals might be a little too delicate and awkward for the free-range bugs that were expected to forage for their own food. They might get torn up and damaged. But I was thinking, as I was working with these, that you might have more than one design, later. Different packages, perhaps, for different microbial synthesis suites."

"Certainly," said Enrique. "Certainly."

"Last one," said Ekaterin, and keyed the vid.

This bug's legs and body parts were a deep, glimmering blue. The carapace halves flared and then swept back in a teardrop shape. Their center was a brilliant yellow, shading immediately to a deep red-orange, then to light flame blue, then dark flame blue edged with flickering iridescence. The abdomen, barely visible, was a rich dark red. The creature looked like a flame, like a torch in the dusk, like a jewel cast from a crown. Four people leaned forward so far they nearly fell off their chairs. Martya's hand reached out. Ekaterin smiled demurely.

"Wow, wow, wow," husked Kareen. "Now *that* is a *glorious* bug!"

"I believe that was what you ordered, yes," murmured Ekaterin.

She touched a vid control, and the static bug came to life momentarily. It flicked its carapace, and a luminous lace of wing flashed out, like a spray of red sparks from a fire. "If Enrique can figure out how to make the wings bio-fluoresce at the right wavelength, they could twinkle in the dark. A group of them might be quite spectacular."

Enrique leaned forward, staring avidly. "Now *there's* an idea. They'd be a *lot* easier to catch in dim locations that way . . . There would be a measurable bio-energy cost, though, which would come out of butter production."

Mark tried to imagine an array of these glorious bugs, gleaming and flashing and twinkling in the twilight. It made his mind melt. "Think of it as their advertising budget."

"Which one should we use?" asked Kareen. "I really liked the one that looked like a flower . . ."

"Take a vote, I guess," said Mark. He wondered if he could persuade anyone else to go for the slick black model. A veritable assassin-bug, that one had looked. "A shareholder's vote," he added prudently.

"We've hired a consultant for aesthetics," Enrique pointed out. "Perhaps we should take her advice." He looked over to Ekaterin.

Ekaterin opened her hands back to him. "The aesthetics were all I could supply. I could only guess at how technically feasible they were, on the bio-genetic level. There may be a trade-off between visual impact, and the time needed to develop it."

"You made some good guesses." Enrique hitched his chair over to the comconsole, and ran through the series of bug vids again, his expression going absent.

"Time is important," Kareen said. "Time is money, time is . . . time is everything. Our first goal has to be to get some saleable product launched, to start cycling in capital to get the basic business up, running, and growing. Then play with the refinements."

"And get it out of Vorkosigan House's basement," muttered Mark. "Maybe . . . maybe the black one would be quickest?"

Kareen shook her head, and Martya said, "No, Mark." Ekaterin sat back in a posture of studied neutrality.

Enrique stopped at the glorious bug, and sighed dreamily. "This one," he stated. One corner of Ekaterin's mouth twitched up, and back down. Her order of presentation hadn't been random, Mark decided.

Kareen glanced up. "Faster than the flower-bug, d'you think?"

"Yes," said Enrique.

"Second the motion."

"Are you sure you don't like that black one?" said Mark plaintively.

"You're outvoted, Mark," Kareen told him.

"Can't be, I own fifty-one percent . . . oh." With the distribution of shares to Kareen and to Miles's cook, he'd actually slipped below his automatic majority. He intended to buy them back out, later . . .

"The glorious bug it is," said Kareen. She added, "Ekaterin said she'd be willing to be paid in shares, same as Ma Kosti."

"It wasn't that hard," Ekaterin began.

"Hush," Kareen told her firmly. "We're not paying you for hard. We're paying you for good. Standard creative consultant fee. Pony up, Mark."

With some reluctance—not that the workwoman was unworthy of her hire, but merely covert regret for the additional smidge of control slipping through his fingers—Mark went to the comconsole and made out a receipt of shares paid for services rendered. He had Enrique and Kareen countersign it, sent off a copy to Tsipis's office in Hassadar, and formally presented it to Ekaterin.

She smiled a little bemusedly, thanked him, and set the flimsy aside. Well, if she took it for play-money, at least she hadn't supplied play-work. Like Miles, maybe she was one of those people who was incapable of any speeds but *off* and *flat-out*. All things done well for the glory of God, as the Countess put it. Mark glanced again at the glorious bug, which Enrique was now making cycle through its wing-flash some more. Yeah.

"I suppose," said Mark with a last longing look at Kareen, "we'd better be going." Time-the-essence and all that. "The bug hunt has stopped everything in its tracks. R and D is at a standstill . . . we're barely maintaining the bugs we have."

"Think of it as cleaning up your industrial spill," Martya advised unsympathetically. "Before it crawls away."

"Your parents let Kareen come here today. Do you think they'd at least let her come back to work?"

Kareen grimaced hopelessly.

Martya screwed up her mouth, and shook her head. "They're coming down some, but not that fast. Mama doesn't say much, but Da . . . Da has always taken a lot of pride in being a good Da, you see. The Betan Orb and, well, you, Mark, just weren't in his Barrayaran Da's instruction manual. Maybe he's been in the military too long. Although truth to tell, he's barely handling *Delia's* engagement without going all twitchy, and she *is* playing by all the old rules. As far as he knows."

Kareen raised an inquiring eyebrow at this, but Martya did not elaborate.

Martya glanced aside to the comconsole, where the glorious bug sparked and gleamed under Enrique's enraptured gaze. "On the other hand—the guard-parents haven't forbidden *me* to go over to Vorkosigan House."

"Martya . . ." Kareen breathed. "Oh, could you? *Would* you?"

"Eh, maybe." She glanced under her lashes at Mark. "I was thinking maybe I could stand to get into some of this share-action myself."

Mark's brows rose. Martya? Practical Martya? To take over the bug hunt and send Enrique back to his genetic codes, without sestinas? Martya to maintain the lab, to deal with supplies and suppliers, to not flush bug butter down the sink? So what if she looked on him as a sort of oversized repulsive fat butter bug that her sister had inexplicably taken for a pet. He had not the least doubt Martya could make the brains run on time. . . . "Enrique?"

"Hm?" Enrique murmured, not looking up.

Mark got his attention by reaching over and switching off the vid, and explained Martya's offer.

"Oh, yes, that would be lovely," the Escobaran agreed sunnily. He smiled hopefully at Martya.

The deal was struck, though Kareen looked as if she might be having second thoughts about sharing shares with her sister. Martya electing to return to Vorkosigan House with them on the spot, Mark and Enrique rose to make their farewells.

"Are you going to be all right?" Mark asked Kareen quietly, while Ekaterin was busy getting her bug designs downloaded for Enrique to carry off.

She nodded. "Yeah. You?"

"I'm hanging on. How long will it take, d'you suppose? Till this mess gets resolved?"

"It's resolved already." Her expression was disturbingly fey. "I'm done arguing, though I'm not sure they realize it yet. I've had it. While I'm still living in my parents' house, I'll continue to hold myself honor-bound to obey their rules, however ludicrous. The moment I've figured out how to be somewhere else without compromising my long-range goals, I'll walk away. Forever, if need be." Her mouth was grim and determined. "I don't expect to be there much longer."

"Oh," said Mark. He wasn't exactly sure what she meant, or meant to do, but it sounded . . . ominous. It terrified him to think that he might be the cause of her losing her family. It had taken him a lifetime, and dire effort, to win such a place of his own. The Commodore's clan had looked to be such a golden refuge, to him . . . "It's . . . a lonely place to be. On the outside like that."

She shrugged. "So be it."

The business meeting broke up. Last chance . . . They were in the tiled hallway, with Ekaterin ushering them out, before Mark worked up the courage to blurt to her, "Are there any messages I can take for you? To

Vorkosigan House, I mean?" He was absolutely certain he would be ambushed by his brother on his return, given the way Miles had briefed him on his departure.

Renewed wariness closed down the expression on Ekaterin's face. She looked away from him. Her hand touched her bolero, over her heart; Mark detected a faint crackle of expensive paper beneath the soft fabric. He wondered if it would have a salutary humbling effect on Miles to learn where his literary effort was being stored, or whether it would just make him annoyingly elated.

"Tell him," she said at last, and no need to specify which *him*, "I accept his apology. But I can't answer his question."

Mark felt he had a brotherly duty to put in a good word for Miles, but the woman's painful reserve unnerved him. He finally mumbled diffidently, "He cares a lot, you know."

This wrenched a short little nod from her, and a brief, bleak smile. "Yes. I know. Thank you, Mark." That seemed to close the subject.

Kareen turned right at the sidewalk, while the rest of them turned left to head back to where the borrowed Armsman waited with the borrowed groundcar. Mark walked backwards a moment, watching her retreat. She strode on, head down, and didn't look back.

Miles, who had left the door of his suite open for the purpose, heard Mark returning in the late afternoon. He nipped out into the hall, and leaned over the balcony with a predatory stare down into the black-and-white paved entry foyer. All he could tell at a glance was that Mark looked overheated, an inescapable result of wearing that much black and fat in this weather.

Miles said urgently, "Did you see her?"

Mark stared up at him, his brows rising in unwelcome irony. He clearly sorted through a couple of tempting responses before deciding on a simple and prudent, "Yes."

Miles's hands gripped the woodwork. "What did she say? Could you tell if she'd read my letter?"

"As you may recall, you explicitly threatened me with death if I dared ask her if she'd read your letter, or otherwise broached the subject in any way."

Impatiently, Miles waved this off. "*Directly*. You know I meant not to ask *directly*. I just wondered if you could tell . . . anything."

"If I could tell what a woman was thinking just by looking at her, would I look like *this*?" Mark made a sweeping gesture at his face, and glowered.

"How the hell would I know? I can't tell what you're thinking just because you look surly. You usually look surly." *Last time, it was indigestion.* Although in Mark's case, stomach upset tended to be disturbingly connected with his other difficult emotional states. Belatedly, Miles remembered to ask, "So . . . how *is* Kareen? Is she all right?"

Mark grimaced. "Sort of. Yes. No. Maybe."

"Oh." After a moment Miles added, "Ouch. Sorry."

Mark shrugged. He stared up at Miles, now pressed to the uprights, and shook his head in exasperated pity. "In fact, Ekaterin did give me a message for you."

Miles almost lurched over the balcony. "What, *what*?"

"She said to tell you she accepts your apology. Congratulations, dear brother; you appear to have won the thousand-meter crawl. She must have awarded you extra points for style, is all I can say."

"Yes! Yes!" Miles pounded his fist on the rail. "What else? Did she say anything else?"

"What else d'you expect?"

"I don't know. Anything. *Yes, you may call on me*, or *No, never darken my doorstep again*, or *something*. A clue, Mark!"

"Search me. You're going to have to go fish for your own clues."

"Can I? I mean, she didn't actually *say* I was not to bother her again?"

"She said, she couldn't answer your question. Chew on it, crypto-man. I have my own troubles." Shaking his head, Mark passed out of sight, heading for the back of the house and the lift tube.

Miles withdrew into his chambers, and flung himself

down in the big chair in the bay window overlooking the back garden. So, hope staggered upright again, like a newly revived cryo-corpse dizzied and squinting in the light. But not, Miles decided firmly, cryo-amnesiac. Not this time. He lived, therefore he learned.

I can't answer your question did not sound like *No* to him. It didn't sound like *Yes* either, of course. It sounded like ... one more last chance. Through a miracle of grace, it seemed he was to be permitted to begin again. Scrape it all back to Square One and start over, right.

So, how to approach her? *No more poetry, methinks. I was not born under a rhyming planet.* Judging from yesterday's effort, which he had prudently removed from his wastebasket and burned this morning along with all the other awkward drafts, any verse flowing from his pen was likely to be ghastly. Worse: if by some chance he managed something good, she'd likely want more, and then where would he be? He pictured Ekaterin, in some future incarnation, crying angrily *You're not the poet I married!* No more false pretenses. Scam just wouldn't do for the long haul.

Voices drifted up from the entry hall. Pym was admitting a visitor. It wasn't anyone Miles recognized at this muffled distance; male, so it was likely a caller upon his father. Miles dismissed it from his attention, and settled back down.

She accepts your apology. She accepts your apology. Life, hope, and all good things opened up before him.

The unacknowledged panic which had gripped his throat for weeks seemed to ease, as he stared out into the sunny scene below. Now that the secret urgency driving him was gone, maybe he could even slow down enough to make of himself something so plain and quiet as her friend. What would *she* like ... ?

Maybe he would ask her to go for a walk with him, somewhere pleasant. Possibly not in a garden, quite yet, all things considered. A wood, a beach ... when talk lagged, there would be diversions for the eye. Not that he expected to run short of words. When he could speak truth, and was no longer constrained to concealment and lies, the possibilities opened up startlingly. There was so much more to say . . . Pym cleared his throat from the doorway. Miles swiveled his head.

"Lord Richars Vorrutyer is here to see you, Lord Vorkosigan," Pym announced.

"That's Lord Vorrutyer, if you please, Pym," Richars corrected him.

"Your cousin, m'lord." Pym, with a bland nod, ushered Richars into Miles's sitting room. Richars, perfectly alive to the nuance, shot a suspicious look at the Armsman as he entered.

Miles hadn't seen Richars for a year or so, but he hadn't altered much; he was looking maybe a little older, what with the advance of his waistline and the retreat of his hairline. He was wearing a piped and epauletted suit in blue and gray, reminiscent of the Vorrutyer House colors. More appropriate for day-wear than the imposing formality of the actual uniform, it nonetheless managed to suggest, without overtly claiming a right to, the garb of a Count's heir. Richars still looked permanently peeved: no change there.

Richars stared around General Piotr's old chambers, frowning.

"You have a sudden need of an Imperial Auditor, Richars?" Miles prodded gently, not best pleased with the intrusion. He wanted to be composing his next note to Ekaterin, not dealing with a Vorrutyer. Any Vorrutyer.

"What? No, certainly not!" Richars looked indignant, then blinked at Miles as though just now reminded of his new status. "I didn't come to see you at all. I came to see your father about his upcoming vote in Council on that lunatic suit of Lady Donna's." Richars shook his head. "He refused to see me. Sent me on to you."

Miles raised his brows at Pym. Pym intoned, "The Count and Countess, having heavy social obligations tonight, are resting this afternoon, m'lord."

He'd seen his parents at lunch; they hadn't seemed a bit tired. But his father had told him last night that he meant to take Gregor's wedding as a vacation from his duties as Viceroy, not a renewal of his duties as Count, carry on boy, you're doing fine. His mother had endorsed this plan emphatically. "I am still my father's voting deputy, yes, Richars."

"I had thought, because he was back in town, he'd take over again. Ah, well." Richars studied Miles dubiously, shrugged, and advanced toward the bay window.

All mine, eh? "Um, do sit down." Miles gestured to the chair opposite him, across the low table. "Thank you, Pym, that will be all."

Pym nodded, and withdrew. Miles did not suggest refreshments, or any other impediment to speeding Richars through his pitch, whatever it was going to be. Richars certainly hadn't dropped in for the pleasure of his company, not that his company was worth much just now. *Ekaterin, Ekaterin, Ekaterin . . .*

Richars settled himself, and offered in what was evidently meant as sympathy, "I passed your fat clone in the hallway. He must be a great trial to you all. Can't you do anything about him?"

It was hard to tell from this if Richars found Mark's obesity or his existence more offensive; on the other hand, Richars too was presently struggling with a relative in an embarrassing choice of body. But Miles was also reminded why, if he did not exactly go out of his way to avoid his Vorrutyer cousin-not-removed-far-enough, he did not seek his company. "Yes, well, he's *our* trial. What do you want, Richars?"

Richars sat back, shaking the distraction of Mark from his head. "I came to speak to Count Vorkosigan about . . . although come to think of it—I understand you've actually *met* Lady Donna since she returned from Beta Colony?"

"Do you mean Lord Dono? Yes. Ivan . . . introduced us. Haven't you seen, ah, your cousin yet?"

"Not yet." Richars smiled thinly. "I don't know who she imagines she's fooling. Just not the real thing, our Donna."

Inspired to a touch of malice, Miles let his brows climb. "Well, now, that depends entirely on what you define as *the real thing*, doesn't it? They do good work on Beta Colony. She went to a reputable clinic. I'm not as familiar with the details as, perhaps, Ivan, but I don't doubt the transformation was complete and real, biologically speaking. And no one can deny Dono is true Vor, and a Count's legitimate eldest surviving child. Two out of three, and for the rest, well, times change."

"Good God, Vorkosigan, you're not *serious*." Richars sat upright, and compressed his lips in disgust. "Nine generations of Vorrutyer service to the Imperium, to come to *this*? This tasteless joke?"

Miles shrugged. "That's for the Council of Counts to decide, evidently."

"It's absurd. Donna *cannot* inherit. Look at the consequences. One of the first duties of a Count is to sire his heir. What woman in her right mind would ever marry her?"

"There's someone for everyone, they say." A hopeful thought. Yes, and if even Richars had managed matrimony, how hard could it be? "And heir-production isn't exactly the only job requirement. Many Counts have failed to spawn their own replacements, for one reason or another. Look at poor Pierre, for example."

Richars shot him an annoyed, wary look, which Miles elected not to notice. Miles went on, "Dono seemed to be making a pretty good impression on the ladies when I saw him."

"That's just the damned women sticking together, Vorkosigan." Richars hesitated, looking struck. "You say *Ivan* brought her?"

"Yes." Just exactly how Dono had strong-armed Ivan into this was still unclear to Miles, but he felt no impulse to share his speculations with Richars.

"He used to screw her, you know. So did half the men in Vorbarr Sultana."

"I'd heard . . . something." *Go away, Richars. I don't want to deal with your smarmy notion of wit right now.*

"I wonder if he still . . . well! I'd never have thought Ivan Vorpatril climbed into that side of the bunk, but live and learn!"

"Um, Richars . . . you have a consistency problem, here," Miles felt compelled to point out. "You cannot logically imply my cousin Ivan is a homosexual for screwing Dono, not that I think he is doing so, unless you simultaneously grant Dono is actually male. In which case, his suit for the Vorrutyer Countship holds."

"I think," said Richars primly after a moment, "your cousin Ivan may be a very confused young man."

"Not about that, he's not," Miles sighed.

"This is irrelevant." Richars impatiently brushed away the question of Ivan's sexuality, of whatever mode.

"I must agree."

"Look, Miles." Richars tented his hands in a gesture of reason. "I know you Vorkosigans have backed the Progressives since Piotr's days ended, just as we Vorrutyers have always been staunch Conservatives. But this prank of Donna's attacks the basis of Vor power itself. If we Vor do not stand together on certain core issues, the time will come when all Vor will find ourselves with nothing left to stand *upon*. I assume I can count on your vote."

"I hadn't really given the suit much thought yet."

"Well, think about it now. It's coming up very soon."

All right, all right, granted, the fact that Dono amused Miles considerably more than Richars did was not, in and of itself, qualification for a Countship. He was going to have to step back and evaluate this. Miles sighed, and tried to force himself to attend more seriously to Richars's presentation.

Richars probed, "Are there any matters you are pursuing in Council at the moment, especially?"

Richars was angling for a vote-trade, or more properly, a trade in vote-futures, since, unlike Miles's, his vote was vapor right now. Miles thought it over. "Not at present. I have a personal interest in the Komarran solar mirror repair, since I think it will be a good investment for the Imperium, but Gregor seems to have his majority well in hand on that one." *In other words, you don't have anything I need, Richars. Not even in theory.* But he added after a moment's further reflection, "By-the-by, what do you think of René Vorbretten's dilemma?"

Richars shrugged. "Unfortunate. Not René's fault, I suppose, the poor sod, but what's to be done?"

"Reconfirm René in his own right?" Miles suggested mildly.

"Impossible," said Richars with conviction. "He's *Cetagandan*."

"I am trying to think by what possible criteria anyone could sanely describe René Vorbretten as a Cetagandan," said Miles.

"Blood," said Richars without hesitation. "Fortunately, there is an untainted Vorbretten line of descent to draw on to take his place. I imagine Sigur will grow into René's Countship well enough in time."

"Have you promised Sigur your vote?"

Richars cleared his throat. "Since you mention it, yes."

Therefore, Richars now possessed the promise of Count Vormoncrief's support. Nothing to be done for René with that tight little circle. Miles merely smiled.

"This delay in my confirmation has been maddening," Richars went on after a moment. "Three months wasted, while the Vorrutyer's District drifts without a hand on the controls, and Donna prances around having her sick little joke."

"Mm, that sort of surgery is neither trivial nor painless." If there was one techno-torture on which Miles was an expert, it was modern medicine. "In a strange sense, Dono killed Donna for this chance. I think he's deathly serious. And having sacrificed so much for it, I imagine he's likely to value the prize."

"You're not—" Richars looked taken aback. "You're surely not thinking of voting *for* her, are you? You can't imagine your father endorsing that!"

"Plainly, if I do, he does. I am his Voice."

"Your grandfather," Richars looked around the sitting room, "would spin in his grave!"

Miles's lips drew back on a humorless smile. "I don't know, Richars. Lord Dono makes an excellent first impression. He may be received everywhere the first time for curiosity, but I can well imagine him being invited back on his own merits."

"Is that why you received her at Vorkosigan House, for curiosity? I must say, you didn't help the Vorrutyers with that. Pierre was strange—did he ever show you his collection of hats lined with gold foil?—and his sister's no improvement. The woman should be clapped in an attic for this whole appalling escapade."

"You should get over your prejudices and meet Lord Dono." *You can leave any time now, in fact.* "He quite charmed Lady Alys."

"Lady Alys holds no vote in Council." Richars gave Miles a sharp frown. "Did he—*she*—charm you?"

Miles shrugged, compelled to honesty. "I wouldn't go that far. He wasn't my chief concern that night."

"Yes," said Richars grumpily, "I heard all about *your* problem."

What? Abruptly, Miles found that Richars had finally riveted his full, undivided attention. "And what problem would that be?" he inquired softly.

Richar's lip turned up in a sour smile. "Sometimes, you remind me of my cousin By. He's very practiced at the suave pose, but he's not nearly as slick as he pretends to be. I'd have thought you'd have had the tactical wits to seal the exits before springing a trap like that." He conceded after a moment, "Though I do think the better of Alexi's widow for standing up to you."

"Alexi's widow?" breathed Miles. "I didn't know Alexi was married, let alone deceased. Who's the lucky lady?"

Richars gave him a don't-be-stupid look. His smile grew odder, as it penetrated that he'd drawn Miles out of his irritating indifference at last. "It was just a *leetle* obvious, don't you think, My Lord Auditor? Just a *leetle* obvious?" He leaned back in his chair, squinting through narrowed eyes.

"I'm afraid you've lost me," said Miles, in an extremely neutral tone. As automatically as breathing, Miles's face, posture, gestures slid into Security mode, unrevealing, unobtrusive.

"Your Administrator Vorsoisson's so-convenient death? Alexi thinks the widow hadn't guessed earlier how—and why—her husband died. But judging from her flaming exit from your proposal-party, all of Vorbarr Sultana figures that she knows now."

Miles kept his expression to no more than a faint, slight smile. "If you are talking about Madame Vorsoisson's late husband Tien, he died in a breath mask accident." He did not add *I was there.* It didn't sound . . . helpful.

"Breath mask, eh? Easy enough to arrange. I can think of three or four ways to do it without even exerting myself."

"Motivation alone does not a murder make. Or . . . since you're so quick at this—what *did* happen the night Pierre's fiancée was killed?"

Richars's chin rose. "*I* was investigated and cleared. *You* haven't been. Now, I don't know if the talk about you is true, nor do I greatly care. But I doubt you'd care for the ordeal either way."

"No." Miles's smile remained fixed. "Enjoyed your part in that inquest, did you?"

"No," said Richars plainly. "Little officious guard bastards crawling all over my personal affairs, none of which were any of their damned business . . . drooling all over myself on fast-penta . . . The proles love having a Vor in their sights, don't you know. They'd piss all over themselves for a shot at someone of *your* rank. But you're likely safe, in the Council up there above us all. It would take a brave fool to lay the charge there, and what would he gain? No win for anyone."

"No." Such a charge would be quashed, for reasons of which Richars knew nothing—and Miles and Ekaterin would have to endure the scurrilous speculation that would follow that quashing. No win at all.

"Except possibly for young Alexi and the widow Vorsoisson. On the other hand . . ." Richars eyed Miles in growing conjecture, "There's a visible benefit to you if someone *doesn't* lay such a charge. I see a possible win-win scenario here."

"Do you."

"Come on, Vorkosigan. We're both as Old Vor as it's possible to be. It's stupid of us to be brangling when we should both be on the same side. Our interests march together. It's a tradition. Don't pretend your father and grandfather weren't top party horse-traders."

"My grandfather . . . learned his political science from the Cetagandans. Mad Emperor Yuri offered him post-graduate instruction after that. My grandfather schooled my father." *And both of them schooled me. This is the only warning you will receive, Richars.* "By the time I knew Piotr, Vorbarr Sultana party politics were just an amusing pastime to him, to entertain him in his old age."

"Well, there you are, then. I believe we understand each other pretty well."

"Let's just see. Do I gather you are offering not to lay a murder charge against me, if I vote for you over Dono in the Council?"

"Those both seem like good things to me."

"What if someone else makes such an accusation?"

"First they'd have to care, then they'd have to dare. Not all that likely, eh?"

"It's hard to say. *All of Vorbarr Sultana* seems a suddenly enlarged audience to my quiet family dinner. For example, where did you encounter this . . . fabrication?"

"At a quiet family dinner." Richars smirked, obviously satisfied at Miles's dismay.

And what route had the information traveled? Ye gods, *was* there a security rupture behind Richars's mouthings? The potential implications ranged far beyond a District inheritance fight. ImpSec was going to have a hell of a time tracking this.

All of Vorbarr Sultana. Ohshitohshitohshit.

Miles sat back, looked up to meet Richars's eyes directly, and smiled. "You know, Richars, I'm glad you came to see me. Before we had this little talk, I had actually been undecided how I was going to vote on the matter of the Vorrutyer's District."

Richars looked pleased, watching him fold so neatly. "I was sure we could see eye to eye."

The attempted bribery or blackmail of an Imperial Auditor was treason. The attempted bribery or blackmail of a District Count during wrestling for votes was more in the nature of normal business practice; the Counts traditionally expected their fellows to defend themselves in that game, or be thought too stupid to live. Richars had come to see Miles in his Voting Deputy hat, not his Imperial Auditor hat. Switching hats, and the rules of the game, on him in midstream seemed unfair. *Besides, I want the pleasure of destroying him myself.*

Whatever ImpSec found in addition would be ImpSec's affair. And ImpSec had no sense of humor. Did Richars have any idea what kind of lever he was trying to pull? Miles manufactured a smile.

Richars smiled back, and rose. "Well. I have other men to see this afternoon. Thank you, Lord Vorkosigan, for your support." He stuck out his hand. Miles took it without hesitation, shook it firmly, and smiled. He smiled him to the door of his suite when Pym arrived to escort him out, and smiled while the booted feet made their way down the stairs, and smiled until he heard the front doors close.

The smile transmuted to pure snarl. He stormed around the room three times looking for something that wasn't an antique too valuable to break, found nothing of that description, and settled for whipping his grandfather's seal dagger from its sheath and hurling it quivering into the doorframe to his bedroom. The satisfying vibrant hum faded all too quickly. In a few minutes, he regained control of his breathing and swearing, and schooled his face back to bland. Cold, maybe, but very bland.

He went into his study and sat at his comconsole. He brushed aside a repeat of this morning's message from Ivan to call him marked *urgent,* and coded up the secured line. A little to his surprise, he was put through to ImpSec Chief General Guy Allegre on the first try.

"Good afternoon, my Lord Auditor," Allegre said. "How may I serve you?"

Roasted, apparently. "Good afternoon, Guy." Miles hesitated, his stomach tightening in distaste for the task ahead. No help for it. "An unpleasant development stemming from the Komarr case—" no need to specify *which* Komarr case—"has just been brought to my attention. It appears purely personal, but it may have security ramifications. It seems I am being accused in the court of capital gossip of having a direct hand in the death of that idiot Tien Vorsoisson. The imputed motive being to woo his widow." Miles swallowed. "The second half is unfortunately true. I have been," *how to put this,* "attempting to court her. Not terribly . . . well, perhaps."

Allegre raised his brows. "Indeed. Something just crossed my desk on that."

Argh! What, for God's sake? "Really? That was quick." *Or else it really is all over town.* Yeah, it stood to reason Miles might not be the first to know.

"Anything connected with that case is red-flagged for my immediate attention."

Miles waited a moment, but Allegre didn't volunteer anything more. "Well, here's my bit for you. Richars Vorrutyer has just offered to nobly refrain from laying a murder charge against me for Vorsoisson's death, in exchange for my vote in the Council of Counts confirming him as Count Vorrutyer."

"Mm. And how did you respond to this?"

"Shook his hand and sent him off thinking he had me."

"And does he?"

"Hell, no. I'm going to vote for Dono and squash Richars like the roach he is. But I would very much like to know whether this is a leak, or an independent fabrication. It makes an enormous difference in my moves."

"For what it's worth, our ImpSec informant's report didn't pinpoint anything in the rumor that looks like a leak. No key details that aren't public knowledge, for example. I have a picked analyst following up just that question now."

"Good. Thank you."

"Miles . . ." Allegre pressed his lips thoughtfully together. "I have no doubt you find this galling. But I trust your response will not draw any more attention to the Komarr matter than necessary."

"If it's a leak, it's your call. If it's pure slander . . ." *What the hell am I going to do about it?*

"If I may ask, what do you plan to do next?"

"Immediately? Call Madame Vorsoisson, and let her know what's coming down." The anticipation made him cold and sick. He could scarcely imagine anything farther from the simple affection he'd ached to give her than this nauseating news. "This concerns—this damages—her as much as it does me."

"Hm." Allegre rubbed his chin. "To avoid muddying

already murky waters, I would *request* you put that off until my analyst has had a chance to evaluate her place in all this."

"Her place? Her place is innocent victim!"

"I don't disagree," Allegre said soothingly. "I'm not so much concerned with disloyalty as with possible carelessness."

ImpSec had never been happy to have Ekaterin, an oath-free civilian not under their control in any way, standing in the heart of the hottest secret of the year, or maybe the century. Despite the fact that she'd personally hand-delivered it to them, the ingrates. "She is not careless. She is in fact extremely careful."

"In your observation."

"In my professional observation."

Allegre gave him a placating nod. "Yes, m'lord. We would be pleased to prove that. You don't, after all, want ImpSec to be . . . confused."

Miles blew out his breath in dry appreciation of this last dead-pan remark. "Yeah, yeah," he conceded.

"I'll have my analyst call you with clearance just as soon as possible," Allegre promised.

Miles's fist clenched in frustration, and unfolded reluctantly. Ekaterin didn't go about much; it *might* be several days before this came to her ears from other sources. "Very well. Keep me informed."

"Will do, my lord."

Miles cut the com.

The queasy realization was dawning on him that, in his reflexive fear for the secrets behind the disasters on Komarr, he'd handled Richars Vorrutyer exactly backwards. *Ten years of ImpSec habits, argh.* Miles judged Richars a bully, not a psychotic. If Miles had stood up to him instantly, he might have folded, backed down, shied from deliberately pissing off a potential vote.

Well, it was way too late to go running after him now and try to replay the conversation. Miles's vote against Richars would demonstrate the futility of trying to blackmail a Vorkosigan.

And leave each other permanent enemies in

Council . . . Would calling his bluff force Richars to make good his threat or be forsworn? *Shit, he'll have to.*

In Ekaterin's eyes, Miles had barely climbed out of the last hole he'd dug. He wanted to be thrown together with her, but not, dear God, at a murder trial for the death of her late husband, however aborted. She was just starting to leave the nightmare of her marriage behind her. A formal charge and its aftermath, regardless of the ultimate verdict, must drag her back through its traumas in the most hideous imaginable manner, plunge her into a maelstrom of stress, distress, humiliation, and exhaustion. A power struggle in the Council of Counts was not a garden in which love was like to bloom.

Of course, the entire ghastly vision could be neatly short-circuited if Richars lost his bid for the Vorrutyer Countship.

But Dono hasn't got a chance.

Miles gritted his teeth. *He does now.*

A second later, he tapped in another code, and waited impatiently.

"Hello, Dono," Miles purred, as a face formed over the vid plate. The somber, if musty, splendor of one of Vorrutyer House's salons receded dimly in the background. But the figure wavering into focus wasn't Dono; it was Olivia Koudelka, who grinned cheerfully at him. She had a smudge of dust on her cheek, and three rolled-up parchments under her arm. "Oh—Olivia. Excuse me. Is, um, Lord Dono there?"

"Sure, Miles. He's in conference with his lawyer. I'll get him." She bounced out of range of the pickup; he could hear her voice calling *Hey, Dono! Guess who's on the com!* in the distance.

In a moment, Dono's bearded face popped up; he cocked an inquiring eyebrow at his caller. "Good afternoon, Lord Vorkosigan. What can I do for you?"

"Hello, Lord Dono. It has just occurred to me that, for one reason and another, we never finished our conversation the other night. I wanted to let you know, in case there was any doubt, that your bid for the Vorrutyer Countship has my full support, and the vote of my District."

"Why, thank you, Lord Vorkosigan. I'm very pleased to hear that." Dono hesitated. "Though . . . a little surprised. You gave me the impression you preferred to remain above all this in-fighting."

"Preferred, yes. But I've just had a visit from your cousin Richars. He managed to bring me down to his level in astonishingly short order."

Dono pursed his lips, then tried not to smile too broadly. "Richars does have that effect on people sometimes."

"If I may, I'd like to schedule a meeting with you and René Vorbretten. Here at Vorkosigan House, or where you will. I think a little mutual strategizing could be very beneficial to you both."

"I'd be delighted to have your counsel, Lord Vorkosigan. When?"

A few minutes of schedule comparison and shifting, and a side-call to René at Vorbretten House, resulted in a meeting set for the day after tomorrow. Miles could have been happy with tonight, or instantly, but had to admit this gave him time to study the problem in more rational detail. He bid a tightly cordial good-bye to both his, he trusted, future colleagues.

He reached for the next code on his comconsole; then his hand hesitated and fell back. He'd hardly known how to begin again *before* this mine had blown up in his face. He could say nothing to Ekaterin now. If he called her to try to talk of other things, ordinary kindly trivial things, while knowing this and not speaking it, he'd be lying to her again. Hugely.

But what the hell was he going to say when Allegre *had* cleared him?

He rose and began to pace his chambers.

Ekaterin's requested year of mourning would have served for more than the healing of her own soul. At a year's distance, memory of Tien's mysterious death would have been softened in the public mind; his widow might have gracefully rejoined society without comment, and been gracefully courted by a man she'd known a decent interval. But no. On fire with impatience, sick with dread of losing his chance with her, he'd had to push and push, till he'd pushed it right over the edge.

Yes, and if he hadn't babbled his intentions all over town, Illyan would never have been confused and blurted out his disastrous small-talk, and the highly-misinterpretable incident at the dinner party would never have occurred. *I want a time machine, so's I can go back and shoot myself.*

He had to admit, the whole extended scenario lent itself beautifully to political disinformation. In his covert ops days, he'd fallen with chortles of joy on lesser slips by his enemies. If he were ambushing himself, he'd regard it as a godsend.

You did ambush yourself, you idiot.

If he'd only kept his mouth shut, he might have gotten away clean with that elaborate half-lie about the garden, too. Ekaterin would still be lucratively employed, and—he stopped, and contemplated this thought with extremely mixed emotions. *Cross-ball.* Would a certain miserable period of his youth have been a shade less miserable if he'd never learned of that benign deceit? *Would you rather feel a fool, or be one?* He knew the answer he'd give for himself; was he to grant Ekaterin any less respect?

You did. Fool.

In any case, the accusation seemed to have fallen on him alone. If Richars spoke truth, hah, the back-splash had missed her altogether. *And if you don't go after her again, it will stay that way.*

He stumbled to his chair, and sat heavily. How long would he have to stay away from her, for this delicious whisper to be forgotten? A year? Years and years? Forever?

Dammit, the only crime he'd committed was to fall in love with a brave and beautiful lady. Was that so wrong? He'd wanted to give her the world, or at least, as much of it as was his to give. How had so much good intention turned into this . . . *tangle*?

He heard Pym down in the foyer, and voices again. He heard a single pair of boots climbing the stairs, and gathered himself to tell Pym that he was Not At Home to any more visitors this afternoon. But it wasn't Pym

who popped breezily through the door to his suite, but
Ivan. Miles groaned.

"Hi, coz," said Ivan cheerily. "God, you still looked
wrecked."

"You're behind the times, Ivan. I'm wrecked all over
again."

"Oh?" Ivan looked at him inquiringly, but Miles waved
it away. Ivan shrugged. "So, what's on? Wine, beer? Ma
Kosti snacks?"

Miles pointed to the recently-restocked credenza by
the wall. "Help yourself."

Ivan poured himself wine, and asked, "What are you
having?"

Let's not start that again. "Nothing. Thanks."

"Eh, suit yourself." Ivan wandered back over to the
bay window, swirling his drink in his glass. "You didn't
pick up my comconsole messages, earlier?"

"Oh, yeah, I saw them. Sorry. It's been a busy day."
Miles scowled. "I'm afraid I'm not much company right
now. I've just been blindsided by Richars Vorrutyer, of
all people. I'm still digesting it."

"Ah. Hm." Ivan glanced at the door, and took a gulp
of wine. He cleared his throat. "If it was about the murder rumor, well, if you'd answer your damned messages,
you wouldn't *get* blindsided. I tried."

Miles stared up at him, appalled. "Good God, not you
too? Does everybody in bloody Vorbarr Sultana know
about this goddamn crap?"

Ivan shrugged. "I don't know about everybody.
M'mother hasn't mentioned it yet, but she might think
it was too crude to take notice of. Byerly Vorrutyer
passed it on to me to pass on to you. At dawn, note.
He adores gossip like this. Just too excited to keep it
to himself, I guess, unless he's stirring things up for his
own amusement. Or else he's playing some kind of
sneaky underhanded game. I can't even begin to guess
which side he's on."

Miles massaged his forehead with the heels of his
hands. "Gah."

"Anyway, the point is, *it wasn't me who started this*. You
grasp?"

"Yeah." Miles sighed. "I suppose. Do me a favor, and quash it when you encounter it, eh?"

"As if anyone would believe me? Everybody knows I've been your donkey since forever. It's not like I was an eyewitness anyway. I don't know any more than anyone else." He asserted after a moment's thought, "Less."

Miles considered the alternatives. Death? Death would be much more peaceful, and he wouldn't have this pounding headache. But there was always the risk some misguided person would revive him again, in worse shape than ever. Besides, he had to live at least long enough to cast his vote against Richars. He studied his cousin thoughtfully. "Ivan . . ."

"It wasn't my fault," Ivan recited promptly, "it's not my job, you can't make me, and if you want any of my time you'll have to wrestle m'mother for it. *If* you dare." He nodded satisfaction at this clincher.

Miles sat back, and regarded Ivan for a long moment. "You're right," he said at last. "I have abused your loyalty too many times. I'm sorry. Never mind."

Ivan, caught with a mouthful of wine, stared at him in shock, his brows drawing down. He finally managed to swallow. "What do you mean, *never mind?*"

"I mean, never mind. There's no reason to draw you into this ugly mess, and every reason not to." Miles doubted there'd be much honor for Ivan to win in his vicinity this time, not even the sort that sparked so briefly before being buried forever in ImpSec files. Besides, he couldn't think offhand of anything Ivan could do for him.

"No *need?* Never *mind?* What are you up to?"

"Nothing, I'm afraid. You can't help me on this one. Thanks for offering, though," Miles added conscientiously.

"I didn't offer anything," Ivan pointed out. His eyes narrowed. "You're up to something."

"Not up. Just down." Down to nothing but the certainty that the next weeks were going to be unpleasant in ways he'd never experienced before. "Thank you, Ivan. I'm sure you can find your own way out."

"Well . . ." Ivan tilted up his glass, drained it, and set it down on the table. "Yeah, sure. Call me if you . . . need anything."

Ivan trod out, with a disgruntled backward look over his shoulder. Miles heard his indignant mutter, fading down the stairs: "No *need*. Never *mind*. Who the hell does he think he is . . . ?"

Miles smiled crookedly, and slumped in his seat. He had a great deal to do. He was just too tired to move.

Ekaterin. . . .

Her name seemed to stream through his fingers, as impossible to hold as smoke whipped away by the wind.

CHAPTER THIRTEEN

Ekaterin sat in the midmorning sun at the table in her aunt's back garden, and tried to rank the list of short-term jobs she'd pulled off the comconsole by location and pay. Nothing close by seemed to have anything to do with botany. Her stylus wandered to the margin of the flimsy and doodled yet another idea for a pretty butter bug, then went on to sketch a revision for her aunt's garden involving the use of more raised beds for easy maintenance. The very early stages of congestive heart failure which had been slowing Aunt Vorthys down were due to be cured this fall when she received her scheduled transplant; on the other hand, she would likely return thereafter to her full teaching load. A container-garden of all native Barrayaran species . . . no. Ekaterin returned her attention firmly to the job list.

Aunt Vorthys had been bustling in and out of the house; Ekaterin therefore didn't look up till her aunt said, in a decidedly odd tone, "Ekaterin, you have a visitor."

Ekaterin glanced up, and stifled a flinch of shock. Captain Simon Illyan stood at her aunt's elbow. All right, so, she'd sat next to him through practically a whole dinner, but that had been at Vorkosigan House, where anything seemed possible. Towering legends weren't supposed to rise up and stand casually in one's own garden in the broad morning as though some passing person—probably Miles—had dropped a dragon's tooth in the grass.

Not that Captain Illyan *towered*, exactly. He was much shorter and slighter than she'd pictured him. He'd seldom appeared in news vids. He wore a modest civilian suit of the sort any Vor with conservative tastes might choose for a morning or business call. He smiled diffidently at her, and waved her back to her seat as she started to scramble up. "No, no, please, Madame Vorsoisson . . ."

"Won't . . . you sit down?" Ekaterin managed, sinking back.

"Thank you." He pulled out a chair and seated himself a little stiffly, as if not altogether comfortable. Maybe he bore old scars like Miles's. "I wondered if I might have a private word with you. Madame Vorthys seems to think it would be all right."

Her aunt's nod confirmed this. "But Ekaterin, dear, I was just about to leave for class. Do you wish me to stay a little?"

"That won't be necessary," Ekaterin said faintly. "What's Nikki up to?"

"Playing on my comconsole, just at present."

"That's fine."

Aunt Vorthys nodded, and went back into the house.

Illyan cleared his throat, and began, "I've no wish to intrude on your privacy or time, Madame Vorsoisson, but I did want to apologize to you for embarrassing you the other night. I feel much at fault, and I'm very much afraid I might have . . . done some damage I didn't intend."

She frowned suspiciously, and her right hand fingered the braid on the left edge of her bolero. "Did Miles send you?"

"Ah . . . no. I'm an ambassador entirely without portfolio. This is on my own recognizance. If I hadn't made that foolish remark . . . I did not altogether understand the delicacy of the situation."

Ekaterin sighed bitter agreement. "I think you and I must have been the only two people in the room so poorly informed."

"I was afraid I'd been told and forgotten, but it appears I just wasn't on the need-to-know list. I'm not quite used to that yet." A tinge of anxiety flickered in his eyes, giving lie to his smile.

"It was not your fault at all, sir. Somebody . . . overshot his own calculations."

"Hm." Illyan's lips twisted in sympathy with her expression. He traced a finger over the tabletop in a crosshatch pattern. "You know—speaking of ambassadors—I began by thinking I ought to come to you and put in a good word for Miles in the romance department. I figured I owed it to him, for having put my foot down in the middle of things that way. But the more I thought about it, the more I realized I have truly no idea what kind of a husband he would make. I hardly dare recommend him to you. He was a terrible subordinate."

Her brows flew up in surprise. "I'd thought his ImpSec career was successful."

Illyan shrugged. "His ImpSec *missions* were consistently successful, frequently beyond my wildest dreams. Or nightmares. . . . He seemed to regard any order worth obeying as worth exceeding. If I could have installed one control device on him, it would have been a rheostat. Power him *down* a turn or two . . . maybe I could have made him last longer." Illyan gazed thoughtfully out over the garden, but Ekaterin didn't think the garden was what he was seeing, in his mind's eye. "Do you know all those old folk tales where the count tries to get rid of his only daughter's unsuitable suitor by giving him three impossible tasks?"

"Yes . . ."

"Don't ever try that with Miles. Just . . . don't."

She tried to rub the involuntary smile from her lips, and failed. His answering smile seemed to lighten his eyes.

"I will say," he went on more confidently, "I've never found him a slow learner. If you were to give him a second chance, well . . . he might surprise you."

"Pleasantly?" she asked dryly.

It was his turn to fail to suppress a smile. "Not necessarily." He looked away from her again, and his smile faded from wry to pensive. "I've had many subordinates over the years who've turned in impeccable careers. Perfection takes no risks with itself, you see. Miles was many things, but never perfect. It was a privilege and a terror to command him, and I'm thankful and amazed we both got out alive. Ultimately . . . his career ran aground in disaster. But before it ended, he changed worlds."

She didn't think Illyan meant that for a figure of speech. He glanced back at her, and made a little palm-open motion with his hands in his lap, as if apologizing for having once held worlds there.

"Do you take him for a great man?" Ekaterin asked Illyan seriously. *And does it take one to know one?* "Like his father and grandfather?"

"I think he is a great man . . . in an entirely different way than his father and grandfather. Though I've often been afraid he'd break his heart trying to be them."

Illyan's words reminded her strangely of her Uncle Vorthys's evaluation of Miles, back when they'd first met on Komarr. So if a genius thought Miles was a genius, and a great man thought he was a great man . . . maybe she ought to get him vetted by a *really good* husband.

Voices carried faintly from the house through the open windows into the back garden, too muffled to make out the words. One was a low-pitched male rumble. The other was Nikki's. It didn't sound like the comconsole or the vid. Was Uncle Vorthys home already? Ekaterin had thought he would be out till dinnertime.

"I will say," Illyan went on, waving a thoughtful finger in the air, "he did always have the most remarkable knack for picking personnel. Either picking or making; I was never quite sure which. If he said someone was the person for the job, they proved to be so. One way or another. If he thinks you'd be a fine Lady Vorkosigan, he's undoubtedly right. Although," his tone grew slightly morose, "if you do throw in your lot with him, I can personally guarantee you'll never be in control of what happens next again. Not that one ever is, really."

Ekaterin nodded wry agreement. "When I was twenty, I chose my life. It wasn't this one."

Illyan laughed painfully. "Oh, twenty. God. Yes. When I took oath at twenty to Emperor Ezar, I had my military career all sketched out. Ship duty, eh, and ship captain by thirty, and admiral by fifty, and retirement at sixty, a twice-twenty-years man. I did allow for being killed, of course. All very neat. My life began to diverge from the plan the following day, when I was assigned to ImpSec instead. And diverged again, when I found myself promoted to chief of ImpSec in the middle of a war I'd never foreseen, serving a boy emperor who hadn't even existed a decade earlier. My life has been one long chain of surprises. A year ago, I could not have even imagined myself today. Or dreamed myself happy. Of course, Lady Alys . . ." His face softened at the mention of her name, and he paused, an odd smile playing on his lips. "Lately, I have come to believe that the principal difference between heaven and hell is the company you keep there."

Could one judge a man by his company? Could she judge Miles that way? Ivan was charming and funny, Lady Alys fine and formidable, Illyan, despite his sinister history, strangely kind. Miles's clone brother Mark, for all his bitter bite, seemed a brother in truth. Kareen Koudelka was pure delight. The Vorbrettens, the rest of the Koudelka clan, Duv Galeni, Tsipis, Ma Kosti, Pym, even Enrique . . . Miles seemed to collect friends of wit and distinction and extraordinary ability around himself as casually and unselfconsciously as a comet trailed its banner of light.

Looking back, she realized how very few friends Tien had ever made. He'd despised his coworkers, scorned his scattered relations. She'd told herself that he hadn't the knack for socializing, or was just too busy. Once past his school days, Tien had never made a new good friend. She'd come to share his isolation; *alone together* was a perfect summation of their marriage.

"I think you are very right, sir."

From the house, Nikki's voice rose suddenly in volume and pitch, yanking her maternal ear: "No! No!" Was he defying his uncle over something? Ekaterin raised her head, listening, and frowned uneasily.

"Um . . . excuse me." She flashed a brief smile at Illyan. "I think I'd better go check something out. I'll be right back . . ."

Illyan nodded understanding, and politely pretended to fix his attention on the surrounding garden.

Ekaterin entered the kitchen, her eyes slow to adjust from the glare outside, and quietly rounded the corner through the dining room to the parlor. She stopped in the archway in surprise. The voice she'd heard was not her uncle's; it was Alexi Vormoncrief's.

Nikki was sitting scrunched up in Uncle Vorthys's big chair in the corner. Vormoncrief loomed over him, his face tense, his hands anxiously crooked.

"Back to these bandages you saw on Lord Vorkosigan's wrists the day after your father was killed," Vormoncrief was saying, in an urgent voice. "What kind were they? How big?"

"I dunno." Nikki gave a trapped shrug. "They were just bandages."

"What kind of wounds did they conceal, though?"

"Dunno."

"Well, sharp slashes? Burns, blisters, like from a plasma arc? Can you remember seeing them later?"

Nikki shrugged again, his face stiff. "I dunno. They were raggedy, all the way around, I guess. He still has the red marks." His voice was constricted, on the verge of tears.

An arrested look crossed Vormoncrief's face. "Hadn't noticed that. He's very careful to wear long sleeves, isn't he? In high summer, huh. But did he have any other marks, on his face perhaps? Bruises, scratches, maybe a black eye?"

"Dunno . . ."

"Are you *sure*?"

"Lieutenant Vormoncrief!" Ekaterin interrupted this sharply. Vormoncrief jerked upright, and lurched around. Nikki looked up, his lips parting in relief. "What are you *doing*?"

"Ah! Ekaterin, Madame Vorsoisson. I came to see you." He waved vaguely around the book-lined parlor.

"Then why didn't you come out to where I was?"

"I seized the chance to talk to Nikki, and I'm very glad I did."

"Mama," Nikki gulped from his chair-barricade, "he says Lord Vorkosigan killed Da!"

"*What*?" Ekaterin stared at Vormoncrief, for a moment almost too stunned to breathe.

Vormoncrief gestured helplessly, and gave her an earnest look. "The secret is out. The truth is known."

"What truth? By *whom*?"

"It's being whispered all over town, not that anyone dares—or cares—to do anything about it. Gossips and cowards, the lot of them. But the picture's getting plainer. Two men went out into the Komarran wilderness. One returned, and with some pretty strange injuries, apparently. *Accident with a breath mask*, indeed. But I realized at once that you couldn't have suspected foul play, till Vorkosigan dropped his guard and proposed to you at his dinner. No wonder you ran out crying."

Ekaterin opened her mouth. Nightmare memories flashed. *Your accusation is physically impossible, Alexi; I know. I found them, out in that wilderness, alive and dead both.* A cascade of security considerations poured through her head. It was a direct chain of very few links from the details of Tien's death to the persons and objects that no one dared mention. "It was not like that at all." That sounded weaker than she'd intended. . . .

"I'll wager Vorkosigan was never questioned under fast-penta. Am I right?"

"He's ex-ImpSec. I doubt he could be."

"How convenient." Vormoncrief grimaced ironically.

"*I* was questioned under fast-penta."

"They cleared you of complicity, yes! I was sure of it!"

"*What* . . . complicity?" The words caught in her throat. The embarrassing details of the relentless interrogation under the truth drug she'd endured on Komarr after Tien's death boiled up in her memory. Vormoncrief was late with his lurid accusation. ImpSec had thought of that scenario before Tien's body was cold. "Yes, I was asked all the questions you'd expect a conscientious investigator to ask a close relative in a mysterious death." *And more.* "So?"

"*Mysterious* death, yes, you suspected something even then, I knew it!" With a wave of his hand, he overrode her hasty attempt to interject an *accidental* in place of that ill-chosen *mysterious.* "Believe me, I understand your hideous dilemma perfectly. You don't dare accuse the all-powerful Vorkosigan, the mutie lord." Vormoncrief scowled at the name. "God knows what retaliation he could inflict on you. But Ekaterin, I have powerful relatives too! I came to offer you—and Nikki—my protection. Take my hand—trust me—" he opened his arms, reaching for her "—and together, I swear we can bring this little monster to justice!"

Ekaterin sputtered, momentarily beyond words, and looked around frantically for a weapon. The only one that suggested itself was the fireplace poker, but whether to whap it on his skull or jam it up his ass . . . ? Nikki was crying openly now, thin strained sobs, and Vormoncrief stood between them. She began to dodge around him; ill-advisedly, Vormoncrief tried to wrap her lovingly in his arms.

"Ow!" he cried, as the heel of her hand crunched into his nose, with all the strength of her arm behind it. It didn't drive his nasal bone up into his brain and kill him on the spot the way the books said—she hadn't really thought it would—but at least his nose began to swell and bleed. He grabbed both her wrists before she could muster aim and power for a second try. He was forced to hold them tight, and apart, as she struggled against his grip.

Her sputtering found words at last, shrieked at the top of her voice: "*Let go of me, you blithering twit!*"

He stared at her in astonishment. Just as she gathered her balance to find out if that knee-to-the-groin thing worked any better than that blow-to-the-nose one, Illyan's voice interrupted from the archway behind her, deadly dry.

"The lady asked you to unhand her, Lieutenant. She shouldn't have to ask twice. Or . . . once."

Vormoncrief looked up, and his eyes widened with belated recognition of the former ImpSec chief. His hands sprang open, his fingers wriggling a little as if to shake off their guilt. His lips moved on one or two tries at speech, before his mouth at last made it into motion. "Captain Illyan! Sir!" His hand began to salute, the realization penetrated that Illyan wore civvies, and the gesture was converted on the fly to a tender exploration of his bunged and dripping nose. Vormoncrief stared at the blood smear on his hand in surprise.

Ekaterin swerved around him to slide into her uncle's armchair and gather up the sniffling Nikki, hugging him tight. He was trembling. She buried her nose in his clean boy-hair, then glared furiously over her shoulder. "How dare you come in here uninvited and interrogate my son without my permission! How dare you harass and frighten him like this! How dare you!"

"A very good question, Lieutenant," said Illyan. His eyes were hard and cold and not kindly at all. "Would you care to answer it for both of our curiosities?"

"You see, you see, sir, I, I, I . . ."

"What *I* saw," said Illyan, in that same arctic voice, "was that you entered the home of an Imperial Auditor, uninvited and unannounced, while the Auditor was not present, and offered physical violence to a member of his family." A beat, while the dismayed Alexi clutched his nose as if trying to hide the evidence. "Who is your commanding officer, Lieutenant Vormoncrief?"

"But she hit—" Vormoncrief swallowed; he abandoned his nose and came to attention, his face faintly green. "Colonel Ushakov, sir. Ops."

In a supremely sinister gesture, Illyan pulled an

audiofiler from his belt, and murmured this information into it, together with Alexi's full name, the date,
time, and location. Illyan returned the audiofiler to its
clip with a tiny snap, loud in the silence.

"Colonel Ushakov will be hearing from General
Allegre. *You* are dismissed, Lieutenant."

Cowed, Vormoncrief retreated, walking backwards.
His hand rose toward Ekaterin and Nikki in one last,
futile gesture. "Ekaterin, please, let me help you . . ."

"You *lie*," she snarled, still gripping Nikki. "You lie
vilely. Don't you *ever* come back here!"

Alexi's sincere, if daunted, confusion was more infuriating than his anger or defiance would have been. Did
the man not understand a word she'd said? Still looking stunned, he made it to the entry hall, and let himself
out. She set her teeth, listening to his bootsteps fade
down the front walk.

Illyan remained leaning against the archway, his arms
folded, watching her curiously.

"How long were you standing there?" she asked him,
when her breath had slowed a bit.

"I came in on the part about the fast-penta interrogation. All those key words—ImpSec, complicity . . .
Vorkosigan. My apologies for eavesdropping. Old habits die hard." His smile came back, though it regained
its warmth rather slowly.

"Well . . . thank you for getting rid of him. Military
discipline is a wonderful thing."

"Yes. I wonder how long it will take him to realize
I don't command him, or anyone else? Ah, well. So, just
what was the obnoxious Alexi blithering about?"

Ekaterin shook her head, and turned to Nikki. "Nikki,
love, what happened? How long was that man here?"

Nikki sniffed, but he was no longer trembling as
badly. "He came to the door right after Aunt Vorthys
left. He asked me all kinds of questions about when
Lord Vorkosigan and Uncle Vorthys stayed with us on
Komarr."

Illyan, his hands in his pockets, strolled nearer. "Can
you remember some of them?"

Nikki's face screwed up. "Was Lord Vorkosigan alone

with Mama much—how would I know? If they were alone, I wouldn't 'a *been* there! What did I see Lord Vorkosigan do. Eat dinner, mostly. I told him about the aircar ride ... he asked me all about breath masks." He swallowed, and looked wildly at Ekaterin, his hand clenching on her arm. "He said Lord Vorkosigan did something to Da's breath mask! Mama, is it *true*?"

"No, Nikki." Her own grip around him tightened in turn. "That wasn't possible. I found them, and I know." The physical evidence was plain, but how much could she say to him without violating security? The fact that Lord Vorkosigan had been chained to a rail by the wrists and unable to do anything to anyone's breath mask including his own led immediately to the question of who had chained him there and why. The fact that there were a myriad of things about that nightmare night Nikki didn't know led immediately to the question of how much more he hadn't been told, why Mama, how Mama, what Mama, why, why, why ...

"They made it up," she said fiercely. "They made it all up, only because Lord Vorkosigan asked me at his party to marry him, and I turned him down."

"Huh?" Nikki wriggled around and stared at her in astonishment. "He *did*? Wow! But you'd be a Countess! All that money and stuff!" He hesitated. "You said *no*? Why?" His brow wrinkled. "Is that when you quit your job too? Why were you so mad at him? What *did* he lie to you about?" Doubt rose in his eyes; she could feel him tense again. She wanted to scream.

"It was nothing to do with Da," she said firmly. "This—what Alexi told you—is just a slander against Lord Vorkosigan."

"What's a *slander*?"

"It's when somebody spreads lies about somebody, lies that damage their honor." In the Time of Isolation, you could have fought a duel with the two swords over something like this, if you'd been a man. The rationale of dueling made sudden sense to her, for the first time in her life. She was ready to kill someone right now, but for the problem of where to aim. *It's being whispered all over town ...*

"But . . ." Nikki's face was taut, puzzled. "If Lord Vorkosigan was with Da, why didn't he help him? In school on Komarr, they taught us how to share breath masks in an emergency . . ."

She could watch it in his face, as the questions began to twine. Nikki needed facts, truth to combat his frightened imaginings. But the State secrets were not hers to dispense.

Back on Komarr, she and Miles had agreed between them that if Nikki's curiosity became too much for Ekaterin to deal with, she would bring him to Lord Auditor Vorkosigan, to be told from his Imperial authority that security issues prevented discussing Tien's death until he was older. She had never imagined that the subject would take *this* form, that the Authority would himself be accused of Nikki's father's murder. Their neat solution suddenly . . . wasn't. Her stomach knotted. *I have to talk to Miles.*

"Well, now," Illyan murmured. "Here's an ugly little bit of politicking. . . . Remarkably ill-timed."

"Is this the first you've heard of this? How long has this been going around?"

Illyan frowned. "It's news to me. Lady Alys usually keeps me apprised of all the interesting conversations circulating in the capital. Last night, she had to give a reception for Laisa at the Residence, so my intelligence is a day behind . . . internal evidence suggests this has to have blown up since Miles's dinner party."

Ekaterin's horrified glance rose to his face. "Has *Miles* heard about this yet, do you think?"

"Ah . . . perhaps not. Who would tell him?"

"It's all my fault. If I hadn't gone charging out of Vorkosigan House in a huff . . ." Ekaterin bottled the remainder of this thought, as sudden distress thinned Illyan's mouth; yes, he imagined he held a link in this causal chain too.

"I need to go talk with some people," said Illyan.

"I need to go talk with Miles. I need to go talk with Miles *right now*."

A calculating look flashed across Illyan's face, to be succeeded by his normal bland politeness. "I happen to have a car and driver waiting. May I offer you a lift, Madame Vorsoisson?"

But where to park poor Nikki? Aunt Vorthys wouldn't be back for a couple of hours. Ekaterin could not have him present for this—oh, what the hell, it was Vorkosigan House. There were half a dozen people she could send him off to be with—Ma Kosti, Pym, even Enrique. *Eep*—she'd forgot, the Count and Countess were home now. All right, *five* dozen people. After another moment of frenzied hesitation, she said, "*Yes.*"

She got shoes on Nikki, left a message for her aunt, locked up, and followed Illyan to his car. Nikki was pale, and growing quieter and quieter.

The drive was short. As they turned into Vorkosigan House's street, Ekaterin realized she didn't even know if Miles would be there. She should have called him on the comconsole, but Illyan had been so prompt with his offer. . . . They passed the bare, baking Barrayaran garden, sloping down from the sidewalk. On the far side of the desert expanse, a small, lone figure sat on the curving edge of a raised bed of dirt.

"Wait, stop!"

Illyan followed her glance, and signaled his driver. Ekaterin had the canopy popped and was climbing out almost before the vehicle had sighed to the pavement.

"Is there anything else I can do for you, Madame Vorsoisson?" Illyan called after her, as she stood aside to let Nikki exit.

She leaned back toward him to breathe venomously, "Yes. *Hang* Vormoncrief."

He offered her a sincere salute. "I shall do my humble best, madame."

His groundcar pulled away as, Nikki in tow, she turned to step over the low chain blocking foot traffic from the site, and strode down into the garden.

Soil was a living part of a garden, a complex ecosystem of microorganisms, but this soil was going to be dead in the sun and gone in the rains if no one got its proper ground cover installed . . . Miles, she saw as she drew nearer, was sitting next to the only plant in this whole blighted expanse, the little skellytum rootling. It was hard to say which of them looked more desperate and forlorn. An empty pitcher sat on the wall next to his knee, and he stared in worry at the rootling and the spreading stain of water on the soil around it. He glanced up at the sound of their approaching steps. His lips parted; the most appalling thrilled look passed over his face, to be suppressed almost instantly and replaced by an expression of wary courtesy.

"Madame Vorsoisson," he managed. "What are you uh, doing . . . um, welcome. Welcome. Hello, Nikki . . ."

She couldn't help it; the first words out of her mouth were nothing she'd rehearsed in the groundcar, but rather, "You haven't been pouring water *over* the barrel, have you?"

He glanced at it, and back to her. "Ah . . . shouldn't I?"

"Only around the roots. Didn't you read the instructions?"

He glanced guiltily again at the plant, as if expecting to find a tag he'd overlooked. "What instructions?"

"The ones I sent you, the appendix—oh, never mind." She pressed her fingers to her temples, clutching for coherence in her seething brain.

His sleeves were rolled up in the heat; the ragged red scars ringing his wrists were plainly visible in the bright sunlight, as were the fine pale lines of the much older surgical scars running up his arms. Nikki stared at them in worry. Miles's gaze finally tore itself from her general *hereness*, and took in her agitated state.

His voice went flatter. "I gather gardening isn't what you came about."

"No." This was going to be hard—or maybe not. *He knows. And he didn't tell me.* "Have you heard about this . . . this monstrous accusation going around?"

"Yesterday," he answered bluntly.

"Why didn't you *warn* me?"

"General Allegre asked me to wait on ImpSec's security evaluation. If this . . . ugly rumor has security implications, I am not free to act purely on my own behalf. If not . . . it's still a difficult business. An accusation, I could fight. This is something subtler." He glanced around. "However, since it's now come to you perforce, his request is moot, and I shall consider myself relieved of it. I think perhaps we'd better continue this inside."

She contemplated the desolate space, open to the sky and the city. "Yes."

"If you will?" He gestured toward Vorkosigan House, but made no move to touch her. Ekaterin took Nikki by the hand, and they accompanied him silently up the path and around through the guarded front gate.

He led them up to "his" floor, back to the cheerful sunny room in which he'd fed her that memorable luncheon. When they reached the Yellow Parlor, he seated her and Nikki on the delicate primrose sofa and himself on a straight chair across from them. There were lines of tension around his mouth she hadn't seen since Komarr. He leaned forward with his hands clasped between his knees and asked her, "How and when did it come to you?"

She gave a, to her ears, barely coherent account of Vormoncrief's intrusion, corroborated by occasional elaborations from Nikki. Miles listened gravely to Nikki's stammering recital, attending to him with a serious respect which seemed to steady the boy despite the horrifying nature of the subject. Although he did have to suck a smile back off his lips when Nikki got to a vivid description of how Vormoncrief acquired his bloody nose—"And he got it all over his uniform, too!" Ekaterin blinked, taken aback to find herself receiving exactly the same look of pleased masculine admiration from both parties.

But the moment of enthusiasm passed.

Miles rubbed his forehead. "If it were up to my judgment, I'd answer several of Nikki's questions here and now. My judgment is unfortunately suspect. *Conflict of interest* doesn't even begin to cover my position in this." He sighed softly, and leaned back on the hard chair in an unconvincing simulation of ease. "The first thing I would like to point out is that at the moment, all the onus is on me. The backsplash of this sewage appears to have missed you. I'd like to see it stay that way. If

we . . . don't see each other, no one will have pretext
to target you with further slander."

"But that would make you look worse," said Ekaterin.
"It would make it look as if I believed Alexi's lies."

"The alternative would make it look as if we had
somehow colluded in Tien's death. I don't see how to
win this one. I do see how to cut the damage in half."

Ekaterin frowned deeply. *And leave you standing there
to be pelted with this garbage all alone?* After a moment
she said, "Your proposed solution is unacceptable. Find
another."

His eyes rose searchingly to her face. "As you
wish . . ."

"What are you talking about?" Nikki demanded, his
brows drawn down in confusion.

"Ah." Miles touched his lips, and regarded the boy.
"The reason, it seems, that my political opponents have
accused me of sabotaging your da's breath mask, is that
I want to court your mother."

Nikki's nose wrinkled, as he worked through this.
"Did you really ask her to marry you?"

"Well, yes. In a pretty clumsy way. I did." Was he
actually reddening? He spared her a quick glance, but
she didn't know what he saw in her face. Or what he
made of it. "But now I'm afraid that if she and I continue to go around together, people will say we must
have plotted together against your da. She's afraid that
if we don't continue to go around together, people will
say that proves she thinks I did—I'm sorry if this dis-
tresses you—murder him. It's called, damned if you do,
damned if you don't."

"Damn them all," said Ekaterin harshly. "I don't care
what any of those ignorant idiots think, or say, or do.
People can go choke on their vile gossip." Her hands
clenched in her lap. "I do care what Nikki thinks." *Rot*
Vormoncrief.

Vorkosigan raised an eyebrow at her. "And you think
this version wouldn't come around to him too, the way
the first one did?"

She looked away from him. Nikki was scrunching up
again, glancing uncertainly from adult to adult. This was

not, Ekaterin decided, the moment to tell him to keep his feet off the good furniture.

"Right," Miles breathed. "All right, then." He gave her a ghost of a nod. She was shaken by a weird inner vision of a knight drawing down his visor before facing the tilt. He studied Nikki a moment, and moistened his lips. "So—what *do* you think of it all so far, Nikki?"

"Dunno." Nikki, so briefly voluble, was drawing in again, not good.

"I don't mean facts. No one has given you enough facts yet for you to make much of. Try feelings. Worries. For example, are you afraid of me?"

"Naw," Nikki muttered, wrapping his arms around his knees and staring down at his shoes rubbing on the fine yellow silk upholstery.

"Are you afraid it might be true?"

"It could not be," said Ekaterin fiercely. "It was physically impossible."

Nikki looked up. "But he was in ImpSec, Mama! ImpSec agents can do anything, and make it look like anything!"

"Thank you for that . . . vote of confidence, Nikki," said Miles gravely. "I think. In fact, Ekaterin, Nikki's right. I can imagine several plausible scenarios that could have resulted in the physical evidence you saw."

"Name one," she said scornfully.

"Most simply, I might have had an unknown accomplice." Rather horribly, his fingers made a tiny twisting gesture, as of someone venting a bound man's oxygen supply. Nikki of course missed both the gesture and the reference. "It elaborates from there. If I can generate them, so can others, and I'm sure some won't hesitate to share their bright ideas with you."

"You foresaw this?" she asked, a little numb.

"Ten years in ImpSec does things to your brain. Some of them aren't very nice."

The tidal wave of anger that had hurled her here was receding, leaving her standing on a very bare shore indeed. She had not intended to talk so frankly in front of Nikki. But Vormoncrief had destroyed any chance of continuing to protect him by ignorance. Maybe Miles was right. They were going to have to deal with this. All three of them were going to have to deal, and go on dealing, ready or not, old enough or not.

"Shuffling facts only takes you so far anyway. Sooner or later, you come down to bare trust. Or mistrust." He turned to Nikki, his eyes unreadable. "Here's the truth. Nikki, I did not murder your father. He went out-dome with a breath mask with nearly empty reservoirs, which he did not check, and then got caught outside too long. I made two bad mistakes that prevented me from being able to save him. I don't feel very good about that, but I can't fix it now. The only thing I can do to make up for it is to take care of—" He stopped abruptly, and eyed Ekaterin with extreme wariness. "To see that his family is taken care of, and doesn't lack for any need."

She eyed him back. His family had been Tien's least concern, judging by his performance while he was alive, or else he would not have left her destitute, himself secretly dishonored, and Nikki untreated for a serious genetic disease. Yet Tien's larger failures, time bombs though they'd been for Nikki's future, had seldom impinged on the young boy. In a pensive moment during the funeral she had asked Nikki what one of his happy memories of his da was. He'd remembered Tien taking them for a wonderful week at the seaside. Ekaterin, recalling that the monorail tickets and reservations for that holiday had been slipped to her as a charity by her brother Hugo, had kept silent. Even from the grave, she thought bitterly, Tien's personal chaos still reached out to disrupt her grasp for peace. Maybe Vorkosigan's bid to shoulder responsibility was not a bad thing for Nikki to hear.

Nikki's lips were tight, and his eyes a little blurry, as he digested Miles's blunt words. "But," he began, and stalled.

"You must be starting to think of a lot of questions," Miles said in a tone of mild encouragement. "What are some of them? Or even just one or two of them?"

Nikki looked down, then up. "But—but—why didn't he check his breath mask?" He hesitated, then went on in a rush, "Why couldn't you share yours? What were your two mistakes? What did you lie to Mama about that got her so mad? Why *couldn't* you save him? How *did* your wrists get all chewed up?" Nikki took a deep breath, gave Miles an utterly daunted look, and almost wailed, "Am I supposed to kill you like Captain Vortalon?"

Miles had been following this spate with close attention, but at this last he looked taken aback. "Excuse me. Who?"

Ekaterin, flummoxed, supplied in an undervoice, "Captain Vortalon is Nikki's favorite holovid hero. He's a jump pilot who has galactic adventures with Prince Xav, smuggling arms to the Resistance during the Cetagandan invasion. There was a whole long sequence about him chasing down some collaborators who'd ambushed his da—Lord Vortalon—and avenging his death on them one by one."

"I somehow missed that one. Must have been off-world. You let him watch all that violence, at his tender age?" Miles's eyes were suddenly alight.

Ekaterin set her teeth. "It was *supposed* to be educational, on account of the historical accuracy of the background."

"When I was Nikki's age, my obsession was Lord Vorthalia the Bold, Legendary Hero from the Time of Isolation." His reminiscent voice took on a rather fruity narrator's cadence, delivering this last. "That started with a holovid too, come to think of it, though before I was done I was persuading my gran'da to take me to look up original Imperial archives. Turned out Vorthalia wasn't as legendary as all that, though his real adventures weren't all so heroic. I think I could still sing all nine verses of the song that went with—"

"Please don't," she growled.

"Well, it could have been worse. I'm glad you didn't let him watch *Hamlet*."

"What's Hamlet?" asked Nikki instantly. He was starting to uncoil a little.

"Another great revenge drama on the same theme, except this one is an ancient stage play from Old Earth. Prince Hamlet comes home from college—by the way, how old was your Captain Vortalon?"

"Old," said Nikki. "Twenty."

"Ah, well, there you go. Nobody expects you to carry out a really good revenge till you're at least old enough to shave. You have several years yet before you have to worry about it."

Ekaterin started to cry *Lord Vorkosigan!* in outraged protest to this line of black humor, till she saw that Nikki looked noticeably relieved. Where was Miles going with this? She held her tongue, and nearly her breath, and let him run on.

"So in the play, Prince Hamlet comes home for his father's funeral, to find that his mother has married his uncle."

Nikki's eyes widened. "She married her *brother*?"

"No, no! It's not *that* racy a play. His other uncle, his da's brother."

"Oh. That's all right, then."

"You'd think so, but Hamlet gets a tip-off that his old man was murdered by the uncle. Unfortunately, he can't tell if his informant is telling truth or lies. So he spends the next five acts blundering around getting nearly the whole cast killed while he dithers."

"That was stupid," said Nikki scornfully, uncoiling altogether. "Why didn't he just use fast-penta?"

"Hadn't been invented yet, alas. Or it would have been a much shorter play."

"Oh." Nikki frowned thoughtfully at Miles. "Can *you* use fast-penta? Lieutenant Vormoncrief . . . said you couldn't. And that it was *very convenient*." Nikki precisely mimicked Vormoncrief's sneer in these last two words.

"On myself, you mean? Ah, no. I have a screwy response to it that renders it unreliable. Which was very handy in my ImpSec days, but isn't so good right now. In fact, it's damned *in*convenient. But I wouldn't be allowed to be publicly questioned and cleared about your da's death even if it did work, because of certain security issues involved. Nor privately, in front of you alone, for the same reason."

Nikki was silent for a little, then said abruptly, "Lieutenant Vormoncrief called you *the mutie lord*."

"A lot of people do. Not to my face."

"He doesn't know I'm a mutie too. So was my da. Doesn't it make you mad when they call you that?"

"When I was your age, it bothered me a lot. It doesn't seem very relevant anymore. Now that there's good gene cleaning available, I wouldn't pass on any problems to my children even if I were a dozen times more damaged." His lips twisted, and he carefully didn't look at Ekaterin. "Assuming I can ever persuade some daring woman to marry me."

"Lieutenant Vormoncrief wouldn't want us . . . wouldn't want Mama if he knew I was a mutie, I bet."

"In that case, I urge you to tell him right away," Vorkosigan shot back, deadpan.

Mirabile, this won a brief, sly grin from Nikki.

Was this the trick of it? Secrets so dire as to be unspeakable, thoughts so frightening as to make clear young voices mute, kicked out into the open with blunt ironic humor. And suddenly the dire didn't loom so darkly any more, and fear shrank, and anyone could say anything. And the unbearable seemed a little easier to lift.

"Nikki, the security issues I mentioned make it impossible to tell you everything."

"Yeah, I know." Nikki hunched again. "It's 'cause I'm nine."

"Nine, nineteen, or ninety wouldn't matter on this one. But I do think it's possible to tell you a good deal more than you know now. I'd like to have you talk to a man who does have authority to decide how many details are proper and safe for you to hear. He also lost a father under tragic circumstances at an early age, so he's been where you stand now. If you're willing, I'll set up an appointment."

Who did he mean? One of the high-ranking ImpSec men, it had to be. But judging from her own unpleasant brushes with ImpSec on Komarr, Ekaterin couldn't imagine any of them voluntarily parting with directions to the Great Square, let alone this.

"All right . . ." said Nikki slowly.

"Good." A little gleam of relief flickered in Miles's eyes, and faded again. "In the meanwhile . . . I expect this slander may come round to you again. Maybe from an adult, maybe from someone your own age who overhears the adults talking about it. The story will likely get garbled and changed around in a lot of strange ways. Do you know how you are going to deal with it?"

Nikki looked briefly fierce. He made a swipe with his fist. "Punch 'em in the nose?"

Ekaterin winced in guilt; Miles caught her cringe.

"I would hope for a more mature and reasoned response from you," Vorkosigan intoned piously to Nikki, one eye on her. Drat the man for making her laugh at a moment like this! Possibly it had been too long since anyone had punched *him* in the nose? Satisfaction twitched his lip at her choke.

He went on more seriously, "May I suggest instead you simply tell whoever it may be that the story isn't true, and refuse to discuss it further. If they persist, tell them they have to talk with your mother, or your uncle or aunt Vorthys. If they still persist, go *get* your mother or uncle or aunt. You don't need me to tell you this is some pretty ugly stuff, here. No thinking, honorable adult should be dragging you into it, but unfortunately all that means is that you're likely to find yourself badgered by unthinking adults."

Nikki nodded slowly. "Like Lieutenant Vormoncrief." Ekaterin could almost see the relief afforded Nikki by being presented with this conceptual slot into which to tuck his late tormentor. *United against a common enemy.*

"To put it as politely as possible, yes."

Nikki fell into a digestive silence. After letting him mull a little, Miles suggested they all repair to the kitchen for a fortifying snack, adding that the box of new kittens had just been moved to what was becoming its traditional place next to the stove. The depth of his strategy was revealed when, after Ma Kosti plied both Nikki and Ekaterin with food-rewards that would produce positive conditioning in rocks, the cook took the boy to the other end of the long room, leaving Miles and Ekaterin an almost-private moment.

Ekaterin, sitting on the stool next to Miles's, leaned her elbows on the counter and stared down the kitchen.

Over by the stove, Ma Kosti and the fascinated Nikki were kneeling over the box of furry mewing bundles. "Who is this man you think Nikki should see?" she asked quietly.

"Let me make sure first he'll be willing to do what we need, and can make the time available," Miles answered cautiously. "You and Nikki will go in together, of course."

"I understand, but . . . I was thinking, Nikki tends to withdraw around strangers. Make sure this fellow grasps that just because Nikki goes monosyllabic doesn't mean he's not desperately curious."

"I'll make sure he understands."

"Does he have much experience with children?"

"Not as far as I know." Miles gave her a rueful smile. "But perhaps he'll be grateful for the practice."

"Under the circumstances, I find that unlikely."

"Under the circumstances, I'm afraid you're right. But I trust his judgment."

The myriad other questions which lay between them had to wait, as Nikki came bouncing back with the news that all newborn kittens' eyes were blue. The near-hysteria which had crumpled his face when they'd first arrived was erased. This kitchen made a fair barometer of his internal state; pleasantly distracted by food and pets, he was clearly much calmer. That he now could *be* so diverted was telling, Ekaterin judged. *I was right to come to Miles. How did Illyan know?*

Ekaterin let Nikki burble on till he ran down, then said, "We should go. My aunt will be wondering what happened to us." The hasty note she'd penned had told where they'd gone, but not why; Ekaterin had been far too upset at the time to even try to include the details. She looked forward without pleasure to explaining this whole hideous mess to her uncle and aunt, but at least they knew the truth, and could be counted upon to share her outrage.

"Pym can drive you," Miles offered immediately.

He made no attempt to trap her here this time, she noted with dark amusement. Not a slow learner, indeed?

Promising to call her when he'd cleared Nikki's

interview, Miles handed them personally into the rear compartment of the groundcar, and watched them out the gates. Nikki was quiet on this trip, too, but the silence was much less fraught now.

After a little, he gave her an odd, appraising look. "Mama . . . did you turn Lord Vorkosigan down 'cause he's a mutie?"

"No," she replied at once, and firmly. His brows bent. If he didn't get a more explicit answer, he would likely make up his own, she realized with an inward sigh. "You see, when he hired me to make his garden, it wasn't because he wanted a garden, or thought I was good at the work. He just thought it would give him a chance to see me a lot."

"Well," said Nikki, "that makes sense. I mean, it did, didn't it?"

She managed not to glower at him. Her work meant nothing to him—what did? If you could say anything to anyone . . . "Would you like it, if somebody promised to help you become a jump pilot, and you worked your heart out studying, and then it turned out they were tricking you into doing something else?"

"Oh." The light glimmered, dimly.

"I was angry because he'd tried to manipulate me, and my situation, in a way I found invasive and offensive." After a short, reflective pause, she added helplessly, "It seems to be his *style*." Was it a style she could learn to live with? Or was it a style he could bloody well learn not to try on her? Live, or learn? *Can we have some of both?*

"So . . . d'you like him? Or not?"

Like was surely not an adequate word for this hash of delight and anger and longing, this profound respect laced with profound irritation, all floating on a dark pool of old pain. The past and the future, at war in her head. "I don't know. Some of the time I do, yes, very much."

Another long pause. "Are you *in love* with him?"

What Nikki knew of adult love, he'd mostly garnered off the holovid. Part of her mind readily translated this question as code for, *Which way are you going to jump, and what will happen to me?* And yet . . . he could not share or even imagine the complexity of her romantic hopes and fears, but he certainly knew how such stories were supposed to Come Out Right.

"I don't know. Some of the time. I think."

He favored her with his Big People Are Crazy look. In all, she could only agree.

CHAPTER FOURTEEN

Miles had obtained copies of archives from the Council of Counts covering all the contested succession debates from the last two centuries. Together with a stack of gleanings from Vorkosigan House's own document room, they spread themselves over two tables and a desk in the library. He was deeply engrossed in a hundred-and-fifty-year-old account of the fourth Count Vorlakial's family tragedy when Armsman Jankowski appeared at the door from the anteroom and announced, "Commodore Galeni, m'lord."

Miles looked up in surprise. "Thank you, Jankowski." The Armsman gave him an acknowledging nod, and withdrew, closing the double doors discreetly behind himself.

Galeni trod across the great library, and regarded the scattering of papers, parchments, and flimsies with an ex-historian's alert eye. "Cramming, are you?" he inquired.

"Yes. Now, you had that doctorate in Barrayaran history. Do any really interesting District succession squabbles spring to your memory?"

"Lord Midnight the horse," Galeni replied at once. "Who always voted 'neigh.' "

"Got that one already." Miles waved at the pile on the far end of the inlaid table. "What brings you here, Duv?"

"Official ImpSec business. Your requested analyst's report, My Lord Auditor, regarding certain rumors about Madame Vorsoisson's late husband."

Miles scowled, reminded. "ImpSec is late off the mark. This would have done a lot more good yesterday. Not a hell of a lot of point to order *me* to back off, and then let Ekaterin and Nikki be subjected to that surprise harassment—in her own home, good God—by that idiot Vormoncrief."

"Yes. Illyan told Allegre. Allegre told me. I wish *I* had someone to tell . . . I was still pulling in informants' reports and cross-checks as of midnight last night, thank you very much, my lord. I wasn't able to calculate anything like a decent reliability score till late yesterday."

"Oh. Oh, no, Allegre didn't put you on this . . . slander matter personally, did he? Sit, sit." Miles waved Galeni to a chair, which the Komarran pulled up around the corner of the table from Miles.

"Of course he did. I was an eyewitness to your ghastly dinner party, which seems to have launched the whole thing, and more to the point, I'm already in the need-to-know pool regarding the Komarr case." Galeni seated himself with a tired grunt; his eye automatically began to scan the documents sideways. "There was no way Allegre would add another man to that pool if he could possibly avoid it."

"Mm, makes sense, I guess. But I'd hardly think you'd have *time*."

"I didn't," said Galeni bitterly. "I've been putting in an extra half shift after dinner nearly every day since I was promoted to head of Komarran Affairs. *This* came out of my sleep cycle. I'm considering abandoning meals and just hanging a food tube over my desk, which I could suck on now and then."

"I'd think Delia would put her foot down, after a while."

"Yes, and that's another thing," Galeni added, in an aggravated tone.

Miles waited a beat, but Duv did not elaborate. Well, and did he really need to? Miles sighed. "Sorry," he offered.

"Yes, well. From ImpSec's point of view, I have excellent news. No evidence has yet surfaced indicating any leak of the classified matters surrounding Tien Vorsoisson's death. No names, no hints of . . . technical activities, not even rumors of financial chicanery. There continues to be a complete and most welcome absence of Komarran conspirators of any stripe from any of the several scenarios of your murder of Vorsoisson."

"*Several* scenarios—! How many versions are circulating—no, don't tell me. It would just raise my blood pressure to no good purpose." Miles gritted his teeth. "So, what, am I supposed to have made away with Vorsoisson—a man twice my size—through some devilish ex-ImpSec trick?"

"Perhaps. In the one version concocted so far where you were not pictured as acting alone, the only henchmen posited were vile and corrupt ImpSec personnel, in your pay."

"This could only have been imagined by someone who never had to fill out one of Illyan's arcane expenditure-and/or-income reports," Miles growled.

Galeni shrugged amused agreement.

"And were there—no, let me tell you," Miles said. "There were no leaks traced from the Vorthys's household."

"None," Galeni conceded.

Miles grumbled a few satisfied swear words under his breath. He knew he hadn't misestimated Ekaterin. "Do me a personal favor and be sure to highlight that fact in the copy of this you send up to Allegre, eh?"

Galeni opened his hand in a carefully noncommittal gesture.

Miles blew out his breath, slowly. No leaks, no treasons: just idle malice and circumstance. And a touch of theoretical blackmail. Upsetting to himself, to his parents when it came to them, as it soon must, upsetting to the Vorthyses, to Nikki, to Ekaterin. They had *dared* to upset Ekaterin with this . . . He carefully ignored his simmering fury. Rage had no place in this. Calculation and implacable action did.

"So what, if anything, is ImpSec planning to do about it all?" Miles asked at last.

"At present, as little as possible. It's not as though we don't have enough other tasks on our plate. We will, of course, continue to monitor all data for any key items that might lead public attention back to where we don't want it. It's a poor second choice to no attention at all, but this murder scenario does us one favor. For anyone who refuses to accept Tien Vorsoisson's death as a mere accident, it presents a plausible cover story, which entirely accounts for no further investigation being permitted."

"Oh, entirely," snarled Miles. *I see where this is going.* He sat back, and folded his arms mulishly. "Does this mean I'm on my own?"

"Ah . . ." said Galeni. He drew it out for a rather long time. Eventually, he ran out of *ah* and was forced to speak. "Not exactly."

Miles bared his set teeth, and waited for Galeni, who waited for him.

Miles broke first. "Dammit, Duv, am I supposed to just stand here and eat this shit raw?"

"Come on, Miles, you've done coverups before. I thought you covert ops fellows lived and breathed this sort of thing."

"Never in my own sandbox. Never where I had to live in it. My Dendarii missions were hit and run. We always left the stink far behind."

Galeni's shrug lacked sympathy. "I must also point out, these are first results. Just because there are no leaks yet doesn't mean none will be . . . siphoned out into the open later on."

Miles exhaled slowly. "All right. Tell Allegre he has his goat. Baaah." He added after a moment, "But I draw the line at pretending to guilt. It was a breath mask accident. Period."

Galeni waved a hand in acceptance of this. "ImpSec won't complain."

It was *good*, Miles reminded himself, that there was

no security rupture in the Komarr case. But this also killed his faint, unvoiced hope that he could leave Richars and his cronies to the untender mercies of ImpSec to be disposed of. "As long as this is all gas, so be it. But you can let Allegre know, that if it goes to a formal murder charge against me in the Council . . ." *Then what?*

Galeni's eyes narrowed. "Do you have reason to think someone will charge you there? Who?"

"Richars Vorrutyer. I have a sort of . . . personal promise from him."

"He can't, though. Not unless he gets a member to lay it for him."

"He can if he beats out Lord Dono and is confirmed Count Vorrutyer." *And my colleagues are like to choke on Lord Dono.*

"Miles . . . ImpSec *can't* release the evidence surrounding Vorsoisson's death. Not even to the Council of Counts."

By the look on Galeni's face, Miles read that as *Especially* not to the Council of Counts. Knowing that erratic body, he sympathized. "Yes. I know."

Galeni said uneasily, "What are you planning to do?"

Miles had more compelling reasons than the strain on ImpSec's nerves to wish to sidestep this whole scenario. Two of them, mother and son. If he worked it right, none of this looming juridical mess need ever touch Ekaterin and her Nikki. "Nothing more—nor less—than my job. A little politicking. Barrayaran style."

Galeni eyed him dubiously. "Well . . . if you really intend to project innocence, you need to do a more convincing job. You . . . *twitch*."

Miles . . . twitched. "There's guilt and there's guilt. I am not guilty of willful murder. I am guilty of screwing up. Now, I'm not alone—this one took a full committee. Headed by that fool Vorsoisson himself. If only he'd—dammit, every time you step off the downside shuttle into a Komarran dome they sit you down and make you watch that vid on breath mask procedures. He'd been living there nearly a year. He'd been *told*."

He fell silent a moment. "Not that I didn't know better than to go out-dome without informing *my* contacts."

"As it happens, no one is accusing you of negligence."

Miles's mouth twisted bitterly. "They flatter me, Duv. They flatter me."

"I can't help you with that one," said Galeni. "I have enough unquiet ghosts of my own."

"Check." Miles sighed.

Galeni regarded him for a long moment, then said abruptly, "About your clone."

"Brother."

"Yes, him. Do you know . . . do you understand . . . what the devil does he *intend*, with respect to Kareen Koudelka?"

"Is this ImpSec asking, or Duv Galeni?"

"Duv Galeni." Galeni paused for a rather longer time. "After the . . . ambiguous favor he did me when we first encountered each other on Earth, I was content to see him survive and escape. I wasn't even too shocked when I learned he'd popped up here, nor—now I've met your mother—that your family took him in. I'd even reconciled myself to the likelihood that we would meet, from time to time." His level voice cracked a trifle. "I wasn't expecting him to mutate into my brother-in-law!"

Miles sat back, his brows rising in partial sympathy. He refrained from doing anything so rude as, say, cackling. "I would point out, that in an exceedingly weird sense, you are related already. He's your foster brother. Your father had him made; by some interpretations of the galactic laws on clones, that makes him Mark's father too."

"This concept makes my head spin. Painfully." He stared at Miles in sudden consternation. "Mark doesn't think of *himself* as my foster brother, does he?"

"I have not so far directed his attention to that legal wrinkle. But think, Duv, how much *easier* it will be if you only have to explain him as your brother-in-law. I mean, lots of people have embarrassing in-laws; it's one of life's lotteries. You'll have all their sympathy."

Galeni gave him a look of Very Limited Amusement.

"He'll be Uncle Mark," Miles pointed out with a slow, unholy smile. "You'll be Uncle Duv. I suppose, by some loose extension, I'll be Uncle Miles. And here I never thought I'd be anybody's uncle—an only child and all that."

Come to think of it . . . if Ekaterin ever accepted him, Miles would become an instant uncle, acquiring *three* brothers-in-law simultaneously, all with attached wives, and a pack of nieces and nephews already in place. Not to mention the father-in-law and the stepmother-in-law. He wondered if any of them would be embarrassing. Or— a new and unnerving thought—if *he* was going to be the appalling brother-in-law . . .

"*Do* you think they'll marry?" asked Galeni seriously.

"I . . . am not certain what cultural format their bonding will ultimately take. I am certain you could not pry Mark away from Kareen with a crowbar. And while Kareen has good reasons to take it slowly, I don't think any of the Koudelkas know *how* to betray a trust."

That won a little eyebrow-flick from Galeni, and the slight mellowing that any reminder of Delia invariably produced in him.

"I'm afraid you're going to have to resign yourself to Mark as a permanent fixture," Miles concluded.

"Eh," said Galeni. It was hard to tell if this sound represented resignation, or stomach cramp. In any case, he climbed to his feet and took his leave.

Mark, entering the black-and-white tiled entry foyer from the back hallway to the lift tubes, encountered his mother descending the front staircase.

"Oh, Mark," Countess Vorkosigan said, in a just-the-man-I-want-to-see voice. Obediently, he paused and waited for her. She eyed his neat attire, his favorite black suit modified by what he trusted was an unthreatening dark green shirt. "Are you on your way out?"

"Shortly. I was just about to hunt up Pym and ask him to assign me an Armsman-driver. I have an interview set up with a friend of Lord Vorsmythe's, a food service fellow who's promised to explain Barrayar's distribution system to me. He may be a future customer—I thought it might look well to arrive in the groundcar, all Vorkosiganly."

"Very likely."

Her further comment was interrupted by two half-grown boys rounding the corner: Pym's son Arthur, carrying a smelly fiber-tipped stick, and Jankowski's boy Denys, lugging an optimistically large jar. They clattered up the stairs past her with a breathless greeting of, "Hello, milady!"

She wheeled to watch them pass, her eyebrows rising in amusement. "New recruits for science?" she asked Mark as they thumped out of sight, giggling.

"For enterprise. Martya had a flash of genius. She put a bounty on escaped butter bugs, and set all the Armsmen's spare children to rounding them up. A mark apiece, and a ten-mark bonus for the queen. Enrique is back to work splicing genes full-time, the lab is caught up again, and *I* can return my attention to financial planning. We're getting bugs back at the rate of two or three an hour; it should be all over by tomorrow or the next day. At least, none of the children seem yet to have hit on the idea of sneaking into the lab and freeing Vorkosigan bugs, to renew their economic resource. I may devise a lock for that hutch."

The Countess laughed. "Come now, Lord Mark, you insult their honor. These are our *Armsmen's* offspring."

"*I* would have thought of that, at their age."

"If it weren't their liege-lord's bugs, they might have." She smiled, but her smile faded. "Speaking of insults . . . I wanted to ask you if you'd heard any of this vile talk going around about Miles and his Madame Vorsoisson."

"I've been head-down in the lab for the last several days. Miles doesn't come back there much, for some reason. What vile talk?"

She narrowed her eyes, slipped her hand through his arm, and strolled with him toward the antechamber to the library. "Illyan and Alys took me aside at the Vorinnis's dinner party last night, and gave me an earful. I'm extremely glad they got to me first. I was then cornered by two other people in the course of the evening and given garbled alternate versions . . . actually, one of them was trolling for confirmation. The other appeared to hope I'd pass it on to Aral, as he didn't dare repeat it to his face, the spineless little snipe. It seems rumors have begun to circulate through the capital that Miles somehow made away with Ekaterin's late husband while on Komarr."

"Well," said Mark reasonably, "you know more about that than I do. Did he?"

Her eyebrows went up. "Do you care?"

"Not especially. From everything I've been able to gather—between the lines, mostly, Ekaterin doesn't talk about him much—Tien Vorsoisson was a pretty complete waste of food, water, oxygen, and time."

"Has Miles said anything to you that . . . that leaves you in doubt about Vorsoisson's death?" she asked, seating herself beside the huge antique mirror gracing the side wall.

"Well, no," Mark admitted, taking a chair across from her. "Though I gather he fancies himself guilty of some carelessness. I think it would have been a much more interesting romance if he *had* assassinated the lout for her."

She sighed, looking bemused. "Sometimes, Mark, despite all your Betan therapist has done, I'm afraid your Jacksonian upbringing still leaks out."

He shrugged, unrepentantly. "Sorry."

"I am moved by your insincerity. Just don't repeat those no doubt honest sentiments in front of Nikki."

"I may be Jacksonian, ma'am, but I'm not a complete loss."

She nodded, evidently reassured. She began to speak again, but was interrupted by the double doors to the library swinging wide, and Miles escorting Commodore Duv Galeni out through the anteroom.

Seeing them, the Commodore paused to give the Countess a civil good-day. The greeting he gave to Mark was just as civil, but much warier, as though Mark had lately erupted in a hideous skin disease but Galeni was too polite to comment on it. Mark returned the greeting in kind.

Galeni did not linger. Miles saw his visitor out the front door, and retraced his steps toward the library.

"Miles!" said the Countess, rising and following him in with an expression of sudden concentration. Mark trailed in after them, uncertain if she'd finished with him or not. She cornered Miles against one of the sofas flanking the fireplace. "I understand from Pym that your Madame Vorsoisson was here yesterday, while Aral and I were out. She was *here*, and I *missed* her!"

"It was not exactly a social call," Miles said. Trapped, he gave up and sat down. "And I could hardly have delayed her departure till you and Father returned at midnight."

"Reasonable enough," his mother said, completing her capture by plunking down on the matching sofa across from him. Gingerly, Mark seated himself next to her. "But when *are* we to be permitted to meet her?"

He eyed her warily. "Not . . . just now. If you don't mind. Things are in a rather delicate, um, situation between us just at the moment."

"Delicate," echoed the Countess. "Isn't that a distinct improvement over a life in ruins with vomiting?"

A brief hopeful look glimmered in his eye, but he shook his head. "Just now, it's pretty hard to say."

"I quite understand. But only because Simon and Alys explained it to us last night. Might I ask why we had to hear about this nasty slander from them, and not from you?"

"Oh. Sorry." He sketched her an apologetic bow. "I only first heard about it day before yesterday myself. We've been running on separate tracks the past few days, what with your social whirl."

"You've been sitting on this for two days? I should have wondered at your sudden fascination with Chaos Colony during our last two meals together."

"Well, I *was* interested in hearing about your life on Sergyar. But more critically, I was waiting on the ImpSec analysis."

The Countess glanced toward the door Commodore Galeni had lately exited. "Ah," she said, in a tone of enlightenment. "Hence Duv."

"Hence Duv." Miles nodded. "If there had been a security leak involved, well, it would have been a whole different matter."

"And there was not?"

"Apparently not. It seems to be an entirely politically motivated fiction, made up out of altogether circumstantial . . . circumstances. By a small group of Conservative Counts and their hangers-on whom I have lately offended. And vice versa. I've decided to deal with it . . . politically." His face set in a grim look. "In my own way. In fact, Dono Vorrutyer and René Vorbretten will be here shortly to consult."

"Ah. Allies. Good." Her eyes narrowed in satisfaction.

He shrugged. "That's what politics is about, in part. Or so I take it."

"That's your department now. I leave you to it, and it to you. But what about you and your Ekaterin? Are you two going to be able to weather this?"

His expression grew distant. "We three. Don't leave out Nikki. I don't know yet."

"I've been thinking," said the Countess, watching him closely, "that I should invite Ekaterin and Kareen to tea. Just us ladies."

A look of alarm, if not outright panic, crossed Miles's face. "I . . . I . . . not yet. Just . . . not yet."

"No?" said the Countess, in a tone of disappointment. "When, then?"

"Her parents wouldn't let Kareen come, would they?" Mark put in. "I mean . . . I thought they'd cut the connection." A thirty-year friendship, destroyed by him. *Good work, Mark. What shall we do for an encore? Accidentally burn down Vorkosigan House? At least that would get rid of the butter bug infestation. . . .*

"Kou and Drou?" said the Countess. "Well, of *course* they've been avoiding me! I'm sure they don't dare look me in the eye, after that performance the night we came back."

Mark wasn't sure what to make of that, though Miles snorted wryly.

"I miss her," said Mark, his hand clenching helplessly along his trouser seam. "I *need* her. We're supposed to start presenting bug butter products to potential major accounts in a few days. I was counting on having Kareen along. I . . . I can't do sales very well. I've tried. The people I pitch to all seem to end up huddled on the far end of the room with lots of furniture between us. And Martya is too . . . forthright. But Kareen is brilliant. She could sell anything to anyone. Especially Barrayaran men. They sort of lie down and roll over, waving their paws in the air and wagging their tails—it's just amazing. And, and . . . I can stay calm, when she's with me, no matter how much other people irritate me. Oh, I want her *back* . . ." These last words escaped him in a muffled wail.

Miles looked at his mother, and at Mark, and shook his head in bemused exasperation. "You're not making proper use of your Barrayaran resources, Mark. Here you have, in-house, the most high-powered potential Baba on the planet, and you haven't even brought her into play!"

"But . . . what could she do? Under the circumstances?"

"To Kou and Drou? I hate to think." Miles rubbed his chin. "Butter, meet laser-beam. Laser-beam, butter. Oops."

His mother smiled, but then crossed her arms and stared thoughtfully around the great library.

"But, ma'am . . ." Mark stammered, "could you? *Would* you? I didn't presume to ask, after all the things . . . people said to one another that night, but I'm getting desperate." *Desperately* desperate.

"I didn't presume to intrude, without a direct invitation," the Countess told him. She waited, favoring him with a bright, expectant smile.

Mark thought it over. His mouth shaped the unfamiliar word twice, for practice, before he licked his lips, took a breath, and launched it into unsupported air. "*Help* . . . ?"

"Why, *gladly*, Mark!" Her smile sharpened. "I think what we need to do is to sit down together, the five of us—you and me and Kareen and Kou and Drou—right here, oh, yes, right *here* in this library, and talk it all over."

The vision filled him with inchoate terror, but he grasped his knees and nodded. "Yes. That is—you'll talk, right?"

"It will be just fine," she assured him.

"But how will you even get them to come here?"

"I think you can confidently leave that to me."

Mark glanced at his brother, who was smiling dryly. *He* did not look in the least dubious of her statement.

Armsman Pym appeared at the library door. "Sorry to interrupt, m'lady. M'lord, Count Vorbretten is arriving."

"Ah, good." Miles jumped to his feet, and hastened around to the long table, where he began gathering up stacks of flimsies, papers, and notes. "Bring him straight up to my suite, and tell Ma Kosti to start things rolling."

Mark seized the opportunity. "Oh, Pym, I'm going to need the car and a driver in about," he glanced at his chrono, "ten minutes."

"I'll see to it, m'lord."

Pym set off about his duties; Miles, a determined look on his face and a pile of documentation under his arm, charged out after his Armsman.

Mark looked doubtfully at the Countess.

"Run along to your meeting," she told him comfortably. "Stop up to my study when you get back, and tell me all about it."

She actually sounded interested. "Do you think you might like to invest?" he offered in a burst of optimism.

"We'll talk about it." She smiled at him with genuine pleasure, surely one of the few people in the universe to do so. Secretly heartened, he took himself off in Miles's wake.

The ImpSec gate guard passed Ivan through to Vorkosigan House's grounds, then returned to his kiosk at a beep from his comm link. Ivan had to step aside while the iron gates swung wide and the gleaming armored groundcar lumbered out into the street. A brief hope flared in Ivan's breast that he had missed Miles, but the blurred shape that waved at him through the half-mirroring of the rear canopy was much too round.

It was Mark who was off somewhere. When Pym ushered him into Miles's suite, Ivan found his leaner cousin sitting by the bay window with Count René Vorbretten.

"Oh, sorry," said Ivan. "Didn't know you were enga— occupied."

But it was too late to back out; Miles, turning toward him in surprise, controlled a wince, sighed, and waved him to enter. "Hello, Ivan. What brings you here?"

"M'mother sent me with this note. Why she couldn't just call you on the comconsole I don't know, but I wasn't going to argue with a chance to escape." Ivan proffered the heavy envelope, Residence stationery sealed with Lady Alys's personal crest.

"Escape?" asked René, looking amused. "It sounded to me as though you have one of the cushiest jobs of any officer in Vorbarr Sultana this season."

"Hah," said Ivan darkly. "You want it? It's like working in an office with an entire boatload of mothers-in-law-to-be with pre-wedding nerves, every one of them a flaming control freak. I don't know where Mama *found* that many Vor dragons. You usually only meet them one at a time, surrounded by an entire family to terrorize. Having them all in a bunch teamed up together is just *wrong*." He pulled up a chair between Miles and René, and sat down in a pointedly temporary posture. "My chain of command is built upside down; there are twenty-three commanders, and only one enlisted. Me. I want to go back to Ops, where my officers don't preface every insane demand with a menacing trill of, '*Ivan*, dear, won't you be a *sweetheart* and—' What I wouldn't give to hear a nice, deep, straightforward masculine bellow of '*Vorpatril!*' . . . From someone other than Countess Vorinnis, that is."

Miles, grinning, started to open the envelope, but then paused and listened to the sound of more persons being admitted into the hall by Pym. "Ah," he said. "Good. Right on time."

To Ivan's dismay, the visitors Pym next gated into his lord's chambers were Lord Dono and Byerly Vorrutyer, and Armsman Szabo. All of them greeted Ivan with repulsive cheer; Lord Dono shook Count René's hand with firm cordiality, and seated himself around the low table from Miles. By draped himself over the back of Dono's armchair and looked on. Szabo took a straight chair like Ivan's a little back from the principals and folded his arms.

"Excuse me," said Miles, and finished opening the envelope. He pulled out Lady Alys's note, glanced down it, and smiled. "So, gentlemen. My aunt Alys writes: *Dear Miles,* the usual elegant courtesies, and then—*Tell your friends Countess Vorsmythe reports René may be sure of her husband's vote. Dono will need a little more push there, but the topic of his future as a straight Progressive Party voter may bear fruit. Lady Mary Vorville also reports comfortable tidings to René due to some fondly remembered military connection between his late father and her father Count Vorville. I had thought it indelicate to lobby Countess Vorpinski regarding a vote for Lord Dono, but she surprised me by her quite enthusiastic approval of Lady Donna's transformation.*"

Lord Dono muffled a laugh, and Miles paused to raise an inquiring eyebrow.

"Count—then Lord—Vorpinski and I were quite good friends for a little while," Dono explained, with a small smirk. "After your time, Ivan; I believe you were off to Earth for that stint of embassy duty."

To Ivan's relief, Miles did not ask for further details, but merely nodded understanding and read on, his voice picking up the precise cadences of Lady Alys's diction. "*A personal visit by Dono to the Countess, to assure her of the reality of the change and the unlikelihood*—unlikelihood is underscored—*of its reversal in the event of Lord Dono obtaining his Countship, may do some good in that quarter.*

"*Lady Vortugalov reports not much hope for either René or Dono from her father-in-law. However,*—hah, get this—*she has shifted the birthdate of the Count's first grandson two days forward, so it just happens to coincide with the day the votes are scheduled, and has invited the Count to be present when the replicator is opened. Lord Vortugalov of course will also be there. Lady Vortugalov also mentions the Count's voting deputy's wife pines for a wedding invitation. I shall release one of the spares to Lady VorT. to pass along at her*

*discretion. The Count's alternate will not vote against his
lord's wishes, but it may chance he will be very late to that
morning's session, or even miss it altogether. This is not a
plus for you, but may prove an unexpected minus for Richars
and Sigur."*

René and Dono were starting to scribble notes.

*"Old Vorhalas has a deal of personal sympathy for René,
but will not vote against Conservative Party interests in the
matter. Since Vorhalas's rigid honesty is matched by his other
rigid habits of mind, I'm afraid Dono's case is quite hopeless there.*

*"Vortaine is also hopeless; save your energy. However, I
am reliably informed his lawsuit over his District's bound-
ary waters with his neighbor Count Vorvolynkin continues
unresolved, with undiminished acrimony, to the mortifica-
tion of both families. I would not normally consider it
possible to detach Count Vorvolynkin from the Conservatives,
but a whisper in his ear from his daughter-in-law Lady
Louisa, upon whom he dotes, that votes for Dono and René
would seriously annoy,* underscored, *his adversary has
borne startling results. You may reliably add him to your
accounting."*

"Now, *that's* an unexpected boon," said René happily,
scribbling harder.

Miles turned the page over and read on, *"Simon has
described to me the appalling behavior of,* well, that's not
pertinent, hum de hum, heh, *extremely poor taste,* underscored, thank you Aunt Alys, here we go, *Finally, my dear
Countess Vorinnis has assured me that the vote of Vorinnis's
District may also be counted upon for both your friends. Your
Loving Aunt Alys.*

*"P.S. There is no excuse for this to be done in a scram-
bling way at the last minute. This Office wishes the prompt
settlement of the confusion, so that invitations may be issued
to the proper persons in a punctual and graceful manner.
In the interest of a timely resolution to these matters, feel free
to set Ivan to any little task upon which you may find him
useful."*

"What?" said Ivan. "You made that up! Let me
see . . ." With an unpleasant smirk, Miles tilted the paper
toward Ivan, who leaned over his shoulder to read the

postscript. It was his mother's impeccable handwriting, all right. Damn.

"Richars Vorrutyer sat right there," said Miles, pointing to René's chair, "and informed me that Lady Alys held no vote in Council. The fact that she has spent more years in the Vorbarr Sultana political scene than all of us here put together seemed to escape him. Too bad." His smile broadened.

He turned to look half over his shoulder as Pym re-entered the sitting room trundling a tea cart. "Ah. May I offer you gentlemen some refreshments?"

Ivan perked up, but to his disappointment, the tea cart held tea. Well, and coffee, and a tray of Ma Kosti delectables resembling a decorative food-mosaic. "Wine?" he suggested hopefully to his cousin, as Pym began to pour. "Beer, even?"

"At this hour?" said René.

"For me, it's been a long day already," Ivan assured him. "Really."

Pym handed him a cup of coffee. "This will buck you up, m'lord."

Ivan took it reluctantly.

"When my grandfather held political conferences in these chambers, I could always tell if he was scheming with allies, or negotiating with adversaries," Miles informed them all. "When he was working with friends, he served coffee and tea and the like, and everyone was expected to stay on his toes. When he was working over the other sort, there was always a startling abundance of alcoholic beverages of every description. He always began with the good stuff, too. Later in the session the quality would drop, but by that time his visitors were in no shape to discriminate. I always snuck in when his man brought the wine cart, because if I stayed quiet enough, people were less likely to notice me and run me out."

Ivan pulled his straight chair closer to the tray of snacks. By took a chair equally strategically positioned on the other side of the cart. The other guests accepted cups from Pym and sipped. Miles smoothed a hand-scribbled agenda out on his knee.

"Item the first," he began. "René, Dono, has the Lord Guardian of the Speaker's Circle set the time and order in which the votes on your two suits go down?"

"Back to back," replied René. "Mine is first. I confess, I was grateful to know I'd be getting it over with as soon as possible."

"That's perfect, but not for the reason you think," Miles replied. "René, when your suit is called, you should yield the Circle to Lord Dono. Who, when his vote is over, should yield it back to you. You see why, of course?"

"Oh. Yes," said René. "Sorry, Miles, I wasn't thinking."

"Not . . . entirely," said Lord Dono.

Miles ticked the alternatives off on his fingers. "If you are made Count Vorrutyer, Dono, you may then immediately turn around and cast the vote of the Vorrutyer's District for René, thus increasing his vote bag by one. But if René goes first, the seat of the Vorrutyer's District will still be empty and will only cast a blank tally. And if René subsequently loses—by, let us say, one vote— you would also lose the Vorbretten vote on your round."

"Ah," said Dono, in a tone of enlightenment. "And you expect our opponents will also be making this calculation? Hence the value of the last-minute switch."

"Just so," said Miles.

"Will they anticipate the alteration?" asked Dono anxiously.

"They are not, as far as I know, quite aware of your alliance," By replied, with a slightly mocking semibow.

Ivan frowned at him. "And how long till they are? How do we know you won't just pipeline everything you see here to Richars?"

"He won't," said Dono.

"Yeah? *You* may be sure which side By's on, but *I'm* not."

By smirked. "Let us hope Richars shares your confusion."

Ivan shook his head, and snabbled a flaky shrimp puff which seemed to melt in his mouth, and chased it with coffee.

Miles reached under his chair and pulled out a stack

of large transparent flimsies. He peeled off the top two, and handed one each to Dono and René across the low table. "I've always wanted to try this," he said happily. "I pulled these out of the attic last night. They were one of my grandfather's old tactical aids; I believe he had the trick from his father. I suppose I could devise a comconsole program to do the same thing. They're seating plans of the Council chamber."

Lord Dono held one up to the light. Two rows of blank squares arced in a semicircle across the page. Dono said, "The seats aren't labeled."

"If you need to use this, you're supposed to know," Miles explained. He thumbed off an extra and handed it across. "Take it home, fill it out, and memorize it, eh?"

"Excellent," said Dono.

"Theory is, you use 'em to compare two related close votes. Color code each District's desk—say, red for no, green for yes, blank for unknown or undecided—and put one atop the other." Miles dropped a handful of bright flow pens onto the table. "Where you end up with two reds or two greens, ignore that Count. You've either no need, or no leverage. Where you have blanks, a blank and a color, or a red and a green, look to those men as the ones to concentrate your lobbying on."

"Ah," said René, taking up two pens, leaning over the table, and starting to color. "How elegantly simple. I always tried to do this in my head."

"Once you start talking maybe three or five related votes, times sixty men, nobody's head can hold it all."

Dono, lips pursed thoughtfully, filled out some dozen or so squares, then moved around next to René to crib the rest of the names versus locations. René, Ivan noticed, colored very meticulously, neatly filling each square. Dono scribbled bold, quick splashes. When they'd finished, they laid the two flimsies a little askew atop one another.

"My word," said Dono. "They do just jump out at you, don't they?"

Their voices fell to murmurs, as they began to develop their list of men to go tag-team. Ivan brushed shrimp puff crumbs off his uniform trousers. Byerly bestirred himself to gently suggest one or two slight corrections to the distribution of marks and blanks, based upon impressions he'd, oh quite casually to be sure, garnered during his sojourns in Richars's company.

Ivan craned his neck, counting up greens and double-greens. "You're not there yet," he said. "Regardless of how few votes Richars and Sigur obtain, no matter how many of their supporters get diverted that day, you each have to have a positive majority of thirty-one votes, or you don't get your Districts."

"We're working on it, Ivan," said Miles.

From his sparkling eye and dangerously cheerful expression, Ivan recognized his cousin in full forward momentum mode. Miles was reveling in this. Ivan wondered if Illyan and Gregor would ever rue the day they'd dragged him off his beloved galactic covert ops and stuck him home. Scratch that—*how soon* they would rue the day.

To Ivan's dismay, his cousin's thumb descended forcefully on a pair of blank squares Ivan had hoped he would overlook.

"Count Vorpatril," said Miles. "Ah, ha." He smiled up at Ivan.

"Why are you looking at me?" asked Ivan. "It's not as though Falco Vorpatril and I are drinking buddies. In fact, the last time I saw the old man he told me I was a hopeless floater, and the despair of my mother, himself, and all other geezer-class Vorpatrils. Well, he didn't say *geezer-class*, he said *right-thinking*. Comes to the same thing."

"Oh, Falco is tolerably amused by you," Miles ruthlessly contradicted Ivan's personal experience. "More to the point, you'll have no trouble getting Dono in to see him. And while you're there, you can both put in good words for René."

I knew it would come to this, sooner or later. "I'd have had to swallow chaff enough if I'd presented Lady Donna to him as a fiancée. He's never had the time of day for Vorrutyers generally. Presenting Lord Dono to him as a future colleague . . ." Ivan shuddered, and stared at the bearded man, who stared back with a peculiar lift to his lip.

"Fiancée, Ivan?" inquired Dono. "I didn't know you cared."

"Well, and I've missed my chance now, haven't I?" Ivan said grumpily.

"Yes, now and any time these past five years while I was cooling my heels down in the District. I was there. Where were you?" Dono dismissed Ivan's plaint with a jerk of his chin; the tiny flash of bitterness in his brown eyes made Ivan squirm inside. Dono saw his discomfort, and smiled slowly, and rather evilly. "Indeed, Ivan, clearly this entire episode is *all your fault*, for being so slow off the mark."

Ivan flinched. *Dammit, that woman—man—person, knows me too bloody well . . .*

"Anyway," Dono went on, "since the choice is between Richars and me, Falco's stuck with a Vorrutyer whatever the case. The only question is which one."

"And I'm sure you can point out all the disadvantages of Richars," Miles interposed smoothly.

"Somebody else can. Not me," said Ivan. "Serving officers are not supposed to involve themselves with party politics anyway, so there." He folded his arms and stood, or at any rate, sat, precariously on his dignity.

Miles tapped Ivan's mother's letter. "But you have a lawful order from your assigned superior. In writing, no less."

"Miles, if you don't burn that damned letter after this meeting, you're out of your mind! It's so hot I'm surprised it hasn't burst into flame all on its own!" Hand-written, hand-delivered, no copy electronic or otherwise anywhere—the destroy-after-reading directive was inherent.

Miles's teeth bared in a small smile. "Teaching me my business, Ivan?"

Ivan glowered. "I flat refuse to go a step farther in this. I told Dono that taking him to your dinner party was the last favor I'd do for him, and I'm standing on my word."

Miles eyed him. Ivan shifted uneasily. He hoped Miles

wouldn't think to call the Residence for a reiteration.
Standing up to his mother seemed safer in absentia than
in person. He fixed a surly look on his face, hunkered
in his chair, and waited—somewhat curiously—for whatever creative blackmail or bribery or strong-arm tactic
Miles would next evolve to twist him to his will. Escorting Dono to Falco Vorpatril was going to be so damned
embarrassing. He was planning just how to present himself to Falco as a thoroughly disinterested bystander,
when Miles said, "Very well. Moving right along—"

"I said no!" Ivan cried desperately.

Miles glanced up at him in faint surprise. "I heard
you. Very well: you're off the hook. I shall ask nothing
further of you. You can relax."

Ivan sat back in profound relief.

Not, he assured himself, profound disappointment.
And most *certainly* not profound alarm. *But . . . but . . .
but . . . the obnoxious little git needs me, to pull his nuts
out of the fire . . .*

"Moving right along now," Miles continued, "we come
to the subject of dirty tricks."

Ivan stared at him in horror. *Ten years as Illyan's top
agent in ImpSec coverts ops . . .* "Don't do it, Miles!"

"Don't do what?" Miles inquired mildly.

"Whatever you're thinking of. Just don't. I don't want
anything to do with it."

"What I was *about* to say," said Miles, giving him an
extremely dry look, "was that *we*, being on the side of
truth and justice, need not stoop to such chicanery as,
say, bribery, assassination or milder forms of physical
diversion, or—heh!—blackmail. Besides, those sorts of
things tend to . . . backfire." His eye glinted. "We do
need to keep a sharp lookout for any such moves on
the part of our adversaries. Beginning with the obvious—
put everyone's full duty roster of Armsmen on high-alert
status, make sure your vehicles are guarded from tam-
pering *and* that you have alternate modes and routes
for reaching Vorhartung Castle the morning of the vote.
Also, detach whatever trusted and resourceful men you
can spare to be certain that nothing untoward happens
to impede the arrival of your supporters."

"If we're not stooping, what do you call that shell game with the Vortugalovs and the uterine replicator?" Ivan demanded indignantly.

"A piece of wholly unexpected good fortune. None of us *here* had anything to do with it," Miles replied tranquilly.

"So it's not a dirty trick if it's untraceable?"

"Correct, Ivan. You learn fast. Grandfather would have been . . . surprised."

Lord Dono looked very thoughtful at this, leaning back and gently stroking his beard. His faint smile gave Ivan chills.

"Byerly." Miles looked across to the other Vorrutyer, who was nibbling gently on a canapé and either listening or dozing, depending on what those half-closed eyes signified. By opened his eyes fully, and smiled. Miles went on, "Have you overheard anything we ought to know on this last head from Richars or the Vormoncrief party?"

"So far, they appear to have limited themselves to ordinary canvassing. I believe they have not yet realized you're closing on them."

René Vorbretten regarded By doubtfully. "Are we? Not by my tally. And when and if they do realize—and I'll bet Boriz Vormoncrief will catch on to it eventually—how d'you think they'll jump?"

By held out his hand, and tilted it back and forth in a balancing gesture. "Count Vormoncrief is a staid old stick. However things fall out, he'll live to vote another day. And another, and another. He's far from indifferent to Sigur's fate, but I don't think he'll cross the line for him. Richars . . . well, this vote is everything to Richars, now, isn't it? He started out in a fury at being forced to exert himself for it at all. Richars is a loose cannon, getting looser." This image did not appear to disturb By; in fact, he seemed to draw some private pleasure from it.

"Well, keep us informed if anything changes in that quarter," said Miles.

Byerly made a little salute of spreading his hand over his heart. "I live to serve."

Miles raised his eyes and gave By a penetrating look; Ivan wondered if this sardonic cooption of the old ImpSec tag-line perhaps did not sit too well with one who'd laid down so much blood and bone in Imperial service. He cringed in anticipation of the exchange if Miles sought to censure By for this minor witticism, but to Ivan's relief Miles let it pass. After a few more minutes spent apportioning target Counts, the meeting broke up.

CHAPTER FIFTEEN

Ekaterin waited on the sidewalk, holding Nikki's hand, while Uncle Vorthys hugged his wife good-bye and his chauffeur loaded his valise into the back of his groundcar. Uncle Vorthys would be going straight from this upcoming morning meeting to the shuttleport and an Imperial fast courier to Komarr, there to deal with what he'd described to Ekaterin as *a few technical matters*. The trip was the culmination, she supposed, of the long hours he'd been spending lately closeted at the Imperial Science Institute; in any case, it hadn't seemed to take the Professora by surprise.

Ekaterin reflected on Miles's penchant for understatement. She'd felt ready to faint, last night, when Uncle Vorthys had sat her and Nikki down and informed them *who* Miles's "man with authority" was, the fellow he thought could talk with understanding to Nikki because he too had lost a father young. Emperor-to-be Gregor had been not yet five years old when the gallant Crown Prince Serg had been blown to bits in Escobar orbit during the retreat from that ill-advised military adventure. In all, she was glad no one had told her till the audience was confirmed, or she would have worked herself into an even worse state of nerves. She was uncomfortably aware that her hand gripping Nikki's was a little too moist, a little too chill. He would take his cue from the adults; she *must* appear calm, for his sake.

They all piled into the rear compartment at last, waved to the Professora, and pulled away. Her eye was becoming more educated, Ekaterin decided. The first time she'd ridden in the courtesy car that the Imperium provided her uncle on permanent loan, she hadn't known to interpret its odd smooth handling as a cue to its level of armoring, nor the attentive young driver as ImpSec to the bone. For all her uncle's deceptive failure to deck himself out in high Vor mode, he moved in the same rarefied circles Miles inhabited with equal ease—Miles because he'd lived there all his life, her uncle because his engineer's eye gauged men by other criteria.

Uncle Vorthys smiled fondly down at Nikki, and patted him on the hand. "Don't look so scared, Nikki," he rumbled comfortably. "Gregor is a good fellow. You'll be fine, and we'll be with you."

Nikki nodded dubiously. It was his black suit that made him look so pale, Ekaterin told herself. His only really good suit; he'd last worn it at his father's funeral, a piece of unpleasant irony Ekaterin schooled herself to ignore. She'd drawn the line at donning her own funeral dress. Her everyday black-and-gray outfit was getting a trifle shabby, but it would have to do. At least it was clean and pressed. Her hair was pulled back with neat severity, braided into a knot at the back of her neck. She touched the lump of the little Barrayar pendant, hidden beneath her high-necked black blouse, for secret reassurance.

"Don't you look so scared either," Uncle Vorthys added to her.

She smiled wanly.

It was a short drive from the University district to the Imperial Residence. The guards scanned them and passed them smoothly through the high iron gates. The Residence was a vast stone building several times the size of Vorkosigan House, four stories high and built, over a couple of centuries and radical changes of architectural styles, in the form of a somewhat irregular hollow square. They drew up under a secondary portico on the east end.

Some sort of high household officer in Vorbarra livery met them, and guided them down two very long and echoing corridors to the north wing. Nikki and Ekaterin both stared around, Nikki openly, Ekaterin covertly. Uncle Vorthys seemed indifferent to the museum-quality décor; he'd trod this corridor dozens of times to deliver his personal reports to the ruler of three worlds. Miles had lived here till he was six, he'd said. Had he been oppressed by the somber weight of this history, or had he regarded it all as his personal play set? *One guess.*

The liveried man ushered them into a sleekly-appointed office the size of most of one floor of the Professor's house. On the near end, a half-familiar figure leaned against a huge comconsole desk, his arms folded. Emperor Gregor Vorbarra was grave, lean, dark, good-looking in a narrow-faced, cerebral fashion. The holovid did not flatter him, Ekaterin decided instantly. He wore a dark blue suit, with only the barest hint of military decoration in the thin side-piping on the trousers and the high-necked tunic. Miles stood across from him dressed in his usual impeccable gray, rendered somewhat less impeccable by his feet-apart posture and his hands stuffed in his trouser pockets. He broke off in midsentence; his eyes rose anxiously to Ekaterin's face as she entered, and his lips parted. He gave his fellow Auditor a jerky little encouraging nod.

The Professor did not need the cue. "Sire, may I present my niece, Madame Ekaterin Vorsoisson, and her son, Nikolai Vorsoisson."

Ekaterin was spared an awkward attempt at a curtsey when Gregor stepped forward, took her hand, and shook it firmly, as though she were one of the equals he was first among. "Madame, I am honored." He turned to Nikki, and shook his hand in turn. "Welcome, Nikki. I'm sorry our first meeting should be occasioned by such a difficult matter, but I trust it will be followed by many happier ones." His tone was neither stiff nor patronizing, but perfectly straightforward. Nikki managed an adult handshake, and only goggled a little.

Ekaterin had met a few powerful men before; they had mostly looked through her, or past her, or at her with the sort of vague aesthetic appreciation she'd bestowed on the knickknacks in the corridor outside. Gregor looked her directly in the eye as if he saw all the way through to the back of her skull. It was at once unnervingly uncomfortable and strangely heartening. He gestured them all toward a square arrangement of leather-covered couches and armchairs at the far end of the room, and said softly, "Won't you please be seated?"

The tall windows overlooked a garden of descending terraces, brilliant with full summer growth. Ekaterin sank down with her back to it, Nikki beside her; the cool northern light fell on their Imperial host's face, as he took an armchair opposite them. Uncle Vorthys sat between; Miles pulled up a straight chair and sat a little apart from them all. He appeared arms crossed and at his ease. She wasn't quite sure how she came to read him as tense and nervous and miserable. And masked. A glass mask . . .

Gregor leaned forward. "Lord Vorkosigan asked me to meet with you, Nikki, because of the unpleasant rumors which have sprung up surrounding your father's death. Under the circumstances, your mother and your great-uncle agreed it was needful."

"Mind you," Uncle Vorthys put in, "I wouldn't have chosen to drag the poor little fellow further into it if it weren't for those gabbling fools."

Gregor nodded understanding. "Before I begin, some caveats—words of warning. You may not be aware of it, Nikki, but in your uncle's household you have been living under a certain degree of security monitoring. At his request, it is usually as limited and unobtrusive as possible. It's only gone to a higher and more visible level twice in the last three years, during some unusually difficult cases of his."

"Aunt Vorthys showed us the outside vid pickups," Nikki offered tentatively.

"Those are part of it," Uncle Vorthys said. The least part, according to the thorough briefing a polite ImpSec officer in plainclothes had given Ekaterin the day after she and Nikki had moved in.

"All the comconsoles are also either secured or monitored," Gregor elaborated. "Both his vehicles are kept in guarded locations. Any unauthorized intruder should bring down an ImpSec response in under two minutes."

Nikki's eyes widened.

"One wonders how Vormoncrief got in," Ekaterin couldn't help darkly muttering.

Gregor smiled apologetically. "Your uncle doesn't choose to have ImpSec shake down his every casual visitor. And Vormoncrief was on the Known list due to his previous visits." He looked again at Nikki. "But if we continue this conversation today, you will perforce step over an invisible line, from a lower level of security monitoring to a rather higher one. While you live in your uncle's household, or if . . . you should ever go to live in Lord Vorkosigan's household, you wouldn't notice the difference. But any extensive travel on Barrayar will have to be cleared with a certain security officer, and your potential off-planet travel restricted. The list of schools you may attend will become suddenly much shorter, more exclusive, and, I'm sorry, more expensive. On the bright side, you won't have to worry much about encounters with casual criminals. On the dark side, any," he spared a nod for Ekaterin, "*hypothetical* kidnappers who did get through would have to be assumed to be highly professional and extremely dangerous."

Ekaterin caught her breath. "Miles didn't mention that part."

"I daresay Miles didn't even think about it. He's lived under exactly this sort of security screen most of his life. Does a fish think about water?"

Ekaterin darted a glance at Miles. He had a very odd look on his face, as though he'd just bounced off a force wall he hadn't known was there.

"Off-planet travel." Nikki seized on the one item in this intimidating list of importance to him. "But . . . I want to be a jump pilot."

"By the time you are old enough to study for a jump pilot, I expect the situation will have changed," said Gregor. "This applies mainly to the next few years. Do you still want to go on?"

He hadn't asked her. He'd asked Nikki. She held her breath, resisting the urge to prompt him.

Nikki licked his lips. "Yes," he said. "I want to know."

"Second warning," said Gregor. "You will not walk out of here with fewer questions than you have now. You will just trade one set for another. Everything I tell you will be true, but it will not be complete. And when I come to the end, you will be at the absolute limit of what you may presently know, both for your own safety and that of the Imperium. Do you still want to go on?"

Nikki nodded dumbly. He was transfixed by this intense man. So was Ekaterin.

"Third and last. Our Vor duties come upon us at a too-early age, sometimes. What I am about to tell you will impose a burden of silence upon you that would be hard for an adult to bear." He glanced at Miles and Ekaterin, and at Uncle Vorthys. "Though you will have your mother and aunt and uncle to share it with. But for what may be the first time, you must give your name's word in all seriousness. Can you?"

"Yes," Nikki whispered.

"Say it."

"I swear by my word as Vorsoisson . . ." Nikki hesitated, searching Gregor's face anxiously.

"To hold this conversation in confidence."

"To hold this conversation in confidence."

"Very well." Gregor sat back, apparently fully satisfied. "I'm going to make this as plain as possible. When Lord Vorkosigan went out-dome with your father that night to the experiment station, they surprised some thieves. And vice versa. Both your father and Lord Vorkosigan were hit with stunner fire. The thieves fled, leaving both men chained by the wrists to a railing on the outside of the station. Neither of them were strong enough to break the chains, though both tried."

Nikki sneaked a look at Miles, half the size of Tien, little bigger than Nikki himself. Ekaterin thought she could see the wheels turning in his head. If his father, so much bigger and stronger, had been unable to free himself, could Miles be blamed for likewise failing?

"The thieves did not mean for your father to die. They didn't know his breath-mask reservoirs were low. Nobody did. That was confirmed by fast-penta interrogation later. The technical name for this sort of accidental killing is not murder, but manslaughter, by the way."

Nikki was pale, but not yet on the verge of tears. He ventured, "And Lord Vorkosigan . . . couldn't share his mask because he was tied up . . . ?"

"We were about a meter apart," said Miles in a flat tone. "Neither of us could reach the other." He spread his hands a certain distance out to the sides. At the motion, his sleeves pulled back from his wrists; the ropy pink scars where the chains had cut to the bone edged into view. Could Nikki see that he'd nearly ripped his hands off, trying, Ekaterin wondered bleakly? Self-consciously, Miles pulled his cuffs back down, and put his hands on his knees.

"Now for the hard part," said Gregor, gathering Nikki back in by eye. It had to feel to Nikki as though they were the only two people in the universe.

He's going to go on? No—no, stop there . . . She wasn't sure what apprehension showed in her face, but Gregor spared it an acknowledging nod.

"This is the part your mother would never tell you. The *reason* your da took Lord Vorkosigan out to the station was because your da had let himself be bribed by the thieves. But he had changed his mind, and wanted Lord Vorkosigan to declare him an Imperial Witness. The thieves were angry at this betrayal. They chained him to the rail in that cruel way to punish his attempt to retrieve his honor. They left a data disc with documentation of his involvement taped to his back for his rescuers to find, to be certain of disgracing him, and then called your mama to come get him. But—not knowing about the low reservoirs—they called her too late."

Now Nikki was looking stunned and small. *Oh, poor*

*son. I would not have tarnished Tien's honor in your eyes;
surely in your eyes is where all our honor is kept. . . .*

"Due to further facts about the thieves that no one
can discuss with you, all of this is a State secret. As far
as the rest of the world knows, your da and Lord
Vorkosigan went out alone, met no one, became separated while on foot in the dark, and Lord Vorkosigan
found your da too late. If anyone thinks Lord
Vorkosigan had something to do with your da's death,
we are not going to argue with them. You may state that
it's not true and that you don't wish to discuss it. But
don't let yourself be drawn into disputes."

"But . . ." said Nikki, "but that's not fair!"

"It's hard," said Gregor, "but it's necessary. Fair has
nothing to do with it. To spare you the hardest part,
your mama and uncle and Lord Vorkosigan told you the
cover story, and not the real one. I can't say they were
wrong to do so."

His eye and Miles's caught each other in a steady
gaze; Miles's eyebrows inched up in a quizzical look,
to which Gregor returned a tiny ironic nod. The
Emperor's lips thinned in something that was not quite
a smile.

"All the thieves are in Imperial custody, in a top-
security prison. None of them will be leaving soon. All
the justice that could be done, has been done; there's
nothing left to finish there. If your father had lived, he
would be in prison now too. Death wipes out all debts
of honor. In my eyes, he has redeemed his crime and
his name. He cannot do more."

It was all much, much tougher than anything Ekaterin
had pictured, had dared to imagine Gregor or anyone
forcing Nikki to confront. Uncle Vorthys looked very
grim, and even Miles looked daunted.

No: this *was* the softened version. Tien had not been
trying to retrieve his honor; he'd merely learned that
his crime had been discovered and was scrambling to
evade the consequences. But if Nikki were to cry out,
I don't care about honor! I want my da back! could she say
he was wrong? A little of that cry flickered in his eyes,
she imagined.

Nikki looked across at Miles. "What *were* your two mistakes?"

He replied steadily, with what effort Ekaterin could not guess, "First, I failed to inform my security backup when I left the dome. When Tien took me out to the station we were both anticipating a cooperative confession, not a hostile confrontation. Then, when we surprised the . . . thieves, I was a second too slow drawing my own stunner. They fired first. A diplomatic hesitation. A second's delay. The greatest regrets are the tiniest."

"I want to see your wrists."

Miles pushed back his cuffs, and held out his hands, palm down and then palm up, for Nikki's close inspection.

Nikki's brow wrinkled. "Was your breath mask running out too?"

"No. Mine was fine. I'd checked it when I'd put it on."

"Oh." Nikki sat back, looking extremely subdued and pensive.

Everyone waited. After a minute, Gregor asked gently, "Do you have any more questions at this time?"

Mutely, Nikki shook his head.

Frowning thoughtfully, Gregor glanced at his chrono and rose, with a hand-down gesture that kept everyone else from popping to their feet. He strode to his desk, rummaged in a drawer, and returned to his seat. Leaning across the table he held out a code-card to Nikki. "Here, Nikki. This is for you to keep. Don't lose it."

The card had no markings at all. Nikki turned it over curiously, and looked his inquiry at Gregor.

"This card will code you in to my personal comconsole channel. A very few friends and relatives of mine have this access. When you put it in the read-slot of your comconsole, a man will appear and identify you and, if I am available, pass you through to the comconsole nearest to me. You don't have to tell him anything about your business. If you think of more questions later—as you may, I gave you a lot to absorb in a very short time—or if you simply need someone to talk to about this matter, you may use it to call me."

"Oh," said Nikki. Gingerly, after turning it over again, he tucked the card into his tunic's breast pocket.

By the slight easing of Gregor's posture, and of Uncle Vorthys's, Ekaterin concluded the audience was over. She shifted, preparing to catch the cue to rise, but then Miles lifted a hand—did he always seize the last word?

"Gregor—while I appreciate your gesture of confidence in refusing my resignation—"

Uncle Vorthys's brows shot up. "Surely you didn't offer to resign your Auditorship over this miserable gibble-gabble, Miles!"

Miles shrugged. "I thought it was traditional for an Imperial Auditor not only to be honest, but to appear so. Moral authority and all that."

"Not always," said Gregor mildly. "I inherited a couple of damned shifty old sticks from my grandfather Ezar. And for all that he's called Dorca the Just, I believe my great-grandfather's main criterion for his Auditors was their ability to convincingly terrorize a pretty tough crew of liegemen. Can you imagine the nerve it would have taken one of Dorca's Voices to stand up to, say, Count Pierre Le Sanguinaire?"

Miles smiled at this vision. "Given the enthusiastic awe with which my grandfather recalled old Pierre . . . the mind boggles."

"If public confidence in your worth as an Auditor is that damaged, my Counts and Ministers will have to indict you themselves. Without my assistance."

"Unlikely," growled Uncle Vorthys. "It's a smarmy business, my boy, but I doubt it will come to that pass."

Miles looked less certain.

"You've now danced through all the proper forms," said Gregor. "Leave it, Miles."

Miles nodded what seemed to Ekaterin reluctant, if relieved, acceptance. "Thank you, Sire. But I wanted to add, I was also thinking of the personal ramifications. Which are going to get worse before they bottom out and die away. Are you quite sure you want me standing on your wedding circle, while this uproar persists?"

Gregor gave him a direct, and slightly pained, look. "You will not escape your social duty that easily. If General Alys does not request I remove you, there you will stand."

"I wasn't trying to escape—! . . . anything." He ran down a trifle, in the face of Gregor's grim amusement.

"Delegation is a wonderful thing, in my line of work. You may let it be known that anyone who objects to the presence of my foster-brother in my wedding circle may take their complaints to Lady Alys, and suggest whatever major last-minute dislocations in her arrangements they . . . dare."

Miles could not quite keep the malicious smile off his lips, though he tried valiantly. Fairly valiantly. Some. "I would pay money to watch." His smile faded again. "But it's going to keep coming up as long as—"

"Miles." Gregor's raised hand interrupted him. His eyes were alight with something between amusement and exasperation. "You have, in-house, possibly the greatest living source of Barrayaran political expertise in this century. Your father's been dealing with uglier Party in-fighting than this, with and without weapons, since before you were born. Go tell *him* your troubles. Tell him I said to give you that lecture on honor versus reputation he gave me that time. In fact . . . tell him I request and require it." His hand-wave, as he rose from his armchair, put an emphatic end to the topic. Everyone rustled to their feet.

"Lord Auditor Vorthys, a word before you depart. Madame Vorsoisson—" he took Ekaterin's hand again "—we'll talk more when I am less pressed for time. Security concerns have deferred public recognition, but I hope you realize you've earned a personal account of honor with the Imperium of great depth, which you may draw upon at need and at will."

Ekaterin blinked, startled almost to protest. Surely it was for Miles's sake that Gregor had wedged open this slice of his schedule? But this was all the oblique reference to the *further* events on Komarr they dared to make in front of Nikki. She managed a short nod, and a murmur of thanks for the Imperial time and concern.

Nikki, modeling himself a little awkwardly upon her, did likewise.

Uncle Vorthys bid her and Nikki good-bye, and lingered for whatever word his Imperial master wanted before he took ship. Miles escorted them into the corridor, where he told the waiting liveried man, "I'll see them out, Gerard. Call for Madame Vorsoisson's car, please."

They began the long walk around the building. Ekaterin glanced back over her shoulder toward the Emperor's private office.

"That was . . . that was more than I'd expected." She looked down at Nikki, walking between them. His face was set, but not crumpled. "Stronger." *Harsher.*

"Yes," said Miles. "Be careful what you ask for. . . . There are special reasons I trust Gregor's judgment in this above anyone else's. But . . . I think perhaps I'm not the only fish who doesn't think about water. Gregor is routinely expected to endure daily pressures that would drive, well, me, to drink, madness, or downright lethal irritability. In return, he overestimates us, and we . . . scramble not to disappoint him."

"*He* told me the truth," said Nikki. He marched on in silence for a moment more. "I'm glad."

Ekaterin held her peace, satisfied.

Miles found his father in the library.

Count Vorkosigan was seated on one of the sofas flanking the fireplace, perusing a hand-reader. By his semiformal garb, a dark green tunic and trousers reminiscent of the uniforms he'd worn most of his life, Miles deduced he was on his way out soon, doubtless to one of the many official meals the Viceroy and Vicereine seemed obliged to munch their way through before Gregor's wedding. Miles was reminded of the intimidating list of engagements that Lady Alys had handed him, coming up soon. But whether he dared try to mitigate their social and culinary rigors by having Ekaterin accompany him was now a very dubious question.

Miles flung himself onto the sofa opposite his father;

the Count looked up and regarded him with cautious interest.

"Hello. You look a trifle wrung."

"Yes. I've just come from one of the more difficult interviews of my Auditorial career." Miles rubbed the back of his neck, still achingly tense. The Count lifted politely inquiring eyebrows. Miles continued, "I asked Gregor to straighten out Nikki Vorsoisson on this slander mess to the limit he judged wise. He set the limit a lot further out than Ekaterin or I would have."

The Count sat back, and laid his reader aside. "Do you feel he compromised security?"

"No, actually," Miles admitted. "Any enemy snatching Nikki for questioning would already know more than he does. They could empty him out in ten minutes on fast-penta, and no harm done. Maybe they'd even bring him back. Or not . . . He's no more a security risk than before. And no more nor less *at* risk, as a lever on Ekaterin." *Or on me.* "The real conspiracy was very closely held even among the principals. That's not the problem."

"And the problem is—?"

Miles leaned his elbows on his knees, and stared at his dim distorted reflections in the toes of his half-boots. "I thought, because of Crown Prince Serg, Gregor would know how—or whether—someone ought to be apprised that his da was a criminal. If you can call Prince Serg that, for his secret vices."

"I can," breathed the Count. "Criminal, and halfway to raving mad, by the time of his death." Then-Admiral Vorkosigan had been an eyewitness to the Escobaran invasion disaster on the highest levels, Miles reflected. He sat up; his father looked him full in the face, and smiled somberly. "That Escobaran ship's lucky shot was the best piece of political good fortune ever to befall Barrayar. In hindsight, though, I regret that we handled Gregor so poorly on the matter. I take it that he did better?"

"I think he handled Nikki . . . well. At any rate, Nikki won't experience that sort of late shock to his world. Of course, compared to Serg, Tien wasn't much worse than foolish and venal. But it was hard to watch. No nine-year-old should have to deal with something this vile, this close to his heart. What will it make him?"

"Eventually . . . ten," the Count said. "You do what you have to do. You grow or go under. You have to believe he will grow."

Miles drummed his fingers on the sofa's padded arm. "Gregor's subtlety is still dawning on me. By admitting Tien's peculation, he's pulled Nikki to the inside with us. Nikki too now has a vested interest in maintaining the cover story, to protect his late da's reputation. Strange. Which is what brings me to you, by the way. Gregor asks—requests and requires, no less!—you give me the lecture you gave him on honor versus reputation. It must have been memorable."

The Count's brow wrinkled. "Lecture? Oh. Yes." He smiled briefly. "So that stuck in his mind, good. You wonder sometimes, with young people, if anything you say goes in, or if you're just throwing your words on the wind."

Miles stirred uncomfortably, wondering if any of that last remark was to his address. All right, *how much* of that remark. "Mm?" he prompted.

"I wouldn't have called it a lecture. Just a useful distinction, to clarify thought." He spread his hand, palm up, in a gesture of balance. "Reputation is what other people know about you. Honor is what you know about yourself."

"Hm."

"The friction tends to arise when the two are not the same. In the matter of Vorsoisson's death, how do you stand with yourself?"

How does he strike to the center in one cut like that? "I'm not sure. Do impure thoughts count?"

"No," said the Count firmly. "Only acts of will."

"What about acts of ineptitude?"

"A gray area, and don't tell me you haven't lived in that twilight before."

"Most of my life, sir. Not that I haven't leaped up into the blinding light of competence now and then. It's sustaining the altitude that defeats me."

The Count raised his brows, and smiled crookedly, but charitably refrained from agreeing. "So. Then it seems to me your immediate problems lie more in the realm of reputation."

Miles sighed. "I feel like I'm being gnawed all over by rats. Little corrosive rats, flicking away too fast for me to turn and whap them on the head."

The Count studied his fingernails. "It could be worse. There is no more hollow feeling than to stand with your honor shattered at your feet while soaring public reputation wraps you in rewards. *That's* soul-destroying. The other way around is merely very, very irritating."

"Very," said Miles bitterly.

"Heh. All right. Can I offer you some consoling reflections?"

"Please do, sir."

"First, this too shall pass. Despite the undoubted charms of sex, murder, conspiracy, and more sex, people will eventually grow bored with the tale, and some other poor fellow will make some other ghastly public mistake, and their attention will go haring off after the new game."

"*What* sex?" Miles muttered in exasperation. "There hasn't *been* any sex. Dammit. Or this would all seem a great deal more worthwhile. I haven't even gotten to *kiss* the woman yet!"

The Count's lips twitched. "My condolences. Secondly, given this accusation, no charge against you that's *less* exciting will ruffle anyone's sensibilities in the future. The near future, anyway."

"Oh, great. Does this mean I'm free to run riot from now on, as long as I stop short of premeditated murder?"

"You'd be amazed." A little of the humor died in the Count's eyes, at what memory Miles could not guess, but then his lips tweaked up again. "Third, there is no thought control—or I'd certainly have put it to use before this. Trying to shape, or respond to, what every idiot on the street believes—on the basis of little logic and less information—would only serve to drive you mad."

"Some people's opinions do matter."

"Yes, sometimes. Have you identified whose, in this case?"

"Ekaterin's. Nikki's. Gregor's." Miles hesitated. "That's all."

"What, your poor aging parents aren't on that short list?"

"I should be sorry to lose your good opinion," said Miles slowly. "But in this case, you're not the ones . . . I'm not sure how to put this. To use Mother's terminology—you are not the ones sinned against. So your forgiveness is moot."

"Hm," said the Count, rubbing his lips and regarding Miles with cool approval. "Interesting. Well. For your fourth consoling thought, I would point out that in *this* venue," a wave of his finger took in Vorbarr Sultana, and by extension Barrayar, "acquiring a reputation as a slick and dangerous man, who would kill without compunction to obtain and protect his own, is not *all* bad. In fact, you might even find it useful."

"Useful! Have you found the name of *the Butcher of Komarr* a handy prop, then, sir?" Miles said indignantly.

His father's eyes narrowed, partly in grim amusement, partly in appreciation. "I've found it a mixed . . . damnation. But yes, I have used the weight of that reputation, from time to time, to lean on certain susceptible men. Why not, I paid for it. Simon says he's experienced the same phenomenon. After inheriting ImpSec from Negri the Great, he claimed all he had to do in order to unnerve his opponents was stand there and keep his mouth shut."

"I worked with Simon. He damned well *was* unnerving. And it wasn't just because of his memory chip, *or* Negri's lingering ghost." Miles shook his head. Only his father could, with perfect sincerity, regard Simon Illyan as an ordinary, everyday sort of subordinate. "Anyway, people may have seen Simon as sinister, but never as corrupt. He wouldn't have been half as scary if he hadn't been able to convincingly project that implacable indifference to, well, any human appetite." He paused in contemplation of his former commander-and-mentor's quelling management style. "But dammit, if . . . if my enemies won't allow me minimal moral sense, I wish they'd at least give me credit for competence in my vices! If I were going to murder someone, I'd have done a much smoother job than that hideous mess. No one would even guess a murder had occurred, ha!"

"I believe you," soothed the Count. He cocked his head in sudden curiosity. "Ah . . . have you ever?"

Miles burrowed back into the sofa, and scratched his cheek. "There was one mission for Illyan . . . I don't want to talk about it. It was close, unpleasant work, but we brought it off." His eyes fixed broodingly on the carpet.

"Really. I had asked him not to use you for assassinations."

"Why? Afraid I'd pick up bad habits? Anyway, it was a lot more complicated than a simple assassination."

"It generally is."

Miles stared away for a minute into the middle distance. "So what you're telling me boils down to the same thing Galeni said. I have to stand here and eat this, and smile."

"No," said his father, "you don't have to smile. But if you're really asking for advice from my accumulated experience, I'm saying, Guard your honor. Let your reputation fall where it will. And outlive the bastards."

Miles's gaze flicked up curiously to his father's face. He'd never known him when his hair wasn't gray; it was nearly all white now. "I know you've been up and down over the years. The first time your reputation took serious damage—how did you get through it?"

"Oh, the first time . . . that was a long time ago." The Count leaned forward, and tapped his thumbnail pensively on his lips. "It suddenly occurs to me, that among observers above a certain age—the few survivors of that generation—the dim memory of that episode may not be helping your cause. Like father, like son?" The Count regarded him with a concerned frown. "*That's* certainly a consequence I could never have foreseen. You see . . . after the suicide of my first wife, I was widely rumored to have killed her. For infidelity."

Miles blinked. He'd heard disjointed bits of this old

tale, but not that last wrinkle. "And, um . . . was she? Unfaithful?"

"Oh, yes. We had a grotesque blowup about it. I was hurt, confused—which emerged as a sort of awkward, self-conscious rage—and severely handicapped by my cultural conditioning. A point in my life when I could definitely have used a Betan therapist, instead of the bad Barrayaran advice we got from . . . never mind. I didn't know—couldn't imagine such alternatives existed. It was a darker, older time. Men still dueled, you know, though it was illegal by then."

"But did you . . . um, you didn't really, um . . ."

"Murder her? No. Or only with words." It was the Count's turn to look away, his eyes narrowing. "Though I was never one hundred percent sure your grandfather hadn't. He'd arranged the marriage; I know he felt responsible."

Miles's brows rose, as he considered this. "Remembering Gran'da, that does seem faintly and horribly possible. Did you ever ask him?"

"No." The Count sighed. "What, after all, would I have done if he'd said yes?"

Aral Vorkosigan had been what, twenty-two at the time? Over half a century ago. *He was far younger then than I am now. Hell, he was just a kid.* Dizzily, Miles's world seemed to spin slowly around and click into some new and tilted axis, with altered perspectives. "So . . . how did you survive?"

"I had the luck of fools and madmen, I believe. I was certainly both. *I* didn't give a damn. Vile gossip? I would prove it an understatement, and give them twice the tale to chew upon. I think I stunned them into silence. Picture a suicidal loon with nothing to lose, staggering around in a drunken, hostile haze. Armed. Eventually, I got as sick of myself as everyone else must have been of me by that time, and pulled out of it."

That anguished boy was gone now, leaving this grave old man to sit in merciful judgment upon him. It did explain why, old-Barrayaran though he was in parts, his father had never so much as breathed the suggestion of an arranged marriage to Miles as a solution to his romantic difficulties, nor murmured the least criticism of his few affairs. Miles jerked up his chin, and favored his father with a tilted smile. "Your strategy does not appeal to me, sir. Drink makes me sick. I'm not feeling a bit suicidal. And I have *everything* to lose."

"I wasn't recommending it," the Count said mildly. He sat back. "Later—much later—when I also had too much to lose, I had acquired your mother. Her good opinion was the only one I needed."

"Yes? And what if it had been her good opinion that had been at risk? How would you have stood then?" *Ekaterin . . .*

"On my hands and knees, belike." The Count shook his head, and smiled slowly. "So, ah . . . when *are* we going to be permitted to meet this woman who has had such an invigorating effect on you? Her and her Nikki. Perhaps you might invite them to dinner here soon?"

Miles cringed. "Not . . . not another dinner. Not soon."

"My glimpse of her was so frustratingly brief. What little I could see was very attractive, I thought. Not too thin. She squished well, bouncing off me." Count Vorkosigan grinned briefly, at this memory. Miles's father shared an archaic Barrayaran ideal of feminine beauty that included the capacity to survive minor famines; Miles admitted a susceptibility to that style himself. "Reasonably athletic, too. Clearly, she could outrun you. I would therefore suggest blandishments, rather than direct pursuit, next time."

"I've been *trying*," sighed Miles.

The Count regarded his son, half amused, half serious. "This parade of females of yours is very confusing to your mother and me, you know. We can't tell whether we're supposed to start bonding to them, or not."

"*What* parade?" said Miles indignantly. "I brought home *one* galactic girlfriend. *One*. It wasn't my fault things didn't work out."

"Plus the several, um, extraordinary ladies decorating Illyan's reports who didn't make it this far."

Miles thought he could feel his eyes cross. "But how

could he—Illyan never knew—he never told you about—
no. Don't tell me. I don't want to know. But I swear
the next time I see him—" He glowered at the Count,
who was laughing at him with a perfectly straight face.
"I suppose Simon won't remember. Or he'll pretend he
doesn't. Damned convenient, that optional amnesia he's
developed." He added, "Anyway, I've mentioned all the
important ones to Ekaterin already, so there."

"Oh? Were you confessing, or bragging?"

"Clearing the decks. Honesty . . . is the only way, with
her."

"Honesty is the only way with anyone, when you'll
be so close as to be living inside each other's skins.
So . . . *is* this Ekaterin another passing fancy?" The
Count hesitated, his eyes crinkling. "Or is she the one
who *will* love my son forever and fiercely—hold his
household and estates with integrity—stand beside him
through danger, and dearth, and death—and guide my
grandchildren's hands when they light my funeral
offering?"

Miles paused in momentary admiration of his father's
ability to *deliver* lines like that. It put him in mind of
the way a combat drop shuttle delivered pinpoint incen-
diaries. "That would be . . . that would be Column B,
sir. All of the above." He swallowed. "I hope. If I don't
fumble it again."

"So when do we get to *meet* her?" the Count
repeated reasonably.

"Things are still very unsettled." Miles climbed to his
feet, sensing that his moment to retreat with dignity was
slipping away rapidly. "I'll let you know."

But the Count did not pursue his erratic line of
humor. Instead he looked at his son with eyes gone
serious, though still warm. "I am glad she came to you
when you were old enough to know your own mind."

Miles favored him with an analyst's salute, a vague
wave of two fingers in the general vicinity of his forehead. "So am I, sir."

CHAPTER SIXTEEN

Ekaterin sat at her aunt's comconsole, attempting to compose a résumé that would conceal her lack of experience from the supervisor of an urban plant nursery that supplied the city's public gardens. She was not, drat it, going to name *Lord Auditor Vorkosigan* as a reference. Aunt Vorthys had left for her morning class, and Nikki for an outing with Arthur Pym under the aegis of Arthur's elder sister; when the door chime's second ring tore her attention from her task, Ekaterin was abruptly aware that she was alone in the house. Would enemy agents bent on kidnapping come to the front door? Miles would know. She pictured Pym, at Vorkosigan House, frostily informing the intruders that they would have to go round back to the *spies'* entrance . . . which would be sprinkled with appropriate high-tech caltrops, no doubt. Controlling her new paranoia, she rose and went to the front hall.

To her relief and delight, instead of Cetagandan infiltrators, her brother Hugo Vorvayne stood on the front stoop, along with a pleasant-featured fellow she recognized after an uncertain blink as Vassily Vorsoisson, Tien's closest cousin. She had seen him exactly once before in her life, at Tien's funeral, where they had met long enough for him to officially sign over Nikki's guardianship to her. Lieutenant Vorsoisson held a post in traffic control at the big military shuttleport in Vorbretten's District; when she'd first and last seen him, he'd worn Service dress greens as suited the somber formality of the occasion, but today he'd changed to more casual civvies.

"Hugo, Vassily! This is a surprise—come in, come in!" She gestured them both into the Professora's front parlor. Vassily gave her a polite, acknowledging nod, and refused an offer of tea or coffee, they'd had some at the monorail station, thank you. Hugo gave her hands a brief squeeze, and smiled at her in a worried way before taking a seat. He was in his mid-forties; the combination of his desk work in the Imperial Bureau of Mines and his wife Rosalie's care was broadening him a trifle. On him, it looked wonderfully solid and reassuring. But alarm tightened Ekaterin's throat at the tension in his face. "Is everything all right?"

"*We're* all fine," he said with peculiar emphasis.

A chill flushed through her. "Da—?"

"Yes, yes, he's fine too." Impatiently, he gestured away her anxiety. "The only member of the family who seems to be a source of concern at the moment is you, Kat."

Ekaterin stared at him, baffled. "Me? I'm all right." She sank down into her uncle's big chair in the corner. Vassily pulled up one of the spindly chairs, and perched a little awkwardly upon it.

Hugo conveyed greetings from the family, Rosalie and Edie and the boys, then looked around vaguely and asked, "Are Uncle and Aunt Vorthys here?"

"No, neither one. Aunt will be back from class in a while, though."

Hugo frowned. "I was hoping we could see Uncle Vorthys, really. When will he be back?"

"Oh, he's gone to Komarr. To clear up some last technical bits about the solar mirror disaster, you know. He doesn't expect to be back till just before Gregor's wedding."

"Whose wedding?" said Vassily.

Gah, now Miles had *her* doing it. She was *not* on a

first-name basis with Grego—with the Emperor, she was *not*. "Emperor Gregor's wedding. As an Imperial Auditor, Uncle Vorthys will of course attend."

Vassily's lips formed a little O of enlightenment, *that* Gregor.

"No chance of any of us getting near it, I suppose," Hugo sighed. "Of course, *I* have no interest in such things, but Rosalie and her lady friends have all gone quite silly over it." After a short hesitation, he added inconsistently, "Is it true that the Horse Guards will parade in squads of all the uniforms they've worn through history, from the Time of Isolation through Ezar's day?"

"Yes," said Ekaterin. "And there will be massive fireworks displays over the river *every* night." A faintly envious look crept into Hugo's eyes at this news.

Vassily cleared his throat, and asked, "Is Nikki here?"

"No . . . he went out with a friend to see the pole-barge regatta on the river this morning. They have it every year; it commemorates the relief of the city by Vlad Vorbarra's forces during the Ten-Years' War. I understand they're doing a bang-up job of it this summer—new costumes, and a reenactment of the assault on the Old Star Bridge. The boys were very excited." She did not add that they expected to have an especially fine view from the balconies of Vorbretten House, courtesy of a Vorbretten Armsman friend of Pym's.

Vassily stirred uncomfortably. "Perhaps it's just as well. Madame Vorsoisson—Ekaterin—we actually came down here today for a particular reason, a very serious matter. I should like to talk with you frankly."

"That's . . . generally best, when one is going to talk," Ekaterin responded. She glanced in query at Hugo.

"Vassily came to me . . ." Hugo began, and trailed off. "Well, *you* explain it, Vassily."

Vassily leaned forward with his hands clasped between his knees and said heavily, "You see, it's this. I received a most disturbing communication from an informant here in Vorbarr Sultana about what has been happening—what has recently come to light—some very disturbing information about you, my late cousin, and Lord Auditor Vorkosigan."

"Oh," she said flatly. So, the circuit of the Old Walls, what remained of them, did not limit the slander to the capital; the slime-trail even stretched to provincial District towns. She had somehow thought this vicious game an exclusively High Vor pastime. She sat back and frowned.

"Because it seemed to concern both our families very nearly—and, of course, because something of this peculiar nature must be cross-checked—I brought it to Hugo, for his advice, hoping that he could allay my fears. The corroborations your sister-in-law Rosalie supplied served to increase them instead."

Corroborations of what? She could probably make a few shrewd guesses, but she declined to lead the witnesses. "I don't understand."

"I was told," Vassily stopped to lick his lips nervously, "it's become common knowledge among his high Vor set that Lord Auditor Vorkosigan was responsible for sabotaging Tien's breath mask, the night he died on Komarr."

She could demolish this quickly enough. "You are told lies. That story was made up by a nasty little cabal of Lord Vorkosigan's political enemies, who wished to embarrass him during some District inheritance in-fighting presently going on here in the Council of Counts. Tien sabotaged himself; he was always careless about cleaning and checking his equipment. It's just whispering. No such actual charge has been made."

"Well, how could it be?" said Vassily reasonably. But her confidence that she'd brought him swiftly to his senses died as he went on, "As it was explained to me, any charge would have to be laid in the Council, before and by his peers. His father may be retired to Sergyar, but you may be sure his Centrist coalition remains powerful enough to suppress any such move."

"I would hope so." It might be suppressed, oh yes, but not for the reason Vassily thought. Lips thinning, she stared coldly at him.

Hugo put in anxiously, "But you see, Ekaterin, the

same person informed Vassily that Lord Vorkosigan attempted to force you to accept a proposal of marriage from him."

She sighed in exasperation. "Force? No, certainly not."

"Ah." Hugo brightened.

"He did ask me to marry him. Very . . . awkwardly."

"My God, that was really *true*?" Hugo looked momentarily stunned. He sounded a deal more appalled at this than at the murder charge—doubly unflattering, Ekaterin decided. "You refused, of course!"

She touched the left side of her bolero, tracing the now not-so-stiff shape of the paper she kept folded there. Miles's letter was not the sort of thing she cared to leave lying around for anyone to pick up and read, and besides . . . she wanted to reread it herself now and then. From time to time. Six or twelve times a day . . . "Not exactly."

Hugo's brow wrinkled. "What do you mean by *not exactly*? I thought that was a yes-or-no sort of question."

"It's . . . difficult to explain." She hesitated. Detailing in front of Tien's closest cousin how a decade of Tien's private chaos had worn out her soul was just not on her list, she decided. "And rather personal."

Vassily offered helpfully, "The letter said that you seemed confused and distraught."

Ekaterin's eyes narrowed. "Just what busybody did you have this—*communication*—from, anyway?"

Vassily replied, "A friend of yours—he claimed—who is gravely concerned for your safety."

A friend? The Professora was her friend. Kareen, Mark . . . Miles, but he would hardly traduce himself, now . . . Enrique? *Tsipis*? "I cannot imagine any friend of mine doing or saying any such thing."

Hugo's frown of worry deepened. "The letter also said Lord Vorkosigan has been putting all sorts of pressure on you. That he has some strange hold on your mind."

No. Only on my heart, I think. Her mind was perfectly clear. It was the rest of her that seemed to be in rebellion. "He's a very attractive man," she admitted.

Hugo exchanged a baffled look with Vassily. Both men had met Miles at Tien's funeral; of course, Miles had been very closed and formal there, and still grayly fatigued from his case. They'd had no opportunity to see what he was like when he opened up—the elusive smile, the bright, particular eyes, the wit and the words and the passion . . . the confounded look on his face when confronted by Vorkosigan liveried butter bugs . . . she smiled helplessly in memory.

"Kat," said Hugo in a disconcerted tone, "the man's a mutie. He barely comes up to your shoulder. He's *distinctly* hunched—I don't know why that wasn't surgically corrected. He's just *odd*."

"Oh, he's had dozens of surgeries. His original damage was far, far more severe. You can still see these faint old scars running all over his body from the corrections."

Hugo stared at her. "*All* over his body?"

"Um. I assume so. As much of it as I've seen, anyway." She stopped her tongue barely short of adding, *The top half*. A perfectly unnecessary vision of Miles entirely naked, gift-wrapped in sheets and blankets in bed, and her with him, slowly exploring his intricacies all the way down, distracted her imagination momentarily. She blinked it away, hoping her eyes weren't crossing. "You have to concede, he has a good face. His eyes are . . . very alive."

"His head's too big."

"No, his body's just a little undersized for it." How had she ended up arguing Miles's anatomy with Hugo, anyway? He wasn't some spavined horse she was considering purchasing against veterinary advice, drat it. "Anyway, this is none of it our business."

"It is if he—if you—" Hugo sucked his lip. "Kat . . . if you're under some kind of threat, or blackmail or some strange thing, you don't stand alone. I know we can get help. You may have abandoned your family, but we haven't abandoned you."

More's the pity. "Thank you for that estimate of my character," she said tartly. "And do you imagine our Uncle *Lord Auditor* Vorthys is incapable of protecting me, if it should come to that? And Aunt Vorthys, too?"

Vassily said uneasily, "I'm sure your uncle and aunt

are very kind—after all, they took you and Nikki in—but I'm given to understand they are both rather unworldly intellectuals. Possibly they do not understand the dangers. My informant says they haven't been guarding you at all. They've permitted you to go where you will, when you will, in a completely unregulated fashion, and come in contact with all sorts of dubious persons."

Their *unworldly* aunt was one of Barrayar's foremost experts on every gory detail of the political history of the Time of Isolation, spoke and read four languages flawlessly, could sift through documentation with an eye worthy of an ImpSec analyst—a line of work several of her former graduate students were now in—and had thirty years of experience dealing with young people and their self-inflicted troubles. And as for Uncle Vorthys—"Engineering failure analysis does not strike me as an especially unworldly discipline. Not when it includes expertise on sabotage." She inhaled, preparing to enlarge on this.

Vassily's lips tightened. "The capital has a reputation as an unsavory milieu. Too many wealthy, powerful men—and their women—with too few restraints on their appetites and vices. That's a dangerous world for a young boy to be exposed to, especially through his mother's . . . love affairs." Ekaterin was still mentally sputtering over this one when Vassily's voice dropped to a tone of hushed horror, and he added, "I've even heard—they say—that there's a high Vor lord here in Vorbarr Sultana who used to be a *woman*, who had her brain transplanted to a *man's body*."

Ekaterin blinked. "Oh. Yes, that would be Lord Dono Vorrutyer. I've met him. It wasn't a brain transplant—ick! what a horrid misrepresentation—it was just a perfectly ordinary Betan body mod."

Both men boggled at her. "You *encountered* this creature?" said Hugo. "Where?"

"Um . . . Vorkosigan House. Actually. Dono seemed a very bright fellow. I think he'll do very well for Vorrutyer's District, if the Council grants him his late brother's Countship." She added after a moment of bitter consideration, "All things considered, I quite hope he gets it. *That* would give Richars and his slandering cronies one in the eye!"

Hugo, who had absorbed this exchange with growing dismay, put in, "I have to agree with Vassily, I'm a little uneasy myself about having you down here in the capital. The family so wishes to see you *safe*, Kat. I grant you're no girl anymore. You should have your own household, watched over by a steady husband who can be trusted to guard your welfare *and* Nikki's."

You could get your wish. Yet . . . she had stood up to armed terrorists, and survived. And *won*. Her definition of *safe* was . . . not so very narrow as that, anymore.

"A man of your own class," Hugo went on persuasively. "Someone who's right for you."

I think I've found him. He comes with a house where I don't hit the walls each time I stretch, either. Not even if I stretched out forever. She cocked her head. "Just what do you think my class is, Hugo?"

He looked nonplused. "*Our* class. Solid, honest, loyal Vor. On the women's side, modest, proper, upright. . . ."

She was suddenly on fire with a desire to be immodest, improper, and above all . . . not upright. Quite gloriously horizontal, in fact. It occurred to her that a certain disparity of height would be immaterial, when one—or two—were lying down . . . "You think I should have a house?"

"Yes, certainly."

"Not a planet?"

Hugo looked taken aback. "What? Of course not!"

"You know, Hugo, I never realized it before, but your vision lacks . . . scope." *Miles* thought she should have a planet. She paused, and a slow smile stole over her lips. After all, *his* mother had one. It was all in what you were used to, she supposed. No point in saying this aloud; they wouldn't get the joke.

And how had her big brother, admired and generous if more than a little distant due to their disparity of age, grown so small-minded of late? No . . . *Hugo* hadn't changed. The logical conclusion shook her.

Hugo said, "Damn, Kat. I thought that part of the

letter was twaddle at first, but this mutie lord *has* turned your head around in some strange way."

"And if it's true . . . he has frightening allies," said Vassily. "The letter claimed that Vorkosigan had Simon Illyan himself riding point for him, herding you into his trap." His lips twisted dubiously. "That was the part that most made me wonder if I was being made a game of, to tell you the truth."

"I've met Simon," Ekaterin conceded. "I found him rather . . . sweet."

A dazed silence greeted this declaration.

She added a little awkwardly, "Of course, I understand he's relaxed quite a lot since his medical retirement from ImpSec. One can see that would be a great burden off his mind." Belatedly, the internal evidence slotted into place. "Wait a minute—*who* did you say sent you this hash of hearsay and lies?"

"It was in the strictest confidence," said Vassily warily.

"It was that blithering idiot Alexi Vormoncrief, wasn't it? Ah!" The light dawned, furiously, like the glare from an atomic fireball. But screaming, swearing, and throwing things would be counterproductive. She gripped the chair arms, so that the men could not see her hands shake. "Vassily, Hugo should have told you—I turned down a proposal of marriage from Alexi. It seems he's found a way to revenge his outraged vanity." *Vile twit!*

"Kat," said Hugo slowly, "I did consider that interpretation. I grant you the fellow's a trifle, um, idealistic, and if you've taken against him I won't try to argue his suit—though he seemed perfectly unobjectionable to me—but I saw his letter. I judged it quite sincerely concerned for you. A little over the top, yes, but what do you expect from a man in love?"

"Alexi Vormoncrief is not in love with me. He can't see far enough past the end of his own Vor nose to even know who or what I am. If you stuffed my clothes with straw and put a wig on top, he'd scarcely notice the change. He's just going through the motions supplied by his cultural programming." Well, all right, and his more fundamental biological programming, and he wasn't the only one suffering from that, now was he?

She would concede Alexi a ration of sincere sex drive, but she was certain its object was arbitrary. Her hand strayed to her bolero, over her heart, and Miles's memorized words echoed, cutting through the uproar between her ears: *I wanted to possess the power of your eyes* . . .

Vassily waved an impatient hand. "All this is beside the point, for me if not for your brother. You're not a dowered maiden anymore, for your father to hoard up with his other treasures. I, however, have a clear family duty to see to Nikki's safety, if I have reason to believe it is threatened."

Ekaterin froze.

Vassily had granted her custody of Nikki with his word. He could take it back again as easily. It was she who'd have to take suit to court—*his* District court—not only to prove herself worthy, but also to prove him unworthy and unfit to have charge of the child. Vassily was no convicted criminal, nor habitual drunkard, nor spendthrift nor berserker; he was just a bachelor officer, a conscientious, duty-minded orbital traffic controller, an ordinary honest man. She hadn't a prayer of winning against him. If only Nikki had been her daughter, those rights would be reversed. . . .

"You would find a nine-year-old boy an awkward burden on a military base, I should think," she said neutrally at last.

Vassily looked startled. "Well, I hope it won't come to *that*. In the worst scenario, I'd planned to leave him with his Grandmother Vorsoisson, until things were straightened out."

Ekaterin held her teeth together for a moment, then said, "Nikki is of course welcome to visit Tien's mother any time she invites him. At the funeral she gave me to understand she was too unwell to receive visitors this summer." She moistened her lips. "Please define the term *worst scenario* for me. And just what exactly do you mean by *straightened out*?"

"Well," Vassily shrugged apologetically, "coming down here and finding you actually betrothed to the man who murdered Nikki's father would have been pretty bad, don't you agree?"

Had he been prepared to take Nikki away this very day, in that case? "I told you. Tien's death was accidental, and that accusation is pure slander." His disregard of her words reminded her horribly of Tien, for a moment; was obliviousness a Vorsoisson family trait? Despite the danger of offending him, she glowered. "Do you think I'm lying, or do you think I'm just stupid?" She fought for control of her breathing. She had faced far more frightening men than the earnest, misguided, Vassily Vorsoisson. *But never one who could cost me Nikki with a word.* She stood on the edge of a deep, dark pit. If she fell now, the struggle to get out again would be as filthy and painful as anything she could imagine. Vassily must *not* be pushed into taking Nikki. *Trying to take Nikki.* And she could stop him—how? She was legally overmatched before she even began. *So don't begin.*

She chose her words with utmost caution. "So what do you mean by straightened out?"

Hugo and Vassily looked at each other uncertainly. Vassily ventured, "I beg your pardon?"

"I cannot know if I have toed your line unless you show me where you've drawn it."

Hugo protested, "That's not very kindly put, Kat. We have your interests at heart."

"You don't even know what my interests are." Not true, Vassily had his thumb right down on the most mortal one. Nikki. *Eat rage, woman.* She had used to be expert at swallowing herself, during her marriage. Somehow she'd lost the taste for it.

Vassily groped, "Well . . . I'd certainly wish to be assured Nikki was not being exposed to persons of undesirable character."

She granted him a thin smile. "No problem. I shall be more than happy to entirely avoid Alexi Vormoncrief in the future."

He gave her a pained look. "I was referring to Lord Vorkosigan. And his political and personal set. At least— at least until this very dark cloud is cleared from his reputation. After all, the man is accused of *murdering* my *cousin.*"

Vassily's outrage was dutiful clan loyalty, not personal

grief, Ekaterin reminded herself. If he and Tien had met more than three times in their lives it was news to her. "Excuse me," she said steadily. "If Miles is not to be charged—and I can't think he will be, on this—how may he be cleared, in your view? What has to happen?"

Vassily appeared momentarily baffled.

Hugo put in tentatively, "I don't want *you* exposed to corruption, either, Kat."

"You know, Hugo, it's the strangest thing," Ekaterin said genially to him, "but somehow Lord Vorkosigan has overlooked sending me invitations to *any* of his orgies. I'm quite put out. Do you suppose it's not the orgy season in Vorbarr Sultana yet?" She bit back further words. Sarcasm was not a luxury she—or Nikki—could afford.

Hugo rewarded this sally with a flat-lipped frown. He and Vassily gave one another a long look, each so obviously trying to divest the dirty work onto his companion that Ekaterin would have laughed, if it hadn't been so painful. Vassily finally muttered weakly, "She's *your* sister . . ."

Hugo took a breath. He was a Vorvayne; he knew his duty, by God. *All us Vorvaynes know our duty. And we'll keep on doing it till we die. No matter how stupid or painful or counterproductive it is, yes! After all, look at me. I kept oath for eleven years to Tien. . . .*

"Ekaterin, I think the burden falls on me to say this. Till this murder rumor business is settled, I'm flat requesting you not to encourage or, or see this Miles Vorkosigan fellow again. Or I will have to agree Vassily is completely justified in removing Nikki from the situation."

Removing Nikki from his mother and her paramour, you mean. Nikki had lost one parent this year, and lost all his friends in the move back to Barrayar. He was just starting to find the city he'd been dropped into less strange, to begin to unfold in tentative new friendships, to lose that wooden caution that had marred his smile for a while. She imagined him ripped away again, denied the chance to see her—for it would come down to that, wouldn't it? it was she, not the capital, Vassily suspected of corruption—plopped down in the third strange place in a year among unknown adults who regarded him not as a child to be delighted in, but as a duty to be discharged . . . no. No.

"Excuse me. I am willing to cooperate. I just haven't been able to compel either of you to say what I'm supposed to be cooperating with. I perfectly see what you are worried about, but *how* is it *to be settled*? Define *settled*. If it's till Miles's enemies stop saying nasty things about him, it could be a long wait. His line of work routinely pits him against the powerful. And he's not the sort to back down from any counterattack."

Hugo said, a bit more feebly, "Avoid him for a time, anyway."

"A time. Good. Now we're getting somewhere. How long exactly?"

"I . . . can hardly say."

"A week?"

Vassily, sounding a bit offended, put in, "Certainly more than that!"

"A month?"

Hugo rolled his hands in a frustrated gesture. "*I* don't know, Kat! Till you forget these odd notions you have about him, I suppose."

"Ah. Till the end of time. Hm. I can't quite decide if that's specific enough, or not. I think not." She took a breath, and said reluctantly, because it was such a long time and yet likely to sound so plausible to them, "To the end of my mourning year?"

Vassily said, "At the very minimum!"

"Very well." Her eyes narrowed, and she smiled, because smiling would do more good than howling. "I shall take you at your name's word, Vassily Vorsoisson."

"I, I, uh . . ." said Vassily, unexpectedly cornered. "Well . . . something should be settled by then. Surely."

I gave up too much, too soon. I should have tried for Winterfair. She added in sudden afterthought, "I reserve the right to tell him—and tell him why—myself, however. In person."

"Is that wise, Kat?" asked Hugo. "Better to call him on the comconsole."

"Anything less would be cowardly."

"Can't you send him a note?"

"*Absolutely* not. Not with this . . . news." What a vile return *that* would be, for Miles's own declaration sealed in his heart's blood.

At her defiant stare, Hugo weakened. "One visit, then. A brief one."

Vassily shrugged reluctant acquiescence.

An uncomfortable silence fell, after this. Ekaterin realized she ought to invite the pair of them to lunch, except that she didn't feel like inviting them to continue breathing. Yes, and she should exert herself to charm and soothe the Vassily. She rubbed her temples, which were throbbing. When Vassily made a feeble motion toward escape from the Professora's parlor by mumbling about *things to do*, she did not impede them.

She locked the front door on their retreating forms, and returned to curl up in her uncle's chair, unable to decide whether to go lie down, or pace, or weed. Anyway, the garden was still stripped of weeds from her last upset about Miles. It would be an hour yet before Aunt Vorthys returned from her class, and Ekaterin could pour out her fury and panic into her ear. Or her lap.

To Hugo's credit, she reflected, he hadn't seemed enticed by the promise of a Countess's place for his little sister at any price, nor had he suggested that was the prize that motivated her. Vorvaynes were above that sort of material ambition.

Once, she had bought Nikki a rather expensive robopet, which he'd played with for a few days and then neglected. It had been forgotten on a shelf until, attempting to clean, she'd tried to give it away. Nikki's sudden frantic protests and heartbroken carryings-on had shaken the roof.

The parallel was embarrassing. Was Miles a toy she hadn't wanted till they'd tried to take him from her? Deep down in her chest, someone was screaming and sobbing. *You're not in charge here. I'm the adult, dammit.* Yet Nikki had kept his robopet . . .

She would deliver the bad news about Vassily's

interdict to Miles's face. But not yet, oh, not quite yet. Because unless this smear upon his reputation was suddenly and spectacularly *settled*, that might be her last look at him for a very long time.

Kareen watched her father sink into the soft upholstery of the groundcar that Tante Cordelia had sent for them, and hitch around restlessly, placing his swordstick first on his lap and then at his side. Somehow, she didn't think his discomfort was all from his old war wounds.

"We're going to regret this, I know we are," he said querulously to Mama, for about the sixth time, as she settled in beside him. The rear canopy closed over the three of them, blocking the bright afternoon sun, and the groundcar started up smoothly and quietly. "Once that woman gets her hands on us, you know she'll have our heads turned inside out in ten minutes, and we'll be sitting there nodding away like fools, agreeing with every insane thing she says."

Oh, I hope so, I hope so! Kareen clamped her lips shut, and sat very still. She wasn't safe yet. The Commodore could still order Tante Cordelia's driver to turn the car around and take them back home.

"Now, Kou," said Mama, "we can't go on like this. Cordelia's right. It's time things were arranged more sensibly."

"Ah! There's that word—*sensible*. One of her favorites. I feel like I already have a plasma arc targeter spot right *there*." He pointed to the middle of his chest, as though a red dot wavered across his green uniform.

"It's been very uncomfortable," said Mama, "and I for one am getting tired of it. *I* want to see our old friends, and hear all about Sergyar. We can't stop all our lives over this."

Yeah, just mine. Kareen's teeth clenched a little harder.

"Well, *I* do not want that fat little weird clone—" he hesitated, judging by the ripple of his lips editing his word choice at least twice "—making up to my daughter. Explain to me why he needs two years of Betan therapy if he isn't half mad, eh? Eh?"

Don't say it, girl, don't say it. She gnawed on her knuckles instead. Fortunately, the drive was very short.

Armsman Pym met them at the door to Vorkosigan House. He favored her father with one of those formal nods that evoked a salute. "Good afternoon Commodore, Madame Koudelka. Welcome, Miss Kareen. Milady will receive you in the library. This way, please . . ." Kareen could almost swear, as he turned to escort them, that his eyelid shivered at her in a wink, but he was playing the Bland Servitor to the hilt today, and he gave her no more clues.

Pym ushered them through the double doors, and announced them with formality. He withdrew discreetly but with a—knowing Pym—deliberate air of abandoning them to a deserved fate.

In the library, part of the furniture had been rearranged. Tante Cordelia waited in a large wing chair perhaps accidentally reminiscent of a throne. At her right and left hands, two smaller armchairs faced one another. Mark sat in one of them, wearing his best black suit, shaved and slick as he'd been for Miles's ill-fated party. He popped to his feet and stood at a sort of awkward attention as the Koudelkas entered, clearly unable to decide whether it would be worse to nod cordially or do nothing. He compromised by standing there looking stuffed.

Across from Tante Cordelia, an entirely new piece of furniture had been placed. Well, *new* was a misnomer; it was an elderly, shabby couch which had lived for at least the past fifteen years up in one of Vorkosigan House's attics. Kareen remembered it dimly from the old hide-and-seek days. Last she'd seen it, it had been piled high with dusty boxes.

"Ah, and there you all are," said Tante Cordelia cheerfully. She waved at the second armchair. "Kareen, why don't you sit right here." Kareen scooted in as directed, clutching the arms. Mark seated himself again on the edge of his own chair, and watched her anxiously. Tante Cordelia's index finger rose like a target seeker, and pointed first to Kareen's parents, then to the old sofa. "Kou and Drou, you sit down—*there*."

Both of them stared with inexplicable dismay at the harmless piece of old furniture.

"Oh," breathed the Commodore. "Oh, Cordelia, this is fighting dirty . . ." He started to swing around and head for the exit, but was brought up short by his wife's hand closing like a vise on his arm.

The Countess's gaze sharpened. In a voice Kareen had rarely heard her use before, she repeated, "*Sit. Down.*" It wasn't even her Countess Vorkosigan voice; it was something older, firmer, even more appallingly confident. It was her old Ship Captain's voice, Kareen realized; and her parents had both lived under military authority for decades.

Her parents sank as though folded.

"There." The Countess sat back with a satisfied smile on her lips.

A long silence followed. Kareen could hear the old-fashioned mechanical clock ticking on the wall in the antechamber next door. Mark gave her a beseeching stare, *Do you know what the hell is going on here?* She returned it in kind, *No, don't you?*

Her father rearranged the position of his swordstick three times, dropped it on the carpet, and finally scooted it back toward himself with the heel of his boot and left it there. She could see the muscle jump in his jaw as he gritted his teeth. Her mother crossed and uncrossed her legs, frowned, stared down the room out the glass doors, and then back at her hands twisting in her lap. They looked like nothing so much as two guilty teenagers caught . . . hm. Like two guilty teenagers caught screwing on the living room couch, actually. Clues seemed to float soundlessly down like feathers, in Kareen's mind, falling all around. *You don't suppose . . .*

"But Cordelia," Mama burst out suddenly, for all the world as though continuing aloud a conversation just now going on telepathically, "we want our children to do *better* than we did. To *not* make the same mistakes!"

Ooh. Ooh. Oooh! Check, and did she ever want the story behind this one . . . ! Her father had underestimated the Countess, Kareen realized. That hadn't taken any more than *three* minutes.

"Well, Drou," said Tante Cordelia reasonably, "it seems to me that you have your wish. Kareen has most certainly done better. Her choices and actions have been considered and rational in every way. And as far as I can tell, she hasn't made any mistakes at all."

Her father shook a finger at Mark, and sputtered, "That . . . *that* is a mistake."

Mark hunched, and wrapped his arms protectively around his belly. The Countess frowned faintly; the Commodore's jaw tightened.

The Countess said coolly, "We'll discuss Mark presently. Right now, allow me to draw your attention to how intelligent and informed your daughter is. Granted, she had not your disadvantage of trying to construct her life in the emotional isolation and chaos of a civil war. You both bought her a better, brighter chance than that, and I doubt you're sorry for it."

The Commodore shrugged grudging agreement. Mama sighed in something like negative nostalgia, not longing for the remembered past but relief at having escaped it.

"Just to pick one example not at random," the Countess went on, "Kareen, didn't you obtain your contraceptive implant before you began physical experimentation?"

Tante Cordelia was so bloody Betan . . . she just belted out things like that in casual conversation. Kareen and her chin rose to the challenge. "Of course," she said steadily. "And I had my hymen cut and did the programmed learning course the clinic gave on related anatomy and physiology issues, and Gran-tante Naismith bought me my first pair of earrings, and we went out for dessert."

Da rubbed his reddening face. Mama looked . . . envious.

"And I daresay," Tante Cordelia went on, "you wouldn't describe your first steps into claiming your adult sexuality as a mad secret scramble in the dark, full of confusion, fear and pain, either?"

Mama's negative-nostalgia look deepened. So did Mark's.

"Of course not!" Kareen drew the line at discussing *those* details with Mama and Da, although she was dying for a comfortable gossip with Tante Cordelia about it all. She'd been too shy to start with an actual *man*, so she'd hired a hermaphrodite Licensed Practical Sexuality Therapist whom Mark's counselor had recommended. The L.P.S.T. had explained to her kindly that hermaphrodites were extremely popular with young persons taking the introductory practical course for just that reason. It had all worked out *really really* well. Mark, anxiously hovering by his comconsole for her post-coital report, had been so pleased for her. Of course, his introduction to his own sexuality had included such ghastly trauma and tortures, it was only natural he be worried sick. She smiled reassuringly at him now. "If that's Barrayar, I'll take Beta!"

Tante Cordelia said thoughtfully, "It's not entirely that simple. Both societies seek to solve the same fundamental problem—to assure that all children arriving will be cared for. Betans make the choice to do it directly, technologically, by mandating a biochemical padlock on everyone's gonads. Sexual behavior seems open at the price of absolute social control on its reproductive consequences. Has it never crossed your mind to wonder how that is enforced? It should. Now, Beta *can* control one's ovaries; Barrayar, especially during the Time of Isolation, was forced to try to control the entire woman attached to them. Throw in Barrayar's need to increase its population to survive, at least as pressing as Beta's to limit its to the same end, and your *peculiar* gender-biased inheritance laws, and, well, here we all are."

"Scrambling in the dark," growled Kareen. "No *thank* you."

"We should never have sent her there. With *him*," Da grumbled.

Tante Cordelia observed, "Kareen was committed to her student year on Beta before she ever met Mark. Who knows? If Mark hadn't been there to, ah, insulate her, she might have met a nice Betan and stayed with him."

"Or it," Kareen murmured. "Or her."

Da's lips tightened.

"These trips can be more one-way than you expect. I haven't seen my own mother face-to-face more than three times in the last thirty years. At least if she sticks with Mark, you may be certain Kareen will return to Barrayar frequently."

Mama appeared very struck by this. She eyed Mark in new speculation. He essayed a hopeful, helpful smile.

Da said, "I want Kareen to be safe. Well. Happy. Financially secure. Is that so wrong?"

Tante Cordelia's lips twisted up with sympathy. "Safe? Well? That's what I wanted for my boys, too. Didn't always get it, but here we are anyway. As for happiness . . . I don't think you can *give* that to anyone, if they don't have it in them. However, it's certainly possible to give *un*-happiness—as you are finding."

Da's frown deepened in a somewhat surly manner, quelling Kareen's impulse to loudly cheer on this line of reasoning. Better let the Baba handle this . . .

The Countess continued, "As for that last . . . hm. Has anyone discussed Mark's financial status with you? Kareen, or Mark . . . or Aral?"

Da shook his head. "I thought he was broke. I assumed the family made him an allowance, like any other Vor scion. And that he ran through it—like any other Vor scion."

"I'm not *broke*," Mark objected strenuously. "It's a temporary cash-flow problem. When I budgeted for this period, I wasn't expecting to be starting up a new business in the middle of it."

"In other words, you're broke," said Da.

"Actually," Tante Cordelia said, "Mark is completely self-supporting. He made his first million on Jackson's Whole."

Da opened his mouth, but then shut it again. He gave his hostess a disbelieving stare. Kareen hoped it would not occur to him to inquire closely into Mark's method for winning this fortune.

"Mark has invested it in an interesting variety of more and less speculative enterprises," Tante Cordelia went on kindly. "The family *backs* him—I've just bought some shares in his butter bug scheme myself—and we'll always be here for emergencies, but Mark doesn't need an allowance."

Mark looked both grateful and awed to be so maternally defended, as if . . . well . . . just so. As if no one had ever done so before.

"If he's so rich, why is he paying my daughter in IOUs?" demanded Da. "Why can't he just draw something out?"

"Before the end of the period?" said Mark, in a voice of real abhorrence. "And lose all that *interest*?"

"And they're not IOUs," said Kareen. "They're shares!"

"Mark doesn't need money," said Tante Cordelia. "He needs what he knows money can't buy. Happiness, for example."

Mark, puzzled but pliable, offered, "So . . . do they want me to pay for Kareen? Like a dowry? How much? I *will*—"

"No, you twit!" cried Kareen in horror. "This isn't Jackson's Whole—you can't buy and sell *people*. Anyway, dowries were what the girl's family gave the fellow, not the other way around."

"That seems very wrong," said Mark, lowering his brows and pinching his chin. "Backwards. Are you sure?"

"Yes."

"I don't care if the boy has a million marks," Da began, sturdily and, Kareen suspected, not quite truthfully.

"Betan dollars," Tante Cordelia corrected absently. "Jacksonians do insist on hard currencies."

"The galactic exchange rates on the Barrayaran Imperial mark have been improving steadily since the War of the Hegen Hub," Mark started to explain. He'd written a paper on the subject last term; Kareen had helped proofread it. He could probably talk for a couple of hours about it. Fortunately, Tante Cordelia's raised finger staunched this threatened flow of nervous erudition.

Da and Mama appeared lost in a brief calculation of their own.

"All right," Da began again, a little less sturdily. "I don't care if the boy has *four* million marks. I care about Kareen."

Tante Cordelia tented her fingers thoughtfully. "So what is it that you want from Mark, Kou? Do you wish him to offer to marry Kareen?"

"Er," said Da, caught out. What he *wanted*, near as Kareen could tell, was for Mark to be carried off by predators, possibly even along with his four million marks in nonliquid investments, but he could hardly say so to Mark's mother.

"Yes, of course I'll offer, if she wants," Mark said. "I just didn't think she wanted to, yet. Did you?"

"No," said Kareen firmly. "Not . . . not yet, anyway. It's like I've just started to find myself, to figure out who I really am, to grow. I don't want to *stop*."

Tante Cordelia's brows rose. "Is that how you see marriage? As the end and abolition of yourself?"

Kareen realized belatedly that her remark might be construed as a slur on certain parties here present. "It is for some people. Why else do all the stories *end* when the Count's daughter gets married? Hasn't that ever struck you as a bit sinister? I mean, have you ever read a folk tale where the Princess's mother gets to do anything but die young? I've never been able to figure out if that's supposed to be a warning, or an instruction."

Tante Cordelia pressed her finger to her lips to hide a smile, but Mama looked rather worried.

"You grow in different ways, afterward," Mama said tentatively. "Not like a fairy tale. Happily ever after doesn't cover it."

Da's brows drew down; he said, in an odd, suddenly uncertain voice, "*I* thought we were doing all right . . ."

Mama patted his hand reassuringly. "Of course, love."

Mark said valiantly, "If Kareen wants me to marry her, I will. If she doesn't, I won't. If she wants me to go away, I'll go—" This last was accompanied by a covertly terrified glance her way.

"No!" cried Kareen.

"If she wants me to walk downtown backwards on my hands, I'll try. Whatever she wants," Mark finished up.

The thoughtful expression on Mama's face suggested that at least she liked his attitude. . . . "Is it that you wish to just be betrothed?" she asked Kareen.

"That's almost the same as marriage, here," said Kareen. "You give these oaths."

"You take those oaths seriously, I gather?" said Tante Cordelia, with a flick of her eyebrow toward the occupants of the mystery couch.

"Of *course*."

"I think it's down to you, Kareen," said Tante Cordelia with a small smile. "What do you want?"

Mark's hands clenched on his knees. Mama sat breathless. Da looked as if he was still worrying about the implications of that happily-ever-after remark.

This was Tante Cordelia. That wasn't a rhetorical question. Kareen sat silent, struggling for truth in confusion. Nothing less or else than truth would do. Yet where were the words for it? What she wanted was simply not a traditional Barrayaran option . . . ah. Yes. She sat up, and looked Tante Cordelia, and then Mama and Da, and then Mark in the eye.

"Not a betrothal. What I want . . . what *I* want—is an *option* on Mark."

Mark sat up, brightening. Now she was speaking a language they both understood.

"*That's* not Betan," said Mama, sounding confused.

"This isn't some weird Jacksonian practice, is it?" Da demanded suspiciously.

"No. It's a new Kareen custom. I just now made it up. But it fits." Her chin lifted.

Tante Cordelia's lips twitched up in amusement. "Hm. Interesting. Well. Speaking as Mark's, ah, agent in the matter, I would point out that a good option is not infinitely open-ended, nor all one-way. They have time limits. Renewal clauses. Compensation."

"Mutual," Mark broke in breathlessly. "Mutual option!"

"That would appear to cover the problem of compensation, yes. What about time limits?"

"I want a year," said Kareen. "To next Midsummer. I want at least a year, to see what we can do. I don't want anything from anybody," she glared at her parents, "but to *back off*!"

Mark nodded eagerly. "Agreed, agreed!"

Da jerked his thumb at Mark. "He'd agree to anything!"

"No," said Tante Cordelia judiciously. "I think you'll find he won't agree to anything that would make Kareen unhappy. Or smaller. Or unsafe."

Da's frown took on a serious edge. "Is that so? And what about her safety *from* him? All that Betan therapy wasn't for no reason!"

"Indeed not," agreed Tante Cordelia. Her nod acknowledged that seriousness. "But I believe it has been effective—Mark?"

"Yes, ma'am!" He sat there trying desperately to look Cured. He couldn't quite bring it off, but the effort was clearly sincere.

The Countess added quietly, "Mark is as much a veteran of our wars as any Barrayaran I know, Kou. He was conscripted earlier, is all. In his own strange and lonely way, he fought as hard, and risked as much. And lost as much. Surely you can grant him as much time to heal as you needed?"

The Commodore looked away, his face grown still.

"Kou, I wouldn't have encouraged this relationship if I thought it was unsafe for either of our children."

He looked back. "You? I know you! You trust beyond reason."

She met his eyes steadily. "Yes. It's how I get results beyond hope. As you may recall."

He pursed his lips, unhappily, and toed his swordstick a little. He had no reply for this one. But a funny little smile turned Mama's mouth, as she watched him.

"Well," said Tante Cordelia cheerfully into the lengthening silence, "I do believe we've achieved a meeting of the minds. Kareen to have an option upon Mark, and vice versa, until next Midsummer, when perhaps we should all meet again and evaluate the results, and consider negotiating an extension."

"What, are we supposed to just stand back while those two just—carry on?" cried Da, in a last fading attempt at indignation.

"Yes. Both to have the same freedom of action that, ah, you two," she nodded at Kareen's parents, "had at the same phase of your lives. I admit, carrying on was made easier for you, Kou, by the fact that all your fiancée's relatives lived in other towns."

"I remember you were terrified of my brothers," Mama recalled, the funny little smile spreading a bit. Mark's eyes widened thoughtfully.

Kareen marveled at this inexplicable bit of history; her Droushnakovi uncles all had hearts of butter, in her experience. Da set his teeth, except that when he looked at Mama his eyes softened.

"Agreed," said Kareen firmly.

"Agreed," echoed Mark at once.

"Agreed," said Tante Cordelia, and raised her brows at the couple on the couch.

Mama said, "Agreed." That quizzical, quirky smile in her eyes, she waited for Da.

He gave her a long, appalled, *You, too?!* stare. "You've gone over to their side!"

"Yes, I believe so. Won't you join us?" Her smile broadened further. "I know we don't have Sergeant Bothari to knock you on the jaw and help kidnap you along against your better judgment this time. But it would've been dreadfully unlucky for us to have tried to go collect the Pretender's head without you." Her grip on his hand tightened.

After a long moment, Da turned from her and frowned fiercely at Mark. "You understand, if you hurt her, I'll hunt you down myself!"

Mark nodded anxiously.

"Your codicil is accepted," murmured Tante Cordelia, her eyes alight.

"Agreed, then!" Da snapped. He sat back grumpily, with a See-what-I-do-for-you-people look on his face. But he didn't let go of Mama's hand.

Mark was staring at Kareen with a smothered elation. She could almost picture the entire Black Gang, jumping up and down in the back of his head, cheering, and Lord Mark hushing them lest they draw attention to themselves.

Kareen took a breath, for courage, dipped her hand into her bolero pocket, and drew out her Betan earrings, the pair that declaimed her implant and her adult status. With a little push, she slipped one into each earlobe. It was not, she thought, a declaration of independence, for she still lived in a web of dependencies. It was more of a declaration of Kareen. *I am who I am. Now, let's see how much I can do.*

CHAPTER SEVENTEEN

Armsman Pym, a little out of breath, admitted Ekaterin to the front hall of Vorkosigan House. He tugged his tunic's high collar into adjustment, and smiled his usual welcome.

"Good afternoon, Pym," Ekaterin said. She was satisfied that she was able to keep any tremor out of her voice. "I need to see Lord Vorkosigan."

"Yes, ma'am."

That *Yes, milady!* in this hall the night of the dinner party had been a revealing slip of his tongue, Ekaterin realized belatedly. She hadn't noticed it at the time.

Pym keyed his wrist com. "M'lord? Where are you?"

A faint thump sounded from the com link, and Miles's muted voice: "North wing attic. Why?"

"Madame Vorsoisson is here to see you."

"I'll be right down—no, wait." A brief pause. "Bring her up. She'll like to see this, I bet."

"Yes, m'lord." Pym gestured toward the back entry. "This way." As she followed him to the lift tube, he added, "Little Nikki not with you today, ma'am?"

"No." Her heart failed her at the prospect of explaining why. She left it at that.

They exited the tube at the fifth level, a floor she

hadn't penetrated on that first, memorable tour. She followed him down an uncarpeted hallway and through a pair of double doors into an enormous low-ceilinged room that extended from one side of the wing to the other. Roof beams hand-sawn from great trees crossed it overhead, with yellowing plaster between. Utilitarian lighting fixtures hung from them along a pair of center aisles created by the high-piled stowage.

Part of it was normal attic detritus: shabby furniture and lamps rejected even from the servants' quarters, picture frames that had lost their contents, spotted mirrors, wrapped squares and rectangles that might be some of the paintings, rolled tapestries. Still older oil lamps and candelabras. Mysterious crates and cartons and cracking leather-bound cases and scarred wooden trunks with long-dead people's initials burned in below their latches.

From there it grew more remarkable. A bundle of rusty cavalry javelins with wrinkled, faded brown-and-silver pennons wrapped about them wedged up against a hand-sawn post. Racks of faded Armsmen's uniforms bunched tightly together, brown and silver. Quantities of horse gear: saddles and bridles and harnesses with rusty bells, with unraveling tassels, with tarnished silver facings, with clacking beads all battered with their bright paint flaking off; hand-embroidered hangings and saddle blankets, with the Vorkosigans' VK and variations of their crest elaborated in thread. Dozens of swords and daggers, thrust randomly into barrels like steel bouquets.

Miles, in shirtsleeves, sat in the debris in the middle of one aisle about two-thirds of the way down the long room, surrounded by three open trunks and several half-sorted piles of papers and flimsies. One of the trunks, apparently just unlocked, was full to the brim with a miscellaneous cache of obsolete energy weapons, their power cartridges, Ekaterin trusted, long gone. A second, smaller case seemed to be the source of some of the papers. He glanced up and gave her an exhilarated grin.

"I told you the attics were something to see. Thank you, Pym."

Pym nodded and withdrew, giving his lord what Ekaterin's eye was now able to decode as a little good-luck salute.

"You weren't exaggerating," Ekaterin agreed. What kind of stuffed bird *was* that, hung upside down in the corner, glaring down at them through malignant glass eyes?

"The one time I had Duv Galeni up here, he nearly had a gibbering fit. He reverted right in front of my eyes back into Doctor Professor Galeni, and raved at me for hours—days—about the fact that we haven't cataloged all this junk. He's still on about it, if I make the mistake of reminding him. I should have thought that my father installing that climate-controlled document room would have been enough." He waved her to a seat on a long polished walnut chest.

She sat, and smiled mutely at him. She should tell him her bad news, and leave. But he was so clearly in an expansive mood, she hated to derail him. When had his voice become a caress upon her ears? Let him babble on just a little longer . . .

"Anyway, what I ran across that I thought might interest you—" His hand started for a lump covered with a heavy white cloth, then wavered over the trunk of weapons. "Actually, *this* is pretty interesting, too, though it might be more in Nikki's line. Does he appreciate the grotesque? I'd have thought it a fabulous find when I was his age. I don't know how I missed it—oh, of course, Gran'da would have held the keys." He held up a coarse brown cloth bag, and poked a little dubiously into its contents. "I *believe* this is a sack of Cetagandan scalps. Want to see?"

"See, maybe. Touch, no."

Obligingly, he held it open for her inspection. The dried yellowing parchmentlike scraps with bits of hair clinging, or in some cases, falling off, indeed looked like human scalps to her. "Eeuw," she said appreciatively. "Did your grandfather take them himself?"

"Mm, possibly, though it seems rather a lot for one man, even General Piotr. I think it's more likely they were collected and brought to him as trophies by his guerillas. All fine, but then what could he do with 'em? Can't throw 'em away, they're *presents*."

"What are you going to do with them?"

He shrugged, and laid the bag back in the trunk. "If Gregor needed to send a subtle diplomatic insult to the Cetagandan Empire, which he doesn't just now, I suppose we could return them with elaborate apologies. Can't think of any other use offhand."

He shut the trunk, sorted through a variety of mechanical keys in the little pile at his knee, and locked it again. He rose to his knees, upended a crate in front of her, hoisted the shrouded object onto it, and pulled back the covering for her inspection.

It was a beautiful old saddle, similar to the old-fashioned cavalry style but more lightly built, for a lady. Its dark leather was elaborately carved and stamped in leaf, fern and flower patterns. The green velvet of its padded and stitched seat was worn half-bald, dried and split, the stuffing peeking out. Maple and olive leaves, carved and delicately tinted in the leather, surrounded a V flanked by a smaller B and K all closed in an oval. More embroidery, its colors surprisingly bright, echoed the botanical pattern in a blanket pad.

"There *ought* to be a matching bridle, but I haven't found it yet," Miles said, his fingers tracing over the initials. "It's one of my paternal grandmother's saddles. General Piotr's wife, Princess-and-Countess Olivia Vorbarra Vorkosigan. She obviously used this one quite a bit. My mother could never be persuaded to take up riding—I never was able to figure out why not—and it wasn't one of my father's passions. So it was left to Gran'da to try to teach me to keep the tradition alive. But I didn't have time to keep it up once I was an adult. Didn't you say you ride?"

"Not since I was a child. My great-aunt kept a pony for me—though I suspect it was as much for the manure for her garden. My parents had no room in town. He was a fat, ill-tempered beast, but I adored him." Ekaterin smiled in memory. "Saddles were a bit optional."

"I was thinking, maybe we could get this repaired and reconditioned, and put it back into use."

"Use? Surely that belongs in a museum! Hand-made—absolutely unique—historically significant—I can't even imagine what it would fetch at auction!"

"Ah—I had this same argument with Duv. It wasn't just hand-made, it was custom-made, especially for the Princess. Probably a gift from my grandfather. Imagine the fellow, not just a worker but an artist, selecting the leather, piecing and stitching and carving. I picture him hand-rubbing in the oil, thinking of *his* work used by his Countess, envied and admired by her friends, being part of this—this whole work of art that was her life." His finger traced the leaves around the initials.

Her guess of its value kept ratcheting up in time to his words. "For heaven's sake get it appraised first!"

"Why? To loan to a museum? Don't need to set a price on my grandmother for that. To sell to some collector to hoard like money? Let him hoard money, that's all that sort wants anyway. The only collector who'd be worthy of it would be someone who was personally obsessed with the Princess-and-Countess, one of those men who fall hopelessly in love across time. No. I owe it to its maker to put it to its *proper* use, the use he intended."

The weary straitened housewife in her—Tien's pinchmark spouse—was horrified. The secret soul of her rang like a bell in resonance to Miles's words. Yes. That was how it should be. This saddle belonged under a fine lady, not under a glass cover. Gardens were meant to be seen, smelled, walked through, grubbed in. A hundred objective measurements didn't sum the worth of a garden; only the delight of its users did that. Only the use made it *mean* something. How had Miles learned that? *For this alone I could love you . . .*

"Now." He grinned in response to her smile, and drew breath. "God knows I need to start doing something for exercise, or all this culinary diplomacy I do nowadays will defeat Mark's attempt to differentiate himself from me. There are several parks here in town with hacking paths. But it's not much fun to ride by myself. Think you'd be willing to keep me company?" He blinked a trifle ingenuously.

"I would love to," she said honestly, "but I can't." She could see in his eyes a dozen counterarguments springing up, ready to charge into the breach. She held up a hand to stop him bursting into speech. She must bring this little self-indulgent ration of pretend-happiness to a close, before her will broke. Her forced agreement with Vassily only permitted her a taste of Miles, not a meal. Not a banquet . . . Back to harsh reality. "Something new has come up. Yesterday, Vassily Vorsoisson and my brother Hugo came to see me. Set on, apparently, by a nasty letter from Alexi Vormoncrief."

Tersely, she detailed their visit. Miles sat back on his heels, his face setting, listening closely. For once, he didn't interrupt.

"You set them straight?" he said slowly, when she paused for breath.

"I *tried*. It was infuriating to watch them just . . . dismiss my word, in favor of all those sordid insinuations from that fool Alexi, of all men. Hugo was genuinely worried about me, I suppose, but Vassily is all wound up in this misconstrued family duty and some inflated ideas about the depraved decadence of the capital."

"Ah," said Miles thinly. "A romantic, I see."

"Miles, they were ready to take Nikki away right then! And I have no legal way to fight for custody. Even if I took Vassily to the Vorbretten District magistrate's court, I couldn't prove him grossly unfit—he's not. He's just grossly gullible. But I thought—too late, last night—about Nikki's security classification. Would ImpSec do something to stop Vassily?"

Miles frowned, his brows drawing down. "Possibly . . . not. It's not as if he wanted to take Nikki off-world. ImpSec could have no objection to Nikki going to live on a military base—in fact, they'd probably consider it a better safe-zone than your uncle's or Vorkosigan House either one. More anonymous. I can't think they'd be too keen about a lawsuit drawing more public attention to the Komarran affair, either."

"Would they quash it? In whose favor?"

He hissed thoughtfully through his teeth. "Yours, if

I asked them to, but it would be just like them to do so in a way that provides maximum support to the cover story—which is how they've classified this murder-slander in their little one-track minds this week. I hardly dare touch it; I'd only make things worse. I wonder if somebody . . . I wonder if somebody anticipated that?"

"I know Alexi's pulling Vassily's strings. Do you think someone's pulling Alexi's strings, trying to bait you into making some ruinous public move?" That would make *her* the last link in a chain by which his hidden enemy sought to yank Miles into an untenable position. A chilling realization. But only if she—and Miles—did what that enemy anticipated.

"I . . . hm. Possibly." His frown deepened. "Better by far that your uncle straighten things out, anyway, privately, inside the family. Is he still due back from Komarr before the wedding?"

"Yes, but that's only if his so-called *few little technical matters* don't get more complicated than he anticipates."

Miles grimaced in sympathetic understanding. "No guarantees then, right." He paused. "Vorbretten's District, eh? If push came to shove, I could quietly call in a favor from René Vorbretten, and have him, ah, arrange things. You could jump over the magistrate's court and take it to him on direct appeal. I wouldn't have to involve ImpSec or appear in the matter at all. That wouldn't work if Sigur holds Countship of the Vorbretten's District by then, though."

"I don't want push to come to shove. I don't want Nikki troubled more at all. It's been ghastly enough for him." She sat tight and trembling, whether with fear or anger or a venomous combination she could hardly say.

Miles scrambled up off his heels, and came round and sat rather tentatively next to her on the walnut chest, and gave her a searching look. "One way or another, we can make it come round right in the end. In two days, both these District inheritance votes come due in the Council of Counts. Once the vote's over, the political motivation to stir up trouble with this accusation against me evaporates, and the whole thing will start to fade." That would have sounded very comfortable, if he hadn't added, "I hope."

"I shouldn't have suggested putting you in quarantine till my mourning year was over. I should have tried Vassily on Winterfair first. I thought of that too late. But I can't risk Nikki, I just can't. Not when we've come so far, survived so much."

"Sh, now. I think your instincts are right. My grandfather had an old cavalry saying: 'You should get over heavy ground as lightly as you can.' We'll just lie low for a little while here so as not to rile poor Vassily. And when your uncle gets back, he'll straighten the fellow out." He glanced up at her, sideways. "Or, of course, you could simply not see me for a year, eh?"

"I should dislike that exceedingly," she admitted.

"Ah." One corner of his mouth curled up. After a little pause, he said, "Well, we can't have that, then."

"But Miles, I gave my word. I didn't want to, but I did."

"Stampeded into it. A tactical retreat is not a bad response to a surprise assault, you know. First you survive. Then you choose your own ground. *Then* you counterattack."

Somehow, not her doing, his thigh lay by hers, not quite touching but warm and solid even through two layers of cloth, gray and black. She couldn't exactly lay her head on his shoulder for comfort, but she might sneak her arm around his waist, and lean her cheek on the top of his head. It would be a pleasant sensation, easing to the heart. *I shouldn't do that.*

Yes, I should. Now and always . . . No.

Miles sighed. "Bitten by my reputation. Here I thought the only opinions that mattered were yours, Nikki's, and Gregor's. I forgot Vassily's."

"So did I."

"My da gave me this definition: he told me reputation was what other people knew about you, but honor was what you knew about yourself."

"Was that what Gregor meant, when he told you to talk to him? Your da sounds wise. I'd like to meet him."

"He wants to meet you, too. Of course, he immediately followed this up by asking me how I stood with myself. He has this . . . this *eye*."

"I think . . . I know what he means." She might curl her fingers around his hand, lying loosely on his thigh so close to hers. Surely it would lie warm and reassuring in her palm . . . *You've betrayed yourself before, in starvation for touch. Don't.* "The day Tien died, I went from being the kind of person who made, and kept, a life-oath, to one who broke it in two and walked away. My oath had mattered the world to me, or at least . . . I'd traded the world for it. I still don't know if I was forsworn for nothing or not. I don't suppose Tien would have gone charging out in that stupid way that night if I hadn't shocked him by telling him I was leaving." She fell silent for a little. The room was very still. The thick old stone walls kept out the city noises. "I am not who I was. I can't go back. I don't quite like who I have become. Yet I still . . . stand: But I hardly know how to go on from here. No one ever gave me a map for this road."

"Ah," said Miles. "Ah. That one." His voice was not in the least puzzled; he spoke in a tone of firm recognition.

"Towards the end, my oath was the only piece of me left that hadn't been ground down. When I tried to talk about this to Aunt Vorthys, she tried to reassure me that it was all right because everyone else thought Tien was an ass. *You* see . . . it has nothing to do with Tien, saint or monster. It was me, and my word."

He shrugged. "What's hard to see about that? It's blazingly obvious to *me*."

She turned her head, and looked down at his face, which looked up at her in patient curiosity. Yes, he perfectly understood—yet did not seek to comfort her by dismissing her distress, or trying to convince her it didn't matter. The sensation was like opening the door to what she'd thought was a closet, and stepping through into another country, rolling out before her widening eyes. *Oh.*

"In my experience," he said, "the trouble with oaths

of the form, *death before dishonor*, is that eventually, given enough time and abrasion, they separate the world into just two sorts of people: the dead, and the forsworn. It's a survivor's problem, this one."

"Yes," she agreed quietly. *He knows. He knows it all, right down to that bitter muck of regret at the bottom of the soul's well. How does he know?*

"Death before dishonor. Well, at least no one can complain I got them out of order ... You know ... " He started to look away, but then looked back, to hold her eye directly. His face was a little pale. "I wasn't exactly medically discharged from ImpSec. Illyan fired me. For falsifying a report about my seizures."

"Oh," she said. "I didn't know that."

"I know you didn't. I don't exactly go round advertising the fact, for pretty obvious reasons. I was trying so hard to hang on to my career—Admiral Naismith was everything to me, life and honor and most of my identity by then—I broke it instead. Not that I didn't set myself up for it. Admiral Naismith began as a lie, one I redeemed by making him come true later. And it worked really well, for a while; the little Admiral brought me everything I ever thought I wanted. After a while I began to think all sins could be redeemed like that. Lie now, fix it later. Same as I tried to do with you. Even love is not as strong as habit, eh?"

Now she did dare to tighten her arm around him. No reason for them both to starve. ... For a moment, he went as breathless as a man laying food before a wild animal, trying to coax it to his hand. Abashed, she drew back.

She inhaled, and ventured, "Habits. Yes. I feel as if I'm half-crippled with old reflexes." *Old scars of mind.* "Tien ... seems never more than a thought away from me. Will his death ever fade, do you suppose?"

Now he didn't look at her. Didn't dare? "I can't answer for you. My own ghosts just seem to ride along, mostly unconsulted, always there. Their density gradually thins, or I grow used to them." He stared around the attic, blew out his breath, and added elliptically, "Did I ever tell you how I came to kill my grandfather? The great general who survived it all, Cetagandans, Mad Yuri, everything this century could throw at him?"

She declined to be baited into whatever shocked response he thought this dramatic statement deserved, but merely raised her brows.

"I disappointed him to death, eh, the day I blew my Academy entrance exams, and lost my first chance at a military career. He died that night."

"Of course," she said dryly, "you were the cause. It couldn't possibly have had anything to do with his being nearly a hundred years old."

"Yeah, sure, I know." Miles shrugged, and gave her a sharp look up from under his dark brows. "The same way you know Tien's death was an accident."

"Miles," she said, after a long, thoughtful pause, "are you trying to one-up my dead?"

Taken aback, his lips began to form an indignant denial, which weakened to an, "Oh." He gently thumped his forehead on her shoulder as if beating his head against a wall. When he spoke again, his ragging tone did not quite muffle real anguish. "How *can* you stand me? I can't even stand me!"

I think that was the true confession. We are surely come to the end of one another. "Sh. Sh."

Now he did take her hand, his fingers tightening around it as warmly as any embrace. She did not jerk back in startlement, though an odd shiver ran through her. *Isn't starving yourself a betrayal too, self against self?*

"To use Kareen's Betan psychology terminology," she said a little breathlessly, "I have this Thing about oaths. When you became an Imperial Auditor, you took oath again. Even though you were forsworn once. How could you bear to?"

"Oh," he said, looking around a little vaguely. "What, when they issued you your honor, didn't they give you the model with the reset button? Mine's right here." He pointed to the general vicinity of his navel.

She couldn't help it; her black laughter pealed out, echoing off the beams. Something inside her, wrapped tight to the breaking-point, loosened at that laugh. When he made her laugh like that, it was like light and air let in upon wounds too dark and painful to touch, and so a chance at healing. "Is that what that's for? I never knew."

He smiled, recapturing her hand. "A very wise woman once told me—you just go on. I've never encountered any good advice that didn't boil down to that, in the end. Not even my father's."

I want to be with you always, so you can make me laugh myself well. He stared down at her palm in his as though he wanted to kiss it. He was close enough that she could feel their every breath, matching rhythms. The silence lengthened. She had come to give him up, not get into a necking session . . . if this went on, she'd end up kissing him. The scent of him filled her nose, her mouth, seemed rushed by her blood to every cell of her body. Intimacy of the flesh seemed easy, after the far more terrifying intimacy of the mind.

Finally, with enormous effort, she sat up straight. With perhaps equal effort, he released her hand. Her heart was thumping as though she'd been running. Trying for an ordinary voice, she said, "Then your considered opinion is, we should wait for my uncle to take on Vassily. Do you really think this nonsense is meant as a trap?"

"It has that smell. I can't quite tell yet how many levels down the stench is coming from. It *might* only be Alexi trying to cut me out."

"But then one considers who Alexi's friends are. I see." She attempted a brisk tone. "So, are you going to nail Richars and the Vormoncrief party, in the Council day after tomorrow?"

"Ah," he said. "There's something I need to tell you about that." He looked away, tapped his lips, looked back. He was still smiling, but his eyes had gone serious, almost bleak. "I believe I've made a strategic error. You, ah, know Richars Vorrutyer seized on this slander as a lever to try and force a vote from me?"

She said hesitantly, "I'd gathered something of a sort was going on, behind the scenes. I didn't realize it was quite so overt."

"Crude. Actually." He grimaced. "Since blackmail

wasn't a behavior I wished to reward, my answer was to put all my clout, such as it is, behind Dono."

"Good!"

He smiled briefly, but shook his head. "Richars and I now stand at an impasse. If he wins the Countship, my open opposition almost forces him to go on to make his threat good. At that point, he'll have the right and the power. He won't move immediately—I expect it will take him some weeks to collect allies and marshal resources. And if he has any tactical wits, he'll wait till after Gregor's wedding. But you see what comes next."

Her stomach tightened. She could see all too well, but . . . "*Can* he get rid of you by charging you with Tien's murder? I thought any such charge would be quashed."

"Well, if wiser heads can't talk Richars out of it . . . the practicalities become peculiar. In fact, the more I think about it, the messier it looks." He spread his fingers on his gray-trousered knee, and counted down the list. "Assassination is out." By his grimace, that was meant as a joke. Almost. "Gregor wouldn't authorize it for anything less than overt treason, and Richars is embarrassingly loyal to the Imperium. For all I know, he really *does* believe I murdered Tien, which makes him an honest man, of sorts. Taking Richars quietly aside and telling him the truth about Komarr is right out. I'd expect a lot of maneuvering around the lack of evidence, and a verdict of Not Proven. Well, ImpSec might manufacture some evidence, but I'm getting pretty queasy wondering what kind. Neither my reputation nor yours will be their top priority. And you're bound to be sucked into it at some point, and I . . . won't be in control of all that happens."

She found her teeth were pressed together. She ran her tongue over her lips, to loosen the taut muscles of her jaw. "Endurance used to be my specialty. In the old days."

"I was hoping to bring you some new days."

She scarcely knew what to say to this, so merely shrugged.

"There is another choice. Another way I can divert this . . . sewer."

"Oh?"

"I can fold. Stop campaigning. Cast the Vorkosigan's District vote as an abstention . . . no, that likely wouldn't be enough to repair the damages. Cast it for Richars, then. Publicly back down."

She drew in her breath. *No!* "Has Gregor asked you to do this? Or ImpSec?"

"No. Not yet, anyway. But I was wondering if . . . you would wish it so."

She looked away from him, for three long breaths. When she looked back, she said levelly, "I think we'd both have to use that reset button of yours, after that."

He took this in with almost no change of expression, but for a weird little quirk at the corner of his mouth. "Dono doesn't have enough votes."

"As long as he has yours . . . I should be satisfied."

"As long as you understand what's likely coming down."

"I understand."

He vented a long, covert exhalation.

Was there nothing she could do to help his cause? Well, Miles's hidden enemies wouldn't be jerking so many strings if they didn't want to produce some ill-considered motions. Stillness, then, and silence—not of the prey that cowered, but of the hunter who waited. She regarded Miles searchingly. His face was its usual cheerful mask, but nerve-stretched underneath . . . "Just out of curiosity, when was the last time you used your seizure stimulator?"

He didn't quite meet her eye. "It's . . . been a while. I've been too busy. You know it knocks me on my ass for a day."

"As opposed to falling on your ass in the Council chamber on the day of reckoning? No. I believe you have a couple of votes to cast. You use it tonight. Promise me!"

"Yes, ma'am," he said humbly. From the odd little gleam in his eye, he was not so crushed as his briefly hang-dog look suggested. "I promise."

Promises. "I have to go."

He rose without argument. "I'll walk you out." They strolled arm in arm, picking their way down the aisle through the hazards of discarded history. "How did you get here?"

"Autocab."

"Can I have Pym give you a lift home?"

"Sure."

In the end, he rode with her, in the back of the vast old armored groundcar. They talked only of little things, as if they had all the time in the world. The drive was short. They did not touch each other, when he let her off. The car pulled away. The silvered canopy hid . . . everything.

Ivan's smile muscles were giving out. Vorhartung Castle was brilliantly appointed tonight for the Council of Counts' reception for the newly arrived Komarran delegation to Gregor's wedding, which the Komarrans persisted in calling Laisa's wedding. Lights and flowers decorated the main entry hall, the grand staircase to the Council Chamber gallery, and the great salon where dinner had been held. The party did dual duty, also celebrating the augmented solar mirror array voted by, or rammed through, depending on one's political view, the Council last week. It was an Imperial bride-gift of truly planetary scope.

The feast had been followed by speeches and a holovid presentation displaying plans not only for the mirror array, vital to Komarr's ongoing terraforming, but unveiling designs for a new jump-point station to be built by a joint Barrayaran-Komarran consortium including Toscane Industries and Vorsmythe Ltd. His mother had assigned Ivan a Komarran heiress to squire about this intimate little soiree of five hundred persons; alas that she was sixty-plus years old, married, and the empress-to-be's aunt.

Unintimidated by her high Vor surroundings, this cheerful gray-haired lady was serene in her possession of a large chunk of Toscane Industries, a couple of thousand Komarran planetary voting shares, and an

unmarried granddaughter upon whom she plainly doted.
Ivan, admiring the vid pix, agreed that the girl was
charming, beautiful, and clearly vastly intelligent. But
since she was also only seven years old, she'd been left
at home. After dutifully conducting Aunt Anna and her
immediate hangers-on about the castle and pointing out
its most salient architectural and historical features, Ivan
managed to wedge the whole party back into the crowd
of Komarrans around Gregor and Laisa, and plotted his
escape. As Aunt Anna, in a voice raised to pierce the
hubbub, informed Ivan's mother that he was a *very cute
boy*, he faded backwards through the mob, angling
toward the servitors stationed by the side walls handing out after-dinner drinks.

He almost bounced off a young couple making their
way down the side aisle, who were looking at each other
instead of where they were going. Lord William
Vortashpula, Count Vortashpula's heir, had lately
announced his engagement to Lady Cassia Vorgorov.
Cassie was in wonderful looks: eyes bright, face becom-
ingly flushed, low-cut gown—dammit, *had* she done
something to augment her bustline, or had she simply
matured a bit over the past couple of years? Ivan was
still trying to decide when she caught his gaze; she
tossed her head, making the flowers wound in her
smooth brown hair bounce, smirked, gripped her
fiancé's arm more tightly, and stalked past him. Lord
Vortashpula twittered a brief distracted greeting to Ivan
before he was towed off.

"Pretty girl," said a gruff voice at Ivan's elbow, making
him flinch. Ivan turned to find his cousin-several-times-
removed Count Falco Vorpatril watching him from
under fiercely bushy gray eyebrows. "Too bad you
missed your chance with her, Ivan. Dumped you for a
better berth, did she?"

"I was not *dumped* by Cassie Vorgorov," said Ivan a
little hotly. "I was never even courting her."

Falco's deep chuckle was unpleasantly disbelieving.
"Your mother told me Cassie had quite a crush on you,
at one time. She seems to have recovered nicely. Cassie,
not your mother, poor woman. Although Lady Alys

seems to have got over all her disappointments in your ill-fated love matches, too." He glanced across the room toward the group around the Emperor, where Illyan attended upon Lady Alys with his usual quiet panache.

"None of my love matches were ill-fated, sir," said Ivan stiffly. "They were all brought to mutually agreeable conclusions. I *choose* to play the field."

Falco merely smiled. Ivan, disdaining to be baited further, made a polite bow to the aged but upright Count Vorhalas, who had come up to his old colleague Falco. Falco was either a progressive Conservative, or a conservative Progressive, a notorious fence-sitter courted by both sides. Vorhalas had been key man in the Conservative opposition to the Vorkosigan-led Centrist machine for as long as Ivan could remember. He was not a Party leader, but his reputation for iron integrity made him the man to whom all others looked to set the standard.

Ivan's cousin Miles came strolling down the aisle just then, smiling slightly, his hands in the pockets of his brown-and-silver Vorkosigan House uniform. Ivan tensed to duck out of the line of fire, should Miles be looking for volunteers for whatever ungodly scheme he might be pursuing at the moment, but Miles merely gave him a half-salute. He murmured greetings to the two Counts, and gave Vorhalas a respectful nod, which, after a moment, the old man returned.

"Where away, Vorkosigan?" Falco inquired easily. "Are you going to that reception at Vorsmythe House after this?"

"No, the rest of the team will be covering that one. I'll be joining Gregor's party." He hesitated, then smiled invitingly. "Unless, perhaps, you two gentlemen would be willing to reconsider Lord Dono's suit, and would like to go somewhere and discuss it?"

Vorhalas just shook his head, but Falco grunted a laugh. "Give over, Miles, do. That one's hopeless. God knows you've been giving it your all—at least, I know *I've* tripped over you everywhere I've been for the past week—but I'm afraid the Progressives are going to have to be satisfied with this soletta gift victory."

Miles glanced around at the dwindling crowd, and

gave a judicious shrug. He'd done a good bit of tearing around on Gregor's behalf to bring this vote off, Ivan knew, in addition to his intense campaigning for Dono and René. Little wonder he looked drained. "We have all done a good turn for our future, here. I think this mirror augmentation will be bearing fruit for the Imperium long before the terraforming is complete."

"Mm," said Vorhalas neutrally. His had been an abstaining vote on the mirror matter, but Gregor's majority had made it of no moment.

"I wish Ekaterin might have been here tonight to see this," Miles added wistfully.

"Yeah, why didn't you bring her?" asked Ivan. He didn't understand Miles's strategy on this one; he thought the beleaguered couple would be far better served openly defying public opinion, and so forcing it to bend around them, than cravenly bowing to it. Bravado would be much more Miles's style, too.

"We'll see. After tomorrow." He added under his breath, "I wish the damn vote was over."

Ivan grinned, and lowered his tone in response. "What, and you so Betan? Half-Betan. I thought you approved of democracy, Miles. Don't you like it after all?"

Miles smiled thinly, and declined to be baited. He bade his seniors a cordial good-night, and walked off a bit stiffly.

"Aral's boy doesn't look well," Vorhalas observed, staring after him.

"Well, he did have that medical discharge from the Service," Falco allowed. "It was a wonder he was able to serve as long as he did. I suppose his old troubles caught up with him."

This was true, Ivan reflected, but not in the sense Falco meant. Vorhalas looked a bit grim, possibly thinking about Miles's prenatal soltoxin damage, and the painful Vorhalas family history that went with it. Ivan, taking pity on the old man, put in, "No, sir. He was injured on duty." In fact, that gray skin tone and hampered motion strongly suggested Miles had undergone one of his seizures lately.

Count Vorhalas frowned thoughtfully at him. "So, Ivan. You know him about as well as anyone. What do you make of this ugly tale going around about him and that Vorsoisson woman's late husband?"

"I think it is a complete fabrication, sir."

"Alys says the same," Falco noted. "I'd say she's in a position to know the truth if anyone is."

"That, I grant you." Vorhalas glanced at the Emperor's entourage, across the glittering and crowded salon. "I also think she is entirely loyal to the Vorkosigans, and would lie without hesitation to protect their interests."

"You are half right, sir," said Ivan testily. "She is entirely loyal."

Vorhalas made a placating gesture. "Don't bite me, boy. I suppose we'll never really know. One learns to live with such uncertainties, as one grows older."

Ivan choked back an irritable reply. Count Vorhalas's was the sixth such more or less oblique inquiry into his cousin's affairs Ivan had endured tonight. If Miles was putting up with *half* this, it was no wonder he looked exhausted. Although, Ivan reflected morosely, it was probable that very few men dared asked him such questions to his face—which meant that Ivan was drawing *all* the fire meant for Miles. Typical, just typical.

Falco said to Vorhalas, "If you're not going on to Vorsmythe's, why don't you come back with me to Vorpatril House? Where we can at least drink sitting down. I've been meaning to have a quiet talk with you about that watershed project."

"Thank you, Falco. That sounds considerably more restful. Nothing like the prospect of vast sums of money changing hands to generate rather wearing excitement among our colleagues."

From which Ivan concluded that the industries in Vorhalas's District had largely missed the boat on this new Komarran economic opportunity. The glazed numbness creeping over him had nothing to do with too much to drink; in fact, it suggested he'd had far too little. He was about to continue his trip to the bar when an even better diversion crossed his vision.

Olivia Koudelka. She was wearing a white-and-beige lace confection that somehow emphasized her blond shyness. And she was *alone*. At least temporarily.

"Ah. Excuse me, gentlemen. I see a friend in need." Ivan escaped the grayhairs, and bore down on his quarry, a smile lighting his face and his brain going into overdrive. Gentle Olivia had always been eclipsed on Ivan's scanner by her older and bolder sisters Delia and Martya. But Delia had chosen Duv Galeni, and Martya had bounced Ivan's suit in no uncertain terms. Maybe . . . maybe he'd stopped working his way down the Koudelka family tree a tad too soon.

"Good evening, Olivia. What a pretty frock." Yes, women spent so much time on their clothes, it was always a good opening move to notice the effort. "Enjoying yourself?"

"Oh, hi, Ivan. Yes, certainly."

"I didn't see you earlier. Mama put me to work buttering up Komarrans."

"We were rather late arriving. This is our fourth stop this evening."

We? "The rest of your family here? I saw Delia with Duv, of course. They're caught over there in that cluster around Gregor."

"Are they? Oh, good. We'll have to say hi before we go."

"What are you doing after this?"

"Going on to that squeeze at Vorsmythe House. It's potentially extremely valuable."

While Ivan was trying to decode this last cryptic remark, Olivia looked up, her gaze caught by someone. Her lips parted and her eyes lit, reminding Ivan for a dizzy moment of Cassie Vorgorov. Alarmed, he followed the line of her glance. But there was no one in it except Lord Dono Vorrutyer, apparently just parting company with his/her old friend Countess Vormuir. The Countess, svelte in a red dress that strikingly complemented Dono's sober black, patted Dono on the arm, laughed, and strolled away. Countess Vormuir was still estranged from her husband, as far as Ivan knew; he wondered what kind of time

Dono might be making with her. The concept made his brain cramp.

"Vorsmythe House, eh?" said Ivan. "Maybe I'll go along. I can about guarantee they'll be trotting out the *good* wine, for this. How are you getting there?"

"Groundcar. Would you like a lift?"

Perfect. "Why, yes, thank you. I would." He'd ridden here with his mother and Illyan, from his point of view to avoid risking his speedster's enamel in the parking cram, from hers so that she could be sure he'd show up for duty as ordered. He hadn't anticipated that the absence of his own car would prove a tactical aid. He smiled brilliantly down upon Olivia.

Dono strode over to them, smiling in a peculiarly satisfied manner that put Ivan disquietingly in mind of the lost Lady Donna. Dono was not a person with whom Ivan cared to be quite so publicly paired. Perhaps he could keep Olivia's hellos brief, and then whisk her off.

"Things look like they're breaking up," said Dono to Olivia. He gave Ivan a nod of greeting. "Shall I call Szabo to bring round the car?"

"We ought to see Delia and Duv first. Then we can go. Oh, I offered Ivan a ride along with us to Vorsmythe's. I think there'll be room."

"Certainly." Dono smiled cheerful welcome.

"Did she take the packet?" Olivia asked Dono, with a glance up at the flash of red now vanishing into the crowd.

Dono's smile broadened briefly to a remarkably evil grin. "Yep."

While Ivan was still trying, and failing, to calculate how to get rid of the person providing the transportation, Byerly Vorrutyer made his way around some tables and descended upon them. Damn. Worse and worse.

"Ah, Dono," By greeted his cousin. "Are you still planning on Vorsmythe's for your last stop of the night?"

"Yes. Do you need a ride too?"

"Not from here to there. I have other arrangements. I'd appreciate if you could drop me home after, though."

"Of course."

"What a long talk you had with Countess Vormuir,

out there on the balcony. Chewing over old times, were you?"

"Oh, yes." Dono smiled vaguely. "This and that, you know."

By gave him a penetrating look, but Dono declined to elaborate. By asked, "Did you manage to get in to see Count Vorpinski this afternoon?"

"Yes, finally, and a couple of others too. Vortaine was no help, but at least with Olivia along he was forced to stay polite. Vorfolse, Vorhalas, and Vorpatril all declined to hear my pitch, unfortunately." Dono shot Ivan a somewhat ambiguous look from under his black brows. "Well, I'm not sure about Vorfolse. No one answered the door; he might really have not been home. It was hard to tell."

"So how's the vote tally doing?" By asked.

"Close, By. Closer than I'd ever dared to dream, to tell you the truth. The uncertainty is now making me quite sick to my stomach."

"You'll get through it. Ah . . . close on which side?" By inquired.

"The wrong one. Unfortunately. Well . . ." Dono sighed, "it will have been a great try."

Olivia said sturdily, "You're going to make history." Dono pressed her hand to his arm, and smiled gratefully at her.

Byerly shrugged, which by his standards qualified as a consoling gesture. "Who knows what might happen to turn things around?"

"Between now and tomorrow morning? Not much, I'm afraid. The die is pretty much cast."

"Chin up. There're still a couple of hours to work on the men at Vorsmythe House. Just stay sharp. I'll help. See you over there. . . ."

And so Ivan found himself not with a private opportunity to make time with Olivia, but rather, trapped with her, Dono, Szabo, and two other Vorrutyer Armsmen in the back of the late Count Pierre's official car. Pierre's was one of the few vehicles Ivan had ever encountered that could beat Miles's Regency relic for both fusty luxury and a paranoid armoring that made its best progress a sort of lumbering wallow. Not that it wasn't *comfortable*; Ivan had slept in space station hostel rooms that were smaller than this rear compartment. But Olivia had somehow ended up seated between Dono and Szabo, while Ivan shared body heat with a couple of Armsmen.

They were two-thirds of the way to Vorsmythe House when Dono, who had been staring out the canopy with little vertical lines scored between his brows, suddenly leaned forward and spoke into the intercom to his driver. "Joris, swing around by Count Vorfolse's again. We'll give him one more try."

The car lumbered around the next corner, and began to backtrack. In a couple of minutes, the apartment building containing Vorfolse's flat loomed into view.

The Vorfolse family had a remarkable record for picking the losers in every Barrayaran war of the last century, including choosing to collaborate with the Cetagandans and backing the wrong side in Vordarian's Pretendership. The somewhat morose present heir, oppressed by his ancestors' many defeats, eked out his life in the capital by renting the drafty old Vorfolse clan mansion to an enterprising prole with grandiose ambitions, and living entirely off the proceeds. Instead of the permitted squad of twenty, he kept only a single Armsman, an equally depressed and rather elderly fellow who doubled as every servant the Count had. Still, Vorfolse's apprehensive refusal to align himself with any faction or party or project, no matter how benign it appeared, at least meant he wasn't an automatic *yes* for Richars. And a vote was a vote, Ivan supposed, no matter how eccentric.

A narrow, multilevel parking garage attached to the building provided spaces for the prole residents to house their vehicles, at a stiff surcharge Ivan had no doubt. Parking space in the capital was normally leased by the square meter. Joris oozed Pierre's groundcar into the meager clearances, then suffered a check when he discovered all the ground-floor visitor parking to be taken.

Ivan, planning to stay in the comfy car with Olivia, revised his plan when Olivia jumped out to accompany

Dono. Dono left Joris waiting for a space to open up, and, flanked by Olivia and his security outriders, strode out through the street-level pedestrian access and around toward the apartment building's front entrance. Torn between curiosity and caution, Ivan trailed along. With a short gesture, Szabo left one of his men to take station by the outer door, and the second by the lift tube exit on the third floor, so that by the time they arrived at Vorfolse's flat they were a not-too-intimidating party of four.

A discreet brass tag was screwed a little crookedly to the door above the apartment's number; it read *Vorfolse House* in a script that was meant to be imposing, but, in context, succeeded mainly in being rather pathetic. Ivan was reminded of his Aunt Cordelia's frequent assertion that governments were mental constructs. Lord Dono touched the chime-pad.

After a couple of minutes, a querulous voice issued from the intercom. The little square of its vid viewer stayed blank. "What do you want?"

Dono glanced at Szabo, and whispered, "That Vorfolse?"

"Sounds like," Szabo murmured back. "It's not qua-very enough to be his old Armsman."

"Good evening, Count Vorfolse," Dono said smoothly into the com. "I'm Lord Dono Vorrutyer." He gestured at his companions. "I believe you know Ivan Vorpatril, and my senior Armsman, Szabo. Miss Olivia Koudelka. I stopped by to talk to you about tomorrow's vote on my District's Countship."

"It's too late," said the voice.

Szabo rolled his eyes.

"I have no wish to disturb your rest," Dono pressed on.

"Good. Go away."

Dono sighed. "Certainly, sir. But before we depart, may I at least be permitted to know how you intend to vote on the issue tomorrow?"

"I don't care which Vorrutyer gets the District. The whole family's deranged. A plague on both your parties."

Dono took a breath, and kept smiling. "Yes, sir, but

consider the consequences. If you abstain, and the vote falls short of a decision, it will simply have to be done over again. And over and over, until a majority is finally reached. I would also point out that you would find my cousin Richars a most unrestful colleague—short-tempered, and much given to factionalism and strife."

Such a long silence issued from the intercom, Ivan began to wonder if Vorfolse had gone off to bed.

Olivia leaned into the scan pickup to say brightly, "Count Vorfolse, sir, if you vote for Lord Dono, you won't regret it. He'll give diligent service to both the Vorrutyer's District and to the Imperium."

The voice replied after a moment, "Eh, you're one of Commodore Koudelka's girls, aren't you? Does Aral Vorkosigan support this nonsense, then?"

"Lord Miles Vorkosigan, who is acting as his father's voting deputy, supports me fully," Dono returned.

"Unrestful. Eh! *There's* unrestful for you."

"No doubt," said Dono agreeably. "I have noticed that myself. But how do you intend to vote?"

Another pause. "I don't know. I'll think about it."

"Thank you, sir." Dono motioned them all to decamp; his little retinue followed him back toward the lift tubes.

"That wasn't too conclusive," said Ivan.

"Do you have any idea how positive *I'll think about it* seems, in light of some of the responses I've gotten?" said Dono ruefully. "Compared to certain of his colleagues, Count Vorfolse is a fountain of liberality." They collected the Armsman, and descended the lift tube. Dono added as they reached the ground foyer, "You have to give Vorfolse credit for integrity. There are a number of dubious ways he could be stripping his District of funds to support a more opulent lifestyle here, but he doesn't choose 'em."

"Huh," said Szabo. "If *I* were one of his liege people, I'd damn well *encourage* him to steal something. It would be better than this miserable miserly farce. It's just not proper Vor. It's not good *show*."

They exited the building with Szabo in the lead, Dono and Olivia somehow walking side by side, and Ivan following, trailed by the two other Armsmen. As they passed through the pedestrian entry to the dim garage, Szabo stopped short and said, "Where the hell's the car?" He lifted his wrist comm to his lips. "Joris?"

Olivia said uneasily, "If somebody else had come in, he'd have had to take the car all the way up, back down, and around the block to let them past. No room to turn *that* car in here."

"Not without—" Szabo began. He was interrupted by a quiet buzz, seemingly out of nowhere, a sound familiar enough to Ivan's ears. Szabo fell like a tree.

"Stunner tag!" bellowed Ivan, and jumped behind the nearest pillar to his right. He looked around for Olivia, but she had dodged the other way, with Dono. Two more well-aimed stunner shots took out the other two Armsmen as they broke right and left, though one got off a wild shot with his own weapon before he went down.

Ivan, crouching between the pillar and a dilapidated groundcar, cursed his unarmed state and tried to see where the shots had come from. Pillars, cars, inadequate lighting, shadows . . . further up the ramp, a dim shape flitted from the shadow of a pier and vanished among the tightly packed vehicles.

Stunner combat rules were simple. Drop everything that moved, and sort them out later, hoping that no one harbored a bad heart condition. Dono's unconscious Armsman could supply Ivan with a stunner, if he could reach it without getting himself zapped. . . .

A voice from up the ramp whispered hoarsely, "Which way did he go?"

"Down toward the entry. Goff'll get him. Drop that damned officer as soon as you get a clear shot."

At least three assailants, then. Assume one more. At *least* one more. Cursing the tight clearances, Ivan retreated backward on his hands and knees from his stunner-bolt-stopping pillar and tried to work his way between the row of cars and the wall, edging toward the entry again. If he could make it out onto the street—

This had to be a snatch. If it had been an

assassination, their attackers would have picked a much deadlier weapon, and the whole party would be well-mixed hamburger on the walls by now. In a slice of vision between two cars, away down the descending ramp to his left, a white shape moved: Olivia's party dress. A meaty thunk came from behind a pillar there, followed by a nauseating noise like a pumpkin hitting concrete. "Good one!" Dono's voice jerked out.

Olivia's mother, Ivan reminded himself, had been the boy-Emperor's *personal* bodyguard. He tried to imagine the cozy mother-daughter instruction rituals in the Koudelka household. He was pretty sure they hadn't been limited to baking cakes together.

A black-clad shape darted.

"There he goes! Get him! No, no—he's supposed to stay *conscious*!"

Running footsteps, scuffling and breathing, a thunk, a strangled yelp—praying everyone's attention would be diverted, Ivan dove for the Armsman's stunner, snatched it up, and ducked again for cover. From the ascending ramp to the right came the *whuff* of a vehicle backing rapidly and illegally down toward them. Ivan risked a peek over a car. The back doors of the battered lift van swung wildly open, as it jerked to a halt at the curve. Two men hustled Dono toward it. Dono was open-mouthed, stumbling, a look of astonished agony on his face.

"Where's Goff?" barked the driver, swinging out to look at his two comrades and their prize. "Goff!" he shouted.

"Where's the girl?" asked one of them.

The other said, "Never mind the girl. Here, help me bend him back. We'll do the job, dump him, and get out of here before she can run for help. Malka, circle around and get that big officer. He wasn't supposed to be in this picture." They pulled Dono into the van—no, only half into the van. One man pulled a bottle from his pocket, flipped off its cap, and placed it ready-to-hand on the edge of the van floor. What the hell . . . ? *This isn't a kidnapping.*

"Goff?" the man detailed to hunt down Ivan called

uncertainly into the shadows, as he crouched and skittered past the cars.

The, under the circumstances, *extremely* unpleasant hum of a vibra knife sounded from the hand of the man bending over Dono. Risking everything, Ivan popped to his feet and fired.

He scored a direct hit on the fellow seeking Goff; the man spasmed, fell, and failed to move thereafter. Dono's men carried *heavy* stunners, and not without cause, apparently. Ivan only managed to wing one of the others. They both abandoned Dono and dashed behind the van. Dono fell to the pavement, and curled up around himself; with all this stunner fire flashing around, probably no worse a move than trying to run for it, but Ivan had a gruesome vision of what would happen if the van backed up.

From further up the ramp, on the far side of the van, two more stunner bolts snapped out in quick succession.

Silence.

After a moment, Ivan called cautiously, "Olivia?"

She responded from higher up the ramp in a breathless sort of little-girl voice, "Ivan? Dono?"

Dono spasmed on the pavement, and vented a moan.

Warily, Ivan stood up and started for the van. After a couple of seconds, probably to see if he would draw any more fire, Olivia rose from her cover and ran lightly down the ramp to join him.

"Where'd you get the stunner?" he inquired, as she popped around the vehicle's side. She was barefoot, and her party dress was tucked up around her hips.

"Goff." Somewhat absently, she jerked her skirts back down with her free hand. "Dono! Oh, no!" She jammed the stunner into her cleavage and knelt by the black-clad man. She raised a hand covered, sickeningly, with blood.

"Only," gasped Dono, "a cut on my leg. He missed. Oh, God! Ow, ow!"

"You're bleeding all over the place. Lie still, love!" Olivia commanded. She looked around a little frantically, jumped up and peered into the dark cavernous emptiness of the van's freight compartment, then determinedly ripped off the beige lace overskirt of her party dress. More quick ripping sounds, as she hastily fashioned a pad and some strips. She began to bind the pad tightly to the long shallow slash along Dono's thigh, to staunch the bleeding.

Ivan circled the van, collected Olivia's two victims, and dragged them back to deposit in a heap where he could keep an eye on them. Olivia now had Dono half sitting up, his head cradled between her breasts as she anxiously stroked his dark hair. Dono was pale and shaking, his breathing disrupted.

"Take a punch in the solar plexus, did you?" Ivan inquired.

"No. Further down," Dono wheezed. "Ivan . . . do you remember, whenever one of you fellows got kicked in the nuts and went over, doing sports or whatever, how I laughed? I'm sorry. I never knew. I'm *sorry* . . ."

"Sh," Olivia soothed him.

Ivan knelt down for a closer look. Olivia's first aid was doing its job; the beige lace was soaked with bright gore, but the bleeding had definitely slowed. Dono wasn't going to exsanguinate here. His assailant had sliced Dono's trousers open; the vibra-knife lay abandoned on the pavement nearby. Ivan rose, and examined the bottle. His head jerked back at the sharp scent of liquid bandage. He considered offering it to Olivia for Dono, but there was no telling what nasty additives it might be spiked with. Carefully, he recapped it, and stared around at the scene. "It seems," he said shakily, "someone was aiming to reverse your Betan surgery, Dono. Disqualify you just before the vote."

"I'd figured that out, yeah," Dono mumbled.

"Without anesthetic. I think the liquid bandage was to stop the bleeding, after. To be sure you'd live through it."

Olivia cried out in revolted horror. "That's *awful*!"

"That's," Dono sighed, "Richars, in all probability. I didn't think he'd go this far. . . ."

"That's—" said Ivan, and stopped. He scowled at the vibra knife, and stirred it with the toe of his boot. "Now,

I'm not saying I approve of what you did, Dono, or of what you're trying to do. But that's just *wrong*."

Dono's hands wandered protectively to his groin. "Hell," he said in a faint voice. "I hadn't even got to try it *out* yet. I was saving myself. For once in my life, I wanted to be a virgin on my wedding night . . ."

"Can you stand up?"

"Are you joking?"

"No." Ivan glanced around uneasily. "Where'd you leave Goff, Olivia?"

She pointed. "Over by that third pillar."

"Right." Ivan went to collect him, seriously wondering where Pierre's car had gone. The thug Goff was still unconscious too, although of a subtly more disturbing limpness than the stunner victims. It was the greenish skin tone, Ivan decided, and the weird spongy lump on his head. He paused along the route, in dragging Goff to join the others, to check Szabo's wrist comm for Joris. No answer, though Szabo's pulse seemed to be bumping along all right.

Dono was stirring, but still not ready to stand. Ivan frowned, stared around, then jogged up the ramp.

Just around the next curve, Ivan found Pierre's groundcar sitting skewed a little sideways across the concrete. Ivan didn't know by what trick they'd lured Joris out of it, but the young Armsman lay in a stunned heap in front of the car. Ivan sighed, and dragged him around to dump in the rear compartment, and backed the car carefully down to the van.

Dono's color was coming back, and he was now sitting up only a little bent over.

"We have to get Dono medical attention," Olivia told Ivan anxiously.

"Yep. We're going to need all kinds of drugs," Ivan agreed. "Synergine for some," he craned his neck toward Szabo, who twitched and moaned but didn't quite claw back to consciousness, "fast-penta for others." He frowned at the heap of thugs. "You recognize any of these goons, Dono?"

Dono squinted. "Never seen 'em in my life."

"Hirelings, I suppose. Contracted through who knows

how many middlemen. Could be days before the municipal guard, or ImpSec if they take an interest, get to the bottom of it all."

"The vote," sighed Dono, "will be over by then."

I don't want anything to do with this. This isn't my job. It's not my fault. But really, this was a political precedent *nobody* was going to favor. This was damned *offensive.* This was just . . . really *wrong.*

"Olivia," Ivan said abruptly, "can you drive Dono's car?"

"I think so . . ."

"Good. Help me get the troops loaded up."

With Olivia's assistance, Ivan managed to get the three stunned Vorrutyer Armsmen laid into the rear compartment with the unfortunate Joris, and the disarmed thugs hoisted rather less carefully into the back of their own van. He locked the doors firmly from the outside, and took charge of the vibra knife, the armload of illegal stunners, and the bottle of liquid bandage. Tenderly, Olivia helped Dono limp over to his car, and settled him into the front seat with his leg out. Ivan, watching the pair, blond head bent over dark, sighed deeply, and shook his head.

"Where to?" called Olivia, punching controls to lower the canopies.

Ivan swung up into the van's cab, and shouted over his shoulder, "Vorpatril House!"

CHAPTER EIGHTEEN

The great Chamber of the Council of Counts had a hushed, cool air, despite the bright dapple of colored light falling through the stained glass windows high in the east wall onto the oak flooring. Miles had thought he was early, but he spotted René at the Vorbretten's District desk, arrived even before him. Miles laid out his flimsies and checklists on his own desk in the front row, and circled around the benches to René's place, second row right.

René looked trim enough in his Vorbretten House uniform of dark green piped with bittersweet orange, but his face was wan.

"Well," said Miles, feigning cheer for the sake of his colleague's morale. "This is it, then."

René managed a thin smile. "It's too close. We're not going to make it, Miles." He tapped a finger nervously on his checklist, twin to the one on Miles's desk.

Miles put a brown-booted foot up on René's bench, leaned forward with a deliberately casual air, and glanced at his papers. "It's tighter than I'd hoped it would be," he admitted. "Don't take our precount as a done deal, though. You never know who's going to change his mind at the last second and bolt."

451

"Unfortunately, that cuts both ways," René pointed out ruefully.

Miles shrugged, not disagreeing. He would plan for a hell of a lot more redundancy in future votes, he decided. *Democracy, faugh.* He felt a twinge of his old familiar adrenaline-pumped prebattle nerves, without the promised catharsis of being able to shoot at someone later if things went really badly. On the other hand, he was unlikely to be shot *at* here, either. *Count your blessings.*

"Did you make any more progress last night, after you went off with Gregor?" René asked him.

"I think so. I was up till two in the morning, pretending to drink and arguing with Henri Vorvolk's friends. I believe I nailed Vorgarin for you after all. Dono . . . was a harder sell. How did things go last night at Vorsmythe's? Were you and Dono able to make your list of last-minutes contacts?"

"I did," said René, "but I never saw Dono. He didn't show."

Miles frowned. "Oh? I'd understood he was going on to the party. I figured between the two of you, you'd have it in hand."

"You couldn't be in two places at once." René hesitated. "Dono's cousin Byerly was hunting all over for him. He finally went off to look for him, and didn't come back."

"Huh." If . . . no, dammit. If Dono had been, say, assassinated in the night, the chamber would be abuzz with the news by now. The Vorbarr Sultana Armsmen's grapevine would have passed it on, ImpSec would have called, something. Miles would have to have heard. Wouldn't he?

"Tatya's here." René sighed. "She said she couldn't stand to wait at home, not knowing . . . if it was still going to *be* home by tonight."

"It will be all right."

Miles walked out onto the floor of the chamber and gazed up at the in-curving crescent of the gallery, with its ornately carved wooden balustrade. The gallery was beginning to fill also, with interested Vor relatives and other people with the right or the pull to gain admittance. Tatya Vorbretten was there, hiding in the back row, looking even more wan than René, supported by one of René's sisters. Miles gave her an optimistic thumb's-up he was by no means feeling.

More men filtered into the chamber. Boriz Vormoncrief's crowd arrived, including young Sigur Vorbretten, who exchanged a polite, wary nod with his cousin René. Sigur did not attempt to stake a claim to René's bench, but sat close under his father-in-law's protective wing. Sigur was neutrally dressed in conservative day-wear, not quite daring a Vorbretten House uniform. He looked nervous, which would have cheered Miles up more if he hadn't known it was Sigur's habitual look. Miles went to his desk and assuaged his own nerves by checking off arrivals.

René wandered over. "Where *is* Dono? I can't hand off the circle to him as planned if he's late."

"Don't panic. The Conservatives will drag their feet for all of us, trying to delay things till they have all their men in. Some of whom won't be coming. I'll stand up and gabble if I have to, but meanwhile, let *them* filibuster."

"Right," said René, and returned to his seat. He laced his hands on top of his desk as if to keep them from twitching.

Blast it, Dono had twenty good Armsmen of his own. He *couldn't* have gone missing with no one to notice. A potential Count should be able to find his way to the Chamber on his own. He shouldn't need Miles to take him by the hand and lead him in. Lady Donna was famous for being fashionably late, and making dramatic entrances; Miles thought she should have dumped those habits with the rest of her baggage back on Beta Colony. He drummed his fingers on his desk, turned a little away from René's line of sight, and tapped his wrist com.

"Pym?" he murmured into it.

"Yes, m'lord?" Pym replied promptly from his station out in the parking area, guarding Miles's groundcar and, no doubt, chatting with all his opposite number Armsmen doing the same duty. Well, not quite all:

Count Vorfolse always arrived alone by autocab. Except that he hadn't, yet.

"I want you to call Vorrutyer House for me and find out if Lord Dono is on his way. If there's anything holding him up, take care of it, and speed him along. All due assistance, eh? Then report back to me."

"Understood, m'lord." The tiny activation light winked out.

Richars Vorrutyer marched into the chamber, looking pugnacious in a neat Vorrutyer House uniform that already claimed his status as a Count. He arranged his notes on the Vorrutyer's District desk in the second row center, looked around the chamber, and sauntered over to Miles. The blue-and-gray fit him well enough, but, as he approached Miles's desk, Miles saw to his secret delight that the side seams showed signs of having been let out recently. Just how many years had Richars kept it hanging in his closet, awaiting this moment? Miles greeted him with a slight smile, concealing rage.

"They say," Richars growled to him in an undervoice, not concealing rage quite so well, Miles fancied, "that an honest politician is one who stays bought. It seems you don't qualify, Vorkosigan."

"You should choose your enemies more wisely," Miles breathed back.

Richars grunted. "So should you. I don't bluff. As you'll find out before this day is over." He stalked away to confer with the group of men now clustered around Vormoncrief's desk.

Miles controlled his irritation. At least they had Richars worried; he wouldn't be going out of his way to be such an ass otherwise. Where the hell was *Dono?* Miles made doodles of mercenary hand weapons in the margin of his check-list, and reflected on just how much he didn't want Richars Vorrutyer sitting back there in his blind spot for the next forty years.

The chamber was filling now, getting warmer and noisier, coming alive. Miles rose and made a circuit of the room, checking in with his Progressive allies, pausing to add a few urgent words in support of René and Dono to men he still had listed as undecided.

Gregor arrived, with a minute to spare, entering from the little door to his private conference chamber in back of his dais. He took his traditional seat on his plain military camp stool, facing all his Counts, and exchanged a nod with the Lord Guardian of the Speaker's Circle. Miles broke off his last conversation, and slid onto his own bench. At the precise hour, the Lord Guardian called the room to order.

Still no sign of Dono, dammit! But the other team was short of men, too. As Miles had predicted to René, a string of Conservative Party Counts called in their two-minute speaking rights, and began handing the Circle off to one another, with lots of long, paper-shuffling pauses between speakers. All the Counts, experienced in this drill, checked chronos, counted heads, and settled in comfortably. Gregor watched impassively, allowing no sign of impatience or, indeed, any other emotion to show on his cool, narrow face.

Miles bit his lip, as his heartbeat intensified. Very like a battle, yes, this moment of commitment. Whatever he'd left undone, it was too late to fix it now. *Go. Go. Go.*

A rush of anxiety clogged Ekaterin's throat when she answered the door chime and discovered Vassily and Hugo waiting on her aunt's porch. It was followed by a rush of anger at them both for so destroying her former pleasure in seeing her family. She kept herself, barely, from leaping into a gabble of protests that she *had too* followed their rules. *At least wait till you're accused.* She controlled her exploding emotions, and said uninvitingly, "Yes? What do you two want now?"

They looked at each other. Hugo said, "May we come in?"

"Why?"

Vassily's hands clenched; he rubbed one damp-looking palm on his trouser seam. He had chosen his lieutenant's uniform today. "It's extremely urgent."

Vassily was wearing his nervous, Help-I-Am-In-The-Corrupt-Capital look again. Ekaterin was strongly tempted to shut the door on them both, leaving Vassily to be killed and eaten by whatever cannibals he imagined populated Vorbarr Sultana's alleyways—or drawing rooms. But Hugo added, "Please, Ekaterin. It really is most urgent."

Grudgingly, she gave way, and motioned them into her aunt's parlor.

They did not sit. "Is Nikki here?" Vassily asked at once.

"Yes. Why?"

"I want you to get him ready to travel immediately. I want to get him out of the capital as soon as possible."

"*What?*" Ekaterin almost shrieked. "Why? *Now* what lies have you been swallowing down whole? I *have not* seen or spoken with Lord Vorkosigan except for one short visit day before yesterday to tell him I was exiled. And you agreed to that! Hugo is my witness!"

Vassily waved his hands. "It's not that. I have a new and even more disturbing piece of information."

"If it's from the same source, you're a bigger fool than I thought possible, Vassily Vorsoisson."

"I checked it by calling Lord Richars himself. I've learned a lot more about this volatile situation in the last two days. As soon as Richars Vorrutyer is voted into the Countship of the Vorrutyer's District this morning, he intends to lay a murder charge in the Council of Counts against Lord Auditor Vorkosigan for the death of my cousin. At that point, I believe the blood will hit the walls."

Ekaterin's stomach knotted. "Oh, no! The fool . . . !"

Aunt Vorthys, attracted by the raised voices, rounded the corner from the kitchen in time to hear this. Nikki, trailing her, muted his enthusiastic cry of *Uncle Hugo!* at the sight of the adults' strained faces.

"Why, hello, Hugo," said Aunt Vorthys. She added uncertainly, "And, um . . . Vassily Vorsoisson, yes?" Ekaterin had given her and Nikki only the barest outline of their previous visit; Nikki had been indignant and a little frightened. Aunt Vorthys had endorsed Miles's opinion that it would be best to wait for Uncle Vorthys's return to attempt to adjust the misunderstanding.

Hugo gave her a respectful nod of greeting, and continued heavily, "I have to agree with Ekaterin, but it only supports Vassily's worries. I can't imagine what has possessed Vorrutyer to make such a move while Aral Vorkosigan *himself* is in town. You'd think he'd at least have the sense wait till the Viceroy returned to Sergyar before attacking his heir."

"Aral Vorkosigan!" cried Ekaterin. "Do you really think *Gregor* will blithely accept this assault on one of his chosen Voices? Not to mention look forgivingly on someone trying to start a huge public scandal two weeks before his wedding . . . ! Richars isn't a fool, he's *mad*." Or acting in some kind of blind panic, but what did Richars have to be panicked about?

"For all I know, he is mad," said Vassily. "He's a Vorrutyer, after all. If this comes down to the sort of internecine street fighting among the high Vor we've seen in the past, no one in the capital is safe. And especially no one they've managed to draw into their orbits. I want to have Nikki well on his way before that vote comes down. The monorail lines could be cut, you know. They were during the Pretendership." He gestured to Aunt Vorthys for confirmation of this fact.

"Well, that's true," she admitted. "But even the open warfare of the Pretendership didn't lay waste to the whole of the capital. The fighting was quite focused, all in all."

"But there *was* fighting around the University," he flashed back.

"Some, yes."

"Did you see it?" asked Nikki, his interest immediately diverted.

"We only located it so as to go round, dear," she told him.

Vassily added a little grudgingly, "You are welcome to accompany us too, Ekaterin—and you too, of course, Madame Vorthys—or better still, take refuge with your brother." He gestured at Hugo. "It's possible, given that it's widely known you've drawn Lord Vorkosigan's attention, that you could become a target yourself."

"And hasn't it crossed your mind yet that you are

being aimed by Miles's enemies at just that target? That you've let yourself be manipulated, used as their tool?" Ekaterin took a deep, calming breath. "Has it occurred to either of you that Richars Vorrutyer may *not* be voted the Countship? That it could go to Lord Dono instead?"

"That crazy woman?" said Vassily in astonishment. "Impossible!"

"Neither crazy nor a woman," said Ekaterin. "And if he becomes Count Vorrutyer, this entire exercise of yours comes to nothing."

"Not a chance I propose to bet my life—or Nikki's—on, madame," said Vassily stiffly. "If you choose to stay here and bear the risks, well, I shall not argue with you. I have an absolute obligation to protect Nikki, however."

"So do I," said Ekaterin levelly.

"But Mama," said Nikki, clearly trying to unravel this rapid debate, "Lord Vorkosigan *didn't* murder Da."

Vassily bent slightly, and gave him a pained, sympathetic smile. "But how do you know, Nikki?" he asked gently. "How does anyone know? That's the trouble."

Nikki closed his lips abruptly, and stared uncertainly at Ekaterin. She realized that he didn't know just how private his private interview with the Emperor was supposed to remain—and neither did she.

She had to admit, Vassily's anxiety was contagious. Hugo had clearly taken a fever of it. And while it had been a long time since strife among the Counts had seriously threatened the stability of the Imperium, that wouldn't make you any less dead if you had the bad luck to be caught in a cross-fire before Imperial troops arrived to shut it down. "Vassily, this close to Gregor's wedding, the capital is crawling with Security. Anyone—of any rank—who made the least move toward public disorder at the moment would find himself slapped down so fast he wouldn't know what hit him. Your fears are . . . exaggerated." She'd wanted to say, *groundless.* But what if Richars did win his Countship, and its concomitant right to lay criminal charges against his new peers in the Council?

Vassily shook his head. "Lord Vorkosigan has made a dangerous enemy."

"Lord Vorkosigan *is* a dangerous enemy!" She bit her tongue, too late.

Vassily stared at her a moment, shook his head, and turned to Nikki. "Nikki, get your things. I'm taking you away."

Nikki looked at Ekaterin. "Mama?" he said uncertainly.

What was it Miles had said about being ambushed by your habits? Time and again, she'd yielded to Tien's wishes over matters pertaining to Nikki, even when she'd disagreed with him, because he was Nikki's father, because he had a right, but most of all because to force Nikki to choose between his two parents seemed a cruelty little short of ripping him apart. Nikki had always been off-limits as a pawn in their conflicts. That Nikki had been Tien's hostage in the peculiar gender bias of Barrayar's custody laws had been a secondary consideration, though it was a wall she'd felt press against her back more than once.

But dammit, she'd never taken an oath of honor to Vassily Vorsoisson. He didn't hold half of Nikki's heart. What if, instead of player and pawn, she and Nikki were suddenly allies, beleaguered equals? What then was possible?

She folded her arms and said nothing.

Vassily reached for Nikki's hand. Nikki dodged around Ekaterin, and cried, "Mama, I don't have to go, do I? I was supposed to go to Arthur's tonight! I don't want to go with Vassily!" His voice was edged with sharp distress.

Vassily inhaled, and attempted to recover his balance and his dignity. "Madame, control your child!"

She stared at him for a long moment. "Why, Vassily," she said at last, her voice silky, "I thought you were revoking my authority over Nikki. You certainly don't seem to trust my judgment for his safety and well-being. How shall *I* control him, then?"

Aunt Vorthys, catching the nuance, winced; Hugo, father of three, also got it. She had just given Nikki tacit permission to go to his limit. Bachelor Vassily missed the curve.

Aunt Vorthys began faintly, "Vassily, do you really think this is wise—"

Vassily held out a hand, more sternly. "Nikki. Come along. We must catch the eleven-oh-five train out of North Gate Station!"

Nikki put his hands behind his back, and said valiantly, "No."

Vassily said in a tone of final warning, "If I have to pick you up and carry you, I will!"

Nikki returned breathlessly, "I'll scream. I'll tell everybody you're kidnapping me. I'll tell them you're *not* my father. And it'll all be true!"

Hugo looked increasingly alarmed. "For God's sake, don't drive the boy into hysterics, Vassily. They can keep it up for *hours*. And everybody stares at you as if you were the reincarnation of Pierre Le Sanguinaire. Little old ladies come up and threaten you—"

"Like this one," Aunt Vorthys interrupted. "Gentlemen, let me dissuade you—"

The harassed and reddening Vassily made another grab, but Nikki was quicker, dodging around the Professora this time. "I'll tell them you're kidnapping me for *'moral purposes'*!" he declaimed from behind this ample barrier.

Vassily asked Hugo in a shocked voice, "How does he know about that sort of thing?"

Hugo waved this away. "He probably just heard the phrase. Children repeat things like that, you know."

Vassily clearly didn't. A poor memory, perhaps?

"Nikki, look," said Hugo, in a voice of reason, bending a little to peer at the boy in his refuge behind the seething Professora. "If you don't want to go with Vassily, suppose you come and visit me and Aunt Rosalie, and Edie and the boys, for a little while instead?"

Nikki hesitated. So did Ekaterin. This ploy might have been made to work, with another push, but Vassily took advantage of the momentary distraction to make another grab at Nikki's arm.

"Ha! Got you!"

"Ow! Ow! Ow!" screamed Nikki.

Perhaps it was because Vassily didn't have the trained parental ear that could instantly distinguish between real pain and noise for effect, but when Ekaterin started grimly forward, he flinched back, his grip unconsciously loosening. Nikki broke away, and ran for the hall stairs.

"I'm not going!" Nikki yelled over his shoulder, scrambling up the stairs. "I'm not, I won't! You can't make me. Mama doesn't *want* me to go!" At the top he whirled to fling frantically back, as Vassily, baited into chasing him, reached the bottom, "You'll be sorry you made my mama unhappy!"

Hugo, ten years older and vastly more experienced, shook his head in exasperation and followed more slowly. Aunt Vorthys, looking very distressed and a little gray, brought up the rear. From above, a door slammed.

Ekaterin arrived, her heart hammering, in the upper hallway as Vassily bent over the door to her uncle's study and rattled the knob.

"Nikki! Open this door! Unlock it at once, do you hear me?" Vassily turned to look beseechingly at Ekaterin. "Do something!"

Ekaterin leaned her back against the opposite wall, folded her arms again, and smiled slowly. "I only know one man who was ever able to talk Nikki out of a locked room. And he isn't here."

"Order him out!"

"If you are indeed insisting on taking custody of him, Vassily, this is your problem," Ekaterin told him coolly. She let *The first of many* stand implied.

Hugo, stumping breathlessly up the stairs, offered, "Eventually, they do calm down and come out. Sooner if there's no food in there."

"Nikki," said Aunt Vorthys distantly, "knows where the Professor hides his cookies."

Vassily stood up, and stared at the heavy wood and old iron hardware. "We could break it down, I suppose," he said hesitantly.

"Not in *my* house, Vassily Vorsoisson!" Aunt Vorthys said.

Vassily gestured at Ekaterin. "Fetch me a screwdriver, then!"

She didn't move. "Find it yourself." She didn't add, *you blundering nitwit* aloud, quite, but it seemed to be understood.

Vassily flushed angrily, but bent again. "What's he doing in there? I hear voices."

Hugo bent too. "He's using the comconsole, I think."

Aunt Vorthys glanced briefly down the hallway toward her bedroom door. From which there was a door to the bath, from which there was another door into the Professor's study. Well, if Aunt Vorthys wasn't going to point out this alternate and unguarded route to the two men now pressing their ears to the door, why should Ekaterin?

"I hear two voices. Who in the world could he be calling on the comconsole?" asked Vassily, in a dismissive tone that didn't invite an answer.

Suddenly, Ekaterin thought she knew. Her breath caught. "Oh," she said faintly, "*dear*." Aunt Vorthys stared at her.

For a hysterical moment, Ekaterin considered dashing around and diving through the alternate doors, to shut down the comconsole before it was too late. But the echo of a laughing voice drifted through her mind . . . *Let's see what happens.*

Yes. Let's.

One of Boriz Vormoncrief's allied Counts droned on in the Speaker's Circle. Miles wondered how much longer these delaying tactics could continue. Gregor was starting to look mighty bored.

The Emperor's personal Armsman appeared from the little conference chamber, mounted the dais, and murmured something into his master's ear. Gregor looked briefly surprised, returned a few words, and motioned the man off. He made a small gesture to the Lord Guardian of the Speaker's Circle, who trod over to him. Miles tensed, expecting Gregor was about to call a halt to the filibuster and command the voting to begin, but instead the Lord Guardian merely nodded, and returned to his bench. Gregor rose, and ducked through the door behind the dais. The speaking Count glanced aside at this motion, hesitated, then carried on. It might not be significant, Miles told himself; even Emperors had to go to the bathroom now and then.

Miles seized the moment to key his wristcom again. "Pym? What's up with Dono?"

"Just got a confirmation from Vorrutyer House," Pym returned after a moment. "Dono's on his way. Captain Vorpatril is escorting him."

"Only *now*?"

"He apparently only arrived home less than an hour ago."

"What was he doing all night?" Surely Dono hadn't picked the night before the vote to go tomcatting with Ivan—on the other hand, maybe he'd wanted to prove something. . . . "Never mind. Just be sure he gets here all right."

"We're on it, m'lord."

Gregor indeed returned in about the amount of time it would have taken him to take a leak. He settled back in his seat without interfering with the Speaker's Circle, but he cast an odd, exasperated, faintly bemused glance in Miles's direction. Miles sat up and stared back, but Gregor gave him no further clue, returning instead to his usual impassive expression that could conceal anything from terminal boredom to fury.

Miles would not give his adversaries the satisfaction of seeing him bite his nails. The Conservatives were going to run out of speakers very soon, unless more of their men arrived. Miles did another head count, or rather, survey of empty desks. The turnout was high today, for this important vote. Vortugalov and his deputy remained absent, as Lady Alys had promised. Also missing, more inexplicably, were Vorhalas, Vorpatril, Vorfolse, and Vormuir. Since three and possibly all four of these were votes secured and counted on by the Conservative faction, this was no loss. He began doodling a winding garland of knives, swords, and small explosions down the other margin of his flimsy, and waited some more.

" . . . one hundred eighty-nine, one-hundred-ninety, one-hundred ninety-one," Enrique counted, in a tone of great satisfaction.

Kareen paused in her task at the laboratory comconsole, and leaned around the display to watch the Escobaran scientist. Assisted by Martya, he was finishing the final inventory of recovered Vorkosigan liveried butter bugs, simultaneously reintroducing them into their newly cleaned stainless steel hutch propped open on the lab bench.

"Only nine individuals still missing," Enrique went on happily. "Less than five percent attrition; an acceptable loss for an accident of this unfortunate nature, I think. As long as I have *you*, my darling."

He turned to Martya, and reached past her to lift the jar containing the queen Vorkosigan butter bug, which had been brought in only last night by Armsman Jankowski's triumphant younger daughter. He tipped the jar and coaxed the bug out onto his waiting palm. The queen had grown some two centimeters longer during the rigors of her escape, according to Enrique's measurements, and now filled his hand and hung out over the sides. He held her up to his face, and made encouraging little kissing noises at her, and stroked her stubby wing carapaces with his fingertip. She clung on tightly with her claws, drawing blood, and hissed back at him.

"They make that noise when they're happy," Enrique informed Martya, in response to her doubtful stare.

"Oh," said Martya.

"Would you like to pet her?" He held out the giant bug invitingly.

"Well . . . why not?" Martya, too, attempted the experiment, and was rewarded by another hiss, as the bug arched her back. Martya smiled crookedly.

Privately, Kareen thought any man whose idea of a good time was to feed, pet, and care for a creature that mainly responded to his worship with hostile noises was going to get along great with Martya. Enrique, after a few more heartening chirps, tipped the queen into the steel hutch to be swarmed over, groomed, cosseted, and fed by her worker-progeny.

Kareen vented a mellow sigh, and returned her attention to deciphering Mark's scrawled notes on the cost-price analysis of their top five proposed food products. *Naming* them all was going to be a challenge. Mark's ideas tended to the bland, and there was no point in asking Miles, whose embittered suggestions all ran to things like *Vomit Vanilla* and *Cockroach Crunch*.

Vorkosigan House was very quiet this morning. Any Armsmen that Miles hadn't borrowed had gone off with the Viceroy and Vicereine to some fancy political breakfast being held in honor of the Empress-to-be. Most of the staff had been granted the morning off. Mark had seized the opportunity—and Ma Kosti, who was becoming their permanent product development consultant—and left to look at a small dairy packaging plant in operation. Tsipis had found a similar packager in Hassadar that was moving to a larger location, and had drawn Mark's attention to their abandoned facility as a possible venue for the pilot plant for bug butter products.

Kareen's morning commute to work had been short. Last night, she'd claimed her first sleepover at Vorkosigan House. To her secret joy, she and Mark had been treated neither as children nor criminals nor idiots, but with the same respect as any other pair of adults. They'd closed Mark's bedroom door on what was no one's business but their own. Mark had gone off to his tasks whistling this morning—off-key, as he apparently shared his progenitor-brother's total lack of musical talent. Kareen hummed under her breath rather more melodically.

She broke off at a tentative knock on the laboratory doorframe. One of the maidservants stood there, looking worried. In general, Vorkosigan House's service staff avoided the laboratory corridor. Some were afraid of the butter bugs. More were afraid of the teetering stacks of one-liter bug butter tubs, now lining the hallway to over head-height on both sides. All had learned that to venture down here invited being dragged into the laboratory to taste test new bug butter products. This last hazard had certainly cut down on the noise and interruptions. This young lady, as Kareen recalled, shared all three aversions.

"Miss Koudelka, Miss Koudelka ... Dr. Borgos, you have visitors."

The maid stepped aside to admit two men to the laboratory. One was thin, and the other was ... big. They both wore travel-rumpled suits in what Kareen recognized from life with Enrique as the Escobaran style. The thin man, youngish-middle-aged or young with middle-aged mannerisms, it was hard to tell, clutched a folder stuffed with flimsies. The big one merely hulked.

The thin man stepped forward, and addressed Enrique. "Are you Dr. Enrique Borgos?"

Enrique perked up at the Escobaran accent, a breath of home no doubt after his long, lonely exile among Barrayarans. "Yes?"

The thin man flung up his free hand in a gesture of rejoicing. "At last!"

Enrique smiled with shy eagerness. "Oh, you have heard of my work? Are you, by chance ... investors?"

"Hardly." The thin man grinned fiercely. "I am Parole Officer Oscar Gustioz—this is my assistant, Sergeant Muno. Dr. Borgos—" Officer Gustioz placed a formal hand upon Enrique's shoulder, "you are under arrest by order of the Cortes Planetaris de Escobar for fraud, grand theft, failure to appear in court, and forfeiture of posted bond."

"But," sputtered Enrique, "this is Barrayar! You can't arrest me here!"

"Oh, yes I can," said Officer Gustioz grimly. He flopped down the file folder on the lab stool Martya had just vacated, and flipped it open. "I have here, in order, the official arrest order from the Cortes," he began to turn over flimsies, all stamped and creased and scrawled upon, "the preliminary consent for extradition from the Barrayaran Embassy on Escobar, with the three intermediate applications, approved, the final consent from the Imperial Office here in Vorbarr Sultana, the preliminary and final orders from the Vorbarra District Count's office, *eighteen* separate permissions to transport a prisoner from the Barrayaran Imperial jump-point stations between here and home, and last but not least, the clearance from the Vorbarr Sultana Municipal Guard, signed by Lord Vorbohn himself. It took me over a month to fight my way through all this bureaucratic obstruction, and I am not spending another *hour* on this benighted world. You may pack one bag, Dr. Borgos."

"But," cried Kareen, "but Mark *paid* Enrique's bail! We bought him—he's *ours* now!"

"Forfeiture of bond does not erase criminal charges, Miss," the Escobaran officer informed her stiffly. "It adds to them."

"But—why arrest Enrique and not Mark?" asked Martya, puzzling through all this. She stared down at the stack of flimsies.

"Don't make suggestions," Kareen huffed at her under her breath.

"If you are referring to the dangerous lunatic known as Lord Mark Pierre Vorkosigan, Miss, I tried. Believe me, I tried. I spent a week and a half trying to get the documentation. He carries a Class III Diplomatic Immunity that covers him for nearly everything short of outright murder. In addition, I found I had only to pronounce his last name correctly to produce the most damn-all stone wall obtuseness from every Barrayaran clerk, secretary, embassy officer and bureaucrat I encountered. For a while, I thought I was going mad. At last, I became reconciled to my despair."

"The medications helped, too, I thought, sir," Muno observed amiably. Gustioz glowered at him.

"But *you* are not escaping me," Gustioz continued to Enrique. "One bag. Now."

"You can't just barge in here and take him away, with no warning or anything!" Kareen protested.

"Do you have any idea the effort and attention I had to expend to assure that he was *not* warned?" said Gustioz.

"But we *need* Enrique! He's *everything* to our new

company! He's our entire research and development department. Without Enrique, there will never be any Barrayaran-vegetation-eating butter bugs!"

Without Enrique, they would have no nascent bug butter industry—her shares would be worth nothing. All her summer's work, all Mark's frantic organizational efforts, would be flushed down the drain. No profits—no income—no adult independence—no hot slippery fun sex with Mark—nothing but debts, and dishonor, and a bunch of smug family members all lining up to say *I told you so* . . . "You can't take him!"

"On the contrary, miss," said Officer Gustioz, gathering up his stack of flimsies, "I can and I will."

"But what will happen to Enrique on Escobar?" asked Martya.

"Trial," said Gustioz in a voice of ghoulish satisfaction, "followed by jail, I devoutly pray. For a long, long time. I hope they append court costs. The comptroller is going to scream when I turn in my travel vouchers. It will be like a vacation, my supervisor said. You'll be back in two weeks, she said. I haven't seen my wife and family in two months . . ."

"But that's utterly wasteful," said Martya indignantly. "Why shut him up in a box on Escobar, when he could be doing humanity some real good *here*?" She was calculating the rapidly dwindling value of her shares too, Kareen guessed.

"That is between Dr. Borgos and his irate creditors," Gustioz told her. "I'm just doing my job. Finally."

Enrique looked terribly distressed. "But who will take care of all my poor little girls? You don't understand!"

Gustioz hesitated, and said in a disturbed tone, "There was no reference to any dependents in my orders." He stared in confusion at Kareen and Martya.

Martya said, "How did you get in here, anyway? How did you get past the ImpSec gate guard?"

Gustioz brandished his rumpled folder. "Page by page. It took forty minutes."

"He insisted on checking every one," Sergeant Muno explained.

Martya said urgently to the maid, "Where's Pym?"

"Gone with Lord Vorkosigan, miss."

"Jankowski?"

"Him, too."

"Anyone?"

"All the rest are gone with m'lord and m'lady."

"Damn! What about Roic?"

"He's sleeping, Miss."

"Fetch him down here."

"He won't like being waked up off-duty, miss . . ." the maid said nervously.

"Fetch him!"

Reluctantly, the maid started to drag herself out.

"Muno," said Gustioz, who'd watched this by-play with growing unease, "now." He gestured at Enrique.

"Yes, sir." Muno gripped Enrique by the elbow.

Martya grabbed Enrique's other arm. "No! Wait! You can't take him!"

Gustioz frowned at the retreating maid. "Let's go, Muno."

Muno pulled. Martya pulled back. Enrique cried, "Ow!" Kareen grabbed the first weaponlike object that came to her hand, a metal meter stick, and circled in. Gustioz tucked his folder of flimsies up under his arm and reached to detach Martya.

"Hurry!" Kareen screeched at the maid, and tried to trip Muno by thrusting the meter stick between his knees. The whole mob was circling around the stretching Enrique as the pivot-point, and she succeeded. Muno released Enrique, who fell toward Martya and Gustioz. In a wild attempt to regain his balance, Muno's hand came down hard on the corner of the bug hutch peeping over the lab bench.

The stainless steel box flipped into the air. One-hundred-ninety-two astonished brown-and-silver butter bugs were launched in a vast chittering madly fluttering trajectory out over the lab. Since butter bugs had the aerodynamic capacity of tiny bricks, they rained down upon the struggling humans, and crunch-squished underfoot. The hutch clanged to the floor, along with Muno. Gustioz, attempting to shield himself from this unexpected air assault, lost his grip on his folder;

colorfully-stamped documents joined butter bugs in fluttering flight. Enrique howled like a man possessed. Muno just screamed, frantically batted bugs off himself, and tried to climb up on the lab stool.

"Now see what you've done!" Kareen yelled at the Escobaran officers. "Vandalism! Assault! Destruction of property! Destruction of a *Vor lord's* property, on Barrayar itself! Are you in trouble now!"

"Ack!" cried Enrique, trying to stand on tiptoe to reduce the carnage below. "My girls! My poor girls! Watch where you put your *feet*, you mindless murderers!"

The queen, who due to her weight had had a shorter trajectory, scuttled away under the lab bench.

"What are those horrible things?" yipped Muno, from his perch on the teetering stool.

"Poison bugs," Martya informed him venomously. "New Barrayaran secret weapon. Everywhere they touch you, your flesh will swell up, turn black, and fall off." She made a valiant attempt to introduce a chittering bug down Muno's trousers or collar, but he fended her off.

"They are not!" Enrique denied indignantly, from tiptoe.

Gustioz was down on the floor furiously gathering up flimsies and trying not to touch or be touched by the scattering butter bugs. When he rose, his face was scarlet. "Sergeant!" he bellowed. "Get down from there! Seize the prisoner! We leave *at once*."

Muno, overcoming his startlement and a little sheepish to be discovered in high retreat by his comrade, stepped carefully off the stool and grabbed Enrique in a more professional come-along style. He bundled Enrique out the lab door as Gustioz scooped up the last of his flimsies and jammed them back any-which-way into his folder.

"What about my one bag?" wailed Enrique, as Muno began to march him down the hall.

"I will buy you a damned toothbrush at the shuttleport," panted Gustioz, scrambling after. "And a change of underwear. I will buy them from my own pocket. Anything, but out, out!"

Kareen and her sister both hit the door at once, and

had to sort themselves out. They stumbled into the corridor as their future biotech fortune was dragged away down it, still protesting that butter bugs were harmless and beneficial symbiotes. "We can't let him get away!" cried Martya.

A stack of bug butter tubs tumbled over on Kareen as she regained her balance, thumping off her head and shoulders and thudding to the floor. "Ow!" She caught a couple of the kilogram-plus cartons, and stared after the retreating men. She zeroed in on the back of Gustioz's head, hoisted a tub in her right hand, and drew back. Martya, fending off cascading tubs from the other wall, stared at her with widening eyes, nodded understanding, and took a similar grip on a missile of her own.

"Ready," gasped Kareen, "Aim—"

CHAPTER NINETEEN

It didn't take ImpSec less than two minutes to arrive at Lord Auditor Vorthys's residence; it took them almost four minutes. Ekaterin, who'd heard the front door open, wondered if it would be considered rude of her to point this out to the stern-featured young captain who mounted the stairs, followed by a husky and humorless-looking sergeant. No matter: Vassily, watched by an increasingly irritated Hugo, was still calling blandishments and imprecations in vain through the locked door. A long silence had fallen in the room beyond.

Both men turned and stared in shock at these new arrivals. "Who did he *call?*" muttered Vassily.

The ImpSec officer ignored them both, and turned to give a polite salute to Aunt Vorthys, whose eyes widened only briefly. "Madame Professora Vorthys." He extended his nod to Ekaterin. "Madame Vorsoisson. Please forgive this intrusion. I was informed there was an altercation here. My Imperial master requests and requires me to detain all present."

"I believe I understand, Captain, ah, Sphaleros, isn't it?" said Aunt Vorthys faintly.

"Yes, ma'am." He ducked his head at her, and turned to Hugo and Vassily. "Identify yourselves, please."

Hugo found his voice first. "My name is Hugo Vorvayne. I'm this lady's elder brother." He gestured at Ekaterin.

Vassily came automatically to attention, his gaze riveted to the ImpSec Horus eyes on the captain's collar. "Lieutenant Vassily Vorsoisson. Presently assigned to OrbTrafCon, Fort Kithera River. I am Nikki Vorsoisson's guardian. Captain, I'm very sorry, but I'm afraid you've had some sort of false alarm."

Hugo put in uneasily, "It was very wrong of him, I'm sure, but it was only a nine-year-old boy, sir, who was upset about a domestic matter. Not a real emergency. We'll make him apologize."

"That's not my affair, sir. I have my orders." He turned to the door, pulled a small slip of flimsy from his sleeve, glanced at a hastily scrawled note thereupon, tucked it away, and rapped smartly on the wood. "Master Nikolai Vorsoisson?"

Nikki's voice returned, "Who is it?"

"Ground-Captain Sphaleros, ImpSec. You are requested to accompany me."

The lock scraped; the door swung open. Nikki, looking both triumphant and terrified, stared up at the officer, and down at the lethal weapons holstered at his hip. "Yessir," he croaked.

"Please come this way." He gestured down the stairs; the sergeant stepped aside.

Vassily almost wailed, "Why am I being arrested? I haven't done anything wrong!"

"You are not being arrested, sir," the ground-captain explained patiently. "You are being detained for questioning." He turned to Aunt Vorthys and added, "*You*, of course, are not detained, ma'am. But my Imperial Master earnestly invites you to accompany your niece."

Aunt Vorthys touched her lips, her eyes alight with curiosity. "I believe I shall, Captain. Thank you."

The captain nodded sharply to the sergeant, who hastened to offer Aunt Vorthys his arm down the stairs. Nikki slipped around Vassily, and grabbed Ekaterin's hand in a painfully tight grip.

"But," said Hugo, "but, but, *why?*"

"I was not told why, sir," said the captain, in a tone devoid of either apology or concern. He unbent just enough to add, "You'll have to ask when you get there, I suppose."

Ekaterin and Nikki followed Aunt Vorthys and the sergeant; Hugo and Vassily perforce joined the parade. At the bottom of the stairs Ekaterin glanced down at Nikki's bare feet and yipped, "Shoes! Nikki, where are your shoes?" A brief delay followed while she galloped rapidly around the downstairs and found one under her aunt's comconsole and the other by the kitchen door. Ekaterin clutched them both in her hand as they exited the front door.

A large, unmarked, shiny black aircar sat impressively wedged into a narrow area on the sidewalk, one corner crushing a small bed of marigolds, the other barely missing a sycamore tree. The sergeant helped both ladies and Nikki to seats in the rear compartment, and stood aside to oversee Hugo and Vassily climb in. The captain joined them. The sergeant slid into the front compartment with the driver, and the vehicle lurched abruptly into the air, scattering a few leaves and twigs and bark shreds from the sycamore. The car spun away at high speed at an altitude reserved for emergency vehicles, passing a lot closer to the tops of buildings than Ekaterin was used to flying.

Before Vassily had overcome his hyperventilation enough to even form the question, *Where are you taking us?*, and just as Ekaterin managed to get Nikki's feet stuffed into his shoes and the catch-strips firmly fastened, they arrived over Vorhartung Castle. The gardens around it were colorful and luxuriant with high summer growth; the river gleamed and burbled in the steep valley below. Counts' banners, indicating the Council was in session, snapped in bright rows on the battlements. Ekaterin found herself searching eagerly over Nikki's head for a brown-and-silver flag. Heavens, there it was, the silver leaf-and-mountain pattern shimmering in the sun. The parking lots and circles were all jammed. Armsmen in half a hundred different District liveries, brilliant as great birds, sat or leaned chatting among their vehicles. The ImpSec aircar came down neatly in a large, miraculously open space right by a side door.

A familiar middle-aged man in Gregor Vorbarra's own livery stood waiting. A tech waved a security scanner over each of them, even Nikki. With the captain bringing up the rear, the liveried man whisked them through two narrow corridors and past a number of guards whose arms and armor owed nothing to history and everything to technology. He ushered them into a small paneled room containing a holovid-conference table, a comconsole, a coffee machine, and very little else.

The liveried man circled the table, directing the visitors to stand behind chairs: "You, sir, you, sir, you young sir, you ma'am." He held out a chair only for Aunt Vorthys, murmuring, "If you would be pleased to sit, Madame Professora Vorthys." He glanced over his arrangements, nodded satisfaction, and ducked out a smaller door in the other wall.

"Where *are* we?" Ekaterin whispered to her aunt.

"I've never actually been in this room before, but I *believe* we are directly behind the Emperor's dais in the Counts' Chamber," she whispered back.

"He *said*," Nikki mumbled in a faintly guilty tone, "that this all sounded too complicated for him to sort out over the comconsole."

"*Who* said that, Nikki?" asked Hugo nervously.

Ekaterin glanced past him as the smaller door opened again. Emperor Gregor, also wearing his own Vorbarra House livery today, stepped through, smiled gravely at her, and nodded at Nikki. "Pray do not get up, Professora," he added in a soft voice, as she made to rise. Vassily and Hugo, both looking utterly pole-axed, came to military attention. He added aside, "Thank you, Captain Sphaleros. You may return to your duty station now."

The captain saluted and withdrew. Ekaterin wondered if he would ever find out why this bizarre transport duty had fallen upon him, or if the day's events would forever be a mystery to him.

Gregor's liveried man, who had followed him in, held out the chair at the head of the table for his master, who remarked, "Please be seated," to his guests as he sank down.

"My apologies," Gregor addressed them generally, "for your rather abrupt translocation, but I really can't absent myself from these proceedings just now. They may stop dragging their feet out there at any moment. I hope." He tented his hands on the table before him. "Now, if someone will please explain to me why Nikki thought he was being kidnapped against his mother's will?"

"Entirely against my will," Ekaterin stated, for the record.

Gregor raised his brows at Vassily. Vassily appeared paralyzed. Gregor added encouragingly, "Succinctly, if you please, Lieutenant."

His military discipline rescued Vassily from his stasis. "Yes, Sire," he stammered out. "I was told— Lieutenant Alexi Vormoncrief called me early this morning to tell me that if Lord Richars Vorrutyer obtained his Countship today, he was going to lay a charge of murder in Council against Lord Miles Vorkosigan for the death of my cousin Tien. Alexi said— Alexi feared that some considerable disruption in the capital would follow. I was afraid for Nikki's safety, and came to remove him to a safer location till things . . . things settled down."

Gregor tapped his lips. "And was this your own idea, or did Alexi suggest it?"

"I . . ." Vassily hesitated, and frowned. "Actually, Alexi did suggest it."

"I see." Gregor glanced up at his liveried man, standing waiting by the wall, and said in a crisper tone, "Gerard, take a note. This is the third time this month that the busy Lieutenant Vormoncrief has come to my negative attention in matters touching political concerns. Remind Us to find him a post somewhere in the Empire where he may be less busy."

"Yes, Sire," murmured Gerard. He didn't write anything down, but Ekaterin doubted he needed to. It didn't take a memory chip to remember the things that Gregor said; you just *did*.

"Lieutenant Vorsoisson," said Gregor briskly, "I'm

afraid that gossip and rumor are staples of the capital scene. Sorting truth from lies supplies full-time and steady work for a surprising number of my ImpSec personnel. I believe they do it well. My ImpSec analysts are of the professional opinion that the slander against Lord Vorkosigan grew not from the events on Komarr—of which I am fully apprised—but was a later invention of a group of, hm, disaffected is too strong a term, disgruntled men sharing a certain political agenda that they believed would be served by his embarrassment."

Gregor let Vassily and Hugo digest this for a moment, and continued, "Your panic is premature. Even *I* don't know which way today's vote is going to fall out. But you may rest assured, Lieutenant, that my hand is held in protection over your relatives. No harm will be permitted to befall the members of Lord Auditor Vorthys's household. Your concern is laudable but not necessary." His voice grew a shade cooler. "Your gullibility is less laudable. Correct it, please."

"Yes, Sire," squeaked Vassily. He was bug-eyed by now. Nikki grinned shyly at Gregor. Gregor acknowledged him with nothing so broad as a wink, merely a slight widening of his eyes. Nikki hunkered down in satisfaction in his chair.

Ekaterin jumped as a knock sounded from the door to the hallway. The liveried man went to answer it. After a low conversation, he stepped aside to admit another ImpSec officer, this time a major in undress greens. Gregor looked up, and gestured him to his side. The man glanced around at Gregor's odd guests, and bent to murmur in the Emperor's ear.

"All right," said Gregor, and "All right," and then, "It's about time. Good. Bring him directly here." The officer nodded and hurried back out.

Gregor smiled around at them all. The Professora smiled back sunnily, and Ekaterin shyly. Hugo smiled too, helplessly, but he looked dazed. Gregor did have that effect on people meeting him for the first time, Ekaterin was reminded.

"I'm afraid," said Gregor, "that I am about to be rather busy for a time. Nikki, I assure you that no one is going to carry you off from your mother today." His eyes flicked to Ekaterin as he said this, and he added a tiny nod just for her. "I should be pleased to hear your further concerns after this Council session. Armsman Gerard will find you places to watch from the gallery; Nikki may find it educational." Ekaterin wasn't sure if this was an invitation or a command, but it was certainly irresistible. He turned a hand palm up. They all scrambled to their feet, except for Aunt Vorthys who was decorously assisted by the Armsman. Gerard gestured them courteously toward the door.

Gregor leaned over and added in a lower voice to Vassily, just before he turned to go, "Madame Vorsoisson has my full trust, Lieutenant; I recommend you give her yours."

Vassily managed something that sounded like *urkSire!* They shuffled out into the hallway. Hugo could not have stared at his sister in greater astonishment if she'd sprouted a second head.

Partway down the narrow hall, they had to go single file as they met the major coming back. Ekaterin was startled to see he was escorting a desperately strung-out looking Byerly Vorrutyer. By was unshaven, and his expensive-looking evening garb rumpled and stained. His eyes were puffy and bloodshot, but his brows quirked with recognition as he passed her, and he managed an ironic little half-bow at her, his hand spread over his heart, without breaking stride.

Hugo's head turned, and he stared at By's lanky, retreating form. "You know that odd fellow?" he asked.

"One of my suitors," Ekaterin replied instantly, deciding to turn the opportunity to good account. "Byerly Vorrutyer. Cousin to both Dono *and* Richars. Impoverished, imprudent, and impervious to put-downs, but very witty . . . if you care for a certain nasty type of humor."

Leaving Hugo to unravel the hint that there might be worse hazards to befall an unprotected widow than the regard of a certain undersized Count's heir, she followed the Armsman into what was evidently a private lift-tube. It carried the party to the second floor and

another narrow hallway, which ended in a discreet door
to the gallery. An ImpSec guard stood by it; another
occupied a matching cross-fire position at the back of
the gallery's far side.

The gallery overlooking the Council chamber was
about three-quarters full, rumbling with low-voiced conversations among the well-dressed women and the men
in green Service uniforms or neat suits. Ekaterin felt
suddenly shabby and conspicuous in her mourning
black, particularly when Gregor's Armsman cleared
spaces in the center of the front row for them by
politely, but without explanation, requesting five young
gentlemen there to shift. None offered a protest to a
man in *that* livery. She smiled apologetically at them as
they filed out past her; they regarded her curiously in
turn. She placed Nikki securely between herself and
Aunt Vorthys. Hugo and Vassily sat on her right.

"Have you ever been here before?" Vassily whispered,
staring around as wide-eyed as Nikki was.

"No," said Ekaterin.

"I was here once on a school tour, years ago," confessed Hugo. "The Council wasn't in session, of course."

Only Aunt Vorthys appeared undaunted by their surroundings, but then, she'd visited Vorhartung Castle's
archives fairly frequently in her capacity as a historian
even before Uncle Vorthys had been appointed an
Imperial Auditor.

Eagerly, Ekaterin scanned the Council floor, spread
out below her like a stage. In full session, the scene was
colorful in the extreme, with all the Counts in the most
elegant versions of their House liveries. She searched
the rainbow-cacophony for a small figure in a uniform
of, by comparison with some, subdued and tasteful
brown and silver . . . there! Miles was just getting up
from his desk, in the front row on the curve to
Ekaterin's right. She gripped the balcony rail, her lips
parting, but he did not look up.

It was unthinkable to call out to him, even though
no one occupied the Speaker's Circle just now; interjections from the gallery were not permitted while the
Council was in session, nor were anyone but the Counts

and whatever witnesses they might call allowed onto the floor. Miles moved easily among his powerful colleagues, walking over to René Vorbretten's desk for some conference. However tricky it had been for Aral Vorkosigan to thrust his damaged heir into this assembly, all those years ago, they'd evidently grown used to him by now. Change *was* possible.

René, glancing up at the gallery, saw her first, and drew Miles's attention upward. Miles's face lifted toward her, and his eyes widened in a mixture of delight, confusion, and, as he took in Hugo and Vassily, concern. Ekaterin dared a reassuring wave, just a little spread of her open hand in front of her chest, quickly refolded in her lap. Miles returned her the odd lazy salute that he used to convey an astonishing array of editorial comment; in this case, a wary irony atop a deep respect. His gaze swept on to meet Aunt Vorthys's; his brows rose in hopeful inquiry, and he gave her a nod of greeting, which she returned. His lips turned up.

Richars Vorrutyer, talking to a Count in the front row of desks, saw Miles's salute of greeting and followed it up to the gallery. Richars was already wearing the blue-and-gray garb of his House, a Count's full livery, taking a lot for granted, Ekaterin thought with sharp disapproval. After a moment, recognition dawned in his eyes, and he frowned malevolently up at her. She frowned back coldly at this coauthor, at the very least, of her current crisis. *I know your type. I'm not afraid of you.*

Gregor had not yet returned to his dais from his private conference room; what were he and Byerly talking about back there? Dono, she realized as her eye inventoried the men below, was not here yet. That energetic figure would stand out in any crowd, even this one. Was there a secret reason for Richars's obnoxious confidence?

But just as a knot of alarm began to grow in her chest, dozens of faces below swiveled around toward the doors to the chamber. Directly beneath her, a party of men walked out onto the council floor. Even from this angle of view, she recognized the bearded Lord Dono.

He wore a blue-and-gray Vorrutyer House cadet's uniform, near-twin to the one Richars wore, but more nicely
calculated, its fittings and decorations those of a Count's
heir. Disturbingly, Lord Dono was limping, moving stiffly
as though in some lingering pain. To her surprise, Ivan
Vorpatril strode in with them. She was less certain of
the other four men, though she recognized some of
their liveries.

"Aunt Vorthys!" she whispered. "Who are all the
Counts with Dono?"

Aunt Vorthys was sitting up with a surprised and
puzzled look on her face. "The one with the mane
of white hair in the blue and gold is Falco Vorpatril.
The younger one is Vorfolse, that very odd fellow
from the South Coast, you know. The elderly gentleman with the cane is, good heavens, Count Vorhalas
himself. The other one is Count Vorkalloner. Next to
Vorhalas, he's considered the stiffest old stick in the
Conservative Party. I expect they are the votes everyone was waiting for. Things ought to start to move
now."

Ekaterin searched for Miles's response. His relief at
the appearance of Lord Dono plainly warred with dismay at the arrival of Richars's most powerful supporters, in force. Ivan Vorpatril detached himself from the
group and sauntered over to René's desk, the most
peculiar smirk on his face. Ekaterin sat back, her heart
thumping anxiously, trying desperately to decode the
interplay below even though only a few words of the
low-voiced buzz around the desks floated up intelligi-
bly to her ear.

Ivan took a moment to savor the look of complete
crogglement on his cousin the Imperial-Auditor-I'm-In-
Charge-Here's face. *Yes, I bet you're having trouble figuring this one out.* He ought, he supposed, to feel guilty
for not taking a moment in the frantic runnings-around
early this morning to give Miles a quick comconsole call
and let him know what was coming down, but really,
it had been too late by then for Miles to make a difference anyway. For a few seconds more, Ivan was one

step ahead of Miles in his own game. *Enjoy.* René Vorbretten was looking equally confused, however, and Ivan had no score to settle with him. Enough.

Miles looked up at his cousin with an expression of mixed delight and fury. "Ivan you idi—" he began.

"*Don't* . . . say it." Ivan raised a hand to cut him off before his rant was fairly launched. "I just saved your ass, again. And what thanks do I get, again? None. Nothing but abuse and scorn. My humble lot in life."

"Pym reported you were bringing in Dono. For which I do thank you," said Miles through set teeth. "But what the hell did you bring *them* for?" He jerked his head at the four Conservative Counts, now filing across the chamber toward Boriz Vormoncrief's desk.

"Watch," murmured Ivan.

As Count Vorhalas came even with Richars's desk, Richars sat up and smiled at him. "About time, sir! Am I glad to see you!"

Richars smile faded as Vorhalas walked past him without so much as turning his head in Richars's direction; Richars might have been invisible, for all the note Vorhalas took of this greeting. Vorkalloner, following close on the heels of his senior, at least gave Richars a frown, recognition of sorts.

Ivan held his breath in happy anticipation.

Richars tried again, as the snowy-haired Falco Vorpatril stumped by. "Glad you made it, sir . . . ?"

Falco stopped, and stared coldly down at him. In a voice which, while pitched low, penetrated perfectly well to the far ends of the floor, Falco said, "Not for long, you won't be. There is an unwritten rule among us, Richars; if you attempt any ploy on the far side of ethical, you'd damned well better be good enough at your game not to get caught. You're not good enough." With a snort, he followed his fellows.

Vorfolse, passing last, hissed furiously at Richars, "How dare you try to draw me into your schemes by using *my* premises to mount your attack? I'll see you taken apart for this." He marched on after Falco, distancing himself from Richars in every way.

Miles's eyes were wide, his lips parted in growing

appreciation. "Busy night, was it, Ivan?" he breathed, taking in Dono's limp.

"You would not believe."

"Try me."

In a rapid undervoice, Ivan filled in both Miles and the startled René. "The short version is, a gang of paid thugs tried to reverse Dono's Betan surgery with a vibra knife. Jumped us coming out of Vorfolse's place. They had a nice plan for taking out Dono's Armsmen, but Olivia Koudelka and I weren't on their list. We took them instead, and I delivered them and the evidence to Falco and old Vorhalas, and let them take it from there. No one, of course, bothered to inform Richars; we left him in a news blackout. Richars may wish he had that vibra knife to use on his own throat before today is done."

Miles pursed his lips. "Proof? Richars has to have worked through multiple layers of middlemen for something like this. If he really had practice on Pierre's fiancée, he's damned sly. Laying the trail to his door won't be easy."

René added more urgently, "How fast can we get our hands on evidence?"

"It would have been weeks, but Richars's stirrup-man has turned Imperial Witness." Ivan inhaled, at the top of his triumph.

Miles tilted his head. "Richars's stirrup-man?"

"Byerly Vorrutyer. He apparently helped Richars set it all up. But things went wrong. Richars's hired goons were tailing Dono, supposed to jump him when he arrived at Vorsmythe House, but they saw what they thought was a better opportunity at Vorfolse's. By was having foaming fits when he finally caught up with me, just before dawn. Didn't know where all his pawns had gone, poor hysterical mastermind. *I'd* captured 'em. First time I've ever seen By Vorrutyer at a loss for words." Ivan grinned in satisfaction. "Then ImpSec arrived and took him away."

"How . . . unexpected. That's not how I'd placed Byerly in this game at all." Miles's brow furrowed.

"I thought you were too damned trusting. There was

something about By that didn't add up for me from the beginning, but I just couldn't put my finger on it—"

Vorhalas and his cronies were now clustered around Boriz Vormoncrief's desk. Vorfolse seemed to be the most emphatic, gesturing angrily, with occasional glances over his shoulder at Richars, who was watching the scene with alarm. Vormoncrief's jaw set, and he frowned deeply. He shook his head twice. Young Sigur looked horrified; unconsciously, his hands closed protectively in his lap and his legs squeezed closed.

All the *sotto voce* debates ended when Emperor Gregor stepped out of the small doorway behind the dais, and mounted it to take his seat again. He motioned to the Lord Guardian of the Speaker's Circle, who hurried over to him. They conferred briefly. The Lord Guardian's gaze swept the room; he walked over to Ivan.

"Lord Vorpatril." He nodded politely. "Time to clear the floor. Gregor's about to call the vote. Unless you are to be called as a witness, you must take a seat in the gallery now."

"Right-ho," Ivan said genially. Miles exchanged a thumb's-up with René, and hurried back to his desk; Ivan turned for the door.

Ivan walked slowly past the Vorrutyer's District desk, where Dono was saying cheerfully to Richars, "Move over, sport. Your thugs missed, last night. Lord Vorbohn's municipal guardsmen will be waiting for you by the door with open arms when this vote is over."

With extreme reluctance, Richars shifted to the far end of the bench. Dono plopped down and crossed his booted legs—at the ankles, Ivan noted—and spread his elbows comfortably.

Richars snarled under his breath, "So you may wish. But Vorbohn will have no jurisdiction over me when I take the Countship. And Vorkosigan's party will be so convulsed over *his* crimes, they'll have no chance to throw stones at me."

"Stones, Richars, darling?" Dono purred back. "You should be so lucky. I foresee a landslide—with you under it."

Leaving the Vorrutyer family reunion behind, Ivan made for the double doors, which the guards opened for him. A job well done, by God. He glanced over his shoulder as he reached them, to find Gregor staring at him. The Emperor favored him with a faint smile, and the barest hint of a nod.

It didn't make him feel gratified. It made him feel *naked*. Too late, he recalled Miles's dictum that the reward for a job well done was usually a harder job. For a moment, in the hall beyond the chamber, he considered an impulse to turn right for the exit to the gardens instead of left for the stairs to the gallery. But he wouldn't miss this denouement for worlds. He climbed the stairs.

"Fire!" cried Kareen.

Two bug butter tubs sailed in high trajectories down the hallway. Kareen expected them to go *thud* on their targets, like rocks only a little more resilient. But all the tubs on the tops of the stacks were Mark's new bargain supply, bought *on sale* somewhere. The cheaper, thinner plastic didn't have the structural integrity of the earlier tubs. They didn't hit like rocks; they hit like grenades.

Upon impact with Muno's shoulders and the back of Gustioz's head, the rupturing tubs spewed bug butter on the walls, ceiling, floor, and incidentally the targets. Since the second barrage was already in the air before the first one landed, the surprised Escobarans turned around just in time to take the next bug butter bombs full in the chest. Muno's reflexes were quick enough to fend off a third tub, which burst on the floor, kneecapping the entire party with white, dripping bug butter.

Martya, wildly excited, was now keening in a sort of berserker howl, firing more tubs down the corridor as fast as she could grab them. The tubs didn't all rupture; some hit with quite satisfying thunks. Muno, swearing, batted down a couple more, but was baited into releasing Enrique long enough to snatch a couple of tubs from the stacks on their end of the corridor and heave them back at the Koudelka sisters. Martya ducked the tub aimed at her; the second exploded at Kareen's feet. Muno's attempt to lay down a covering fire for his party's retreat backfired when Enrique dropped to his knees and scrambled away down the hall toward his screaming Valkyriesque protectors.

"Back in the lab," cried Kareen, "and lock the door! We can call for help from there!"

The door at the far end of the corridor, beyond the Escobaran invaders, banged open. Kareen's heart lifted, momentarily, as Armsman Roic staggered through. Reinforcements! Roic was fetchingly attired in boots, briefs, and a stunner holster on backwards. "What t' hell—?" he began, but was interrupted as a last unfortunate round of friendly fire, launched unaimed by Martya, burst on his chest.

"Oh, sorry!" she called through cupped hands.

"What the *hell* is going on down here?" Roic bellowed, scrabbling for his stunner on the wrong side of his holster with hands slippery from their coating of bug butter. "You woke me up! 'S the *third time* somebody's woke me up this morning! I'd *just got to sleep.* 'Swore I'd *kill* the next sonuvabitch who woke me up—!"

Kareen and Martya clung together for a moment of pure aesthetic appreciation of the height, the breadth of shoulder, the bass reverberation, the generous serving of athletic young male Roic presented; Martya sighed. The Escobarans, naturally, had no idea who this giant naked screaming barbarian was who'd appeared between them and the only exit route they knew. They retreated a few steps backward.

Kareen cried urgently, "Roic, they're trying to kidnap Enrique!"

"Yeah? Good." Roic squinted blearily at her. "Make sure they pack all his devil bugs along with him . . ."

The panicked Gustioz tried to lunge past Roic toward the door, but caromed off him instead. They both slipped in the bug butter and went down in an arcing flurry of highly official documentation. Roic's trained, if sleep-deprived, reflexes cut in, and he attempted to pin his accidental assailant to the floor, not easy given that they were both now coated with quantities of lubricant. The faithful Muno, in a crouching scramble, braved another barrage of bug butter tubs to grab again for Enrique, making contact with a flailing arm trying to bat him away. They both skidded and went down on the treacherous footing. But Muno got a good grip on one of Enrique's ankles, and began sliding him back up the corridor.

"You can't stop us!" panted Gustioz, half under Roic. "I have a proper warrant!"

"Mister, I don't *want* to stop you!" yelled Roic.

Kareen and Martya dove to grab Enrique's arms, and pulled in the other direction. Since nobody had any traction, the contest was momentarily inconclusive. Kareen risked letting go of an arm, and hopped around Enrique to place a well-aimed kick to Muno's wrist; he howled and recoiled. The two women and the scientist scrambled over each other and back through the laboratory door. Martya got it jammed shut and locked just before Muno's shoulder banged into it from the other side.

"Comconsole!" she gasped over her shoulder to her sister. "Call Lord Mark! Call *somebody*!"

Kareen knuckled bug butter from her eyes, dove for the station chair, and began tapping in Mark's personal code.

Miles twisted his head around and watched, hopelessly out of earshot, as Ivan arrived in the front row of the gallery and ruthlessly evicted an unfortunate ensign. The younger officer, outranked and outweighed, reluctantly gave up his prime spot and went off searching for standing room in the back. Ivan slid in beside Professora Vorthys and Ekaterin. A low-voiced conversation ensued; from Ivan's expansive gestures and self-satisfied smirk, Miles guessed he was favoring the ladies with an account of his last night's heroic adventures.

Dammit, if I had been there, I could have saved Lord Dono just as well . . . Or maybe not.

Miles had recognized Ekaterin's brother Hugo and Vassily Vorsoisson, flanking her on the other side, from their brief encounter at Tien's funeral. Had they arrived in town to harass Ekaterin about Nikki again? Now, listening to Ivan, they looked thoroughly taken aback. Ekaterin said something fierce. Ivan laughed uneasily, then turned around to wave at Olivia Koudelka, just taking a seat in the back row. It wasn't fair for someone who'd been up all night to look that fresh. She'd changed clothes, from last night's party dress into a loose silk suit featuring fashionable Komarran-style trousers. Judging from her wave and smile, at least she hadn't been injured in the fight. Nikki asked an excited question, which the Professora answered; she stared down coolly and without approval at the back of Richars Vorrutyer's head.

What the devil was Ekaterin's whole family doing up there with her? How had she persuaded Hugo and Vassily to cooperate with this visit? And what hand did Gregor have in it? Miles swore he'd seen a Vorbarra Armsman, turning away after escorting them to their seats. . . . On the floor of the Council, the Lord Guardian of the Speaker's Circle banged the butt of a cavalry spear bearing the Vorbarra pennon onto the wooden plaque set in the floor for that purpose. The *clack-clack* echoed through the chamber. No time now to dash up to the gallery and find out what was going on. Miles tore his attention from Ekaterin, and prepared to tend to business. The business that would decide if they were both to be plunged into dream or nightmare. . . . The Lord Guardian called out, "My Imperial Master recognizes Count Vormoncrief. Come forward and make your petition, my lord."

Count Boriz Vormoncrief stood up, patted his son-in-law on the shoulder, and strode forward to take his place in the Speaker's Circle under the colorful windows, facing the semi-circle of his fellow Counts. He made a short, formal plea for the recognition of Sigur as the rightful heir to the Vorbretten's District, with reference to René's gene scan evidence, already circulated among his colleagues well before this vote. He made no comment on Richars's case, waiting in the queue. A shift from alliance to distancing, yes by God! Richars's face, as he listened, was set and stolid. Boriz stood down.

The Lord Guardian banged the spear butt again. "My Imperial Master recognizes Count Vorbretten. Come forward and claim your right of rebuttal to this petition, my lord."

René stood up at his desk. "My Lord Guardian, I yield the Circle temporarily to Lord Dono Vorrutyer." He sat again.

A little murmur of commentary rose from the floor. Everyone followed the swap and its logic; to Miles's deep and concealed satisfaction, Richars seemed taken by surprise. Dono stood, limped forward into the Speaker's Circle, and turned to confront the assembled Counts of Barrayar. A brief white grin flashed in his beard. Miles followed his glance up into the gallery just in time to see Olivia standing on her seat and making a sweeping thumb's-up gesture.

"Sire, My Lord Guardian, my lords." Dono moistened his lips, and launched into the formal wording of his petition for the Countship of the Vorrutyer's District. He reminded all present that they had received certified copies of his complete medical report and the witnessed affidavits to his new gender. Briefly, he reiterated his arguments of right by male primogeniture, Count's Choice, and his prior experience assisting his late brother Pierre in the administration of the Vorrutyer's District.

Lord Dono stood legs apart, hands clasped behind the small of his back in an assertive stance, and raised his chin. "As some of you know by now, last night someone attempted to take this decision from you. To decide the future of Barrayar not in this Council Chamber, but in the back streets. I was attacked; luckily, I escaped serious injury. My assailants are now in the hands of Lord Vorbohn's guard, and a witness has given evidence sufficient for the arrest of my cousin Richars for suspicion of conspiracy to commit this mutilation. Vorbohn's men await him outside. Richars will depart this chamber either into their arresting arms, or placed by you above their jurisdiction—in which case, judgment of the crime *will* fall upon you later.

"Government by thugs in the Bloody Centuries gave Barrayar many colorful historical incidents, suitable for high drama. I don't think it's a drama we wish to return to in real life. I stand before you ready and willing to serve my Emperor, the Imperium, my District, and its people. I also stand for the rule of law." He gave a grave nod toward Count Vorhalas, who nodded back. "Gentlemen, over to you." Dono stood down.

Years ago—before Miles was born—one of Count Vorhalas's sons had been executed for dueling. The Count had chosen not to raise his banner in rebellion over it, and had made it clear ever since that he expected like loyalty to the law from his peers. It was a kind of moral suasion with sharp teeth; *nobody* dared oppose Vorhalas on ethical issues. If the Conservative Party had a backbone that kept it standing upright, it was old Vorhalas. And Dono, it appeared, had just put Vorhalas in his back pocket. Or Richars had put him there for him . . . Miles hissed through his teeth in suppressed excitement. *Good pitch, Dono, good, good. Superb.*

The Lord Guardian banged his spear again, and called Richars up for his answer to Dono's petition. Richars looked shaken and angry. He strode forward to take his place in the Speaker's Circle with his lips already moving. He turned to face the chamber, took a deep breath, and launched into the formal preambles of his rebuttal.

Miles's attention was diverted by some rustling up in the gallery: more latecomers arriving. He glanced up, and his eyes widened to see his mother and father, in the row directly behind Ekaterin and the Professora, murmuring a negotiation for seats together and apologies and thanks to a startled Vor couple who instantly made way for the Viceroy and Vicereine. They'd evidently got away from their breakfast meeting in time to attend this vote, and were still formally dressed, Count Aral in the same brown-and-silver House uniform Miles wore, the Countess in a fancy embroidered beige ensemble, her red-roan hair in elaborate braids wreathing her head. Ivan craned around, looked surprised, nodded a greeting, and muttered something under his breath. The Professora, intent on hearing Richars's words, shushed him. Ekaterin hadn't looked behind her; she gripped the balcony rail and stared intently down at Richars as though willing him to pop an artery in the speech centers of his brain. But he droned on, coming to the summation of his arguments.

"That I have always been Pierre's heir is inherent in his lack of acknowledgement of any other in that place. I grant there was no love lost between us, which I always considered unfortunate, but as many of you have reason to know, Pierre was a, ah, *difficult* personality. But even he realized he could have no other successor but me.

"Dono is a sick joke of Lady Donna's, which we here have tolerated for too long. She is the very essence of the sort of galactic corruption," his glance, and his hand, flicked to mutie-Miles, as though to suggest his enemy's body was an outward and visible form of an inward and invisible poison, "against which we must fight, yes, I say fight, and I say it boldly and aloud, for our native purity. She is a breathing threat to our wives, daughters, sisters. She is an incitement to rebellion against our deepest and most fundamental order. She is an insult to the honor of the Imperium. I beg you will finish her strutting charade with the finality it deserves."

Richars glanced around, anxiously seeking signs of approval from his dauntingly impassive listeners, and continued, "With respect to Lady Donna's feeble threat to bring her claimed attack—which might in fact have come from any quarter sufficiently outraged by her posturing—onto the floor of this chamber for judgment. I say, bring it on. And who would be her stalking horse, to lay the case before you, in that event?" He made a broad gesture at Miles, sitting at his desk with his booted feet out and listening with as little expression as he could maintain. "One who stands accused of far worse crimes himself, even up to premeditated murder."

Richars was rattled; he was trying to set off his smokescreen *way* too early. It was a smoke Miles choked on all the same. *Damn you, Richars.* He could not let this pass unchallenged here, not for an instant.

"A point of order, my Lord Guardian." Not changing his posture, Miles pitched his drawl to carry across the chamber. "I am not accused; I am slandered. There is an unsubtle legal distinction between the two."

"It will be an ironic day when *you* try to lay down a criminal accusation here," Richars parried, stung, Miles hoped, by the implied threat of countersuit.

Count Vorhalas called out from his place in the back row, "In the event, Sire, my Lord Guardian, my lords, having viewed the evidence and listened to the preliminary interrogations, I should be pleased to lay the charge against Lord Richars myself."

The Lord Guardian frowned, and tapped his spear suggestively. Historically, permitting men to start speaking out of turn had quickly led to shouting matches, fist fights, and, in prior eras when weapons scanners hadn't been available, famous melees and duels to the death. But Emperor Gregor, listening with very little expression himself, made no move to intervene.

Richars was growing yet more off balance; Miles could see it in his reddening face and heavy breathing. To Miles's shock, he gestured up at Ekaterin. "It's a bold villain who can stand unashamed while his victim's own wife looks down at him—though I suppose she could hardly look up at him, eh?"

Faces turned toward the pale black-clad woman in the gallery. She looked chilled and frightened, jerked out of her safe observer's invisibility by Richars's unwelcome attention. Beside her, Nikki stiffened. Miles sat upright; it was all he could do to keep himself from launching himself across the chamber at Richars's throat and attempting to throttle him on the spot. That wouldn't work anyway. He was compelled to other means of combat, slower, but, he swore, more effective in the end. How dare Richars turn on *Ekaterin* in this public venue, invade her most private concerns, attempt to manipulate her most intimate relationships just to serve his power-grab?

Miles's anticipated nightmare of defense was here, now. Already he would be forced to turn his attention not just to truth but to appearances, to check every word out his mouth for its effect on the listeners who could become his future judges. Richars had put himself one-down through his botched attack on Dono; could he scramble back up over Miles's and Ekaterin's bodies? It seemed he was about to try.

Ekaterin's face was utterly still, but white around the lips. Some prudent back part of Miles's brain couldn't help making a note of what she looked like when she was *really* angry, for future reference. "You are mistaken, Lord Richars," she snapped down at him. "Not your first mistake, apparently."

"Am I?" Richars shot back. "Why else, then, did you flee in horror from his public proposal, if not your belated realization of his hand in your late husband's death?"

"That's no business of yours!"

"One wonders what pressures he has brought to bear since to gain your compliance . . ." His smarmy sneer invited the listeners to imagine the worst.

"Only if one is a damned fool!"

"Proof is where you find it, madame."

"That's your idea of proof?" Ekaterin snarled. "Fine. Your legal theory is easily demolished—"

The Lord Guardian banged his spear. "Interjections from the gallery are *not* permitted," he began, staring up at her.

Behind Ekaterin, the Viceroy of Sergyar stared down at the Lord Guardian, tapped his index finger suggestively against the side of his nose, and made a small two-fingered sweeping gesture taking in Richars below: *No; let him hang himself.* Ivan, glancing over his shoulder, grinned abruptly and swiveled back. The Lord Guardian's eyes flicked to Gregor, whose face bore only the faintest smile and little other cue. The Lord Guardian continued more weakly, "But direct questions from the Speaker's Circle may be answered."

Richars's questions had been more rhetorical, for effect, than direct, Miles judged. Assuming Ekaterin would be safely silenced by her position in the gallery, he hadn't expected to have to deal with direct answers. The look on Richars's face made Miles think of a man tormenting a leopardess suddenly discovering that the creature had no leash. Which way would she pounce? Miles held his breath.

Ekaterin leaned forward, gripping the railing with her knuckles going pale. "Let's finish this. Lord Vorkosigan!"

Miles jerked in his seat, taken by surprise. "Madame?" He made a little half-bow gesture. "Yours to command . . ."

"Good. Will you marry me?"

A kind of roaring, like the sea, filled Miles's head; for a moment, there were only two people in this chamber, not two hundred. If this was a ploy to impress his colleagues with his innocence, would it work? *Who cares? Seize the moment! Seize the woman! Don't let her get away again!* One side of his lip curled up, then the other; then a broad grin took over his face. He tilted toward her. "Why, *yes*, madame. Certainly. Now?"

She looked a little taken aback at the vision this perhaps conjured of his abandoning the chamber instantly, to take her up on her offer this very hour, before she could change her mind. Well, he was ready if she was. . . . She waved him down. "We'll discuss that later. Settle this business."

"My pleasure." He grinned fiercely at Richars, who was now gaping like a fish. Then he just grinned. *Two hundred witnesses. She can't back out now. . . .*

"So much for *that* line of reasoning, Lord Richars," Ekaterin finished. She sat back with a hand-dusting gesture, and added, by no means under her breath, "*Twit*."

Emperor Gregor looked decidedly amused. Nikki, beside Ekaterin, was jittering with enthusiasm, mumbling something that looked like *go-go-mama*. The gallery had broken into half-choked titters. Ivan just rubbed his mouth with the back of his hand, though his eyes were narrowed with laughter. He glanced again behind Ekaterin, where the Vicereine looked as though she was

choking, and the Viceroy turned a bark of laughter into
a discreet cough. In a sudden flush of self-consciousness,
Ekaterin shrank in her seat, hardly daring even to look
at her brother Hugo or Vassily. She looked down at
Miles, though, and her lips softened with a helpless
smile.

Miles grinned back like a loon; Richars's blackest
glare in his direction slid off him as though deflected
by a force field. Gregor made a brief gesture to the Lord
Guardian to move things along.

Richars had entirely lost the thread of his argument
by now, as well as the momentum, center stage, and the
sympathy of his audience. Anyone's attention that wasn't
fixed on Ekaterin was aimed at Miles, with an amusement grown impatient with Richars's ugly drama. Richars
finished weakly and incoherently, and left the Circle.

The Lord Guardian called the voice vote to begin.
Gregor, who fell early in the roll as Count Vorbarra,
voted *Pass* rather than an abstention, reserving the right
to cast his ballot at the end, should a deciding vote be
required, an Imperial privilege he didn't often invoke.
Miles started to track the vote, but by the time the roll
came around to him, had taken to jotting repeated
iterations of *Lady Ekaterin Nile Vorkosigan* intertwined
with *Lord Miles Naismith Vorkosigan* in his fanciest handwriting down the margins of his flimsy. René Vorbretten,
grinning, had to prompt him to the correct response,
which got another muffled laugh from the gallery.

No matter: Miles could tell when the magic majority of thirty-one had passed by the rustling that grew
on floor and gallery, as others keeping the tally concluded that Dono was in. Richars was left with a poor
showing of some dozen votes, as several of his counted-
upon Conservative supporters called abstentions in the
wake of Count Vorhalas's sturdy vote for Lord Dono.
Dono's final total was thirty-two, not exactly an overwhelming victory, but with a vote to spare above the
minimum for binding decision. Gregor, with obvious
satisfaction, cast the Vorbarra vote as an abstention,
affecting the outcome not at all.

A stunned-looking Richars climbed to his feet at the

Vorrutyer's District desk, and cried desperately, "Sire, I appeal this decision!" Really, he had no other choice; tying the case up for another round was the only move that could now save him from the municipal guard lying patiently in wait for him outside the chamber.

"Lord Richars," Gregor responded formally, "I decline to hear your appeal. My Counts have spoken; their decision stands." He nodded to the Lord Guardian, who had the chamber's sergeants-at-arms swiftly escort Richars out the doors to his waiting fate before he could recover from his shock sufficiently to burst into futile protests or physical resistance. Miles's teeth clenched in savage contentment. *Cross me, will you, Richars? You're done.*

Well . . . really, Richars had done himself, when he'd struck at Dono in the middle of the night and missed. Thanks were due to Ivan, to Olivia, and, in a back-handed way Miles supposed, to Richars's secret supporter Byerly. With friends like By, who needed enemies? And yet . . . there was something about Ivan's version of last night's events that just didn't add up right. *Later. If an Imperial Auditor can't get to the bottom of that one, no one can.* He'd start by interrogating Byerly, now presumably safely in custody of ImpSec. Or better still, maybe with . . . Miles's eyes narrowed, but he had to give over the line of thought as Dono rose again to his feet.

Count Dono Vorrutyer entered the Speaker's Circle to give calm thanks to his new colleagues, and to formally return the speaker's right to René Vorbretten. With a small, very satisfied smile, he returned to the Vorrutyer's District desk and took sole and undisputed possession. Miles was trying very hard not to crank his head over his shoulder and stare up into the gallery, but he did keep stealing little glances up Ekaterin's way. So it was he caught the moment when his mother finally leaned forward between Ekaterin and Nikki to convey her first greetings of the morning.

Ekaterin swiveled, and turned pale. Both her future parents-in-law smiled at her in perfect delight, and exchanged, Miles trusted, suitably enthusiastic welcomes.

The Professora turned too, and made some exclamation of surprise; she, however, followed it up by a handshake with the Vicereine exhibiting all the air of some secret sisterhood revealed. Miles was slightly unnerved by the older ladies' attitude of cheerful maternal conspiracy. Had intelligence been flowing in a hidden channel between their two households all this time? *What has my mother been saying about me?* He thought about trying to debrief the Vicereine later. Then he thought better of the idea.

Viceroy Vorkosigan too extended his hand, somewhat awkwardly, over Ekaterin's shoulder, and gripped her hand warmly. He glanced down past her at Miles, smiled, and made some comment that Miles was just as glad he couldn't hear. Ekaterin rose gracefully to the challenge, naturally, and introduced her brother and a nicely stunned-looking Vassily all round. Miles made the instant decision that if Vassily tried to give Ekaterin any more trouble about Nikki, Miles would throw him ruthlessly and without compunction to the Vicereine for a dose of Betan therapy that would make his head spin.

The riveting pantomime was alas interrupted when René Vorbretten rose to take his place in the Speaker's Circle. The occupants of the gallery turned their attention back to the floor of the Council. With Ekaterin's warm eyes upon him, Miles sat up and tried to look busy and effective, or at least attentive. He was sure he didn't fool his father, who knew damned well that at this point in a normal Council vote it was all over but the posturing.

René made a valiant attempt to pull his speech together, not easy after the previous rousing events. He stood by his record of ten years' faithful service in his Countship, and his grandfather's before him, and drew his colleagues' attention to his late father's military career and death in battle in the War of the Hegen Hub. He made a dignified plea for his reconfirmation, and stood down, his smile strained.

Again, the Lord Guardian called the roll, and again, Gregor passed rather than abstaining. This time, Miles managed to follow the tally. In a firm voice, Count Dono cast his very first vote ever in the name of the Vorrutyer's District.

Sigur did better than Richars's debacle, but not quite good enough; René's count hit thirty-one at almost the very end of the call. There it stood. Gregor abstained, having a deliberately null effect on the outcome. Count Vormoncrief rather perfunctorily called his appeal, and to no one's wonder, Gregor declined to hear it. Vormoncrief and a surprisingly relieved-looking Sigur rose to a much better showing in defeat than Richars had, going up to shake René's hand. René took the Circle again to briefly thank his colleagues, and returned it to the Lord Guardian. The Lord Guardian tapped his spear on the plank, and declared the session closed. Chamber and gallery broke into a swirl of motion and noise.

Miles restrained himself from leaping across tables and chairs and over the backs of his crowd of colleagues to get up to the gallery only because the family party there rose themselves, and began to make their way up the stairs toward the back doors. Surely his mother and father could be relied upon to pilot Ekaterin down here to him? He found himself trapped anyway in a crowd of Counts offering him a barrage of congratulations, comments, and jokes. He barely heard, processing them all with an automatic *Thank you . . . thank you,* occasionally entirely at odds with what had actually been said to him.

At last, he heard his father call his name. Miles's head snapped around; such was the Viceroy's aura that the crowd seemed to melt away between them. Ekaterin peered shyly into the mob of uniformed men from between her formidable outriders. Miles strode over to her, and gripped her hands painfully hard, searching her face, *Is it true, is it real?*

She grinned back, idiotically, beautifully, *Yes, oh, yes.*

"You want a leg up?" Ivan offered him.

"Shut up, Ivan," Miles said over his shoulder. He glanced around at the nearest bench. "D'you mind?" he whispered to her.

"I believe it is customary . . ."

His grin broadened, and he jumped up on it, wrapped her in his arms, and gave her a blatantly possessive kiss. She embraced him back, just as hard, shaking a little.

"Mine to me. Yes," she whispered fiercely in his ear.

He hopped back down, but did not release her hand.

Nikki, almost eye to eye with him, stared at Miles measuringly. "You *are* going to make my mama *happy*, aren't you?"

"I'll surely try, Nikki." He returned Nikki a serious nod, with all his heart. Gravely, Nikki nodded back, as if to say, *It's a deal.*

Olivia, Tatya, and René's sister arrived, fighting their way through the departing crowd, to pounce on René and Dono. Panting in their wake came a man in Count's livery of carmine and green. He stopped short and stared around the chamber in dismay, and moaned, "Too late!"

"Who's that?" Ekaterin whispered to Miles.

"Count Vormuir. He seems to have missed the session."

Count Vormuir staggered off toward his desk on the far side of the chamber. Count Dono watched him go by with a little smile.

Ivan drifted up to Dono, and said in an undervoice, "All right, I have to know. How'd you sidetrack Vormuir?"

"I? I had nothing to do with it. However, if you must know, I believe he spent the morning having a reconciliation with his Countess."

"All morning? At his age?"

"Well, she had some assistance from a nice little Betan aphrodisiac. I believe it can extend a man's attention span for *hours*. No nasty side effects, either. Now you're getting older, Ivan, you might wish to check it out."

"Got any more?"

"Not I. Talk with Helga Vormuir."

Miles turned to Hugo and Vassily, his smile stiffening just a shade. Ekaterin gripped his hand harder, and he returned a reassuring squeeze. "Good morning, gentlemen. I'm glad you could make this historic Council session. Would you be pleased to join us all for lunch at Vorkosigan House? I feel sure we have some matters to discuss more privately."

Vassily seemed well on his way to permanently stunned, but he managed a nod and a mumbled *thank you*. Hugo eyed the grip between Miles and Ekaterin, and his lips twisted up in a bemused acquiescence. "Perhaps that would be a good idea, Lord Vorkosigan. Seeing as how we are to, um, become related. I believe that betrothal had enough witnesses to be binding. . . ."

Miles tucked Ekaterin's hand in his arm, and pulled her close. "So I trust."

The Lord Guardian of the Speaker's Circle made his way over to their group. "Miles. Gregor wishes to see you, and this lady, before you go." He gave Ekaterin a smiling nod. "He said something about a task in your Auditor's capacity . . ."

"Ah." Not loosening his grip on her hand, Miles towed Ekaterin through the thinning crowd to the dais, where Gregor was dealing with several men who were seizing the moment to present concerns to his Imperial attention. He fended them off and turned to Miles and Ekaterin, stepping down over the dais.

"Madame Vorsoisson." He nodded to her. "Do you think you will require any further assistance in dealing with your, er, domestic trouble?"

She smiled gratefully at him. "No, Sire. I think Miles and I can handle it from here, now that the unfortunate political aspect has been removed."

"I had that impression. Congratulations to you both." His mouth was solemn, but his eyes danced. "Ah." He beckoned to a secretary, who drew an official-looking document, two pages of calligraphy all stamped and sealed, from an envelope. "Here, Miles . . . I see Vormuir finally made it. I'll let you hand this off to him."

Miles glanced over the pages, and grinned. "As discussed. My pleasure, Sire."

Gregor flashed a rare smile at them both, and

escaped his courtiers by ducking back through his private door.

Miles reordered the pages, and sauntered over to Vormuir's desk.

"Something for you, Count. My Imperial Master has considered your petition for the confirmation of your guardianship of all your lovely daughters. It is herewith granted."

"Ha!" said Vormuir triumphantly, fairly snatching the documents from Miles. "What did I say! Even the Imperial lawyers had to knuckle under to ties of blood, eh? Good! Good!"

"Enjoy." Miles smiled, and drew Ekaterin rapidly away.

"But Miles," she whispered, "does that mean Vormuir wins? He gets to carry on that dreadful child-assembly-line of his?"

"Under certain conditions. Step along—we really want to be out of the chamber before he gets to page two . . ."

Miles gestured his lunch guests out into the great hall, murmuring rapid instructions into his wristcom to have Pym bring up the car. The Viceroy and Vicereine excused themselves, saying they would be along later after they had a short chat with Gregor.

All paused, startled, as from the chamber, a voice echoed in a sudden howl of anguish.

"Dowries! *Dowries!* A hundred and eighteen *dowries . . .*"

"Roic," said Mark ominously, "why are these trespassers still *alive?*"

"We can't go round just shooting casual visitors, m'lord," Roic attempted to excuse himself.

"Why not?"

"This isn't the Time of Isolation! Besides, m'lord," Roic nodded toward the bedraggled Escobarans, "they do seem to have a proper warrant."

The smaller Escobaran, who'd said his name was Parole Officer Gustioz, held up a wad of sticky flimsies as evidence, and shook it meaningfully, spattering a few last white drops. Mark stepped back, and carefully flicked the stray spot from the front of his good black suit. All three men appeared to have been recently dipped headfirst into a vat of yogurt. Studying Roic, Mark was put dimly in mind of the legend of Achilles, except that his bug butter marinade seemed to extend to both heels.

"We'll see." If they had hurt Kareen . . . Mark turned, and knocked on the locked laboratory door. "Kareen? Martya? Are you all right in there?"

"Mark? Is that you?" Martya's voice came back though the door. "At last!"

Mark studied the dents in the wood, and frowned, narrow-eyed, at the two Escobarans. Gustioz recoiled slightly, and Muno inhaled and tensed. Scraping noises, as of large objects being dragged back from the entryway, emanated from the lab. After another moment, the lock tweetled, and the door stuck, then was yanked open. Martya poked her head through. "Thank heavens!"

Anxiously, Mark pressed past her to find Kareen. She almost fell into his offered embrace, then they both thought better of it. Though not as well-coated as the men, her hair, vest, shirt and trousers were liberally splattered with bug butter. She bent, carefully, to greet him with a reassuring kiss instead. "Did they hurt you, love?" Mark demanded.

"No," she said a bit breathlessly. "We're all right. But Mark, they're trying to take Enrique away! The whole business will go down the toilet without him!"

Enrique, very disheveled and gummy, nodded frightened confirmation.

"Sh, sh. I'll straighten things out." Somehow . . .

She ran a hand through her hair, half her blond curls standing wildly upright from the bug butter mousse, her chest rising and falling with her breathing. Mark had spent most of the morning finding the most remarkably obscene associations triggered in his mind by dairy packaging equipment. He'd kept his mind on his task only by promising himself an afternoon nap, not alone, when he'd got home. He'd had it all planned out. The romantic scenario hadn't included Escobarans. Dammit, if *he* had Kareen and a dozen tubs of bug butter, he would find more interesting things to do than rub it in her hair. . . . And so he did, and so he might, but first he had to get rid of these bloody unwelcome Escobaran skip-tracers.

He walked back out into the corridor, and said to them, "Well, you can't take him. In the first place, I paid his bail."

"Lord Vorkosigan—" began the irate Gustioz.

"Lord Mark," Mark corrected instantly.

"Whatever. The Escobaran Cortes does not, as you seem to think, engage itself in the slave trade. However it's done on this benighted planet, on Escobar a bond is a guarantee of court appearance, not some kind of human meat market transaction."

"It is where I come from," Mark muttered.

"He's Jacksonian," Martya explained. "Not Barrayaran. Don't be alarmed. He's getting over it, mostly."

Possession was nine-tenths of . . . something. Until he was certain he could get Enrique back, Mark was loath to let him out of his sight. There had to be some way to legally block this extradition. *Miles* would likely know, but . . . Miles had made no secret of how he felt about butter bugs. Not a good choice of advisors. But the Countess had bought shares . . . "Mother!" said Mark. "Yes. I want you to at least wait till my mother gets home and can talk to you."

"The Vicereine is a very famous lady," said Gustioz warily, "and I would be honored to be presented to her, some other time. We have an orbital shuttle to catch."

"They go every hour. You can get the next one." Mark just bet the Escobarans would prefer not to encounter the Viceroy and Vicereine. And how long had they been watching Vorkosigan House, to seize this unpopulated moment to make their snatch?

Somehow—probably because Gustioz and Muno were good at their job—Mark found that the whole conversation was moving gently and inexorably down the hallway. They left a sort of slime trail behind them, as if a herd of monstrous snails were migrating through Vorkosigan House. "I must certainly examine your documentation."

"My documentation is entirely in order," Gustioz declared, clutching what looked like a giant spit-wad of flimsies to his glutinous chest as he began to climb the stairs. "And in any case, it has nothing whatever to do with *you!*"

"The hell it doesn't. I posted Dr. Borgos's bond; I have to have some legal interest. I paid for it!"

They reached the dining room; Muno had somehow wrapped a ham hand around Enrique's upper arm. Martya, frowning at him, took preemptive possession of the scientist's other arm. Enrique's look of alarm doubled.

The argument continued, at rising volume, through several antechambers. In the black-and-white tiled entry hall, Mark dug in his heels. He nipped around in front of the pack and stood between Enrique and the door, spread-legged and bulldoggish, and snarled, "If you've been after Enrique for two bloody months, Gustioz, another half hour can make no difference to you. You *will* wait!"

"If you dare to impede me in the legal discharge of my duties, I will find some way to charge you, I guarantee it!" Gustioz snarled back. "I don't care who you're related to!"

"You start a brawl in Vorkosigan House, and you'll damned well find it matters very much who I'm related to!"

"You tell him, Mark!" Kareen cried.

Enrique and Martya added their voices to the uproar. Muno took a tighter grip on his prisoner, and eyed Roic warily, but Kareen and Martya more warily. As long as the reddening Gustioz was still bellowing, Mark reasoned, he had him blocked; when he took a deep breath and switched to forward motion, it would then descend to the physical, and then Mark was not at all sure who would be in control anymore. Somewhere in the back of Mark's head, Killer whined and scratched like an impatient wolf.

Gustioz took a deep breath, but suddenly stopped yelling. Mark tensed, dizzy with the loss of center/self/safety as the *Other* started to surge forward.

Everybody else stopped yammering, too. In fact, the noise died away as though someone had cut the power line. A breath of warm summer air stirred the hairs on the back of Mark's neck as the double doors, behind him, swung wide. He wheeled.

Framed in the doorway, a large party of persons paused in astonishment. Miles, resplendent in full Vorkosigan House livery, stood in the center with Ekaterin Vorsoisson on his arm. Nikki and Professora Vorthys flanked the couple on one side. On the other, two men Mark didn't know, one in lieutenant's undress greens and the other a stoutish fellow in civvies, goggled at the butter-beslimed arguers. Pym stared over Miles's head.

"Who is that?" whispered Gustioz uneasily. And there just wasn't any question which *who* he referred to.

Kareen snapped back under her breath, "Lord Miles Vorkosigan. *Imperial Auditor* Lord Vorkosigan! Now you've done it!"

Miles's gaze traveled slowly over the assembled multitude: Mark, Kareen and Martya, the stranger-Escobarans, Enrique—he winced a little—and up and down the considerable length of Armsman Roic. After a long, long moment, Miles's teeth unclenched.

"Armsman Roic, you appear to be out of uniform."

Roic stood to attention, and swallowed. "I'm . . . I was off-duty. M'lord."

Miles stepped forward; Mark wished to hell he knew how Miles did it, but Gustioz and Muno automatically braced too. Muno didn't let go of Enrique, though.

Miles gestured at Mark. "This is my brother, Lord Mark. And Kareen Koudelka, and her sister Martya. Dr. Enrique Borgos, from Escobar, my brother's, um, houseguest." He indicated the group of people who'd trailed him in. "Lieutenant Vassily Vorsiosson. Hugo Vorvayne," he nodded at the stoutish man, "Ekaterin's *brother*." His emphasis supplied the undertext, *This had better not be the sort of screwup it looks like.* Kareen winced.

"Everyone else, you know. I'm afraid I haven't met these other two gentlemen. Are your visitors, by chance, on their way out, Mark?" Miles suggested gently.

The dam broke; half a dozen people simultaneously began to explain, complain, excuse, plea, demand, accuse, and defend. Miles listened for a couple of minutes—Mark was uncomfortably reminded of how appallingly smoothly his progenitor-brother handled the multitracking inputs of a combat command helmet—then, at last, flung up a hand. Miraculously, he got silence, barring a few trailing words from Martya.

"Let me see if I have this straight," he murmured. "You two gentlemen," he nodded at the slowly drying Escobarans, "wish to take Dr. Borgos away and lock him up? Forever?"

Mark cringed at the hopeful tone in Miles's voice.

"Not forever," Parole Officer Gustioz admitted regretfully. "But certainly for a good long time." He paused, and held out his wad of flimsies. "I have all the proper orders and warrants, sir!"

"Ah," said Miles, eyeing the sticky jumble. "Indeed." He hesitated. "You will, of course, permit me to examine them."

He excused himself to the mob of people who'd accompanied him, gave a squeeze to Ekaterin's hand—wait a minute, hadn't they been not talking to each other? Miles had walked around all day yesterday in a dark cloud of negative energy like a black hole in motion; just looking at him had given Mark a headache. Now, beneath that heavy layer of irony, he frigging *glowed*. What the hell was happening here? Kareen, too, eyed the pair with growing surmise.

Mark abandoned this puzzle temporarily as Miles beckoned Gustioz to a side table beneath a mirror. He plucked the flower arrangement from it and handed it off to Roic, who scrambled to receive it, and had Gustioz lay down his extradition documents in a pile.

Slowly, and Mark had not the least doubt Miles was using every theatrical trick to buy time to think, he leafed gingerly through them. The entire audience in the entry hall watched him in utter silence, as if enspelled. He carefully touched the documents only with his fingertips, with an occasional glance up at Gustioz that had the Escobaran squirming in very short order. Every once in a while he had to pick up a couple of flimsies and gently peel them apart. "Mm-hm," he said, and "Mm-hm," and "All eighteen, yes, very good."

He came to the end, and stood thoughtfully a moment, his fingers just touching the pile, not releasing them back to the hovering Gustioz. He glanced up questioningly under his eyebrows at Ekaterin. She gazed rather anxiously back at him, and smiled wryly.

"Mark," he said slowly. "You did pay Ekaterin for her design work in shares, not cash, as I understand?"

"Yes," said Mark. "And Ma Kosti too," he hastened to point out.

"And me!" Kareen put in.

"And me!" added Martya.

"The company's been a little cash-strapped," Mark offered cautiously.

"Ma Kosti too. Hm. Oh, dear." Miles stared off into space a moment, then turned and smiled at Gustioz.

"Parole Officer Gustioz."

Gustioz stood upright, as if to attention.

"All the documents you have here do indeed appear to be legal and in order."

Miles picked the stack up between thumb and forefinger, and returned them to the officer's grasp. Gustioz accepted them, smiled, and inhaled.

"However," Miles continued, "you are missing one jurisdiction. Quite a critical one: the Imp Sec gate guard should not have let you in here without it. Well, the boys are soldiers, not lawyers; I don't think the poor corporal should be reprimanded. I will have to tell General Allegre to make sure it's part of their briefing in future, though."

Gustioz stared at him in horror and disbelief. "I have permissions from the Empire—the planetary local space—the Vorbarra District—and the City of Vorbarr Sultana. What other jurisdiction *is* there?"

"Vorkosigan House is the official residence of the Count of the Vorkosigan's District," Miles explained to him in a kindly tone. "As such, its grounds are considered Vorkosigan District soil, very like an embassy's. To take this man *from Vorkosigan House*, in the city of Vorbarr Sultana, in the Vorbarra District, on Barrayar, in the Imperium, you need all those," he waved at the tacky pile, "and also an extradition authorization, an order in the Count's Voice—just like this one you have here for the Vorbarra's District—from the Vorkosigan's District."

Gustioz was trembling. "And where," he said hoarsely, "can I find the nearest Vorkosigan's District Count's Voice?"

"The nearest?" said Miles cheerily. "Why, that would be me."

The Parole Officer stared at him for a long moment. He swallowed. "Very good, sir," he said humbly, his voice cracking. "May I please have an order of extradition for Dr. Enrique Borgos from, the, the Count's Voice?"

Miles looked across at Mark. Mark stared back, his lips twisting. *You son of a bitch, you're enjoying every second of this. . . .*

Miles vented a long, rather regretful sigh—the entire audience swayed with it—and said briskly, "No. Your application is denied. Pym, please escort these gentlemen off my premises, then inform Ma Kosti that we will be sitting, um," his gaze swept the entry hall, "ten for lunch, as soon as possible. Fortunately, she likes a challenge. Armsman Roic . . ." He stared at the young man, still clutching the flowers, who stared back in pitiful panic. Miles just shook his head, "Go get a *bath*."

Pym, tall, sternly middle-aged, and in full uniform, advanced intimidatingly upon the Escobarans, who broke before him, and weakly let themselves be cowed out the doors.

"He'll have to leave this house sometime, dammit!" Gustioz shouted over his shoulder. "He can't hole up in here forever!"

"We'll fly him down to the District in the Count's official aircar," Miles called back in cheery codicil.

Gustioz's inarticulate cry was cut off by the doors swinging shut.

"The butter bug project is really very fascinating," said

Ekaterin brightly to the two men who'd come in with her and Miles. "You should see the lab."

Kareen signaled a frantic negative. "Not now, Ekaterin!"

Miles passed a grimly warning eye over Mark, and gestured his party in the opposite direction. "In the meantime, perhaps you would enjoy seeing Vorkosigan House's library. Professora, would you be so kind as to point out some of its interesting historical aspects to Hugo and Vassily, while I take care of a few things? Go with your aunt, Nikki. Thank you so much . . ." He held onto Ekaterin's hand, keeping her by him, as the rest of the party shuffled off.

"Lord Vorkosigan," cried Enrique, his voice quavering with relief, "I don't know how I can ever repay you!"

Miles held up a hand, dryly, to cut him off in midlaunch. "I'll think of something."

Martya, a little more alive to Miles's nuances than Enrique, smiled acerbically and took the Escobaran by the hand. "Come on, Enrique. I think maybe we'd better start working off your debt of gratitude by going down and cleaning up the lab, don't you?"

"Oh! Yes, of course . . ." Firmly, she hauled him off. His voice drifted back, "Do you think he'll like the butter bugs *Ekaterin* designed . . . ?"

Ekaterin smiled down fondly at Miles. "Well played, love."

"Yes," said Mark gruffly. He found himself staring at his boots. "I know how you feel about this whole project. Um . . . thanks, eh?"

Miles reddened slightly. "Well . . . I couldn't risk offending my cook, y'know. She seems to have adopted the man. It's the enthusiastic way he eats my food, I suppose."

Mark's brows lowered in sudden suspicion. "*Is* it true that a Count's Residence is legally a part of his District? Or did you just make that up on the spot?"

Miles grinned briefly. "Look it up. Now if you two will excuse us, I think I'd better go spend some time calming the fears of my in-laws-to-be. It's been a trying morning for them. As a personal favor, dear brother, could you *please* refrain from springing any more crises upon me, just for the rest of today?"

"In-laws-to . . . ?" Kareen's lips parted in thrilled delight. "Oh, Ekaterin, good! Miles, you—you rat! When did this happen?"

Miles grinned, a real grin this time, not playing to the house. "She asked me, and I said yes." He glanced up more slyly at Ekaterin, and went on, "I had to set her a good example, after all. You see, Ekaterin, that's how a proposal *should* be answered—forthright, decisive, and above all, positive!"

"I'll keep it in mind," she told him. She was poker-faced, but her eyes were laughing as he led her off toward the library.

Kareen, watching them go, sighed in romantic satisfaction, and leaned into Mark. All right, so this stuff was contagious. This was a problem? Screw the black suit. He slipped an arm around her waist.

Kareen ran a hand through her hair. "I want a shower."

"You can use mine," Mark offered instantly. "I'll scrub your back . . ."

"You can rub everything," she promised him. "I think I pulled some muscles in the tug-of-Enrique."

By damn, he might salvage this afternoon yet. Smiling fondly, he turned with her toward the staircase.

At their feet, the queen Vorkosigan-liveried butter bug scuttled out of a shadow and waddled quickly across the black-and-white tiles. Kareen yipped, and Mark dove after the huge bug. He skidded to a halt on his stomach under the side table by the wall just in time to see the silver flash of her rear end slide out of sight between the baseboard and a loose paving stone. "God *damn* but those things can flatten out! Maybe we ought to get Enrique to make them, like, taller or something." Dusting his jacket, he climbed back to his feet. "She went into the wall." Back to her nest in the walls somewhere, he feared.

Kareen peered doubtfully under the table. "Should we tell Miles?"

"No," said Mark decisively, and took her hand to mount the stairs.

EPILOGUE

From Miles's point of view, the two weeks to the Imperial wedding sped past, though he suspected that Gregor and Laisa were running on a skewed relativistic time-distortion in which time went slower but one aged faster. He manufactured appropriate sympathetic noises whenever he encountered Gregor, agreeing that this social ordeal was a terrible burden, but, truly, one that everyone must bear, a commonality of the human condition, chin up, soldier on. Inside his own head, a continuous counterpoint ran in little popping bubbles, *Look! I'm engaged! Isn't she pretty?* She *asked* me. *She's smart, too. She's going to marry* me. *Mine, mine, all mine. I'm engaged! To be married! To this woman!* an effervescence that emerged, he trusted, only as a cool, suave smile.

He did arrange to dine over at the Vorthys's three times, and have Ekaterin and Nikki to meals at Vorkosigan House twice, before the wedding week hit and all his meals—even breakfasts, good God—were bespoken. Still, his timetable was not as onerous as Gregor's and Laisa's, which Lady Alys and ImpSec between them had laid out in one-minute increments. Miles invited Ekaterin to accompany him to all his social obligations. She raised her brows at him, and accepted a sensible and dignified three. It was only later that Kareen pointed out that there were limits to the number of times a lady wanted to be seen in the same dress, a problem which, had he but realized it existed, he would gladly have set out to solve. It was perhaps just as well. He wanted Ekaterin to share his pleasure, not his exhaustion.

The cloud of amused congratulation that surrounded them for their spectacular betrothal was marred only once, at a dinner in honor of the Vorbarr Sultana Fire Watch which had included handing out awards for men exhibiting notable bravery or quick thinking in the past year. Exiting with Ekaterin on his arm, Miles found the door half blocked by the somewhat drunken Lord Vormurtos, one of Richars's defeated supporters. The room had mostly emptied by that time, with only a few earnestly chatting groups of people left. Already the servers were moving in to clean up. Vormurtos leaned on the frame with his arms crossed, and failed to move aside.

At Miles's polite, "Excuse us, please," Vormurtos pursed his lips in exaggerated irony.

"Why not? Everyone else has. It seems if you are Vorkosigan enough, you can even get away with murder."

Ekaterin stiffened unhappily. Miles hesitated a fractional moment, considering responses: explanation, outrage, protest? Argument in a hallway with a half-potted fool? No. *I am Aral Vorkosigan's son, after all.* Instead, he stared up unblinkingly, and breathed, "So if you truly believe that, *why are you standing in my way?*"

Vormurtos's inebriated sneer drained away, to be replaced by a belated wariness. With an effort at insouciance that he did not quite bring off, he unfolded himself, and opened his hand to wave the couple past. When Miles bared his teeth in an edged smile, he backed up an extra and involuntary step. Miles shifted Ekaterin to his other side and strode past without looking back.

Ekaterin glanced over her shoulder once, as they

made their way down the corridor. In a tone of dispassionate observation, she murmured, "He's melted. You know, your sense of humor is going to get you into deep trouble someday."

"Belike," Miles sighed.

The Emperor's wedding, Miles decided, was very like a combat drop mission, except that, wonderfully, *he* wasn't in command. It was Lady Alys's and Colonel Lord Vortala the Younger's turn for nervous breakdowns. Miles got to be a grunt. All he had to do was keep smiling and follow orders, and eventually it would all be over.

It was fortunate that it was a Midsummer event, because the only site large enough for all the circles of witnesses (barring the stunningly ugly municipal stadium) was the former parade ground, now a grassy sward, just to the south of the Residence. The ballroom was the backup venue in the event of rain, in Miles's view a terrorist plan that courted death by overheating and oxygen deprivation for most of the government of the Imperium. To match the blizzard that had made the Winterfair betrothal so memorable, they ought to have had summer tornadoes, but to everyone's relief the day dawned fair.

The morning began with yet another formal breakfast, this time with Gregor and his groom's party at the Residence. Gregor looked a little frayed, but determined.

"How are you holding up?" Miles asked him in an undervoice.

"I'll make it through dinner," Gregor assured him. "Then we drown our pursuers in a lake of wine and escape."

Even Miles didn't know what refuge Gregor and Laisa had chosen for their wedding night, whether one of the several Vorbarra properties or the country estate of a friend or maybe aboard a battle cruiser in orbit. He *was* sure there wasn't going to be any sort of unscheduled Imperial shivaree. Gregor had chosen all his most frighteningly humorless ImpSec personnel to guard his getaway.

Miles returned to Vorkosigan House to change into
his very best House uniform, ornamented with a careful selection of his old military decorations that he
otherwise never wore. Ekaterin would be watching him
from the third circle of witnesses, in company with her
uncle and aunt and the rest of his Imperial Auditor
colleagues. He likely wouldn't see her till the vows were
over, a thought that gave him a taste of what Gregor's
anxiety must be.

The Residence's grounds were filling when he arrived
back. He joined his father, Gregor, Drou and Kou,
Count Henri Vorvolk and his wife, and the rest of the
first circle in their assigned staging area, one of the
Residence's public rooms. The Vicereine was off somewhere in support of Lady Alys. Both women and Ivan
arrived with moments to spare. As the light of the
summer evening gilded the air, Gregor's horse, a gloriously glossy black beast in gleaming cavalry regalia,
was led to the west entrance. A Vorbarra Armsman
followed with an equally lovely white mare fitted out for
Laisa. Gregor mounted, looking in his parade red-and-
blues both impressively Imperial and endearingly nervous. Surrounded by his party on foot, he proceeded
decorously across the grounds through an aisle of
people to the former barracks, now remodeled as guest
quarters, where the Komarran delegation was housed.

It was then Miles's job to pound on the door and
demand in formal phrases that the bride be brought
forth. He was watched by a bevy of giggling Komarran
women from the wide-flung flower-decked windows
overhead. He stepped back as Laisa and her parents
emerged. The bride's dress, he noted in the certainty
that there would be a quiz later, included a white silk
jacket with fascinating glittery stuff over various other
layers, a heavy white silk split skirt and white leather
boots, and a headdress with garlands of flowers all
cascading down. Several tensely smiling Vorbarra
Armsmen made sure the whole ensemble got loaded
without incident aboard the notably placid mare—Miles
suspected equine tranquilizers. Gregor shifted his horse
around to lean across and grip Laisa's hand briefly; they

smiled at each other in mutual amazement. Laisa's father, a short, round Komarran oligarch who had never been near a horse in his life before he'd had to practice for this, valiantly took the lead line, and the cavalcade wound its stately way back through the aisles of well-wishers to the south lawn.

The marriage pattern was laid on the ground in little ridges of colored groats, hundreds of kilos of them altogether, Miles had been given to understand. The small central circle awaited the couple, surrounded by a six-pointed star for the principal witnesses, and a series of concentric rings for guests. First close family and friends—then Counts and their Countesses—then high government officials, military officers, and Imperial Auditors—then diplomatic delegations; after that, people packed to the limit of the Residence's walls, and more in the street beyond. The cavalcade split, bride and groom dismounting and entering the circle each from opposite sides. The horses were led away, and Laisa's female Second and Miles were handed the official bags of groats to pour upon the ground and close the couple in, which they managed to do without either dropping the bags, or getting too many groats down their respective footwear.

Miles took his place upon his assigned star point, his parents and Laisa's parents on either hand, Laisa's Komarran female friend and Second opposite. Since *he* didn't have to remember Gregor's lines for him, he occupied the time as the couple repeated their promises—in four languages—by studying the pleasure on the Viceroy and Vicereine's faces. He didn't think he'd ever seen his father cry in public before. All right, so some of it was the sloppy sentiment overflowing everywhere today, but some of it had to be tears of sheer political relief. That was why he had to rub water from *his* eyes, certainly. Damned effective public theater, this ceremony. . . .

Swallowing, Miles stepped forward to kick the groats aside and open the circle to let the married couple out. He seized his privilege and position to be the first to grab Gregor's hand in congratulations, and to stand on

tiptoe to kiss the bride's flushed cheek. And then, by
damn, it was party time, he was done and off the hook,
and he could go and hunt for Ekaterin in all this mob.
He made his way past people scooping up handfuls of
groats and tucking them away for souvenirs, craning his
neck for a glimpse of an elegant woman in a gray silk
gown.

Kareen gripped Mark's arm and sighed in satisfaction. The maple ambrosia was a *hit*.

It was rather clever, Kareen thought, how Gregor had
shared out the astronomical cost of his wedding reception among his Counts. Each District had been invited
to contribute an outdoor kiosk, scattered about the
Residence grounds, to offer whatever local food and
drink (vetted, of course, by Lady Alys and ImpSec)
they'd cared to display to the strolling guests. The effect
was a little like a District Fair, or rather, a Fair of Districts, but the competition had certainly brought out the
best of Barrayar. The Vorkosigan's District kiosk had a
prime location, at the northwest corner of the Residence
just at the top of a path that went down into the sunken
gardens. Count Aral had donated a thousand liters of
his District wine, a traditional and very popular choice.

And at a side table next to the wine bar, Lord Mark
Vorkosigan and MPVK Enterprises offered to the
guests—tah dah!—their first food product. Ma Kosti and
Enrique, wearing Staff badges, directed a team of
Vorkosigan House servitors scooping out generous portions of maple ambrosia to the high Vor as fast as they
could hand them across the table. At the end of the
table, framed by flowers, a wire cage exhibited a couple
of dozen bright new Glorious Bugs, glowing in blue-red-
gold, together with a brief explanation, rewritten by
Kareen to remove both Enrique's technicalities and
Mark's blatant commercialism, of how they made their
ambrosia. All right, so none of the renamed bug butter being distributed had actually been made by the new
bugs, but that was a mere packaging detail.

Miles and Ekaterin came strolling through the crowd,
along with Ivan. Miles spotted Kareen's eager wave, and

angled toward them. Miles was wearing that same blitzed, deliriously pleased look he'd been sporting for two weeks; Ekaterin, at this her first Imperial Residence party, looked a trifle awed. Kareen darted aside and grabbed a cup of ambrosia, and brandished it as the trio came up.

"Ekaterin, they love the Glorious Bugs! At least half a dozen women have tried to steal them to wear as hair ornaments with their flowers—Enrique had to lock down the cage before we lost any more. He said, they are supposed to be a *demonstration*, not *free samples*."

Ekaterin laughed. "I'm glad I was able to cure your customer resistance!"

"Oh, my, yes. And with a debut at the Emperor's wedding, everyone will want it! Here, have you had the maple ambrosia yet? Miles?"

"I've tried it before, thank you," said Miles neutrally.

"Ivan! You've got to taste this!"

Ivan's lips twisted dubiously, but with amiable grace he lifted the spoon to his mouth. His expression changed. "Wow, what did you lace this with? It's got a notable kick to it." He resisted Kareen's attempt to wrest back the cup.

"Maple mead," said Kareen happily. "It was Ma Kosti's inspiration. It really works!"

Ivan swallowed, and paused. "Maple mead? The most disgusting, gut-destroying, guerilla attack-beverage ever brewed by man?"

"It's an acquired taste," murmured Miles.

Ivan took another bite. "Combined with the most revolting food product ever invented . . . How did she make it come out like *this*?" He scraped up the last of the soft golden paste, and eyed the cup as though considering licking it out with his tongue. "Impressively efficient, that. Get fed *and* drunk simultaneously . . . no wonder they're lining up!"

Mark, smiling smugly, broke in. "I just had a nice little private chat with Lord Vorsmythe. Without going into the details, I can say that our startup money shortage looks to be solved one way or another. Ekaterin! I am now in a position to redeem the shares I gave you for the bug design. What would you say to an offer of twice their face value back?"

Ekaterin looked thrilled. "That's wonderful, Mark! And so timely. That's more than I ever expected—"

"What you say," Kareen broke in firmly, "is, *no, thank you.* You hang on to those shares, Ekaterin! What you do if you need cash is set them as collateral against a loan. Then, next year when the stock has split I don't know how many times, sell *some* of the shares, pay back the loan, and keep the rest as a growth investment. By the time Nikki's ready, you might well be able to put him through jump-pilot school with it."

"You don't *have* to do it that way—" Mark began.

"That's what I'm doing with mine. It's going to pay my way back to Beta Colony!" She wasn't going to have to beg so much as a tenth-mark from her parents, news they'd found a little more surprising than was quite flattering. They'd then tried to press the offer of a living allowance on her, just to regain their balance, Kareen thought, or possibly the upper hand. She'd taken enormous pleasure in sweetly refusing. "I told Ma Kosti not to sell, either."

Ekaterin's eyes crinkled. "I see, Kareen. In that case . . . thank you, Lord Mark. I will think about your offer for a little while."

Foiled, Mark grumbled under his breath, but, with his brother's sardonic eye upon him, didn't continue his attempted hustle.

Kareen flitted back happily to the serving table, where Ma Kosti was just hoisting up another five-liter tub of maple ambrosia and breaking the seal.

"How are we doing?" Kareen asked.

"They're going to clean us out in another hour, at this rate," the cook reported. She was wearing a lace apron over her very best dress. A large and exquisite fresh orchid necklace, which she'd said Miles had given her, fought for space on her breast with her Staff badge. There was more than one way to get in to the Emperor's wedding, by golly. . . .

"The maple mead bug butter was a great idea of yours for soothing down Miles about this," Kareen told her. "He's one of the few people I know who actually *drinks* the stuff."

"Oh, that wasn't *my* idea, Kareen lovie," Ma Kosti told her. "It was Lord Vorkosigan's. He owns the meadery, you know. . . . He's got an eye to channeling more money to all those poor people back in the Dendarii Mountains, I think."

Kareen's grin broadened. "I *see*." She stole a glance at Miles, standing benignly with his lady on his arm and feigning indifference to his clone-brother's project.

In the gathering dusk, little colored lights began to gleam all through the Residence's garden and grounds, fair and festive. In their cage, the Glorious Bugs began to flip their wing carapaces and twinkle back as if in answer.

Mark watched Kareen, all blonde and ivory and raspberry gauzy and entirely edible, returning from their bug butter table, and sighed in pleasure. His hands, stuffed in his pockets, encountered the gritty grains she had insisted he store there for her when the wedding circle had broken up. He shook them from his fingers, and held out his hand to her, asking, "What are we supposed to do with all these groats, Kareen? Plant them or something?"

"Oh, no," she said, as he pulled her in close. "They're just for remembrance. Most people will put them up in little sachets, and try to press them on their grandchildren someday. *I was at the Old Emperor's wedding, I was*."

"It's miracle grain, you know," Miles put in. "It multiplies. By tomorrow—or later tonight—people will be selling little bags of supposedly-wedding groats to the gullible all over Vorbarr Sultana. Tons and tons."

"Really." Mark considered this. "You know, you could actually do that legitimately, with a little ingenuity. Take your handful of wedding groats, mix 'em with a bushel of filler-groats, repackage 'em . . . the customer would still get *genuine* Imperial wedding groats, in a sense, but they'd go a lot farther . . ."

"Kareen," said Miles, "do me a favor. Check his

pockets before he gets out of here tonight, and confiscate any groats you find."

"I wasn't saying *I* was going to!" said Mark indignantly. Miles grinned at him, and he realized he'd just been Scored On. He smiled back sheepishly, too elated by it all tonight to sustain any emotion downwards of *mellow*.

Kareen glanced up, and Mark followed her gaze to see the Commodore in his parade red-and-blues, and Madame Koudelka in something green and flowing like the Queen of Summer, making their way toward them. The Commodore swung his swordstick jauntily enough, but he had a curiously introspective look on his face. Kareen broke away to cadge more ambrosia samples to press on them.

"How are you two holding up?" Miles greeted the couple.

The Commodore replied abstractedly, "I'm a little, um. A little . . . um . . ."

Miles cocked an eyebrow. "A little um?"

"Olivia," said Madame Koudelka, "has just announced her engagement."

"I thought this was awfully contagious," said Miles, grinning slyly up at Ekaterin.

Ekaterin returned him a melting smile, then said to the Koudelkas, "Congratulations. Who's the lucky fellow?"

"That's . . . um . . . the part it's going to take some getting used to," the Commodore sighed.

Madame Koudelka said, "Count Dono Vorrutyer."

Kareen arrived back with an armload of ambrosia cups in time to hear this; she bounced and squealed delight. Mark glanced aside at Ivan, who merely shook his head and reached for another ambrosia. Of all the party, his was the one voice that didn't break into some murmur of surprise. He looked glum, yes. Surprised, no.

Miles, after a brief digestive pause, said, "I always did think one of your girls would catch a Count."

"Yes," said the Commodore, "but . . ."

"I'm quite certain Dono will know how to make her happy," Ekaterin offered.

"Um."

"She wants a big wedding," said Madame Koudelka.

"So does Delia," said the Commodore. "I left them arm wrestling over who gets the earlier date. And the first shot at my poor budget." He stared around at the Residence grounds, and all the increasingly happy revelers. As it was still early in the evening, they were almost all still vertical. "This is giving them both grandiose ideas."

In a rapt voice, Miles said, "Ooh. I *must* talk to Duv."

Commodore Koudelka edged closer to Mark, and lowered his voice. "Mark, I, ah . . . feel I owe you an apology. Didn't mean to be so stiff-necked about it all."

"That's all right, sir," said Mark, surprised and touched.

The Commodore added, "So, you're going back to Beta in the fall—good. No need to be in a rush to settle things at your age, after all."

"That's what we thought, sir." Mark hesitated. "I know I'm not very good at family yet. But I mean to learn how."

The Commodore gave him a little nod, and a crooked smile. "You're doing fine, son. Just keep on."

Kareen's hand squeezed his. Mark cleared his suddenly inexplicably tight throat, and considered the novel thought that not only could you have a family, you might even have more than one. A wealth of relations . . . "Thank you, sir. I'll try."

Olivia and Dono themselves rounded the corner of the Residence then, arm in arm, Olivia in her favorite primrose yellow, Dono soberly splendid in his Vorrutyer House blue and gray. The dark-haired Dono was actually a little shorter than his intended bride, Mark noticed for the first time. All the Koudelka girls ran to tall. But the force of Dono's personality was such that one hardly noticed the height differential.

They arrived at the group, explaining that they'd been told by five separate people to go try the maple ambrosia before it was gone. They lingered, while Kareen collected another armload of samples, to accept congratulations from all assembled. Even Ivan rose to this social duty.

When Kareen returned, Olivia told her, "I was just talking to Tatya Vorbretten. She was so happy—she and René have started their little boy! The blastocyst just got transferred to the uterine replicator this morning. All healthy so far."

Kareen, her mother, Olivia, and Dono all put their heads together, and that end of the conversation became appallingly obstetrical for a short time. Ivan backed away.

"It's getting worse and worse," he confided to Mark in a hollow voice. "I used to only lose old girlfriends to matrimony one at a time. Now they're going in *pairs*."

Mark shrugged. "Can't help you, old fellow. But if you want my advice—"

"*You're* giving *me* advice on how to run my love life?" Ivan interjected indignantly.

"You get what you give. Even I figured that one out, eventually." Mark grinned up at him.

Ivan growled, and made to slope off, but then paused to stare, startled, as Count Dono hailed his cousin Byerly Vorrutyer, just passing by on the walk leading to the Residence. "What's *he* doing here?" Ivan muttered.

Dono and Olivia excused themselves and left, presumably to share their announcement with this new quarry. Ivan, after a short silence, handed his empty cup to Kareen and trailed after them.

The Commodore, scraping the last of his ambrosia out of his cup with the little spoon provided, stared glumly after Olivia clinging joyfully to her new fiancé. "Countess Olivia Vorrutyer," he muttered under his breath, obviously trying to get both his mouth and his mind around the novel concept. "My son-in-law, the Count . . . dammit, the fellow's almost old enough to be Olivia's father himself."

"Mother, surely," murmured Mark.

The Commodore gave him an acerbic look. "You understand," he added after a moment, "just on principles of propinquity, I always figured my girls would go for the bright young officers. I expected I'd end up owning the general staff, in my old age. Though there is Duv, I suppose, for consolation. Not young either, but bright enough to be downright scary. Well, maybe *Martya* will find us a future general."

At the bug butter table, Martya in a mint-green gown had stopped by to check on the success of the operation, but stayed to help dish out ambrosia. She and Enrique bent together to lift another tub, and the Escobaran laughed heartily at something she said. When Mark and Kareen returned to Beta Colony, they had agreed Martya would take over as business manager, going down to the District to oversee the startup of the operations. Mark suspected she would end up with a controlling share of the company, eventually. No matter. This was only his first essay in entrepreneurship. *I can make more.* Enrique would bury himself in his development laboratory. He and Martya would both, no doubt, learn a lot, working together. Propinquity . . .

Mark tested the idea on the tip of his tongue, *And this is my brother-in-law, Dr. Enrique Borgos* . . . Mark moved so as to place the Commodore's back to the table, where Enrique was regarding Martya with open admiration and spilling a lot of ambrosia on his fingers. Gawky young intellectual types were noted for aging well, Kareen had told him. So if one Koudelka had chosen the military, and another the political, and another the economic, it would complete the set for one to select the scientific . . . It wasn't just the general staff Kou looked to own in his old age, it was the world. Charitably, Mark decided to keep this observation to himself.

If he was doing well enough by Winterfair, maybe he'd give Kou and Drou a week's all-expenses-paid trip to the Orb, just to encourage the Commodore's heartening trend toward social liberality. That it would also allow them to travel out to Beta Colony and see Kareen would be an irresistible bribe, he rather thought. . . .

Ivan stood and watched as Dono finished his cordial conversation with his cousin By. Dono and Olivia then entered the Residence through the wide-flung glass doors from which light spilled onto the stone-paved promenade. Byerly collected a glass of wine from a passing servitor's tray, sipped, and went to lean pensively on the balustrade overlooking the descending garden paths.

Ivan joined him. "Hello, Byerly," he said affably. "Why aren't you in jail?"

By looked around, and smiled. "Why, Ivan. I'm turned Imperial Witness, don't you know. My secret testimony has put dear Richars into cold storage. All is forgiven."

"Dono forgave what *you* tried?"

"It was Richars's idea, not mine. He's always fancied himself a man of action. It didn't take much encouragement at all to lure him past the point of no return."

Ivan smiled tightly, and took Byerly by the arm. "Let's take a little walk."

"Where to?" asked By uneasily.

"Someplace more private."

The first private place they came to down the path, a stone bench in a bush-shrouded nook, was occupied by a couple. As it happened, the young fellow was a Vorish ensign Ivan knew from Ops HQ. It took him about fifteen captainly seconds to evict the pair. Byerly watched with feigned admiration. "Such a man of authority you're turning into these days, Ivan."

"Sit down, By. And cut the horseshit. If you can."

Smiling, but with watchful eyes, By seated himself comfortably, and crossed his legs. Ivan positioned himself between By and the exit.

"Why are you *here*, By? Gregor invite you?"

"Dono got me in."

"Good of him. Unbelievably good. I—for example— don't believe it for a second."

By shrugged. "S'true."

"What was *really* going on the night Dono was jumped?"

"Goodness, Ivan. Your persistence begins to remind me horribly of your short cousin."

"You've lied and you're lying, but I can't tell about *what*. You make my head hurt. I'm about to share the sensation."

"Now, now . . ." By's eyes glinted in the colored lights,

though his face was half shadowed. "It's really quite simple. I told Dono that I was an *agent provocateur*. Granted, I helped set up the attack. What I neglected to mention—to Richars—was that I'd also engaged a squad of municipal guardsmen to provide a timely interruption. To be followed, in the script, by Dono staggering into Vorsmythe House, very shaken up, in front of half the Council of Counts. A grand public spectacle guaranteed to cinch a substantial sympathy vote."

"You convinced Dono of this?"

"Yes. Fortunately, I *was* able to offer up the guardsmen as witnesses to my good intentions. Aren't I clever?" By smirked.

"So—I reflect—is Dono. Did he set this up with you, to trip Richars?"

"No. In fact. I meant it to be a surprise, although not quite as much of a surprise as, ah, it turned out. I wished to be certain Dono's response was absolutely convincing. The attack had to actually start—and be witnessed—to incriminate Richars, and eliminate the 'I was only joking' defense. It would not have had the proper tone at all if Richars himself had been merely—and provably—the victim of an entrapment by his political rival."

"I'll swear you weren't faking being distraught as hell that night when you caught up with me."

"Oh, I was. A most painful memory. All my beautiful choreography was just ruined. Though, thanks to you and Olivia, the outcome was saved. I should be grateful to you, I suppose. My life would be . . . most uncomfortable right now if those nasty brutal thugs had succeeded."

Just exactly how uncomfortable, By? Ivan paused for a moment, then inquired softly, "Did Gregor order this?"

"Are you having romantic visions of plausible deniability, Ivan? Goodness me. No. I went to some trouble to keep ImpSec out of the affair. This impending wedding made them all so distressingly rigid. They would, boringly, have wanted to arrest the conspirators immediately. Not *nearly* as politically effective."

If By was lying . . . Ivan didn't want to know. "You

play games like that with the big boys, you'd better make damn sure you win, Miles says. Rule One. And there is no Rule Two."

Byerly sighed. "So he pointed out to me."

Ivan hesitated. "*Miles* talked to you about this?"

"Ten days ago. Has anyone ever explained the meaning of the term *déjà vu* to you, Ivan?"

"Reprimanded you, did he?"

"I have my own sources for mere reprimand. It was worse. He . . . he *critiqued* me." Byerly shuddered, delicately. "From a covert ops standpoint, don't you know. An experience I trust I may never repeat." He sipped his wine.

Ivan was almost lured into sympathetic agreement. But not quite. He pursed his lips. "So, By . . . who's your blind drop?"

By blinked at him. "My what?"

"Every deep cover informer has a blind drop. It wouldn't do for you to be seen tripping in and out of ImpSec HQ by the very men you might, perhaps, be ratting on tomorrow. How long have you had this job, By?"

"What job?"

Ivan sat silent, and frowned. Humorlessly.

By sighed. "About eight years."

Ivan raised a brow. "Domestic Affairs . . . counterintelligence . . . civilian contract employee . . . what's your rating? IS-6?"

By's lip twitched. "IS-8."

"Ooh. Very good."

"Well, I am. Of course, it *was* IS-9. I'm sure it will be again, someday. I'll just have to be boring and follow the rules for a while. For example, I will have to report this conversation."

"Feel free." Finally, it all added up, in neat columns with no messy remainders. So, Byerly Vorrutyer was one of Illyan's dirty angels . . . one of Allegre's, now, Ivan supposed. Doing a little personal moonlighting on the side, it appeared. By must certainly have received a reprimand over all his sleight-of-hand on Dono's behalf. But his career would survive. If Byerly was a bit of a loose screw, just as certainly, down in the bowels of ImpSec HQ, there was a very bright man with a screwdriver. A Galeni-caliber officer, if ImpSec was lucky enough. He might even drop in to visit Ivan, after this. The acquaintance was bound to prove interesting. Best of all, Byerly Vorrutyer was *his* problem. Ivan smiled relief, and rose.

Byerly stretched, picked up his half-empty wineglass, and prepared to accompany Ivan back up the path.

Ivan's brain kept picking at the scenario, despite his stern order to it to stop now. A glass of wine of his own ought to do the trick. But he couldn't help asking again, "So who *is* your blind drop? It ought to be someone I know, dammit."

"Why, Ivan. I'd think you'd have enough clues to figure it out for yourself by now."

"Well . . . it has to be someone in the high Vor social milieu, because that's clearly your specialty. Someone you encounter frequently, but not a constant companion. Someone who also has daily contact with ImpSec, but in an unremarkable way. Someone no one would notice. An unobserved channel, a disregarded conduit. Hidden in plain sight. Who?"

They reached the top of the path. By smiled. "*That* would be telling." He drifted away. Ivan wheeled to catch a servitor with a tray of wineglasses. He turned back to watch By, doing an excellent imitation of a half-drunk town clown not least because he *was* a half-drunk town clown, pause to give one of his little By-bows to Lady Alys and Simon Illyan, just exiting the Residence together for a breath of air on the promenade. Lady Alys returned him a cool nod.

Ivan choked on his wine.

Miles had been hauled away to pose with the rest of the wedding party for vids. Ekaterin tried not to be too nervous, left in Kareen and Mark's good company, but she felt a twinge of relief when she saw Miles again making his way down the steps from the Residence's north promenade toward her. The Imperial Residence was vast and old and beautiful and intimidating and crammed with history, and she doubted she'd ever emulate the way Miles seemed to pop in and out of side doors as though he owned the place. And yet . . . moving in this amazing space was easier this time, and she had no doubt would be still easier the next visit. Either the world was not so huge and frightening a place as she'd once been led to believe, or else . . . she was not so small and helpless as she'd once been encouraged to imagine herself. If power was an illusion, wasn't weakness necessarily one also?

Miles was grinning. As he took her hand and gripped it to his arm again, he vented a sinister chuckle.

"That is the most *villainous* laugh, love . . ."

"It's too good, it's just too good. I had to find you and share it at once." He led her a little away from the Vorkosigans' wine kiosk, crowded with revelers, around some trees to where a wide brick path climbed up out of Old Emperor Ezar's north garden. "I just found out what Alexi Vormoncrief's new posting is."

"I hope it's the ninth circle of hell!" she said vengefully. "That nitwit very nearly succeeded in having *Nikki* taken from me."

"Just as good. Almost the same thing, actually. He's been sent to Kyril Island. I was hoping they'd make him weather officer, but he's only the new laundry officer. Well, one can't have everything." He rocked on his heels with incomprehensible glee.

Ekaterin frowned in doubt. "That hardly seems punishment enough . . ."

"You don't understand. Kyril Island—they call it Camp Permafrost—is the worst military post in the Empire. Winter training base. It's an arctic island, five hundred kilometers from anywhere and anyone, including the nearest women. You can't even swim to escape, because the water would freeze you in minutes. The bogs will eat you alive. Blizzards. Freezing fog. Winds that can blow away groundcars. Cold, dark, drunken, deadly . . . I spent an eternity there, a few months once. The trainees, they come and go, but the *permanent* staff is stuck. Oh. Oh. Justice is *good. . . .*"

Impressed by his evident enthusiasm, she said, "Is it really that bad?"

"Yes, oh, yes. Ha! I'll have to send him a case of good brandy, in honor of the Emperor's wedding, just to start him off right. Or—no, better. I'll send him a case of *bad* brandy. After a while, no one there can tell the difference anyway."

Accepting his assurances for the present and future discomfort of her recent nemesis, she sauntered contentedly with him along the edge of the sunken garden. All the principal guests, including Miles, would be called in for the formal dinner soon, and they would be separated for a time, he to the high table to sit between Empress Laisa and her Komarran Second, she to join Lord Auditor Vorthys and her aunt again. There would be tedious speeches, but Miles laid firm plans for reconnecting with her right after dessert.

"So what do you think?" he asked, staring speculatively around at the party, which seemed to be gaining momentum in the dusk. "Would you like a big wedding?"

She now recognized the incipient theatrical gleam in his eye. But Countess Cordelia had primed her on how to handle this one. She swept her lashes down. "It just wouldn't feel appropriate in my mourning year. But if you didn't mind waiting till next spring, it could be as large as you like."

"Ah," he said, "ah. Fall is a nice time for weddings, too . . ."

"A quiet family wedding in the fall? I would like that."

He would find some way to make it memorable, she had no fear. And, she suspected, it might be better not to leave him time for over-planning.

"Maybe in the garden at Vorkosigan Surleau?" he said. "You haven't seen that yet. Or else the garden at Vorkosigan House." He eyed her sidelong.

"Certainly," she said amiably. "Outdoor weddings are going to be the rage for the next few years. Lord and Lady Vorkosigan will be all in the mode."

He grinned at that. His—her—*their*—Barrayaran garden would still be a bit bare by fall. But full of sprouts and hope and life waiting underground for the spring rains.

They both paused, and Ekaterin stared in fascination at the Cetagandan diplomatic delegation just climbing the brick steps that wound up from the reflecting pools. The regular ambassador and his tall and glamorous wife were accompanied not only by the haut governor of Rho Ceta, Barrayar's nearest neighbor planet of the empire, but also by an actual haut woman from the Imperial capital. Despite the fact that haut ladies were said never to travel, she had been sent as the personal delegate of Emperor the haut Fletchir Giaja and his Empresses. She was escorted by a ghem-general of the highest rank. No one knew what she looked like, as she traveled always in a personal force bubble, tonight tinted an iridescent rose color for festivity. The ghem-general, tall and distinguished, wore the formal blood-red uniform of the Cetagandan emperor's personal guard, which ought to have clashed horribly with the bubble, but didn't.

The ambassador glanced at Miles, waved polite greeting, and said something to the ghem-general, who nodded. To Ekaterin's surprise, the ghem-general and the pink bubble left their party and strolled/floated over to them.

"Ghem-general Benin," said Miles, suddenly on-stage in his most flowing Imperial Auditor's style. His eyes were alight with curiosity and, oddly, pleasure. He swept a sincere bow at the bubble. "And haut Pel. So good to see you—so to speak—once more. I hope your unaccustomed travel has not proved too wearing?"

"Indeed not, Lord Auditor Vorkosigan. I have found it quite stimulating." Her voice came from a transmitter in her bubble. To Ekaterin's astonishment, her bubble grew almost transparent for a moment. Seated in her float chair behind the pearly sheen, a tall blonde woman of uncertain age in a flowing rose-pink gown appeared momentarily. She was staggeringly beautiful, but something about her ironic smile did not suggest youth. The concealing screen clouded up once more.

"We are honored by your presence, haut Pel," Miles

said formally, while Ekaterin blinked, feeling temporarily blinded. And suddenly horribly dowdy. But all the admiration in Miles's eyes burned for her, not for the pink vision. "May I introduce my fiancée, Madame Ekaterin Nile Vorvayne Vorsoisson."

The distinguished officer murmured polite greetings. He then turned his thoughtful gaze upon Miles, and touched his lips in an oddly ceremonious gesture before speaking.

"My Imperial Master the haut Fletchir Giaja had asked me, in the event that I should encounter you, Lord Vorkosigan, to extend his *personal* condolences for the death of your close friend, Admiral Naismith."

Miles paused, his smile for a moment a little frozen. "Indeed. His death was a great blow to me."

"My Imperial Master adds that he *trusts* that he will remain deceased."

Miles glanced up at the tall Benin, his eyes suddenly sparkling. "Tell your Imperial Master from me—I *trust* his resurrection will not be required."

The ghem-general smiled austerely, and favored Miles with an inclination of his head. "I shall convey your words exactly, my lord." He nodded cordially at them both, and he and the pink bubble drifted back to their delegation.

Ekaterin, still awed by the blonde, murmured to Miles, "What was *that* all about?"

Miles sucked on his lower lip. "Not news, I'm afraid, though I'll pass it on to General Allegre. Benin just confirms something Illyan had suspected over a year ago. My covert ops identity was come to the end of its usefulness, at least as far as its being a secret from the Cetagandans was concerned. Well, Admiral Naismith and his various clones, real and imagined, kept 'em confused for longer than I'd have believed possible."

He gave a short nod, not dissatisfied, she thought, despite his little flash of regret. He took a firmer grip on her.

Regret . . . And what if she and Miles had met at twenty, instead of she and Tien? It had been possible;

she'd been a student at the Vorbarra District University, he'd been a newly minted officer in and out of the capital. If their paths had crossed, might she have won a less bitter life?

No. We were two other people, then. Traveling in different directions: their intersection must have been brief, and indifferent, and unknowing. And she could not unwish Nikki, or all that she had learned, not even realizing she was learning, during her dark eclipse. *Roots grow deep in the dark.*

She could only have arrived here by the path she'd taken, and here, with Miles, *this* Miles, seemed a very good place to be indeed. *If I am his consolation, he is most surely mine as well.* She acknowledged her years lost, but there was nothing in that decade she needed to circle back for, not even regret; Nikki, and the learning, traveled with her. Time to move on.

"Ah," said Miles, looking up as a Residence servitor approached them, smiling. "They must be rounding up the strays for dinner. Shall we go in, milady?"

PRAISE FOR
LOIS MCMASTER BUJOLD

What the critics say:

The Warrior's Apprentice: "Now here's a fun romp through the spaceways—not so much a space opera as space ballet.... it has all the 'right stuff.' A lot of thought and thoughtfulness stand behind the all-too-human characters. Enjoy this one, and look forward to the next." —Dean Lambe, *SF Reviews*

"The pace is breathless, the characterization thoughtful and emotionally powerful, and the author's narrative technique and command of language compelling. Highly recommended." —*Booklist*

Brothers in Arms: " ... she gives it a genuine depth of character, while reveling in the wild turnings of her tale.... Bujold is as audacious as her favorite hero, and as brilliantly (if sneakily) successful." —*Locus*

"Miles Vorkosigan is such a great character that I'll read anything Lois wants to write about him.... a book to re-read on cold rainy days." —Robert Coulson, *Comic Buyer's Guide*

Borders of Infinity: "Bujold's series hero Miles Vorkosigan may be a lord by birth and an admiral by rank, but a bone disease that has left him hobbled and in frequent pain has sensitized him to the suffering of outcasts in his very hierarchical era. ... Playing off Miles's reserve and cleverness, Bujold draws outrageous and outlandish foils to color her high-minded adventures." —*Publishers Weekly*

Falling Free: "In *Falling Free* Lois McMaster Bujold has written her fourth straight superb novel.... How to break down a talent like Bujold's into analyzable components? Best not to try. Best to say: 'Read, or you will be missing something extra-ordinary.' " —Roland Green, *Chicago Sun-Times*

The Vor Game: "The chronicles of Miles Vorkosigan are far too witty to be literary junk food, but they rouse the kind of craving that makes popcorn magically vanish during a double feature." —Faren Miller, *Locus*

MORE PRAISE FOR
LOIS MCMASTER BUJOLD

What the readers say:

"My copy of *Shards of Honor* is falling apart I've reread it so often. . . . I'll read whatever you write. You've certainly proved yourself a grand storyteller."
—Lisa Kolbe, Colorado Springs, CO

"I experience the stories of Miles Vorkosigan as almost viscerally uplifting. . . . But certainly, even the weightiest theme would have less impact than a cinder on snow were it not for a rousing good story, and good story-telling with it. This is the second thing I want to thank you for. . . . I suppose if you boiled down all I've said to its simplest expression, it would be that I immensely enjoy and admire your work. I submit that, as literature, your work raises the overall level of the science fiction genre, and spiritually, your work cannot avoid positively influencing all who read it."
—Glen Stonebraker, Gaithersburg, MD

" 'The Mountains of Mourning' [in *Borders of Infinity*] was one of the best-crafted, and simply best, works I'd ever read. When I finished it, I immediately turned back to the beginning and read it again, and I can't remember the last time I did that."

—Betsy Bizot, Lisle, IL

"I can only hope that you will continue to write, so that I can continue to read (and of course buy) your books, for they make me laugh and cry and think . . . rare indeed."
—Steven Knott, Major, USAF